The McKenna Legacy...
A Legacy of Love

To my darling grandchildren,

I leave you my love and more. Within thirty-three days of your thirty-third birthday — enough time to know what you are about — you will have in your grasp a legacy of which your dreams are made. Dreams are not always tangible things, but more often are born in the heart. Act selflessly in another's behalf, and my legacy will be yours.

Your loving grandmother,
Moira McKenna

P.S. Use any other inheritance from me wisely and only for good, lest you destroy yourself or those you love.

Dear Reader,

We all know that wonderful feeling of being part of a family—the special warmth we feel in its welcoming embrace, the strength we derive from its unconditional support. But in the McKenna clan, three of Grandmother Moira's adult grandchildren have gone astray. With the help of her very extraordinary legacy, will Keelin, Skelly and Kate find their way home?

Longtime popular author Patricia Rosemoor brings you the very special stories of these three McKennas in her newest trilogy, THE McKENNA LEGACY. In *See Me In Your Dreams* she introduces you to this dynamic family. Uncover the secrets and share the adventures of all the McKennas as Pat continues with *Tell Me No Lies*. *Touch Me in the Dark* comes to you next month.

Look for all THE McKENNA LEGACY titles!

Regards,

Debra Matteucci
Senior Editor & Editorial Coordinator
Harlequin Books
300 E. 42nd St.
New York, NY 10017

Tell Me No Lies
Patricia Rosemoor

Harlequin Books

TORONTO • NEW YORK • LONDON
AMSTERDAM • PARIS • SYDNEY • HAMBURG
STOCKHOLM • ATHENS • TOKYO • MILAN
MADRID • WARSAW • BUDAPEST • AUCKLAND

To my enthusiastic editor, Bonnie Crisalli.
Thanks for encouraging me to develop
The McKenna Legacy, a project dear to my heart.

And to Cathy Andorka and Rosemary Paulas
for your years of support.

ISBN 0-373-22386-2

TELL ME NO LIES

Copyright © 1996 by Patricia Pinianski

This edition published by arrangement with Harlequin Books S.A.

® and TM are trademarks of the publisher. Trademarks indicated with
® are registered in the United States Patent and Trademark Office, the
Canadian Trade Marks Office and in other countries.

Printed in U.S.A.

McKENNA FAMILY TREE

Descendants of MOIRA KELLY McKENNA

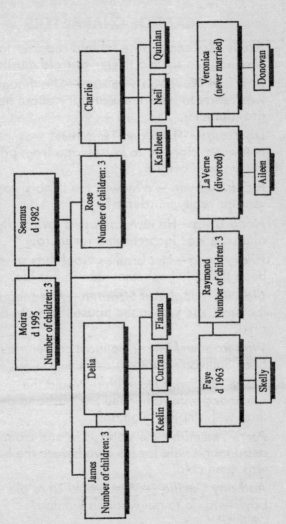

CAST OF CHARACTERS

Skelly McKenna—The tabloid reporter took the challenge to solve a thirty-year-old murder.

Rosalind (Roz) Van Straaten—She thought she was ready to hear the real story about her grandmother.

Lily Lang—"The Blond Temptress" was notorious, right up to her escape from prison thirty years before.

Frank Sullivan—Why was the Illinois state senator really murdered?

Noah Lang—He never stopped loving Lily even after she was incarcerated for murder.

Hilary Lang—Her brother Noah has always been the only important man in her life.

Claudia (Lang) Van Straaten—A teenager at the time, she was in the house the night Sullivan died.

Walt Rogowski—His political career was made after Sullivan's death.

Diane (Sullivan) Nesmith—Would the estranged wife rather see her husband dead than with another woman?

Perry Nesmith—He stepped in and claimed the dead man's wife for his own before the body was even cold.

Anthony Cavillo—What would Lily's old boyfriend do to get what he wanted?

Prologue

June 1963

Lily Lang stared out at the fog blanketing the river valley as the church clock below struck eleven. With a shrug of her shoulders, her dinner dress slithered down her full hips and puddled around her sling-backed high heels.

A fog of unhappiness was choking the very breath from her.

How had it come to this? Her life was in the dumper. Her divorce from Noah was to be finalized within the week. No matter how much she still loved him, she couldn't put it off any longer. His monstrous jealousy was too frightening. And news of the public fight she'd had with Frank earlier that evening was undoubtedly already spreading like wildfire.

What else would she expect? The citizens of her hometown had always been hypercritical of her, no matter how highly she was regarded by the rest of the country.

Maybe she never should have left Hollywood.

But if she'd never left, Claudia wouldn't have been born.

Thinking about the pretty, shy daughter who—to her constant amazement—was a budding young woman, brought a bittersweet smile to her lips, anguish to her heart. Noah had threatened that unless she gave up on what he called her "crazy divorce idea," he would seek sole custody of their only child. With his old family money and social position, no doubt he would succeed. He would name every man she'd ever been seen with during their several separations. And the courts would believe the worst of her, even as he did. Even as the town did.

Once notorious, always notorious.

Who was she to be a role model for an impressionable thirteen-year-old?

Claudia's mother, that's who, Lily reminded herself.

Tears slipped down her cheeks as she crossed to the dresser in the dark, finding her brush and stroking the long tresses for which she'd become known. Her nearly waist-length silver blond hair was not only her vanity, but it had made her famous.

Perhaps if it hadn't...

Lily threw the brush down to the dresser. She needed a good cry. She deserved one. About to indulge herself, she went wide-eyed instead when a sharp noise emanated from below.

A gunshot?

Heart pounding, she rushed to the bedroom door and threw it open even as a second shot rang out.

Fingers curling into the hand-carved landing rail, her mouth too dry to call out, Lily looked down to the first floor. She could see nothing from where she stood. The staircase and foyer below were as dark as her bedroom had been. Only half considering the advisability of facing someone with a loaded weapon, dressed as she was in a satin slip, Lily tore down the stairs, her treacherous heels making her stumble as she neared the bottom.

Catching hold of the banister to steady herself, she noted a light shone from beneath the pocket doors of the front parlor.

Holding her breath, Lily crept forward and listened intently. Through the wooden panels, she could hear nothing but the tortured sound of choked sobs. With shaking hands, she slid open the double doors...

...unprepared for the horrific sight on the other side....

Chapter One

Chicago
June 1996

"Thirty years ago today, Lily Lang, better known as 'the Blond Temptress' to her fans, escaped the Dwight Correctional Center for Women."

Rosalind Van Straaten paced before the television set. "Can you believe this atrocity?" she asked her father, who calmly sat watching from the cream-on-cream sofa in the day spa's office. "After all these years, someone had to go and dig up the old scandal."

That someone being Skelly McKenna of "The Whole Story," a tabloid news program. His office had contacted her, requesting an interview—one she had turned down in no uncertain terms—so at least she had been forewarned. She glared at the image of the too-good-looking, too-assured, dark-haired man.

"People don't care how old a story is," Rip Van Straaten said, "as long as it's juicy."

"A pleasant if not great talent, Hollywood starlet Lily Lang earned her fame and nickname during

World War II, when she became a poster girl for our boys overseas.''

The on-screen shot was the infamous black-and-white photograph of a stunning blonde reclining on a chaise, satin tap shorts and a sequined halter top hugging her lush curves. Her waist-length hair curled along the right side of her face and waterfalled over her shoulder. A mole at the left corner of her mouth punctuated full lips that were parted, as if in invitation to a kiss.

''Amazing how very much you look like your grandmother,'' her father mused, irritating Rosalind further.

''Shh!''

''After the war, Lily returned to her home state of Illinois only to reveal that she had married Lieutenant Noah Lang in a secret ceremony before he was shipped off in 1943. Lily retired from movie stardom, and with her Winnetka-based husband, founded a hair-product-and-cosmetics empire—none other than Temptress.''

''I can't believe it!'' Rosalind cried. ''Not only is he dragging our family through the muck again, but his spotlighting the company is bound to ruin my day spa before it has a chance to get off the ground.''

''Don't complain. Free publicity.''

''Publicity's fine, Father. Notoriety's not.''

Skelly McKenna went on, his expression serious, as though he had a personal stake in the union.

''While Temptress flourished, the Lang marriage did not. After years of upheaval, the Langs first separated in 1959. Lily took their daughter Claudia, then nine, back to her hometown of Galena.''

Rosalind clenched her jaw and only hoped no one had been distasteful enough to suggest her mother tune in. Claudia Van Straaten never talked about that time in her life, acted as if nothing untoward had ever happened.

''Lily and Noah tried reconciling several times, but four years later in 1963, divorce was imminent on that fateful day when state Senator Frank Sullivan entered the Langs' Galena home for the last time.''

Rosalind stared at the photograph of the politician and his aide, a young man whose face was strikingly familiar. When the image dissolved to lurid shots of a bloody Sullivan sprawled across the parlor floor, she glanced away, unable to stomach the sight.

''Frank Sullivan was shot to death just before midnight. Lily Lang herself called the authorities and confessed to the heinous murder of her latest lover.''

Her grandfather had told Rosalind that despite the confession, his Lily had been innocent. And she'd always done her best to believe him. Rosalind didn't want to have any doubts, for his or her mother's sake. Or for her own, she had to admit. Even though she'd only heard from her grandmother a few times in her life—and that, years before—she felt an inexplicable bond with the now-elderly woman.

''Her sentence . . . life imprisonment. Lily accepted her punishment without objection. But on the third anniversary of her incarceration, the Blond Temptress staged a daring escape. Working in the laundry, she stole a dress belonging to one of the employees. She waited until dusk, at which time she went over the twelve-foot fence topped with barbed wire, changed into the dress and wrapped a scarf around her famous hair.

"So disguised, the Blond Temptress hitchhiked a ride, the unsuspecting driver of the car taking her nearly one hundred miles south of the prison."

Rosalind again focused on the so-called reporter, wondering if he derived real satisfaction from digging up muck that could still hurt several people she loved.

What kind of a human being was this smooth-tongued devil who played word games with other people's lives for ratings and profits? A three-decade-old murder was entertainment, not hard news. Did he have a conscience—would he even care if he realized his words might be reopening old wounds? Why couldn't he have left them in peace?

"The escape was executed thirty years ago, and to this day, Lily Lang has eluded authorities—"

Rosalind took the satisfaction of zapping off the television on a close-up of Skelly McKenna's pretty face. "This could kill Grandfather," she said, her voice shaky.

"Noah's a crusty old devil."

"With a bad heart."

"He'll survive."

"And what about Mother?"

"I'm certain whatever Claudia thinks, she will keep her opinion to herself."

The change of inflection in his tone wounded Rosalind. An only child, she wanted to be part of a real family, an impossible wish when her parents had slept in separate bedrooms, lived separate lives, for as long as she could remember. They were achingly polite to one another. They never argued, for heaven's sake. But they might as well be strangers.

The only time Claudia Van Straaten seemed to remember she had a husband was when she accompanied him to obligatory business functions. Rosalind knew her father had seen other women from time to time and, as much as she hated the very notion of infidelity, she could hardly blame him.

She sank into the chair behind her desk. "How to handle this?"

"I'd advise you to ignore the whole thing. If anyone brings it up, tell them it's ancient history—nothing to do with you. Say it with a smile. No one will hold this against you, sweetheart. Or against your pet project here. So cheer up and take me on that tour you promised."

Rosalind knew her father was trying to distract her. A warm, supportive man, always quick to smile or laugh, he was the very opposite of her mother.

Humoring him, she rose and crossed to the door, forcing a half smile. "Sure. Let's start with the wet areas." She led the way, her pride in her accomplishment wiping away her distress for the moment.

The day after she'd earned her MBA, Rip Van Straaten had made Rosalind his personal assistant so she could quickly learn Temptress inside and out. The company gave them more than a comfortable living, but she'd soon realized her father was far better at employee relations than innovation. He hadn't made any significant changes in product lines or services since her grandfather had retired.

Young and ambitious, Rosalind had decided the day spa was the very thing to move the company into the future. The new venture would give her a chance to expand Temptress, to build a niche that was uniquely hers. Her concept was to make pampering accessible even to women of moderate means. Services would range from hair and nail care to facials, from various massage encounters to eucalyptus inhalation and water therapy. The beauty products used in the spa would, of course, be manufactured by Temptress.

The Gold Coast site was the first of three planned Chicago-area locations and was barely two weeks away from its grand opening—workmen were still seeing to critical details.

Rosalind was aware of more than one male head turning in her direction as she and her father arrived at the ceramic-tiled area. The attention embarrassed her. She might look something like her notorious grandmother had at the same age, but she certainly was no blond temptress.

"Whirlpool...sauna...inhalation-therapy rooms," she said as they passed a painter who was adding another cloud to the sky blue walls in the wet area. "The wooden planters will be filled with tropical greenery, and a couple of tables will be equipped with colorful umbrellas."

Her father was inspecting the free-form whirlpool that reminded Rosalind of a miniature lagoon. "I'm sure it'll be very classy. Very you." His warm smile was catching.

"You always know how to make me feel better."

He slipped an arm around her shoulders and gave them a squeeze. "You really shouldn't worry about old scandals, honey."

"But I am worried," she admitted, her smile fading. "Thanks to Skelly McKenna."

He was the one who'd dredged up the past.

Therefore, Rosalind decided, *he* was the one who would have to fix things.

SKELLY LEANED BACK in his chair, feet up on his black-lacquer desk. He was editing copy for the next day's show, wishing for a story to end all stories that he could personally bring home. His network had a new prime-time magazine show in the works, and he was under consideration for a promotion. The other candidates had one up on him because they were all part of *legitimate* news teams.

Prime time.

Respect.

His father's approval.

Skelly was wondering what they would feel like when his office door opened to reveal a welcome visitor—his cousin, Keelin McKenna.

"Hey, cuz, do all brides-to-be look as beautiful as you do?" He set his feet on the floor and rose to greet her with a big hug.

"You're full o' the blarney, Skelly McKenna," Keelin said, her lilt more pronounced than usual.

"Not this time."

In truth, his Irish cousin looked radiant. Soft color flooded her cheeks. Her gray eyes sparkled. And her cloud of auburn hair appeared positively fiery against the yellow of the gauzy dress that floated around her, its long skirts brushing the tops of her ankle boots.

"Tyler sends you his greetings."

Tyler Leighton was Keelin's fiancé. Skelly held out a chair for her opposite his own. "So, how are things with Cheryl?" he asked, referring to Tyler's daughter, who had gone through a terrible ordeal the week before.

"She acts as though the kidnapping was nothing. But Tyler's taking no chances. The two have already started family-therapy sessions together."

"She's okay with the wedding? I mean, considering how fast it's all happening."

Keelin was determined to stick to the schedule defined by what Skelly thought of as the McKenna legacy—Moira's bequest to her grandchildren being lifelong happiness to be achieved by the thirty-third day after their thirty-third birthday. Not that Skelly believed in such prophecies.

"It seems Cheryl has accepted me," Keelin was saying. "She's a very loving fourteen-year-old. And she's needed a woman in her life for a very long time."

"She couldn't get a better stepmom, cuz."

"I shall try my best."

Skelly shook his head. What a delightful surprise his sweet, soft cousin had turned out to be. She'd certainly taken his heart by storm. He hadn't even known her two weeks before, and now he felt as if they'd been fast friends forever.

"So how are the plans for the wedding coming?"

"Your sister is a wonder. She's helped me arrange everything."

Skelly laughed. "Aileen does get things done when she sets her mind to it."

"The only thing we still need is a best man."

"I suppose Brock Olander is out of the question."

Keelin heaved a sigh. "Tyler's business partnership with Brock is being dissolved even as we speak . . . or he would be here to ask you himself."

"Ask me what?"

"To be his best man, of course."

Skelly started. "No 'of course' about it. I was under the distinct impression that Tyler's got a pretty low opinion of tabloid journalists."

"He considers you an exception after the restrained way you handled the follow-up story about Cheryl's kidnapping."

"Listen, about that story—the network execs were pretty impressed. I'm being considered for a huge promotion. An anchor desk on a prime-time magazine. Your cuz may go legit yet."

Keelin's smile lit the room. "Skelly, congratulations. If that's what you want."

He'd never planned on working in tabloid news—the fates had merely pushed him in that direction. Not that he was ashamed of what he did, but he was ready for a change and he had neither the guts nor the heart to resurrect old dreams.

"It's the best opportunity I've ever had. You bet I want the job."

"Then I'll pray you succeed."

"Thanks. Now, about the best-man thing. Are you sure you didn't coerce Tyler into the invitation?"

"Oh, Skelly, Tyler will never forget all the help you gave me in finding his daughter. Asking you to be his best man comes directly from his heart. From both our hearts."

"Then how can I refuse?"

The cousins grinned at each other.

"Good," Keelin said. "That's settled, then."

"So, who's going to give the bride away?"

Skelly assumed Keelin hadn't yet informed her family in Ireland that she was about to be married. Their aunt's rebellious marriage to a man who wasn't Catholic had caused the beginning of a thirty-some-year rift in the family—a rift Keelin was determined to heal. Skelly knew Keelin feared her father's reaction when he learned that she, too, had chosen true love above the religious strictures of her church. Not that she herself would ever be anything but Catholic.

"I called them, Skelly. It took a great deal of courage, but I could not marry without them knowing."

"And?"

A small cloud passed over her visage. "Da didn't take it well. And even if he did, he's in no shape to be traveling. My mother will stay to take care of him, but she wants what's best for me. Curran's most valuable horse is racing next weekend, so he cannot come, either. Flanna will be here, though, as my maid of honor."

His sweet cousin certainly had the courage of a giant. "So you're giving yourself away?"

"Truth be told...I've asked Uncle Raymond to escort me. I thought him the appropriate choice to stand in for Da."

Especially since his father, her father and Aunt Rose were triplets. "Good. Maybe giving you away will soften him up for the reunion idea."

Keelin grinned again. "What better thing to ask as my wedding gift?"

"What a clever con artist," he said admiringly.

She sobered. "Only because I want our families to be reunited, for Da and Uncle Raymond and Aunt Rose to forgive one another and be truly happy."

Skelly knew the impetus for Keelin's quest had been his uncle James's heart attack. Keelin had told him her father had asked for Raymond and Rose on what he'd thought was his deathbed. The man must be as stubborn as Skelly's own parent, though, for once he knew he would survive, James had denied wanting any such thing. Healer of the spirit, as well as the body, Keelin had been compelled to act, in secret, of course—she'd told her family she was coming to the United States on business when really she'd come to see Raymond and Rose.

Skelly suspected Keelin would have a lot to account for to her father, her judgment day being not too far off. He only hoped it didn't all blow up in her face. If history were to repeat itself...the consequences didn't bear considering.

Besides, she would at least have Tyler, Skelly reminded himself. "I'm happy for you, cuz."

"Thank you, Skelly. Now I must go. I promised to take Cheryl shopping. She insists I need a new look, though I cannot for the life of me fathom what is wrong with the one I have." Still smiling, she shrugged and stood. "Tyler will ring you with the details about the wedding. And Skelly...about Moira's legacy..."

"What about it?"

"Believe in it, Skelly. You cannot have much time, either. If I remember correctly, your birthday didn't fall far behind mine."

Though he had recently turned thirty-three himself, Skelly merely laughed. As if he had time to worry about romance when a career opportunity was on the line. "I'll keep my antennae out for Ms. Right."

"You do that. You deserve a woman who can make you happy."

Giving him a swift kiss on his cheek, Keelin swept out the door, leaving Skelly staring after her. What an innocent his cousin was. What a wishful thinker. Her meeting Tyler right now had been sheer luck, nothing more. No hocus-pocus. No magic. Just dumb luck that it had happened within their grandmother's time frame.

Even as he stared at the copy he was supposed to be editing, Skelly couldn't quite put Keelin's admonishment from his mind. He'd never put much thought into finding Ms. Right—he'd been too busy working, building a career. He'd assumed it would happen to him some day, though he'd never put a timetable to starting a family life. But suddenly he wondered if he were missing something.

Keelin's happiness made him feel . . . empty.

Another knock at the door made him think she'd forgotten something. "That you, cuz? C'mon in."

When the door opened to reveal the most beautiful woman he'd ever laid eyes on, Skelly went slack jawed with a sense of déjà vu.

"Skelly McKenna." No uncertainty in her husky-voiced query.

"That'd be me."

"We need to talk." She stepped inside and closed the door behind her.

Silver blond hair pulled back in a soft twist revealed perfect features, sky blue eyes dusted by dark lashes and a tiny mole punctuating the left corner of her luscious mouth. Dressed in a powder blue business suit, the skirt short enough to reveal the extraordinary length of her legs, she was a knockout.

And too incredibly familiar for her appearance to be coincidence . . .

When she held out her perfectly manicured hand and said "Rosalind Van Straaten," he wasn't in the least surprised.

"Lily Lang's granddaughter," he mused. "What can I do for you?"

"Retract your story."

She was certainly direct—he'd give her that. "Retract the truth. Hmm, now there's an interesting concept."

With a placid smile, she said, "I'm not certain you would know the truth if it bit you."

Smothering a laugh, Skelly sat and indicated Rosalind should do the same. She stood where she was, feet seemingly rooted to the spot, and crossed her arms over her chest. Those baby-blues were glaring at him.

"All right, what do you take issue with?" he asked. "My calling your grandmother the Blond Temptress? Documenting the troubles between her and your grandfather? Or recapping the murder, her conviction and subsequent flight?"

"Yes."

Skelly threw up his hands. "But all of the above is true."

"Tarnished truth," she argued. "And you didn't have to rehash any of it. Besides, you don't really know what happened in the Galena house that night."

"I do my research."

"No one ever proved my grandmother killed anyone."

"They didn't have to. She voluntarily confessed."

"That's not the same as the authorities looking into Sullivan's death—they took her at her word."

"Sounds reasonable to me. Why should they have turned elsewhere? And what motive would Lily Lang have had to lie when her freedom was on the line?"

"I don't know." The husky voice was tight with emotion. "We all have our own motivations for doing what we do. Yours is money, isn't it?"

Skelly suspected he should be insulted, but he couldn't quite work up the steam. He was too intrigued by Rosalind Van Straaten. "I get paid for what I do."

"Doing another piece on my grandmother...one more favorable than the last—at least offering reasonable doubt as to her guilt...how much would that take?"

His eyebrows shot up. "You're trying to bribe me!" he said with mock indignation.

She made an impatient sound. "I'm simply offering to pay you for what you do. What do you care what copy you read as long as someone writes the check?"

Now he was insulted. He didn't fabricate stories. He didn't knowingly perpetuate lies. "Let me see if I have this straight," he said, fighting his clenching jaw muscles. "You want to pay me to whitewash your family's dirty laundry."

Though she flushed, Rosalind persisted. "How much?"

"Not interested, Roz." He deliberately allowed his gaze to wander up the length of her long legs. "Taking money from you wouldn't be ethical."

Her berry-tinted mouth gaped. She drew herself up to her full height. "Your telecast wasn't ethical."

"I didn't embellish the facts—they've all appeared in print for everyone to read."

"But how much personal research did you do?"

"The murder happened more than thirty years ago—"

"Exactly!"

"So I did what I could," he continued. "Used documented knowledge. Oh...and I had my assistant con-

tact you, as well as others germane to the case. I'm sure
you'll remember you turned down her request for an interview with me. No one wanted to talk.''

She paled and sank into the chair he'd offered earlier.
''Who else did you contact? Surely not my mother.''

''Your own mother didn't tell you about our offer?
Curious. What about your grandfather?''

Her breathing was as unnatural as her color. She didn't
answer immediately. She appeared almost ill . . . and as if
the wheels in her head were spinning wildly.

Finally, as if to convince herself, as well as him, she
said, ''Undoubtedly they thought to spare me.''

His momentary irritation with her fled. ''I don't understand. You weren't even born when this all happened. What's your stake?''

Her blue eyes widened. ''My family's reputation and
standing in the community are my stake. And what about
the innocent people involved here? My grandfather and
mother are flesh-and-blood human beings, you know,
and they have been hurt enough.''

Her eyes had to be the most beautiful in the world,
Skelly thought, mesmerized by their transparency. In
them, he read pride. Resentment. Determination.

She wasn't going to let him alone until he agreed to do
something—but why? To soothe some emotional hurt he
might have caused? She wasn't the naive type. She
couldn't believe that journalists based professional decisions on personal feelings—not even on their own.
Could be she knew something he didn't about the case. . . .
A thought that intrigued him.

The brass had been impressed with his level of involvement with the Cheryl Leighton case. That had led
to his being considered for the promotion. He'd been
wishing for a ripe story . . . and this could be it. Should he

grab the opportunity and if it panned out, his career would get another boost in a direction that might make him happier... might even make his father proud.

Skelly decided he wouldn't mind being badgered by Rosalind Van Straaten. Contrary to her assumption as to his character, he couldn't be bribed. Though he worked in a segment of the television industry that sometimes played fast and loose with hard news, "The Whole Story" never knowingly ran an untruth.

Besides, he had his own brand of integrity.

"Give me something significant to run with," he said, "and I'll consider doing a follow-up."

"That's *your* job. You're the reporter. For once in your life, give your audience the real 'whole story.' Give them the unvarnished truth."

Rather, a version of the truth that she wanted to hear, Skelly thought cynically.

Skelly figured he was in a win-win situation. He might get the story that would make his career. And if not, at least he would spend some quality time with a woman who was as interestingly strong willed as she was beautiful. Both attributes turned him on.

"I'm a reasonable man." He stared into that stunning face, and a weird feeling washed through him. Part of him wished the McKenna legacy was more than fiction even as the cynic in him resisted believing it might be. Keelin had gotten to him good with her not-so-subtle romantic prodding. "I'll dig for the truth... but only if you'll cooperate."

"How?" Her expression grew immediately cautious.

"You'll have to work with me. And not censor me. That could very well mean exposing your family and its past to even more unfavorable public scrutiny."

Chapter Two

Rosalind forced herself to breathe normally. She obviously hadn't thought through the situation carefully enough before going to see Skelly McKenna. Browbeating and bribing him into reporting a more favorable angle on the story hadn't worked, so she'd somehow found herself challenging him to dig up the unvarnished truth. She only hoped that hadn't been a big mistake.

He'd made one valid point. How else could he proceed without involving her family further, perhaps to everyone's detriment?

As for working with him...

"I hardly think you need my input," she said, trying to circumvent a direct, negative response. It wouldn't do to provoke McKenna again—not when she almost had him where she wanted him.

"Getting cold feet?"

"That's not the issue."

"Then what is? That you would rather not soil your pretty hands—"

"I work hard, thank you very much."

"—or your social position by associating with a tabloid reporter?"

"My reputation is above reproach."

"Then it must be something else that's stopping you." He arched his eyebrows. "I do tend to be a little intimidating at times...."

His slow grin forced a dimple in his right cheek, giving him a roguish air. Rosalind started and blinked, for a moment forgetting they were opponents. Skelly McKenna was a devastatingly handsome man. Black hair tousled onto a high forehead. Intense blue eyes. Wicked smile. And though she wore three-inch heels, he was still a bit taller, seemed athletically built....

Realizing where her thoughts were headed, she steered her wayward mind back on track. "I'm rarely intimidated, Mr. McKenna."

More often, she was irritated with men like him. Cocky. Mocking. Seemingly unflappable.

"'Skelly.' And I'll call you Roz." Before she could object to the wretched nickname, he rolled on. "Being so formal is a little ridiculous when two people are working closely together, don't you agree?"

"I never agreed to—"

"And if you want a more positive follow-up soon enough to counter whatever you deemed disagreeable about the original story, we need to get moving immediately."

Even knowing he was keeping the upper hand, Rosalind stilled any further objection. She did want that follow-up. Enough to chance what Skelly might find.

Irritated with herself now—how much more damage could be done to her family, after all?—she promptly buried any vague doubts that lingered at the back of her mind. However, she did admit her being part of the investigation would be a smart move. Alongside Skelly, she would learn everything he did, when he did. He couldn't gloss over anything he found that might point away from her grandmother.

And on the slight, unthinkable possibility that he dug up information that could be construed as damaging, she'd be there to stop him from capitalizing on it.

"All right," Rosalind acceded. "You win. So we'll start first thing tomorrow?"

She didn't supervise the day-to-day work being done on the spa, merely checked every nuance at intervals. Knowing how to delegate authority meant she could afford to take time off when necessary.

"Actually I'm taping two shows tomorrow morning. I'm off Monday, since Tuesday is a holiday." If he spent it with her, the Fourth of July wouldn't be just another day as usual. "I had this evening in mind. We can start over dinner. Dress casual."

Noting he was staring at her legs again, Rosalind decided she would wear a pants outfit. "Where and what time?"

"I'll pick you up at six-thirty." He poised a pen over a notebook. "I'll need your home address."

"I'd rather meet you at the restaurant."

While Skelly gave her another of his wicked smiles, he didn't taunt her as she expected he might. "Make it seven, then. Six Shillings on Lincoln Avenue—do you know it?"

"I know where it is. I'll be there."

With that, Rosalind swept herself out of Skelly's office and kept going until she was out on the street, where she hailed a taxi. It wasn't until she slipped behind the driver and gave him her Lincoln Park address that she allowed herself to think of the commitment she'd made.

And to hope that this was one time she wouldn't regret sticking her nose where it didn't belong.

WITH AN HOUR TO KILL before having to be at the restaurant, Skelly turned on the television and kicked back in his favorite leather chair, beer in hand. Feet propped on the hassock, television tuned to nationwide news anchored by one of his competitors for the promotion, he watched without anything registering. A few slugs of the lager quenched his thirst.

If only he could assuage his other needs as easily.

Damn Keelin for provoking him. Damn Rosalind Van Straaten for showing up before he'd had the time to forget his cousin's visit.

Rosalind Van Straaten. The name as classy as the lady. Definitely as strong. Nearly as beautiful. Unfortunately he doubted the beautiful, strong, classy lady had any kind thoughts for him.

Still, it was weird how she'd shown up right after Keelin had gotten him to thinking about his future.

Exchanging his bottle for an envelope that he'd laid on the coffee table, he turned and touched the thick, cream-colored paper as though he could discern some magic inside. His name and address were written in a distinctly foreign hand. The stamp proclaimed the delivery to be from Eire. And though he was familiar with its contents, he pulled the letter from within and reread his grandmother's heartfelt wish for him.

To my darling Skelly,
I leave you my love and more. Within thirty-three days after your thirty-third birthday—enough time to know what you are about—you will have in your

grasp a legacy of which your dreams are made. Dreams are not always tangible things, but more often are born in the heart. Act selflessly in another's behalf, and my legacy shall be yours.

> Your loving grandmother,
> Moira McKenna

P.S. Use any other inheritance from me wisely and only for good lest you harm yourself or those you love.

Cynic that he was, Skelly had thought the letter so much nonsense when he'd first received it, had even suspected the grandmother whom he'd never met had been a bit out-to-lunch—after all, she *had* been ninety-plus when she'd written the missive.

But something made him keep her last letter to him.

And something made him read it, over and over again, until he knew the words by heart.

His cousin Keelin certainly believed in the legacy, was its staunchest promoter after having met and fallen in love with Tyler Leighton. Both of his siblings and his other cousins—nine of them altogether—had each received an identical letter from their grandmother.

Smoothing his fingers over her signature, he asked softly, "So, Moira, my dear, what do you have in store for me?" half hoping she would answer.

He had no visitation, heard no voices in his head. Moira was keeping mum for the moment.

Skelly shook his head at his detour into fantasy and carefully slipped the letter back into its sheath. Then he checked his watch and realized he now had little more than fifteen minutes to get over to Six Shillings. His future awaited him. Professional future, he reminded himself as images of Roz flitted through his wayward mind.

He'd already traded his work clothes for a pair of jeans and a chambray shirt, its sleeves rolled to the elbows. He slipped his feet into worn running shoes and, with his fingers, combed back the hair spilling onto his forehead.

Locking the door of his town house behind him, he could hardly wait to see Roz... and whatever it was the cosmetics heiress considered casual wear.

NOT KNOWING what to expect either from Skelly McKenna or the place they were to meet, Rosalind entered Six Shillings with a sense of trepidation. She was pleasantly surprised—at least by the restaurant. The wainscoted walls and hand-carved bar were remnants of the past century. Classical music played softly in the background, while video footage of art pieces rather than some rough-and-tumble sporting event played on the monitors suspended in each corner of the room.

"Can I help you?" asked a young woman in cotton walking shorts and a camp shirt.

"I'm looking for...oh, there he is." She spotted Skelly. "I can seat myself."

Skelly was sprawled across a booth in an alcove lit by a brass wall sconce. His attention was, for the moment, on his notebook. He was scribbling an entry. An enticing blue-black lock of hair caressed his high forehead. As if sensing her presence, he glanced up, his suddenly wide-eyed, subtly amused expression making her check her royal blue silk tunic and pants and matching nubuck sandals to see if something were amiss. She shrugged—everything appeared to be intact.

And when she raised her gaze to Skelly's, it was to recognize male appreciation.

Rosalind was appreciative herself. The reporter looked better in chambray than he did in starched linen—virile and somehow more appealing—but she hoped he couldn't tell what she was thinking. She was seeking justice for a grandmother she'd never met, not a date.

She slid into the booth across from him. "Am I late?"

He checked his watch. "Mmm, about fifteen seconds."

"I'll do better next time."

"Why, Roz, is that a promise...or do you actually have a sense of humor?"

"Only when I'm not worked up about something."

"I'll keep that in mind."

"Do." Wondering how she could discourage him from abbreviating her name, Rosalind noticed the approaching waitress, as well as the menus Skelly had discarded to the side of the table. "Did you have a look?"

"I probably know the list by heart. I only live a few blocks from here."

While she barely lived a mile away. In a city the size of Chicago, that practically made them neighbors.

"So, what do you recommend?"

"A big, fat, juicy burger with fries."

Which translated to greasy. "I think I'd better give the menu a look myself."

In the end, Rosalind chose a grilled-chicken-breast sandwich with a salad and a glass of spring water with lime, while Skelly went for the burger and a lager. With a promise to deliver their drinks shortly, the waitress departed to place their orders.

And Skelly consulted the scribbling in his notebook. Rosalind tried to read upside down the notes he'd made to himself, but either his penmanship was atrocious or he was operating in shorthand. She could barely make out a word here or there.

Suddenly nervous now that they were getting down to it, she asked, "So, how do we begin?"

"By talking." Skelly leaned back against the padded booth, arms spread across the booth top on each side of him. "You telling me what you know about the murder that I don't."

"I doubt anything."

"Try me. You must have picked up some hearsay from your parents over the years. Claudia was in the Galena house when Frank Sullivan died."

She shook her head. "Mother was a child."

"She was thirteen years old. Hardly a child, Roz."

Rosalind flushed and admitted, "She simply doesn't talk about that night."

"What about Grandpa Noah?"

"Grandfather wasn't there."

Skelly gave her a look that sent a chill up her spine, but before he could pursue a direction she didn't want to take, the waitress arrived with their drinks.

"Thanks," he said with a wink, making the waitress flush and grin.

"Your food will be up in a few minutes, Skelly."

When the waitress turned to another table, Rosalind noted, "She knows your name."

"I told you I was a regular."

And a popular one, at least with the young women, she decided, caught again by his wicked smile and dimpled cheek. Annoyed, not wanting to notice anything personal about the man—not wanting to humanize him—Rosalind reminded herself of her mission.

He held out his glass toward her. "To the truth . . . no matter what it happens to be."

The truth. Rosalind picked up her water glass and tried to hide the uneasiness that flashed through her. "To success in clearing my grandmother's name," she murmured, adding to herself, *And all her family members*.

Rosalind sipped at her drink to relieve her suddenly dry mouth. She watched Skelly over the rim of her glass and assured herself that she had not opened a Pandora's box. She figured he would pursue the line of questioning about her grandfather's whereabouts the night of the murder. And was surprised when he didn't.

"So what does Noah Lang have to say about Frank Sullivan's death and about your grandmother's incarceration?" he asked instead. "Off-the-record, that is."

"Exactly what he told the press at the time. Grandfather insists his Lily didn't do it, that she wasn't capable of murdering anyone."

"And you believe him?"

"I believe he's a good judge of character. I assume you'll remember he demanded the authorities scrutinize the people around Frank Sullivan carefully. Any number of people might have had motives. But, of course, they didn't. As far as the police were concerned, they had an open-and-shut case. Maybe that's where we should start."

"Did Noah ever mention any specific person he suspected?"

"If he has an opinion, he's never shared it with me."

Rosalind noticed Skelly was doodling in his notebook, underlining what she discerned as names and drawing arrows and other symbols in the margins. As if he were talking to himself in code.

But Skelly looked directly at her when he said, "Noah Lang was also in love with his soon-to-be ex-wife."

So he wasn't letting it go. She said, "They had their problems. Every married couple does."

"Every married couple doesn't separate—several times—before applying for divorce."

"My grandmother was a warm, giving woman. Too warm and giving to others, I think. Grandfather wanted all of her attention for himself."

"You mean he was jealous."

"I wasn't there."

"But you have opinions."

Her grandfather could be controlling, as she personally knew, but Rosalind didn't want to get into this. "Any man would be possessive of a woman he loved."

"And Lily was amazingly beautiful," Skelly said, gazing intently at her. "She rated scads of attention from other men. She and Noah Lang were married during the war. She used his name when she went to Hollywood, yet she kept her marriage secret. Thousands of men in the service must have been drooling over her photograph. That was no secret. How do you think it made your grandfather feel?"

"How would you feel if you were in a similar situation?"

"I've never been madly in love with a woman. What about you?"

Her voice tight with her growing tension, she tried to make light of an uncomfortable subject. "I've never been in love with a woman, either."

Skelly laughed. "Hmm, you do have a sense of humor. Great avoidance technique. But you do know what I mean."

Of course she did. And she *had* been in love before. Once. Rosalind still didn't understand her own actions, but she knew that she'd been the one to sabotage the relationship. She'd always been more comfortable keeping men at an emotional distance.

"You're being a bit personal." Part of the reason Skelly had agreed to follow up on Lily's story, she was certain. She wasn't oblivious to his interest. But she had her own agenda, one that did not include sharing anything of herself with a tabloid-television reporter. "My feelings have nothing to do with our investigation."

"Your feelings have everything to do with it." His expression turned serious. "If they didn't, you wouldn't have stormed into my office, ready to bite off my head."

"Granted."

Their food arrived. While they ate, Rosalind went over anything she'd ever heard that related to Frank Sullivan's death, but as she'd predicted, she was able to add nothing new to Skelly's information bank.

And when the check came an hour later, Rosalind insisted on paying, quickly whipping out her gold card. God forbid she let him pay, lest he think of their dinner as being more than a business meeting.

"Trying to bribe me again?" Skelly asked after the waitress disappeared.

"Making certain we understand each other," Rosalind clarified.

"I already got the picture, Roz."

"That's 'Rosalind.'"

Raising her eyebrows, she silently dared him to argue the point. He didn't. Finishing the last of his lager, he merely stared at her, his expression amused.

Or was it smug?

Rosalind was relieved when the waitress returned with her credit card and receipt.

"About little Claudia," Skelly mused as she placed the loose items in her purse. "Sometimes children are aware of more details than adults give them credit for...or want to know about.''

Rosalind's heart skipped a beat. "What are you suggesting?''

"That we pay your mother a visit.''

"When?''

"Now.''

"It's late.''

"It's not even eight-thirty," Skelly argued. "We can be in Winnetka around nine. Unless you don't want me to talk to your mother.''

"No, of course not." She ignored the feeling of uncertainty that shot through her.

"Good. I live a few blocks from here. Let's go." When she hesitated, he added, "To get my car.''

Rosalind let Skelly take the lead. For the moment, she'd lost control and would have to be satisfied going along for the ride.

WORKING ON AN UPCOMING fund-raising event for Be Kind to Kids, the charitable organization she'd helped found a dozen years before, Claudia Van Straaten was sorting through the papers strewed the length of her twenty-foot dining-room table when the doorbell rang.

Now, who could that be?

Not pleased at being interrupted, she removed her reading glasses and rose. Her view was blocked by the stained-glass panels hanging before the mullioned windows of the cathedrallike sunken dining room. A second buzz quickened her step up the three stairs to the foyer and the front door. A glance through the glass inset revealed her daughter with a stranger.

Puzzled, she swung open the heavy wooden panel. "Rosalind, did I forget you were supposed to be here tonight? Your father's not home."

"No, Mother, we didn't have anything planned."

Claudia offered her cheek for her daughter's kiss. "I must look a fright."

"You look wonderful, as usual."

Nevertheless, Claudia fingered a few loose strands of the light brown hair, precision cut into a youthful style, and wished she'd changed out of her leggings and knee-length shirt after working out. Not that she wasn't proud of her figure, as slim as a girl's. She merely liked to be presentable, especially when meeting a stranger.

"And who might this young man be?"

"His name is Skelly McKenna."

Rosalind made the pronouncement as if she should recognize the man. Claudia didn't even know any Mc-Kennas. "A new beau? How nice."

"No, Mother, he's not. We need to talk to you about something important."

Frowning, Claudia looked back on the work that was her life these days. She supposed she could spare a *few* minutes for her daughter.

"Well, let's sit for a moment, then."

Larger than the dining room, the living room was L shaped and divided into three distinct seating areas. Claudia led them to her favorite—a grouping of a couch and two chairs right outside the conservatory, whose myriad plants provided her with some distraction from her more important daily pursuits. She sat in one chair and noticed that her daughter made a point of taking the other. The young man settled in the middle of the couch.

Curiosity piqued, she asked, "What is it, then?"

Rosalind exchanged glances with her companion. "Skelly is a television reporter, Mother. You know what day today is, don't you?"

The word *reporter* sent Claudia into a tizzy. Her breath quickened even as her head went light. Of course she knew what day it was. She wasn't senile. Not that she wanted to be reminded.

"You know I try not to think of anything unpleasant," she snapped at her daughter. She glared at the dark-haired young man. "And I do not speak to reporters."

"Then talk to *me,* Mother," Rosalind begged. " 'The Whole Story' did a segment on Lily's escape from Dwight, but Skelly has agreed to do a follow-up. Something more favorable. But he needs some information."

"How would I know about her escape?"

"Not the escape," the reporter said. "The murder. The circumstances surrounding Frank Sullivan's death."

Her blood ran cold. "I couldn't tell you anything even if I wanted to."

"Wouldn't you like to see your mother's name cleared?"

"But she confessed."

"The case was never investigated," Rosalind reminded her.

"And your daughter feels there's some doubt as to her grandmother's guilt."

The room began closing in on her. Claudia tried not to panic.

"I cannot help you. I don't remember anything." She aimed an accusatory glare at her daughter. "You know that. I've told you that many times before."

"But, Mother—"

"How dare you bring this jackal into my home? Haven't I suffered enough?" Claudia's pulse was racing.

She could feel the panicky rush throughout her body. "His kind doesn't care about the truth—"

"You don't know me well enough to generalize," the reporter interrupted. "I don't make up my stories. I don't tell lies, at least not purposely. If there's more to know about the murder—something that will put things in a new light for Lily Lang—then I want to set the record straight."

"You prey on the weak. On the young, who can't defend themselves!"

"Mother!"

Claudia realized she was on the verge of ranting. She tried swallowing, but her throat muscles didn't want to cooperate. Her heart was banging painfully against her ribs...just as it did every time she thought about that horrible night more than thirty years before. She broke out into a cold sweat.

This wouldn't do. Wouldn't do at all.

Claudia took a deep, slow breath and visualized as she'd been taught to do.

Mere seconds later, under control, she said, "I'm sorry, Mr. McKenna. If Rosalind vouches for you, then of course you must be above the crowd." Though her breath was still shaky, she was feeling a bit better. More like herself. "But I simply have nothing to tell you."

He persisted. "Perhaps if we re-created the events leading up to that murder..."

Claudia's laugh was brittle. "A well-known psychiatrist prodded and probed, but he couldn't get inside my head. You're an amateur, my dear." Phantoms racing through her mind, pretending as if nothing were wrong, she stood. She gave her visitors her most practiced smile, her smoothest voice, both meant to assuage. "I am sorry, but I must get back to my work. Now. Be Kind to Kids is holding a fund-raiser next month, and I'm in charge."

"Of course you are." Her expression blank, Rosalind rose and gestured for the reporter to do the same. "I'm sorry we bothered you, Mother."

But Claudia's thoughts had already drifted back to the dining room and her proposal. She had to keep focused. Keep in mind who she was and what she was about.

Then she would remain safe from the demons of the past that had for so long threatened to smother her.

"I DID WARN YOU Mother wouldn't be able to tell you anything," Rosalind said shortly after they'd driven away from her parents' Winnetka property.

"That you did."

Though Skelly wasn't certain that her mother had been completely truthful with them. In his experience, a person often buried what he or she didn't want others to know about. And from the physical signs—changes in her respiration, pupils and skin tone—Claudia Van Straaten certainly had been hiding *something* from them.

Not that he would say as much to Roz. Not now. He needed her cooperation if he was to delve straight into the past for a journalist's dream of a story...and to get closer to the woman herself. He was beginning to think both objectives were equally important. His interest in the thirty-three-year-old murder was piqued...as was his growing attraction to Roz herself. He didn't want to put her off by sharing suspicions that might have no basis in fact.

He turned the conversation away from her mother. "I seem to remember someone else was staying in the Galena house. Your aunt Hilary."

"She wasn't home at the time of the murder."

"So she said."

He could feel Roz's gaze bore into him when she asked, "Are you naturally suspicious?"

"Suspicion is a key weapon in a journalist's arsenal."

"A famous quote?"

"A personal observation." Skelly waited a beat before pressing the issue. "So, tell me about your aunt."

"She's a warm, kind woman. A bit eccentric but completely loyal." Roz sounded defensive. "She's devoted her life to this family."

Giving Skelly the impression that she was devoted to Hilary Lang in return... and making him wonder exactly how close they were. Family loyalty. His cousin Keelin had it. So did Roz. Another thing he'd missed out on.

"So Hilary took care of *your* family rather than having one of her own?"

"Not every woman wants to marry and have children."

"What about you?"

"We're not talking about me."

"We are now."

He glanced at her. She was staring out the side window as if inspecting the properties they were passing. It was too dark to see anything beyond the pools of golden light cast by the old-fashioned street lamps. He'd pushed her buttons, and she was avoiding an answer. Because she didn't know? Or because she didn't care to share anything of herself with him?

He couldn't help himself.

"So, what about you, Roz?" he prodded, vaguely aware her answer was more important to him than it should be.

"I haven't decided."

"What's the holdup?"

"I have my reasons."

"Now you're really making me curious."

"Not suspicious?" she asked, her gaze finding him in the dark once more.

Skelly glanced her way with a rueful smile. "They do go hand in hand." He wasn't going to wring any personal confessions out of her at the moment, so he got back to business.

"Where does Aunt Hilary say she was when Frank Sullivan died?" For, if he'd come across the information in his research materials, he hadn't retained as much.

"She was out for a walk."

"At midnight?"

"Frank Sullivan died *before* midnight," she reminded him.

She was splitting hairs. "How long a walk did she take?"

Roz was beginning to sound a bit exasperated when she said, "You'd have to ask *her*."

An invitation he was eager to accept.

"Good idea. She doesn't claim any lapses in memory, does she?" He didn't have to look Roz's way to sense her immediate displeasure. "I was only asking."

"I'm sure Aunt Hilary will be happy to tell you whatever she can. She's a night owl, so we could call her when we get back to the city."

"I was thinking about talking to her in person."

"That's impossible. She lives with Grandfather in Galena—at least a three-hour drive."

"I didn't mean tonight. But I can get away tomorrow, as soon as I'm done taping. As luck would have it, I'm free for the entire holiday weekend."

"I don't know—"

He swept through her halfhearted objection. "Galena is the murder site, after all. Investigating long-distance could prove...unrewarding."

He could tell she was uncomfortable with the idea. Was she afraid of what he might learn? Or was it the thought of being alone with him so far from home? The second option both titillated and amused him.

"So, what about it?" he prompted.

"You're not thinking of taking a camera crew, are you?"

"Not now. Not until I'm certain there's reason. For the present, it'll just be you and me." To lessen the impression that he wanted to spend some time alone with her—which, of course, he did—he added, "Unless your mother wants to come along," perfectly aware that Claudia Van Straaten would never agree.

Roz seconded that notion. "I'm sure she won't. Though I will call and tell her what we're doing. After which I'd best call Grandfather. He would pitch a fit if he was the last to know what was going on. I, uh, don't know how he'll feel about a reporter coming to stay."

"Even if he knows my intentions are to help you clear his darling Lily's name?"

"That might make the difference," she admitted.

To devil her, he said, "Then again, we don't have to stay at the family homestead."

"That's right," she returned smartly. "*You* could get a motel room."

Touché.

"What's the matter, Roz...does being around me make you nervous?" he teased.

"Of course not." Her voice was tight. "Irritable, perhaps, but not nervous."

Skelly laughed. So he did have some effect on her. "That's a start."

"For what?"

"A promising relationship."

"You must be joking."

"*Working* relationship," he clarified, gratified when she shifted in her seat. "Although you never know what could come out of it. Take my friend Gary. He was partnered on an advertising campaign with the last woman in the world he wanted to work with—he and Cynthia had been rubbing each other the wrong way for months."

"And their supervisor didn't notice?"

"Their boss was taking a chance those sparks would electrify the campaign," Skelly explained. "He was absolutely correct." He thought to pull Roz's leg a bit to see where it got him. "And in the process, Gary and Cynthia found some personal electricity, as well."

"Sounds like a recipe for disaster."

"Not in their case," he fibbed. "It's five years and two kids later, and they're still in love."

"What's the point?"

"That sometimes you find the unexpected in the least likely places."

Roz smothered a choked sound but didn't come up with a return. Having finished the story with a whopper—Gary would kill him if he ever learned how he'd been defamed, for he still detested Cynthia—Skelly grinned, content to keep silent as they whipped along.

Once back in the city, he said, "I'm not a mind reader. You'll have to give me your address unless you want me to leave you at a bus stop."

Her reluctance to comply was palpable—as if he would have power over her merely because he knew where she lived.

"Don't worry," he assured her, "I'm not the type of guy who drops over whenever he feels like it."

"You wouldn't get past the doorman if you did." After a short pause, she said, "Sheridan and Diversey."

"We're almost neighbors."

Roz ignored the observation. "Tomorrow *I'll* drive."

"Uncomfortable with me at the wheel?"

"There's nothing wrong with your driving. I know the route. I know the town. I'm being practical. So I'll pick you up at the station at one sharp."

Practical, his Aunt Fanny. Biting back a retort, Skelly let her have her way. It was obvious that Rosalind Van Straaten, cosmetics heiress, was used to control, and he'd bet that trait wasn't limited to her professional life. He had a strong feeling that she didn't like surprises much. His enthusiasm for the long weekend growing, Skelly decided he'd have to teach her different, hoping that all the surprises would be pleasant ones for her, of course, and therefore pleasant for him.

He'd never met anyone quite like Roz. Not that he hadn't been with his share of beautiful women. Smart ones, too. But something more—her complexity, the challenge she represented—set her apart from the others. And then there was the family loyalty that reminded him of Keelin.

Enough reasons to want to know Roz better, Skelly decided, even if the investigation turned out to be a bust.

Chapter Three

"Yesterday we updated you on the thirtieth anniversary of the Blond Temptress's escape from the Dwight Correctional Center for Women," Skelly said at the close of Friday's show. "As a result, I received a tip that, contrary to her voluntary confession, Lily Lang was innocent of state senator Frank Sullivan's murder."

He turned to his close-up camera.

"I plan on investigating this claim firsthand. If there's a story, I'll find it," he promised. "And *whatever* I learn about Frank Sullivan's untimely death, you'll get it here, on 'The Whole Story,' next week. Stay tuned."

Skelly froze until he got the all-clear signal from the floor director. The first taping of the morning complete, he relaxed. The show would air early that afternoon—he'd already be on the way to Galena with Roz.

A sound man removed his wireless microphone, and as Skelly rose, he stripped off his suit jacket and loosened his tie. He'd have to change for the second program. As was typical in the industry, he never wore the same clothing on camera twice.

"Good show, people," came the director's voice over the studio speaker. "Go mainline some caffeine."

Knowing he had an hour before they began taping Monday's show, Skelly headed for his office, where he could relax in private and do some thinking about the long weekend ahead. He hadn't been able to get Roz out of his mind for more than a few minutes at a time. He grinned when he thought of her reaction to the nickname that suited her better than the prissy-sounding "Rosalind." Truth be known, he'd been walking around with a smile all morning. He couldn't remember when he'd looked forward with such enthusiasm to seeing a woman—even though this one wasn't exactly under his spell.

The challenge definitely excited him.

"Hey, Skelly, wait up."

The research assistant he'd grabbed first thing that morning ran after him, waving a sheaf of papers.

"Results so soon? I'm impressed."

An attractive young woman right out of journalism school, Heidi was more ambitious than most. Skelly could always count on her to get what he needed.

"Frank Sullivan wasn't exactly a retiring politician," she said. "He seemed to thrive on photo ops. I found more than a dozen articles covering his political activities in the months before his death." She handed him the fruits of her research. "Hope this helps."

"It's a start. I'll probably need more."

"I'm with you. I'll be in town all weekend. My business card's right there," she said, indicating that she'd clipped it to the top of the stack. "I scribbled my home phone number on the back. Feel free to call any time."

Skelly had the distinct impression that Heidi would welcome his call . . . business or not. "I may have to take you up on that."

Before he could retreat, she said, "Hey, congratulations on the prime-time spot."

"I don't have the inside track yet."

"You will. I have a feeling this story is going to push you right over the top. And, uh, when you do get the promotion, I assume you can hand pick your staff...."

"*If* any of this happens, I'll keep you in mind."

"Thanks." With a thousand-watt smile, Heidi backed off, her gaze glued to his face.

Skelly turned away, his mind already on the possibilities in hand.

A few minutes later, settled in his office, sucking up some strong black coffee, he scanned the headlines, looking for any topic that might jump out at him. Sullivan had been involved in the usual stuff.

Budget...school crisis...zoning.

Heidi had been right about the photo-opportunity thing. Sullivan's good-looking mug highlighted nearly every article. One picture particularly caught Skelly's attention—the state senator accompanied by one of his aides, who looked oddly familiar. Skelly remembered using a similar shot of the two of them in yesterday's broadcast. But the sense of recognition went beyond that.

Skimming the story for a name to go with the youthful face, he did a double take when he found it: *Walt Rogowski.* No wonder the young aide looked so familiar. Having been a state senator for more than twenty years, Rogowski had retired from politics a while back, supposedly to concentrate on his law practice. No one had been much surprised when he'd announced his candidacy for the upcoming gubernatorial election.

So the would-be governor of Illinois had gotten his start with Frank Sullivan, Skelly mused, quickly putting pieces together. Rogowski had been working for the state senator at the time of his demise. And within a half-dozen years, he'd taken over Sullivan's old seat.

A fact that was definitely of interest.

On impulse, Skelly grabbed the phone and punched in his father's home number. Currently a U.S. congressman, Raymond McKenna had been involved in politics since emigrating from the old sod.

"Top of the morning," came the familiar voice with its slight Irish lilt.

"Dad, it's Skelly."

"Ah, boyo—calling about your cousin's wedding?"

"Actually I need some help with a story I'm working on."

Something he'd never before thought of asking of his father. But, as much as he disliked running up against his only parent's disapproval, Skelly knew that his father might have—or be able to get—an inside track through his political cronies.

"And what might that be?"

"What do you know about Frank Sullivan's murder?"

A short pause was followed by his father's denial. "Probably not as much as you do, I'm guessing. I was barely off the boat from Eire when the man died."

Then he did know something, Skelly figured. And for some reason, was reluctant to get into it.

"I was born in 1963, the same year Sullivan died. That means you'd been here for a year, Dad. Weren't you working for the ward committeeman?"

"Aye. Running errands. I didn't have a say in any of the party's doings, especially those outside the city. I never even met Frank Sullivan."

"But I'm sure you kept your ears open between running errands. Scandals don't die as easily as a man. Being that you hung out with Sullivan's colleagues, I thought you might have picked up on the talk...."

"You mean rumors? Sensationalism is *your* business, not mine."

Skelly's hand clenched around the receiver. He should be used to that critical tone after thirty-three years— nothing he did ever met his father's exacting standards—but the old man still had the power to wound him.

"There's usually a basis to rumors," he said more calmly than he was feeling. "I don't report anything that I can't check out."

"I haven't so much as heard the man's name in decades," his father insisted. "Not until you dragged it out on your program."

Skelly started. He hadn't been aware his father even watched his show. He'd never admitted as much before.

"What about Walt Rogowski?"

An uncomfortable pause was followed by his father's "What does Rogowski have to do with your story?"

"Maybe nothing. He was working for Sullivan at the time of his death, though. He had to know what the senator was up to...who his enemies were."

"If he'll tell you."

"What? You don't think he's honest?"

"Now, you wouldn't be hearing that from me, boyo."

A roundabout confirmation, Skelly realized. "Listen, I know you've got to have party loyalty, but—"

"In truth, I can't fathom why the party is supporting Rogowski for governor."

His father's statement put Skelly on alert. "You don't like him, do you?"

"A man doesn't need to like everyone he works with."

"Why? What do you know?"

"Nothing that has to do with Sullivan's murder. Now, about your cousin's wedding—I've agreed to give her away, and I hear you're to be the best man."

Frustrated but knowing he wasn't going to get anything more from his father at the moment, Skelly caved in and let him change the subject. Congressman Raymond McKenna was obviously impressed with his niece. More impressed than he was with his own son, Skelly realized bitterly.

His mind only half on the conversation, he was relieved when a production assistant poked her head in the office and asked him to report to wardrobe. He promised his father he'd call when he got back to town.

And wondered if Walt Rogowski still called Galena home.

Before leaving his office, he called Heidi and asked her to find out.

ROSALIND HAD TAKEN this route to Galena so many times she could practically drive it blindfolded. All except for the last stretch, that was, when the flat land and boring straight road suddenly exploded into rolling green hills and dangerous curves that engaged all her senses.

"Almost like we've been transported out of Illinois," Skelly commented.

"That's the way I feel about this corner of the state. And this is my favorite part of the drive . . . as long as it's daylight."

"The dark scares you?"

"No, but the fog does. And there's plenty of it around here at night."

Rosalind shifted back to second as her Thunderbird rolled through a big dip and down an incline. Even so, a little thrill shot through her, and she had to keep herself in check so she didn't throw caution to the wind and accelerate as she felt like doing. She sensed it would behoove her to remain cautious in all things while she was around Skelly McKenna.

"What else scares you?" he suddenly asked.

She could feel his gaze on her, but she wouldn't give him the satisfaction of acknowledging that awareness.

"Getting too complacent." Not wanting to give him an opening to interrogate her as he seemed wont to do at every opportunity, she took the offensive. "Isn't your family going to miss you this weekend?"

"My sister always moans about our not spending more holiday time together, but she'll be with her mother's people." He clarified, "Aileen is my *half* sister."

"At least you have a sibling. Being an only child isn't all it's cracked up to be."

"Two siblings, actually. We have a half brother, as well—same father, yet another mother. Donovan never particularly cared for me or Aileen."

Or Skelly for Donovan—that implication was clear. "What about your parents?"

"My mother died when I was born. Dad has always suspected it was my fault."

A revealing statement, Rosalind thought. "Sorry."

"Not as sorry as I am."

Always having known she was well loved by her father, grandfather and great-aunt—even by her mother, who was too-often withdrawn—Rosalind really did feel a little sorry for Skelly. He made it sound as if he'd never had a sense of family or the kind of closeness that had prompted her to do something about his Blond Temptress story. If the day spa had been her only concern, she might have let it alone.

"So, do you use your job to fill in the blank spaces?"

"Spaces in what?"

"Your life."

"What makes you think there are any?"

"You don't exactly have a big, loving family. You're not married." Or so she assumed. "You're not, are you?"

"Not at present."

"Divorced?"

"I've never been so much as tempted."

But he was staring at her again, in a way that made the delicate skin along her neck bump. She couldn't help but be reminded of the story he'd spun the night before. His telling her about Gary and Cynthia turning negative sparks into positive wasn't reassuring.

A bit agitated, she said, "So, no serious lady, either. What's left?"

"Friends."

"You spend a lot of time with them? Doing what?"

"Suddenly you're awfully interested in *my* personal life. Am I missing something here?"

"I'm merely trying to have a normal conversation."

"Or maybe you think I'm the most fascinating man you've ever met," he suggested in a low voice that sent her hormones scrambling.

Rosalind sniffed. "Don't flatter yourself."

"Challenging, then."

She didn't disagree.

Skelly's smothered laughter got to her. Rosalind glanced his way, was caught for a second by the sparkle in his blue eyes. His wicked grin sent a flush straight through her. His dimpled cheek invited her to reach out and connect with him. She forced her gaze back to the road just in time to take another switchback curve.

"I once read a story about a woman who was a lot like you," Skelly said.

"How so?"

"She was beautiful, smart, talented. Kept herself busy all the time so she didn't have to deal with her *real* problems."

Annoyed at the last, Rosalind said, "That doesn't sound like me at all." Did it? Hesitating only a moment, she asked, "What problems?"

"Distrust. Fear. Loneliness."

"Definitely not me."

"You are *definitely* distrustful," he argued. "And everyone has secret fears."

She tried turning the tables on him. "So what are yours?"

But he wasn't biting. "And everyone is lonely at times, some more than others."

She wondered if he was thinking of her ... or of himself. No mother. Distant father. A half sister whose loyalties were split between two households. She imagined his spending too much time by himself.

Certain he would never admit to being lonely, she asked, "So how did the woman's story end?"

"She met a man—"

"—who solved all her problems?" She should have figured where he was going with this.

"Who was there for her when she needed him. She grew to trust him, count on him. Her fears grew less important. And as she let herself grow closer to him ... become attached ... her life felt fuller. More satisfying."

Now, why did this story sound like something Skelly made up? Did he really think she'd see herself in this fictitious woman and open up to him? She wouldn't put it past him to try a head trip on her.

Rosalind glanced his way, expecting that he would be smirking at her, but to her surprise, his expression was quite serious. Thoughtful. A strange feeling she couldn't identify shot through her, leaving her a little breathless. She swallowed hard and tried concentrating on the road ahead.

Skelly McKenna confused her. When she'd stormed into his office, she'd assumed he was arrogant and unscrupulous. Now she suspected he was far more complex than the cliché tabloid reporter she'd expected. She shouldn't like him, didn't want to like him, but it seemed her rational self had no say in the matter. Despite her initial animosity toward him, Skelly was getting to her on a very primal level, something she couldn't seem to control.

A fact that made Rosalind decidedly edgy.

GALENA WAS A HILLY TOWN divided by a ribbon of river. At the foot of one of the steepest inclines, Roz turned onto busy Main Street, where couples strolled hand in hand and parents rushed their children along.

"Tourists are already out in full force for the holiday," Skelly said, noting the decorations—bunting and flags galore.

"It's pretty much like this every summer weekend. I'm going to stop at the drugstore before heading up to the house. Need anything?"

"Not that I can think of." When she pulled into a parking spot, he said, "I'll stay here to make a call." He fetched his cellular phone from his briefcase. "Handy little things."

"Personally I wouldn't have one. Life is already too rushed and stressful. So you'll be here?"

"Or browsing shop windows."

"Don't go too far."

"I don't think I can get lost."

"I meant that I'll only be a minute."

Remembering the exchange in his office, Skelly arched his brows and checked his watch in challenge.

"Oh, for heaven's sake! Do you have to take things so literally?"

She left the car, slipped a coin into the meter and hurried toward the drugstore. Grinning as he watched her progress, he realized she turned a few heads—no doubt because of her stunning looks.

Skelly called his voice mail at work. Only one message—something he could handle next week.

He decided to browse.

Strolling down the street, he admired the refurbished buildings which were home to shops selling antiques, art, jewelry and souvenirs. He'd visited Galena before, and so he was acquainted with its history. Galena once had been a major commercial center, fortunes amassed in the 1840s through mining, smelting and steamboating. Ulysses S. Grant and eight other Union generals of the Civil War had called the area home. Then, with the arrival of the railroad and the Galena River becoming silted in from soil erosion, the town declined. By the turn of the century, Galena suffered complete economic shock. Only over the past few decades had the charming town recovered, renovated and become a popular tourist spot.

Skelly stopped before a window display that attracted him. Yesterday's Treasures offered intricately designed old jewelry and other accessories—painted fans, beaded bags, lace gloves—laid out in charming disarray across the top of a mirrored vanity of inlaid wood. Wondering if Roz ever wore such trinkets, he realized he was being scrutinized. He looked up.

Several yards behind the plate-glass window, a rugged man with craggy features crowned by a too-obvious toupee stared at him intently. But the moment their gazes meshed, the other man turned his attention back to his clipboard. Skelly assumed he was the owner in search of a potential customer.

"There you are," Roz said, sounding breathless. "You lose."

"It's been more than a minute."

"That's because I had to come looking for you." She was stuffing a small paper bag into her purse. "Ready to go?"

Though he could stand there indefinitely fencing with her, Skelly nodded. And as they walked off, he glanced back into the antique shop. The owner was staring at them.

Once back in the car, he asked Roz, "How much time do you spend in Galena?"

"Not all that much—I haven't had the time since I was a kid. I always manage a weekend here and there, though. I know the town pretty well, if not many of the people."

A few minutes later, they were overlooking Main Street from the intersection of Hill and High. Below rose several church steeples and dozens of homes in a variety of old styles, including Greek Revival, Federal and Italianate.

"We're here," Roz said, turning into a diagonal parking space at the foot of another incline below Lang House.

Skelly alighted from the Thunderbird, beating her to the open trunk. He lifted both their bags and climbed the stepped walkway, Roz quickly catching up. He admired the mansion's Queen Anne architecture, the cream, rose and federal blue trim of the wraparound porch, windows and turret, as well as the stained-glass and beveled windows. Even though the structure was mostly brick rather than wood, Skelly thought the finishing touches made Lang House a "painted lady" in the very best tradition.

As his foot hit the top step, Skelly said, "You're certain I'm welcome to stay here."

"Grandfather and Aunt Hilary are expecting you."

Which sounded like an evasion. He figured the elderly brother and sister had agreed only under pressure from Roz. That made him uncomfortable, but he knew he didn't have much choice of where to bunk, considering this was a holiday weekend. Roz had said something about the town's tourist facilities being maxed out.

Before they could cross the porch, the front door swung open to reveal a short, generously rounded woman who squealed in delight as she flew to greet them. "Rosalind!" She threw her arms around her much taller grand-niece for a big hug.

Skelly could hardly believe Hilary Lang was in her late sixties. Her warm brown hair with its scattered threads of gray was pulled back in a modern twist from a barely lined, still-pretty face. He found no clouding in the alert blue eyes that turned to inspect him.

Her arm slipping possessively around the older woman's shoulders, Roz said, "Aunt Hilary, this is Skelly McKenna. Skelly, my aunt Hilary."

"How nice to meet you. What a fine-looking young man." Hilary gave Roz an arch look. "About time you got some sense into that hard head of yours and found an interesting man to keep you stimulated."

"Aunt Hilary, I told you—"

"I know. I know. You're here to do research." Her forehead creased. "Well, what are we doing standing out on the porch when I've put the kettle on for some tea?"

Hilary scurried inside, Roz following, Skelly bringing up the rear. He left their bags at the foot of the stairs and followed the women through the antique-filled foyer and dining room. As he went, he glanced into both front and back parlors, wondering which had been the crime scene.

"What would you like with your tea?" Hilary asked Skelly when he entered the modernized kitchen. She was already pulling mugs from a wooden tree. "Cookies or scones?"

"You don't need to go to any trouble."

"Pish-tosh. I enjoy doing for others."

"A scone sounds great, then." In truth, Skelly's stomach was growling, since Roz had shown up before he had a chance to grab lunch.

"Rosalind?"

"Have I ever turned down your homemade scones?"

Hilary put three in the toaster oven to warm.

"Where's Grandfather?"

"Your guess is as good as mine, honey. We watched 'The Whole Story' after lunch." Hilary turned her bright-eyed gaze on Skelly. "After you divulged that you were following up on the murder and that you would share *whatever* information you found with your viewers, Noah was seething."

Skelly noticed Hilary herself didn't appear any too happy.

"Skelly, you didn't!"

He turned to find Roz glaring at him. "That's what you wanted from me—to do a follow-up piece on your grandmother. Isn't it?"

"You didn't have to make some big announcement that'll have people salivating for the details beforehand." She sucked in her breath. "Not to mention the press. We don't need them descending on us and interfering."

Suspecting her problem really was that, if what they found wasn't to her liking, Roz might not want him doing a follow-up after all, he said, "I doubt you have anything to worry about with the press at this point."

"Really. I was worried about *you* after I turned down your assistant's request for an interview. And I was right, wasn't I?"

Unable to argue with her logic, Skelly didn't try.

"Grandfather is all right, isn't he?" Roz asked, forehead furrowed.

"I'm certain he is," her great-aunt reassured her. "But he's in one of his moods. He raced out of here, mumbling to himself. Hasn't even called to tell me what time he'll be home for supper."

Hilary set the mugs, small plates and a pot of tea in the center of the table. "So, how long have you two kids known each other?"

"I met your charming niece yesterday."

"She is charming," Hilary agreed. "Smart. And a knockout. You could do worse."

"Aunt Hilary!"

Skelly smothered a grin at her obvious matchmaking.

Hilary ignored her niece's outrage. "If there's anything you want to know about Rosalind, feel free to ask me," she continued, fetching fresh lemon, a pitcher of cream and an assortment of preserves from the refrigerator. "I raised her, you know."

"You did?" It was the first he'd heard of it.

"I mean, I helped Claudia," Hilary quickly amended. "For years, we all lived in the Winnetka house together—Noah and me, Claudia, Rip and Rosalind. I know my niece's faults, as well as her virtues, though the virtues outweigh everything else, of course."

"Can we change the subject?" Roz pleaded.

Skelly noted she was avoiding looking at him.

Hilary sighed. "If we must."

"My aunt is a confirmed romantic," Roz muttered through her teeth.

"What's wrong with that?" Skelly whispered. "She's very sweet. Besides, I wouldn't mind hearing more about those faults of yours."

Her blue eyes widened and connected with his. A becoming flush stole up her neck. Skelly decided he liked putting her off balance.

As if Roz could read his mind, she muttered, "Oh, stuff it!"

Clucking to herself, Hilary fetched the scones from the toaster oven and joined them at the table. For a few moments, everyone concentrated on the refreshments. Pouring tea. Preparing their scones. Skelly took a big bite and washed it down with hot Earl Grey. His complaining stomach thanked him profusely.

He noticed that, while Hilary went through the motions, she didn't put a thing to her mouth.

"So, you really think you can find some evidence to exonerate Lily at this late date?" she asked.

She was running her forefinger around and around the rim of her mug as if she were bothered by something.

"At least to cast some doubt on the verdict," Roz chimed in.

"What do you think?" Skelly asked the older woman. "Was Lily telling the truth when she confessed?"

"My sister-in-law might have been a lot of things, but to my knowledge, she was not a liar."

Hilary was hedging . . . and something in her eyes put Skelly on alert. He wondered what she meant by *a lot of things*. "What were you doing staying in Lily's house?"

"Lily's house? Oh, no. Noah bought and renovated this place after he came back from the war front. Lily'd had a difficult time here as a girl, and Noah wanted the people in her past to sit up and take notice of what she'd become. She visited once, made a big splash, then didn't feel the need to return . . . not until years later when she wanted some distance from her marriage. At any rate, after he and Lily were reunited, Noah didn't need me the way he used to."

"So you moved from Winnetka to Galena."

"Why not? There was no room for me in Lily's household. Figuratively speaking. She was still the star Hollywood made her even if she had retired from moviemaking. Besides, I loved it here."

Roz said, "So you were living here permanently when Lily left Grandfather," as if she hadn't realized it before.

Hilary nodded. "And I stayed through all of her comings and goings, dragging that poor child with her, when she couldn't make up her mind about the divorce. I only moved back to Winnetka afterward."

Skelly mulled over the information that was new to him, duly noting the undercurrent of animosity Hilary had for her sister-in-law. Roz had told him that after Noah's retirement, he'd insisted on moving to Galena— to be closer to Lily's memory—and Hilary had naturally accompanied him. She'd never mentioned her great-aunt's love of the place, possibly because Hilary never had revealed it before. How curious.

And the fact that Hilary moved from Winnetka to Galena because of Lily, then back to Winnetka after Lily was incarcerated, said a lot about their relationship. Skelly figured Hilary couldn't have been too happy when her sister-in-law chose to invade what she must have thought of as *her* territory.

He backtracked a bit. "So Lily was poor before she met Noah?"

Hilary nodded. "And a bit wild, or she never would have gone to Hollywood while he was off fighting a war. Small-town people don't approve of wild."

And Skelly had the distinct feeling that Hilary included herself in the consensus. "What do you remember about the night Frank Sullivan died?"

"I made dinner for me and Claudia while Frank and Lily ate at a restaurant in town. After Claudia went upstairs to bed, I took a long walk. She *was* thirteen and very mature," Hilary added, as if she'd received criticism from someone about leaving the girl alone.

"Why a 'long' walk?"

"I had some thinking to do." Her voice quavered. "About personal things. I didn't return until after the sheriff's men arrived."

Skelly wondered. Hilary now had a death grip on her mug. Because the memory of what she'd found was so upsetting? Or could there be something more? . . .

"Did you notice anything unusual?" he asked. "Out of place?"

"I didn't *usually* have a dead body sprawled over my parlor floor—"

A thunderous voice interrupted. "What's going on here? Why are you giving my sister the third degree?"

Skelly turned to the doorway as Roz shot out of her chair.

"Grandfather, there you are!" She stood on tiptoe to kiss his weathered cheek.

While Hilary looked younger than sixty-something, Skelly decided Noah Lang looked every bit of seventy-five. White haired. Old-age thin. A back too stiff to be natural. Arthritic hands.

But continuing to be the focus of Noah's angry glare, Skelly knew not to underestimate the power of this man, no matter his advanced years.

"WE'RE DOING ONLY WHAT we came to do," Skelly said, rising. "I thought you were in agreement."

Noah tightened his jaw. He never would have agreed to anything if Rosalind hadn't been so convincing. She'd assured him she and that so-called newsman would research other people who'd known Frank Sullivan to see if they could dig up possible suspects or motives for his murder. Rosalind said all she wanted was to place reasonable doubt in the minds of Skelly McKenna's audience if not in the authorities. How could he have refused her without arousing her suspicions?

"I didn't agree to a circus, young man, and that's what you're turning this story into. We've already been through that once."

"You're being unfair, sir. All I did was alert my viewers that I was taking another look into the facts."

"Bah!" Noah waved Skelly off. "Sensationalism is sensationalism. I should have known better."

"Grandfather, Skelly did agree to research the story personally on my urging." His granddaughter looked up at him with a worried expression. "I thought that would make you happy."

"The only thing that'll make me happy is having my darling Lily at my side for whatever little time I have left on this earth."

"If we can find the real killer, that might be possible," the reporter said. "That is...*if* she's actually innocent."

"You can count on that. Lily never killed anyone, no matter what foolishness she spouted."

A pang of regret stabbed Noah in the heart for the millionth time. He hadn't had his wits about him or he wouldn't have gone along with it. He would have figured some other way out. He never should have let Lily plead guilty.

He never should have let her be locked up for something that he knew she hadn't done.

Chapter Four

Rosalind hoped she hadn't made a mistake in pursuing the past, that her convincing Skelly to investigate wouldn't cause her grandfather more heartache than if she'd ignored his story about Lily. They got through an early dinner in a civilized manner. Taking her lead in keeping the conversation away from the reason they were here, Skelly kept to questions about the Galena area. He might have been a curious tourist.

Afterward they gathered in the front parlor...the scene of the crime.

Rosalind had never found anything sinister about the room, perhaps because, shortly after the murder, her great-aunt had ordered it stripped and totally redecorated. The room had been repainted since, but not much else had changed, at least not that she could remember. Nearly forty years old and reminiscent of a much earlier era, the cream, blue and rose decor remained timelessly elegant.

Her grandfather sat in the wing chair closest to the fireplace, which could only be fueled by coal. Skelly made himself comfortable in the matching chair, while she and her great-aunt shared the couch facing both men.

And within a matter of seconds, Rosalind saw Skelly change from affable guest to dogged reporter.

"We need to get back to the reason we're here," he told her grandfather. "If you really believed Lily didn't murder Sullivan, did you try to convince her to change her story?"

Bony hands gripping the arms of his chair, Noah said, "She was utterly determined in her path."

"Did she give you a reason for killing him?"

"No."

"My grandmother never explained her actions to anyone," Rosalind said.

"Because she didn't do it!"

"Noah, calm down," Hilary pleaded. "You know too much excitement isn't good for you."

"Bah!"

Her great-aunt's warning sent a renewed wave of worry washing through Rosalind. Her grandfather put on a good show, but she wasn't sure he was as healthy as he would like people to believe. He'd retired not because he was unable to run Temptress, but because he'd had a heart attack. A mild one, but who knew how serious the next one could be.

"Grandfather, we're on your side." At least, she was. Skelly was a loose cannon, though she wouldn't say so in front of her elderly relatives. "Please remember that. We need your help if we're ever going to get to the truth."

She noticed her grandfather's fingers tightened around the chair arms.

And Skelly continued, "You obviously still cared for your wife even though she was determined to divorce you."

"I *loved* Lily. I'll love her until the day I die."

"Then surely you hired a private investigator in an effort to clear her name."

"No."

"I don't understand. You're a man of means—"

"Lily didn't want me to interfere. She insisted I leave well enough alone."

"But a man in love would go to any lengths to prove his lady innocent."

"A man respects the wishes of the woman he loves."

The line of questioning was making Rosalind uneasy. This wasn't like her grandfather. He'd bullied her into line often enough while she was growing up. He never gave up when he wanted something. And more than anything, he'd wanted his Lily....

Attempting to turn the conversation in a less disturbing direction, she asked, "Is there someone in particular you suspected of the crime?"

"I wasn't here much, so I didn't know many of the locals. But it could be anyone," her grandfather said. "Political enemies. Someone in Sullivan's own party who was jealous of him. And then there's the widow."

Hilary quickly added, "Diane Sullivan remarried real fast, a few months after the trial—Perry Nesmith, antique-shop owner. They still run the shop together. A person could get the impression Diane didn't grieve at all for her husband's death. Then again, if she knew Frank wasn't faithful to her..."

"Why should she be loyal to him?" Rosalind finished.

Skelly asked her great-aunt, "Were there any signs of a break-in that night?"

"None. Most of the windows were open, but that wasn't anything unusual."

Rosalind looked at the bay windows that were even now wide open. "Was there a screen missing?"

"All of them. The man I occasionally hired to do chores kept promising to put them up, but he never got around to it."

"Open windows. No screens. Easy entry and exit." Skelly ticked off the points on his fingers and nodded. "That gives us opportunity for practically anyone. By the way, Mr. Lang, when did you arrive on the scene?"

"Got into Galena first thing in the morning. A little after six."

"That was approximately a half-dozen hours after the body was discovered. Fast work. Who put the call in to you?"

Rosalind shifted. What was Skelly's point?

"The sheriff, of course."

"In the middle of the night?"

"I *was* still her husband." Noah rose. "If you have no other questions . . ."

For a moment, Rosalind thought Skelly was going to object. Then his expression changed subtly. "They can wait."

"I'll come up with you, Noah."

And Rosalind couldn't help but note the subtle change in her great-aunt as Hilary joined her brother . . . almost as if she were nervous about something.

"Before you go," Skelly said as they moved to the doorway. "It's not too late to visit the widow if one of you can give us the Nesmith address."

"As far as I know, they still live in the limestone mansion Frank Sullivan bought for Diane shortly before his death," Hilary said. "On the other side of Route 20." She gave them directions if not an exact address.

"We'll find it," Rosalind assured her great-aunt.

She fetched her purse, and a few minutes later, they were on their way.

"So what do you expect we'll get out of Diane Nesmith?" she asked Skelly once they were in the Thunderbird, with her behind the wheel again.

"Information about any cronies who might have been jealous or had a grudge against Sullivan."

"If she remembers after all this time. Besides, he may not have brought his work home with him."

"If nothing else . . . a reaction."

She pulled the car out of the parking spot and nosed it south. "More than thirty years later?"

"Trust me. If she's been hiding anything, her nerves will tell."

His statement sent yet another wave of uneasiness through Rosalind. Surely Aunt Hilary wouldn't hide anything from her. Nor would Grandfather. Going over their every reaction to the situation since they'd arrived that afternoon, she wasn't focused on her driving.

"A Stop sign."

She stomped the brake pedal, which had more give than usual. The car slid to a stop in the middle of the intersection.

"I guess you shouldn't have bothered."

"We should have stopped sooner." Accelerating, Rosalind glanced at the dash. "The brake light is on. I must be a little low on fluid."

"I assume gas stations are open this late, even in a small burg like this one."

"You're not worrying about your safety in my hands, are you?" she joked.

"If I was actually *in* your hands . . ."

A glance at Skelly made Rosalind flush. He was leering at her, but the sparkle in his eyes told her he was teasing. Or was he? Conscious of his continuing gaze on her, she noted they were approaching the next Stop sign.

She stepped on the brake, but the pressure on the pedal diminished. It seemed like forever before they came to a complete stop. Still, she was confident that she could get as far as the gas station on Route 20, or she never would have accelerated again.

Her mistake.

The rest of the ride was downhill all the way, the incline one of the steepest in Galena. From a distance, she saw another vehicle's lights sweep the cross street. She applied her brakes in what she hoped was plenty of time.

Her foot went straight to the floor.

And rather than slowing, the Thunderbird picked up speed on the downward pitch.

"Omigod! The brakes are gone!"

She stomped on the pedal hard, to no avail. Her only reward was a sharp twinge across her foot and ankle.

"Throw the car into a lower gear," Skelly said more calmly than she was feeling.

Rosalind shifted into first. The other vehicle came to a stop at the intersection. The Thunderbird bucked, slowed a bit, but kept right on rolling.

"Don't move. Don't move!" she implored. As if she were close enough for the other driver to hear.

"Whatever you do, don't panic," Skelly said grimly.

But now Rosalind could see that the small car held a woman and several kids. A sick feeling filled her. The other vehicle crept into the intersection. Even in first, the Thunderbird accelerated because of the steep grade.

"Oh, get moving, please!"

She flashed her brights rapidly. Like a wild animal mesmerized by the unexpected, the other car stopped dead, the driver staring their way. And Rosalind's short life flashed through her mind. She yanked the wheel and swerved to the right. As if goosed, the other car suddenly shot off. The Thunderbird cleared its tail by inches.

Screaming voices followed her.

"You did it." Skelly placed a hand on her thigh and squeezed. "Now keep your head and we'll be all right."

Hard to do when they were shooting down the steep grade, the speedometer still climbing.

"The emergency brake," she muttered.

"We're going too fast."

"Tell me about it. What choice do I have?"

Stomach churning, her left foot found the emergency-brake pedal. She shoved down hard. Again the Thunderbird lurched and slowed. Then a heavy metallic smell permeated the car, and the great *thunk* that followed, accompanied by another lurch, told her the cable had snapped. Though the hill was leveling out to flat ground, the Thunderbird's speed was barely affected.

"Damn!" Straight ahead at the end of the incline, she could see bright lights and traffic. Her adrenaline shot up another notch. "The highway!"

"You can do this."

Skelly was no longer trying to disguise his anxiety. Rosalind had the distinct suspicion that more than anything in the world, he wished he could take control of the car as easily as he had her. She gave him credit that he didn't try to wrest the steering wheel from her grip.

"I'll turn right and aim for the shoulder," she told him.

"Good thinking."

To give herself the best shot possible, she steered into the opposing traffic's lane. Sweat prickled her skin, and her stomach twisted itself into a big, fat knot.

The highway fast approached.

Trying to breathe normally, Rosalind inched the wheel to the right, nosing the Thunderbird at an angle across the street so the abrupt turn wouldn't be so sharp. Close enough to hear the highway traffic, she chanced a quick look over her shoulder. An eighteen-wheeler whizzed by. The next vehicle appeared to be some distance behind.

"You've got enough room to maneuver," Skelly confirmed.

As the Thunderbird's nose shot across the stop line, she aimed for the shoulder and, because she couldn't slow down, prayed they wouldn't take the turn on two wheels.

"You've almost got it," Skelly said, voice tight.

The car careered around the corner, then straddled the line dividing the right lane from the shoulder. The flat ground being in their favor, their speed decreased discernibly. Rosalind checked her rearview mirror and noticed the driver of the fast-approaching vehicle was flashing his brights as he closed in on her. A little fancy steering, and the Thunderbird weaved a bit... then settled onto the shoulder just in time.

"Thank you," she whispered, suddenly drained.

A pickup shot by them, horn blasting repeatedly, driver leaning toward the passenger side to aim an obscene gesture her way. Anger added to fear, Rosalind wished she could tell him what he could do with himself.

"Idiot!" Skelly muttered.

A small incline cut their speed even more. She threw the transmission into Neutral. Within seconds, the Thunderbird was barely rolling, so she shifted into Park. They jerked to a stop.

"We made it. Thank God."

She cut the engine. Then, both hands gripping the wheel, heart in her throat, she tried to get her breath.

"Good driving, Roz." Skelly sounded like himself again. "Ever think of turning pro?"

Considering the hilly, winding approach to Galena that always tempted her to let it all out, she returned, "Not anymore."

Adrenaline leaving her in a rush, her head suddenly spinning, her body hot and clammy, Rosalind rested her forehead against the steering wheel. A wave of nausea washed through her, and she had to keep taking deep breaths and swallowing hard so she wouldn't lose it.

"Hey, you okay?" Skelly asked.

Rosalind heard his seat-belt release and was aware of his scooting closer. "I'm trying not to be sick," she groaned.

He reached across her and released both her seat belt and door. Turning her shoulders toward the opening, he said, "Get it over with and you'll feel better."

His touch calming, she was starting to feel better already. The nausea was receding as quickly as it had come over her. "I'll be all right."

"You're shaking."

Skelly pulled her to him and gathered her in his arms. She wasn't even tempted to push at him and move away. The experience had jolted the sense out of her, she supposed. She allowed her body rather than her head to do the thinking. Somehow, leaning on Skelly—a man she wouldn't normally give the time of day—seemed right.

He stroked her hair, rubbed her neck, trailed his hand down her spine. She nestled closer, inhaling the scent that lingered along his jawline—after-shave mixed with a trace of fear—and wondered if he weren't holding on to her for his own comfort as much as hers.

"What a freak thing to happen," she murmured.

"Freak. Right."

But he didn't sound as if he thought so.

ALL DAY, SKELLY had wanted to get his hands on Roz, but not like this. Not because she was upset. Thank God she wasn't hurt. That neither of them had been killed. Freak occurrence? He only hoped so.

He gave her one last hug, then reluctantly released her and gazed into her shadowed face. "Nerves steady?"

"Much better."

"Unfortunately I left my cell phone at the house." He wanted some answers from a professional mechanic. "The gas station isn't too far. Can you make it?"

Roz nodded and slid to the other side, leaving Skelly feeling as if he'd misplaced some important part of himself. Upon stepping outside, she made a muffled sound and grabbed on to the door.

He popped out of the car. "What?"

"My foot." Grimacing, she faced him, closing her door in the process and leaning against the car's body. "I stomped on the brake too hard and felt kind of a zing. I guess I twisted something."

"Are you sure nothing's broken?" Skelly asked, slamming his door and rushing to her side. "Does Galena have a hospital?"

"You're getting ahead of yourself. I probably aggravated a tendon or something. I'm not going to see a doctor, when all I need is some ice."

"Still . . . you'd better wait for me here, while I go for help. The driver of the tow truck can bring you home before dealing with the Thunderbird. Don't worry, I'll stay with him and take care of everything."

He reached for the door handle, intending to help her back inside, but she put a hand on his arm.

"No. I'd rather stay with you. It isn't far. We can see the gas station from here, for heaven's sake."

Even in the dim light of the highway, he could see Roz's face. Her too-wide eyes and clenched jaw told him she was afraid to be alone. Against his better judgment, Skelly caved in.

"Stubborn woman." He snaked his arm around her waist. "At least lean on me, then."

"If you insist."

Roz shifted her weight. Skelly was aware of every soft curve pressed against him. They started walking. Rather, he walked while she limped along. Despite the hazardous situation—or perhaps because of it—he was having trouble thinking clearly and remaining alert to any other possible dangers. He was too intent on the woman at his side. She slid an arm around his shoulders and adjusted herself, drawing even closer, loose strands of her silky hair caressing his neck and cheek. Wild imaginings raced through his head—all having to do with him and Roz in some intimate situation.

"I can't believe the brakes giving out like that," she said, jolting him out of the fantasy. "Not on a vehicle that's barely a year old."

"Cars are full of surprises." Skelly kept his tone neutral. He didn't want to worry Roz until he was certain they had something to worry about. Thinking he knew how to distract her, he said, "Kind of like women."

Reacting immediately, Roz demanded, "Are you comparing me to my car?"

Skelly deliberately inspected her. "Let's see. Eye-catching detail. Long, sleek lines. Quality workmanship. Exciting when the motor's revved up." Unable to help himself, he stared down at her foot and added, "But not so perfect that you don't break down once in a while.''

Roz smacked him in the chest. "Beast." But she was smothering a smile.

Making his heart beat faster. "It could be dangerous to mistreat your crutch."

She laughed aloud, and Skelly was lost. He'd been playing games with her from the first, testing her reactions, seeing if he could get under her skin. The joke was on him. At that moment, he knew he wanted Rosalind Van Straaten too much for his own comfort.

They were nearly opposite the gas station. Skelly watched for a break in traffic, then balancing more of her weight on himself, hurried Roz across. She clung to him, nails biting into the flesh of his arm, stirring him yet again. He was glad when they reached the other side and he could all but let go of her. He couldn't take much more close contact without doing something about it.

"Hey, Limp-along, any damage?"

"No new nicknames, please. 'Roz' is bad enough."

"'Roz' suits you." Skelly pulled a face. "How much do you hate it?"

"I'm adjusting."

"Good thing, because I wasn't planning on changing my tune."

"What a surprise," she muttered as they moved beneath the station's lit canopy.

Moments later, Skelly gave Jarvis Wiggs, the owner, an abbreviated version of their plight. After aiming a puzzled look at Roz, the man immediately led them to the tow truck. Skelly helped her into the cab and slid in beside her, while Jarvis hopped up behind the wheel.

"So how long do you think it will take to fix my car?" Roz asked.

"Can't do nothing but haul it in tonight."

"Could you at least give the brakes a look?" Skelly asked. "We'd like to know the extent of the damage."

"Yup. I can do that."

Which relieved Skelly immensely. That way, he'd know if he needed to be on guard.

The tow truck nosed to the edge of the highway. A break in traffic sent them careering directly into the left lane. Skelly quickly glanced at Roz, fearing the motion would make her sick again, but she seemed to be holding up.

"You folks from around here?"

"We're visiting for a few days," Roz said, pressing her elbow into Skelly's ribs, giving him the distinct impression that she didn't want the man to know more. "We're staying with my relatives."

"Holiday weekend. Good time for a visit. From the big city, huh?"

"We had to get away."

Thunderbird in sight, Skelly said, "There's the car."

Jarvis nodded. "So it is. Be sure not to miss the Main Street parade on the morning of the Fourth. Everyone turns out for the festivities." He whipped the tow truck into a U-turn, pulling up directly in front of the Thunderbird. "Walt Rogowski will even have his own float. You know—he's running for governor. Local boy."

"So I've heard," Roz said.

Heidi had already informed Skelly that Rogowski not only still lived in Galena, but that his main campaign office was located in the heart of town. He hadn't yet shared with Roz any information he'd gathered about the man who'd begun his political career as Sullivan's aide. Now wasn't the time to do so, either.

That particular revelation could wait.

Chapter Five

Finished inspecting the Thunderbird, Jarvis wiped his greasy hands on his cover-up and lumbered toward them. Rosalind noticed his forehead was furrowed. Her stomach flip-flopped.

"Brake line was damaged."

"You mean it was cut," Skelly said, putting her even more on edge.

"More like punctured. Curious. Most of the line's still intact. You folks musta left a trail of fluid behind you."

She asked, "How exactly was it damaged?"

"Couldn't say for sure." The station owner rubbed a grimy hand through his thinning hair. "Coulda been something sharp flying off the road, I reckon."

But he didn't sound convinced, Rosalind decided. And Skelly certainly didn't *look* convinced. They both thought... She didn't want to face the truth until she and Skelly could talk privately.

"So, will you be able to fix both the brake line and the emergency tomorrow?" she asked, mind whirling with the implications.

"Your car'll be ready in the afternoon, Miss Van Straaten. Can't say what time for sure. The auto-parts store here in town don't always have stock for newer cars.

Might have to send someone over to Dubuque to get what I need.''

Rosalind nodded. "If you run into any problems, please call.'' She'd given him her grandfather's address and phone number.

"Will do.'' Jarvis nodded. "Now hop back in the truck, and I'll run you home.''

Throughout the five-minute drive, Jarvis and Skelly kept up a running dialogue, Jarvis being something of an unofficial if enthusiastic guide to his hometown.

Rosalind couldn't concentrate on their conversation. Her thoughts were spinning with the possibility that someone could have booby-trapped her brakes. Never before having been a target, she was having difficulty accepting the concept. Surely it was equally possible that no one but the fates were responsible.

Wasn't it?

When Jarvis stopped the tow truck in front of Lang House, he peered out at the mansion a moment, then stared at her intently, his bushy eyebrows arched in surprise. She figured he now knew who she was—and probably was doing some quick calculating. Hopefully he wasn't on the local grapevine, or the entire town would hear about the incident by morning.

And they barely had started their investigation.

Rosalind wished she dare ask the gas-station owner to keep whatever he knew or assumed to himself lest he set off warning bells among the very people she and Skelly meant to question. Forewarned was forearmed, after all, and Galena was a small town. Undoubtedly more than a few of its citizens watched "The Whole Story.'' If people figured out what they were up to in advance, they might close ranks and shut her and Skelly out.

In the end, she merely said, "Thanks for the lift," and with Skelly's help, slid out of the truck.

"See you tomorrow." With a wave, Jarvis drove off.

Rosalind limped up the sidewalk, Skelly's arm again supporting her. The house was dark, and she guessed both her grandfather and great-aunt were asleep. She pulled keys from her trouser pocket and unlocked the door.

As they stepped inside, she announced, "I need a stiff drink."

"What you need is ice."

"That, too."

They proceeded to the rear parlor, where the liquor was kept. She turned on a small table lamp with a lovely stained-glass shade. Golden light pooled around them. Enough for her to see Skelly's expression grow deadly serious when he stared into her eyes.

Her skin pebbled, and her head went light. "What?"

"Sit while I get some ice for that foot."

Not in the mood to argue and relieved at the momentary reprieve, Rosalind settled into the room's most comfortable chair and put her feet up on the matching ottoman. She was facing the coal fireplace, above which hung the oil portrait of a young Lily that had always dominated the room.

"There's an ice bag in the cabinet above the refrigerator," she said.

"Back in a minute."

Skelly headed for the kitchen, leaving her alone. Her and Lily and the shadowy mental image of a murdered man. Never having been afraid in the old house before, Rosalind suddenly found herself scanning the shadows. Listening for unusual noises. Not a pleasant pastime.

"What really happened in this house that night?" she asked the painted Lily.

Her grandmother didn't seem to be in tune with her thoughts, however, for she received no answer.

True to his word, Skelly was back in a flash. Twirling the ice bag, he stared down at her foot. "This isn't going to do much good through leather."

"I wasn't thinking..." She started to reach for her shoe, but he stopped her.

"Allow me." Sitting on the edge of the ottoman, Skelly loosened the laces and removed the shoe. "Maybe I should take a better look." Carefully he rolled down her sock and slid it off her foot, his fingertips then gently exploring her ankle. "A little swollen, but not bad," he pronounced. "Does it hurt to the touch?"

Surprised by the sensation that shot up her leg from the spot where fingers met flesh—definitely not pain—Rosalind shook her head and made an incoherent sound that she covered with a forced cough.

She couldn't take her eyes from him.

Never having debated that he was a handsome man—though she had thought of him as a pretty face—Rosalind took a moment to savor Skelly while his attention was focused on his ministrations.

The lock of blue-black hair splashing his high forehead.

Lashes thick and long, brushing his strong cheekbones when he blinked.

His mouth.

The mouth caught her. A very sensual mouth that easily turned up into a wicked smile. An irresistible mouth that tempted her into fantasizing—

"How about here?" Skelly's low tone broke into her unexpected imaginings.

He drew his palm over the top of her foot. Tingling blossomed into a more urgent sensation that threatened her.

"It's fine," Rosalind choked out. "Uh, the ice—maybe you'd better put it on and get us that drink. Over there." She pointed to the corner of the room, where the cart stood directly in his line of sight.

Flashing her a smile that made her insides curl, Skelly molded the ice bag around her ankle and over the top of her foot, then snugged it in place by wrapping all with a dish towel that he'd brought from the kitchen.

"How does that feel?"

As if she were being tortured by his touch, Rosalind thought, relieved when he finally removed his hand from her leg. What she said was, "Cold."

"Then I've done my job." He rose. "What's your preference?"

"Brandy. And don't be stingy."

For a moment, Skelly had made her forget about everything but him, but now her mind flew back to the hellish ride that could have killed them both. When he handed her a bulbous glass holding more than a generous splash of brandy, she took a large swallow, grateful for the instant, steadying warmth that soothed her nerves, if not her growing fear.

"I'm afraid it was my fault," Skelly said, expression again sober. "If I hadn't announced my intentions to personally investigate the Sullivan murder on 'The Whole Story,' I wouldn't have forewarned whoever messed with the brake line." He set himself down on the ottoman facing her. "If Grandpa Noah and Aunt Hilary caught the update today, you can bet a lot of other people around here did, as well."

Having already come to that conclusion, Rosalind admitted, "Gossip is a favorite pastime in a small town." Another swallow of brandy helped her face the probable truth. "You think the miscreant and the person who killed Frank Sullivan are one and the same."

"Maybe. Whoever damaged the brake lines might be trying to protect the real murderer—even a potential suspect." Skelly was leaning forward, cupping his drink with both hands. He was staring into the goblet as intently as if the glass were a crystal ball that would give up the perpetrator's identity. "Loyalty is more important to some people than justice."

"Important enough to put innocent lives in danger?" Thankful the brandy was oozing its way through her entire system, brain included, Rosalind murmured, "Unbelievable," in a perfectly calm voice.

Skelly flashed her a look that spoke more volumes than his terse "Believe it."

Which shot a chill through her. "But how? When? The car was parked right in front of the house in the open."

"Open to whose view? Not ours, certainly—not if we were on the first floor."

True, the hill itself half hid parked cars. "But we have neighbors—"

"Whose houses aren't exactly cheek by jowl like in a big city. All the trees, bushes and fences in between preclude a straight line of sight. Whoever tampered with your car would have figured that out."

Though she knew he had a point, Rosalind hadn't given up on playing devil's advocate. "All right. Let's agree the word of your follow-up today did get around. 'The Whole Story' was televised only a couple of hours before we arrived in town. Who actually knows you're in Galena, not to mention your being here at Lang House with me? My grandfather... my aunt... and now Jarvis Wiggs... none of whom could possibly have tampered with the brakes.''

She disliked whatever it was about Skelly's gaze that made her feel he thought her naive. Warmth stole up her neck. Surely he couldn't really believe either of the people she loved so dearly was capable of hurting her? So Grandfather had sounded a bit defensive... and Aunt Hilary had seemed a little nervous. Bringing up old hurts couldn't be easy for them. They'd gone through hell with Lily once, and that had been when they were younger and in good health.

"Can you be so sure either Noah or Hilary didn't spill the beans to someone?" Skelly asked. "They've known we were coming since last night, right?"

"Yes, but they wouldn't tell anyone what we were up to—not even good friends. The situation is too sensitive.''

Skelly finished his drink and leaned forward to set the glass on a decorative table, his hip and thigh brushing her leg provocatively. For a moment, as another measure of warmth stole through her—this one induced by neither brandy nor embarrassment—Rosalind lost track of the conversation. But if Skelly had any like awareness, she couldn't tell.

"Are you forgetting the stop we made in town?" he continued. "*Anyone* could have seen us on Main Street and could have recognized me from 'The Whole Story.'" He twisted around, and she knew he was staring at the portrait. "And if you aren't the spitting image of Lily..."

He could have something there. She *had* noticed a few people staring both in the drugstore and on Main Street, though she hadn't given them another thought until this moment. She often received more attention than was comfortable.

"So we can assume your presence is no secret," she agreed. "That someone who wanted to stop you knew where to find you through me."

"The same someone who messed with your brakes."

Rosalind took an uneasy breath. *So, what now?*

The next step was clear enough, but only with a great deal of reluctance did she say, "I guess it's time to bring in the authorities."

Skelly gave her another of those don't-be-so-naive looks. "How wise would that be when we can't even prove the brakes were tampered with?"

"Jarvis thought they were."

"Though he wouldn't commit himself," he reminded her.

"Maybe if he were pressed to give an opinion..."

"Which would open a whole can of worms. The authorities will want to know who could possibly have it in for you. You'll have to explain the reason we're here. And then we'll probably be told to cease and desist any private investigation—even though the official inquiry will probably go no further than their dusting the car for prints and talking to the neighbors for witnesses. In the meantime, someone will be bound to leak the information to the press."

"And the tabloid reporters will be down on us like the vultures they are."

Skelly's expression blanked, and Rosalind realized he'd taken the criticism personally. A pang of regret at being so loose-mouthed washed through her. There was no denying she *had* thought him less than ethical at first...but her getting to know him personally confused the issue.

As did her attraction.

When Skelly had held her in his arms after their narrow escape, she'd melted inside. He'd been so tender. So comforting.

So unlike the image he'd projected while doing his story on her grandmother.

Avoiding his eyes, she said, "I wasn't generalizing. Not everyone associated with tabloid news fills that description. I'm willing to judge a person on his actions." The best she could do for an apology, considering she still had some doubts about him. She waited in vain for a response. "Well. I guess we ought to sleep on whether or not we involve the authorities." She took the last sip of brandy and set her glass next to his on the table. "Maybe we'll have a whole new perspective in the morning."

"Yeah, maybe," he said, not sounding convinced. "But first let's see to your injury. You've been iced long enough, at least for now." He unwound the dish towel and removed the ice bag. "So, how's the foot?"

She tested. "Numb."

"Then I'd better give you a hand." He stood and did just that.

Rosalind's fingers engulfed by his, she rose carefully. The room danced a bit—an aftereffect of the brandy. And when she took a step, her shoulder barely brushing against Skelly set off warning signals. She wished she could blame the liquor for that, as well.

Proceeding into the foyer without so much as a twinge, she headed for the staircase. "It's feeling pretty good." And kept going, up several steps.

"It's *looking* pretty good, too."

Unable to ignore the smooth tone that told her Skelly was appreciating something other than her foot, Rosalind glanced back at him while continuing to climb. Her mistake. The foyer whirled around her, and she suddenly found herself clutching the railing.

He rushed to her side, his arm hooking around her middle. "I had no idea you were such a cheap date."

She blinked him into precise focus. "Excuse me?"

"You know—a woman who can only handle one drink is considered a cheap date."

"You poured me a double."

"And you're definitely flying."

Irritated at his teasing, especially with him breathing down her neck, she said, "I am *not* flying," with as much dignity as she could muster. "My feet are firmly planted on the ground—rather, the stairs—thank you very much."

"Not for long."

Before Rosalind knew what he was about, Skelly slid his other arm under her legs and, with a grunt, hoisted her like a sack of potatoes.

"I can walk!" she protested.

"Not up two flights—not in your condition," he argued, breathlessly conquering one step, then another. "If you lose your balance again, you might hurt that foot. Or worse. You'd have to see a doctor and would probably end up on crutches or confined to bed. Then who would help me conduct this investigation?"

He was exaggerating, of course, but she couldn't help herself. Choosing to accept his logic despite her good sense, to stay right where she was for a little while—as close to Skelly as she dared—she slid her arms around his neck and settled against his chest. Eyelids drifting half-closed, she allowed her head to gravitate toward his shoulder. He sucked in his breath but didn't say anything.

Something was happening to her, Rosalind thought
hazily, something she neither understood nor wanted.
Skelly's appeal for her was growing, making her forget
about being cautious. Wrapped in a cocoon of warmth,
she was content to remain in his embrace. Reality receded, including their reason for being there. The only
thing she could think of was the man cradling her against
him. She was vaguely aware of their moving past the
landing and onto the darkened staircase that led to the
only bedroom not on the second floor.

Lily's attic sanctuary.

When visiting, even as a girl, she had told Skelly, Rosalind had always made the turreted bedroom her own.

They reached the upper level, and she expected Skelly
to set her down. Instead, he opened the door and carried
her into the spacious hideaway, dark but for the moonlight that shone through myriad windows. He kept going until he reached the edge of the bed, and though he
released her legs, he continued to hold fast to her waist.

Feet connecting with the floor, Rosalind made no move
to unwind her arms from around his neck. She merely
turned within his shelter, the better to see him. The friction of her body moving against his provoked a disturbing throb that quickly spread. Her breath caught in her
throat and remained trapped there when they came face-
to-face.

Moonshine silvered Skelly's mysterious expression. His
eyes were half-closed, focused on her through taut slits
and thick lashes. From what she could see, they appeared to be filled with a blend of confusion and yearning that mirrored her own mixed feelings.

Seconds multiplied, and still he didn't put her from
him. Only his labored breathing broke the silence be-

tween them. Was he winded from the climb? Or from anticipation?

Seconds spilled into moments. Her pulse raced faster and faster. She recognized its insistent throb throughout her body, all the way to her fingers and toes. Senses heightened, she imagined his heart beat in rhythm with her own.

All thoughts not having to do with Skelly receded until she was surrounded by him, filled with him.

His strength. His heat. His scent.

"Roz," he whispered.

His husky voice sent a thrill through her. "Mmm." She pressed closer, sliding a hand along the nape of his neck, threading her fingers through his thick hair.

"I should leave. *Now.*"

"Not yet. Stay a moment." *Long enough to kiss her.* What would it hurt to compare reality with fantasy? "Just a tiny moment."

"You don't know what you're doing."

"I always know."

"But you're tipsy."

"Not really."

As she raised her chin, offering him her mouth, her head swam, though not from the brandy. He hesitated only a moment, then with a groan, accepted. His lips parted hers, his tongue thrusting, a sensual invader. Welcome. Exciting. Making her yearn for more.

The reality won over the imagining by a mile.

Swamped by sensation, limbs turned to mush, Rosalind hung on to Skelly for all she was worth. Breasts crushed into his chest, hips against hips, she felt more alive than she could ever remember. She fisted his hair and nipped the inside of his lip, then trembled when he deepened the kiss. His hands crept downward, cupping her derriere and pulling her more tightly into him. Excitement escalated.

Halfway to nirvana, she recognized his need and realized he was as electrified as she.

A little voice inside her head told her to cool down. To stop before she let things go too far. She'd only wanted a kiss, and that to satisfy her curiosity. Or so she'd thought.

Now it seemed she didn't know what she wanted.

Wondering how to harness enough energy to be sensible, she was surprised when Skelly settled the issue, a groan tearing from his throat as he grabbed her arms and pushed her a safe distance away from him.

For a moment, they stood frozen, panting, gazes locked.

Reality check!

Rosalind was more than a little shocked at her own outlandish actions. What had come over her? Was still over her? She'd never, ever played the seductress. Yet, even now, she yearned for the feel of Skelly's arms anchoring her to him . . . was tempted to continue enticing him.

Until he said, "I'd better let you get to bed." His voice was tight. Distant. "That whole episode with the car was more emotionally draining than you probably realize . . . and we have a long day ahead of us tomorrow."

He sounded so damn rational that she took a big step back—and not only physically. "Of course." She tried to sound as casual as he did, as if the kiss hadn't shaken her up good. "And we need to get an early start."

"The earlier the better. Good night."

She watched him go, watched the darkness swallow him, heard rather than saw the door close. If only she could leave her churning thoughts behind as easily as he'd left her... Impossible.

For heaven's sake, she'd thrown herself at a man and couldn't even blame the brandy, because she really had been sober, if a little too relaxed. And yet she'd acted totally out of character. No wonder Skelly had assumed she was in an emotional state over their nightmare ride. Perhaps he had a point. Perhaps mortal danger made her bold enough—or vulnerable enough—to succumb to ridiculous fantasies.

She turned on a nightstand lamp, willing its soft golden glow to open her eyes and bring her back to her senses. Skelly might be attracted to her, Rosalind conceded, but all he really cared about was getting the story behind the murder.

As did she, of course.

Moving to the turret, she stared out the windows overlooking the river valley and began unbuttoning her shirt. The night view was glorious. A moonstruck sky sparkling with a million stars above. Warmly lit houses perched on every hill. A glowing aura running the length of Main Street below. And a tentative fog rising lazily from the river to caress its banks.

She removed the shirt. The silk swishing over her skin made her breasts ache and her belly tighten. She was still aroused. That single kiss persisted in tormenting her in a dozen ways. *No big deal,* Rosalind told herself. It didn't mean anything, not in the context of male-female relationships. She'd merely been celibate too long.

More than two years too long.

The blouse puddled to the floor, followed by her single shoe and sock, then her belt and trousers, leaving her in a lacy satin camisole and tap pants... and with memories she'd rather not consider.

Shortly before graduating with her MBA, she'd ruined her relationship with Timothy Hayes, the only man she'd ever loved. The man she'd thought she might marry. Tim had asked her. Rather than accepting right off, however, she'd begged for time, saying that she wanted to be sure she was ready. He'd been wonderfully understanding.

But the marriage thing had unglued her. She'd lain awake nights in a sweaty panic. She'd seen Tim differently, her view of him enveloped in a haze of fright.

To feel better, she'd begun making demands of Tim—their purpose, to convince her of his devotion. He'd taken her unusual behavior in stride for a while until those demands became unrealistic, impossible for him to meet and still remain the person he was. He hadn't stayed the distance, hadn't called her bluff. Instead, he'd retreated.

No big surprise.

No secret that life was easier and safer without romantic entanglements.

To hear Grandfather tell it, he and his darling Lily had loved each other madly, yet they'd managed to break each other's hearts. She'd always seen beyond his smile to his sadness. Aunt Hilary had once admitted to being in love with a man for many years, and yet she'd never married him, though she hadn't said why. And her parents had lived separate lives ever since she could remember, while pretending to be devoted in public for the sake of his business and her charities. Now, there was a fine example of what a marriage should *not* become.

Rosalind wondered if all the women in her family were doomed to inherit some cursed gene that denied them lifelong, loving relationships.

Not that any of her genes had a thing to do with Skelly McKenna. He was merely a catalyst, she assured herself. A sexy man who'd nudged her slumbering libido awake. Since Tim had walked out on her, she'd been so careful about choosing escorts who were safe that she'd become complacent when it came to recognizing a potential problem.

She'd underestimated Skelly.

She hadn't seen him coming.

Pulling pins from her hair, Rosalind shook the mass free so that it cascaded around her shoulders. Absently she finger-combed tangles out of the long tresses.

And made a vow that she wouldn't mistakenly confuse physical hunger with anything even faintly serious.

THE GOLDEN GLOW FLITTING through the tower room that threw Rosalind into silhouette had clarified her every move as she'd stripped to her undergarments before the windows. Now she was fussing with her cloud of long blond hair.

Just as Lily had that fateful night.

Rosalind... Lily. Lily... Rosalind. They might be interchangeable.

Like seeing a vision from the past.

A ghost... only Lily wasn't dead.

So what did one do with a nosy woman if she refused to be scared off?

A haunting question.

Chapter Six

After straightening up the mess they'd left in the parlor, Skelly set Roz's shoe and sock at the bottom of the staircase. Now what? Too revved up to sleep anytime soon, he was thinking of calling Keelin. But involving his cousin in another dangerous situation when she had imminent nuptials on her mind didn't quite sit right.

He stuck his hands in his pockets and wandered into the shadowy front parlor, where his thoughts roamed back to the attic room and Roz. Though he'd realized she'd been warming up to him, he'd been unprepared for her capitulation.

Skelly paced to work off his subsequent frustration.

He could hardly believe Roz had seduced him into kissing her. He could still feel the imprint of her lush body against his, could still taste the sweetness of her mouth. And his imagination wouldn't give him any peace about what might have happened if he hadn't abruptly stopped them both.

So why had he?

Skelly couldn't put a name to what he felt for Roz. That he wanted her was clear enough. But he wouldn't take advantage of any woman not in her right mind. Roz had claimed she wasn't drunk, but he was certain she'd been high on the adrenaline of a near-death experience.

Seeking a distraction, Skelly noted the old brass telescope mounted on a wooden tripod. Drawn to the instrument, which was set before a window, he hunched over to see through its single eye. Shards of light exploded through the magnifying lenses. He focused, then shifted to check on the source—a security light attached to someone's home a few blocks away.

Who would ever guess a town this size needed security lights?

Then again, who would ever guess someone would try to hurt, if not kill, him and Roz just because he'd publicly run off at the mouth about investigating the past? Lily Lang was looking pretty innocent at the moment. At least of Frank Sullivan's murder, Skelly conceded.

Before he could resume his pacing, a furtive movement from across the street caught his attention. Someone seemed to be lurking among the trees and bushes. Dwellings on that side were a ways downhill, so it was highly unlikely that the person was doing anything but keeping watch on Lang House. The shadowy figure was too distant and the night too dark for him to make out any details.

Skelly quickly tilted the telescope in the new direction, but by the time he refocused, there was nothing to see. And he began to wonder if the person had been any more threatening than a neighbor walking his dog.

Shaking his head in disgust, Skelly hoped he wouldn't be seeing potential murderers in every shadow. Thinking about someone plotting against him and Roz would keep him up all night unless he talked to someone with a calming influence. It didn't take long to decide to call Keelin, after all, if only to hear a friendly voice.

In the rear parlor, he found an old-fashioned phone behind the stained-glass lamp. Snatching it, he plunked himself down on the ottoman and dialed her hotel—sensitive to the feelings of Cheryl, Tyler's teenage daughter, Keelin wouldn't move in with the man she loved until after the wedding. No sooner had he snapped off the light in hopes the dark would relax him, than the hotel clerk answered and put through his call.

His cousin picked up on the first ring. "The hour is late," came her lovely lilt. "Speak your piece."

"Hey, cuz, it's me."

"Ah, Skelly, I'm truly sorry if I was rude. Tyler was supposed to call earlier, and I thought I would vex him a bit for being so negligent of his bride-to-be."

"Sorry to disappoint you."

"No, not at all," she assured him cheerfully. "Um, you sound a bit odd."

"Could be the phone or the connection," he fibbed. "I'm not at home."

"The connection is grand, but I'm hearing something desperate in your voice...." She paused, obviously waiting for an affirmation, but when he gritted his teeth and held himself back, she quickly changed the subject. "So, where have you taken yourself to?"

"Galena—that's in northwestern Illinois," he explained, figuring she wouldn't have a clue. "Guess who's investigating a murder?"

For the next few minutes, he got her up to speed on the prospective story that had brought Roz into his life and the two of them to Galena. He still hesitated unfolding the evening's main event.

"I did catch part of the Blond Temptress the other day," Keelin admitted. "So... this Lily Lang may not have been guilty. Interesting, but... don't you normally leave research up to your staff? Unless you have some *personal* interest in the story that's worth giving up your holiday weekend for," she mused.

Laughing, Skelly insisted, "I really am here because of the story—if the outcome's good, it could cinch my promotion to a prime-time spot with the network and take me out of the tabloid game."

"I knew you had it in you." Then, in a sly tone, Keelin asked, "Now, what about this Roz?"

"Well...Roz isn't too hard on the eyes," he hedged. "She looks a lot like Grandma Lily did at the same age."

"Aha! So a romantic involvement is a possibility."

Envisioning the kiss they'd shared, Skelly couldn't deny it. "How did you learn to read me so well in such a short time, cuz?"

"'Tis a gift."

A little envious of her true gift, Skelly sighed. If only he, too, had inherited one of Moira's special abilities in addition to her heartfelt wishes. Though Keelin had insisted he'd acquired his storytelling talent from their grandmother, it wasn't quite the same as having a little paranormal help if he and Roz found themselves in another potential tight spot.

But Keelin had it.

He'd been skeptical about her self-professed ability to see through another's eyes in dreams until he'd personally witnessed the results of her using the gift to rescue Cheryl Leighton from her kidnappers. He might as well tell her everything—he couldn't help himself. In a way, she'd brought up the subject. And he really did need someone other than Roz with whom he could talk freely.

"Speaking of gifts...you wouldn't have had any weird dreams about me lately?"

"About *you?* Skelly, now you have me worried. Tell me, for heaven's sake!"

He took a big breath and said rapidly, "The brakes on Roz's car went out tonight, and fate didn't do the dirty work. Someone punctured the brake-fluid line."

"Dear God, you could have been killed! Why would someone do such a thing?"

"To interfere with our investigation. We'll keep on, of course. Cautiously. The up side is that I now know for sure I didn't come all this way on a fool's mission."

"Merely a dangerous one. What did the local constable have to say?"

"We didn't alert the authorities. We don't need interference."

"But you could use the protection."

"That's where you come in. If you have one of your dreams, you can do something, get help right away."

He didn't want to acknowledge his darkest thought— that if the worst happened to him while Keelin was tuned in, she would be witness. Not that anything that dire would happen to him.

"But, Skelly, you know my dreams don't foretell the future. They merely allow me to see through another's eyes at a time of crisis. If you find yourself in trouble, I will not know until it happens. What if I'm too late? What if whoever I call does not believe me? What if I don't see anything at all?"

"Cuz, whoa! I didn't mean to get you crazy." Nor load her with guilt—she'd had enough of that. "I just figured someone ought to know what's going on here."

"You said you're staying with the young woman's family. What about them?"

"Someone I trust," he amended.

For in truth, after talking to Noah Lang, he had some serious doubts about the old man.

"God in heaven, if anything happens to you . . . I shall never forgive you."

Skelly grinned. "I know it'd be tough finding a new best man at the last minute."

"'Tis not my marriage I'm thinking on, Skelly Mc-Kenna, but your well-being," she said irritably.

"I love you, too."

He spent the next few minutes getting Keelin to talk about plans for her wedding the following weekend. Everything on that end seemed to be running smoothly, courtesy of his half sister. Aileen always had been able to charm her way through life's little curves.

By the time he hung up, the tension in Keelin's voice had dissipated, though he knew he hadn't lessened her worry. Still, he couldn't help but feel better that she was aware of what was going on. She'd proved herself to be a woman a person could not only trust but could count on in a crisis. He only hoped it wouldn't come to that.

With some of the burden off his shoulders, Skelly was about to head for his bedroom at last. What sounded like a soft shuffle of footsteps on the porch delayed him. Listening intently, he thought the sounds died at the front door.

Had someone been watching the house, after all, and was now ready to break in?

Silently he rose and flattened himself against the wall even as the lock jiggled. His mind raced, searching for something he could use as a weapon if he needed one. *The fireplace poker.* Peering around the edge of the doorway, he could see through the front parlor to the entryway as the door opened and the foyer light snapped on. An amazed Skelly watched as Hilary Lang slipped inside, carefully locked the door and tiptoed up the stairs.

THE NEXT MORNING, Rosalind felt like her old self—in complete control. Her summer pantsuit reflected her strictly business mood. Skelly appeared for breakfast dressed a bit more casually, a silk T-shirt beneath his lightweight sports jacket. They managed to avoid the topic of car brakes in front of her aunt. When Hilary inquired after the night before, Rosalind merely told her they hadn't yet succeeded in talking to Diane Nesmith. Skelly's look of relief both surprised and puzzled her.

"I'll get the dishes so you kids can be on your way," Hilary offered. "Will you be home for lunch?"

"I doubt it." Rosalind kissed her great-aunt's cheek. "I'm not certain about dinner, either."

"Make sure you don't get so caught up in this investigation business that you don't eat. You know how you get on an empty stomach."

Skelly's eyebrows arched. "And how is that?"

"Let's get going." She pushed him into the dining room. Then, when she heard the water running from the kitchen, she whispered, "We can walk down to Main Street."

"Your foot—"

"Is fine. If we ask to borrow a car, we'll have to explain ourselves, something I don't intend to do."

A few minutes later, they were outside, making their way down the steep incline to the street below. With her being extra careful, going was slow.

"It'll be easier when we get to the steps." She indicated the long, steep staircase that would take them close to the heart of town. "When we get to Main Street, I'll head for the widow's shop." Having awakened with the

first streaks of dawn, she'd had plenty of time to think
things through and plan a course of action. "You see
what you can find in the newspaper morgue."

"Now, wait a minute—"

"Anything before the murder," she went on, her mind
made up. "Lily was certain to have been featured on the
society pages a few times while she was here. And maybe
you'll be able to dig up something new on Sullivan, as
well."

"I appreciate your telling me how to do my job,
but—"

"You're welcome."

"—I think we should stick together."

"That won't be necessary."

"After what almost happened last night?"

Starting down the staircase that clung to the side of the
hill, she considered both what had happened to her car
and what had happened between them . . . and couldn't
make up her mind which was the more dangerous for her.

"Last night took me by surprise." Meaning both incidents. "Now I'm warned." Splitting up at least for a
while would serve several purposes, including giving her
some breathing room. "Besides, it's broad daylight and
there'll be hundreds of people on the streets." Many of
whom were already strolling in and out of open shops.

"That doesn't mean something couldn't happen to
you."

His words sent a shiver of unease through her.
"Please—don't appoint yourself my guardian. I've been
taking care of myself for quite a while now. I'm merely
being logical, trying to make up for the time we lost last
night."

Relieved when he didn't continue arguing, Rosalind
wondered if Skelly's giving in hadn't been too easy. But

if he was up to something, she couldn't tell from his expression. Whatever might be rolling around in that devious mind of his, he wasn't giving her a clue.

They took the last of the stairs and headed into the growing crowd of tourists.

"The *Clarion* office is about a block and a half north," she said, pointing past the red-white-and-blue bunting that cut across the street.

"Aren't you going to march me to the door?"

When Skelly aimed one of his wicked smiles at her, he rendered her speechless for a moment. That she'd convinced herself to straighten up her act and keep things between them strictly business didn't seem to matter. She cursed the hormones that didn't give a fig about being sensible.

"I trust you'll find the newspaper office on your own." Her tone was purposely clipped. "And I'll find you after I talk to Diane Nesmith."

Skelly gave her a mock salute and left. Rosalind set off in the opposite direction, glancing over her shoulder when she was halfway down the block. She caught sight of him weaving through the crowd, still headed in the right direction. *Good.* Breathing more easily now that she was on her own, she zeroed in on the antique store, whose address she'd gotten from a local directory that morning.

After an admiring glance at the display of old jewelry and accessories in the window, she gazed beyond the plate glass. At the far end of the store, a lone woman was busy working at a handsome buffet. An old-fashioned lace-trimmed dress covering her too-thin body, light brown hair fluffed out and so sprayed a tornado couldn't muss it, she appeared sixtyish—the right age for Frank Sullivan's widow.

Taking a deep breath to calm her suddenly jangling nerves, Rosalind entered Yesterday's Treasures.

DIANE NESMITH WAS rearranging a display of cut crystal to make room for a newly arrived pitcher and matching stemmed glasses when the tinkle of the bell at the door alerted her. A glance to the front of the store disclosed a woman's indistinct form, the blur caused by the thick prescription lenses she needed for close-up work.

"Perry, we have a customer."

Her husband was in the storeroom, unpacking a crate of items from the 1890s that he'd recently bought at an estate sale. He didn't answer. As usual when involved with something that fascinated him, he was tuned out to everything else, even her. Not wanting to interrupt her own task lest she forget her plan for rearranging the pieces—her short-term memory was already failing her— she called out again.

"Perry!"

But her raised voice was for naught—he still didn't answer. And, as she had hundreds of times before, she reminded herself that a woman could do worse than be married to a man who disappeared into his own world once in a while.

A pleasant if husky female voice directly behind her said, "Excuse me, but I'm looking for Diane Nesmith."

Affixing a smile to her lips, gingerly cradling a stemmed water glass in one hand, Diane turned. "You found her. How can I help? . . ."

The polite greeting died on her lips, and her fingers went slack. Crystal shattered around her feet. For a moment, Diane hoped something was wrong with her glasses, for her eyes seemed to be playing tricks on her.

She blinked and refocused, but the image, while a bit distorted, remained the same.

Long silver blond hair...perfect figure...mole dotting the corner of her mouth... The room started spinning. Diane swayed and clutched at a highboy for support.

"Are you all right?" the Lily Lang look-alike asked, grasping on to her arm.

Her face practically in that of the other woman, she opened her mouth to speak, but no words would form.

"Here, you'd better sit down." The young woman gently guided her to a nearby upholstered chair.

Once seated, Diane tried to regain her breath. She was still a bit light-headed, and her ears were buzzing. Worse, blood was pumping far too rapidly through her body. She had to calm down. She had to. With shaking hands, she removed her glasses.

"I could get you some water."

"Please. In the back..."

But just then, Perry wandered into the shop, proclaiming, "What an incredible find! You won't believe it, my dear." As he focused first on the customer, then on her, his eyes went round. "Diane?"

"Dizzy," she forced out.

"Your pills! I'll get them." He flew back the way he'd come.

The blonde's forehead was furrowed. "I didn't mean to startle you. I'm Rosalind Van Straaten."

"I can see who you are...that woman's kin."

"Lily's granddaughter."

Now that the initial shock was wearing off, Diane drew her scattered thoughts together. "Why are you here? What do you want from me?"

"To talk."

Obviously about the murder. She'd assumed the past was dead and buried with Frank. That displeasing memories began crowding her mind angered her. Why couldn't she forget the past instead of the things that were important to her in the present?

"We have nothing to talk about, Miss Van Straaten. Your family has done enough."

"I have reason to believe my grandmother *didn't* kill your husband."

Rosalind had picked up a silver hairbrush and was running her fingers over the design on the back. Fingers that shook slightly. Realizing that Lily's granddaughter was nervous put Diane more at ease. Undoubtedly she merely needed to hear the story firsthand. Not that Diane would ever admit the trouble had started because she hadn't been able to conceive Frank's child. Heartbroken, she'd turned her husband away from her bed rather than acknowledge her failure.

What she said was, "*I* have good reason to believe Lily *did* kill Frank. I knew he was cheating on me for years—I even suspected with her—but I tolerated it because he was discreet." Frank hadn't gone without his comforts for long, she remembered bitterly. Less than a year. Whenever the urge took him, he'd slipped away for the night. "Those last several weeks, though, he was careless. People saw him with Lily."

"He was unfaithful for years?" Rosalind set down the brush and folded her arms over her chest. "And you stayed with him all that time?"

"He wouldn't agree to any kind of separation. His political career. Voters wouldn't have it. Getting a divorce wasn't so easy in those days, especially if both parties didn't agree. Nothing like it is now."

And she'd asked first for an annulment, then a divorce after realizing Frank was only going through the motions of caring about her in public for the voters' sakes. They'd had nothing tender left between them. A woman needed tenderness from a man. Even a barren woman. She'd begged him to let her go. His continual refusals had made her turn to Perry. She'd assumed Frank's male pride would come before all—and that, once he figured things out, he'd change his mind.

Only he hadn't.

"You think your husband's unwillingness to divorce is the reason my grandmother killed him?"

The sickening memories threatened to choke her, but Diane wouldn't let on. Because of Frank, she'd learned to hide her true feelings from the world. She'd become expert at it.

"Lily was making a clean break from your grandfather at last. Everyone knew it. I guess she finally made up her mind which man she wanted. My husband. But when Frank didn't agree to leave me for her . . ."

"That's all your assumption, though, isn't it?" Rosalind asked, sounding aghast.

"What's going on here? Can't you see my wife is ill?" Perry boomed as he rushed back into the shop and to her side. "Here, my dear, take your medication." He handed her a pill and water, which he watched her take. Then he glared at Rosalind. "My wife has high blood pressure that's very difficult to control. Are you trying to kill her?"

"No, of course not."

"Then I suggest you get out of here. Now."

Rosalind nodded and backed away. "I'll go. I didn't mean for you to be so upset, Mrs. Nesmith. I really am sorry."

That's what Lily had said to her all those years ago, Diane remembered, watching the granddaughter leave. Frank had committed the ultimate betrayal by telling that harlot about the disaster of their private lives. And then Lily'd had the presumption to speak to her about her inability to conceive.

To feign sympathy.

"Are you feeling any better now, my dear?"

"Yes, thanks to you, as always."

She stared up at Perry, his craggy features stark with worry under that salt-and-pepper toupee he'd taken to wearing. Silly man. Always trying to look younger—for *her,* he said—when she was already content with him. But that was Perry. He'd always done what he thought essential for her happiness ever since the day she'd turned to him.

Diane never doubted how much *this* husband cared about her.

He never gave her reason to regret Frank's untimely death.

THOUGH SKELLY HAD FOUND several references to Lily in the year before the murder—mostly on the society pages, as Roz had expected—he still hadn't come across any information that raised his reporter's antennae. No matter. He kept at the task, scrutinizing one microfiche after another. Time-consuming work, but the owners of the *Clarion* had only fully embraced computer technology a few years ago—that being the reason Heidi hadn't pulled any of her research from the Galena weekly.

Trading one microfiche for the next, Skelly wondered if Roz was doing any better than he. If she was trying to control Diane Nesmith as she had him earlier, he doubted it. What had gotten into her? Either she'd rolled off the wrong side of the bed or she'd had trouble sleeping.

If the latter, Skelly certainly hoped he was to blame.

His grin faded when he remembered seeing Hilary sneak inside right after he'd imagined someone was watching the house. He hesitated telling Roz. He knew she wasn't ready to suspect either of the elderly Langs.

His musing was interrupted when Sara—office manager, columnist and proofreader—poked her head into the small back room that served as the morgue. With her light brown ponytail and her freckled nose, the young woman didn't look mature enough to handle so much responsibility.

"How's it going, Skelly? Making any progress?"

She'd not only recognized him, but had been aware of his purpose in town. He'd immediately received the red-carpet treatment and an unsolicited promise that his visit to the *Clarion* would remain confidential.

"Only a few issues to go."

"I have a little free time. If you tell me what exactly you're looking for, maybe I can help."

"Thanks, but it's one of those I'll-know-it-when-I-see-it predicaments."

"Gotcha. Yell if you need anything."

"Will do."

Skelly scanned through the next microfiche so quickly that he almost passed up the story covering the Historical Society Ball. He backed up. The annual fund-raiser had been held barely a month before the murder. From the spread of photographs, he gathered the whole town had turned out. On closer inspection, one of the shots in particular piqued his interest.

Lily being very friendly with a man who was neither Noah Lang nor Frank Sullivan.

Skelly took stock of the burly man in his expensive-looking tuxedo—most others had settled on suits. He appeared to be fortyish, sported a receding hairline and was chomping on a cigar. While his arm was wrapped possessively around Lily's waist, she was leaning into him, wide-eyed, her smile dazzling. The caption identified the man as Anthony Cavillo.

Centering the photo in the frame, Skelly made a copy, which he took to the reception desk, where Sara was focused on her computer until she spotted him.

"Recognize this guy?" he asked, setting the copy on her desk.

"Anthony Cavillo." Her eyebrows shot up. "Sure, everyone knows the owner of River Bluff—that's a combination resort and vacation-housing development."

"Where?"

"A few miles southwest of Galena, along the Mississippi bluffs. Take Blackjack Road and follow the signs. Oh, and he's part of a syndicate operating *River Star,* a riverboat casino operation."

At last, Skelly's antennae went on alert. "Thanks."

Sara handed him the photocopy and said, "Anthony Cavillo has helped boost the local economy for decades. People around here like him. A lot."

"I'll keep that in mind."

Skelly figured he was warned—he'd better be cautious when sniffing around for information about the eminent businessman. He couldn't help but wonder about the syndicate running *River Star,* so the first thing he did back in the newspaper morgue was pull out his cellular telephone and Heidi's card. He called her home number, but her machine answered.

"Skelly here. I need whatever you can get on one Anthony Cavillo from the early sixties up to the present."

He shared the little he already had and asked her to get back to him as soon as possible. Hesitating only a moment, he decided to give her the Langs' number, as well, in case he couldn't be reached on his cell phone.

Then he returned to the microfiche. Unfortunately the next few issues of the *Clarion* revealed no pearls of new information. He scanned the details of Lily's arrest, confession, subsequent trial and incarceration.

When he found the name of the man who'd been sheriff at the time, he scribbled it into his notebook. He assumed Orville Galt had been long retired. A local telephone directory gave him Galt's number and address. Talking to him might shed some light on a few things, not the least of which was whether or not he'd alerted Noah Lang of Lily's arrest in the middle of the night as the old man had claimed.

He'd barely recorded the information when he heard Roz in the reception area. Not wanting her to know he was checking on her grandfather's story, he slipped the notebook into his pocket and hurriedly replaced the directory. When she found him, he was straightening up the desk around the microfiche machine.

"Looks like my timing was perfect," she said from the doorway.

"Yup." Still stinging from her impression of a prison commandant, he couldn't help needling her. "I was almost ready to come looking for you."

A deep line appeared between her eyebrows. "Why? I told you I'd find you here."

"'Told' as in 'dictated.' And to make sure you could keep the upper hand, you chose not to tell me where you were going."

"You knew I was planning to talk to Diane Nesmith."

"But you withheld the name of her shop."

The frown deepened. "An oversight."

"Then you won't mind telling me now."

With an exasperated sigh, she said, "Yesterday's Treasures."

Giving Skelly a gut-wrenching start.

Chapter Seven

Tension lay thick between them as they traded the cool newspaper office for the late-morning heat. Skelly's questions concerning her whereabouts had annoyed Rosalind, but his tight-lipped silence put her on edge. She was debating whether or not to leave it alone when he took the choice from her.

Hooking her arm and pulling her around a corner onto a side street where they were apart from the crowd, he demanded, "So why the hell didn't you tell me the name of Diane Nesmith's shop earlier?"

His delayed reaction astounded Rosalind, as did his irate expression. He was truly angry. Not having a clue as to his point—other than his being ticked because she had taken charge of the investigation—she resented his trying to make her feel culpable.

"I don't get it," she protested, extracting her arm from his grip. "What's your problem?"

"When you came looking for me after your detour to the drugstore, I was standing directly in front of Yesterday's Treasures."

"If you say so." She shrugged and settled against an iron railing that protected the stairway to a basement entrance. "I wasn't really paying much attention to anything but finding you. As for this morning, I may have been assertive in delegating tasks, but if you think I purposely withheld information from you, you're mistaken.''

To her relief, some of the tension drained from Skelly, and his features softened from angry to concerned. Another surprise, one she didn't want to examine too closely. Remaining annoyed with him was infinitely more comfortable.

''While you were there,'' he began calmly, ''did you happen to run into an older guy wearing an odd-looking toupee?''

She waited until a couple passed by them before saying, ''Perry Nesmith, Diane's husband.''

''That's it, then,'' he muttered, jaw clenched. ''Nesmith saw us yesterday afternoon—and he recognized us, Roz. So at least one person who could know something about the murder was aware that we were in town.''

Unease replaced annoyance. The man hadn't indicated he knew who she was, not even when they'd been face-to-face. ''Are you certain?''

''I was admiring the goods in the front window when I felt someone watching me. I caught Nesmith at it, and he suddenly got real busy. Then you found me. As we walked off, I glanced back inside and caught him staring after us. At first, I thought he'd just been interested in us as customers. Now I'd swear he knew exactly who we were.''

Finally the reason Skelly was so troubled hit her. ''The brakes!''

''Perry Nesmith is definitely a candidate,'' he agreed. ''What did he say to you?''

''He ordered me to leave.'' And he'd been pretty hostile, Rosalind remembered, her pulse surging. She waited for more people to pass by. "Diane nearly had a stroke when she took a good look at me. Literally. Perry was being very protective of her."

Skelly swore under his breath. "So you didn't get anywhere with the widow."

"I didn't say that. Diane did some talking while her husband was in back, fetching her medication." But Rosalind felt unsettled—vulnerable—continuing the conversation in the street. She pulled away from the railing. "Let's finish this inside somewhere."

He canvased the area as if making certain no one was observing them. "Okay."

A nearby bakery provided tables and chairs for hungry shoppers who wanted a fast energy boost. A peek through the window assured Rosalind the place wasn't too busy yet, so they could have some privacy...*if* they managed to keep their voices down.

Entering, she directed Skelly to claim a table off in the corner while she went up to the bakery counter. The bear claws were calling her name, so she bought a couple to go with their coffees.

She'd barely slid the tray onto the table before Skelly asked, "So, what did you get out of the widow?"

Wanting a moment to settle down inside, Rosalind sat, serenely unloaded their refreshments and placed the tray on an empty chair. She took a swallow of coffee for good measure.

By contrast, Skelly was a mass of impatience. His expression tight. His posture stiff. His fingers uncharacteristically drumming the tabletop.

Rosalind decided she liked bringing out this side of Skelly. His obvious frustration at not having the upper hand humanized him somehow, made him more appealing...if that were possible. She had to admit he certainly couldn't have been more appealing than he had been the night before. Though she'd like to pretend her tiny romantic digression hadn't happened, memories of that kiss kept nagging her at inopportune moments.

She pushed the mug and plate that Skelly had been ignoring closer to him. "Have some coffee while it's still hot. And these bear claws are to die for."

"Ro-o-oz."

Taking a hint from his warning tone, she figured it was time to stop pushing his buttons. "All right. Diane knew her husband had been cheating on her for years, and she wanted a divorce that he wouldn't even consider."

"Sullivan was looking out for his political career."

"She, of course, claims the divorce issue prompted the murder. Because Lily had finally decided to make her separation from Grandfather final, Diane figures she expected Frank to do likewise."

"Then killed him when he wouldn't agree to leave his wife for her?"

"In a fit of passion."

A thoughtful Skelly took a big slug of coffee, then shook his head. "Doesn't make sense. If Lily loved Sullivan so much, why did she keep reconciling with Noah? Could be Diane killed her husband to get out of the marriage . . . or Nesmith did the dirty work for her."

"I'd say we have ourselves a couple of genuine suspects, as Grandfather suggested," she agreed without enthusiasm.

Able to imagine all the years of misery Diane had gone through—knowing her husband was cheating on her and having no way out—Rosalind felt sorry for the poor woman. If Diane *had* killed Frank Sullivan, the heinous act certainly had been one of desperation.

She took some comfort in her bear claw and coffee before changing the subject. "So, did you come up with anything from the *Clarion?*"

Skelly pulled a piece of paper from his jacket pocket, unfolded it and handed it to her. Though his fingers brushed hers only briefly, Rosalind was reminded of the way he'd touched her the night before. Immediately self-conscious, feeling her neck warm, she focused all her attention on the copy of the old newspaper photograph. Of course, she recognized her grandmother if not the man.

"Who is he?" she asked.

"I thought you might know."

She read the caption. "Anthony Cavillo. Cavillo. I recognize the name . . . though not because it was linked with Lily's."

"He's a big shot around here."

Skelly told her about the resort and gambling boat— Rosalind had heard of both. She gathered he found some fault with Cavillo's second business. Gambling was always suspect, but the riverboats were a fairly new venture begun long after Lily had disappeared. She didn't see what gambling had to do with her grandmother.

"So Lily knew him. What's the big deal?"

"Roz, wake up and take a closer look. Lily *knew* him." He arched his eyebrows at her. "And this photo was taken mere weeks before the murder."

Lily and Cavillo did appear to have more than a passing acquaintance, Rosalind realized, a lump settling in the pit of her stomach. A new scenario involving a love triangle occurred to her. She didn't like imagining one man killing another over Lily any more than she liked believing Lily could be a murderess. She handed the copy back to Skelly.

"We can only guess whether or not they were having an affair."

"Or we could ask *him*," Skelly suggested, tapping his finger against the likeness of Anthony Cavillo. "I know you're not thrilled thinking the woman Grandpa Noah worshiped could have been involved with even one man outside of her marriage, but—"

She cut him off. "But I'm trying to be realistic. And nonjudgmental. Lily's marriage to Grandfather had been rocky for several years." And perhaps her grandmother had destroyed it even as Rosalind had destroyed her own love relationship—though her grandfather had been more determined than Tim to hang on to the woman he loved. "Perhaps we should pay Mr. Cavillo a visit later, after we collect the Thunderbird. What do we do in the meantime?"

Only after posing the question did Rosalind realize that, despite her vow to manage the situation, she'd handed control back to Skelly. A quick look at him assured her that at least he wasn't gloating.

He said, "I think we should glad-hand the local candidate for the governor's seat."

"Walt Rogowski?" Starting to feel as if she were out of the loop, Rosalind had to remind herself that being a reporter made Skelly a professional investigator of sorts. His instincts were more finely honed than hers. "What in the world does *he* have to do with anything?"

"Rogowski was working for Frank Sullivan at the time of the murder. A few years later, he was sharp enough to win Sullivan's seat in the state senate. That's not the kind of man who misses things."

Rosalind agreed. "He would have known exactly what had been going on in the political arena around Sullivan."

Now, if only they could convince the candidate to share any information he might have stored away in his memory...

WALT ROGOWSKI FINISHED proofreading a new promotional flyer that was ready to be printed and distributed at the parade on Tuesday. He handed the clipboard back to Kim, a perky seventeen-year-old volunteer. Planning on being a political-science major, she would work for his campaign the entire summer until she had to leave for college.

"Looks good," he said, meaning her, as well as the copy. He wasn't too old to appreciate her dark beauty... or her youthful innocence.

"I'll take it to the printer personally."

Walt nodded, then dismissed her, after which he searched for Eddie Turner, the not-too-bright but brawny fellow he'd hired to see to his continued good health. He spotted his bodyguard in the midst of several winsome volunteers making paper flowers for the Fourth of July float. The incongruous sight of something delicate coming from those menacing hands amused Walt. Eddie was turning out to be a man of many talents.

The outer office abuzz with activity and noise, he retreated to his antique-lined inner sanctum to work on his Fourth of July speech in peace and quiet. He planned to make it a humdinger, one that would get the entire town behind him, get everyone's juices flowing. Not to mention a substantial amount of cash. He wasn't ignorant of the cost of the governor's seat, and over the years, he'd grown expert at finagling campaign contributions even out of die-hard penny-pinchers.

Opening the folder, Walt went over the bare bones he'd already written. He'd created his own version of "family values" that would be part of his platform. Not bad. He was recording some thoughts about where to expand and what to add, when a knock at his door rattled his focus.

Vexed, he said, "Come in," though he continued to write so he wouldn't forget anything.

Footsteps stopped directly opposite his desk. "Mr. Rogowski?"

"Call me Walt." He looked up to match the face with the unfamiliar if intriguing husky voice. Hiding his instant hostile reaction took every bit of the finesse he'd developed as a politician. "What can I do for you folks?"

He aimed a winning smile at Lily's granddaughter and that tabloid scum who accompanied her. He'd been angry when he was informed of McKenna's first broadcast, furious when he'd caught the second himself. Forewarned was forearmed . . . but even so, he couldn't believe his luck. The past had finally come knocking at his door precisely when he was reaching for the pinnacle of his political career.

The blonde gave him a winning smile. "We'd like a few minutes of your time."

"I'm always available to my constituents," he said expansively, as if he didn't want to be rid of them both—and the sooner the better. "Sit. Please."

As they took the armchairs opposite him, Walt leaned his head against the padded leather of his chair. He'd long ago perfected the art of appearing relaxed even when he was fuming inside. He should damn well have received more than one Academy Award for best performance over the years. Though he knew why the couple had come to see him, it wouldn't do to show his hand. He waited for one of them to speak.

"This is Skelly McKenna," the woman began, "and I'm Rosalind Van Straaten. I believe you knew my grandmother—Lily Lang."

Since there was no point in being anything but truthful, he said, "You look like her."

"So I've been told."

"Not that I knew her well." He faced the lout whose visage was nearly as familiar. "McKenna...Skelly McKenna...hmm, where...I have it! You're on that afternoon newsmagazine show, aren't you?"

"'The Whole Story.' You also know my father, Raymond McKenna."

Now, *that* took him by surprise. "You're Ray's boy? Well, now." Walt's mind spun, wondering how he could use that information to his advantage. Ray McKenna had never quite warmed up to him, but they were connected by the same political party. That counted for something. "You give your daddy my best."

"I'll do that. And I hope you can do something for me, as well." The reporter glanced at Lily's granddaughter. "I mean for us."

"Name it."

"Roz is a little upset with me because I did a follow-up story on her grandmother's escape from prison."

"Follow-up?" So the reporter was keeping his inquisition low-key. Two could play the same game. "But that had to be some twenty-odd years ago."

"Thirty this week," Rosalind said.

Though he didn't appreciate being corrected, Walt gave her a rueful smile. "The years do get away from a person."

"Roz doesn't think Lily killed Frank Sullivan." And with a casual shrug, McKenna added, "I promised I would take this weekend to ask around, see if I could dig up anything that justifies her position."

He said this as if he were only playing at investigating to pacify the woman—because he wanted her?—but Walt wasn't so sure he believed that. As he well knew from decades of personal experience, reporters could be as crafty as politicians when it came to winning.

He steepled his fingers and stared down the other man. "And how does that involve me?"

"You worked for Sullivan. We thought you might remember some of his colleagues...and adversaries. Anyone with a grudge. Or a reason to be jealous."

"Thirty years is nearly half a lifetime."

"But a man was murdered," Rosalind reminded him, as if he could ever forget. "Surely you must have had some speculations of your own at the time."

"An ambitious man always makes enemies. Frank was no exception. But murder as a solution to political disagreement? If that were the case, I would hate to think of how many times I might have been killed over the years."

"Whatever you say stays with us," the reporter promised. "I protect my sources."

As if tabloid reporters had integrity. But determined to seem agreeable and cooperative, Walt frowned and struck a thoughtful pose.

"I do remember a couple of men who didn't like Frank for one reason or another. State Representative Richard Hardy—God rest his soul—was very ambitious, and always in Frank's shadow. And John Melling was relieved of a prestigious appointment after an investigation by a committee Frank headed. Melling made some vague threats when he left Springfield, but no one took him seriously."

McKenna was busy scribbling in a small notebook. "This Melling—is he still alive?"

"As far as I know."

"Where can we find him?"

Yearning to know what was in that little black book—especially any entries specifically about him—Walt had to force his attention on the conversation. "I believe Melling was originally from Rockford, but I'm afraid he's someone I've had no reason to keep up with."

"If we don't succeed here," the woman told the reporter, "on the way back to Chicago, we can stop in Rockford to track down John Melling."

Why couldn't the two of them go on a wild-goose chase and get out of his hair *now?* Walt wondered, seething inside. Why had they chosen to open this Pandora's box even as the gubernatorial race was gearing up? He was in the spotlight nearly every moment, for God's sake. He didn't need to deal with any more damage control.

Rosalind leaned forward. "How well did you know Frank Sullivan personally?"

"Frank was more than a dozen years older and a whole lot more sophisticated than I was way back then. We didn't run in the same social circles."

"You mean with my grandmother."

"I meant anyone with money."

"Then you wouldn't know whether or not he had any personal enemies?"

"Other than your grandfather?"

Rosalind blanched and fell back into her chair. That shut her up. And it brought out McKenna's protective instincts, Walt noticed. The reporter slipped a hand over hers and gave it a squeeze. A friendly squeeze? Or something more intimate? He made a mental note to remember that.

"Any other thoughts?" the reporter asked him in a tight voice.

His own patience stretched, Walt spread his hands and shrugged. And when his interrogators rose, he took his first deep breath since the cross-examination had begun.

"Thank you for your cooperation," Rosalind said. "Please call me if you think of anything else that might be helpful."

"Of course, my dear." A brilliant idea striking him, Walt let them get to the door before he said, "Wait a minute. I do remember something else." He gazed at Skelly McKenna. "Professional privilege?"

"You've got it."

"Frank did have an ongoing dispute with a local businessman over zoning."

"Someone who still lives in the Galena area?"

"Indeed. His name is . . ." Walt paused for dramatic effect, so he would seem torn about revealing the man's identity. Having done the bastard a *big* favor, he never had felt that he'd received equal compensation. And he would tell him so when they met at River Bluff later that evening. "His name is Anthony Cavillo."

STILL STINGING from the comment about her grandfather, Rosalind waited until they were well away from Rogowski's office before asking, "So, what do you think?"

"That we're on the right trail."

"What about Walt Rogowski himself? Do you suppose he knows anything he didn't tell us?"

"Hard to say. He's real slick."

"I didn't like him, either."

Skelly gave her a surprised look. "At least we agree on something."

She hadn't thought they'd disagreed on much since he'd consented to help her. Their squabbles basically reflected their continuing struggle for authority rather than how to proceed or what to think about whom.

"I assume we're agreed that we need to get to Cavillo as soon as possible," she said.

"Okay. So we agree on two things."

Rosalind spotted a store that had a public telephone. "I'm going to find out if the car is ready."

When she picked up her pace, Skelly said, "You're limping again."

So she was. "But not badly."

"Not yet."

He put a hand on her arm to slow her, reminding Rosalind of the way he'd touched her in the politician's office. Her pulse quickened. Either Skelly was protecting her . . . soothing her . . . or seeing to her hurts.

She stopped dead in her tracks.

What kind of a business relationship was that?

Though she'd tried her best to put it out of mind, she recalled the way she'd gotten to her bedroom the night before. "Are you going to carry me up *those* stairs, too?" she asked, indicating the ones built into the hill.

"Depends on how badly you want me to." Skelly's wicked grin dimpled his cheek.

Ignoring the thrill that shot straight through her, she answered tartly, "Depends on how much you irritate me in the next few minutes."

Skelly snorted and their gazes met. Rosalind realized she was grinning idiotically. Worse, her heart was thumping for absolutely no reason . . . that was, no reason other than her locking wits with a man who'd wormed his way through her defenses. She was finding it difficult to remember they'd ever been adversaries.

"Here." He shoved his hand into his jacket pocket and whipped out his cellular phone. "Make that call."

A nearby bench was available, so Rosalind took a seat and punched in the number. Jarvis answered. To her disappointment, he told her the Thunderbird wouldn't be ready for a couple of hours. The kid he'd sent to Dubuque to fetch a part was only on his way back now. Discouraged at being stopped cold for the moment—they'd been on a roll so far—she shared the bad news with Skelly.

"So we'll have lunch, then hang around Lang House."

Unable to think of a better proposal, she contented herself with choosing the place to eat. Barely an hour later, when Skelly suggested they call a taxi, she insisted on walking. A course she soon came to regret. Though she negotiated the steep staircase with care, hardly feeling a dull ache in her foot, the ache eventually turned into an annoying twinge.

Which Skelly observed. "You really are limping."

Exhausted both by the climb and the soaring midday heat, she conceded her mistake. "I guess a taxi would have been the thing."

Skelly removed his jacket and hooked the garment over one shoulder. Perspiration glued his silk T-shirt to his chest. He might have been half-naked, Rosalind thought, mesmerized.

"Maybe you'll listen to me next time."

Expression intent, he shifted the jacket into one arm and came at her as if he meant to scoop her up in his arms and carry her uphill. She reacted by instinct, placing a hand square against his damp, hot chest.

"Don't even think about it," she warned. "You'll regret the hernia by the time we get to the front steps, and then you'll be blaming me for the demise of your manhood. It's only another block. I'll survive.''

"Hey, you're the boss," he said with a straight face.

Feeling his heart palpating against her palm—not to mention the wet heat of exertion—she snatched her hand away, grumbling, "Remember that."

Grateful when they reached the grounds, Rosalind noticed no cars sat in the parking area. Grandfather and Aunt Hilary were both out for the day. She limped up the walkway, hobbled up the steps and threw herself into one of the flower-cushioned wicker porch chairs. Skelly tossed his jacket onto another chair, grabbed a third, twirled it around and sat facing her.

This time, a bit self-conscious beneath his gaze, she was the one to draw off her shoe and sock. Her ankle and foot weren't even half as puffy as they had been the night before. Carefully she tested them, rotating and stretching. Barely a twinge.

"Not too bad."

"Let me see."

On alert when Skelly reached for her leg, she stiffened. He lightly grasped her calf and ankle and guided her resisting foot into his lap.

"Roz, loosen up."

How could she when warning signals were going off inside her head? "This is as loose as I get."

Glancing at her through thick black lashes, he murmured, "Now, why don't I believe that?"

Rosalind grew even more flustered as his hand slid beneath her pant leg toward her calf. The thrill of his touch didn't stop there, but kept traveling all the way up her leg. She failed to ignore the sensation. He gently massaged her calf muscles, and ever so slowly worked his way down to her heel.

"That's not where it hurts," she finally protested. Though he was creating an ache of a very different kind in her, it wouldn't do to elaborate.

Repeating the disturbing maneuver, he asked, "Haven't you ever had a massage before?"

"Of course. I'm opening a day spa in two weeks, for heaven's sake." Though she hadn't given her business a thought since she'd left Chicago. "I'm personally familiar with all the services we're going to offer."

"Then you should know how important it is to relax the muscles around the injured area first."

Theory was one thing, practice another—she wasn't relaxing at all. Now he was working on her heel. Squeezing. Pressing. Making her antsy.

Trying to sound natural, she asked, "What makes you such an expert?"

"My sister, Aileen, is a massage therapist. She taught me some of her tricks."

"And I'll bet you take every available opportunity to use them."

"If I can be of help..." He shrugged modestly and attended to her arch. "I remember that time last year when Ursula foolishly miscalculated the difficulty of a jump and banged herself all the way down..."

Down where? Rosalind wondered. Some ski slope? Visions of Ursula, probably some bikinied ski bunny, intruded.

"No broken bones or anything," Skelly continued. His thumbs were probing the ball of her foot now—her weakness. "But it would have been a miracle if she'd come out of the accident unscathed."

Part of her was turning into a lump of putty in his hands—while the sane part had every intention of putting an end to his subtle manipulation. Somehow she couldn't manage getting up and running into the house as she'd like.

Trying to retain a cool facade, she forced herself to say, "And you ministered to poor Ursula's needs."

"Of course. I laid her out on the table and went over her entire body, inch by inch. Her spine. The back of her neck. Her limbs."

Imagining his doing the same to her, Rosalind squirmed in her chair. "I get the picture."

"She especially liked it when I worked on her toes."

He demonstrated, one toe at a time, gently squeezing the tips and working his way down. Then he advanced along the sides of her foot toward her ankle. Finally he arrived at the injured area, but when he touched her, the twinges were all pleasurable ones.

"Ursula was so pleased that she flipped onto her back and offered me her tummy."

An image she didn't want to conjure. "Don't hold your breath," she muttered.

Though each stroke was seducing her into an altered state of mind.

Rosalind felt as if Skelly were making love to her in full view of anyone who might pass by. Embarrassed as she might be, she was also glued to her chair.

"Yup, you should have heard her purr in appreciation."

Purr?

"As in Ursula the cat?"

"Last time I looked. I was house-sitting for Aileen and took Urs outside for some fresh air. The poor darling got herself up onto a garage roof and came down the wrong way." Skelly's blue eyes twinkled as he asked innocently, "Why? What did you think I was talking about?"

"Exactly what you wanted me to."

Straightening in her chair, Rosalind pulled her foot free and glared into his fraudulent expression. At the moment, he was working on innocence. Ursula the ski bunny, indeed. He'd done it to her again—inveigled her with one of his stories. Undoubtedly the other tales, while having some grain of truth, had been twisted to suit his purposes, as well.

"Charlatan," she muttered under her breath, glad she was finally wise to him. Somehow she'd find a way to give as good as she got. "I think I'd better get that ice."

"Need some cooling down, do you?"

Rosalind repressed the desire to eradicate that smug smile from his lips. "Oh-h-h . . . get over yourself!"

She swiped her shoe and sock from the porch floor, popped out of the chair and over to the door. Breaking the close connection gave her a sense of triumph disproportionate to the simple action.

After glancing at his watch, Skelly followed suit, retrieving his jacket, though he seemed to be heading for the steps rather than the door.

"We probably have another hour to kill," he said. "Why don't you lie down, get some rest?"

She realized he didn't mean to come inside. "What about you?"

"I'm going for a walk."

"You haven't stretched your legs enough for one day?"

"I thought about getting a good look at the neighborhood. While it's still light."

The simply stated intention held sinister overtones. "The door will be locked," she said, realizing that sounded more like a threat than a point of information.

Skelly didn't seem to notice. He was already scoping out the area to the north and west. "I can manage the bell." He gave her a distracted smile and indicated the front door. "Well, go ahead. What kind of gentleman would I be if I didn't see you safe inside?"

Any retort died at his "safe." He didn't think she was. Underneath all her bravado, she didn't think she was, either, Rosalind realized. Then again, neither was he.

"And who's going to watch over you?" she asked.

He parted his suit jacket, giving her a glimpse of the cell phone. "I can always dial 911, ma'am."

He made her smile. And relax.

"Don't get lost," she warned anyway.

But once inside, Rosalind realized the only thing that made her feel truly safe was being near Skelly.

Chapter Eight

"A man can't even read his newspaper in peace," Orville Galt grumbled to himself.

Rising, his arthritic fingers hanging on to the section containing the *Police Blotter,* he opened the door. A sultry summer breeze swept over him. The man on the other side appeared hot and winded, but Orville was glad to be wearing a flannel shirt.

Squinting over his dime-store half-moon glasses at the familiar face, he asked, "Can I help you?"

"You can if you're Orville Galt, retired sheriff."

"Don't tell me I won some kinda sweepstakes." He poked his head out the door and peered around. "Nope. No Prize-mobile." Then he inspected the TV tabloid reporter more closely. "And if you're tryin' to sell me brushes, you forgot your sample case."

"I'm Skelly McKenna from 'The Whole Truth.'"

"Hmm, so you are."

"Could you spare a few minutes to talk to me?"

"I'll prattle to anyone who'll listen. Keeps me from makin' friends with the walls. C'mon in if you don't mind the mess. Can't afford a cleaning lady more'n once a month, and it's darn near that now."

His place was tired-looking like him, magazines and books stacked on every horizontal surface, but it was home. He closed the door and claimed his La-Z-Boy.

"Place hasn't been the same since Agatha died." Orville added the newspaper to the growing pile next to his recliner. "Keeping up with chores has never been my strong suit."

"But I gather law enforcement was."

"Forty-odd years." With a resigned sigh, he removed the magnifying glasses and set them down on a rickety occasional table. "But that's enough small talk. Sit and let's get down to business."

Springs squealed in protest, and the middle cushion sagged alarmingly when the reporter took the couch. He slid to one side, where he hung on to the arm to keep from being swallowed whole.

"How well do you remember the Frank Sullivan murder?" McKenna began.

"Figured that's what you were about." Orville couldn't help his resentment at the younger man's having free rein to dig into the case when his own hands had been tied. "Murder's a major event around here—not like in the big city. In all my years on the force, I had maybe a dozen homicides."

"I suspect this was your most prominent case."

"By far. So, what is it you're wanting from me?"

"I'm beginning to believe Lily Lang was innocent. And I figured if anyone could help me make up my mind, it would be you."

A little flattered despite the bitterness, he grunted. "I gotta admit Lily's confession made the case easy on us. I've always wondered if it wasn't too damn easy."

McKenna jumped on that. "Then why didn't you hold off until you investigated other suspects?"

"Lily confessed! The highly experienced D.A. believed her. I was only the sheriff."

Orville clenched his jaw at having to defend himself. He was still ticked that he hadn't had the clout to run the investigation the way his gut told him.

"Were you at the crime scene?"

"First to arrive. Lily wasn't herself, granted. She was subdued...like the light had gone outta her. But she told me what she'd done...and handed over the gun nice as you please."

"And that made it too easy?"

"Not that exactly...it's not the only time a murderer stuck around and confessed. Seems a woman's more prone to giving herself up, especially when she's killed a man she loved because he was a threat."

McKenna started. "Are you saying Lily was roughed up?"

Orville shook his head. "Didn't look it. Darn curious, too. Signs of a struggle all over the room. A table knocked over. Broken lamp. Sofa outta line. But Lily...why, she was perfectly dressed, every hair in place...like she was gonna step in front of the cameras any minute. Not a sign of blood on her, neither."

"But Sullivan was shot. Why should Lily have had blood on her?"

"Didn't even think about it then." Drawing on a memory, he frowned. "Couldn't see 'em in that light, but the lab found traces of blood on the gun. Sullivan's blood. Always did puzzle me how there could be blood on the weapon but not on her hands."

"She could have washed them."

"After wiping the gun clean...or trying to," he agreed. "But why would Lily go to that trouble if she planned to confess anyhow? And why would she claim she'd never left the room after shooting Sullivan . . . except to make the call from the other parlor, of course.''

"You're certain she wiped the weapon clean?"

"Must've, 'cause the technician couldn't find no other prints, only the one set where she was hanging on to the gun when she turned it over to me. Funny thing, though. Whatever she used to wipe the dang thing clean . . . we never did find hide nor hair of it.''

"Did you ask her to explain?"

"Asked her lots of things she wouldn't answer. Just kept on saying over and over she'd killed Frank Sullivan. No details. No motive. No regret.''

"Can you remember anything else that didn't make sense?" McKenna asked with relish, as if his juices were flowing.

Orville started. Why should he lay out everything he knew or suspected for some reporter who meant nothing to him? He'd said too much already.

"I'd reckon that was enough to haunt me for a long time afterward, until Lily escaped Dwight, anyhow. Can't say I was sorry to hear she was free.''

"One more thing about the night of the murder . . . after Lily turned herself in, who did she make her one phone call to?''

The question surprised Orville into answering. "Why, no one. Her sister-in-law arrived back at the house. She went right upstairs, made sure little Claudia didn't wake while we took her mama away.''

"What about a lawyer?"

"Against my advice, Lily refused to phone for counsel," he said, growing ticked at himself for continuing to blab. "Said she'd take a court-appointed lawyer. I believe she would've, too, if that husband of hers hadn't insisted on bringing in some hotshot. And him a step away from divorce court. Hiring that big-city lawyer was a waste of his good money, though...considering..."

"That Lily wouldn't cooperate in defending herself," McKenna finished.

"If she would've furnished some extenuating circumstances, he mighta been able to get her a reduced sentence."

"So, *you* placed the call to her husband."

"No, sir, that I didn't."

"One of your deputies?"

"Not without orders from me. I imagine his sister let Lang know what was going on."

And that was all he was going to say. McKenna could dig for the rest. Orville was looking forward to seeing what a big-city reporter could do with the rumors and innuendos rife in a small town.

SKELLY LEFT the retired sheriff's modest two-story frame house surrounded by older, grander neighbors with better-tended grounds, certain that, before he and Roz were through with their personal investigation, he was going to have his hooks in the story of a lifetime. A damn career maker. The big boys at the network would definitely sit up and take notice.

The bonanza of information he'd never expected to unearth when he'd sought out Galt stunned him.

Self-defense was something he hadn't considered before. How could there have been a struggle with Lily showing no signs of it? And from Galt's description of her appearance...it almost sounded as if she'd prepared herself to give the performance of her life.

Something was wrong there, big time.

A conspiracy of silence surrounded Sullivan's death. The authorities had held back information from the press, while Lily had held back information from the authorities. Why? Had someone with connections in a high place had it in for her? And whom had she been trying to protect?

If he'd had any doubts that Lily Lang was innocent of murder, they certainly had vanished, Skelly admitted.

He suspected that Orville Galt harbored a secret guilt for his own participation in the Sullivan case...rather, for his decided lack thereof. He'd had plenty of years to forget the details, and yet he hadn't. If only the man would prove cooperative later, when he was putting together the segment for 'The Whole Story.' Skelly could imagine the impact of a televised interview with the retired sheriff.

He picked up his pace, Lang House being only a few blocks away. What was he going to tell Roz? He hadn't wanted her to know he was checking on her grandfather, and Galt certainly hadn't corroborated the old man's story.

Noah had insisted the sheriff—not Hilary—had called him. Why would he have lied? And why had his sister gone along with him? Unless Noah had said the first thing that came to mind, and Hilary chose to protect him from whatever truth he was hiding. For Roz's sake, Skelly wished he didn't have to acknowledge the only obvious conclusion he could draw.

That Noah Lang had already arrived in Galena *before* Frank Sullivan drew his last breath.

ROSALIND WAVERED between worried and impatient. Where was Skelly? She couldn't believe how long he'd been gone. He didn't seem the type who would lose himself in Galena's past by taking in its diverse architecture on a foot tour. She was certain he'd chosen to investigate the neighborhood so he would be familiar with his surroundings in case they ran into more trouble.

The top-floor turret windows would afford her a better view of the blocks adjacent than those on the first floor. The trip to her bedroom was maddeningly slow. Disappointment pricked her when she saw no sign of the man. She whipped away from the windows and began to pace.

The bed reminded Rosalind of Skelly's suggestion that she get some rest, but she was too keyed up to continue doing nothing. Besides, lying against the coverlet's plush folds thinking about him might provoke fantasies she'd rather not have. Even now, she imagined she could feel the mattress pressed into the back of her legs as she kissed him....

"No, you don't, Skelly McKenna," she muttered. "Stop sneaking up on me like that."

But what to do with herself? Neither Aunt Hilary nor Grandfather had returned home.

Her gaze wandered the room, stopping at an inside wall. A corner portion was actually a slanted door that would open to a storage area nestled under the eaves. Not having investigated the treasure trove since childhood, she wondered if Lily's belongings still waited there intact . . . as Grandfather had so long ago mandated.

Only one way to find out, she thought, glad to have a distraction. Maybe Lily herself had left some inadvertent clue as to what had prompted her to lie that fateful night.

Why hadn't she thought of this before?

The door opened easily, and the light switch still worked. Two bare bulbs illuminated a space that was a dozen feet long but only half as wide, the outer wall being slanted and making it impossible for her to stand up-right.

A rod the length of the enclosure still sagged from hanger upon hanger of glamorous clothing, all sealed in zipped plastic bags. Boxes of all sizes and descriptions both below and lining a narrow shelf above held more of Lily's possessions. Halfway along the outer wall, a dormer window with a cushioned seat awaited. As a child, Rosalind had spent hour after hour sitting there, sorting through boxes and albums of souvenirs from her grandmother's Hollywood days.

Everything looked exactly as she remembered. Indeed, it looked as if nothing had been touched in thirty years. But, of course, Rosalind knew that wasn't true.

No dust. The place was obviously cleaned on a regular basis, undoubtedly Grandfather's doing. Heart hurting for him, she suspected he spent too much time alone in here with his beloved's things, immersing himself in the past.

She began by eliminating containers of shoes or other accessories, as well as those filled with the movie-star memorabilia she'd once been so fond of. What she dragged to the floor space around the window were several plain cardboard cartons, a flowered hatbox holding some loose black-and-white photographs and a small trunk.

Hatbox first.

Though she'd never done more than take a quick look at these particular photographs before, Rosalind instantly identified them as being a record of her grandmother's growing-up years in Galena. Whether faded from age or in soft focus because the camera had been cheap, Lily was nonetheless recognizable because of her silvery hair and tiny mole.

Even as a toddler, she'd charmed the camera. A tomboy at age six or seven, she'd posed at the top of a narrow fence, tongue sticking out boldly at the lens. By the time she was twelve or thirteen, she'd turned self-conscious…yet the camera had gone on loving her. And as a teenager, she'd been absolutely breathtaking. That her clothes were inexpensive and often worn didn't detract from her natural charisma.

Or prevent boys from being infatuated with her.

Spreading out a number of photographs like a hand of cards, Rosalind more closely examined Lily's companions. The same two dark-haired boys appeared in several shots taken over a period of years, the last of which had probably been taken at a prom. Lily was dancing with one of them—they were obviously caught up in each other romantically by this time—while the second watched on from the sidelines, his expression wistful. She could be wrong, but she thought the loner bore a strong resemblance to Frank Sullivan. As for Lily's dancing partner—he also seemed familiar, though she couldn't quite place him.

Rosalind slipped the photo into her pocket and next sorted through the cardboard cartons, unfortunately finding nothing of interest. She quickly went on to the last item.

The small trunk was filled with keepsakes of a later time. An album of photos recorded the years of Lily's marriage. And of her own mother's childhood. Rosalind contemplated with longing the shots of her grandparents and mother, all so happy together. It seemed that Claudia Lang had been as loving and demonstrative a child as the grown-up Claudia Van Straaten was cool and distant.

What had happened to make her change so?

A lump in her throat, Rosalind abandoned the reminders of what she'd missed growing up in a divided household. Despite hearing the muffled sounds of more than one car pulling up outside—her aunt and grandfather must both be home—she picked up a container whose wooden surface was intricately carved with tiny leaves and flowers.

When she tried to open the box, however, it thwarted her. The lid stayed firmly in place, and no matter how thoroughly she looked, she could find no visible latch.

Below, the front door slammed, but Rosalind wasn't ready to give up on the box yet.

The catch had to be hidden, so she ran her fingers along every carved surface, testing here, pressing there, searching for anything that would give. The box got away from her, bouncing off the trunk with a loud thunk. Saving it from hitting the floor, she tried again. She doubled her efforts, finally discovering that one of the tiny carved flowers felt slightly higher than the others.

Though she gave it her full attention, the carving wouldn't push. Nor would it slide in any direction. But, to her satisfaction, it did turn slightly... the subtle twisting movement followed by a click.

The lid popped open to reveal the box's contents—a leather-bound diary, 1963 embossed in gold on its cover.

The year Frank Sullivan died and Lily had been incarcerated.

A thread of triumph surged through Rosalind as she imagined the insights Lily's written thoughts might give her. Before she could even turn back the cover to take a peek, however, she heard her name yelled from below.

"Rosalind, are you home, honey?"

"Yes, Aunt Hilary," she returned. "I'll be down in a minute."

But her aunt's slow tread continued up the stairs. Frustrated—not wanting to share her discovery before she could give it a thorough examination herself—Rosalind secreted the diary and replaced the wooden box in the trunk. She didn't have enough time to put everything back the way she'd found it, so she hurried from the storage area, making do with switching off the light and closing the door behind her. She left the bedroom even as her red-faced great-aunt puffed up to the landing.

"I thought I heard you rummaging around, but I didn't see the Thunderbird."

"That's because I left it at a gas station. The brakes needed some adjustment." An understatement, perhaps, but rather a grain of truth than an outright lie.

"Better safe than sorry, especially on these hills."

Her stomach knotting at the memory of the close call, she changed the subject. "I should come down to talk to you and Grandfather."

"Noah's not here, honey. He must have gone out while I was at the supermarket."

Curious…Rosalind was certain she'd heard more than one car pull up. "Where is he, then?"

Her great-aunt glanced away. "He did one of his disappearing acts."

"Again?" Two days in a row?

"He goes off alone for a while when the whim takes him, usually a few times a week. His strike for independence, I guess. Nothing to worry about."

But Hilary herself sounded worried, Rosalind thought. And her great-aunt was acting as nervous as she had under Skelly's questioning the night before.

So when the older woman started down the stairs, she followed. "I'll help you unpack the groceries."

"You're such a dear. Are you certain I can't convince you to have dinner with us? I'm making your favorite."

"Roast pork and pan-roasted potatoes?" Mouth watering already, Rosalind figured she'd better consult Skelly before committing them in case he felt they needed to be elsewhere. "I'm not sure yet, but as soon as Skelly gets back..." Hearing the downstairs door open again, she didn't finish. "Maybe that's him now."

A breathy Hilary stopped at the second-floor landing. "Actually I believe that's Claudia coming in with more groceries. She arrived a few minutes after you and Skelly left this morning."

"Mother is here? You didn't tell me she was coming." And why wouldn't her mother have mentioned it? Rosalind had called specifically to let her know what she and Skelly were up to.

"She took me by complete surprise. Said she decided to come at the last minute because she realized she needed a few days of rest and relaxation."

That didn't sound right. Her mother didn't have a spontaneous bone in her body. And she'd always maintained relaxation was for other people who didn't know what to do with their lives. Besides, she'd been so involved with the details of her upcoming charity event the other night that she'd hardly spared her own daughter a few minutes of her precious time.

No, if her mother was here, the visit had purpose.

Only Rosalind wasn't certain she wanted to know its significance.

SKELLY DECIDED dinner at Lang House was a fine idea until he learned that Claudia Van Straaten had arrived unannounced.

Though he'd hoped to drop some of the information he'd gathered from Orville Galt to see how Noah and Hilary would react, he didn't feel comfortable doing so while Roz's mother was at the table. He couldn't forget how young Claudia had been at the time of the murder—the tragedy had affected her so deeply that even her psychiatrist couldn't trigger memories her subconscious had repressed.

Or so she'd said.

He also couldn't forget being convinced that she'd lied about what she did or did not remember.

Her unexpected appearance already suspect, Claudia compounded Skelly's distrust when she didn't say a single word to him. She even avoided looking at him directly. Roz wasn't faring much better treatment. It was as if Claudia chose to forget they were present . . . or at the very least, to forget their reason for being here.

Provoking her hostility again would merely upset everyone, so Skelly chose to wait for a more opportune moment to see what he could get from Noah and Hilary.

Roz's grandfather was the one to bring up the investigation.

"So, was your day productive?" Noah asked her halfway through dinner.

"I had an interesting encounter with Diane and Perry Nesmith."

When Roz finished detailing her visit, Noah said, "I told you the widow was a likely candidate. Not that you can prove anything. And what would pointing a finger at her now serve? She'd probably have that stroke her husband must be worried about, and that would be that."

Skelly exchanged a look with Roz. From her expression, he figured she was as baffled as he. While her grandfather maintained Lily was innocent—while he'd included the widow among the possible suspects—he certainly didn't sound as if he really wanted them to do anything about it.

No more than he'd tried to prove his darling Lily's innocence before her incarceration, Skelly thought.

"We're not through by any means, Grandfather." Finished with her dinner, Roz placed her flatware on her plate and set her napkin on the table. "As a matter of fact, we have another lead we'll be following up in a little while."

"Tonight?"

Noah's white hair seemed to bristle in disapproval. Hilary merely appeared troubled. And Claudia was picking at her food, acting as if she hadn't heard a word.

Skelly said, "That's when we might be able to find Anthony Cavillo over at River Bluff."

After they'd picked up the Thunderbird, he'd called the resort and had been informed that the owner wasn't around but would be later that evening. Roz had agreed they should head out directly after dinner.

"Cavillo?" Hilary echoed, now appearing puzzled. "He's never been involved in politics. What does he have to do with anything?"

"Cavillo and Sullivan were locked in a long-term dispute over zoning," Roz informed her family. "At least, that's what Walt Rogowski told us."

Noah frowned. "You talked to Rogowski about this?"

An obviously distressed Claudia suddenly threw down her fork and popped out of her chair. "I don't know why you insist on ruining a fine dinner with this horrid topic, Rosalind! I certainly taught you better!" Trembling under the surprised stares her family gave her, she took a deep breath, and within seconds, her visage smoothed. Suddenly smiling as if she'd never been upset at all, she patted Hilary's hand. "Since you did all the cooking, I insist on handling the cleanup."

What a turnabout, Skelly thought, even as he realized that the normally cool Claudia doted on her aunt. Hilary had claimed she'd practically raised Roz. He suspected she'd done the same with Claudia after Lily was imprisoned.

Expression strained, Hilary murmured, "How thoughtful of you, dear."

"I'll help clear," Roz volunteered, standing and gathering dishes.

"I am not helpless, Rosalind." Claudia's frosty blue eyes focused on her daughter. "You run along with your friend and play detective if you must."

Mother and daughter locked gazes. Something subtle passed between them, and Roz backed off.

"Fine."

While she didn't show it, Skelly knew Roz was hurt by her mother's uncaring attitude toward her. From her nonchalant demeanor, he also understood she was used to Claudia's indifference and had cultivated an uncaring facade in self-defense.

Heart going out to Roz, wishing like hell he could hold her in his arms and take away the hurt, he suggested quietly, "Let's get out of here."

Before he said something to her mother that he wouldn't be able to take back.

BECAUSE THEY DIDN'T NEED to leave for River Bluff immediately, Rosalind talked Skelly into visiting her attic room.

"You want to be alone with me, is that it?" he murmured in her ear as they reached the second-floor landing.

Her heart thumped at his suggestive tone. "Down, boy. I'm not the diversion."

"Then what is?"

"Grandfather couldn't tolerate being without keepsakes to remind him of Lily." Excitement quickening her step, she raced up the last flight. "I went through her things, hoping to find some clue to help us."

"And?"

"How about a diary dated 1963..."

Skelly whistled.

"...which I haven't had a look at yet because Aunt Hilary interrupted me." Entering her room with Skelly right behind, she went straight for the closet and switched on the light. "Careful of your head."

One look at the half-open hatbox, in addition to the bit of delicate material sticking out from under the trunk's lid, made her stop cold. Skelly ran right into her.

"Roz?"

"Someone's been up here since this afternoon." Her chest tightened, and she had trouble taking a normal breath. "This isn't the way I left things."

"The diary?"

Fear in her soul, she hastened to the trunk and flipped open the lid. A gauzy scarf she hadn't even noticed before sat on top. She dug down and found the carved box, which had been dumped on its side. Hands trembling, she picked it up and triggered the catch. Only when she saw the leather book inside did she allow herself to breathe normally.

"It's here."

"The perpetrator obviously didn't know what to look for."

"Then why?"

''To see what you were up to. If you were interested in Lily's things, you must have had a reason. *Someone* wanted to know what that was.''

She was thankful he didn't further voice his suspicions. Her grandfather, great-aunt and mother were the only ones with access to her room, she conceded uneasily. Any one of them could have searched it while she and Skelly retrieved the Thunderbird from Jarvis Wiggs. But why? She didn't want to believe a person she loved had anything to hide.

Diary in hand, Rosalind slid onto the window seat, where Skelly joined her. A tight squeeze. Too aware of his presence, she opened the leather cover and flipped through the initial entries—three or four per week—reading bits and pieces here and there.

''Lily and Grandfather were together at the beginning of the year.'' She flew through several more weeks, stopping at the Ides of March. Brow furrowing, she read aloud. '' 'Noah is driving me to the edge with his jealousy. He is certain all men desire me as much as he does. Maybe in my youth.... Even so, why doesn't he trust me?' ''

''That doesn't sound like a woman having an affair with another man,'' Skelly said.

''No.'' Rosalind skimmed the next few pages. ''Hmm. The pattern's clear. When Lily couldn't tolerate Grandfather's jealousy anymore, she left him ... this time, though, it was for good.'' She pointed. '' 'I know I must press the divorce. My heart breaks.' Poor Lily. She still loved him.''

''Maybe she turned to Frank Sullivan in despair.''

''But his widow said they'd been having an affair off and on for years,'' Rosalind related, scanning for any details about the dead man. ''Here. 'I am disappointed in Frank. His actions are not worthy of the boy he once was. I've pleaded with him, but I doubt he will stop.'"

"Stop what?"

"She doesn't say."

"This could be it. Whatever Sullivan was into that she disapproved of could have gotten him killed."

Rosalind nodded, next reading from the middle of June, less than two weeks before the murder. "'Noah arrived in Galena unannounced once more. He keeps hoping to catch me with my lover.'" That her grandfather had been in the habit of showing up unpredictably made her uneasy. "'He means to have custody of Claudia. He says my low behavior is upsetting her. How is that possible when I have never betrayed him?'" The import hitting her, she caught her breath and locked gazes with Skelly. "Do you realize what this means?"

"She and Sullivan *weren't* lovers."

"No matter what his wife and everyone else believed." She read on from the same passage. "'It's true, Claudia has not been herself lately. Not since arriving in Galena. She won't tell me what's troubling her. When I broach the subject, she turns away from me. I seldom see the warm, happy girl I raised. She is becoming withdrawn. Unpredictable. Another worry on my heart. All my fault. Divorce must be terribly frightening to a child, even though I think of her as a very mature thirteen. A young lady.'"

Lily's self-incriminating thoughts haunted Rosalind. She'd seen the photographs showing her mother to be a normal, loving child. Here Lily indicated that her daughter changed. *Withdrawn. Unpredictable.* She'd often thought of her mother in those same terms.

"Are you all right?"

Appreciating Skelly's concern, she admitted, "I'm a little sad. It never occurred to me that Mother was permanently scarred from the emotional upheaval between her own parents."

"Some children are affected more than others."

"I'm certain you're right."

Did that include him? She remembered Skelly hadn't had a secure upbringing himself, what with his mother dying in childbirth and his father holding his affections at bay in unfair retribution. Quickly skimming the final half-dozen entries that appeared to be more of the same, she closed the diary, glad to be done with it for the moment.

"We don't have to see Cavillo tonight if you don't want to," Skelly said, sliding a comforting arm around her shoulders.

She leaned into him as if it were natural to her. "Of course we do. The rest can wait."

Getting out of the house and forgetting the suspicions fomenting in the back of her mind were exactly what she needed.

...Noah arrived in Galena unannounced once more... keeps hoping to catch me with my lover...

Rosalind locked the diary away, wishing she could lock away the memory of those words with equal ease.

PERRY NESMITH HAD BEEN waiting across from Lang House for what seemed like hours before Lily's granddaughter exited with that gossipmonger. He pulled himself together and rushed across the street as they approached the parking area.

He yelled, "Miss Van Straaten!" hoping to give her as good a start as she'd given Diane that morning.

"Mr. Nesmith, what can I do for you?"

"You can damn well stay away from my wife!"

"I appreciate your concern—"

"You couldn't possibly!" If anything, his anger had doubled since that morning. "Diane is a very sick woman. She doesn't need your kind stirring her up."

"Now, wait a minute!" the reporter growled, taking a step toward him.

The blonde put out a hand to hold him back. "Skelly, let me handle this." She seemed sincere enough when she said, "Mr. Nesmith, again let me apologize for upsetting your wife. I only want the truth. My whole family's been upset for thirty-some years."

"That was your grandmother's doing."

"She didn't kill Frank Sullivan. She had no motive."

He didn't argue the point. "Lily nearly killed Diane, seducing Frank with her Hollywood ways."

"My grandmother was his friend. Tell your wife she was wrong. They were never lovers."

"That's a damn lie!" he shouted, shaking inside.

It had to be...or how could he justify what he and Diane had done?

Chapter Nine

The sun dipped low in the sky by the time they drove beneath the tastefully lit sign announcing the entryway to River Bluff. The private road paralleling the Mississippi River ran through a sparsely forested area.

Wondering how long Perry Nesmith had been waiting for them to leave the house, Skelly asked Roz, "What do you think Nesmith *really* wanted?"

She gave him a surprised glance. "A promise that we'd leave his wife be."

"If that's all, he could have come up to the house and rung the bell."

"Maybe he was working up his nerve."

Skelly noted a few vacation homes scattered among the foliage along the way. And additional side roads led through thicker woods, probably to more-distant tracts of the development.

"Someone was watching the house last night, too," he informed her.

"What?"

"Could've been Nesmith. He saw us in town, remember." Skelly tried out a theory to see if it would wash. "What if Nesmith messed with the brakes, then waited outside the house later to see the results of his handi-work?''

"It sounds plausible," she admitted. "Why didn't you say something before?"

"I thought I was mistaken. I was trying to get a better look through the telescope when the person disappeared. I figured a neighbor could have been walking a dog."

And then Hilary had sneaked into the house, and he'd wondered if *she'd* had reason to skulk around outside. Another thing he wouldn't share with Roz—at least not yet. Though she put on a brave front, he knew some of the entries she'd read in the diary had upset her. The last thing in the world he wanted was to make her feel worse. That was bound to happen, though, sooner or later.

For Skelly couldn't rid himself of the bad taste in his mouth every time he thought about Noah's certain antipathy for Frank Sullivan.

Nearly a mile from the entrance, the heart of the complex dominated the clearing. Sprawling along the river bluff, the massive lodge constructed of stone and timber was reminiscent of the edifices erected in state parks by the Civilian Conservation Corps during the Depression.

"Check it out," Skelly said. "Pretty impressive."

"Exactly what I was thinking. Now I wish I'd made the effort to get out here under more auspicious circumstances."

The parking lot was nearly bursting at the seams, but Roz found a spot near a light standard. By the time they departed, Skelly figured it would be dark, and she was justifiably paranoid about leaving the Thunderbird where people could see it. Not that either one of them had figured out a way to keep the car safe overnight.

Hopefully lightning wouldn't strike the same vehicle twice.

Once out of the car, Roz complained, "I don't want to lug a purse around." She threw it into the trunk, then slipped the car keys into her trousers pocket.

They started toward the lodge. Skelly gazed around, absorbing the incredible setting, until his attention was caught by a familiar figure leaving the building via the grand entrance. A tall, trim man wearing a two-thousand-dollar suit, slashes of silver enhancing his precisely cut brown hair, swept down the walkway.

"Whoa!" Skelly stopped. "That *is* who I think it is, right?"

"Walt Rogowski."

"Well, well, well."

"A little odd to find him *here*."

"Unless he's soliciting campaign contributions. Though I didn't get the impression that Rogowski considered Cavillo his bosom buddy."

"Me, neither."

The gubernatorial candidate disappeared into the rear of a Lincoln Towncar. A burly young man, his fair hair tousled by the breeze shooting off the river, closed the door and hopped behind the wheel. The tinted rear window slid open. Still some distance away, Skelly could barely make out Rogowski reclining against the plush interior . . . and yet he swore that, for a moment, the politician looked straight through them.

Then the long black car crept away.

Next to him, Roz shivered.

Skelly rubbed the middle of her back to soothe her, even as he said, "Why don't I feel good about this?"

He started off again, noting that Roz kept glancing over her shoulder. To make certain Rogowski's car stayed gone?

Distracted, she managed to bump into a timbered fence. She gripped the top rail to steady herself. Skelly followed her wide-eyed gaze and faced the descent to the wide river below. A soft incline was broken by a natural path about a dozen feet down. Then the pitch steepened dangerously, promptly becoming a sheer drop to the water.

Looking as if her stomach were doing a jig, Roz hurried him toward the lodge's entrance.

He held the door open for her. "Here's hoping Cavillo won't clam up on us."

"Let's think positive. Rogowski could have been here to see anyone."

Anticipation at meeting Anthony Cavillo quickened Skelly's step. He nearly collided with a little boy who was screaming and running away from his exasperated mother.

"Sorry," the harried woman said, grabbing her son's hand and pulling him back into the noisy throng milling about.

Both the lobby and the equally crowded restaurant beyond matched the lodge's exterior. Timbered beams and two see-through stone fireplaces graced the open space, where a peaked ceiling rose about forty feet high in the center. Couch and chair cushions encased in colorful materials of bold design complemented rough-hewn furniture.

"There's the registration desk," Roz said.

"Let me handle this...if that's all right with you."

"Knock yourself out."

Evidently she wasn't in the mood to bicker.

Though the lobby was packed, traffic at the desk was slow. As Skelly approached the brunette behind the counter, Roz fell behind him. He swiftly inspected the employee's identification tag.

"Good evening, Miss Jerina," he said smoothly. "I called earlier and was told Mr. Cavillo would be in his office about now."

He gave the woman a winning smile, and her ruby red lips curved in response. Then her eyes widened.

"Aren't you Skelly McKenna?"

"Guilty as charged."

"I thought so." Seeming impressed, she leaned toward him across the desk in an intimate manner. "Mr. Cavillo was here, but you just missed him. Something important came up, and he left in a hurry."

Before he could ask how long the owner would be gone, Roz piped up, "Will he be back tonight?" She'd obviously forgotten she'd agreed to let him handle the situation.

Miss Jerina blinked and stared at Roz as if she hadn't noticed her before. "Well, yes—"

"Good," Skelly interrupted. He gave her another smile, hopefully even more winning. "We can wait."

"Unfortunately Mr. Cavillo said he didn't know how long he'd be gone."

"We'll check back in a while."

"We're having our fireworks to celebrate the Fourth tonight. They'll start as soon as it's dark."

Skelly winked at her. Then he took Roz's arm and drew her to the doors opposite the main entrance. Halfway across the room, she slowed and glanced around.

"What?"

"I have the oddest feeling, as if someone is watching us."

But when Skelly gazed through the crowd, not even Miss Jerina was looking their way.

Outside, a deck clung to the length of the building, and a wide stairway ran down to the dock and a busy outdoor café. Its name in flashing lights, the *River Star* navigated offshore, and some distance from it, a fireworks barge was setting anchor.

"So, did Rogowski warn off Cavillo?" Skelly mused as a family of five passed them. "Or was he here on a fishing expedition?"

"Maybe business brought Cavillo to the casino." Roz's attention was glued to the riverboat.

"Could be." Skelly took a leisurely look around. "With or without the gaming operation, Cavillo's got himself a gold mine here."

"The view alone would be worth the stay."

A burnished ball of fire, the sun quickly sank below the horizon—green-black vegetation growing along the far, opposite bank of the Mississippi. Swirls of color skated along the moving waters, which lapped at myriad foliage-covered sandbars. A picture-perfect setting.

The breeze kicked up from the river, and Roz shivered. "Goose bumps." She rubbed her arms. "I could use a walk to stay warm." Skelly welcomed the cool night after the heat of the day. He glanced down at Roz's foot. "Tempting fate?"

"A *short* walk," she clarified, "to someplace private. Besides, this time, I taped up my ankle for support."

Passing a group of oldsters jabbering about their wins and losses on the riverboat, they descended the stairs to the first of several landings. An abbreviated wood-chip path led only as far as a fenced cul-de-sac that held several benches . . . one of which was occupied by a pair of lovers locked in an embrace.

Immediately envisioning Roz in his arms, Skelly wondered what she'd do if he kissed her again.

The fantasy tortured him. He knew he should leave her be until this hunt for a murderer was finished, not because he had anything against mixing business and pleasure, but because he was holding back.

She wouldn't want to hear that Noah had lied, that he suspected the old man could have been in Galena to get rid of his supposed rival. Voicing his suspicions now would not only hurt Roz, but would put immediate distance between them. And he could only imagine how she would feel later if he pointed a finger at her grandfather.

"Feeling adventurous?" he asked her, indicating the natural path that he'd noticed earlier.

"Looks safe enough. Sure."

Skelly climbed through the rails of the fence and offered her a helping hand. At the contact, his senses flared. He was certain Roz felt the connection, too. Like a scared rabbit, though, she scrambled to the other side.

Dusk surrounded them as they started off, but the sky was clear and filled with swirls of stars that would grow brighter as the sky darkened to night.

Rather than letting go of her, he wrapped an arm lightly around her shoulders.

Rather than pulling free, she leaned into him.

Making Skelly want to forget about everything but a growing certainty that only Roz could fulfill Moira's legacy.

"I HOPE WE'RE NOT WASTING our time," Rosalind said as they put distance between them and the lodge. "What if we wait for Cavillo for nothing?"

"Then we come back tomorrow. Besides, I don't know what else we can do at the moment. I was counting on his giving me some new leads."

Skelly's determined tone was gratifying. No doubt about it—he was committed to smoking out the real murderer. Rosalind figured finding the diary had reinforced his commitment. Learning that Lily and Sullivan hadn't been lovers had eliminated her motivation for killing him.

Now, if only they could figure out why her grandmother was upset with Sullivan...

What had the politician been up to? Maybe she'd better read the diary in more detail when she got home. If only she could figure it out, Rosalind was sure they'd have the motive for his murder.

"We *are* at a standstill," she admitted, appreciating Skelly's experience at digging for the truth. "The only suspects we have so far are Diane and Perry Nesmith."

She looked to Skelly for an affirmation. When he said nothing, her stomach knotted. Surely he couldn't suspect anyone close to her. Even as she formed the denial, she thought about the way her grandfather and great-aunt had been acting. About her mother's showing up unannounced.

Pushing those ugly misgivings away, she said, "We have lots of bits and pieces of information with no way of sorting them out."

"Give it time. We keep talking to people, and the information will sort itself out."

Skelly's promise made her feel a bit better. "I'm sure you're correct, though I feel as if I've led you on a wild-goose chase."

"You don't hear me complaining."

"Not at the moment." Increasingly amazed by the turn their contentious partnership had taken, she murmured, "Funny how things change."

"As in?"

"You, for one. I thought I would throttle you before you agreed to investigate Sullivan's murder for yourself—"

"And *I* thought you would throttle me when I coerced you into working with me."

"I knew you wouldn't do a thing if I didn't agree. Honest," she added, "I, uh, suspected you had designs on me."

"I did." His fingers tightened on the soft flesh below her shoulder. "I still do."

The intensity of his statement shook her, as did his expression. He was looking at her as if... "But you're doing serious work here," she said, a lump in her throat. "That can't be merely to impress me."

"Truth is, I feel like a real investigative reporter again."

"Again?"

"I didn't start out wanting to sensationalize the news—not that *I* have a problem with what I do for a living," he assured her. "I do have ethics, and I put in an honest day's work like the next guy."

"What did you want to do?"

"Actually, as a kid, I thought I'd be a different kind of writer altogether," he admitted. "I used to make up stories, tell them to my friends—"

"Even now, you have a flair for storytelling," she noted dryly, thinking of the fables he'd spun for her over the past few days.

Skelly grinned down at her, his dark hair fluttering in the breeze, his too-handsome face washed by moonlight. His appeal never stronger, Rosalind couldn't resist succumbing. Her pulse fluttered and her knees felt weak. If she were the kind of woman who swooned...

A loud pop was followed by a spray of color across the sky. River Bluff's fireworks had begun. Skelly removed his arm from her back, took her hand and pulled her toward a grassy area in the midst of a thicket.

"Looks comfortable enough." He dropped to the ground and gave her arm a tug so she joined him.

"I see." She gave him a knowing look. "*You're* the one who's done too much walking today."

On the way over to the resort, Skelly had informed her of his visit with Orville Galt. He'd used her hurt foot as his excuse for not sharing his plans beforehand—he'd feared she'd insist on coming along when she needed to take it easy. He was probably right.

Rosalind had been heartened to learn the retired sheriff doubted her grandmother's confession. And she'd been outraged that he hadn't had the gumption to speak up about the blood issue if nothing else.

Thinking about the unfairness of what her family had suffered made her tremble.

"Actually I thought we could watch the fireworks." Skelly scooted closer so they were shoulder to shoulder, hip to hip. "Warm?"

"Plenty." Heat seeped through her everywhere they touched. Savoring the delicious sensation without knowing what she wanted to do about it, she asked, "Where were we?" as golden stars sprayed across the night sky. His intense gaze leaving her no doubt as to what *he* wanted, she swallowed hard and prompted, "You were saying something about the kind of writer you hoped to be."

"Oh, right." He sighed. "By the time I got to high school, I had dreams of writing short stories and novels for a living, spinning tales that would touch people. Keelin says I inherited my storytelling ability from our grandmother."

Skelly had told her about the Irish cousin who'd inherited her mysterious extrasensory sight from Moira McKenna. Somehow Rosalind was reassured that Skelly had one of his grandmother's more down-to-earth qualities.

"I might have given fiction writing a serious chance...if I'd had any encouragement."

"So your father disapproved of your ambitions."

"Good guess. He convinced me fiction writing was impractical, that I could never make a living at it. I always tried so hard to please him...."

Just as she had tried in vain to please her own mother, Rosalind thought, empathizing. She shifted and rested more fully against Skelly, enjoying the columns of white shooting high above the river, followed by whining rockets and tiny bursts of additional light. When her hair brushed his cheek, he turned his head, his breath drifting down her neck. Savoring the sensation, she let her eyes flutter closed for a moment.

"I compromised and worked at a degree in journalism," he continued softly. "Then, for several years, I was employed by what even you would consider a legitimate newspaper. I worked the inner city on the crime beat, sometimes undercover. I made a bare-bones living when I deserved combat pay."

"So you changed jobs for more money," she said, hoping she didn't sound disapproving. She wanted in the worst way to understand him.

"The choice wasn't mine. A story about a drug operation that I'd been working on for months went belly-up. Given my not-too-cooperative attitude when I got a bone between my teeth, my editor decided that it was my fault. That I'd blown it. So he fired me. And writing for a tabloid was the only job I could find. I told myself I would only do it until I could get back into the mainstream."

"Did you ever try?"

"I found I was good at tabloid news. I was successful. Money *can* be seductive if you haven't had a lot," he admitted. "Not to mention how satisfying being in the spotlight can be. When opportunity knocked, I jumped at the chance to be an investigative reporter for a televised tabloid that's now defunct. That led to the anchor desk on 'The Whole Story.' Not only does my current job put me in another tax bracket, but it's also safe. No more pavement pounding. No more rubbing shoulders with the criminal element."

"Until now."

He ignored her reminder, saying, "The change felt good at first. I didn't realize how quickly 'safe' could get old."

His confiding in her made Rosalind feel closer to Skelly. "You can always make a move in another direction if that's what you really want."

"I've certainly been thinking about it a lot lately," he confessed. "Would you respect me if I went legit?"

She glanced at him and was surprised by his perfectly sober expression. "I respect you now, Skelly." Staring at his profile limned by a bloom of sparkling red, she realized it was true. "You didn't have to help me. You could have told me never to darken your doorstep again. But you didn't. You agreed to look into my claim, unfounded as it might have been. Giving up your holiday and putting yourself out for something you didn't believe was pretty selfless.''

He was staring straight out at the river, his jaw muscles clenched. "I only wish that were true."

She cupped his chin and turned his head so he was looking at her. "Maybe you took the challenge I offered because you needed to prove something to yourself. Whatever your motive, I don't care."

Skelly started to say something, then shook his head and remained silent. Rosalind examined his face lit by the layered colors of a series of fireworks. His expression mirrored his quandary. She couldn't decide which was the stronger of his warring emotions—hope or regret—but she had no doubt of the clear-cut desire that shone from his eyes.

An insistent inner voice warned her that she shouldn't succumb. *Keep your mind on business!*

"Oh, do be quiet," she murmured.

"I didn't say anything."

"Not you."

Though his forehead wrinkled in puzzlement, his gaze continued to hold her fast, and Rosalind braved a discomfiting truth.

Respect wasn't the only thing she felt for Skelly.

She wouldn't put a name to the longing that filled her. Neither would she beat it away by trying to control this connection growing between them . . . nor by trying to control *him*. She was weary of being too careful. And alone. And no matter her logic, no matter the cursed gene she imagined the women of her family had been bequeathed, she didn't feel alone with Skelly.

He drew closer. Unflinching, she sighed and parted her lips in invitation.

One he answered.

The first brush of his mouth across hers was light, undemanding, as if he were allowing her a chance to change her mind. Her fingers grazed his chin, slid around his jaw and stroked the length of his neck. He sucked in his breath and kissed her properly, if not with the same intensity he'd shown the last time.

Skelly's holding himself in check frustrated Rosalind. Thinking she'd entice him into showing a bit more enthusiasm, she playfully nipped his bottom lip and drew back so that he had to come after her. The maneuver gave him leverage, and before she knew what was happening, his weight shifted and pressed her to the ground. Grass prickled her bare arms as he lay half-atop her, one hand tangling in her hair.

Another kiss, this one deeper.

He assaulted her senses every bit as sharply as the bright heat that lit the night sky.

The inside of his mouth tasted as sweet as any forbidden fruit. She inhaled his earthy, provocative scent. The low sounds he made deep in his throat struck a responsive chord inside her. And when he traced her curves . . . hip to waist to belly . . . her flesh vibrated with expectancy. Eyes closed, she could nevertheless see them.

Together.

A growing ache filled her and clamored for attention. An agonizing eternity passed before he so much as palmed her breast. Immediately her nipple tightened, and her flesh swelled against his hand. The need for further intimacy made her restless and bold.

She explored him in the opposite direction . . . waist to hip to buttocks. Probing further, she stroked him so that he filled her hand.

But before they could be swept away to the heavens, where they'd meld with the brilliant colors that laved them, Skelly rolled to his back, taking her with him.

"You are beautiful, Roz," he whispered, looking up at her, "and not only on the surface."

A compliment no man, not even Tim, had ever paid her. Touched, Rosalind experienced a rush of warmth and pleasure foreign to her.

"Maybe you bring out the best in me."

He laughed softly. "Mostly I irritate you."

"That, as well," she admitted.

"You stimulate me, too."

Skelly shifted and rolled again. Laughing softly, she landed under him, their bodies sharing a more intimate connection. Even through double layers of clothing, Rosalind acknowledged his arousal against the inside of her thigh. Her response natural and spontaneous, she arched against him, a hiss of desire whistling through her teeth as a series of rockets burst behind him in increasing crescendo.

"What are we going to do about this?" she asked.

Sounding every bit as breathless, he teased, "Why, Miz Van Straaten, we *are* in a public place."

To emphasize his statement, a long series of blasts issued from the river.

"The *River Star*..."

The fireworks had ended, and the floating casino was pulling into the dock. She couldn't believe such lousy timing. Not that they would have consummated their passion right there. But at least they could have shared their feelings about doing so at a more appropriate time.

Instead, Skelly was shifting away from her, his attention already refocused. "It's docking now."

The riverboat left its berth every hour and a half, the short sessions designed for people who gambled on a limited budget. Nothing as unprofitable as passengers whose gaming allotment had already gone bust, Rosalind thought sardonically, rising also. She swiped at the bits of grass that clung to her bottom and, for the moment, appreciated the draft that cooled down her heated flesh.

"If Cavillo did board the *River Star*," she said, "he'll be back at the lodge soon."

"And we can be waiting for him."

They retraced their steps along the pathway and soon had a clear view of the stairs leading to the dock. Swarms of people were descending, and by the time they reached the area, swarms more would be making their way up to the lodge. In fighting the crowd, they might miss the very man they meant to confront.

"Maybe we'd better watch for a shortcut," she suggested, hoping for a feasible route to the walkway above.

"The slant softens ahead."

Giving the vicinity Skelly indicated a once-over—they'd have to get past some pretty rocky places—she muttered, "Great trail for Bigfoot."

The going was a lot easier than Rosalind feared, however, and Skelly helped her over the few tough spots.

An unexpected sound overhead—like the spray of pebbles beneath a careless foot—made her pause a moment. The skin along her neck crawled. Unable to ignore the creepy feeling of hostile eyes on her, she scanned their surroundings, but a cloud cover was settling over the night sky, methodically blotting out the moon and stars. Even so, she recognized the towering silhouettes of black-on-black as being trees.

The air around her suddenly kicked up, and a chill whistled down her blouse. *The wind,* she realized with relief, rushing to catch up to Skelly.

Nothing more sinister.

A moment later, they climbed through the fence onto the walkway and stopped to catch their breaths.

"Just in time," Skelly said.

She followed his gaze. Disembarked passengers were already halfway up the lit staircase. "Do you see anyone who could be Cavillo?"

"Too far away to recognize him. Let's see if we can find him up close and personal."

But out in the open, the wind had turned insistent and the temperature had dropped several degrees. The air hung heavy with the threat of rain. And despite the recent exertion, Rosalind was chilly. Gooseflesh spread along her bare arms as had happened earlier.

"Skelly, you go ahead." She easily located the Thunderbird beneath the light standard. "I'm going to fetch a sweater from the trunk."

"I can wait."

"And let Cavillo give us the slip? Don't be silly. I'll catch up to you."

After a second's hesitation, Skelly headed for the lodge at a trot. Rosalind veered in the opposite direction.

Trying to ignore the lingering notion that hostile eyes were following her.

EVEN FROM A DISTANCE, Rosalind's trepidation was evident from the way she kept glancing over her shoulder while cutting across the parking lot. Too bad she wasn't scared enough to run all the way to Chicago and never look back. Her taking on a burden that didn't belong to her had been her big mistake. Foolish, foolish young woman. What had to be done was repugnant, yet her determination to get at the truth left no options.

No one could ever know why Frank Sullivan had to die....

Once at the Thunderbird, Rosalind shoved a hand into her pocket but came up empty. She checked the other pocket, withdrew what looked like a slip of paper, then thrust the thing back where she'd found it. Her frustration was evident.

Seeming torn for a moment, she hurried back toward the bluff's edge.

The last mistake she would ever make.

THAT HER KEY RING HAD slipped from her pocket while she and Skelly had been rolling on the ground was the only conclusion Rosalind could come to. Without the darn car keys, they would be on foot again. Exactly what she needed—having to make another emergency call to the gas station.

Though she'd prefer waiting until Skelly could come with her, she also knew that might be some time if Cavillo actually showed. And if it rained hard, the keys could wash right into the mighty Mississippi, never to be seen again.

She had no options.

Once again a weird sensation made her look behind her. People were now straggling through the parking lot toward their cars, though they paid her no mind.

Her imagination.

Rosalind hiked herself through the timbers of the fence. On the other side, she carefully began retracing her steps. Descending was a bit easier than climbing, though she had to sit her way down in several places ... one danger reminding her of another.

But no one had sabotaged her car this time, she assured herself, even as a big, fat raindrop splashed the tip of her nose. The predicament was entirely of her own making. In the heat of passion, she'd managed to lose her keys.

So why couldn't she shake the ominous feeling that stuck to her like a shadow? Once she found the key ring, Rosalind vowed, she'd return the safe way, would take the stairs back to the lodge. Forget the sweater.

If only she could forget the impending rain. Drops hit her with increasing regularity.

She was thankful when she touched down on the open path and hurried toward the trysting spot. And yet her nerves wound tight as the sounds around her amplified. Leaves rustling. A stone shooting down the incline. Water lapping at the bluff's base. Sounds that had been there all along, she was certain. Being alone was scaring her.

Not wanting to lose her nerve now, she kept on while replaying bits and pieces of the moments in Skelly's arms to distract herself from darker thoughts. How weird fate could be. If he hadn't done the story on Lily, she never would have burst into his office to challenge him, and they wouldn't have ended up together in Galena.

They never would have met at all.

But they had met, and Rosalind knew her life would never be the same. A few short days, and Skelly had become essential. He made her laugh. He turned her on. He banished her loneliness and made her feel safe.

If only she felt safe now... That creepy feeling was sneaking up on her again. The eerie sensation and the steady drizzle forced her into hurrying, the faint glow from the lodge and parking-lot lights her only orientation. When she had a sense of the foliage on the rim side above becoming denser, she knew this was the place. She slowed, barely able to make out the familiar clearing against the thicket of bushes and small trees.

Exposed skin now slick with rain, damp clothes clinging to her flesh, Rosalind took the few steps to the wet grass. There she dropped to her knees, hands blindly searching the ground, quickly covering the area where she and Skelly had shared those intimate moments.

Unfortunately she came up empty-handed.

Sitting back on her haunches, Rosalind took a deep breath. "The keys have to be here *somewhere*. Don't panic or you'll never find them. Concentrate, damn it!"

For part of her continued to be distracted by something she couldn't see.

She began again, slower this time, more methodical, her senses attuned not only to the search but to her surroundings and that elusive shadow. The grass yielded no cache other than a few rocks. Could the keys have flown farther than she'd thought? She widened the search area to include the pockets of earth beneath the bushes. She even checked the base of several small trees.

All she got for her trouble was wet.

Wetter, she amended, getting to her feet even as she heard a sound she couldn't put a name to.

Chilled to the bone from both rain and nerves, she wrapped her arms around herself and backed off. No sense in denying the inevitable. She knew when she was beaten. Jarvis Wiggs to the rescue.

Better him than the bogeyman she kept conjuring, Rosalind thought, hurrying.

The slippery mud caught her off balance, and she did a fancy dance to stay upright. In the process, her foot struck an object that shifted with a muffled sound.

Could it be?

Back on her knees, she felt the rain-soaked path beneath her feet with both hands. The muck oozed around her fingers until she grazed something unyielding. Something not a rock. Hooking the ring, she rescued her keys from the mud, wiped them against a clump of wet grass and shoved them deep into her pocket.

Triumph died an immediate death, however, when she heard a sucking sound behind her. Her heart skipped a beat. A shoe pulling free of the mud? Adrenaline charged, she tried shooting to her feet.

Whoever was behind her was faster.

Hit hard in the middle of her back before she could straighten, a horrified Rosalind screamed as she shot out into nothingness.

Chapter Ten

Heart pounding with misgiving, he leapt down the slick incline, by some miracle avoiding the rocks and staying on his feet.

What could Roz have been thinking?

Instinct pushed him to speed up. And when he heard a woman's terrified scream, his blood ran cold. He ran like hell, trusting luck rather than sight....

Keelin whipped straight up in bed, fists locked around the covers, her body drenched in sweat.

"Skelly!" she whispered.

She'd been dreaming through his eyes. Her cousin was in desperate straits...rather, the woman was.

Not knowing where they were or what to do, she closed her eyes, determined to see more. Normally the visions came to her without warning. Without welcome. Without involving someone she loved. Thank God she'd learned a bit about lucid dreaming.

Seeking a light hypnotic state, she concentrated....

FEAR THREATENED to choke him when he heard the sharp slap-slap of feet running away. His chest squeezed tight until a faint cry from the riverside assured him that Roz was alive. He had to get to her and fast. Envisioning her

*in free-fall and plunging into the Mississippi made his
stomach twist in knots.*

Nothing could happen to her.

Not to the woman he only just found.

*He called out. "Roz, where are you?" Though she had
to be close, he barely heard her over the heaving of his
own breath.*

"Can't . . . hang on . . ."

Bile welled in his throat. He pushed it down.

*"You hang on, or so help me, the entire country will
know what a wimp you turned out to be!"*

*He hoped to make her mad enough to want to hit him.
Mad enough to hold on so that she could.*

*The rain was letting up, and his eyes were adjusting. He
got a vague impression of the clearing even as he heard a
series of twiglike cracks, followed by a swallowed scream
coming almost directly from his left. Wasting no time, he
threw himself down face first, his stomach skimming the
ground as his head and shoulders thrust over the edge.
Her pale shirt caught his eye—she was directly below
him.*

*He could hear her panting . . . her body slipping . . . her
fingers scrabbling to keep her tenuous hold.*

*He pushed forward as far as he dared—his shoulders
and upper torso hanging over the edge.*

"I'll get you!" he yelled.

*But the clump of shrubbery she hung on to broke free
of the wet earth. She started to slide. His arm shot toward her, his hand clamping around her wrist. Though
he was bracing himself, he wasn't ready for the power of
her weight jerking at him. Searing pain stunned him, and
his shoulder felt as if it were torn from its socket, but he
hung on to her for all he was worth.*

"Roz, you've got to help me!"

"... trying..."

Though her body was flush against the slope, the pitch of the incline was so great that she might have been dangling free. He knew she was fighting gravity, valiantly seeking a hold of some kind. Gritting his teeth, he took a mental step beyond the pain. Finally her jerky movements subsided. For a moment, they remained immobile, panting in unison.

"Found a toehold," she gasped out. *"What now?"*

"Now I switch arms."

He wasn't certain how a limb could be both numb and throbbing with such pain at the same time. Tricky business, transferring her substantial weight from one hand to the other.

"Find something to grab on to above your head," he ordered.

He knew the last thing she wanted was to move, but she was no quitter. He felt her carefully adjusting, sliding. Heard her hand clawing, fingers digging in.

"It's more slippery mud than rock."

"It'll hold you," he assured her. It had to. *"Do the same with your free foot."*

More desperate noises. Not a particularly religious man, he prayed as he never had before. He vowed to go to Mass every Sunday... participate in novenas... make a pilgrimage to the Holy Land.

Anything if only she would be all right.

Finally she croaked, *"Got it!"*

"You push up and I'll back off. Together!"

He managed to retreat several inches, enough to give himself more leverage. Hope lent him strength he hadn't known he had. They repeated the process until he could grab both of her wrists and maintain his balance. Pain meant nothing as he dragged her up and onto him.

Throwing her arms around his neck, she clung to him as if she'd never let go.

He'd never had such reason for thanks in his entire life.

THE VISION DISSIPATED, and Keelin opened her eyes, feeling as if the burden had been hers in truth. Her heart was thumping, her breath short. The room was near-dark, the glowing hands of the clock on the mantel reading half-past ten.

"Keelin?" came the sleepy voice next to her. "What is it?"

"A dream."

Tyler immediately sat up and placed a comforting arm around her shoulders. "What sort of dream?"

Though she was certain he didn't have to ask. A normal dream wouldn't upset her so. "Skelly."

"He's in trouble?"

"Aye. Desperate trouble. Though he's safe for the moment."

Certain that the woman hadn't merely fallen, Keelin had no way of knowing whether or not someone was waiting to finish them both off. The uncertainty was the hardest part to bear.

Tyler pulled her close and stroked her hair. Keelin snuggled into him, thankful she wasn't alone in her hotel room. They'd shared hours of passion before falling asleep. She wished he could stay with her, hold her all night, but she knew he had to get home for Cheryl's sake.

"When did the visions start?" he asked.

"This is the first." She'd already told her husband-to-be about Skelly's call of the night before. "He's been on my mind all day. I tried lucid dreaming to tune in to him several times, alas to no avail." Because he hadn't been in danger then. Only the strongest of emotions made the connection. "But now I have...and I wish..." She couldn't say that she wished she hadn't seen through her cousin's eyes when she might make a difference. "I'm afraid for him, Tyler. And for the woman. He cares about her...as much as I do you."

"Moira strikes again," he said softly.

Gran's words were burned into her memory.

Dreams are not always tangible things, but more often are born in the heart. Act selflessly in another's behalf, and my legacy shall be yours....

Keelin wondered if part of the bargain was that all of them—her cousins, as well as her own siblings—would be tested by great danger before happiness was within their grasp. She certainly had been. And now Skelly. What was to say they all would come out unscathed?

At the moment, she could take no comfort in the McKenna legacy.

Glad as she was that Skelly had Gran's bequest within reach, she prayed God that his life wouldn't be forfeit. Once again, she felt the burden of her special inheritance weighing down her very soul.

What to do?

"WHAT WERE YOU thinking of—coming back here alone in the dark?" Skelly asked, his tone calm, though he was feeling anything but.

His good arm wrapped around Roz's waist as they took the easy route back toward the lodge. He kept glancing around, peering through the continuing drizzle, trying to spot anything untoward. Just in case.

"That if I didn't find my car keys, we'd be doing some serious walking tonight," she returned. "The next time you roll me around on the ground, we'd better check to see if anything is missing before you let me up."

Her voice was shaky, and yet she was trying to joke. He couldn't believe she had a sense of humor after what she'd been through. Or maybe she was clinging to anything that would prevent her from breaking down.

Aware that, had he arrived on the scene thirty seconds later, he might have lost this woman who'd stormed his heart, Skelly tightened his hold on her. Had he known of the real dangers awaiting them, he never would have agreed to investigate. At least, he hoped he had that much sense. Her life for his promotion was *not* an acceptable trade.

What he'd like to do was tell Roz the deal was off and insist on driving her back to Chicago now, but he figured the gesture would be futile. With or without him, she wouldn't stop digging for the truth. At least, if he stayed around, he might be able to protect her.

Thinking about driving made him ask, "Did you ever find those keys?"

Roz patted her pocket and let out a long breath. "Still there, thank goodness."

"Did it even cross your mind that you should have waited for me to come with you?"

Sounding defensive, she said, "I was trying to get to the keys before the rain got to them. We might never have found them later. How was I to know that someone would take the opportunity to help me over the edge?"

Skelly had already figured out what happened, though hearing Roz say the words made him sick to his stomach all over again. "I heard someone running away, but I couldn't see anything in this weather. What about you?"

"Afraid not. I'd barely found the keys and *bam!* There I went," she said, trembling renewed. "How did you know to come looking for me?"

Skelly held her closer, wanting in the worst way to take her in his arms and kiss away her remaining fears. But how could he when the villain was on the loose?

"I was waiting near the doors," he said, "keeping one eye out for Cavillo, the other on you. I couldn't believe it when you crawled through that fence. I waited a couple of minutes, assuming you'd be right back. Then I had this really bad feeling and came after you."

"Thank God for weird feelings. Now, if only I'd listened to mine..."

Skelly remembered she'd thought someone was watching them in the crowded lobby. Perry Nesmith? A member of her own family? Anthony Cavillo himself? Though neither of them had seen a familiar face, anyone could have been hiding within the horde, keeping out of their line of sight.

A few minutes later, they climbed back onto the now-empty cul-de-sac. The rain had stopped, but it had done its damage. They sloshed through puddles and huddled together against the chill of the wind. With its bright lights and aura of warmth and safety, the lodge beckoned to him.

He only *hoped* the place was safe.

For, being in no shape to go anywhere—wet and filthy and as exhausted as they both were—Skelly insisted, "We should stay here for the night."

"If rooms are available, which I doubt," Roz agreed more readily than he'd expected. "I hate the thought of going home looking like this. Grandfather and Aunt Hilary would have heart failure if they saw us."

He noticed she didn't include her mother in the statement. He knew Claudia's reactions weren't necessarily what one might expect, but did Roz really believe her mother wouldn't care if she were hurt? As problematic as

Skelly breathed deep and wondered exactly how tough the carpeted floor could be on a sore shoulder.

Trying not to think about anything but the moment, he emptied his pockets, shucked his wet clothes and slid into the robe, only momentarily regretting that the fresh garment was clean while he was not. The thick material instantly warmed him.

And in the bathroom, the shower continued to run.

A bit concerned, he knocked at the door. "Are you all right in there?"

"I'm in heaven," Roz called, sounding more like her old self. "I may stay in here until the hot water runs out."

But someone from housekeeping would be by to pick up their clothing in a few minutes.

Flirting with danger, Skelly asked, "Then can I get in there long enough to haul out your wet things? I mean . . . without offending you?"

"You want me to run around the room naked?"

"Interesting idea." He couldn't help but grin. "A skimpy towel wouldn't be bad, either . . . unless you want the luxurious terry robe I brought you."

"You've thought of everything."

And then some, when it came to her, though he didn't intend to elaborate.

"Do you want clean, dry clothing in the morning or not?" he demanded, fetching her robe. "Someone will be by to collect them any minute now."

"In that case...come on in. My things are on the floor right outside the shower."

Clouds of steam rolled over Skelly, practically blinding him, as he cracked open the bathroom door. If that weren't sufficient to keep him from playing Peeping Tom, the shower stall's textured glass provided an even more efficient barrier. He could make out no more than a vague if voluptuous silhouette, yet even the suggestion of Roz's nudity triggered his imagination.

Only half joking, he asked, "Need someone to wash your back? I still have one good hand."

"Sorry. The management thought of everything, too, including a long-handled brush."

Mesmerized for a moment as Roz lifted her face to the spraying water and made a contented sound that shuddered through him, he cursed the staff's efficiency. Thankfully he quickly found what he'd come for.

Protecting his injured shoulder, he retrieved her wet clothes with the other arm, then backed off fast, saying, "I'll hang the robe on the door." And managed the feat without causing himself too much pain.

"Thanks. I'll be out in a minute."

The image of Roz stepping out of the shower, a gloriously naked Aphrodite, was more than Skelly could handle. He got the hell out of the bathroom.

After what they'd been through, sex should be the last thing on his mind, but making love to Roz was all he could think about. Skelly was too aware of the danger she'd been in. He'd almost lost her without ever having had the opportunity to hold her in his arms through the night. If the reality even half matched his imagination...

A knock at the door dashed his fantasies.

"Be right there," he called.

The car keys already lay on the dresser. Thinking Roz might have been carrying a wallet, he checked her pockets, but all he came up with was an old, damp photo. Grabbing his own things, he used the peephole to make sure the person on the other side was in uniform before surrendering the mess.

Afterward he picked up the faded, water-washed photograph. The young Lily was instantly recognizable, but what was the point of Roz's carrying around what appeared to be a prom shot of her grandmother? A better look at the two young men enlightened him. Standing to the side, a teenage Frank Sullivan watched the dancing couple with envy. And the dark-haired boy who held Lily in his arms?

Skelly stared for a moment, then retrieved the copy of the newspaper photograph that he'd pulled from his pocket. Unfolding the piece of paper, he smoothed it out and laid it on the dresser directly beneath the table lamp. Then he set the old photo next to the copy. A fast comparison convinced him of the young man's identity.

Lily had been dancing with Anthony Cavillo.

HEARING THE MUFFLED RING of a telephone coming from the other room, Rosalind figured the efficient Miss Jerina was probably checking up on them. Or informing Skelly the *real* guest had shown and they had to vacate the room. That wouldn't be so bad, she supposed, if only they had their own clothing...preferably dry, of course.

A long, hot shower, and she felt as if she'd been reborn. Not that she'd given Skelly the same opportunity. Clean and warm, her body encased in thick terry, she wrapped a fresh towel around her head turban-style and left the bathroom.

"Skelly, is that...?"

He held up a hand that stopped her question midsentence. "I wish I could tell you what was coming next," he was saying. "Or better yet, that you could tell me."

While listening to the other person on his cell phone, he gave her an appreciative once-over. Who would have called him on a Saturday night? she wondered.

A friend? A *female* friend?

Telling herself she was not bothered by the possibility, Rosalind wandered to the dresser and, while pretending interest in towel-drying her hair, covertly watched him through the mirror. Stretched across the bed, his long legs bare, his chest half exposed by the robe he'd so carelessly donned, Skelly was tempting enough to grace the cover of a romance novel. No matter that he was decorated with a little mud...she unashamedly wanted to see more of him.

And it piqued her that Skelly was so absorbed in his phone call until he said, "Thanks for tuning in, cuz. I knew you could do it if you tried."

Cuz. Another woman, but not what she'd assumed. The warmth of embarrassment flooded her cheeks, and Rosalind covered by ducking her head. She worked the towel along her hairline so that it draped in front of her face without blocking her view of his mirror image.

"If I get any bright ideas, I'll let you know." Skelly paused, obviously listening. He nodded. "I promise to be more careful." A shorter pause. "And I'll call you tomorrow."

He clicked off the cell phone and tossed it on a nightstand, grimacing with the motion. Hurting, and all because of her, she knew. Rosalind stopped messing with her hair and perched on the edge of the bed.

"That was Keelin?"

Rotating his shoulder pulled another grimace from him. "She was out there on the bluff with us."

A shiver shot through her as she remembered his explanation of his cousin's gift—that Keelin could see through another's eyes in her dreams. "Spooky...and hard to believe." And downright scary, considering one of those dreams supposedly had left Keelin the only witness to a man's death.

"Spooky? I guess. But I'm glad she's able and willing to catch my wavelength. Until recently, she suppressed her ability rather than developing it."

"What made her change her mind?"

"I simply asked. I figured another pair of eyes wouldn't hurt. It's the first time she's forced the issue...at least, in her choice of subjects."

"And she succeeded. You and she must have a special connection."

"Keelin's the special one. She has a bigger heart than anyone I've ever met. Except...maybe you."

Surprised by the unexpected homage, she said, "You'll make me blush."

He stroked her cheek. "I already have."

Flustered, Rosalind stared at Skelly expectantly. Her pulse thrummed, and her flesh quickened. And then, when he rose from the bed, her growing anticipation foundered.

"My turn." He started for the bathroom. "I hope you left me some dry towels."

"There may be a hand towel or two," she teased.

"Then I guess I'll have to air dry."

"Or you could use a hair blower for efficiency," she suggested, deciding to retrieve it and some other amenities the resort provided.

"Hey!" he exclaimed when she squeezed by him. "You've hogged the bathroom long enough."

Grabbing the dryer and a basket of after-shower hair and body products only took a second. "I'm out."

But Skelly was blocking her exit, his shoulder wedged against the doorjamb. Her breath caught in her throat, and her pulse skittered with sudden tension. He gazed through half-lowered lids, as if trying to mesmerize her.

"And here I thought you were taking pity on me—" he indicated his sore shoulder "—and volunteering to wash *my* back."

Thinking she could be convinced, Rosalind was about to challenge him with a tart response when Skelly moved aside to let her pass.

"I know. The long-handled brush," he said with a resigned sigh. And when she didn't immediately leave, he added, "It probably wouldn't be a bad idea to let someone at Lang House know we won't be back tonight. Though I'd prefer you didn't announce our exact whereabouts."

Her mellow mood immediately tempered by the inference that someone at Lang House couldn't be trusted, Rosalind said, "Of course," and waltzed by him.

But she waited until the shower was running before picking up the phone. When no one answered at the other end after a dozen rings, she wondered if she should be concerned. Or suspicious.

Choosing to be neither, she hung up and concentrated on her hair, starting with a leave-on conditioner that would allow her to work out the tangles. Though she longed for her wide-toothed comb, her purse was locked in the trunk of her car, so she made do with finger-combing it.

When her hair was dry and swirling wildly around her shoulders, she turned off all room lights but the small one on the dresser. Exhausted, she should be ready to climb into bed, but instead she was wide-eyed. So, after turning down the covers, she crossed to the window and opened the drapes. Located on the floor above the lobby, the room had a great view, even at night. The rain had stopped, and lights from the stairway and riverboat gleamed through the dark.

Confused thoughts whirled through her head.

The attraction she'd felt for Skelly from the first had grown into something deeper. Brighter. Hotter. Not only did she respect him—and, yes, desire him more than any man she'd ever known—but she owed him her life.

That someone like Skelly McKenna would ever be her hero had never occurred to her, but there it was. He hadn't hesitated to rescue her, though she might have pulled him to his death. That she'd ever believed she could keep him at a professional distance amazed her. That she'd only known him for days seemed inconsequential.

So, when his spell was not immediately upon her— when she had time to think as she did now—why did she instinctively want to hold herself back? She could conjure no reason other than fear that came from deep within.

The same fear that had made her drive Tim away, Rosalind supposed.

The bathroom door opened, and Skelly emerged. Her heart skipped a beat, and she stared blindly into the night. What to do? Reflected movements in the plate glass caught her attention. He was working the shoulder again. Her own bruises and aching muscles were nothing serious—her ankle had even held up okay—but he might not be so lucky. A combination of guilt and gratitude wiped out any hesitation she might have about going to him.

Sympathetic, she asked, ''Are you certain a doctor shouldn't take a look at your shoulder?''

''It'll work itself out.''

Was he trying to mask his pain for her sake? *Macho idiot.*

"Maybe it could use some help. Sit and show me a little flesh," she said, then realized that sounded more provocative than teasing.

When Skelly's piercing gaze bore into her, Rosalind feared he could delve into her mind and read the longing she was trying to repress. And it seemed that he had when he untied and dropped the robe altogether. Her breath caught in her throat until she realized a bath towel hung low on his hips, leaving him a hint of modesty. He made himself comfortable on the edge of the bed, but not before she glimpsed the feathering of dark hair that rose from the cloth to his flat stomach. A sudden inner warmth made her mouth go dry.

And her voice was a little shaky when she said, "The management *did* think of everything, even body lotion," while fetching the bottle from the basket.

"I wouldn't care if it was horse liniment."

She released a nervous laugh. "You might. Have you ever smelled the stuff?"

"I'll take your word for it."

Climbing onto the bed behind him, she squirted the freesia-scented cream into one palm, then rubbed it briskly against the other. Even so, his flesh quivered beneath her hands as she spread the warmed lotion along the muscles between neck and arm. Gently, she made a pass over his shoulder to his chest. With each stroke, she widened her area of concentration.

Nerves made her prattle. "If I do something wrong, tell me. I didn't have a sister to teach me technique." She couldn't help adding, "No Ursula to practice on, either."

"Trust me, you're doing fine."

He didn't sound fine. She thought she'd at least get a snort out of him at the Ursula remark, but he sounded as tense as his muscles felt beneath her fingertips. Knowing exactly what was happening to him, she was at a loss as to how to prevent it.

If that's what she really wanted.

"Work with me here, Skelly," she choked out. "Try to loosen up a little."

More warmed lotion on his upper arm and back didn't do the trick. With each stroke, his muscles grew tighter. And within seconds, every breath he took held a ragged edge. No sooner had Rosalind realized she wasn't immune to his response than Skelly grabbed her wrist, stopping her from continuing.

His back to her, he asked, "What is it you want, Roz?"

"To make you feel better."

"You're driving me crazy." He glanced over his shoulder, lids hooded.

Licking her lips, she concentrated on his wing bone. "Sorry."

"No, you're not. Are you?"

Swallowing hard, she met his gaze and slowly shook her head.

Skelly turned and raised his legs to the bed. Looping an arm around her waist, he gave her no choice but to come with him as he stretched out.

"Now, what was it you wanted?" he asked again.

If she couldn't tell him, her body could. Her back arched, her hips tilted and her thighs whispered against his as she settled along his length.

A low groan was followed by his murmured "That's what I was hoping."

Even as Skelly found her mouth and teased it open, he untied her robe and drew back one side of the garment so that her flesh was exposed to his hand. His kiss was slow and deep and dizzying. She had not the slightest urge to act coy as he rode every curve, explored every silken crevice. She did want this, had known it was a possibility from the moment he'd suggested they stay the night.

In his arms, making love to him, was exactly where she wanted to be.

Danger had made her reckless. And honest with herself. Anything could happen to one if not to both of them. This might be their only chance to be together.

If only Skelly weren't so excruciatingly slow. Rosalind knew she was ready for him within moments of his first touching her. She unfastened the towel, pulled it from his hips and tossed it away. Scraping her nails down his stomach, she urged him to take her.

But Skelly drew out the pleasure, tortured her with the waiting. When he dipped his hand between her thighs, she gladly opened to him, thinking that now was the moment. Though she stroked him seductively, he remained where he was, pleasuring her until she was completely fluid inside. Her pulse met each of his short thrusts, and soon her hips prompted a more demanding rhythm.

Tearing her mouth from his, she begged, "Now, Skelly, please."

He ignored her plea and intently watched her face as he explored deeper and faster until she clutched at him, no longer able to hold back her climax. Lights fractured behind her eyes, and she shuddered against him. He caught her cry with another deep, soulful kiss, and she arched high and hard against his hand. Only when her hips settled back to the mattress did he cover her, his sex hard and throbbing at her entry.

"*Now* you're ready for me," he whispered, easily slipping inside.

Caught unawares by the mind-shattering need that immediately renewed itself, Rosalind dug her nails into his back and arched again, as if she could go even higher.

"Work with me here, Roz." He teased her by echoing her own words. "Try to loosen up a little."

But from his intense expression, she knew that he wasn't far from the edge himself. She slid along his length, over and over, changing the tempo with every stroke of her hips. His breath ragged, he matched her. Tuned in to every nuance of his features, she took him higher and higher, until suddenly he rolled, taking her with him. She straddled his hips. On his back, he offered her complete control.

Despite the need to reach completion with him inside her, she drew out his pleasure as he had hers. She lifted herself high and slow, then lowered herself with equal precision. Again and again, she repeated the torturous motion.

Beneath her, Skelly found her breasts, first with his hands, then with his mouth. With him suckling at first one nipple, then the other, pressure built swiftly and urgently. He slid a hand between them and stroked, within seconds coaxing a wild response from her.

Their bodies shuddered together.

Pulling her down on him, Skelly held her fast, his face in her hair, and whispered, "I love you, Roz."

Making her fight the fear once more.

Chapter Eleven

Bright sunlight streamed into the room, reflecting Rosalind's upbeat mood as she combed and twisted her hair into a loose knot. Their clothes had been delivered first thing—nearly as good as new—and Skelly had fetched her purse from the car before jumping into the shower. His off-key voice rising above the sound of running water made her grin.

Then again, her misgivings laid to rest at least for the moment, his astonishing declaration of love echoing in her mind, she hadn't been able to stop smiling since she'd awakened in Skelly's arms.

He hadn't taken his hands off her all night.

A sharp ring startled her from further contemplating the love issue. Skelly's cell phone. She fetched it from the nightstand. Expecting his cousin Keelin was checking up on him, she was a little unsettled when the woman on the other end identified herself as Heidi Neville.

Wondering what the woman's relationship with Skelly was, she said, "He's unavailable at the moment."

"Darn. I really need to talk to him and I'm leaving in a few minutes. Will he be long?"

"He's in the *shower,*" Rosalind informed her, then realized that, in a not-so-subtle way, she was staking her claim.

"Oh."

"I can take a message."

"I suppose that'll have to do." Heidi sounded disappointed. "Tell Skelly that I spent last evening researching Anthony Cavillo, like he asked."

"Excuse me?"

"This *is* Rosalind Van Straaten, right?"

"Well, yes—"

"I just figured Skelly would have told you I was working backup. I'm a researcher for 'The Whole Story.'"

Rosalind felt both foolish... and relieved. "I have so much on my mind that I wasn't thinking," she hedged. "Let me find something to write on." She pulled a pad of paper and pen from a drawer. "Go ahead."

"I found several more articles about Cavillo locking horns with Frank Sullivan over zoning for River Bluff. They certainly were adversarial. Some of the quotes were real personal and just short of being lawsuit material. I also dug up the name of the man who finally got the zoning pushed through several years later. Walt Rogowski."

"Rogowski," Rosalind echoed, immediately on alert.

"Right. And a few years back, Rogowski was responsible for influencing the legislature to give Cavillo's cartel an okay to start their riverboat-gambling operation."

Rocked by the implication, she said, "Heidi, I hope they pay you what you're worth."

"They don't, but I'm confident Skelly will come through for me."

"You deserve a raise."

"I'm hoping for a whole lot more. If Skelly can break the story he's after, his competition will fall by the way-side. Then that promotion to the prime-time slot will be his, and he'll take me with him."

"I see." Though she *didn't* see why Skelly had never mentioned a possible promotion. Or Heidi. "Anything else?"

"That's it. Tell him to get in touch if he wants me to fax him the articles. Or to dig deeper."

Replacing the cell phone, Rosalind realized no shower sounds were coming from the bathroom. The door opened and Skelly exited, wearing only his trousers and towel-drying his hair. Desire flared anew deep inside her, and she wondered if she would ever get enough of him.

Hooking the towel around his neck, he indicated the pad of paper. "What's up?"

Unbelievable how easily he could distract her from something so important. "You had a call while you were in the shower."

She handed him her scribbles and relayed her conversation with Heidi in detail . . . all but the promotion part.

"Interesting," he said, "considering Rogowski led us to Cavillo."

"That's what I thought. Why would he have cooperated with the man in the past, only to point a finger at him now?"

"Maybe he's learned something about Cavillo that doesn't sit well. Something that—if he went public—might make voters question his judgment."

"But he might not be averse to letting someone else do the dirty work."

Standing in front of the dresser, Skelly picked up the photograph she'd taken from the hatbox. "What if Sullivan blocked Cavillo's zoning request because he wanted to even an old score?''

"What kind of score?"

He flipped the photo around. "How about Lily?"

Then it hit her. "The boy she's dancing with is Anthony Cavillo."

No wonder he'd looked familiar—she'd seen the photocopy, though the mature Cavillo had far less hair.

"You didn't realize that before?"

"I'm afraid not. I did recognize Sullivan and meant to show the photo to you, though." Taking it from Skelly, she said, "Cavillo and Sullivan go way back, even before this. Lily kept photos of the three of them together from the time they were all kids."

"The Three Musketeers?" He pulled a face and nodded. "Our conversation with Cavillo should prove to be interesting, wouldn't you say? This could be the break we've been waiting for."

Or the break he'd *been waiting for...*

As he finished dressing, Rosalind flashed on her conversation with Heidi and the importance of Skelly's getting a hot story. He'd led her to believe he'd been intrigued by the challenge, as well as by her. But he hadn't admitted to the whole truth—that an important promotion hung on the outcome of their investigation.

The omission filled her with doubt about the nature of Skelly's feelings for her.

ANTHONY CAVILLO STOPPED watering his maidenhair fern long enough to get a good look at the visitors his receptionist escorted into his office. What piece of misfortune led Rosalind Van Straaten and Skelly McKenna to *his* door? They had nerve—he'd give them that—sticking around after what had gone down the night before.

"Sit."

Rolling the unlit cigar to the corner of his mouth, he indicated the modern leather couch indicative of his personal decorating taste. His office was a welcome refuge from the rest of the overly rustic lodge.

"Mr. Cavillo, how nice of you to see us on a Sunday," Rosalind said.

As they made themselves at home, he stared for a moment at the Lily Lang look-alike, conjuring memories of his first love—most of them good.

Ah, Lily, why'd you have to leave?

She'd been his kind of woman. So vibrant. Outgoing. Outrageous. Sexy. Irresistible. The Blond Temptress—the moniker fit her perfectly.

The granddaughter seemed more reserved, not a flamboyant bone in her body. Yet he wondered if it wasn't her physical similarity to Lily that had prompted her to dig into ancient history that had nothing to do with her. She'd never even had a chance to meet her infamous grandmother, so why else would she be going to all this trouble?

Keeping a sharp eye on both of them, he said, "I hope the accommodations were to your liking."

Rosalind pulled a face. "How did you know we stayed here last night?"

Attending to his cup-and-saucer vine, he said, "Nothing goes on around River Bluff without my knowing. Not much in Jo Daviess County does."

"Good," McKenna said. "Then you should be a fount of information for us."

For the moment finished with his plants—the calming hobby helped keep his volatile temper in check—Anthony claimed the deep leather chair opposite the couch. He removed the cigar from his mouth.

"Can't even light one of these things anymore. Heart attack." He dropped it into an ashtray on a nearby occasional table. "Don't get old if you can help it." Changing gears, staring at the other man, he asked, "What makes you think I intend to tell you anything?"

"Why wouldn't you cooperate...unless you have something to hide?"

Exactly the reason he couldn't have some damn reporter sniffing around.

Beating him to a response, Rosalind stated diplomatically, "Anything you can tell us about Frank Sullivan's death would be helpful."

Big surprise. "Thirty years is a long time."

"But you and he were friends."

Anthony regarded her. "Were we?"

"My grandmother's old photographs say so."

"As kids, we all hung out together."

"What ended the friendship?" She clarified, "Between you and Sullivan."

"Lily left town. Frank and me decided we didn't have anything in common."

McKenna shifted impatiently. "Are you sure it wasn't because Sullivan was jealous of you and Lily?"

Shrugging, Anthony said, "Her and me—we were simpatico, maybe because people treated us both like we were worthless. White trash. Frank was from the other side of the tracks. He had whatever his heart desired. Except for Lily." Remembering the old days made him nostalgic. "We had drive, though. Both made something of ourselves. Lily was always a looker. Probably every red-blooded male in the county was jealous."

"But not every male had the opportunity to get even by trying to stop you from building River Bluff on state-owned land."

The corner of his eye twitched at the reminder of the devil's pact he'd made to get the clearance. "Only one small tract was state owned."

"One small tract that split your land in two and kept you from building a commercial operation."

The reporter was ticking him off, but Anthony had learned to deal with rabble like him. "What's your point?"

"Just an observation."

Observation, his ass. McKenna was trying to rattle him, but he'd gone up against bigger, more-powerful men and had come out the winner . . . one way or another.

Rosalind cleared her throat. "People believe my grandmother and Frank Sullivan were lovers."

"That's the problem with people," Anthony said wryly. "They open their yaps when they don't know what they're talking about." He barked a laugh. "Lily treated Frank like the brother she never had. That wasn't going to change just because she decided to divorce her old man."

"And you know this . . . how?" McKenna asked.

In an attempt to neutralize the negative effect the reporter was having on him, Anthony envisioned himself in his conservatory, surrounded by flamingo plants, Italian bellflower and weeping figs.

"Galena's a small town," he said. "Lily and I weren't strangers." He narrowed his gaze. "What was it you came to see me about again?"

The reporter's nostrils flared, as if he was gearing himself up for something.

"Mr. Cavillo," Rosalind cut in nervously, "do you know of any reason my grandmother had to be upset with Frank? Something she was trying to talk him out of for some time, actually... probably the same something they argued about publicly over dinner the night he died.''

"If Lily had a problem with Frank, she didn't confide in me. We weren't lovers, either.''

"So you don't have a clue as to what the argument was about?'' the reporter reiterated.

"You oughta get a hearing aid. I already said not.''

"I talked to the widow,'' the woman went on in a rush. "She believes they were arguing over her. That Lily wanted Frank to leave Diane for her, but that Frank wouldn't do it because a divorce would hurt his career.''

"Yeah, I heard that theory before. It holds about as much water as Lily killing Frank. More likely his career would've been ruined if anyone had investigated why a couple of kids quit their volunteer work for him.''

"Kids?'' she echoed.

"Teenagers.'' He couldn't hide his feelings of disgust on this one. "Underage girls.'' Schoolmates of his daughter.

Their expressions stunned, she and the reporter stared at each other. Obviously they hadn't had a clue. Not really surprising. A small town could be a hotbed of gossip...but it could also close ranks to outsiders faster than a speeding bullet.

McKenna asked, "Did these girls or their parents make official complaints against Sullivan?''

"Now, what do you think?'' He hadn't figured the big-city honcho for being naive. "Back then, you had no such thing as sexual-harassment laws. A girl had a pass made at her—or worse—she hushed it up or it would be *her* reputation. Besides, money smooths out a lot of kinks.''

"These girls,'' Rosalind said, her voice trembling, "do you know their names?''

"One of 'em I can't recall. But the other I couldn't forget. Barbara Pohl was the daughter of a real nice woman who worked for me."

A woman he'd had more than a passing acquaintance with. He loved his wife in his own way, but she'd never been what Anthony would consider exciting.

"Do you know what happened to the daughter?" the other man asked.

"Last I heard, Barbara was running a bed and breakfast in one of the smaller towns east of here. Took good care of her mother, too, until the poor woman died of cancer a few years back." He checked his watch and stood. "I'm afraid our social hour is over. I've got business to attend to." He gave the reporter a pointed look and added, "Business which does not concern you."

"Thanks again for seeing us," Rosalind said as she rose.

"You may be seeing us again."

Anthony glowered. "I don't like threats, McKenna."

"Threats? I was talking about the Fourth of July parade on Tuesday morning." His expression innocent, the reporter asked, "You will be there, won't you?"

Though he knew the other man was backpedaling, he let it slide. "Right in the middle of the parade. Now, if you'll excuse me..."

They finally took the hint. Grabbing his cigar from the ashtray, he shoved it in his mouth and ground down on it. Once the door closed behind them, he made for his desk and the phone, where he quickly tapped out a number.

"It's me," he grunted when the other party answered. "You won't believe who just left my office."

"I CAN'T BELIEVE no one mentioned those girls before," Skelly said as they left River Bluff behind.

The revelation had thrown him for a loop. That Sullivan had developed a taste for underage girls opened up a whole new can of worms in their investigation. And new suspects.

"Obviously the situation was hushed up."

"In a small town?"

"Hard to believe, isn't it?" Roz mused as she turned onto Blackjack Road. "Unless . . ."

"What?"

"People in the know were protecting someone."

"You mean the girls," he said.

"And possibly one of their parents. What if Sullivan did more than just make a pass at them?" Her voice was tight with disgust. "And what if there were others? Who knows how far a parent might have gone to avenge his or her child?"

He could almost hear her add, *And who could blame them?* An echo of his own thoughts.

Not that either of them would condone vigilantism in place of the justice system. But Cavillo had been right on about there being little recourse in sexual cases of any kind thirty years before. Without current legal protections, the accuser rather than the defendant would have been on trial.

Skelly wondered how they were going to follow up on this one. Unfortunately Barbara Pohl's mother was dead—Cavillo hadn't said anything about a father—and they didn't even have the name of the second girl.

"Why would people who knew better let an innocent woman go to jail?" he murmured.

"A woman the whole town considered to be white trash."

Skelly knew Cavillo's frank remark had stung Roz. "I'd bet a dime to a dollar that all changed when Lily came back from Hollywood as the Blond Temptress."

"Don't count on it. Most people have long memories. And opinions that don't change easily."

"Oh, I don't know. *You* changed your opinion about *me.*"

He expected a humorous response, but Roz didn't react at all. Her mind was elsewhere. He gave her some space and did some thinking himself, especially about that entry in the diary that had stumped them. Lily had written that she was disappointed in Sullivan, that his actions weren't worthy of him. She'd also said that she'd pleaded with him to stop, but doubted that he would.

Stop what? Hitting on his volunteers?

Nearing town, he said, "About those girls. I wonder what Rogowski could tell us."

Her expression hopeful, Roz glanced at him. "Working for Sullivan, he'd have to know what happened."

"And maybe give us the other name."

"*If* he remembers. And if she and her parents haven't died or moved to God-knows-where. It's worth a try."

When they approached his campaign office, the storefront looked deserted but for a dark-haired young woman who sat with her back to the window. At the sound of the door, she jumped and whirled around, dark eyes wide, mouth trembling.

"Can I help you?"

Skelly glanced at her name badge. "You sure can, Kim. You can tell Mr. Rogowski we're here to see him."

"Mr. Rogowski's not here right now. He's making an appearance in front of the Old Market House along with the rest of the staff."

"We'll find him," Roz said. Once they were outside, she glanced back through the window. "I hope she's okay."

"She's probably upset because everyone went off to have fun without her."

"Or maybe she's scared at being left alone."

"In broad daylight?"

He and Roz walked the few blocks to the Greek Revival building that was now a state historic site and a hub for visitors. Accompanied by the same fair-haired man who'd driven Rogowski away from the lodge the evening before—a bodyguard? Skelly wondered, noting the size of the man—the politician stood near the entrance. He was greeting as many tourists as would stop to shake his hand and take a piece of campaign literature from him.

To get to Rogowski, they passed one of his workers stationed on the adjacent street corner, handing out flyers.

"Ah, Rosalind Van Straaten and Skelly McKenna," the politician said with a heartiness Skelly figured could only be fake. "Eddie, you recognize Mr. McKenna, don't you?"

The fair-haired man flexed his muscles as he stepped to his employer's side. "Seen him on TV."

But Eddie was staring at Roz, a fascinated glint in his eyes. And Skelly had to take hold of himself so he wouldn't pop those eyes back in the too-large head.

"My associate, Eddie Turner. He sees to my welfare," Rogowski said as if issuing a friendly warning. "So, you're playing tourist today, are you, folks? There's a wonderful Fourth of July exhibit inside, including flags that date back to 1776."

"We didn't come to see any flags," Skelly stated.

While Roz—as usual—was more diplomatic. "Could you possibly spare us a few minutes?"

"Of course. I always have time for my constituents." He broke away for a moment to glad-hand a couple of others. Then he turned back to Skelly. "What is it today, young man?"

"Away from here."

Annoyance crossed the politician's face so quickly that Skelly almost thought he imagined it.

"I really can't leave my post. My appearance here has been scheduled for weeks. But I can take a short break." He turned to the hulk and handed him the campaign literature. "Eddie, hold down the fort for a few minutes."

"Sure thing, boss." Eddie's eyes again strayed to Roz.

Only this time, Skelly registered the look he gave her. Rather than undressing her with his eyes as he'd imagined before, he sensed a different kind of tension. As if Eddie were sizing her up, but not in a sexual manner.

His thoughts were broken by Rogowski's "This way."

Skelly wrapped a protective arm around Roz's waist and followed the man around the side of the building to a less trafficked spot. They'd have at least a modicum of privacy, though behind the Old Market House, several floats for Tuesday's parade were being worked on.

Figuring there was no use beating around the bush, Skelly went right to it. "We've been to see Anthony Cavillo."

"Really." Rogowski's expression relayed only a subdued interest. "So you followed up on the zoning thing."

"And learned something even more interesting, something we weren't expecting." He watched the subtle change in the other man's features and wondered what the gubernatorial candidate feared they *had* learned. "It seems that Frank Sullivan had a penchant for a couple of young girls who worked for him.''

"That." Pulling a disgusted face, Rogowski shook his head. "A terrible thing, especially for any man holding the public trust."

"Then you knew about it?" Roz asked, sounding shocked.

"Unfortunately."

"And helped cover it up?"

"You give me more power than I had at the time."

"But you didn't talk," Skelly rephrased.

A flare of something dark subtly colored the man's features. "We all make mistakes."

Roz said, "But it's not too late to correct yours."

"I appreciate your outrage, my dear. But you're referring to something that happened long, long ago. Too long to besmirch the name of a dead man who did this state much good." His temper was beginning to show when he asked, "For pity's sake, can't you two let Frank rest in peace?"

"Sullivan may be dead," Skelly stated flatly, "but his murderer is still free. No matter that she confessed, Lily Lang didn't do it. His molesting underage girls may be the motive we've been searching for—"

Rogowski suddenly interrupted. "You're chasing your tail! You'll never get the proof you need. You'll never get anyone to talk to the authorities."

Meaning him, Skelly figured.

"Did my grandmother know about the girls?" Roz asked.

"I have no idea," the politician snapped. "Lily was Frank's friend, not mine."

"They were *only* friends," she emphasized, "not lovers."

"I never said they were."

The too-easily issued statement jarred Skelly. The last time they'd faced Rogowski, he'd indicated the only enemy he knew Sullivan had was Roz's grandfather. He'd implied Noah Lang had good reason to hate the man he'd considered his rival. And now the politician was backing off.

Wanting Rogowski's thoughts on the subject to be perfectly clear, he asked, "You're saying you don't believe Sullivan and Lily were lovers?"

"It never even crossed my mind, not when I knew Frank was in love with another woman and had been for years."

Skelly was remembering the politician's saying that he didn't know his employer very well because of their differences both in age and social standing. And that he'd attempted to distance himself from any special knowledge where Frank Sullivan was concerned. While he was wondering how best to use the conflicting statements, an intense Roz beat him to it.

"The identity of the other woman...who was she?"

"You really don't have any idea?"

"Not a clue. How would I?"

Rogowski gave her a look of pity. "Because, my dear, the other woman was Hilary Lang."

TOO UPSET TO DRIVE, Rosalind gave over the wheel to Skelly. Thankfully he respected her feelings enough to give her a few, much-needed moments of silence.

Aunt Hilary and Frank Sullivan...was it possible?

In all these years, the woman who'd been more of a mother than her own had never said a word. Not to her. Rather...not exactly.

Hilary had spoken of a man she'd loved with all her heart, though she'd never married him. Frank Sullivan? If that were true, why had she held back his identity, even now? Not that Hilary owed *her* that. But she did owe Lily. No public records indicated that she'd ever stood up for her own sister-in-law by countering the widow's accusations with the truth.

If truth it was.

Could she believe Walt Rogowski?

Rosalind certainly didn't want to. Acceptance would lead to other, more-horrible possibilities. She'd have to consider her great-aunt a murder suspect. She'd have to believe her great-aunt could be responsible for the brakes . . . and her near-fatal fall from the bluff.

She couldn't.

Wouldn't.

And that's all there was to it.

Besides, she hadn't given up on Sullivan's murder being related to his penchant for teenagers. If only they'd gotten the name of the second girl before being distracted by Rogowski's astonishing revelation.

"Anything I can say to cheer you up?" Skelly asked as he parked below Lang House.

"I doubt it." Grandfather's and Mother's cars were in their spots, she noticed, but Hilary's was gone. "Not even one of your exaggerated stories would lighten my mood."

"How about a hug and a kiss and a declaration of my love and support?"

Tears that she refused to shed stung the backs of her eyelids. "I'd like that."

Skelly gathered her in his arms, gave her a sympathetic squeeze and stroked her hair. His kiss was filled with great affection rather than the passion she'd come to expect. Exactly what she needed at the moment, Rosalind realized, as if he could read her mind. She did feel better in the shelter of his arms.

Just as she always felt safer.

It suddenly came to her that, while she'd tried to avoid thinking directly about it, she had fallen in love with Skelly McKenna. And now wasn't exactly the moment to tell him so, not when her heart was heavy with other matters. He had to sense desire for each other wasn't the only thing they shared.

And she *would* tell him that she loved him... at the right moment.

Sighing, she said, "Maybe we should go in."

"Are you going to say anything to Hilary?"

"I'll have to. Eventually. I need a little time."

His head against hers, he nuzzled her hair. "Give her a chance to explain, too, Roz. One thing might not have anything to do with the other."

Meaning the fact that Hilary had been Sullivan's lover wasn't evidence that she'd killed him?

Rosalind nodded. "Of course."

"In the meantime, I'll make some calls and try to find out whether or not Barbara Pohl still owns a bed and breakfast in the area."

Skelly kissed her forehead and let go of her long enough to exit the car. Then he held her hand up the walk, fingers intertwined, until they entered the house.

"Rosalind?"

She followed the shaky voice to the front parlor, where her grandfather sat staring down at the floor. More specifically, at the spot where Frank Sullivan had died. A shiver ran through her until Skelly moved close behind her, fingers gripping her upper arms. Drawing strength from his touch, she leaned back into him, glad for his support.

"What's wrong, Grandfather?"

"I must speak with you. Alone."

"Whatever you have to tell me...you can do so in front of Skelly."

Sitting half-hidden in the afternoon shadows, he appeared shrunken, less imposing. And though she could sense rather than see his eyes, she knew they were focused inward rather than meeting hers.

"What is it?" she asked when he didn't immediately respond. "Are you feeling well?"

"No."

Alarmed, she pulled free of Skelly's grip and made for the rear parlor. "I'll call the doctor."

He held out a staying hand. "I don't need medical attention."

"But if you're not feeling well—"

"I need you to promise me that you'll stop. Both of you. Now."

Her heart thundered in her breast. She didn't have to ask what he meant. A glance at Skelly assured her that he would let her handle this.

"We can't stop, Grandfather. Not until we get to the truth. That's what you want, isn't it? To clear Lily's name after all these years?"

"The truth." His laugh stung with irony. "You don't understand. The truth is part of a house of cards waiting to tumble. Pluck it out and..." He lifted his gaze to her and finally focused as if seeing her for the first time. "I warn you, Rosalind, if you persist, you'll destroy everything you ever cared about."

A sick feeling welled inside her, and her throat didn't want to work. "What do you mean?"

Without answering, he rose and shuffled past Skelly toward the stairs, for once looking every bit his age.

"Grandfather?"

Useless. He didn't so much as glance her way.

"What could he have meant, Skelly?" she whispered.

He took her in his arms as if to brace her, then said what she already knew in her heart.

"That he's been hiding the truth from you all along."

Chapter Twelve

After a muted dinner, Rosalind announced the first thing that came to mind, that she and Skelly were heading for nearby Appleton—he'd learned the location of Barbara Pohl's bed and breakfast. Not that they were actually headed there. They left the house with three sets of accusing eyes following them.

A conspiracy?

Anything was possible, a disillusioned Rosalind now knew. Therefore, she and Skelly had worked out a plan based on her suspicions. Not that she'd explained all to him. For once, he hadn't plagued her with questions or arguments. He'd chosen to cooperate blindly, to trust that she knew what she was doing, and for that she was grateful.

She drove the Thunderbird down the street, but once out of line of sight of Lang House, pulled over and parked. The weeping willow overhead would help camouflage the distinctive car. That and the creeping dusk.

"How long do you think we'll have to wait?" she asked, nerves twisting and turning.

"As long as it takes."

She felt hollow inside, and who could blame her? Her grandfather had turned her world upside down. ...*if you persist, you'll destroy everything you ever cared about*...

"Why did he go along with my plan?" She'd been asking herself the same thing over and over, and only one answer came to mind. "Why didn't he tell me to forget it?"

"Now, that would have worked," Skelly said dryly.

She could hardly miss his sarcasm. "But I did this for *him*."

"Did you?"

"All right, for them. Grandfather... Aunt Hilary... Mother." When Skelly didn't respond, she asked, "Why else?"

"How about for yourself?"

"I never even met Lily—" Rosalind decided she owed Skelly the truth "—though she did write to me a few times."

"She what?"

"During my debutante season, she saw my photograph in the society pages and wanted me to know how proud she was of me. The letters came about once a year and always from a different part of the country. I felt her love... and her underlying sadness...." she said, remembering how those missives had always touched her.

"Nice of you to let me in on all the facts."

"I didn't trust you to begin with, remember, and it's not like I could have told you anything that would have helped," she added defensively. "The last time I heard from Lily was right before I started graduate school."

"That was what? Four years ago?"

"Nearly five. Suddenly there were so many changes in my life." Like Tim, another subject she was reluctant to broach, though Rosalind knew it was inevitable. "Grandfather had his heart attack and retired. Aunt Hilary insisted they move back to Galena. Father took over Temptress and planned for me to follow in his footsteps even before I had my MBA." Not for the first time, she wondered if she'd done what she wanted with her life or what had been expected of her. "I didn't think much about Lily until your broadcast. And then I couldn't think about anything else."

"So you wanted to clear Lily's name because she touched you in those letters."

"Partially, yes."

Though deep inside, she was looking for explanations, Rosalind realized. And justifications. And hope for the future. She didn't want to inherit some cursed gene, to find unhappiness in love, to be cut off from her deepest emotions as were the other women in her family. Lily. Hilary. Mother. She didn't want to continue the self-destructive pattern she'd started with Tim. She'd been looking for another chance at love and life, and she'd found it.

With Skelly.

Before she could put any of those feelings into words, he said, "Here comes a car."

She glanced into her rearview mirror and confirmed it. "Grandfather."

Aunt Hilary had told her about his frequent disappearing acts. Having a good guess at his activities, Rosalind had figured he would steal off at the first opportunity. Well, he'd kept his secret long enough. She gave him a head start, then followed. At the highway, he turned west. Fifteen miles out of town, he crossed the Mississippi and drove through Dubuque.

She was beginning to wonder if he would keep going straight through Iowa when he turned north on an unlit county road. Fearing she would lose him in the dark, she sped up to close the gap between them. Several more miles, and he turned again, this road gravel. Stomach knotted as rock spewed around them, she kept him in sight until he swooped onto a long asphalt driveway, a lit house at its end.

"A farm," Skelly noted.

"Nothing else out here."

"But who...?"

Rosalind cut her lights and coasted onto the property. Nearing the house, she brought the car to a stop. Her heart was racing. She sat and stared at the neat white building, wondering if all her questions would be answered inside.

"Maybe I ought to check things out first," Skelly said.

But a rush of adrenaline was already urging her out of the car. Her long-legged stride quickly ate up the distance to the house. Skelly flew up right behind her even before she rang the bell.

"What is it you expect to find here, Roz?" he murmured, tone ripe with suspicion.

Breath caught in her throat, she fought a surge of nerves as the door opened to reveal an older if lovely woman with stylish, chin-length silver hair, pale blue eyes and a mole decorating the corner of her mouth....

Her grandmother, Lily Lang, in person.

LILY'S HEART nearly stopped. "Rosalind." Without hesitating, she wrapped her arms around the unresisting young woman who could have been her reflection thirty years before and took measure of the man who was staring at her, looking decidedly unsurprised. "And you're Skelly McKenna." She released her granddaughter and stood back from the door. "Come in, both of you."

Rosalind seemed rooted to the spot, as if she didn't know how to act around her. Who could blame the child?

"Why couldn't you leave it alone?" Noah growled out. He gripped the arms of his chair and stared accusingly at his granddaughter.

As Skelly drew Rosalind into the living room, Lily said softly, "Noah, please. She had a right."

"*He* has no rights," her husband said of Skelly. "He wouldn't care what really happened unless he could squeeze a sensational story out of it."

But Lily sensed something more between her granddaughter and the young man who held on to her so possessively.

"Please, sit." She indicated the couch. "I was about to make a pot of tea."

"No tea." Rosalind spoke at last, and when she faced Noah, it was with a sad face. "If you didn't want me to investigate in the first place, why didn't you just say so?"

Swallowing hard, Lily was the one to answer. "You can stop now," she said, hoping. "Return to Chicago, content in knowing that I am at peace."

"People believe—"

"I don't care what people think."

"But you didn't kill Frank Sullivan," Skelly stated, no doubt shading his voice.

"It doesn't matter anymore."

"It does," Rosalind insisted. "If the authorities ever got wind of your being here, you'd be back in prison in a flash. Why did you lie? Who are you still protecting?"

And Lily knew that the secret was not hers to keep any longer. Hers and Noah's. Rosalind did have a right. And something in her granddaughter's fearful expression told her that the girl already suspected. Not knowing would eat at her, and in the end, she would force the issue because she was who she was. Hers and Noah's grandchild—her looks, his temperament.

Aware that she had no choice, Lily took a deep breath and sat on the arm of her husband's chair, clasping his hand for courage. She would tell all.

Then their granddaughter would have to decide what to do with the truth.

"I was getting ready for bed when I heard a gunshot," she began calmly....

THE TORTURED SOUND of choked sobs filtered through the wooden panels as, hands shaking, Lily slid open the parlor's double doors to a horrific sight....

"Claudia!"

The soft light from a table lamp illuminated her thirteen-year-old daughter, who stood over a body. Blood streaked her nightgown, her hands and the gun she held awkwardly.

"Claudia, what have you done?" Lily cried, rushing to the man's side.

He lay facedown, perfectly still, a pool of blood seeping from beneath his chest over the floorboards. Only when she was on her knees did she recognize him. Frantic, she checked his vital signs.

There were none.

Frank Sullivan, her lifelong friend, was dead.

Lily stared up at her daughter through stricken, disbelieving eyes. Claudia had been jealous of Frank, had assumed he was responsible for the breakup of her parents' marriage, had refused to have him for a father. She had assured her child that none of this was true, that she still loved Noah but couldn't bear his possessiveness any longer, that Frank was no more than a good friend. But obviously...

Lily's thoughts scattered when she realized that, while Claudia's sobs had stopped, she was standing stiff as a statue...eyes lifeless...nightgown torn.

Her nightgown was torn! Around her were signs of a struggle.

Panicked anew, she flew to her daughter, touched her cold face. "Baby, what...?" Remembering the rumors she'd heard about those young girls who'd worked for Frank—rumors she'd disbelieved—she was horrified all over again. "Claudia, did Frank touch you? Did he try to make you do something you didn't want to do?"

She gripped the girl's shoulders and gave them a shake. Her daughter stared at her as if hypnotized, through eyes devoid of any clarity. "Mama? What happened?" Haunted eyes that told her Claudia truly didn't remember anything. That she was in shock.

Standing between her daughter and the dead man who'd molested her, Lily sheltered the girl from the sight, as well as from the memory. She removed the gun from Claudia's hand and set it down, cupped her daughter's head against her breast and led her from the room.

"It'll be all right, baby. You didn't do anything wrong. Whatever you think happened...it was a dream. All a bad dream."

She led Claudia upstairs and removed her torn nightclothes, nearly gagging when she imagined what Frank might have done to the girl. She smothered a cry of despair. Dear God, her fault. All her fault. She'd convinced Claudia to trust Frank. Guilt eating at her, she steeled herself against the tears that threatened to cloud her thinking. She cleaned up her daughter, helped her into a fresh nightgown and settled her in bed.

Then she sat with Claudia, stroking her daughter's brow and whispering, "It's good that you forget, baby. Forget everything that happened tonight. You went to bed early and had a bad dream is all. A bad dream..."

You never have to tell anyone about it.... You don't even have to think about it.... Nothing but a bad dream...

Over and over, she whispered the bidding until her daughter's brow cleared, her eyes fluttered closed and her breathing deepened. Claudia finally fell asleep.

Lily gathered the evidence and wadded it into a ball that she stuffed into a trash bag. Noting that she, too, was soiled by some of Frank's blood, she did the same with her owned ruined garments. Then she washed and dressed and applied her makeup as carefully as if she were appearing before the cameras... as if preparing to play the ultimate role.

For that's exactly what she intended to do.

"LUCKILY, NOAH SHOWED UP unexpectedly, even as I placed the call to the police."

Rosalind sat passively, aware of every word her grandmother had uttered, wondering how she could be so devoid of emotion now that she knew the truth. Her mother's attitudes over the years suddenly made perfect sense. Claudia might not be able to remember consciously what had happened, but subconsciously... No wonder she'd been so content with a bedroom separate from her husband, and had turned a blind eye to his mistresses. No wonder she'd had mixed feelings toward her own daughter... conceived in an act she must have despised.

"I arrived too late to talk my darling Lily out of the scheme," her grandfather was saying, "but in enough time to get rid of the evidence against Claudia."

"A little detail that might have tripped me up."

"Maybe you should have gotten rid of the gun while you were at it," Skelly said.

"What would have been the point?"

"It didn't belong to Frank."

"It wasn't *registered* to Frank," Noah corrected. "Buying guns on the street isn't a new phenomenon."

"Especially if you live in a big city like Chicago."

Not seeing there was a purpose to the debate, Rosalind interrupted. "No wonder you didn't move heaven and earth to prove Lily's innocence, Grandfather. The two of you conspired to hide the truth. To protect Mother."

"But you did help Lily escape later, right Noah?" Skelly asked, ever the vigilant reporter.

"She wouldn't hear of it, not at first."

"I thought I could bear my sentence," Lily confirmed, "and hoped I would get off early for good behavior. That way, I could eventually be with the people I loved. I was wrong about the bearable part."

Noah pulled up her hand and kissed it. "Thank God I had the money to smooth the way."

"So you knew where Lily was all along?" Rosalind asked, not quite comfortable calling the near-stranger *Grandmother.*

"Of course. I made all the arrangements. Moved her from place to place every six months or so."

"Thank God you had the money," Skelly echoed her grandfather, an ironic twist to his words. "And that your company business trips were never questioned."

"I would have gone crazy without Noah," Lily admitted. "Even changing disguises with every move, I couldn't chance on getting too close to anyone in case I was recognized. So Noah was all I had."

Ironic that her grandfather finally got what he wanted.

Rosalind met Skelly's gaze and swore that had occurred to him, as well. He sank into a thoughtful silence. And she told herself not to draw any conclusions. Rosalind asked her grandmother, "When did you move here?"

"After Noah had his heart attack." Lily fondly stroked his hand. "He couldn't travel to see me the way he used to, so I came to him."

Though Rosalind had argued with her father that Skelly's broadcast would kill her grandfather, she'd known it hadn't been true. While any heart attack was serious, the doctor had assured them Noah's attack had been relatively mild, and that after a recuperation period, he could get back to business as usual. Only he hadn't. He'd retired and had moved to Galena instead.

"So what will you do now that you know the truth?" her grandfather asked Skelly.

"I haven't decided."

Oddly removed, wanting to accept things as they'd been given to her, Rosalind stood. "We have to go now."

"So soon?" Lily appeared rebuffed.

"But I'll be back. I've always wanted to know you better, and now I'll have the chance."

Lily flashed a look at Skelly, who was making for the door. She didn't say anything. Sensing her grandmother's uncertainty, Rosalind gave her a quick, awkward hug.

"I will be back," she promised.

But a pall of silence hung over the room as she left it. And when they drove off, Skelly seemed immersed in his own thoughts. She held her tongue until they were on the highway, through Dubuque, across the Mississippi and quickly eating miles toward Galena.

"What now?" she asked quietly.

"I need to think things through."

What was there to think about?

"Skelly, your job is done."

"Is it? Everyone in the country still believes Lily is a murderess."

"But she doesn't care."

"But I thought *you* did. Wasn't that the point?"

"For God's sake, Lily's protecting my mother!"

"Who was a child when Sullivan died," he said reasonably. "If Claudia pulled the trigger, it was because she was protecting herself."

If? Hadn't he been listening? "Playing devil's advocate has its place. This isn't it," Rosalind argued. "Lily has taken the blame for thirty-three years and—"

"Don't you think that's long enough? Isn't it time the truth came out so your grandmother can live a normal life again?"

"She is living a normal life!"

"Hiding on some farm? Depending on Noah as a lifeline to the real world?"

The thought bothered Rosalind, as well, but she rationalized that perhaps Lily liked what she had. "You're talking about pointing the finger at my mother, the very person Lily gave up a normal life to protect."

"Your mother won't be going to prison," he said tightly.

"She might as well be. If the truth comes out, she'll be smeared in all the tabloids!"

Sensing Skelly stiffen at the reference, Rosalind gripped the steering wheel so hard that her knuckles hurt. Only a few more miles, she told herself. She had to convince him. Though her remark had been insensitive, she rationalized that Skelly didn't have anything but a job at stake here. And while she'd always known her mother's moods were unpredictable, she now feared for her mental health.

"What if Mother can't handle the truth? What if it pushes her over the edge?" When Skelly didn't respond, Rosalind swallowed hard, and her chest tightened painfully. "You're going to do it, aren't you? You've already made up your mind."

"My mind's not made up about anything yet," he assured her. "There are questions to consider."

But she didn't believe him. "You won't be able to resist. Not with a promotion hanging in the balance."

"How do you know about the promotion?"

"It doesn't matter. I thought *I* mattered to you."

"You do matter," he insisted, practically yelling, "I love you!"

"Then tell me you'll forget about doing the story."

"I can't."

"If you really love me, you can and you will."

"Don't go there, Roz."

"Where?"

"Don't try to control me. Trust me to do the right thing, instead."

"How can I trust you when you didn't tell me why this story was so important to you?"

"Because I'm telling you my priorities have changed."

"In less than a week?"

"How long does it take to fall in love, Roz? Maybe I should be asking how long it takes *you* to fall in love. You've never said how you feel about me."

"Of course I love you!" Not exactly the way she'd meant to tell him.

"No 'of course' about it. How do I know you're not trying to manipulate me into dropping the story?"

"That's the most insulting thing anyone's ever said to me!"

"And your thinking I'm putting a promotion above you isn't? I've tried to tell you from the beginning that I have my own brand of integrity. That hasn't changed...although I admit I'm more willing to take responsibility than I used to be. Be proud of that, Roz, because it's your doing."

Close to tears, she said, "Then I wish I could undo it."

"You wanted the truth. You demanded I be ethical and find the truth and share it with the world. You forgot to tell me the only-as-long-as-whatever-you-say-suits-me part. Remember my condition, that I wouldn't be censored. Now you're doing just that. You want me to suppress the truth...again, for you. Well, you can't have it both ways."

Furious, she yelled, "The only thing you care about are ratings and some damn promotion!"

"What about you, Roz? Do you care about how anyone else feels? What they want? Or is having control over every aspect of your life so damn important that you're willing to throw away the promise of a future together?"

"I'm not the one throwing it away."

An angry silence permeated the already close atmosphere in the car for the rest of the drive. Rosalind was relieved when they entered Galena. And calmer. Wanting to give Skelly another opportunity to be reasonable, she waited until after pulling into her parking space.

Taking a deep breath, she said, "You've had time to think, Skelly, and I'm willing to give you another chance—"

"Another chance at what?"

"To prove that you love me." Though she kept her voice even, desperation filled her. "Please, tell me you won't involve my family in another story that would hurt the very people I was trying to protect."

"I love you more than life itself, Roz," Skelly said all too calmly. "I'm asking you to trust me to do what's right."

"If you can't agree, then you might as well leave," she choked out. "Get your things and go. Take my car." She tossed him the keys and threw open her door. "I'll arrange to have it picked up from the studio later in the week.''

"Roz!"

She was already out of the car and running up the walk. Running away from Skelly. From another relationship.

No, that wasn't quite right, she assured herself. Even if he did love her, Skelly was pushing her away. He didn't love her enough.

The family curse had struck again.

BLIND FURY DROVE Skelly through the dark along fog-laced curves and hills. At least there weren't many other vehicles. A few drivers heading west gave him a wide berth, and the car lights that had been behind him since leaving Galena stayed at a safe distance. All around, a growing quantity of eerie white stuff sucked the black out of the night. His high beams briefly illuminated a green sign announcing three miles to Woodbine. He remembered Roz saying she didn't like to drive this strip of road after dark because the fog scared her and there was plenty of it. He remembered everything Roz had said to him from the first moment he met her.

Unbelievable!

First she'd looked down on him and what he did for a living because she'd assumed he had no ethics. Now, after admitting that she was wrong—and that she respected him—she wanted him to throw away those same ethics that had seemed so important to her. Though he'd known she was controlling, he hadn't considered she'd ditch a once-in-a-lifetime love if she couldn't come out on top.

If he *was* her once-in-a-lifetime, Skelly thought, doubt creeping over him.

To be fair, more than Roz's own ego was involved here. One of the things that had attracted him was her sense of family loyalty. He couldn't fault her for that. And Lily had put them in quite a predicament with her confession.

If Lily knew everything there was to know.

If only Roz had given him time to sort things out. What they knew for certain. What they thought they knew. What they suspected. At least, what *he* suspected. As far as he was concerned, there was more to the big picture.

Like the brakes.

And the bluff.

And the identity of the person responsible for what could have passed for accidents if Roz had been killed.

A cold lump settled in his stomach. Now that he was thinking clearly again, Skelly realized what he'd done. He'd gone and left Roz alone. Vulnerable. And damn it all...unsuspecting! Whoever had started the job was bound to try to finish it.

Before he could find a pull-over where he could turn around and go back, his cell phone rang. He anticipated this would be Keelin, ready to chew his butt for not calling as he'd promised.

"Hey, cuz, you get to hang me by my toes."

The answering Irish lilt was not the one he was expecting. "Ah, boyo, I've been doing some soul-searching."

His father's voice came as a shock. "Dad, are you all right?"

"Not after talkin' to your cousin. What a mess you've gotten yourself into. Keelin confided in me even if you wouldn't."

"I tried to...."

"We never did communicate well, did we, boyo? Not too late to be fixing that, though."

"No," Skelly said, a lump in his throat. "It isn't."

And listened in amazement to what his father had called to tell him.

ROSALIND STOOD BEFORE the front-parlor windows long after Skelly had driven beyond the range of the brass telescope. Her hopes that he would turn around and drive back to her dashed, she felt numb.

And she realized that she'd done exactly the thing she'd feared most. She'd continued the pattern she'd begun with Tim. As she had with her college fiancé, she'd pushed too hard, had expected too much. She'd wanted tangible proof of Skelly's love. Something she could hold up and say, *See, he really does love me.* She'd tried to force him to prove it in a way that was not worthy of either of them.

And if he had gone along with her, how would she have felt about him then?

He wouldn't be the man he was.

A good man, deserving of her respect, and who, God help her, could be trusted to do the right thing.

If only she could tell him—

"He's gone?" came a voice from the dark behind her.

"Aunt Hilary, you startled me." The first floor had been empty when she had entered a while ago, and Rosalind had assumed both her great-aunt and mother had retired. "Yes, Skelly's gone. I'm afraid I drove him off."

And, as if she didn't have enough on her mind, she wondered when Grandfather would return. What he would say. How he would act. How *she* would act. Negative thoughts about her grandfather that Skelly had stirred with his questions kept surfacing.

Hilary drew closer and slipped a comforting arm around her waist. "He wasn't worth it, then, if he could be scared off so easily."

"Worth it?" Rosalind echoed.

"We don't really choose who we love, do we? Fate does that for us. But I have no regrets."

"You don't regret loving Frank Sullivan?" After what Lily had told her?

"So you know." Appearing only slightly surprised, Hilary shook her head. "Maybe that makes me immoral...loving another woman's husband. But Diane shouldn't have turned him away from her bed. He didn't care that she couldn't give him a child. But she made him into a lonely man who needed a woman's arms around him. *My* arms."

Wondering if her aunt was deluding herself, she asked, "Are you certain you were the only one?"

"He never slept with Lily!" Hilary insisted, her tone strident. "He loved *me*...if not enough to destroy his career with a divorce."

She was defending her lover rather than her sister-in-law, and Rosalind faced a fact that had been in front of her nose all along. "You disliked my grandmother, didn't you?"

"Lily was so judgmental where I was concerned." Hilary let go of Rosalind and wandered from the windows. "For years, she interfered with my life. More than once, she convinced Frank to stop seeing me so he could try to reconcile with Diane. That's what they fought about the night he...died. First she came between Noah and me, then did the same with Frank."

Uneasy at the implication of Hilary's possessiveness toward her own brother, Rosalind said, "But in the end, Frank wasn't worth it, Hilary. He did awful things." Remembering that her great-aunt had raised her mother after Lily's incarceration, she said, "Surely at some point you had to guess something was wrong." But if Hilary knew what had happened to Claudia, she wasn't admitting it, Rosalind noted, continuing to push. "At the very least, you must've heard about the teenage girls who quit working for him."

"Old lies! Who's fed you that poison?"

"I've heard it from more than one person."

Hilary shook her head. "I would have known. Here." Placing a hand over her heart, her voice ascending a notch, she insisted, "Frank was a God-fearing man! He would never have sunk so low. Someone wanted to destroy his good name. Someone set him up."

Rosalind felt sick that her grandfather came immediately to mind. His obsessive jealousy would have made him hate Frank Sullivan, because he'd no doubt assumed that the politician was having an affair with Lily.

But would he have tried to destroy the man's career— or worse, his very life?

"Why couldn't Frank have left Diane and married me?" Hilary murmured. "Then everything would have been different."

Her great-aunt sounded a bit delusional, reminding her of Grandfather when he started on Lily. He'd always made it sound as if he'd lost the most precious thing in his life even while he'd had exactly what he wanted . . . ultimate control over the woman he loved.

Control . . .

The same way she'd tried to control Skelly.

Sick inside at the comparison—she was too much like her grandfather for her own comfort—Rosalind wished she could take her demands back. She wished she could see Skelly face-to-face and tell him she'd been wrong. She would do that when she saw him in Chicago, she promised herself, even as unease stole over her. Skelly had wanted to think things over, had said he had questions to consider.

So did she.

"I thought I understood everything," Rosalind murmured. "But I don't. Aunt Hilary, are you certain Frank couldn't have molested those girls?"

"I knew him better than anyone, dear. He never would have touched a child. If I'd ever thought that was true," Hilary swore, eyes filling, "I would have killed him myself!"

A SHORT STOP IN APPLETON, and Skelly was flying back to Galena through a glowing cloud of white. Adrenaline pumped through his arteries, urging him to go faster, even though the fog's tentacles had embraced everything in its path, swallowing objects whole.

Houses . . . trees . . . road.

All gone.

Though he'd switched on his brights, the high beam barely cut a swath through the cloying, damp cotton. Considering the conditions, he was driving recklessly and he knew it, but he couldn't think about his own safety.

Not when he'd left Roz a sitting duck.

A thin beam caught him in the rearview mirror. Another car creeping up on him as he swerved around a bend that he spotted right at the last second. He wasn't the only one driving like a crazy man. Probably the only one who didn't know the road, though.

His stomach churned, and a fist closed around his heart when he thought of the woman he loved, alone and vulnerable, undoubtedly not even considering the danger she might be in. She'd been as upset as he. Maybe more. She'd been unreasonable, too.... They would deal with that later. For now, he could concentrate on one thing only. Getting to her side as fast as possible.

If anything happened to Roz . . .

He'd never forgive himself, Skelly swore, noting the distance between the Thunderbird and the dark car be-

hind him had narrowed. Was the driver nuts? Skelly
tapped his brake pedal lightly a few times in warning, but
either the other driver wasn't aware of the flashing red
lights or was ignoring them. Up an incline and around a
curve, the other vehicle stayed with him until he pressed
on the accelerator.

Gaining speed down the sharp incline did as much
damage to his stomach as any roller coaster, but at least
he'd put the other vehicle a bit behind.

Part of him concentrated on the drive. The other part
drifted back to the bed and breakfast in Appleton. It had
taken some doing, but he'd pried through the false sense
of security with which Barbara Pohl had surrounded
herself for more than thirty years. He'd told her about
the brakes…the bluff…the danger to anyone who knew
too much.

She'd talked.

And, armed with the truth, Skelly only hoped he
wouldn't be too late.

Fear filled him, not for himself, but for the woman he
loved. Roz was a gutsy lady. But she didn't know what
she was up against. Unfortunately he did.

The vehicle following him zoomed forward again,
more quickly this time, as if the other driver were intent
on passing him in the fog. Realizing the potential danger, Skelly scanned the side of the road for a widening.
A pull-over. But what met his eyes instead was the impression of a drop-off. Not that he could see beyond his
brights.

Or into those of the truck coming the other way.

Blinded for a moment, he swerved to the right, his
wheels nearing the edge of the road, too close for comfort, as the truck lumbered by. He pulled the Thunderbird back a bit, not quite to the center line, giving the
driver following him a chance to pass. But while the gap

narrowed dangerously, the other vehicle stayed directly behind him.

Gut clenching, Skelly knew...

Roz wasn't the only one in trouble.

He sensed the other driver didn't want to pass, after all, even before the jolt whipped him forward. Though he was unprepared for a game of bumper tag, his seat belt prevented his chest from being crushed against the wheel. A curve came on him too fast. He muscled the car around it even as he was rammed again, harder this time.

Skelly was ready. Braced. His neck snapped and his head flew back slightly, but he got a quick glance in the rearview mirror. For an instant catching sight of a familiar silhouette in the other car, he managed a moment of triumph before a third hit sent the Thunderbird careering out of his control.

Chapter Thirteen

Sitting in the darkened rear parlor, not knowing what exactly she was waiting for, Rosalind jumped when the telephone shattered the midnight silence. She fumbled the receiver to her ear.

"Skelly?"

"I fear he'll be needing you as quick as you can get to him," came a frantic voice from the other end.

"Keelin." Already sliding into her shoes, she knew this had to be his cousin...and that Keelin had seen something terrible happen to Skelly in one of the visions he'd described. "Tell me, please!"

"The road he was traveling writhes within a dense fog. He left an old house...a bed and breakfast...to return for you. He feared for your safety...only he didn't think of his own."

Rosalind's head was whirling as she accepted Keelin's word without doubt. Bed and breakfast? *Appleton?* Knowing he must have spoken to Barbara Pohl, she flew to her feet. "You're saying that Skelly had an accident on the road?"

"I'm saying someone forced him off a curve."

Her heart climbed to her throat. "He is alive?"

"I cannot see." Keelin sounded as if she were still trying. "He flew through a white blanket...objects rushing along on either side . . . and then nothing. Blackness. Jesus, Mary and Joseph . . . I tried to call him on that portable phone he carries around with him, but he did not answer.''

Trying not to panic, Rosalind said, ''I'm on my way!''

Hanging up, she raced into the kitchen, where she grabbed her great-aunt's spare car keys. She was flying down the steps when she realized her mother was standing in the street, her face pinched into the oddest expression.

Her transfixed gaze suddenly refocusing on her daughter, Claudia asked, ''Rosalind, where in the world are you off to at this late hour?''

''No time to talk.'' She unlocked the big old Buick. ''Skelly's had an accident.''

Even as she jumped behind the wheel, the passenger door opened and her mother slid in on the other side. ''You shouldn't be alone.''

Rosalind put the car in gear and made like an Indy 500 driver, infinitely thankful that the late hour meant traffic was light. Only when the town's limits were behind them did it occur to her that the hour was also late for her mother to be out and about. And that her perceptible concern for her daughter—not to mention a man she disliked—was definitely out of character for her.

''Where were you coming from, Mother?''

Her question was countered by a soft-spoken demand. ''Tell me what happened tonight.''

At the moment unable to deal with her mother's reaction to anything that she and Skelly had learned earlier, Rosalind merely said, ''We had a fight and I told Skelly to go back to Chicago. I gave him the keys to the Thunderbird.''

''Then how do you know he had an accident? Did he call you and ask you to come pick him up? Where is he?

Did he stay with the car? Or did someone get him to the county trauma center?''

Only half registering her mother's rapid-fire questions, Rosalind murmured, "Dear Lord, I didn't think to summon help before I left." He had to be unconscious if Keelin had lost her connection to him...or at least he had been. "Skelly's cousin called after seeing him being forced off the road...retribution for prying into Frank Sullivan's death...."

Realizing whom she was talking to, Rosalind let it drop. According to Lily, she'd taken advantage of her young daughter's shock to help her forget. *If* she'd really pulled the trigger. And if she remembered now, would she really do *anything* to keep her secret? Though they didn't have an ideal relationship, Rosalind couldn't believe that her mother would hurt *her*.

Though someone would.

Someone who knew about brakes and wasn't afraid to go skulking around river bluffs.

Uneven breathing pricked the silence. Rosalind chanced a glance toward the passenger side. Her mother sat stiff and staring through the windshield, seemingly in another world. Her fingers plucked at her skirt, and her head shook slightly.

Bumps crawled along Rosalind's arms and down her spine; she dodged the creepy feeling.

Swallowed whole by a blanket of white, the night was eerie enough. And the car was nosing onto the stretch of road that might thrill her in the brilliance of day, but that frightened her in the fog of night. Still, she didn't slow down around the hair-raising curves, not even as she chanced frequent glances at the other side of the road. Her heart hammered in her breast as she waited for a glimpse of a wreck.

And her mind raced ahead. *Who?* Who could be evil enough to force Skelly off the road?

Next to her, her mother trembled harder. Because she was guilty? Claudia Van Straaten might dislike Skelly, but she wasn't a violent woman. She devoted her life to charity work, especially singling out children.

Rosalind's thoughts raced faster.

Aunt Hilary had sworn Frank Sullivan hadn't molested anyone. If he hadn't touched those girls, if he hadn't touched the thirteen-year-old Claudia, then who had? *Who?* Surely Lily couldn't have been mistaken about what had happened to her own daughter.

She'd barely latched on to a theory when a faint light suddenly cut through the miasma ahead. Light not aimed at them. Not focused on anything.

"That's it."

A definite glow told her the Thunderbird sat somewhere directly below the road. She slowed down. How to get to it? The graded land to her right held no prospects for a quarter of a mile. Then she caught sight of a dirt turnoff. Good enough. Gingerly maneuvering the big Buick around what had to be a private road, she was startled by headlights swooping out of nowhere, another vehicle passing them with mere inches to spare.

Shaking at the close call, Rosalind glanced at her mother, who didn't seem as if she'd noticed, then finished the turn and fled the way they came. When she relocated the motionless glow, she knew she had no choice. She parked the car as close to the edge of the road as possible and turned on the flashers.

"You'll have to get out, Mother. This car's a sitting duck. I have to get to Skelly."

But the older woman didn't so much as move a muscle while Rosalind flew out the door and around to the trunk. She grabbed an emergency flare and one of the flashlights. First starting the flare, she stuck it in the soft shoulder at the rear of the Buick.

Then, with another, less patient warning to her mother, she approached the drop-off, steeling herself as she clambered down the steep grade toward the wreck below. From the direction of the car's beam, she could tell the Thunderbird was tilted awkwardly.

"Skelly!" she yelled, refusing to imagine what she might find inside. "Say something, please!"

Though it was doubtful that anyone more than a few feet away could hear. Her voice stopped dead as if hitting an impenetrable barrier. She didn't let that stop her from talking, however. She kept up her one-sided conversation, voicing encouragement that she didn't really feel.

Cold and still inside with fear, she opened the passenger door. Her softer "Skelly" went unrewarded. A streak of light around the interior told her why.

The car was empty.

Her heart jerked her around. He couldn't have gotten far. Not by himself. But if he wasn't in the car, she assured herself, at least he was alive.

He had to be alive.

Because if he wasn't, it would be all her fault. She'd sent him away in anger. She'd been wrong and she knew she deserved to be reproved, but not, please God, by losing the man she loved forever.

She was circling the surrounding area, her flashlight hitting pockets of clear air—the fog seemed to be lifting gradually—when she heard a low groan to her right. Instinct drew her straight to Skelly. He was stretched out on the ground some distance from the car. The left side of his face awash in blood, he was attempting to push himself to a sitting position. She practically threw herself at him.

"My God, don't move," she said, landing on her knees at his side. She aimed her flashlight at his forehead. A cut slashed through his hairline, but the bleeding had stopped. "Something might be broken."

"Don't...think so...got myself this far," he said, and with another groan, finished sitting up.

"Stay right there," she ordered. "I'll find your cell phone and call for an ambulance."

Before he could respond, the crunch of a foot on dry earth told her they weren't alone.

Rosalind whipped around, her flashlight catching her mother by surprise. Claudia briefly lifted a hand to her eyes . . . and Rosalind swore she got a glimpse of a small handgun.

"Mother?"

"I can't let it happen again!" the older woman said, voice rising, her gaze searching for something that Rosalind couldn't see.

A cold ball formed in the pit of her stomach. "Let what happen?"

"It's my fault Frank died. All my fault."

Had her mother killed him, then? Had Hilary been blind to her lover's proclivities?

Lump square in her throat, she said, "Mother, you're not making any sense. Calm down, and we'll sort this out later. I'm calling an ambulance."

"Forget it." Skelly sucked in the clear air around him. "I need a minute is all."

"Don't argue with me."

A growing apprehension that all was not right forced her away from him and back to the Thunderbird through entrails of thinning fog. It didn't make sense that someone would try to kill Skelly and not finish the job. She needed to find the cell phone and fast.

"Wait!" he yelled after her. "It's not necessary!"

A glance over her shoulder gave her nothing more than a glimpse of the soupy blanket billowing between them. Mentally focusing on the one item that would link them to civilization and the authorities spurred her on. But a few more hurried steps ran her straight into an immovable object that meant to keep her from her goal.

She smothered a yelp and tried to back off. A band of steel wrapping around her wrist trapped her where she stood.

"You should have hightailed it back to Chicago when you had the chance," a disembodied voice whispered. "Now you've gone and complicated everything."

Her heart thundering loud enough to deafen her, she swept the flashlight upward to confirm what she'd already guessed. She met Walt Rogowski's evil gaze before he knocked her hand away with something hard.

A gun.

"So, you *are* the one." Her voice was as shaky as her knees. Simultaneously frightened and relieved, she said, "You're to blame for everything. The brakes. The bluff. The accident. *You* killed Frank Sullivan!"

"Rosalind? What's going on?" Skelly called.

What to do? Skelly was in no shape to help. If she yelled a warning, he would certainly fly to her rescue . . . and Rogowski would simply shoot him dead.

"Tell him you're making the call," the politician instructed in a low voice, tightening his grip around her wrist.

Rosalind complied. "I'm trying to get through to the paramedics!" Then she managed to choke out another whispered question. "What were you doing in Lang House the night you killed Sullivan?"

She wanted Rogowski talking while she calmed down and prepared for the fight of her life. He had a weapon while she only had a flashlight. Dismal odds, at best.

"Me, kill him? Frank and Lily had that big public argument," Rogowski reminded her. "About Hilary, as usual. He came back to the office. I was there, working late. After a while, he decided he had to see Hilary. I drove because he didn't have his car with him. Frank used his keys to get into the house."

"And then you went inside—" thoughts of escape on hold for the moment, Rosalind went for the whole truth "—where you attacked my mother."

"You don't know what you're talking about."

Bracing herself, she said, "You don't think I'm the only one who knows, do you? And all the pieces we've turned up have been exposed to many others. The truth will out if something happens to us."

His laugh chilled her. "I'll stop *anyone* who gets in my way. Eddie!"

Horrified, she heard his bodyguard answer "Here, boss" as the massive young man stepped out of the fog.

"Finish McKenna any way you have to." Rogowski cocked the gun. "I'll take care of the woman myself."

A knife suddenly appeared in Eddie's hand. He took the direction from which she'd come—where Skelly sat like a sitting duck. Her considerable adrenaline wound tight like a spring, Rosalind let loose and shoved her shoulder into the bastard's chest.

"Skelly! Watch out!" she yelled.

Rogowski stumbled and his weapon discharged, the blast eerily dull. For a man in his late fifties, however, he was possessed of extraordinary strength. Desperation, no doubt. While she was able to drag him a few feet, he didn't even loosen his grip on her wrist.

Vaguely aware of muffled sounds that indicated another struggle—Eddie and Skelly—she stopped abruptly, in one smooth motion turning and lifting her thigh to hip level. She snapped her lower leg, kicking out and making contact hard enough to break a kneecap. Pain shot along her foot, around her ankle and up her shin. But, hallelujah, the death grip around her wrist slipped, and she hobbled off.

Metal clattering to rock was followed by Skelly's "That's for the brake line!" Then she imagined hearing his knuckles smashing into softer flesh. "And this is for River Bluff!"

Renewed hope and Eddie's unexpected grunt of pain pushing her on, she quickly reached the wrecked car in hopes of finding the blessed phone. But Rogowski was directly behind her, kneecap intact, and grabbed her by the waistband of her trousers.

He swung her around full circle. Off balance, Rosalind flew straight into the crooked beam of the car's headlights and landed against the grille. The Thunderbird rocked and protested with a metallic wail, and she knew it wouldn't take much to send the car hurtling downhill. She staggered upright and faced Sullivan's murderer, who now had a clear shot at her.

"You sanctimonious bitch!" he yelled, stalking her, gun pointed directly at her face. "Had to put your nose where it didn't belong, just like your grandmother!"

A sharp whine accompanying a split-second bright flash stopped him cold. His eyes opened wide as he stared down at his side, slowly blooming with dark color.

His blood, Rosalind realized, her stomach turning.

"You keep your hands off my daughter!" Claudia snarled, stepping out of the dark, preceded by the small handgun Rosalind had noticed earlier. It shook in her hands. "I was too young to stop you from getting what you wanted all those years ago," she said, "but I'll be damned if I let you hurt anyone else now!"

Her threat shocking Rosalind immobile.

"Claudia..." Rogowski's voice took on a sickening, coaxing tone. "Sweetheart, did you forget what we had together?"

"You took advantage of me! I needed affection...*fatherly* affection."

"And I gave you what you wanted. Remember?"

Sick at heart, Rosalind held her breath as her mother spoke.

"I remember now...after Frank left the house looking for Hilary, you slipped inside so you could get to me again. I tried to make you stop, but you wouldn't. Then Frank caught you, and I ran. But I didn't go far, Walt. I heard everything...saw everything...now I remember it all."

"You were too young to understand—"

"I understood Frank realized *you* were the reason those girls quit working for him. He threatened to expose you, to end your political career right there. He said he'd see you in jail."

Finally Rogowski broke. "I couldn't let him ruin everything! I had my whole future ahead of me. So I fixed things!"

"Fixed things?" Rosalind echoed, aghast. "You make it sound like you repaired a boiler rather than killed a man!" Furious at what he'd done to her mother—at what he'd done to her, for now she knew why her mother had always kept her father at an emotional, as well as physical, distance—she snapped, "What irony! A child molester running for governor on a *family-values* ticket!"

"The public does seem to like that hoo-ha."

"The public isn't going to like *you* for much longer," she promised.

"None of you will be able to say anything if you're all dead." A desperate sound issued from deep within

Rogowski, and he lurched toward Claudia, who tried to aim her weapon.

Panicked that he would hurt her mother again, Rosalind threw herself between the two, blindly swinging out toward the murderer with the heavy flashlight. Her first strike sent his gun flying. Her second caught him in the side of the head. Rogowski teetered, his expression wild as another explosion of noise—an unconscious Eddie's dead weight smashing into the Thunderbird's trunk— split the air.

"Roz, out of the way!" Skelly yelled.

Without hesitating, she flew back, dragging her mother, even as the heavy car swayed and tilted and, with a metallic groan, bounced toward the villainous gubernatorial candidate.

Before Rosalind's amazed eyes, justice played itself out in slow motion.

Rogowski's hands reaching for the vehicle...

His expression of horror when he realized he couldn't stop its forward momentum...

His body jerking as the heavy metal plowed into him...

Rosalind turned away from the final denouement. Bad enough she could hear the metallic thumps and screeches over his screams.

Suddenly she was enveloped in familiar arms and opened her eyes to the face she knew nearly as well as her own. She covered it with thankful kisses even as she tried to explain herself.

"Skelly, I thought...I never would have...I'm sorry...I love you."

She only hoped that when she told him about the imagined curse and how she'd almost made the same mistake twice, he would understand and forgive her.

"I love you, too, Roz, more than life itself."

He captured her mouth and, with a single, heart-wrenching kiss, convinced her.

For a dizzying moment, Rosalind even thought the swelling wail of sirens was part of the magic he always created in her. But all too soon, she realized the sounds were real. Above them, tires screeched and vehicle doors slammed.

"Down here!" Skelly yelled before saying, "I tried to tell you. I called the authorities the moment I regained consciousness. I must have lost the phone somewhere around here."

"Why didn't you say so?"

"You didn't give me a chance."

"So it's my fault?"

"You could learn to listen once in a while."

"Maybe you'll have to learn to speak up—"

"Rosalind, do stop going on," her mother interrupted. "I would guess your young man's head already aches."

"Uh, yes, Mother."

Skelly nuzzled her ear and whispered, "We can finish this later. I never want to stop arguing with you...not for as long as I live."

"...thirty years after her escape, Lily Lang, the Blond Temptress, is finally back where she belongs...."

ON THE TELEVISION screen, the silver-haired Lily sat on a paper-flower-festooned float that brought up the rear of Galena's Fourth of July parade. Decked out in one of her old glamorous dresses that had been altered to her more mature waistline, she was waving to the cheering crowd.

". . . exonerated and firmly in the hearts of the people who love her."

Those in the living room of the Langs' Winnetka home all cheered, as well, as Skelly stopped the preview tape. He'd been nervous about their reactions. Lily. Noah. Claudia. Rip. Hilary. His own father and sister, Aileen. Keelin, Tyler and Cheryl, his cousin's soon-to-be stepdaughter.

And most of all, he'd been worried about Roz's reaction. A quick check assured him that she was beaming with happiness.

"It'll air tomorrow," he said, relieved that everyone seemed to approve.

"You did a wonderful job." Eyes shining with love and more, Roz moved closer. "I'm so proud of you. Mother is, too."

Though he'd been willing to withhold names, to skirt around the fact that Claudia herself had been molested by Walt Rogowski, she'd insisted on his sticking to the facts. Many of the children supported by her pet charity, Be Kind to Kids, had been abused in one way or another. Claudia had seen this as an opportunity to open honest communications with the philanthropists she approached for funding. Now they would see her as more than a do-gooder who had no experience with sordid matters.

The very idea that he and Roz were investigating the past had stirred Claudia's private monsters—the reason she'd shown up unexpectedly in Galena. The truth had come back to her in unwelcome bits and pieces. Her witnessing Rogowski's threatening her daughter's life had brought back the past in startling clarity.

Though she'd been hiding in the rear parlor, Claudia

had witnessed the shooting. Once Rogowski had fled the scene, she'd picked up the gun and had tried to awaken her mother's friend, only to realize he was dead. In her child's mind, Claudia had asked for Rogowski's sexual attention; therefore, she was responsible for Frank Sullivan's death.

The two incidents combined were enough to leave her in deep shock. Lily's comforting her had been hypnotic, her suggestions welcome, and Claudia truly had forgotten everything on a conscious level. Unfortunately the incidents had worked on her subconsciously—hence, her difficulty with closeness.

Skelly admired Claudia's newfound courage and hoped that she would be able to mend the breach between her and her husband, Rip, as she'd said she wanted to do. He knew she and Roz had already vowed to work at becoming closer.

Realizing the time was slipping away, he looked for courage of his own to make the announcement that would be a surprise to most of the people in the room.

"It's time," Roz said, nudging him and leaving him with no choice.

Skelly took a deep breath. "Everyone raise your glasses if you would." He lifted his own. "To Keelin and Tyler and—" The rest of what he planned to say was cut off by more cheers.

"Keelin and Tyler!"

"Hear! Hear!"

Everyone toasted and sipped at champagne.

"And to Skelly and Rosalind!" Keelin added loudly, giving him one of her looks. "I'm proud to be telling you the McKenna legacy has claimed another pair of hearts. We'll be having a double wedding on Sunday."

Then each member of their families had to congratulate and hug them both, starting with Keelin and Tyler and Cheryl.

"Hey, thanks for your help, cuz," he told Keelin as they hugged. "I owe you."

"I think 'tis even we are."

Keelin stepped back between the man she loved and his pretty, teenage daughter, wrapping an arm around each of their waists. Though the wedding wasn't until Sunday, they already looked like a happy family.

"Don't you let this man get away," a teary-eyed Hilary told Roz next. "A woman only has one once-in-a-lifetime love."

Roz hugged her great-aunt, then faced her grandmother.

"Hilary is right." Lily gave the man whose arm was possessively wrapped around her shoulders a loving glance. To Skelly, she said, "Make her as happy as Noah has made me."

"I'll make her happier," Skelly promised.

His gaze locked with Noah's. He would make certain Roz always knew how much he loved her without smothering her, Skelly vowed. And if she ever tried that controlling trick to distance herself from him again . . . well, he was no Tim Hayes. The older man was the first to look away.

Claudia and Rip were next. While Roz's mother gave her a quick kiss on the cheek and a pat on the arm, her father enveloped her in a bear hug.

"You be happy, sweetheart," he ordered. "Don't let work or anything else get in the way of your marriage."

"I won't," she promised.

Rip shook Skelly's hand. "That goes for you, as well, son."

"We'll be making decisions *together*. Right, Roz?"

Reassured, her parents moved away. Skelly noticed Rip's taking Claudia's arm and her smiling in return. He knew their attempt to start anew pleased Roz, who'd always been close to her father and wanted the same with her mother. Maybe now it would be possible.

"I can't believe you kept this from me," Aileen said, enveloping them both in a big hug and yards of colorful material that reflected her shining personality. "My brother...married! I can hardly take it in."

"You won't be long behind," Roz assured her.

"Me?" Aileen laughed. "No man would have me."

"A special man would," Skelly assured her. "It's Moira's legacy."

At last he faced his father. Always his nemesis.

"So, you're to change your ways, are you?" Raymond asked, his expression serious.

"I love Roz more than anything, Dad. Whether or not you approve—"

His father held up his hand. "This is your finest hour, boyo. Don't spoil it." He looked to Roz. "If he lets you down, he'll be hearing from me."

"He won't. He couldn't," Roz said with such surety that Skelly's already overflowing heart filled with even more love.

Raymond cleared his throat. "Now, about your wedding present..."

"You eased the way for my grandmother to remain free while the legal system slowly grinds away," Roz said. "That was the best present anyone could give me."

His father had surprised him, too, Skelly thought, remembering the call on his cell phone when he was driving back to Chicago. He'd talked about the sexual-misconduct rumors—ones aimed at Rogowski rather than Sullivan. He hadn't said anything before because of his loyalty to the party. Skelly now knew the pervert had never stopped, that the girl named Kim had been his latest victim. She was willing to swear to it at Lily's new hearing, as was Barbara Pohl.

Rogowski was beyond earthly payment for his crimes, but Skelly was certain that he'd already answered to a higher power. And Eddie Turner would soon be judged by his peers for his participation in the attempted murders of three people.

Skelly realized his father was staring at him . . . almost as if he didn't know his own son.

"What about you, boyo? What is it *you'll* be wanting?"

That was easy. "I'm of one mind with Keelin. Our family reunited."

"Then you have it. I've already agreed to return to Ireland for the birthday reunion that Keelin's planning. I only hope Rose will be as amenable after what James and I put her through."

Knowing that his cousin and her new husband would stop to see Aunt Rose in South Dakota while on their honeymoon, Skelly asked, "How can anyone refuse Keelin anything?"

"Aye. She's something, that one. A real McKenna . . . like you."

Winking, his father left them alone and joined the throng gathered around the buffet table.

"Whew!" Skelly kissed Roz lightly. "That went better than I thought."

"He's always loved you."

"He hasn't always been proud of me."

"After the piece on Lily airs, you'll be offered that promotion. He'll have no reason to criticize then."

"Trust me, he can find one." Skelly knew he had to say something more. "Um, Roz, I've been meaning to talk to you about the prime-time spot. Assuming I am offered the job, would you be terribly disappointed if I turned it down?"

Her expression didn't change when she asked, "You'd rather stay with 'The Whole Story'?"

"I'd rather try chasing a dream . . . for a little while, at least. Maybe a year or so? I have a wonderful idea for a novel. A woman is incarcerated for a murder that she didn't commit, and—"

"This sounds familiar."

"A writer should write what he knows."

"Do I get to read as you create?"

"Only if you don't try to censor me."

She subtly rubbed up against him. "Can I try to influence you, then?"

Skelly grinned. "Anytime, Roz. Anytime." He glanced up, imagining his own grandmother chuckling with satisfaction as she drifted through the clouds. "Thank you, Moira, my dear," he whispered.

And hoped that each and every McKenna grandchild would find an equally wonderful legacy.

Merry Christmas, Baby!

A romantic collection filled with the magic of Christmas and the joy of children.

SUSAN WIGGS, Karen Young and Bobby Hutchinson bring you Christmas wishes, weddings and romance, in a charming trio of stories that will warm up your holiday season.

MERRY CHRISTMAS, BABY! also contains Harlequin's special gift to you—a set of FREE GIFT TAGS included in every book.

Brighten up your holiday season with *MERRY CHRISTMAS, BABY!*

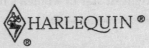

Available in November at your favorite retail store.

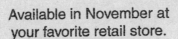

HARLEQUIN ®

®

Look us up on-line at: http://www.romance.net

MCB

REBECCA

43 LIGHT STREET

YORK

FACE TO FACE

*Bestselling author Rebecca York returns to "43 Light Street"
for an original story of past secrets, deadly deceptions—and
the most intimate betrayal.*

She woke in a hospital—with amnesia…and with child.
According to her rescuer, whose striking face is the last
image she remembers, she's Justine Hollingsworth. But
nothing about her life seems to fit, except for the baby
inside her and Mike Lancer's arms around her. Consumed
by forbidden passion and racked by nameless fear, she
must discover if she is Justine…or the victim of some mind
game. Her life—and her unborn child's—depends on it….

Don't miss *Face To Face*—Available in October, wherever
Harlequin books are sold.

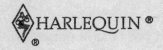

HARLEQUIN ®

®

43FTF

HARLEQUIN®

I N T R I G U E®

THAT'S INTRIGUE—DYNAMIC ROMANCE AT ITS BEST!

Harlequin Intrigue is now bringing you more—more men and mystery, more desire and danger. If you've been looking for thrilling tales of contemporary passion and sensuous love stories with taut, edge-of-the-seat suspense—then you'll *love* Harlequin Intrigue!

Every month, you'll meet four new heroes who are guaranteed to make your spine tingle and your pulse pound. With them you'll enter into the exciting world of Harlequin Intrigue—where your life is on the line and so is your heart!

Harlequin Intrigue—we'll leave you breathless!

INT-GEN

Meet the family staying at
SUMMER HOUSE *Jewel*

• **BEN GILBERT.** The patriarch of the family, he's been proud of his strength—until a stabbing pain makes him re-examine his values. Not only does he long to see his four children together again, he's anxious to choose someone to run Benjamin Gilbert Associates, the company he started thirty years ago.

• **PAT GILBERT.** All Ben's wife wants is a joyous reunion with their strong, confident children. But some of them resent her love; others—beneath the veneer of success—are desperately hanging on to their sanity.

• **JULIE GILBERT KANE.** She's a successful television celebrity, a beautiful and statuesque blonde, a wife and mother of an adorable baby boy. She has it all, plus a sophisticated life in New York City—but something is going wrong. . . .

Please turn the page

• BRAD KANE. Julie's handsome husband, he's a wealthy real-estate tycoon, and a celebrity in his own right. But lately, he's been drinking too much. . . .

• KATY GILBERT. As long as she can remember, Katy has been compared—unfavorably—to her sister Julie. Brilliant, but overweight and self-destructive, Katy's held more jobs than she can count and is desperately trying to find a way to turn her life around. . . .

• WES GILBERT. He was a "nerd" in high school, a computer wizard who surprised everyone when he became a huge corporate success. Now he'll give anything to make his wife love him again. . . .

• BARBARA BOUCHER. Beautiful and poised, she is Wes's wife—and a successful financial analyst. But lately she's been running scared—and now she wants out. . . .

• MICHAEL GILBERT. The "perfect" son, he has always done the right thing. He became a prominent lawyer, married a quiet, domestic woman, has two nice kids. Why is he finding it so hard to come home. . . .

• LYNN GILBERT. She's been married to Michael for seventeen years, and has seemed content to raise their children and keep their home—until now. . . .

SUMMER
HOUSE

Cynthia Blair

BALLANTINE BOOKS • NEW YORK

To Tama

Acknowledgments

I would like to thank Dr. Robert J. Cody of the Department of Cardiology, New York Hospital/Cornell Medical School, for his creative input as well as his medical expertise. I would also like to thank Diane Rothschild for her assistance.

In addition, I would like to thank Henry Blair for his help with golfing terminology and Richard Smith for similar guidance in the area of boating.

As ever, special thanks to my editor, Pamela Strickler, and my agent, Diane Cleaver.

Prologue

It was a perfect June day, one of the precious few awarded those of the Northeast who had endured another bleak winter, another rainy spring. The early morning sun was warm and energizing and a light breeze, carrying with it the fragrance of honeysuckle, sweetened the air. Everywhere the pale green buds that had emerged only weeks earlier were exploding into voluptuous bursts of color, rich reds, yellows, and pinks.

It was the kind of day that brought to mind the word *rebirth.* In fact, it was this very word that kept echoing through Ben Gilbert's mind as he jogged down Emerson Road, totally lost in his own thoughts, absorbed in an exuberant mood. He loved being one of the few people out on the streets of this quiet Westchester suburb early in the morning. He barely noticed the even row of meticulously maintained houses that he passed, the staid brick colonials, charming salt boxes, whimsical Tudors, or occasional ranch house.

He breathed deeply, feeling a surge of satisfaction at his own strength and stamina as he cut across the sidewalk that ran the length of the elementary school, then continued on toward the Harrington Town Library. He was pushing himself just a bit harder than usual.

Fifteen minutes before, he'd left his silent house, wide awake even though his wife was still in bed asleep. As always, just slipping on a pair of running shorts and a T-shirt had invigorated him. After five minutes of stretching out on

1

the front lawn, he'd eased into a slow, steady jog along the same route that he'd been running almost every morning for the past twelve years, ever since his fiftieth birthday.

He always thought of Monday mornings as a time to rev up into full gear all over again, after a two-day hiatus. After this jog, he would follow the same routine he followed every weekday morning. He would hurry back into the house to gulp down coffee and spend a few minutes with his wife. Then he would shower, shave, and don a business suit, all in time to catch the 8:11 bound for Grand Central Station.

He loved his work, presiding over the company he had started some thirty-five years earlier. Benjamin Gilbert Associates was a small but successful promotional firm, consisting of a staff of a dozen or so creative men and women who came up with clever ways of promoting clients' products: running a sweepstakes for a leading laundry soap, putting a free package of a new flavor of gum into a popular children's cereal, coming up with a gimmicky giveaway for a major fast-food chain. He also employed a handful of marketing types who executed the plans, along with some sales representatives who helped bring in new clients. Once a client had signed, all he had to do was write a check and then sit back and bask in the glory—as well as the increased sales and profits.

B.G.A. was Ben's baby. It was his life's work, a little piece of himself that managed to thrive in the competitive field of marketing and sales promotion alongside big names like Donnelly and Synergistics and D. L. Blair. And he loved every aspect of it, from coaching his people before they made a sales pitch to a prospective client, to running numbers on his calculator, to listening to one of the new kids breathlessly present his latest brainstorm.

Even so, the early morning was still his favorite part of the day. The streets were empty, the air was fresh, the world was silent except for the chirping of birds and the rhythmic slapping of his blue and white Nikes against the concrete sidewalk.

That sound turned to a dull thudding as Ben veered off onto the manicured front lawn of the town library, ignoring the KEEP OFF THE GRASS sign. Hell, no one was around to see him, anyway. There was one other sound that accompanied him: the huff, puff of his breath as he pushed toward the end of the three-mile course he'd plotted out for himself a dozen years earlier when he'd decided, once and for all, to fight against the approach of old age.

At first, Ben had used this time to think about the day ahead. The appointments to go to, the memos to write, the decisions to make. After a while, however, he had taught himself to relax as he ran. Now he allowed himself the luxury of letting his mind drift over much more pleasant, relaxing topics.

His wife, Pat, for example. Today he was trying to decide what he could possibly get her as a gift for their wedding anniversary at the end of August. Forty-two years. That certainly sounded like a very long time. Why, then, he wondered, did it now seem as if the whole thing had sped by?

As he jogged through the town where all four of his and Pat's children had grown up, he passed a hundred different reminders of them. There, in front of the elementary school, was the curb where his oldest son Michael, then barely six years old, had fallen off his bicycle. Over here was the town library, where at the ribbon-cutting ceremony three decades before, Julie had read a poem she'd written. Behind the library, on Maple Drive, Ben could pick out the houses that had been on the paper route of his third child Wesley. And there was the home of the nice woman who had once bought a dozen boxes of Girl Scout cookies from Katy. Little Katy— now, it was difficult to believe, thirty-three years old.

Yes, those four children—now four adults with jobs and homes and families of their own—gave him a lot to think about. Summer was coming, and he wondered if he'd get to see them. He hoped that at least once over the next two or three months they'd manage to squeeze in a visit, find the time to travel out to the Gilberts' summer house on Shelter Island, off the eastern end of Long Island. They were all so busy.

Suddenly, as he veered off onto Pickwick Lane, the turn that signified that he had just begun his third mile, Ben felt a stabbing pain in his chest and down his left arm. He was having trouble catching his breath and, at the same time, he broke into a cold sweat. He stopped, doubling over, stricken with pain, overcome with fear.

Oh, my God, I'm having a heart attack!

Ben's mind was racing.

I'm dying! Oh, Lord, I'm dying, and there's no one around to help me. . . .

The pain lasted for what seemed an awfully long time, although in retrospect he would realize it was no more than

five minutes. He dropped to the curb, the corner of someone's front lawn, someone he didn't even know. He clenched
his eyes shut and just sat there waiting, waiting. . . .

And then, it was over. The pain stopped. The fear melted
just as abruptly. He began to feel like himself again.

I'm alive, he thought. My God, I'm alive! Ben was so
relieved and so happy that tears actually sprung to his eyes. I
had a heart attack and I survived. I survived! I'm still alive!

More than anything, he wanted to see Pat.

His wife's face loomed ahead of him, clear in his mind's
eye, as he shuffled home, his hand covering his heart in the
same way a person who'd fallen might have cushioned a
scraped elbow. He could see her as clearly as if he were
looking at a photograph of her: her broad smile; her even if
unremarkable features; her green eyes; her wavy blond hair
streaked only slightly with gray, cut just at the jawline.

His sudden need for her bordered on desperation. All he
knew was that he wanted her to console him, to tell him
everything would be all right, to reassure him that the danger
was over. Only she was in his thoughts as he stumbled on
toward home.

He quickened his pace as soon as he saw the familiar white
colonial-style house up ahead, with its welcoming front porch,
slate blue shutters, and vibrant marigolds and zinnias. He
went around to the back door, into the kitchen.

How comforting it was to see Pat in their large kitchen, the
place where she always seemed most comfortable. It was a
pleasant room, large and sunny, one that managed to retain its
air of homey friendliness even though it was outfitted with
every modern appliance and cooking aid available: a compli-
cated-looking food processor, a microwave, a sleek white
toaster oven that had always looked suspiciously futuristic to
him.

As usual, Pat was the picture of efficiency, humming softly
as she worked, looking as if she had everything under control. Indeed, she had the coffeepot perking, the toaster oven
glowing, the butter softening. And in the midst of it all, she
stood at the counter next to the sink, still dressed in her
bathrobe and slippers, absorbed in slicing a cantaloupe in
half.

She was a strong, competent woman, one who had weathered her share of bad news and hardships. Yes, she would see
him through this, forge ahead without tears, without useless

emotionalism, considering such frivolities a mere waste of everyone's time. She would supply the strength he needed, strength which, at the moment, seemed to have totally eluded him. After all, if their forty-two years together had taught him anything it was that taking charge was one of the things that Pat Gilbert did best.

"Good morning, dear." She glanced up from her work space, the square of butcher block that was set into the Formica counter, only long enough to ascertain that it was, indeed, her husband who'd just come in through the screen door.

"Coffee'll be ready soon. Did you have a nice run? Oh, this melon is perfect. I just love summer fruits, don't you? Peaches, plums, strawberries, melons, of course . . . Or do you want to take a shower first?"

She looked up then, as if she were surprised that he hadn't said anything or moved across the kitchen to help himself to some coffee. When she saw the look on his face, she gasped.

"Ben! What's wrong? You look awful. You're as white as a ghost! What happened?"

"Oh, God, Pat," he cried, sinking into a chair and burying his face in his hands. "I think I just had a heart attack."

"Oh, no!" She dropped the knife onto the butcher block and rushed over to him. "What happened? Are you sure? Should I drive you to the emergency room—or call Dave Jennings? . . ."

"No, no, don't do that. Don't call Jennings. I'm fine now. Really."

Haltingly he told her what had just happened: the pain he'd suddenly experienced while running, the tingling sensation in his arm, the shortness of breath. Pat interrupted with questions every so often, in between punctuating his report with a distraught "Oh, my God!" or "Oh, no, Ben!"

"Is there anything I can do?" she asked when he had finished. "I don't know what to say. . . . What do you want me to do?"

Her voice was soft and meek, like a scared little girl's. He would never have expected her to react this way, with such vulnerability, with such naked fear. Seeing her like this made Ben even more frightened than he had been before.

"Just hold me, Pat," he said in a hoarse voice, his arms already reaching for her. "All I want is for you to hold me."

* * *

That evening, while Pat was showering in the bathroom off the master bedroom, Ben sat on the edge of their queen-sized bed. Even though he was perched right in front of the television, he hadn't turned the set on. Instead, he was just staring, without seeing anything that was in front of him.

He didn't see the room around him, an elegant if impersonal collection of sleek modern furniture, tasteful fabrics in shades of brown and beige, and a sense of harmony that brought credit to the keen eye of an experienced interior designer. He didn't see the gray-haired man in the blue-and-white-striped cotton pajamas reflected in the dark TV screen, handsome with his salt-and-pepper hair and tanned, even features, despite the lines around the eyes, the haggard look around the mouth.

He didn't even see Pat, at first, when she came out of the bathroom. She looked fresh and almost girlish in the flowing peach chiffon nightgown she had just put on, a flattering garment whose soft color accented her pale hair and made her green eyes even greener. She had tried to look her best this evening.

Between his failure to notice her and the look on his face, she knew immediately that her husband was a million miles away.

"A penny for your thoughts," she chirped. All day long she had been trying to be cheerful. She hadn't even protested very much when he continued to refuse to see a doctor or even let her telephone Dave Jennings, a longtime friend and golf buddy who just happened to be an internist. He kept insisting that he was fine now, that he just needed to rest, to take a couple of days off from work. Hell, maybe he'd even imagined the whole thing, misread what was nothing more than a muscle spasm or a sudden wave of tiredness, something that served him right for pushing himself so damned hard. Sure, he'd see Jennings, or maybe some other doctor . . . but not quite yet.

After she'd spoken, Ben looked at her as if he didn't recognize her. "Hmm? Oh, sorry, Pat. I was just thinking."

"Obviously you were thinking." Smiling, she sat down next to him on the beige quilted bedspread and draped her arm lightly around his shoulders. "I was just wondering what you were thinking about."

"I was thinking about what happened today." He spoke in a monotone.

"Of course." Her smile faded. She thought for a few moments, then spoke in a voice hoarse with emotion. "I just don't understand it, Ben. You're so—so youthful. Look at you—especially compared to all our friends. And you've always been the picture of health. Why, you were a swimming champion in college, and then a track star."

"Right," he remembered with a grimace. "Until that stupid injury put me out of commission."

"But that was just a short-term thing. Your neck and your shoulder healed so quickly that even the doctors were impressed, remember? Goodness, you must have told that story a million times."

"That was a long, long time ago, Pat. I'm an old man now." At least, I'm beginning to feel old, he thought ruefully.

"Ben, what about the children?" Pat reminded him gently. "They'll have to be told, of course."

"No!" he barked, so abruptly and so unexpectedly that she started.

"I just thought that—"

"No, I don't want to tell them." This time, Ben's tone was much more gentle. "I don't want them to know. Not yet."

"All right." Pat studied her hands.

"But I have been thinking about them. The children, I mean. I'd like to see them all this summer. You know, have sort of a family reunion. All the kids, all their spouses, all our grandchildren. Out at the beach house on Shelter Island. For a week, maybe two . . ."

"Why, that's a marvelous idea!"

Pat was relieved. Given what had happened earlier that day and how pensive he'd been ever since, he could have come up with all kinds of dreadful ideas: selling the house and moving into a condo; emigrating to some retirement village down in Florida; even dragging out his will again and agonizing over every detail, just as he had a few months earlier when he'd read that magazine article quoting the latest life-expectancy statistics.

But a family reunion—that was something *nice*. Automatically, she started planning, calculating: who would sleep in which room, what meals she'd prepare for such a large group, how best to keep her three grandchildren entertained. . . .

"That wasn't all I was thinking about," Ben went on, sounding almost guilty. "I was also thinking about the business."

"Of course. The business. Perhaps you should take a few weeks off, Ben. Lord knows you're due for a vacation. Some time to yourself, especially now . . ."

"No, no. What I mean is, I was thinking about B.G.A.'s future." He spoke hesitantly. "There's something I have to do, Pat. Something I've been putting off for a long time—for too long."

"Why don't you worry about all that tomorrow?" Pointedly Pat pulled back the covers and climbed into bed. "What you need right now, Ben Gilbert, is a good night's rest."

Ben, however, said nothing. In fact, he seemed to have forgotten that Pat was even in the room with him as he drifted back into his reverie once again.

Yes, he was thinking, it's time to bring the whole family together. So what if they're busy, so what if they've got their own reasons for preferring not to find the time to visit. It's something we can't put off any longer. We've got work to do. For the family business . . . and for ourselves. It's time for me to see them all together, and this summer is when I have to do it. After all, this may turn out to be my last chance.

Chapter One

*N*o matter how early she went to bed, the five o'clock radio alarm was always an unwelcome intrusion. As Julie Gilbert Kane was dragged into consciousness, she wondered, just as she did every weekday morning, if she was crazy to have a career that forced her out of bed at such an ungodly hour.

At least you're not going off to some boring, dead-end job, she reminded herself, turning over and burying her face in her soft down pillow. After all, being cohost on WCBC's "New Day, New York" is a dream career, one that you worked for and fantasized about ever since you graduated from Wheaton College and moved to the city to begin your research job at the station.

Besides, this is your last day of work before vacation. Think of it: three weeks off! Three long, glorious, carefree, relaxing weeks . . .

"It's going to be another hot one," the deejay said cheerfully. "Temperatures in the low nineties, humidity at eighty-seven percent, winds out of the southwest at six miles per hour."

Inwardly, Julie groaned. High temperatures, high humidity—typical for a New York August, and not exactly ideal weather for a three-hour car trip. Good thing the air-conditioning in the BMW had just been repaired.

"Today, the White House is expected to issue a statement—"

She snapped off the radio, then glanced over at the other side of the king-sized bed to make sure the deejay's chirpy voice hadn't woken her husband up. Little danger of that; as usual, he was lost in a deep sleep, the lavender-and-blue-striped sheets pulled way up over his head. Brad still had a good two hours of sleep ahead of him, and his posture made it clear that he had every intention of taking full advantage of them.

As for Julie, she was wide awake by now. She had even forgotten her resentment over being roused so early. Automatically she fell into her routine, one which—hopefully, God and network willing—she would continue to perform hundreds of times more.

After climbing out of bed, she retrieved her French cotton bathrobe, pale yellow dotted with sprigs of white flowers, from the chair. She slipped it on over its matching night-gown, and buttoned a few of the tiniest buttons she had ever seen.

How serene her bedroom looked, with its mauves and lavenders and pale blues against a backdrop of rich cream, the colors even more subdued in the dim morning light that snuck in through the narrow slats of the blinds, concealing the large French windows. She'd decorated it herself a year and a half earlier, when she and Brad had first moved into this luxurious three-bedroom co-op that overlooked the East River. Just being in this room made her feel good. It was such a calming environment, exactly what she needed before rushing off to the studio. Certainly, being cohost on a weekday morning television talk show was the job she had always longed for. Even so, it wasn't easy.

No, it was pressured, exhausting, demanding. But that didn't mean that Julie Kane didn't relish every moment.

She flicked on the bathroom light and found herself in another delightful room—once again, a reflection of her handi-work. Cornflower blue Laura Ashley wallpaper; ruffled curtains; baskets filled with scented soaps in pastel colors; a framed lithograph of plump, smiling cherubs.

She noted all of it with pleasure before studying her reflection in the mirror above the sink. She was relieved to see that this morning there were no obvious flaws that needed disguising. No puffy eyes, no blemishes, no pallor to her fair skin. What was it those fashion magazines used to call it, back in the early sixties when she had clung to every word as if it were the gospel truth? Oh, yes, "porcelain complexion." As ridiculous as that expression may have been, it was actually fairly accurate in her case, she thought, not without satisfaction. And it showed off so well the high cheekbones, the small chiseled nose, the slightly pointed chin, and the inquisitive green eyes.

Julie ran her fingers through her straight, shoulder-length blond hair. Its shade was naturally light, but its ash-blond color was lightened—and its occasional gray strands banished—with subtle platinum streaks. Highlights, or so hairdressers always liked to call them. Well, whatever they were called, they certainly did their part to help Julie Kane look every inch the Golden Girl.

It was just the right look for the female half of the "New Day" show's team. The perfect image for a morning talk show host, whose job it was to interview whomever happened to be famous that week—politicians and bestselling authors and actors. It was all done to inform and entertain her audience, the sleepy early birds of the New York metropolitan area, who were gulping down their breakfast coffee and blow-drying their hair and searching, panic-stricken, for the final draft of that big report they'd been working on all night.

Julie was out of the bathroom in less than ten minutes, after washing her hair in the shower and brushing her teeth. The finishing touches would be taken care of at the studio—the natural-looking makeup and the curl and body that would be added to her blunt-cut hair, thanks to electric rollers and gobs of hair spray and the never-erring meticulousness of Mr. Nevins. All she had to do was show up.

The one exception was her clothes. These were up to her. Stepping stealthily around the pastel-colored bedroom, she slipped on the outfit she'd already decided to wear: a pale pink suit with a perky square-cut jacket and a hip-hugging straight skirt; a coordinated blouse in an even paler shade of pink; and, of course, a colorful scarf, today's selection a flattering collage of pinks and lavenders. A jaunty square of silk, tied differently every day, had become Julie Kane's trademark.

With twenty minutes left before the studio car was to arrive, Julie was faced with a choice. She could go into the kitchen and make herself a cup of coffee. The alternative to that was waiting until she reached her office at the WCBC studios, where her secretary, Meg, would be more than happy to ply her with all the caffeine she wanted, as well as anything else—muffin, donut, Danish—she could talk her boss into consuming. She was positively motherly, that one, always concerned that Julie, with her slender five-foot-ten frame, wasn't eating enough. A second possibility was using the extra time to go through her notes, brush up on the backgrounds of the guests she would be speaking with later on that morning.

Today, however, as she so often did, Julie bypassed both these options. Instead, she crept down the carpeted hallway and silently slipped into the bedroom at the very end. Joshua's room.

As soon as she went in, she was overcome with such strong feelings that her heart felt as if it had been folded in half. It was a type of surrender, a giddiness, a kind of love she had never experienced before giving birth to her only child two and a half years earlier. She barely noticed the room itself; the simple, well-designed wooden furnishings from Workbench; the colorful Marimekko wallpaper and matching curtains; the countless toys and games and stuffed animals piled up all around the nursery. She only had eyes for her Josh, the little golden-haired angel asleep in his bed, both hands tucked sweetly underneath his round cheeks.

She knew her presence might wake him, but she didn't care. As it was, she felt as if she never got enough of being with this little boy. Not that there could ever be such a thing as *enough*. The moments passed much too quickly, with frightening, almost supernatural speed: days turned into weeks, weeks into months. . . .

He was practically a little boy already, and Julie couldn't help marveling over how quickly the time had passed. Was it possible that her baby was already a walking, talking individual, making friends and insisting upon a certain kind of cereal for breakfast and happily relating, in a kind of jibberish that only she could fully understand, exactly how he'd spent every second of the time they'd been apart? As trite as it sounded, it seemed like only yesterday that he was born.

She sat down on his bed, and he stirred slightly. She was courting danger, she knew; even so, she couldn't resist placing her hand lightly on his head. So what if he woke up? That was what Mrs. Pearl was for.

Josh sighed contentedly, as if, even in his deep sleep, he knew his mother was with him—and that he was safe. That was so important to her, especially now, with all the subtle and not-so-subtle tensions that were clouding up their family life. Satisfied, Julie tore herself away. She had lingered longer than she'd meant to, and it was time to throw on her jacket, pick up her burgundy leather Mark Cross briefcase, and hurry downstairs to meet her car.

"Good morning, Mrs. Kane!" The doorman bowed slightly as she strode out of the elevator, toward the glass front doors of East River Towers.

Julie couldn't help smiling to herself, even as she politely returned his greeting and made a comment about what a warm day it promised to be. She was the building's only television celebrity, and both the co-op's employees and the other residents always treated her with deference. At one time it had made her feel uncomfortable. By now she was used to it.

The doorman, her husband, and even little Josh were pushed into the back of her mind as she climbed into the studio limousine. She thanked Gregory, her usual chauffeur, for opening the car door, and then immediately turned to the papers in her briefcase. It was only a fifteen-minute ride to Midtown Manhattan at this hour, when the streets of the city were, thankfully, still practically deserted, but that was just the right amount of time for her to ease herself into the day, to do the homework she had put off until this moment.

Leaning back against the plush blue velvet upholstery, Julie buried herself in her notes, prepared for her days in advance by a crackerjack team of researchers. Once she had been one of those researchers; now, she was the person in front of the camera who called upon their background work in order to speak with confidence and authority about each guest's particular field of interest.

As she read through the typed pages, she saw that today's show would be pretty routine. Her first guest would be a relatively unknown hopeful who planned to run for the Senate in the fall. Next there was the author of a diet book that, despite the absurdity of its basic premise, was breaking all kinds of sales records in the publishing industry. The show would end with an interview with the victim of a mugging who had joined forces with other victims in his neighborhood to form a citizens patrol force. It promised to be an interesting two hours, without being too taxing.

Once she had assured herself that she was in control, Julie put away her papers, stared out the window at the rows of bright flowers that had sprung forth all along the median of Park Avenue as far as the eye could see, and let her mind wander. Not to today's show, not to Josh . . .

No, it was time she forced herself to do some thinking about her husband—even though the mere thought caused an uncomfortable knot to form in her stomach.

Bradford Kane was known around town as the perfect guest at dinner parties. And it was not only because of the impressive stream of real estate coups he had pulled off, no small feat in a cutthroat city like New York, where land and buildings were more valuable than diamonds and gold. True, he was the epitome of success in the realm of wheeling and dealing, the quintessential entrepreneur of the 1980s—at least, that was the label that *New York* magazine had approvingly awarded him a few months earlier when his picture graced their cover.

But that was only part of it. In addition, Brad Kane was intelligent, well-read, charismatic, clever, and articulate. He knew all the right people, wore perfectly fitted suits from Giorgio Armani and Yves St. Laurent, had a craggy face handsome enough to turn heads even at Lutèce and "21." He was the type of man who could talk to anyone and make him or her feel like the most important person in the room.

And he had a knack for acquiring the things he decided that he wanted: that choice piece of land opposite Bloomingdale's, the Stuyvesant Building, a Louis Quatorze table that everyone at the Parke-Bernet auction was drooling over. And the beautiful, glamorous cohost of "New Day, New York."

Stop it! Julie immediately reprimanded herself. There I go again. Being negative. Being cynical. Brad loves me . . . and I love him. We're just going through a rough period, that's all. It happens to every couple . . . doesn't it?

Fortunately, before she had too much of a chance to dwell on the uncomfortable feelings about her husband that had begun to nag at her lately, the sleek black limo pulled up in front of WCBC studios.

"Here we are, Mrs. Kane," announced the driver.

"Thank you, Gregory," she said graciously as she slid out of the car. He accepted the smile she offered him as if it were a gift.

It was just after six as Julie strode into her office. She was already in full gear: her movements energetic, her mind clicking away, her mood one of impatience for the day to get underway. She belonged here, in this vibrant world, where things changed daily, where the emphasis was always on what was new. This was her world, her milieu, the place where she thrived. This was what she did best.

"Good morning, Julie." Meg greeted her with a smile. The younger woman, a bit on the plump side but always fashionably dressed and impeccably groomed, had a steaming mug of coffee in one hand and a pile of pink telephone messages in the other. She followed her boss into her office, already having launched into a friendly monologue about all the things that had already happened in the ten minutes since she'd arrived at work: "New Day's" producer's latest brainstorm; a meeting that had been scheduled for later that morning; some last-minute changes in the show's format.

Poor Meg, Julie thought kindly. She gets here even before I do—and she comes in on the subway, all the way from Brooklyn!

Even so, she knew that her secretary—or, as she thought of her, her right hand—loved her work. Her loyalty, to both the station and to Julie, did not go unnoticed. Julie tried to show her appreciation as best she could, in the little ways she knew counted so much: a pretty silk blouse brought back from a vacation in Paris, a novel she overheard Meg mention that she'd been wanting to read, a bouquet of flowers on her birthday or her anniversary with the station or even just for the hell of it.

The two women had a good relationship, based on a mutual commitment to make "New Day" the best show it could possibly be, as well as a natural liking for each other. Julie often wondered what on earth she—*and* the show—would ever do without Meg.

". . . Oh, and Ron says be sure to ask this diet guru about the effects of exercise on the body's metabolism."

Meg chattered away in her usual animated fashion as Julie hung up her jacket and got settled in at her desk. It was really a glass and chrome Parsons table, which fit in perfectly with the clean, simple lines of the office that Julie herself had decorated in the subdued shades of pink and mauve and blue that she loved so much.

"Apparently he's a real nut about those little trampolines," Meg went on. "You know, the kind that people buy, use once, and then store in their closets for the next twenty years, constantly feeling guilty about not using them. Anyway, give him a chance to do his spiel about those. Oh, before I go, there's one more thing—''

"Don't tell me," Julie interrupted with a smile. "You're going to try to talk me into eating one of those two blueberry muffins that are sitting out there on your desk, the ones that are about six thousand calories each.''

"Nope." Meg blushed slightly. "You're off the hook, for once. I thought I'd bring one over to that cute new guy in accounting. You know, the one who just started here last week." She shrugged and, with a loud sigh, added, "Hey, it's worth a try, right? Don't forget—I'm not getting any younger.''

Don't rush into marriage! Julie was tempted to warn. But then she realized how impulsive—and how silly—saying something like that would be. Just because things between her and Brad weren't perfect at the moment was no reason to start overreacting to every little thing. . . .

"Anyway, what I wanted to mention was your vacation.''

"Uh-oh. Don't tell me the station has changed its mind about letting me go for a full three weeks." Julie was only half kidding.

"Bite your tongue! No, nothing like that. Actually, I just wanted to tell you that I hope you have a terrific time. You and that handsome husband of yours deserve some time off together.''

She forced a smile. "Thanks, Meg.''

She's right, Julie insisted to herself when she was left alone once again. Brad and I do deserve a break. And that's probably all we need—a chance to talk, to enjoy each other, to have some fun.

Yes, she vowed, this time, everything will be perfect.

In fact, she already had the fantasy all worked out in her mind. The three of them—Julie, Brad, little Josh—piling into the red BMW, laughing and teasing each other as they got started on a carefree three weeks. The very picture of the happy family. Yes, this vacation would be good for them.

"Julie! There you are!" The show's assistant producer came rushing into Julie's office, and daydreaming about the next three weeks had to be put on hold. It was time for Julie Kane, the professional, to step in, and her appearance on the scene left little room for anything else.

*   *   *

As soon as the show was over, Julie hurried back to her office, anxious to tie up any loose ends that still remained so she could be on her way. As usual, there was a newly delivered pile of paper in her in-box, a fresh stack of messages, and a telephone that refused to stop ringing. Dutifully she began plowing through this new onslaught of obligations, pushing aside her growing reluctance as she hurried to finish up.

When the phone rang for the tenth time since she'd come back to her desk, Julie picked it up and, irritated by still one more interruption, barked, "Julie Kane."

There was a long pause at the other end of the line.

"Well, that's a hell of a greeting," snorted a familiar voice.

"Oh, Brad. Hi!" Her tone softened immediately. In fact, she sounded almost apologetic. "I didn't expect it to be you. Well," she went on brightly, "all set to sneak out of the city nice and early? I'm pretty sure I can be out of here by noon."

"Listen, Julie. I'm afraid I've run into kind of a snag."

Brad cleared his throat in the casual way he always did when he was about to deliver bad news.

"Look, something's come up. It's that new project I've been working on. You know, the Colony Building. It looks like I'm not going to be able to get out of the city today, after all."

Julie was determined to fight back the tears that were already blurring her vision.

"Well, then, I'll just wait for you. We can drive out to Shelter Island first thing tomorrow morning. Look, it's only Wednesday. We'll still have a head start on all the others. . . ."

"No. You and Josh go on ahead. I'll join you later." He hesitated. "Probably on Friday. Or Saturday morning at the very latest."

Julie swallowed hard.

You're being childish, she told herself. It's not Brad's fault he's gotten tied up with business. He can't help it.

She fought against the other voice inside her, the one that was crying, But it *always* happens! Something always gets in the way of us being together as a family! Business always comes first . . . and Josh and I always come last.

Aloud, in a surprisingly even voice, she said, "All right. If you're sure. I'll pack up the car and leave as soon as I can, just as we'd been planning.

"Besides," she added brightly, trying to convey an optimism she didn't really feel, "this way Josh and I will have some extra time alone together. And I'll get to have my parents to myself for a few days, before the rest of the horde descends."

She paused, hoping for an apology for the way things had worked out, or at least a confirmation that they would all be able to make up for lost time once they got out to Shelter Island.

But Brad just said, "Look, I've got to run. My other phone is ringing. See you—whenever!"

Julie's cheeks were burning as she hung up the phone. She felt bewildered, disoriented—just as she always did whenever Brad changed their plans or offhandedly wriggled his way out of some commitment he'd made. She had been looking forward to a leisurely three-hour ride out to eastern Long Island, a chance to be alone with her husband while Josh dozed in the backseat.

Now, not only would they miss out on that chance to spend time together; suddenly she had to take care of a million details by herself. Orchestrate the packing and the loading of the car. Fill up the gas tank and have the water and the oil checked. And then, battling the Long Island Expressway traffic by herself, driving for three solid hours. All that, when she'd been up since five.

She wondered if perhaps she should wait for her husband, if maybe she should postpone the trip. That way, she would have a couple of days to get herself together. She could take it easy here in the city: do some shopping, catch up on her sleep, take Joshie to the park. Then, of course, Brad could make the trip out to Shelter Island with them, whenever he was free.

But he was expecting her to go on ahead without him, she reminded herself. To wait around for him would seem like a reproach. Besides, her parents were counting on her. It was all set up. And since Katy wasn't arriving until sometime Friday afternoon, and Michael and his family planned to roll in sometime early on Saturday, she felt responsible to them.

No, proceeding with the original plan—minus Brad, of course—would be best.

With a resolute sigh, Julie stood up, as if to make official her sudden feeling that the workday was now over. The stack of mail and memos on her desk no longer held the least bit of interest for her. She simply wanted to get out, to escape, to get on with her vacation.

Vacation—what a lovely word! she reflected, calculating how long it had been since the last time she had taken some time off to really relax. And Shelter Island was the ideal locale for doing just that. Lying in the sun, drinking icy lemonade, gazing at the calm blue water, listening to the distant sound of motorboats and sea gulls, not having a care in the world . . . Suddenly it all seemed so enticing that putting it off for even another minute was simply intolerable.

More important, she was growing more and more anxious to be with her family again with every passing second. Michael and Wes and Katy—and, of course, her parents. Just thinking about seeing Mom and Dad caused a wave of serenity, of feeling safe, to wash over her. She could taste that sense of *belonging*, of being surrounded by people who cared about her, who wanted the best for her, who would do whatever they could to make sure she got it.

Yes, thought Julie, picking up her purse and heading for the door, no longer able to wait another moment, it's good to be going home.

Chapter Two

*B*y *the time* the red BMW came barreling off the ferry, having just crossed over to Shelter Island from Long Island's North Fork, Julie was feeling as if she had just shed all her bad feelings. In the backseat, Josh was fast asleep, so quiet that she kept forgetting he was there. Meanwhile, the radio was softly playing a string of golden oldies, songs that were as comfortable as an old worn-out college sweatshirt. This was the first time in ages that she could remember being completely on her own, an event that was so rare in her life these days that whenever she did manage to experience it, she was a little bit startled by how good it felt.

What a relief it was, enjoying the restful monotony of riding in a car, yet not being en route to some obligation or other: rushing off to the television station so early in the morning; hurrying home to Josh and Brad after putting in a long, tiring day; going off to some social event when what she really felt like doing was taking a long, hot bubble bath or settling into bed with a good book.

It had been three years since her last visit to Shelter Island, yet as the narrow winding road led her away from the ferry dock and into the town of Shelter Island Heights, Julie was struck by how little everything had changed. After passing a handful of charming Victorian houses, their pastel colors and the adorable turrets and widow's walks and gingerbread trim like something out of a book of fairy tales, she saw the imposing white-shingled facade of the Chequit Inn looming up ahead. The somewhat dilapidated hotel, with its green shutters, haphazard array of white wrought-iron tables and chairs outside, and generally droopy appearance, reminded her of a resort hotel in one of England's seaside towns, something out of a movie, a home away from home that was all the more homey for its simplicity and dowdiness.

Beyond the Chequit was the commercial center of the island, an odd combination of the most basic of stores intermingled with a sprinkling of boutiques that sold nothing that could possibly be considered a necessity. To Julie, this mixture had always represented the two types of people who braved the ferry trip in order to come to Shelter Island: the summer residents, who owned houses here on the island, and the short-term visitors, renting a room at the Chequit or the Pridwin for a week, staying at a friend's beach house, or just stopping in for the day.

Just about everything necessary for a summer's stay was available here in this little group of shops, thanks to the cluttered shelves and display cases of the Shelter Island Heights Pharmacy, the hardware store, the marine supply shop, and, off one of the side streets that led to the town dock, Bliss's Department Store. Stocked here was an unexpected mishmash of merchandise, the most eclectic inventory imaginable. Sewing notions and underwear, suntan lotion and plastic beach toys, sun hats and Topsiders—they were all crammed into this delightful store that was reminiscent of an old-fashioned five-and-ten, complete with long display counters that ran its entire length, rough wooden floors that were just the tinest bit uneven, and that unmistakable smell of plastic bags, laundry starch, and newness, the one that always pushed one back into one's childhood, if only for a moment.

Side by side with such no-nonsense establishments were those few gift shops and clothing boutiques, offering slightly overpriced housewares and sportswear that more often than not sported a sailboat, a whale, or, at the very least, a red, white, and blue color scheme. While Julie was comfortable enough in the utilitarian shops, stores in which she could locate just about any item in a few seconds flat, even after her three years' absence, she had never even been inside most of the places that featured serving platters, guest towels, and wraparound skirts, all with their annoying nautical theme.

She continued along the familiar route, out of town and

past the scenic duck pond set alongside the road amidst lush greenery, past the golf course that always reminded her of someone with a fresh crew cut. Perhaps she'd find time for a few rounds of golf while she was here. After all, her father was positively passionate about the game. She turned right at the Tuck Shop, the informal ice-cream parlor that catered mainly to the island's teenaged visitors.

How peaceful it is here on the island, she reflected with a sigh. She turned off the air-conditioning and rolled down the window, wanting to inhale the fresh clean air. And how odd that it's managed to remain so untouched by crowds and commercialism. Especially since it's so close to New York City, not much further than the Hamptons or Fire Island.

At the moment, she was grateful that Shelter Island was as much of a secret as it was. Just being here, surrounded by the natural beauty of this place, made Julie's muscles relax, her breaths deepen, her mind let go of tensions she hadn't even been aware were plaguing her. Yet rather than lingering, Julie leaned on the accelerator. Now that she was so close to her parents' house, she was more anxious than ever to get there.

And then she was pulling into the circular driveway, noticing with amusement that the momentousness of having finally arrived was entirely lost on little Josh, now snoring softly in his car seat. She studied the wooden A-frame that her mother and father had had built for themselves almost fifteen years before. It was a delightful house, made even more welcoming by the fact that it reflected her parents much more than their house in Harrington.

To a large degree, the house reflected Julie's taste, as well. After all, she had been her parents' right hand during much of the planning, helping them work out details with the architect, discussing with them endlessly where the kitchen windows should go, where the bathrooms belonged, how large the closets should be. Then, after the house was completed, Pat had consulted with her almost daily, calling upon her daughter's natural good taste to help conquer the daunting task of decorating a completely empty four-bedroom house.

And so Julie always took particular pride in the understated colors of the house—the beige living room, the pastel-colored bedrooms, the pale yellow kitchen with its modern, airy feeling. And having had a hand in its creation, this house had always felt like home to her, from the very first day she had walked inside.

Now she was back. Julie felt almost giddy as she struggled with the limp body of her sleeping son, holding him close against her as he let out an indignant cry at having had his rest disturbed, even if only to be relocated to a more comfortable place. She carried Josh inside and got him settled in one of the bedrooms, then went off in search of her parents.

As she expected, she found them outside on the patio.

"Here she is! Here's our girl!" chortled Ben, rising from his deck chair to greet his daughter.

"Why, Julie! We didn't even hear you come in!" Pat, too, came over to give her daughter a hug. "My, don't you look wonderful!" she said admiringly, holding her at arm's length and studying her with cool objectivity.

"You, too, Mom. And Dad, you look as if this salty sea air agrees with you. Been getting much golf in?"

Pat, as if suddenly remembering where she was in time, placed her hand on Julie's arm. "Goodness, where's Josh? And where's that dashing husband of yours?"

"Oh, Josh is asleep in the blue room. And Brad—well, he won't be able to make it out for a few more days." Julie grimaced. "Tied up with some business deal. A new office building, one of those fifty-story monstrosities."

Pat frowned, but only for a moment. "Well, then," she said gaily, "so much the better. We'll have you all to ourselves, at least for a little while."

She gestured for her daughter to have a seat, then sat down at the round table opposite her, all the while looking at Julie intently.

"Ben," she said, her eyes still on her daughter, "be a dear and get Julie a cold drink, will you? She must be parched after that long drive. And as for you, dear, I want you to tell me every wonderful thing you've been doing since the last time I saw you."

As always, Julie was only too happy to comply.

Pat Gilbert felt a genuine surge of satisfaction as she gazed at the spread of food she had just laid out all over the kitchen. She was surrounded by bowls and platters and clear plastic containers with beige tight-fitting covers, filled with homemade delectables that would keep her family well fed for a large portion of the next two weeks. Casseroles, salads, cakes so high she was concerned about fitting them into her freezer. It had been a lot of work, planning and preparing that had gone on for weeks, but now that it was done, she could appreciate the rewards of her impressive productivity.

It wasn't as if this were a first, of course. Certainly she had had her share of experience in dealing with large crowds. After all, she was both the mother of four and a seasoned hostess. Even so, a houseful of people was something to reckon with, no matter how much experience one had behind her.

As always, she had risen to the occasion with flying colors. She had been the epitome of organization in getting ready. In the days immediately preceding her family's reunion, she was a woman possessed, making lists and charts and schedules, planning menus and sleeping arrangements, thinking up diversions besides the usual sailing excursions, golf games, and trips to the beach.

Planning for such an onslaught of company was a particular challenge here on Shelter Island, where there were only a handful of food stores. Availability was only one issue; a second, of great importance to Pat even though her financial situation could easily be described as "comfortable," was cost. The island's only supermarket, George's I.G.A., routinely added twenty or thirty or fifty cents onto the cost of each item, a surcharge that was allegedly meant to make up for the additional expense of transporting everything over on the ferry, but which Pat suspected was really nothing more than a way to get the most out of the island's well-to-do summer residents.

But Pat Gilbert was not one to be taken advantage of. So, like so many of her cost-conscious counterparts, she loaded up the car on the mainland whenever she left the island, arriving back at the house with six or eight heavy supermarket bags piled upon the backseat, feeling pleased, indeed, that she had managed to circumvent the system.

That Wednesday morning, a few hours before Julie was due to arrive, Pat had purposefully taken the station wagon across on the ferry, over to Greenport and into Riverhead. There she stocked up on some of the basics she would be needing. Twelve people, seventeen days. That was a real test. She at least wanted to get a good head start.

After filling two carts there, she moved on to the Beverage Barn for beer and soda. Then, to one of the produce stands along Sound Avenue, to fill every available cubic inch of the backseat and trunk. Finally, one last stop: Briermere Farms, for homemade pies that practically made baking at home obsolete—one peach, one raspberry, two Dutch apple.

She was methodical in her preparations, thinking not about the pleasure that the pies might bring or the smiles that her special potato salad recipe might elicit, but approaching it all as a duty, matter-of-factly fulfilling the tasks that she had set out for herself. She gained great satisfaction as she ticked them off on the list she'd written out and stuck on the refrigerator with a magnet decorated with a hand-carved wooden sea gull in flight.

Actually, it was all quite impersonal, as if filling the white ceramic bowls with salads and putting all her appliances to work was an end in itself, rather than a means of celebrating the impending arrival of her children and her grandchildren. She worked through the day not in anticipation of having her family all together again, but as if it were merely the excuse she needed to busy herself with the projects she'd set forth for herself, satisfying in that they were finite and produced such tangible results.

Reacting this way was not at all uncommon for Pat. While she took it for granted that she loved her children—in fact, would have been appalled if anyone had ever dared to suggest that a mother, any mother, didn't automatically have those feelings—she had never been the type of person to get all emotional about them. Or anything else, for that matter. She believed now, as she had throughout her life, that remaining in control was of the utmost importance.

Perhaps it was because early in life, she had experienced firsthand what it meant to have no control. She had started out with a relatively protected childhood in a small town in Indiana, where she had learned long before beginning school that following the rules was the easiest way of getting by. The fact that those rules were rather plentiful never occurred to her, since she had nothing with which to compare her parents' rigidity.

And then, everything changed. As the Depression progressed, her parents lost everything, including the prosperous hardware store that for years had placed them among the town's most admired citizens. At age seven she was sent to live with her aunt and uncle in Chicago, an experience that, while supposedly "for her own good," as she was told with irritating frequency, made her feel terribly abandoned. She clung to those rules and rigidities that had served her so well before more ferociously than ever.

During this time, Pat learned that another form of control was also essential in order to survive: controlling one's emotions. She discovered that dwelling on how much she missed her mother and father only made her feel worse about this situation that had been thrust upon her without her having had the least bit of say in the matter. Instead, she hardened her heart, maintaining an affection for her distant parents without letting her feelings for them get in the way of her day-to-day survival.

While her separation lasted only two years, after which her father was able to send for her once again, the difficult lessons she had learned were to stick with her forever. Yes, she could love, but not without reservation, the unforgettable understanding that anything that could be cared about could also be taken away deeply ingrained.

Perhaps her early experiences had also led her to decide that it was important that she have a large family. When she met Ben Gilbert and considered marrying him, his ready agreement with her on that issue made him even more attractive to her. A houseful of happy children—that was what they were both certain they wanted.

Her first son, Michael, and her first daughter, Julie, fit perfectly into the image she had of what she wanted her adult life to be like. They were both such golden children, both of them "easy babies," cheerful and bright during their early childhood, then well-disciplined achievers once they started school. Every one of their teachers made a point of taking her and Ben aside to exclaim, "If only all the children I teach were like yours!"

As for Wesley and Katy, things were not quite as smooth. Pat discovered early on that there was a side to each of her two younger children that she simply couldn't understand. While she had always been one to accept the rules without question, a trait that she seemed to have passed on to Julie and Michael, both Katy and Wes were born rebels, Katy by choice, Wes by happenstance. Neither of them ever fit in very well.

Pat's frustration over her inability to understand, much less to help, manifested itself in an irritation, a distance that she maintained without even meaning to. She even went so far as to resent them, in a way, for spoiling her picture of that merry household she had envisioned so long before.

Despite whatever disappointment she might have felt, despite her confusion, Pat raised all four of her children with the same conscientiousness. She made sure they all had balanced meals and clean clothes. She drove them here and there, to Boy Scouts and Girl Scouts and sports meets and clubs and friends' houses, whatever each one of them required. And she tried not to let her emotions run her, to allow her to stray too far from her image of what a good mother should be.

But while she knew that no amount of restraint or self-discipline could enable her, or anyone else, to fake what they did not really feel, deep down inside, she was not about to let down her guard. For now, as for the rest of her career as a mother, she would continue to *try*, to go through all the motions, the way she had for this family reunion. After all, it was really the only way she knew.

To that end, she began picking up the plates and bowls and placing them where they belonged, in the refrigerator or the freezer or the cabinets high above. Her children were coming, and she wanted to feed them in whatever ways she could.

The house was so quiet that Julie was certain she was the first one up as she padded downstairs in her pink cotton nightgown, trimmed with white eyelet, her hair pulled back unceremoniously in a low ponytail at the base of her neck. Even though seven o'clock may have seemed early by some people's standards, even on a Thursday morning, she felt as if she had slept late. She was relaxed and well rested. Even her discomfort about Brad's delayed arrival, something that had nagged at her the entire evening before, had faded. On a morning like this, when the air itself was intoxicating, a delightful comingling of the sweet fragrance of the grass and flowers and the saltiness of the sea, it was impossible to feel anything but exuberant.

She planned to tiptoe into the kitchen and make herself a cup of coffee, then take it outside where she would make it last as long as she could. But when she went into the kitchen, she was startled. Not only was a fresh pot already made, filling the room with that unmistakable early morning smell; her mother was sitting at the table, drinking coffee and perusing the local newspaper, the *Shelter Island Reporter*.

"Mom! You're up early." After placing a peck on Pat's

slightly weathered cheek, Julie poured herself some coffee, filling the navy blue mug with a red and white sailboat on the side and wondering, amused at her own observations of the day before, if her mother had picked it up here on the island.

"Well, I realized last night that I've still got a lot to do before the others show up," Pat replied cheerfully. "Tomorrow is Friday already, and Katy's due in sometime in the afternoon. Meanwhile, I've got a refrigerator full of vegetables to cut up into crudités, and I want to make some ice cream. . . . Vanilla, I suppose. I got a couple of Dutch apple pies from Briermere yesterday, which I popped in the freezer first thing. I don't think they'll suffer for it. They're Michael's favorite, you know."

"Yes, I know." And it's obvious that Michael is our mother's "favorite," Julie thought with an indulgent smile, secure in the knowledge that she ran a very close second. She sat down at the table opposite her mother. "Listen, if there's anything I can do to help . . ."

"Oh, no. This is your vacation, remember? I want you to enjoy yourself. Spend some time with your son. Not to mention that gorgeous husband of yours—whenever he gets here, that is."

Julie made a point of not taking that comment as a criticism.

"Besides," Pat went on, "I enjoy doing all this. Getting the house in shape, doing some of the cooking in advance, having everything run smoothly once I've got a house full of people. . . . Of course, I'll get the night off on Saturday. We're planning to barbecue, and that means your father will insist on running the show."

She thought for a moment, then sighed. "I just hope everyone is here by then. Not only Brad, but all the others, as well. Your father has really been looking forward to having the whole clan together. You know what a sentimental old fool he can be sometimes."

"Unlike you, of course," Julie teased gently.

"Well . . ." Pat drained her coffee cup, then stood up to get herself a refill. "You know I'm always happy when you're all here. And not only because Dad and I get to see you all, either. It's important that you kids see each other every now and then, too. Oh, I know you're all busy with your own lives. Even so, it's important for us to get together every once in a while. After all, we're *family*."

Julie was silent, contemplating the meaning of that word, as Pat sat down again.

"Oh, by the way, Julie," she said abruptly, looking as if she'd just remembered that there was something she'd made a mental note to tell her daughter, "you'll never guess who's living on the island now."

"Who, Mom?"

"That boy you used to go out with in high school. You know, the blond one. Tall, rather good-looking . . ."

Julie chuckled. "I can think of five boys who fill that description."

"Paul, wasn't it? Yes, that's it. Paul something."

Immediately Julie made the connection. And she felt as if someone had just hit her in the stomach.

Pat went on, not noticing that all the color had just drained out of her daughter's face. "Paul Dickson? Dickerson? I recognized the name right away when I heard it. Ginny Nesbitt gave me his business card a few weeks ago, when I was admiring the new addition they've just had built onto the house. Now, where did I put that card?" She got up and started riffling through one of the drawers in the kitchen counter.

"Not Paul Dereksen?" Julie tried to sound casual.

"Why, here it is. I *knew* I put it in here. Yes, Paul Derekson—that's it."

She handed the card to her daughter, who took it gingerly, almost as if she were afraid to handle it. Sure enough, the simple business card was printed with PAUL DEREKSEN, CARPENTRY, with a Shelter Island address and telephone number.

Julie swallowed hard. Paul Dereksen. Imagine him turning up again, after all these years, and right here on the island, too. Yes, she had gone out with him in high school, as her mother remembered. But he had been more than just another boyfriend. Much more. Paul had been the one true love of her life—until Brad, of course, she hastened to remind herself. But now, sitting here in the kitchen and holding his business card in her hand, staring at his name again, it was as if Brad didn't exist, as if time had reversed itself and she was seventeen again, back in high school.

Paul Dereksen. No one, not even her mother, knew the truth about the two of them. Just as no one knew how her heart had broken when things didn't turn out the way that she and Paul had been planning for so long.

"Claridge Street. Where exactly is that?" Julie was surprised at how offhanded she was managing to sound.

"Oh, you know. It's in the Heights. Right behind that hardware store. You know the one I mean. It's right across from the Grapevine."

Julie nodded. "Oh, yes. Now I know. So Paul and his wife—Sally, isn't it?—they live here year-round now?"

"Well, Paul does. I know that because after I finished raving about Ginny's new family room, she started raving about him, saying that he'd worked right through Christmas week in order to get it done in time for her big New Year's Eve party. I don't know about any wife, though."

Yes, there's a wife, Julie thought bitterly. And her name is Sally. Sally Horner—also known as "Horny Sally," at least back in high school. She'd been after Paul the whole time he and Julie had been going out together. Of course, he always denied that she was the least bit interested in him every time Julie or one of his buddies teased him about the girl who wore too much eye makeup and skirts that were much too short, the one who'd been bleaching her hair ever since the seventh grade.

What was it he used to say about her? Oh, yes; pretty much the same thing that everybody else used to say about her, that Sally Horner was hot for anything in pants. But Julie always knew that she thought Paul Dereksen was special, that he was the one she really wanted. And, in the end, she was the one who got him. Ruined his life, too, at least as far as two-thirds of the population of Harrington had been concerned. Including Julie. And it was all because of that stupid argument that Julie and Paul had had, some dumb thing that she had probably started because she was always so sensitive where he was concerned, so afraid of losing him, this boy she truly cared about, the only one she'd ever really loved. . . .

"At any rate," Pat interrupted her thoughts, "if you intend to invite Paul and his wife over, please give me some notice. There are already so many people here, and it's impossible to keep track of how much soda there is in the house, not to mention cheese and things for hors d'oeuvres."

"Don't worry, Mom. I won't be asking Paul and his wife over." She looked at the card one more time, letting her eyes linger on the telephone number printed in black on the lower left-hand corner. Then she handed it back to her mother.

"Here, put this away. Who knows? You might decide that you want an addition on your house, too."

She resolved to forget all about him. To pretend that after all these years the hurt was gone, that even her curiosity about him had faded. To act as if knowing that he was so close, right here on this tiny island, would not make it hard for her to think about anything else.

But even as she made a point of moving the conversation on to other topics, she knew that her resolution was going to be difficult to keep.

Chapter Three

"*A*w *right! Now* that's music!"

Katy Gilbert leaned forward to turn up the volume of the car radio. She was hoping that filling the blue interior of her 1979 Volkswagen Rabbit with John Sebastian's "Summer in the City" would help improve her mood. And her mood was certainly in need of some improvement.

It was late Friday afternoon, just past five-thirty, as the white Rabbit sped past Exit 72 on the Long Island Expressway. Traffic was heavy, even this far out east, and the sun was hot. And as if that weren't bad enough, she had been driving since noon and every one of her muscles was hell-bent on getting back at her.

But it was more than the ordeal of the six-hour car trip between upstate New York and Shelter Island that was responsible for the heaviness in her heart and the butterflies in her stomach. It was the prospect of seeing her family once again. And the closer she got to the Gilberts' beach house, the more noticeable and annoying those two physical manifestations of her apprehension grew.

She wasn't dreading seeing *all* of them, of course. If it had been that bad, she wouldn't have come at all. She'd have come up with some excuse, some lie about job obligations or personal ties that, regrettably, forced her to miss out on the Gilberts' very first formalized family reunion. By now, Katy was an expert at making excuses, thinking up rationalizations, explaining away just about anything at such length and with such creativity that the original issue could well become lost in her rhetoric—more often than not her intention, anyway.

There are some compensations, she reminded herself. I'm actually looking forward to seeing some of them. Dad, of course, and Wes—and it'll be fun to see my nephew and my niece Beth.

Yeah, some of them are okay, I guess, Katy reflected, a bit begrudgingly. Too bad the less savory members of the clan will also be present. Like good old Michael, Number One Son, and that wishy-washy wife of his, Lynn. At the mere thought of her sister-in-law, she let out a contemptuous snort.

And then there's Mom. Good old Mom. After all, if it weren't for her, who would I have to remind me how imperfect I am?

Even so, Katy could tolerate all of them. The only person she was really apprehensive about seeing was her older sister Julie. It seemed inevitable that things between them would always be strained. Even now, after all these years . . .

Suddenly the expressway showed signs of coming to an end, and Katy veered off to the right. The Greenport exit, already. Another couple of miles and she'd pass by Stachiw's gas station—one of the most bizarre names of all times, she noted every time she rode past the dilapidated old building— then what used to be a regularly scheduled stop on this trip, Dunkin' Donuts. That is, until it was closed by the Board of Health. Now she would have to seek some other spot for a breather—like the brand-new Carvel just a few doors down.

She could almost taste one of their creamy chocolate, soft ice-cream cones as she drove past Carl's Equipment and its competitor, Tryac Truck and Equipment, establishments that made no bones about the fact that this part of Long Island, the eastern end on the North Fork, was farmland. Fortunately, it wasn't entirely a wasteland: just past the rotary was an enclave of civilization—Burger King and Pizza Hut and Arby's. Those, too, were all possibilities for a pit stop.

Even as she contemplated her options, however, Katy knew she wouldn't be stopping. Not while she was on her way to see the sister to whom she had been comparing herself ever since she was old enough to realize that the fact that she had brown hair and Julie had blond was, and always would be, a major factor in both their lives.

God, I wish I'd taken off fifteen pounds this summer. Well, ten, anyway . . .

Suddenly terribly self-conscious, she glanced down at the outfit she had chosen specifically for her arrival: a pair of jeans and a new shirt, an orange-and-red patchwork number she'd picked up at the Rheinbeck craft fair in upstate New York. Funny, it had looked so flattering in the mirror at home. The jeans had seemed to slenderize her ample hips and thighs, the bright, busy fabric of the shirt to draw the eye upward. Now, however, she felt the outfit was bizarre—and that it made her look dumpy.

"Damn," she breathed. "Damn, damn, damn."

She could just imagine the outfit that Julie would show up in. Something terribly stylish, no doubt. And expensive. Clothes that looked as if she had simply thrown them on without a thought, but that showed off her five-foot-ten frame, her trim, well-toned figure, her chiseled features that rivaled those of any model.

I don't know why I even try to compete with Julie, Katy thought with a self-pitying grimace. Angrily she turned the dial of the radio in a desperate search for a song that would cheer her up. It's a losing battle, anyway.

"Well, fellow members of the Gilbert clan," she said aloud, "I'm afraid you'll just have to take me the way I am, extra pounds and all."

Suddenly feeling sorry for herself, and very much in need of some instant comfort, Katy reached for something to eat. It was an automatic reaction. She bypassed the brown paper bag filled with sweet, fragrant peaches and plums that she had packed that morning with the noblest of intentions. Instead, she opened up the glove compartment, where her emergency reserves were stored.

She used her teeth and one free hand to tear open the cheerful yellow bag of M&M peanuts. As she popped five or six into her mouth, chewing and swallowing without really tasting them, she resolved to watch what she ate while she was out on Shelter Island. And then, she would start a diet right after Labor Day, as soon as she got back home. A strict one, this time. One that would really work. And one she would stick to, for a change.

Well, if that's what I've got to look forward to after this deadly "vacation" at the old sod, Katy thought with chagrin, I might as well start getting psyched up for two weeks of the home version of "Family Feud." I'll try concentrating on the fact that this little sojourn of mine will give me a chance to see Wes again. And that, she reminded herself, is no small consolation.

Katy and her brother had always been close. Perhaps it was because they were the two babies of the family, perhaps because they were only three years apart. More likely it was because each of them had always had an older sibling of the same sex to compete with—one who excelled at just about everything.

Yes, while she had constantly been following in Julie's footsteps, never able to come close to the Golden Girl's achievements, beauty, and popularity, Wesley had grown up in their brother Michael's shadow. Michael Gilbert, class president, captain of the football team, the senior class' "Ugly Man," their high school's male counterpart to the Homecoming Queen. So what that Wesley, five years his junior, was probably a mathematical genius. Not only did that distinction pale beside Mike's accomplishments—Wes's reputation as the school math whiz was, by comparison, almost an embarrassment. And so that constant struggle, the uphill battle to be *as good as* the older Gilbert children, had bonded Wes and Katy together all their lives.

The difference, however, Katy thought with a loud sigh, is that Wesley has gone ahead and surpassed his older brother. In the long run, he won. Sure, Michael is a successful lawyer, with a wife, two daughters, and a suburban split-level house in Wilmington, Delaware, that epitomizes the American Dream. But Wes did even better for himself, always chalking up his achievements and acquisitions right after his older brother, as if waiting to see the standard Michael set before going about the task of bettering him.

It was true that Michael had a shining career as a legal eagle. But Wes was the star at Tek-Life, a small computer firm right outside Boston staffed by fellow M.I.T. graduates, making a small fortune off his ability to treat obscure high-tech problems as mere computer games.

Then there were their wives. Michael's wife, Lynn, was like something out of the pages of the *Ladies' Home Journal*, keeping their home spotless, routinely baking cookies and pies from scratch, and sewing most of the clothes that she and her two children wore, though not skillfully enough to hide that fact.

Wes, however, had surprised and dazzled them all by snagging Barbara Boucher, a high-powered financial analyst at one of Boston's top investment firms, the idealized "Woman of the Eighties" who was written up in the *Globe* and the *New York Times* almost as frequently as Lynn made those cinnamon-pecan rolls of hers. And as if her career achievements weren't impressive enough, Barbara also happened to be as polished as a five-carat diamond—and as flawlessly beautiful. Katy was proud of both her brothers, of course. But when it came right down to it, she enjoyed Wes's successes as if they were her own, viewing each one as a kind of personal triumph.

Not that it really helps my position any, she thought morosely, digging into the candy once again. Even though her jaws hurt from chewing, she continued to devour them mindlessly. After all, the bag wasn't empty yet.

At age thirty-three, Katy Gilbert had yet to decide upon a career. Or a life-style. Or, for that matter, any clear-cut direction at all. She had tried many things, and each of them seemed to be the solution to all her problems—at least, for a little while.

She had transferred from Middlebury College to the University of Wisconsin during her junior year, convinced that changing from a small women's school in New England to a large coed university in the Midwest would give her some motivation—or at least help her decide upon a major. And, indeed, it did, albeit a bit circuitously. Psychology, economics, sociology, political science—she tried them all before settling upon anthropology.

Once she discovered that she was interested in the field of studying groups of people from afar, without actually being a part of their comings and goings, she stayed on at Wisconsin to work toward a Ph.D. She'd almost finished it, too. She'd gotten through the comps and the orals, and her dissertation was half written. But in her mid-twenties, she'd decided to "take some time away from it," hoping to regain some of the interest in the subject she was researching, an interest that had at one time bordered on obsession, yet which suddenly began to wane. And she'd never gone back.

Just as well, she'd rationalized it then, as she still did today. I'm not cut out for the academic life, anyway.

Next she'd tried a variety of jobs, in a variety of locations. Public relations assistant in Chicago, real estate salesperson in

Westchester County, market research analyst in New York. She'd even tried teaching at a private girls' school up near Syracuse. None of them had worked out. Not the jobs, and not the life-styles that went with them.

Now, at thirty-three, she was living in a rented house on the outskirts of Albany, in a town that went from being suburban to rural over the course of just a few miles. It was a big, funky place, actually an old farmhouse that was on a generous plot of land, almost four acres. "Ramshackle" was the way she liked to describe it.

The fact that it was only a mile or so from suburbia was a contrast she always found delightful. She would drive through the regimented rows of boxy tract houses with their manicured lawns laid out as evenly as the squares in a patchwork quilt, and then, when the paved street forked, veer off onto a dirt road. Suddenly, instead of lawns there were endless empty lots left entirely to their own devices, a wild profusion of tall grass and weeds and purple and yellow wildflowers. To Katy, this change of terrain was always a signal that she was on her way home.

The house at the end of the road, her house, was three-stories high. It was impossible to tell whether the faded gray of the shingles was the result of anyone painting them that color, or if that particular nondescript shade had simply evolved on its own over the years. There was a sagging porch in front, complete with two unmatched rocking chairs, one wicker and one wood, strewn with potted plants.

Inside, the furnishings were as eclectic as the house's inhabitants—and they changed with almost the same frequency. At the moment, the living room contained a threadbare rust-colored velour couch that belonged to Steve, the philosophy graduate student at the university. It was also decorated with other pieces that were from his dowry: the stereo, the brown Naugahyde ottoman held together on top with masking tape, and the mock Oriental rug.

The beanbag chair had arrived along with Natalie, the potter who worked as a cocktail waitress on weekends. The dark, forbidding oil paintings accompanied Jason and Lisa, who spent their weekends riding dirt bikes and their weekdays working at whatever odd jobs they could find. They were also the owners of four of the five cats who lived there, the fifth having arrived on her own from places unknown. Like the others, Katy had contributed her fair share, including the yellow butterfly chair, the bamboo plant stand, and the two rocking chairs out on the porch.

As for her current job, she had fallen into it with the same randomness with which she had surrounded herself with mismatched furniture and mismatched roommates. The friend of a friend had hooked her up with a woman who needed someone to help out at her gourmet shop and catering service, a small but prosperous business that handled everything from a take-out lunch of cold pasta salad for one to a seven-course dinner party for one of the city's wealthiest, most status-conscious hostesses, to an office party for thirty held to celebrate the retirement of a much-loved department head.

The work itself was only part of the reason she had decided to try her hand at fluting quiche crusts by the dozen and making decorative roses out of pink salmon pâté. She had hoped that working in something like gourmet catering would help her meet some interesting people. Or, to be totally accurate, some interesting men. As it turned out, however, the only men who called up such services were inevitably married. A case in point was Nicholas Somers. . . .

By now, the radio was giving the six o'clock news report and the Rabbit was chugging past the Greenport 7-Eleven. Katy considered stopping off for something to drink. After all, the M&Ms had made her thirsty, coating her teeth and mouth with a film of sugar that, now that all the candy was gone, was surprisingly unpleasant. Her stomach was jumpy, too, and she thought that a Coke—a *diet* Coke—might calm it down.

She kept driving, though. Now that she was only a few blocks away from the ferry, it didn't make much sense to prolong any further what had already been an excruciatingly long trip. Besides, she suspected that it wasn't really the M&Ms that were upsetting her stomach.

Pretend you're going out to Shelter Island just to see Josh. Yes, that's it. Concentrate on seeing little Joshie again.

She felt better already.

Katy hadn't seen her little nephew since—was it really since Christmas? The chance to spend some time with the precocious two-year-old was enough, in itself, to make this trip worthwhile. Joshua Kane was always so happy to see his Aunt Katy, giggling uncontrollably whenever she suggested that he might be in for an attack by the Tickle Monster, showing her the pretty stones and shells he'd collected by the seashore. . . .

Yes, her nephew, Josh, and Wes, were the two people in her family who loved her as she was. Nothing mattered to the two of them, not the ten or fifteen extra pounds, not the lack of a man in her life, not her inability to choose one single direction in life and stick to it. They never passed judgment. Never disapproved. Never communicated, sometimes with a mere glance or the downturn of a corner of the mouth, that she was in some way letting them down.

Now, Katy thought ruefully as the ferry attendant waved her on toward the flat white elephant of a boat, if only everyone else in that family felt the same way.

Katy was surprised by how pleasant it felt to drive through the small, meandering town of Shelter Island Heights. She especially enjoyed seeing the delightful Victorian houses that greeted the cars that came rolling off the ferry. She viewed them in a new light now that she was living in a house herself and had newfound respect for what the upkeep of such a monster was all about.

One day I'll get my house looking like that, she thought.

Even so, she knew perfectly well that she would never invest the time, money, or effort required to match the effect of the homes she was driving past—so slowly that she feared the people inside might be tempted to call the police. Not when she was only renting. But that was one of the problems with a temporary life. There wasn't very much that *was* worth investing in.

The good mood that was building up in her as she passed so many familiar places, however, was short-lived. She could feel a sense of doom descending over her as she drove into the graveled circular driveway in front of the Gilberts' summer home. She pretended she was the heroine in a horror movie, on her way into a haunted house for what was bound to turn into a harrowing stay. But as she glanced at the house warily before getting out of the car, she had to admit that it looked pretty innocuous.

This one was too modern, for one thing. To be really scary, a house had to be more than fifteen years old. And a wooden A-frame with a circular driveway and a large deck on the second floor, outfitted with white wrought-iron tables and bold yellow-and-white-striped lawn furniture, lacked much of

the mystery of one of Alfred Hitchcock's gloomy Victorian
creations.

Even so, an eerie tune in a minor key seemed to be playing
in the background of Katy's brain as she opened the car door,
grabbed her fringed blue suede carryall from the seat beside
her, and tromped up the three steps that led to the front door.
Bracing herself against the scene that was to come, she
waltzed in bravely.

"Anyone home?" she called. "Or did everyone skip town
when they heard I was coming?"

"Hey, Katy's here!" she heard her father boom. "Katy,
we're out back. Come on out!"

She glanced around the living room, noting without surprise that absolutely nothing had changed since her last visit a
couple of years earlier. Everything was still done in those
pale colors that Julie had helped their mother pick out,
characterless beiges and washed out pastels that were guaranteed not to offend anyone. Except for Katy, of course. She
found such blandness reprehensible.

The interior of the house appeared to be deserted, so she
sauntered out to the back, pushing open the sliding screen
doors that separated the living room from the concrete patio.
Here, at least, was a little bit of color, like the lone crocus
pushing its way out of the ground amidst brown dirt and dead
leaves. The patio was covered with an awning with the same
yellow-and-white stripes that appeared in the lawn furniture
that was carefully arranged out there, furniture that was identical to the chairs and chaise longues placed on the second-
floor deck.

There were other signs of life out here, as well; namely,
her mother, relaxing on a chaise lounge with a cold drink in
her hand.

"The prodigal daughter returns—whatever that means!"
Katy quipped, stepping outside. "At the risk of sounding
trite, hi, Mom!"

Pat Gilbert smiled dryly as she surveyed her younger daughter. "Really, Katherine, you didn't have to dress just for us."

Katy snickered, glad that, years and years earlier, she had
learned not to get defensive around her mother. "I knew
you'd be wearing something smashing, Mom, and I didn't
want to steal the spotlight." She looked around anxiously.
"Where's Daddy? Didn't I just hear his voice?"

He appeared from around the corner. "Here I am, baby. I

just snuck out for a second to turn off the sprinkler. How's my girl?'' He walked toward her, ready to give her a big hug.

But Katy froze. "Daddy, what's wrong? You look *terrible*!''

"Now what kind of greeting is that for your old dad?'' Ben joked with forced heartiness. "You're supposed to tell me how splendid I look.''

Katy frowned. "Maybe your other children lie to you, but I don't. Tell me what's going on. You look as if you've aged twenty years since I last saw you.''

"Katy!'' her mother reprimanded her. "That's no way to talk to your father!''

"Oh, come on.'' Katy was exasperated. All her resolve about not letting her family get to her had already vanished. "There's obviously something wrong here. What's the point of trying to cover it up?'' She scrutinized her father through narrowed eyes. "Are you sick?''

"No, of course he's not sick!'' Pat sputtered.

"I asked *him*, not *you*! Daddy, will you please tell me what the hell is going on?''

Ben put a comforting arm around Katy. "I have been feeling a bit under the weather lately, Katy, now that you mention it. I even saw Dr. Jennings,'' he lied. "But he assured me that it's nothing. Just the years taking their toll.''

"Maybe you should get a second opinion,'' Katy countered. "You look tired. There are big bags under your eyes. . . . And you look like you've lost weight. Daddy, have you been eating enough?''

"Really, Katy. I'm fine.''

"What is *wrong* with everybody in this house? Why can't we try admitting, just once, that maybe everything isn't just 'fine'?''

"Oh, Katy, it's so like you to be negative,'' Pat scolded. "Trying to ruin everything . . .''

"What's going on?'' Julie appeared at the sliding doors in a pink terry-cloth bathrobe, her hair wrapped up in an olive green bath towel. "Katy! When did you get here?'' With a conspiratorial grin, she added, "And how did you manage to stir up trouble so fast?''

By this point, Katy had given up. "Hi, Julie.'' Defeat was reflected in her tone. "How's it going?''

"Great. How about you?''

"Oh, fantastic. Things couldn't be better.'' She decided,

then and there, to phase out everyone around who was over the age of three. "Hey, where's Josh?"

"He's right here. Come on out, Joshie. Don't you want to say hello to your Aunt Katy?" Julie led out a blond little boy whose hands, face, and shirt were smeared with chocolate ice cream. "Here he is."

"Is that Joshua Kane?" Katy cried, dropping to a squatting position. "Come on over here, big guy, and give me a kiss. Just wait till you see what I bought you. You're gonna love it. Hey, wait a minute—you *do* like trucks, don't you?"

Holding the little boy against her, not caring in the least if she, too, became covered with chocolate ice cream, was the best thing she'd done all day. And noticing that the tension among the four adults was rapidly dissipating helped cheer her up. Even so, Katy was already wondering if she had made a mistake in coming.

Chapter Four

"*So*, Julie, how's life in the fast lane?" There was real belligerence underlying Katy's seemingly cheerful tone, as if what was masked as a casual question was actually a challenge.

Julie just smiled. She understood that Katy felt competitive toward her, that, indeed, she could hardly help it. After all, it was old hat by now, simply a continuance of a pattern that had been set up many, many years before.

Even so, it did hurt, just a little bit. Julie had always wished that the two of them could be friends, appreciating each other's differences rather than constantly being at odds because of them. Katy had so much going for her: she was smart, she was witty, she had a sense of flamboyance that she would have been amazed to learn her big sister admired. If only she could celebrate the things she had, rather than lamenting those she was so sure she lacked.

"Things are going okay." Julie took a small sip of the gin and tonic that her father had served up to the three women lounging outside on the patio, taking some time to relax before dinner. As usual, it was much too strong—the dear man never had been able to mix a decent drink. "The show's doing all right, and I've just signed another contract."

"I guess we're talking some pretty big bucks, huh?"

Julie made a point of ignoring that remark. "How about you, Katy? It sounds like you're doing some interesting things these days. The catering business, hmm? A far cry from anthropology. How did you ever get involved in something like that?''

"Oh, you know me. Good old fly-by-night Katy. Just flitting around, playing the dilettante. . . ."

"Come on. Be fair. I wasn't being sarcastic. I was sincerely interested." This time, Julie really was hurt. Wasn't her little sister ever going to be prepared to call a truce? Couldn't the two of them even carry on a normal conversation, without all that other stuff getting in the way?

"Well, I know it's only small potatoes—if you'll excuse the pun." Katy had just decided, with the help of the gin, that acting civil might not be such a bad idea. After all, she still had two full weeks of family togetherness ahead of her—an amount of time which, from where she was sitting, seemed formidable indeed. "Actually, it's a pretty neat place. Foodstuffs, it's called. It was started by a woman named Leslie Marr who used to be a social worker. One day, she just got sick of figuring out solutions to other people's problems, especially when what she really wanted to be doing was making chili for thirty. . . ."

Isn't this nice, thought Pat Gilbert. She sat back in the cheerful yellow-and-white canvas chaise lounge and let the soothing effects of an overly potent gin and tonic wash over her. She didn't normally drink, but this was a special occasion. After all, both her daughters were home together for the first time in ages. Her family was coming together again. It was going to be just like old times—for the next two weeks, anyway.

It was pleasant, sitting out on the patio, comfortably dressed in a bright red, white, and blue pants-and-blouse set. She was enjoying hearing the voices of Julie and Katy as they chatted, without really listening. Oh, every so often she tuned in to what they were saying. Was it possible that Katy was really working for a caterer? Why, that girl could hardly boil an egg! And was she really sharing a dilapidated old farmhouse with four roommates and five cats?

Of course, nothing that Julie was saying surprised her in the least. As always, she was full of reports—couched in modesty though they were—of how well her show was doing, how quickly Josh was learning new things, how successful Brad's real estate ventures were. The rest was just a blur, details and anecdotes that became nothing more than a background to the dreamlike state that Pat was slowly drifting into.

No, it wasn't important to listen to every word they said. What mattered was that they were here, that she was with her two daughters. After all, mothers and daughters always experienced a special bond, didn't they?

When the telephone rang, deep inside the house, it snapped Pat abruptly out of her agreeable reverie. Every one of her muscles tightened up in what was by now a reflex action.

"Oh, I'll get it." Reluctantly she dragged herself out of her comfortable lounge chair, reflecting momentarily that this was one of those times that she was feeling her age. "It's probably for me, anyway."

"I'm sure it's not for me," Katy quipped. "Nobody knows where I am. Nope, this time I managed to cover my tracks nicely."

Pat cast a look of disdain in Katy's direction.

Heavens, she thought, why is that daughter of mine so . . . perverse?

She tried to tell herself, as she had for years, that her youngest child simply had a bizarre sense of humor. And that was certainly true enough. Even so, it was so hard not to become irritated by a contrariness she simply could not understand.

"Hello?" Pat's voice was cheerful as she picked up the beige wall phone in the kitchen.

"Well, well, well. If it isn't the incomparable Pat Gilbert. How's my favorite lady doing?"

She was surprised to hear Brad at the other end of the line. Julie had sounded so vague about his plans, making it sound as if they might not see him for days.

"Why, hello, Brad. I'm just dandy, and waiting around for my favorite son-in-law to show up. But wait, hold on a minute. I'll get Julie."

It never would have occurred to her to take a message, or even to chat with him for a minute. For one thing, he was such a busy man, and Pat couldn't help being slightly in awe of him, even though he was her son-in-law. But even more important was her belief that husbands and wives should talk to each other, not to mettlesome in-laws. Summoning Julie right away, without wasting time making small talk, was simply the right thing to do.

As she slid open the glass doors and passed from the

air-conditioned house to the muggy open-air patio, she realized that her gin and tonic had already started to get to her. Ben was such an inexperienced bartender, invariably making his drinks too strong.

"It's for you, Julie," she said, dropping back into her chair. "It's Brad." Goodness, it felt good to sit down.

Julie looked surprised, but she hesitated for only a moment. She bolted from her chair, calling to her mother, "Thanks, Mom. Will you watch Josh for me?" over her shoulder.

As she rushed to the phone in the kitchen, she nearly tripped on one of Pat's scatter rugs in her effort not to keep her husband waiting.

"Hello, Brad?"

"Julie. I'm here in Sag Harbor. I just flew into East Hampton. God, that was certainly an ordeal. A crazed pilot in a toy plane. But at least I made it in one piece. Anyway, I'm just about to get on the ferry."

Julie was hurt by his impersonalness. It wasn't what he said as much as what he didn't say.

For heaven's sake, what do you want? she scolded herself. Storybook romance, twenty-four hours a day?

"I'll pick you up at the ferry dock," she told him. "Just give me five minutes."

As she hung up the phone, she was surprised to find her mother at her elbow.

"I'm so glad he managed to make it this evening," Pat said, giving her daughter's shoulder a squeeze. "I just love seeing the three of you together. You, Brad, Josh . . . You're the perfect little family."

Julie smiled wanly. If we're so "perfect," she was thinking, how did we manage to start out what's supposed to be a family vacation by arriving two days apart?

"Well, now, you scurry over to the ferry. You don't want to keep Brad waiting, do you? And I'd better start dinner. Goodness, is it already seven? I hope I remembered to take the butter out of the refrigerator to let it soften. . . ."

The effects of her drink vanished as she suddenly busied herself with the role of hostess. After all, Brad was coming.

As was so often the case, both Brad and Julie were on their best behavior as they rode back together to the Gilberts' house. Brad talked about the series of emergency meetings that had been scheduled all week, part of a full-scale effort to get the Colony Building off the ground, once and for all. And he complained some more about his flight from Manhattan to East Hampton.

Julie just listened, nodding and trying to look sympathetic.

What about my day? she was thinking. Aren't you interested in how things went with me? Not to mention Josh, your son . . .

But a less sensitive, and, as she saw it, a more sensible side of her prompted her to keep her complaints to herself.

You're acting like a baby, she told herself. Brad's had a tough day, and he deserves a little coddling. Don't forget that while he was flying across Long Island, risking his life in one of those prop planes that's like something out of a cereal box, you were sipping gin and tonics out on the patio, catching up with Katy. He's hot and tired and probably stressed to the limit. . . .

Proof of that was manifested when Brad paraded into the Gilberts' house. He immediately headed for the bar.

"God, do I need a drink. What a day. And, boy, is it hot."

"Brad! There you are, you naughty thing, you." Pat came sweeping into the living room. She had changed out of her pants and blouse into a summery dress whose formality was much more becoming on her than the sportier look. "Keeping all of us waiting for you for days on end like that!"

"Well, here I am. Live and in person. Hey, where do you folks keep the gin, anyway?"

"Oh, here." Pat handed him what had been her drink. "Help yourself to this gin and tonic. If you don't mind a little melted ice, that is. Ben made it for me, but, well, one really is my limit."

"Thanks, Pat." Now that he had a drink in his hand, Brad was suddenly much more congenial. "You always did know how to treat a guest."

Pat blushed with pleasure over his compliment as he took a gulp.

"Hey, this is pretty weak, isn't it? That brings me back to my original question: where do you folks keep the gin?"

Pat was taken aback, but only for a moment. Cheerfully she found the bottle for him, left on top of a bookcase by her absentminded husband.

"Now, Brad, dear, I hope you'll forgive me if I abandon you. I simply have to see to dinner, or else we'll never get to eat. I know I'm leaving you in good hands, though.

"Besides," she added, her eyes shining, "you and I have two weeks to catch up. But a soufflé has absolutely no patience at all!"

"It looks like all the action has shifted inside," Katy observed, coming into the living room through the sliding doors just as her mother was exiting. When she saw her brother-in-law, she couldn't help grimacing. "Oh. Hi, Brad."

"My, my. If it isn't little Katy. The famous Julie Gilbert Kane's kid sister." He came over and made a grand show of giving her a kiss on the cheek. "Hey, kid sister, can I make you a drink? It looks like I've been nominated for bartender."

He gestured toward his own glass, into which he had just poured another healthy shot of gin. Before she'd even had a chance to answer, he gulped it down as if it were nothing more than a glass of water.

"Thanks, Brad, but I think I'll just have a club soda." More to herself than anyone else, she added, "I've been making a conscious effort to watch what I eat lately."

"Oh, really?" Brad's lips curled into a sneer. "You could have fooled me."

Julie cast him a scathing look, but he made a point of not noticing. Instead he concentrated on dropping ice cubes into two glasses that he'd just taken down from the shelf above the bar.

"I'll take the liberty of making you a drink, as well, my little cabbage." He nodded in his wife's direction. "As for me, I think it's time to switch to Scotch. No ice, no water. Scotch in its pure, unadulterated form, just the way God intended for it to be consumed."

Julie placed her hand gently on her husband's arm. "Don't you think one drink is enough for now, Brad?"

Her voice was soft and casual, but the look in her eyes was one of fierce condemnation. Or perhaps it was one of fear. Katy, who was watching her closely, couldn't tell.

"After all, you don't want to fill up and have your dinner ruined. I understand my mother is cooking up quite a feast for tonight's little reunion."

"You've got it all backwards," Brad returned coldly. "What I'm afraid of is that your mother's dinner might fill me up and ruin my drinking."

He proceeded to down a good portion of his Scotch in a few swallows, all the while watching his wife, a look of open defiance in his dark brown eyes.

Katy stood behind the off-white upholstered living room chair, looking from Julie to Brad and back to Julie again. She had never seen her sister look like that before. Angry, frightened—aware of how powerless she really was.

Katy had never liked Brad; even so, she felt particularly uncomfortable standing there, and part of her longed to flee. But, surprisingly, another part compelled her to stay, to protect her sister—one reaction she never would have expected, not in a million years. The urge to play peacemaker, or at least to smooth over what were all of a sudden some very rough edges, was irresistible.

"Well, I must say," she commented, sounding more agreeable than she had been since she had entered the same room as Brad, "Josh is certainly getting cuter by the minute. And from what I can see, he's smart as a whip. It must be so much fun having a little guy like that around all the time."

"Oh, yeah, 'fun' is definitely the word for it," Brad returned sarcastically. "Especially if you like having your dinner interrupted every night like clockwork, and finding that your favorite cuff links from Cartier's have been dropped into the bottom of the toilet, and constantly tripping over the eighteen million toys that are stuffed into every corner in the apartment. . . . By the way, where is the little tyke, anyway?"

"With his grandfather," Julie replied quietly. "The two of them went across the street. Ben wanted to show him the neighbors' new puppy."

"Good. It's nice to have some peace and quiet for a change."

It was all that Katy could do to keep from making a sarcastic remark of her own, one about how refreshing it was to see an example of the "new man" in action, one of the 1980s' breed of sensitive, caring fathers who considered raising their children a very high priority. But she was afraid it would only worsen the friction between him and Julie.

Fortunately, Pat came bustling back into the living room then, insisting that Katy set the table and Julie help her decide which wine she should serve with dinner. Brad was left on his own—and Katy was removed from the temptation of telling her brother-in-law exactly what she had always thought of him, ever since the day that she came to New York to meet her sister's brand-new fiancé, the one that Julie had so proudly described on the phone as "too good to be true."

She felt that she was the one person who had seen through

him from the start. Especially after the incident, something that, even now, disgusted her whenever she thought about it. Not that she'd said anything about it at the time, of course. After all, Julie was so much in love with this man. And she'd never mentioned it since, although she remembered every time she looked at Brad. And, she suspected from the constant jeering look in his eyes whenever he saw her, he remembered it, also—all too well.

Yes, she'd known what kind of man he was right from the very beginning. But there was little satisfaction to be gained from making that observation now. In fact, as she saw in Julie's eyes a pained look that she had never seen before, Katy was astonished to find that she actually felt a little bit sorry for her sister.

Chapter Five

She stands alone behind the counter at Foodstuffs, shoveling tricolored pasta salad into a plastic take-out container, when a man around forty comes into the shop. He has brown hair, charmingly sparse on top, and eyes so blue that they practically glow. He reeks of the cavalier attitude—toward money, toward detail, toward excess—that characterizes so many of the trendy shop's customers.

"Just throw together a little dinner party for eight," he commands with a nonchalant wave of his hand. "Anything—whatever you think. And you take American Express, don't you?"

Dutifully, busily, Katy puts together a perfect combination of delectable goodies, chooses and measures and packs with practiced efficiency, then deposits a heavy shopping bag on the counter.

"Anything else?" she asks politely.

"Why, yes, as a matter of fact." With that, Nicholas Somers comes around behind the counter, takes her in his arms, and presses his wet, hungry mouth against hers. . . .

It was a delicious fantasy, at least as delicious as Foodstuffs' cheese tortellini with pesto. Katy lay in her bed—or, to be more precise, the cot that was set up at the foot of the twin beds in which her nieces Chrissie and Beth would be sleeping after tonight—relishing the relative quiet of the house so early on this Saturday morning. The window had been left

51

open, her act of defiance against the sterile, albeit comfortable, air-conditioning that homogenized the rest of the house. Through it drifted a cool breeze, a hint of freshness in what were otherwise stifling surroundings. She could hear the sounds of summer—the lapping of waves, the cry of sea gulls—and smell the salty air.

She closed her eyes and ran her hands over her body, ignoring, for once, the occasional excess of flesh they encountered here and there. She felt so sensual this morning, as if not touching or kissing a man within the next five minutes was guaranteed to result in extreme consequences. That was why she was thinking about Nicholas Somers, who she had indeed first met over the counter at Foodstuffs—although not at all as dramatically or as memorably as the scene her brain had just conjured up with such imagination and eagerness. Or perhaps thinking about him was what got her started in the first place.

Yes, that was much more likely, she decided. After all, it'd been happening more and more lately.

Their relationship had begun as a simple business transaction, rapidly graduating to a flirtation. Then to a quick drink after work one evening. And then dinner at a somewhat seedy Mexican restaurant nearby. Now, she and Nicholas were on the verge of moving on into territory that was even hotter than the second-rate enchiladas they'd consumed together at La Tablita Mexicana.

Thinking about what had happened so far was the fun part. The part that was not quite as much fun was reminding herself that somewhere, back at the ranch, readying the microwave for the reheating of Foodstuffs' finest, was a *Mrs.* Somers.

Katy moved her hands, suddenly anxious to test for love handles, and wondered, for the millionth time since Mr. Somers had made it clear what his intentions were, just how much she should let that little fact affect her behavior over the next few weeks. Before she'd met Nicholas, she would have found the idea of having an affair with a married man abhorrent. But now, given his availability, his attentiveness, and, of course, the fact that there wasn't much else around these days, she was prepared to reconsider.

Oh, well, she concluded, suddenly bored with lying in bed brooding, I don't have to decide anything right now. Instead,

I should be concentrating on something important—like getting a tan.

She dragged herself out of bed, glanced at the clock and saw that it was almost ten, and went down to the kitchen in search of a breakfast that would fortify her for a morning of lying on the upstairs deck, a full fifteen feet closer to the sun, as she pursued what she had just designated as her number-one priority.

The kitchen was empty, she was relieved to discover. Contentedly she moseyed around, pouring herself a mug of coffee and popping an English muffin into the toaster. Then she stood staring at the contents of the refrigerator for a full three minutes, debating the issue of whether or not to smear her muffin with strawberry jam. The Briermere Farms label was definitely a persuasive factor. But in the end, reminding herself that Nicholas Somers might soon be caressing her naked flesh led her to choose a more Spartan route.

She had just sat down at the kitchen table with her coffee and muffin *sans* preserves, and was about to pick up the copy of the *Reporter* that some earlier riser had apparently left behind, when her mother strode into the kitchen carrying a cardboard box filled with cauliflower, broccoli, mushrooms, and carrots.

"Good morning, Katy. Sleep well?" Pat cast her daughter an odd look and then headed for the sink with her bounty.

"Do you mean 'well'—or do you mean 'late'?" Katy countered. Before her mother had a chance to come up with a snappy reply, she went on, "Where is everybody, anyway?"

"Well, assuming that I'm not 'anybody,' Julie took Josh over to Shell Beach, your father's working on the Sunfish, and Brad—"

"Oh, goody. I can't wait to hear what good old Brad is up to."

Pat frowned as she began unpacking, sorting, and rinsing off the vegetables with frightening efficiency. "He's upstairs, on the phone. Some big real estate deal that's real hot."

"Or some tart, anyway. Although I wouldn't doubt that *she's* really hot, too!"

"Katy, what on earth is wrong with you?" Pat picked up a paring knife and attacked a carrot with a viciousness that startled Katy. "Can't you ever be civil? Look, it's so rare that we're all together under one roof these days—I just want everyone to have a nice time. Besides, I don't think your father could stand . . .''

"Could stand what, Mom? Would you mind telling me what the hell is going on with him? I told you yesterday that he looks like walking death. What is going on around here?''

Pat set her lips firmly into a straight line. "I'll have none of your swearing, Katy, and I'll have none of your freshness. If you don't want to stay here—and no one's forcing you— then feel free to leave. But if you do stay, I'd appreciate it if you'd keep your nastiness to yourself.''

"Fine. Great. So much for the Welcome Wagon." Angrily Katy stood up and flounced out of the room.

There was a terrible gnawing feeling in Pat's stomach as she watched her daughter walk out of the room. She hadn't meant for their first interaction of the day to end up so—so catastrophic. Then again, she never intended to let any of her deep-rooted anger show. Not where her children were concerned. But somehow, whenever Katy was around, it was as if something inside her just snapped.

It's her own fault, Pat insisted to herself, turning back to her vegetables. She goes out of her way to antagonize me, that girl. She always has, ever since she was a little girl.

Suddenly, without warning, she found herself thinking back to an earlier time, her mind suddenly filled with the memory of an event from long ago, something she hadn't thought about for years. It was the day of Katy's Flying Up ceremony, when she and the other ten-year-old girls from Troop 118 were to cross the small wooden bridge, constructed by one of the handier fathers, to signify their graduation from Brownies to Girl Scouts.

As with all such ceremonies held by the Scouts, it was imperative that she be impeccably groomed, that her uniform be freshly washed and pressed and that all the extras that went along with it—the orange tie worn at the neck, the brown knee socks with the scouting insignia embroidered on the side in white, the brown felt beanie—be just right. Katy had spent days nagging Pat about every little detail, wanting to make sure that nothing be overlooked.

The only thing she didn't remember was white gloves. They, too, were part of the full-dress uniform, and propriety demanded that they, like everything else, be sparkling clean. Pat decided to surprise Katy by taking care of this one item that the little girl was bound to forget.

Sure enough; the Friday evening of the ceremony, as Katy was excitedly donning her uniform, she suddenly froze.

"Mom!" she wailed, looking over from the mirror, her face suddenly twisted with distress. "I forgot the white gloves! Oh, no! What am I going to do? Does this mean I can't go?"

Pat was almost giddy about the little surprise she had up her sleeve, pleased that, for once, she would be able to do something nice for this independent daughter of hers.

"Of course, you can still go. Fortunately, I didn't forget." Smiling, Pat brought out from behind her back a pair of white cotton gloves, freshly washed and bleached, guaranteed to provide just the right finishing touch. "Will these do?"

Katy nearly melted with relief. "Gee, thanks, Mom! You remembered! When did you buy these?"

"Oh, I didn't buy them. When I realized that the ones you've been wearing were beyond saving, I tracked down this old pair of Julie's. I washed them, and look! They're as good as new!"

Pat never did understand the hysteria that followed, nor did she have any patience with Katy's insistence that she no longer wanted to go—that, in fact, she didn't want to have anything more to do with scouting at all. In the end, it was Ben who drove Katy to the ceremony, cheering her on and snapping her photograph as she crossed that wooden bridge, hesitating only for a split second before marching over it.

Another opportunity for mother and daughter to be close, to share a special moment, had been ruined. Pat stayed behind, pretending to be reading as she holed up in her bedroom, but, in reality, spending the evening agonizing over what had transpired, trying to figure out what was so terrible about what she had done.

That same feeling was back, the distress so great that her stomach felt as if it were being wrenched by a strong pair of hands. It was as if she had suddenly sped twenty years back in time. So nothing had changed, even though Katy was now an adult herself, and Pat was trying to cope with another whole generation of Gilberts. The words may have been different, the situations updated, but those same old feelings still remained.

Katy, too, had to cope with a torrent of angry feelings that plagued her long after she had stomped up to her bedroom. After throwing on a pair of baggy shorts and a T-shirt, she raced to the sanctuary of her car, determined to head anywhere that wasn't her mother's house.

Damn it! she thought, her eyes filled with tears as she drove. As she passed a group of bathing suit–clad teenaged girls walking alongside the road, probably no older than her niece Beth, she slowed down, having just realized that she was driving too fast. Why am I always treated like the black sheep of the family? What did I ever do? Just because I'm not thin and gorgeous and successful like Julie . . .

She slowed to a halt for a Stop sign then, and a hand-lettered sign posted on a telephone pole a few yards away caught her eye.

GARAGE SALE TODAY, it read. BOOKS, FURNITURE, CLOTHES, ETC. Underneath was an address, the name of the street one that Katy recognized. Having no place else to go, and certain that she wasn't ready to go back home yet, she headed in that direction.

There were quite a few people browsing among the discards of someone else's life as Katy parked her Rabbit alongside the road and joined them.

See, there are lots of people around here with nothing else to do on a Saturday morning, she thought grimly.

Ordinarily, she stayed away from this kind of thing, finding it depressing looking through other people's worn-out shoes, broken lamps, and ugly souvenirs from vacation trips that had probably turned out badly. She didn't really expect to find anything halfway decent. But then she spotted a springform pan, almost hidden between a rusty cheese grater and a food processor that she was willing to bet had more than half its parts missing.

Inspiration! she thought, experiencing a surge of glee for the first time since she'd hit the road early the day before. I'll whip up one of my famous chocolate hazelnut cheesecakes. Well, not mine, exactly . . . But who'll know that it's really Foodstuffs' recipe? Maybe showing my beloved family that there *are* some things that old Katy can do well will help convince them that I'm not the failure they all seem to think I am.

Yes, the chocolate hazelnut cheesecake was bound to make

a hit. She decided to save it for a special occasion—her parents' wedding anniversary dinner would be perfect. And no one would ever have to know how simple the recipe was, that it only took a few minutes to whip the thing up in the blender. . . .

"Hey, wait a second! What do you think you're doing?"

When Katy was about three feet away from the table, someone suddenly reached over and picked up the springform pan—*her* springform pan. Her first impulse was to grab it out of his hands. Instead, she faced him head on and cried, "You can't buy that! It's mine! I saw it first!"

The man looked at her in surprise. "What are you talking about?"

"That pan. You've got to let me have it. I need it desperately. My entire sense of self-worth, not to mention my dignity, is resting in that pan. Besides, you're probably just going to bring it home to your wife. If you don't say anything about it, she'll never even know she missed out on a fifty-cent springform pan."

"In the first place," the man said calmly, "I was just looking at the thing because I've never seen one before, and I was just trying to figure out what the heck it was. And in the second place, I don't even *have* a wife."

"You don't? Oh. Well." Katy was now sheepish. "Gee, I'm sorry. It's just that when I saw this stupid springform pan, all of a sudden—oh, never mind."

"Here, take it. With my compliments."

Gratefully, and still more than a little embarrassed, Katy took the cake pan from the stranger.

"You must be quite a cook," he said with a grin. "I mean, not only do you know what that contraption is, you obviously plan to put it to good use."

"Oh, sure. I make a mean cheesecake. Hazelnut, with little ribbons of chocolate running through it."

"Wow! Sounds fantastic!"

"Yeah, well, I work for this gourmet shop and catering service."

"No kidding! So where do I go to buy one of these decadent cheesecakes?"

"Sorry, they're not for sale. I mean, not around here, anyway. I live up near Albany. I'm just here on Shelter Island for a couple of weeks."

"Ah. A fellow tourist, like me."

"Really? Out here for the summer?"

The man shook his head. "Afraid not. Only three weeks. See, I work for a bank in the city, and one of its main attractions is the four-week vacations they give us." He shrugged. "I had three of them left, and a pal of mine and his wife, the Cotters, have a house out here. So I invited myself out."

Katy laughed. "Wow. That's quite a visit, three weeks. This pal of yours must be quite a pal."

"Actually, I'm doing my best to keep out of Mark and Wendy's hair." His arms made a sweeping gesture. "That's how I managed to make the yard sale circuit in the first place. It's not something I'd do ordinarily, but you can only play tennis and go to the beach so many times. Especially since I'm already courting disaster, just by being out in the sun this morning." Self-consciously he stroked his nose, red from sunburn and already starting to peel.

Despite the current condition of his nose, however, he wasn't at all unattractive, Katy noted. He was short and what might be called stocky (or, by the less diplomatic, beefy), with dark blond hair cut very short—Wall Street-style, Katy surmised. His face was friendly, if not particularly memorable. He had nice hazel eyes, alert and intelligent. And he was dressed exactly the way a banker on vacation on a resort island would be expected to dress: kelly green Izod sport shirt, khaki shorts which revealed humorous knees, battered Topsiders with no socks. It didn't make any sense at all, but Katy liked him.

"Well," she said boldly, "if you're looking for ways to keep out of the house, I'd be happy to take you on the fifty-cent tour of the island sometime."

"Fifty-cent tour, huh? Is it just a coincidence that that happens to be the price of the pan you just talked me out of? Maybe you're feeling a little guilty, huh?"

Katy laughed. "It's the least I can do. And to tell you the truth, I'm staying with my folks while I'm here. As a matter of fact, my entire family has descended upon the house, like a pack of vultures. Getting out of the house a little isn't such a bad idea."

"I just might take you up on your offer, then. Hey, by the way, I'm Randy Palmer."

"Is that Randy as in Randolph?"

"Randy as in Randall."

"Figures."

"What's that supposed to mean?"

"Oh, I don't know. Somehow, it just all fits. But don't take it personally. . . . I'm Katy Gilbert. Katy as in Katherine."

"Okay, then. How about if I look you up one of these days? I'm sure my host would only be too happy to point me in the direction of the Gilbert residence."

"Sure," Katy said, smiling a funny half-smile that she was pretty sure could be perceived as alluring. "You do that."

Chapter Six

"**I** *don't* see what we have to go to dumb old Shelter Island for," whined Chrissie Gilbert, staring out the car window and scowling. "I'm gonna be, like, so-o-o bored!"

The pretty sixteen-year-old petulantly folded her arms across her chest, covering up the word BENETTON that was printed boldly across the front of her baggy bubble-gum-pink shirt. "I mean, here it is, the last two weeks of summer vacation, and you guys insist on dragging me away from all my friends and making me go sit around Grandma and Grandpa's with absolutely *nothing* to do. God, Heather could, like, hardly believe it when I told her."

"Oh, come on, Chrissie. It won't be so bad," insisted Beth, her thirteen-year-old sister. "It might even be fun. We can go swimming, and biking . . . there'll be lots of stuff we can do."

" 'We'? Are you kidding? You actually think I'm gonna hang out with *you* for the next two weeks? No *way*!"

"Hey, chill out, you two, will you?" interrupted the girls' father, Michael Gilbert, his tone pleading. He hunched even further over the steering wheel and kept his eyes fixed on the crazed drivers of the Belt Parkway. "Chrissie, try being a little nicer to your sister, okay? It won't kill you, you know."

He sighed deeply as he peered at his two daughters through the rearview mirror. "Look, we've all been in this car for over two hours already, and we've still got quite a ways to go. So how about if we try making the rest of our trip something along the lines of pleasant?''

This car trip was, indeed, a minor ordeal. Their five-hour haul from Lawrenceville, New Jersey, to Shelter Island, New York, had begun at seven-thirty that morning, when Michael, his wife Lynn, and their two daughters had stuffed themselves into their Mercedes along with five suitcases, three tennis rackets, and what seemed like an endless collection of useless junk. Between the glaring early morning sun, the heavy Saturday traffic, and the crowdedness of the car, it was inevitable that the four Gilberts drive each other at least a little bit crazy. And they still had a long stretch ahead of them.

Lynn glanced over at her husband, noticing how tightly his jaw was clenched. She knew that he'd been wreaking havoc with his teeth lately, grinding them day and night with such force that their family dentist had warned him that he was wearing them down. She was tempted to reach across the front seat to touch him reassuringly, to squeeze his arm or take his hand. But something stopped her.

Besides, the moment had already passed.

"I don't think it's healthy for us to be spending so much time together," Chrissie's wheedling voice went on. "Heather says she read somewhere that hanging around your parents too much can be harmful to a girl's growth and maturity. Especially during the teenage years. Heather says it can be *dangerous*, even!''

"Yeah, what about the girl's parents?" Michael countered. "It seems to me that last time I saw Heather's mother at a PTA meeting, she'd put on at least thirty pounds."

"Oh, Daddy." Chrissie rolled her eyes upward, as if the comment her father had just made was the stupidest group of words ever uttered. She picked up the oversized cobalt blue Sportsac she was using as a purse these days, crammed with makeup and wallets and Lord knew what else, and began sifting through it. "Well, at any rate, I can't believe you're actually making me go through with this." She found a stick of sugarless gum and popped it into her mouth. "I mean, God, two whole weeks! I'll be, like, a total basket case by the time I get out of there!''

"Yeah, well, you may not be the only one," Michael muttered. Then, as if remembering the role he was expected to play, he said, "Look, let's think positive for a change.

You'll get in some swimming, some tennis, maybe a little bit of sailing—and I think we could all use a change of scenery.''

"If we ever get to Shelter Island, that is. Are we almost there, Daddy?" Chrissie demanded. "My legs are killing me. Doesn't sitting too long cause varicose veins? God, that's the last thing I need. Heather says—"

"Could we please do without another quote from Heather, if you don't mind?" Lynn interrupted her daughter impatiently.

Like her husband, she was feeling the strain of the long trip. She reached up and massaged the muscles at the back of her neck. They were as tight as the strings on those dusty tennis rackets she had finally found in the basement early that morning, after scrounging around for the better part of an hour. No doubt that tension was responsible for the headache that had first crept up on her on the New Jersey Turnpike, just south of Newark, and had been growing worse with each passing mile.

"Nobody ever listens to me!" Chrissie cried.

"How can we help it?" returned her little sister nastily.

"Please, let's just stop all this bickering, okay?" Lynn pleaded.

As if she didn't already have enough to deal with, she could feel her sinuses starting to fill up. She reached into her purse and shuffled through it until she found a tiny green plastic bottle. She sorted through the pills, white aspirins and pale blue Valium and dark blue Pyridium and yellow antihistamines, until she found her pink pills for sinus headaches.

Then she took a can of iced tea out of the shopping bag at her feet and popped it open. Not surprisingly, the term *iced* was a gross misnomer. After being out of the refrigerator for several hours on one of the hottest days of the summer, even in an air-conditioned car, the tea was lukewarm.

It was also dietetic, meaning it tasted like liquid chemicals. She gulped down enough to get two sinus tablets into her stomach, then held the warm can in her lap. She knew that she was now committed to holding on to it until they reached her in-laws' summer house—another couple of hours, at least.

"Anybody want something to eat?" she suggested for the eighteenth time. "I've got cookies here, and some sandwiches."

"Come on, Mom. You know I'm on a diet." Predictably, Chrissie was irritated over the mere suggestion that she consume food that wasn't either diet cola or lettuce.

"Michael?"

"Hmm? Oh, no thanks, hon."

It was obvious to Lynn that he was tuning them all out. She could see it in his very posture, in the way his facial muscles tightened, in the glazed, distant look in his eyes.

Not that I blame him, she thought, quick to rush to his defense.

After all, she reminded herself, in addition to the exasperating cacophony of his family's voices, he'd been dealing with brutal highway traffic for the past two hundred miles.

"Beth?" Lynn tried again. "Do you want anything?"

"No, thanks. . . . Um, what kind of cookies?"

"There's some fruit, too, babe. How about a banana? Or I've got some plums . . ."

Behind her, in the backseat, Beth stiffened, then grew silent. "No, thanks. Changed my mind."

Lynn had insulted her. Again. She was learning that having a chubby daughter was a no-win situation. Offer her cookies, and you were helping her stay fat. Encourage her to eat fruit instead, and you were insinuating that she was less than perfect. Sure, Lynn felt sorry for her. But she had also begun to feel sorry for herself as of late, deflated by her glaring inability to help even her own child.

As a matter of fact, Lynn had been thinking about her various inadequacies quite a bit recently. Her younger daughter, Beth, was withdrawing from her more and more as adolescence crept up on her. She was overweight, unhappy, often surly—and impossible to either comfort or help. Her older daughter, Chrissie, meanwhile, considered her mother her worst enemy.

What hurt the most, however, was the fact that her husband had of late begun following Beth's patterns. Despite the excuses she was constantly making for him, the fact remained that Michael was withdrawing into himself more and more.

His distance this morning was just one more example of his newfound skill. It was becoming a way of life with him. Routinely he answered her chirping questions with a curt "Yes" or "No." Made it clear that he preferred reading a spy novel over conversing with her. Fell asleep on the couch, drifting off in front of the eleven o'clock news, so that even attempting to initiate lovemaking would have been a reproach.

Not that that was an area in which she felt particularly confident, anyway. When it came to the bedroom department, her shortcomings were more glaring than ever—at least, as far as she was concerned. Even when she did make a move, it was with an air of defeat, as if she didn't really expect anything to come of it, anyway.

Even so, whatever tensions and insecurities had existed in their marriage all along were so much more pronounced lately that she scarcely dared think about it. How much of it was her, how much was Michael, and how much was the simple fact that they had been married for seventeen years, she didn't know.

What she did know was that Michael had become a very different person. It used to be that she was charmed to the point of infatuation by her husband's boyish face—with the intelligent green eyes, handsome features, and tousle of dark brown hair that he always wore just a bit too long in front. His expression was one of confidence that bordered on smugness.

And why shouldn't Michael Gilbert be smug? she thought whenever she looked at him without him realizing he was being watched, across a room at a party or while he was talking to someone on the telephone. After all, the good-looking, successful attorney and upstanding citizen of Lawrenceville that she was lucky enough to have as her husband had everything going for him. He was one of those people that everyone had always known would do well. Ever since high school, no one had ever doubted that with his brains, looks, and personality he couldn't help but come out on top. And so she could hardly fault him for thinking of himself in those same terms. Expecting the best, and expecting it to come easily.

Lynn Gilbert, by contrast, placed herself in an entirely different category. She was one of a breed that was growing increasingly rare. She was, in a word, a housewife. Every morning, her husband drove off to his job, her two teenaged daughters, arguing loudly, rushed off to school, and Lynn was left behind in a spacious four-bedroom house with three bathrooms, a wood-paneled basement elevated to the status of playroom, and wall-to-wall carpeting in every room except the kitchen.

And there was nothing ahead of her for the rest of the morning except breakfast dishes to stack in the dishwasher and damp towels to shove into the washing machine. With Lucy, the housekeeper, coming in three days a week to deal with making beds, shopping for food, and flicking on the countless appliances that kept the house in shipshape, there was very little for Lynn to do until four o'clock, when Beth and Chrissie came home from school, still arguing—although this time about something entirely different.

With little in the way of responsibilities to fill up her days, Lynn Gilbert did what any other self-respecting, upper-middle-class housewife would do: shop.

Every other morning, as soon as Lucy showed up at the house and began busily juggling cans of Comet and boxes of Spic and Span, Lynn climbed into her silver Toyota Camry and headed for one of the malls in the area. She preferred department stores, where the wide variety of merchandise allowed her to wander, searching for something to study and admire and perhaps buy.

When her daughters were younger, she always enjoyed browsing in the children's clothing departments, or getting some inexpensive toy that she thought one of them might like. Or she would shop for fabric, then come home and whip up new curtains for their bedrooms or skirts and jumpers for the beginning school year.

Now that they were older, however, picking out something that would suit their tastes was much more difficult. Impossible, in fact. Beth always tried to look pleased when Lynn presented her with a new blouse or the latest bestselling paperback, thanking her profusely and insisting that it was exactly what she'd been wanting—but a look of disappointment invariably showed up in her eyes. The novel was one she'd already read, the sweater was a color she hated, the belt made her look too fat. A few days later, Lynn would find the new item hidden away, stuck in the back of the closet or at the bottom of a drawer.

As for Chrissie, her reaction was also usually negative, but in a way that was much more direct.

"Oh, Mom," she would wail. "This is so *babyish*!" Or, "God, nobody's wearing these anymore!"

Without the girls to buy for, Lynn had to find other goals for her endless shopping sprees. Michael was useful in that there was always something he needed: black socks; a white shirt; on a good day, a gift for his secretary's birthday or his assistant's new baby. There was always Lynn herself, of course, but she felt guilty about spending money on herself.

That left one option: the house. She could always buy something new for the house. And so she did—frequently.

The linen closets were stuffed to ridiculous levels with sheets and towels in coordinated colors. The drawers of the dining room buffet were overflowing with place mats, tablecloths, and napkins. No fewer than six different sets of dessert dishes were stuffed into the kitchen cabinets.

Of course, she didn't need any of the things she bought. Indeed, once she got them home, she was never even certain that she liked them. Occasionally she offered one of her brand-new purchases to Lucy, who was always more than happy to take them off her hands, carrying her newest gift off like a prize won at a church drawing.

The acquisition of all these things should have made Lynn feel some sense of satisfaction, or at least security. Instead, they were like scars, visible proof of her squandered hours, her aimless days, the futility with which she was spending the bulk of her time. They filled her closets, her cupboards, her shelves, her drawers, constant reminders from which she couldn't escape.

All things considered, Lynn should have been looking forward to a break. A two-week vacation on Shelter Island, surrounded by Michael's family, "a long overdue family reunion," in her mother-in-law's words, that coincided with Ben and Pat's forty-second wedding anniversary.

Instead, she was dreading it. She always felt so inadequate in the presence of the Gilbert women. Julie, of course, was the star, the superwoman who, with her celebrity career, successful husband, and beautiful son always made her feel like a sinkful of dishwater—boring in its grayness, slovenly in its functionality, something that was best discarded.

Katy, too, was intimidating. Although she lacked her older sister's panache, she was what Lynn always thought of as colorful. A bit too loud, perhaps, a trifle outrageous in her choice of garish clothing. A lost soul. But, in her own way, a strong, independent woman, with no one to answer to except herself. Smart, too. Lynn didn't know many other people who had worked toward their Ph.D.s.

Her third sister-in-law, Barbara, was as awesome as the other two, even though she, of course, wasn't a Gilbert by birth. Lynn saw Wes's wife as an Ice Maiden: cold, impenetrable, almost inhuman in her perfection.

Then there was Pat, who Lynn always thought of as the matriarch of the family, the queen bee who summoned all the others to her side at will. A whole new set of built-in insecurities emerged whenever Lynn's mother-in-law was concerned. She felt constant pressure to please Michael's mother, to prove to her that her firstborn son hadn't made a mistake, that he hadn't married beneath him. The fact that Pat was such a cold person made the whole thing even harder. She could never help taking her formality personally, as if there were something inherent in Lynn that caused Pat to distance herself.

Besides, she couldn't stop thinking about the fact that something was wrong with her marriage. She knew Michael well enough to sense it. Some deep, dark secret was hovering overhead constantly, like a little black cloud. Coming between them, creating an impassable distance, a no-man's-land. She wished the two of them could have some time alone. These two weeks would have been the perfect time to get away—but this command performance had gotten in the way.

Well, she thought, noticing that her sinus medication had begun to take effect at least a little bit, I might as well try to relax. I've still got a couple of hours' reprieve before I become a Christian dropping in for a friendly visit at the lions' den. She took another sip of her iced tea, determined that, once again, she would try to make the best of a situation in which she had very little control.

"Hi-i-i!" she called gaily a few hours later as she waltzed into the Gilberts' summer house. "We're here! Anybody home?"

Even as she made her grand entrance, Lynn was painfully aware that her skirt was wrinkled and her shoulder-length brown hair had frizzed in the late August humidity. As if that weren't enough, the torn shopping bag she was lugging, containing a homemade chocolate layer cake and two dozen of her cinnamon-pecan buns, completed the picture. She found herself wondering why she hadn't taken the time to get her hair cut or buy a new outfit. Or at least bother to put on some makeup in the car.

Surprisingly, no one was around. But it only took her a moment to realize that on this fine Saturday afternoon, the rest of the family would be lounging on the back patio. She glanced over in that direction. There they all were, on the other side of the glass doors.

Then she heard Julie cry, "Ooh, look, everybody! Michael's here!"

The glass doors slid open and Julie stepped into the house, looking like an ad for some liquor that carried with it a sophisticated image, with her soft blond hair, cool white sundress, and icy drink in hand. "Hi, Lynn! Need any help?"

An appropriate question, Lynn thought wryly. Especially coming from Julie.

Aloud, she said, "I think Michael's got everything under control. Wait—here he comes."

Michael, carrying heavy suitcases in both hands, shoved open the front door with his shoulder. Beth and Chrissie were right behind him, both of them making a token effort to help unload the car. Beth swung a small overnight case that Lynn estimated weighed all of five pounds; Chrissie, two tennis rackets. Both girls looked surly. Lynn wondered what Julie must think of her children—especially now that Julie was a mother herself, with an appropriately darling, bright, well-behaved little boy.

But then she noticed how dramatically Chrissie's mood changed the instant she saw her aunt.

"Julie!" she cried, dropping the tennis rackets onto a bench in the foyer and scrambling toward her. "God, it's like, so great to see you. Ooh, I love your nail polish. What shade is it? Can I borrow it? And can you teach me how to French-braid my hair?"

By this point the other Gilberts were filing into the living room from the patio.

"Chrissie," Julie said, slinging a sisterly arm around her shoulders, "I'll *give* you this nail polish, if you like it that much. And I'd be happy to do your hair, the very first chance we get."

Lynn felt a stab of jealousy. Why couldn't her teenaged daughter look to her for advice on things like makeup and hair? Why couldn't *they* be buddies? After all, she, like Julie, had been a teenaged girl once.

But just looking at Julie gave her the immediate answer. Of course, Chrissie wanted to be more like Julie; who wouldn't? She was beautiful, successful, stylish. . . . Lynn smiled to herself wryly as she considered asking Julie for beauty advice herself.

Julie, I want to lighten my mousey brown hair a little. You know, get rid of the gray. Can you recommend which product to use?

Julie, no matter how carefully I plan what I'm going to

wear, I always end up feeling dowdy. Would you help me pick out some new clothes?

Julie, my husband has been acting as if I've got the plague lately. You and Brad have always seemed to have the perfect marriage. . . .

"Hey, Beth! How's it going?" Katy's loud voice broke through Lynn's ridiculous fantasy. She saw that the rest of the clan was ambling in. "Boy, kid, you must have grown at least six inches since the last time I saw you!"

"Nah, I'm still the same." Beth was obviously pleased by her favorite aunt's compliment.

"Well, anyway, it's great to see you. And Michael, you look like the centerfold of *G.Q.*, as usual. Still setting the legal world on fire down in Lawrenceville?"

Michael smiled at his youngest sister indulgently. "Hey, Katy, it's great to see you." He leaned forward and kissed her cheek. He was, at the moment, feeling much too hassled to match double-edged witticisms with her. Instead he moved on to Julie and Josh, gave them both a big hug, and then turned to his parents.

"Mom. Dad. You both look terrific. Nice tan, Dad."

Ben nodded stiffly. "Son," he pronounced formally, extending his hand for a hearty handshake. "Glad you and the family could make it."

Lynn's heart went out to her husband as she watched his expression change, almost indiscernibly, to reflect the disappointment that this reunion with Ben elicited. While she could see the love and admiration that Ben felt for his oldest son, she knew that Michael saw only that his father approached him from a distance, from the other side of some barrier that came from the belief that men kept their feelings to themselves, stashing needs and wants and insecurities underneath a shield of confidence and control.

But the moment faded almost as quickly as it had come when Pat came rushing over to give her son a big hug.

"Michael!" she sighed, sounding almost relieved. "It's so good to see you!"

It was as if Pat had forgotten that there was anyone else in the room. She saw only Michael, her eyes glowing.

"Hi, Mom." Her fervor made him a bit sheepish. For a moment, he was an eight-year-old boy, embarrassed by his mother's obvious love and concern as she showed up at the door of his classroom waving a forgotten bag lunch or a pair of galoshes.

"You must be famished," Pat went on. "Come on into the kitchen. I've made your favorite potato salad."

"With dill? Oh, great! I'll tell you, I could use something to drink, too."

"We've got beer on ice, and soda and lemonade. . . . Come on into the kitchen. I'll make you some lunch."

Their arms around each other, mother and son sauntered into the kitchen, with Pat exclaiming over how wonderful he looked and how happy she was to see him.

No matter what happens, Lynn thought as she watched the two of them disappear into the other room, Michael will always be perfect, as far as his mother is concerned.

Instead of being happy for her husband, however, that thought made Lynn feel even more dejected than she had all day.

Chapter Seven

Saturday evening was cool, more like spring than summer. The air was light, not at all clouded by the steaminess that often plagues Long Island. Everywhere there were bright primary colors, like a kindergarten classroom: green grass, yellow sunshine, blue water. It was as if even Mother Nature were anxious for the Gilberts' family barbecue to be a success.

Pat was in her element. While it was Ben who was in charge of cooking the steaks over the burning coals, it was she who orchestrated all the other details of the dinner for twelve. She had spent the better part of the day preparing food: enough crudités for an Italian wedding; a cauldron of the dilled potato salad that, up until the dinner hour, only her son Michael had been privileged enough to sample; and feathery baking-powder biscuits, more like little clouds than something as ordinary as food.

As the dinner hour approached, marked by the delicious smells that began emanating from the barbecue that Ben was tending, she left the more mundane tasks like setting the table to Chrissie and Beth. Pat, meanwhile, dramatically paraded out to the patio with her culinary creations, allowing time for each to be applauded before bringing out the next.

"Anything I can do to help?" Julie asked, coming out through the sliding doors with Josh in her arms. For the occasion, she had dressed her son in a blue-and-white-striped seersucker sunsuit made from the same fabric as the sundress she was wearing.

"No, dear. My, don't you two look darling! No, I've got everything under control, thanks to my two little helpers."

Beth, busily folding yellow paper napkins, looked over at her grandmother and beamed. Chrissie, meanwhile, rolled her eyes and went back to her slow-motion sorting of knives, forks, and spoons, her reluctant movements punctuated periodically by loud, resentful sighs.

"Besides," Pat went on, "you've got Josh to deal with. Why don't you go sit down and help yourself to some of my herb dip? I don't think you've had it before."

After stopping off for a polite taste of something she was certain was dangerously fattening, Julie gracefully lowered herself into the empty deck chair next to Lynn. From where she was sitting, Julie could keep an eye on Josh, who was absorbed in marveling over the thick green moss he had just come across at the edge of Pat's flower bed.

"So, Lynn, how have you been?"

Lynn, already having run out of things to say to her in-laws, had been hiding there at the edge of the patio, hoping to blend in with the scenery so that no one would call upon her to be scintillating. Self-consciously she swallowed the half-chewed piece of cauliflower in her mouth. "Oh, fine. Everything's fine."

Panicked, she searched for something more interesting to report. Let's see: I signed up for an adult education course in CPR at the local public high school, since the classes in both low-impact aerobics and quilting were filled. I got rave reviews from everyone, even Chrissie, with the new baked-chicken-with-tarragon recipe I found in *Redbook*. Last week my hairdresser told me that I have very few gray hairs for a woman of thirty-nine. . . .

But somehow, none of these events seemed worth reporting to a woman whose daily "routine" consisted of talking to the rich, the famous, and the important, all under the adoring eyes of millions of television viewers all over the New York metropolitan area.

So the best she could come up with was, "Michael's been working really hard lately." Lynn smiled apologetically, aware of how pathetic it was that the best she could come up with was a boring comment about her husband.

"Poor Michael! And here comes the workhorse now."

Michael strolled onto the patio just then, he and Brad having just taken a tour of the shrubs and trees that they knew were Ben's pride and joy.

"Yeah, well, there's been a lot going on at the office lately," Michael was saying. "I've been spending so much time there lately that I'm thinking of setting up a cot in my office."

"Ah, yes. We know all about the workaholic syndrome," Julie commented lightly. She made a point of not looking at her husband.

Brad, however, was busy making himself another drink. His third in the last hour, or perhaps his fourth, Julie noted with chagrin. She decided just to ignore him, hoping, of course, that he kept his mouth shut and didn't ruin this family gathering. At the moment, at least, he seemed content to leer at Chrissie's curvacious nymphet body, displayed a bit too well by the girl's clingy peach-colored tank top and her peach-and-white, Hawaiian-print short-shorts.

Back in my day, Julie thought wryly, we referred to those as "hot pants." She turned back to Lynn, this time determined to have a real conversation with her.

Katy, meanwhile, was out in front, using the pretext of the patch of flowers along the driveway desperately needing weeding as an excuse to avoid her family for at least a little while longer. The little scene between her and her mother, earlier that morning, still left a bad taste in her mouth. Sure, she'd get over it. But for now, she still needed more time to cool down.

When she heard the distinctive sound of tires crunching against the gravel in the circular driveway, she automatically looked up, wondering as she did if perhaps it was Randy. But, she was pleased to discover, it was someone even better than that.

"Wes!" Katy dropped the trowel and scrambled to her feet. "Hey, Wes! Wes!" She ran over to his car, a snazzy dark blue Volvo, as it rounded the bend of the driveway and came to a halt.

"Katy!" Wesley climbed out of the car and gave his younger sister a big hug. "It's so great to see you! How the hell are you?"

"I'm terrific!" She returned his hug enthusiastically. "Hey, nice car. Looks new. Expensive, too."

Wesley laughed self-consciously. "The computer business has been good to me."

"See that? Being a brain has finally paid off."

"You mean being a *nerd* has paid off." Affectionately he slung his arm around Katy's shoulders.

"Hey, where's Barbara?" For the first time since she'd spotted him, the fact that his wife wasn't with him had registered.

"Oh, uh, that's sort of a long story. She's kind of tied up with this big deal she's been working on for weeks. You know those financial types. Something's always about to break."

"That's too bad." Secretly, Katy was pleased. She always got the feeling that Barbara didn't really like her. Or at least that she didn't approve of her. Besides, this way she would have Wes all to herself for a while. "Is she coming out soon?"

"I, uh, don't know. It depends on her job."

"Oh, you yuppies. Busy, busy, busy," Katy quipped. "But listen, I bet everybody's dying to see you. We're having this huge barbecue tonight, so you're just in time. Can I help you carry anything?"

"Nah, I'll get it all later. I'm anxious to go say hi to everybody."

As they rounded the corner of the house and approached the patio, a round of surprised and enthusiastic greetings welcomed Wesley.

"Wes! You made it!"

After the inevitable hugs, questions about the trip down from Boston, and comments about how healthy he was looking these days, the issue of his absent wife predictably arose once again.

"Where's Barbara?" his mother asked, glancing over his shoulder as if he were perhaps hiding her somewhere.

"She, uh, got tied up."

"So she's coming later?" Pat persisted.

"She's not sure. It depends on whether or not she can get away. . . ."

"But surely whatever's got her occupied can't keep her in Boston for two whole weeks!"

Katy couldn't help smiling. She couldn't tell if her mother's outburst of disappointment was rooted in sincere regret over her daughter-in-law's absence, or something much more trivial, like the possibility that there might be one individual serving of chocolate mousse unaccounted for, or a hand-lettered place card rendered useless. She suspected it was the latter: Pat and Barbara had always been civil enough to each other, but with both women naturally aloof, there was very little opportunity for anything even vaguely resembling warmth to develop between them.

"I'm sure she'll show up within a few days," Wes assured her.

"How about something cold to drink, Wes?" Lynn smiled at him shyly. She had always liked Wesley, finding him the least threatening member of the entire Gilbert family. While he was successful in every sense of the word, he was the kind of person who never used his own achievements to set himself apart from others. Instead, he was friendly, down-to-earth—one of the few people with whom she felt she could be herself.

The other Gilbert with whom Lynn felt comfortable came over just then and slung his arm around Lynn's shoulders.

"Let me take care of that," said Ben, giving her a fatherly squeeze. "What was that old McDonald's commercial? 'You deserve a break today'? You spend enough time taking care of other people's needs."

Lynn smiled at him gratefully. Maybe this family reunion wasn't going to be so dreadful, after all. . . .

"Now, we're all here," said Pat, beaming as she looked fondly at the crowd surrounding her. "Let's dig in, shall we?"

As she shepherded Chrissie and Wes and Lynn toward the copious display of food, laid out buffet-style, she added, "All the Gilberts, together again. Oh, isn't it marvelous? I just know that for the next two weeks, we're all going to have a wonderful time!"

I'm having a *lousy* time, thought Beth grumpily. Sure, all the old folks are happy to hang around, shooting the breeze for hours on end and drinking like fish. And Chrissie will manage; she always does. In fact, she'll probably have found a new best friend by the end of the day or something.

But the prospects for a thirteen-year-old girl were pretty paltry. Beth was too young to drive anywhere, too old to be content just hanging around the house. And given the way she looked in a bathing suit, she wasn't about to make a habit of catching rays at the beach, either.

There was always sailing, of course. Nowadays, she was just about old enough to start playing around with her grandfather's Sunfish, a thirteen-foot lateen-rigged dinghy just big enough for one or two, or the faster Lightning, another small sailboat. But being uncoordinated as well as chubby made that option unattractive, too.

Good thing I brought a suitcase full of books, she thought. Already she was wondering if the dozen paperbacks she'd packed were going to last her the next fifteen days.

Besides, hiding from the world inside the pages of a book wasn't something she could get away with twenty-four hours a day. Like right now, for instance. Everybody in the entire family was out on the patio, trying to look like they were enjoying themselves. And Beth was expected to put in an appearance, if not actually manage to make it look as if she were having a good time, too.

But no one was about to miss her if she slipped away for just a couple of minutes. She wanted to see if the rock garden she had built the summer before was still around, over on the side of the house near the Burtises'. Maybe it wasn't much—just a bunch of stupid rocks and shells she had thought were kind of neat-looking at the time—but it would be fun if they were still there. Like a sign that Beth Gilbert had passed through here, making her mark, however small, on the world.

She ambled around the corner of the house, preparing herself for the fact that she might well find nothing left of the project that had obsessed her the summer before, after she'd gone through every book in the house and learned the hard way that Shelter Island didn't have a bookstore. But then she spotted it: almost one hundred rocks and seashells, some speckled, some white and smooth, some delicate shades of pink and lavender and cream, arranged like one of the images from a kaleidoscope, there in the middle of the strip of flower beds that ran the length of the Gilberts' house.

"Oh, wow!" she breathed aloud, scurrying over to get a better look.

"Hey, what'd you find over there, buried treasure?"

Beth whirled around, startled by the unexpected sound of a voice she didn't recognize—and embarrassed at having been caught off-guard. Over on the other side of the low hedges, in the driveway of the Burtises' house, was a tall, lean young man washing a car. She could feel her cheeks growing as red as the back fender he was hosing down as she took in the easy grin, the sandy blond hair that needed cutting, the expanse of tanned male flesh scarcely covered by the only clothes he was wearing: a bleached-out pair of cutoff jeans.

"What are you looking at?" he said.

It wasn't clear to Beth if he was referring to the rock garden—or to him. At any rate, she remained tongue-tied.

But the boy didn't seem to be bothered by her reticence. "You're Beth, aren't you? I guess you don't remember me. I'm Danny Burtis. I was away at camp the last couple of summers, but you and I used to hang around together, back when we were both little kids."

"Sure, I remember you." That is, she did now. Up until he'd explained who he was, Beth had found it impossible to link up the gawky boy next door she used to play with and this mature—and in her eyes, Adonis-like—creature. He was older, Chrissie's age, in fact, yet he had always singled Beth out, recognizing in her right from the start a kindred spirit. Besides, her big sister never could be bothered with him, a fact that had always been just fine as far as Beth was concerned.

"Then I guess you remember that time we caught those two frogs and stuck 'em inside your sister's top drawer."

"Sure, I remember that." Beth chuckled. Yes, that was back in the old days, when she had actually had fun while visiting her grandparents out on Shelter Island. She and Danny had spent practically every day together. Going into business with a Kool-Aid stand that earned them each a total of about seven cents. Putting together model airplanes from the kits Danny always had on hand. Gunkholing in his parents' dilapidated old wooden rowboat, the predecessor of their new motorboat, packing a lunch in the morning and taking to the seas together in search of pirates, adventure—and buried treasure. "Yeah, we had a lot of fun together, didn't we?"

"We sure did. Hey, come on over and help me wash this car, will ya?"

"I can't." Woefully Beth looked back over her shoulder. Everyone in her family had just burst into laughter at some comment she couldn't hear—probably something cute her sister had just said. "Well, maybe for just a couple of minutes . . ."

"So how've you been, Beth?" Danny was still busy with

the car, scrubbing some unseen dirt off the roof, but he managed to glance over at Beth and wink.

She felt as if her heart was about to burst as she stood nervously on the edge of the driveway, so overcome with adoration that her usual shyness had expanded into a state bordering on catatonia.

"I'm fine."

"That's good. Are you out here with your whole family?" Beth nodded.

"Oh, yeah? So your sister's here, too, huh?"

"Yeah, Chrissie's here." Beth grimaced, but Danny's face was turned away and he didn't notice.

"I bet she's pretty grown up by now. She's about sixteen, right?"

"Sixteen's not too old to get frogs put in your top drawer."

Danny chuckled. "We'll see about that," he commented mysteriously, almost as if he were talking to himself.

"Boy, you sure look a lot different," Beth ventured bravely.

Danny laughed again. "Yeah, would you believe I've grown six inches in the last year and a half? I'm almost as tall as my dad now." He tossed the hose across the lawn and stood back to admire his handiwork. "There. Looks pretty good, don't you think? Hey, how about coming inside for a Coke? I bet my mother'd be thrilled to see you."

"Thanks, but I'd better get back. We're having this big family thing tonight."

"Oh, I see. Okay, then, I guess I'll be seeing you around, Beth." Flashing another one of the smiles that turned Beth's plump knees to water, Danny waved and disappeared into the garage.

"Oh, by the way," Pat said casually as she joined Chrissie in clearing the table. Dinner was over, and it was time to bring out the juicy husks of watermelon, the homemade vanilla ice cream, and the apple pies warmed in the microwave. "Did I tell you that Danny Burtis asked me about you last week?"

"Who on *earth* is Danny Burtis?" Despite the surliness of her tone, Chrissie's ears pricked up. Even though she didn't know who her grandmother was talking about, the fact remained that he was a boy. And he had been asking about her. . . . He automatically got points for that.

"You remember Danny. His family lives right next door.

Why, he used to play with Beth, back when they were both kids.''

"Oh, *that* guy.'' Already the sparkle had disappeared from her clear blue eyes, their color echoed by a smudge of blue eye shadow worn exactly the same way as the model on the cover of that month's issue of *Glamour*.

"Now, now, Chrissie, don't write him off entirely," Pat scolded cheerfully. "It just so happens that Danny has grown up into a fine young man. Why, he's almost six feet tall, and quite good-looking. And is he smart! His mother told me he wants to go to Carnegie-Mellon, to major in electrical engineering. . . .''

"What's this?'' Julie came over then, carrying a cup of coffee in one hand and a tiny slice of watermelon in the other. "Did I hear someone say something about a potential romance? . . .''

"No.'' Chrissie cast her a desperate look. "Grandma's trying to match me up with this—this *nerd* next door!''

"Hey, if he's the guy with the blond hair and the cute legs I noticed washing the car a few minutes ago, I'd check him out!''

Chrissie just rolled her eyes. It was true that she had her eye out for someone—especially now, ever since she'd come up with her brainstorm. She'd had an idea that would impress everyone. *Especially* Heather. And finding a boy was certainly a key step in carrying it out. But she was after much bigger game than some egghead from next door. She wanted someone older. Someone *cooler*. And, most important, someone with some real experience.

But before she had a chance to register even further protestations, she was distracted.

"Attention! Attention, fellow Gilberts!''

Chrissie and the others glanced up as they heard someone banging a spoon against a glass. Wesley was standing at the edge of the patio, obviously trying to get their attention. Everyone else looked interested; Chrissie was just bored. She noticed Beth coming around the corner, her cheeks so flushed that she wondered what she could have possibly been up to. She watched with disgust as her sister headed straight for the table, hesitated as if torn, and then cut herself a huge slice of apple pie and topped it with an obscene glob of ice cream before sitting on a chaise lounge over at the back corner of the patio where she was least apt to be noticed.

"Now that I've got you all enraptured," Wes went on, "I am pleased to announce our guest speaker for the evening. Ben Gilbert needs no introduction."

"Wesley, when I asked you to help me get some attention, this isn't exactly what I had in mind." Ben looked rather sheepish as he stood up, right behind his son. He even seemed a bit nervous.

He cleared his throat loudly. "You know," he began, looking at all the members of his family one by one as he spoke, "getting you all together like this is the best darned idea I've had in ages. And this is coming from a guy whose *job* it is to think up good ideas!

"But, seriously, I only wish it hadn't taken me so long to make sure you all got out here at the same time. Oh, sure, you've all been straggling in over the years, a week here, a week there. But except for a couple of days every Christmas, this is the first time we've all been under one roof in as long as I can remember. And to be perfectly honest," he went on, his eyes becoming clouded for a moment, "I hope we start making this a family tradition—one that's long overdue."

"Hear, hear!" Michael clinked his coffee cup with a spoon, and everyone laughed.

"Now that I've got all the mushy stuff out of the way, as Chrissie would say, I'll get to the point. I know you all well enough to realize that you'd much rather be digging into Pat's homemade ice cream than listening to me. But the truth is, I got you all out here for more than just a family reunion."

By now, everyone was listening closely. Even Josh, silently gorging himself on the tiny spoonfuls of ice cream that Beth kept feeding him, seemed to recognize that something important was going on around him.

"I guess you're all aware that the old man is sixty-two years old now—"

"And getting better every year!" Pat interrupted with a smile.

"Hear, hear!" This time, several spoons were clinked against coffee cups.

"I sure hope so! Anyway, I'm getting to the point where I'm realizing that I'm not going to be around to head up Benjamin Gilbert Associates forever. It's a thriving company, one I'm really proud of. Hell, you all know that. But what's occurred to me lately is that I'd better start looking for somebody to take over. After all, I'm getting to an age where I'm starting to look forward to a long, happy retirement.

"The point is, it would really mean a lot to me if one of you were interested in coming into the business with me." He looked around again, at Michael, at Wes, at his daughters, at Brad and Lynn. "Sure, I know you've all got your own lives to lead. Your own careers, your own families . . . But if I could pass the baton to another Gilbert—well, I think you can guess that nothing would make me happier.

"And now—enough of the serious stuff! That ice cream must be starting to melt something fierce by now. That is, if Beth and Josh have left any for the rest of us!"

Loud talking and laughing erupted from Ben's audience then, as descending upon the dessert and coffee became the top priority. Even so, the significance of his words did not go unheeded.

Chapter Eight

"**S**o, tell me, Julie. What did you think of Dad's little speech last night?" Michael's mouth was twisted into a wry smile as he bent slightly at the waist and prepared to tee off.

Although it was barely past seven on this Sunday morning, the Gardiner's Bay golf course was already crowded. Michael and the rest of the foursome—Julie, Brad, and Ben—had been lucky that they'd forced themselves out of bed and out of the house early.

True, they'd had to ignore the slight hangovers that reminded them that the family barbecue of the night before had dissipated into a wild beer bash. All four of them, as well as most of the others, had stayed up into the wee hours, swatting at mosquitoes and laughing hilariously at the most ridiculous things. Then, the crowd suddenly thinned out around one, when the diehards—including these four—finally settled down for a raucous game of Trivial Pursuit.

"Aha!" Michael cried, shielding his eyes from the early morning sun with his hand. "Right down the middle of the fairway! Not bad for somebody who hasn't played golf in, what is it, a whole year now?"

"Not bad at all," Julie agreed. "Guess I'm up next. But brace yourself. I'm not promising much, since I can't even remember the last time I held a golf club in my hand."

"Good," her older brother countered. "That'll make it that much easier for me to win."

"Wait a minute. Don't get carried away, Michael, dear. You know what they say—'It ain't over 'til it's over.'

"But let's get back to your question," she continued, anxious to finish the conversation her brother had started but lowering her voice so that their father wouldn't overhear. Fortunately, at the moment Brad was monopolizing his father-in-law, trying to impress him, as usual, with what a high roller he was in the real estate world, pulling off this coup and buying that piece of property for a song and bettering this guy in that deal.

"I guess I'm not that surprised by what Dad said," Julie went on. "After all, he is in kind of a spot. Sure, he wants to hand the family business over to one of us. The problem is, I can't see that any of us *wants* it. I, for one, am much too involved in my own career to have time for anything that demanding."

"And I'm a lawyer, not a businessman."

"Wes would be a natural, but he's got his hands full with his high-tech computer business. I certainly don't think he's willing to give that up."

"Guess that leaves Katy." Michael grinned. "Think she's ready to tackle Corporate America?"

Julie was hurt on her little sister's behalf, and she automatically rushed to her defense. "It's possible. She's got a good head on her shoulders, don't forget."

"Yeah, too bad she never managed to figure out what to do with it."

Before Julie had a chance to reply, Michael called to his father, "Come on, Dad! Better tee off before we get into a gang war with those guys coming up behind us. Here, want to use my driver?"

It wasn't until the fourth hole that Ben managed to hone in on the conversation that Michael and Julie had been having.

"I couldn't help overhearing your conversation," he said casually. "About B.G.A., I mean."

"Oh, yeah." Michael glanced over at his brother-in-law, who was taking a few practice strokes with a three-iron in preparation for his turn. Brad was winning—not that surprising, since he was approaching this game as if it were a life-or-death situation rather than a friendly family excursion, a chance to get out of the house and get a bit of exercise. But then again, Brad Kane was someone who approached everything he did with that same attitude. "And here I thought old Brad was talking your ear off."

Ben smiled. "I have X-ray hearing. At least, when it comes to my children."

"Ah. So then you heard me when I told Julie here that I wasn't cut out to be a businessman. At least, not at this point in my life."

Ben fixed his gaze on the fourth hole, some four hundred yards away, pretending to watch where Brad's ball was heading. "You know, Michael, I never told you this before, but back when you graduated from Williams, I was kind of hoping you'd express an interest in coming to work at B.G.A."

Michael kept his eyes on Brad's golf ball, as well. Julie, meanwhile, feigned interest in the scenery, even though she was taking in every word.

"Yeah," said Michael, "I remember having the feeling at the time that that was what you wanted me to do."

"Of course, I was anxious for you to pick whatever made you happy. Medical school, law school, whatever. It's just that I *hoped* . . ."

"I know, Dad. Sure, I thought about it. I mean, it did occur to me that it would have been one of the easiest things for me to do."

"Oh, I wouldn't have made it easy for you, Michael." It was Ben's turn then, and he paused long enough to slice one into the woods. He muttered under his breath, then turned to his son, wearing a grin. "But at any rate, I don't mind telling you I was a little bit disappointed. After all, you were the oldest, and I'd always expected great things from you. . . . Everybody did."

Ben's honesty was coming as a surprise to Julie. While father and daughter had always been close, she knew that Ben and Michael had always maintained a certain formality. Yet here was Ben, confessing a twenty-year-old resentment, something that had been troubling him for all these years, something that Michael hadn't even suspected. . . .

"I hope I didn't disappoint any of my fans." Michael's comment was offhanded as usual, one of the glib responses that appeared to be habit by now. Julie felt sorry for her father.

But Ben didn't seem to be offended in the least.

"Well, I'd better go track down that ball," Ben said, nodding at Julie as if to say he knew perfectly well that he was releasing his son from a topic of conversation that, for some reason, suddenly seemed to be making him uncomfortable. "Just remember, Michael. It's never too late to make a change. I think you'd make a great businessman. At least think about it, will you?"

Before Michael had a chance to respond, Brad came sauntering over.

"Come on, guys, you going to play golf or you going to stand around watching the grass grow?" He slapped his father-in-law on the back.

Julie looked over at Michael and saw that he actually looked relieved.

"Yeah, Brad," he replied, picking up his driver so he could play the seventh hole. "Let's play golf."

The redwood deck on the second floor of the Gilberts' summer house offered a magnificent view of West Neck Bay, a popular spot with the owners of sailboats. On a day like this, when the sun was bright, the humidity down, and the breeze perfect, they were out in impressive numbers, their graceful vessels gliding lazily across the waves. The red and blue and yellow sails of Sunfishes and Hobi Cats, along with the smaller splashes of color atop sailboards, were like bright birds, their fiery plumage set off by a backdrop of tranquil blue.

Just gazing out at the water was relaxing—hypnotizing, even. Katy could feel herself being lured into a delicious dazed state as she lay across a chaise lounge, her eyes fixed on the spectacular view. She had decided over breakfast that soaking up some of the intense August sun—after having conscientiously lathered up with sun block Number Eight, of course—was the best way to spend this Sunday morning. She had made a point of not making any plans and, in fact, relished the idea of total freedom as she watched some of her heartier kin trek off to the golf course for some physical exertion.

She was still considering this afternoon's social event: an excursion to the beach, "just us girls," as her mother had quipped. But for now, she had decided that it was high time she started cultivating the fine art of doing absolutely nothing. And so the latest issue of *Newsweek* lay on the deck beside her, along with a stack of the mail-order catalogues that seemed to accumulate in her mother's house like dust. Instead of forcing herself to be productive, she was just letting her mind wander.

She was about to construct another one of her fantasies, this one involving that new guy she'd run across yesterday, that Randy Palmer, when one of the glass doors leading into the house was slid open. Her brother Wes emerged, dressed in a navy blue sport shirt and a pair of cutoffs. And, she was pleased to see, he was carrying two tall glasses of lemonade.

"If you're planning to get serious about this sun-bunny business," he said, deadpan, "I suggest that you keep in mind the vital importance of replenishing one's supply of liquids. After all," he added, "the idea is to look gorgeous, not prune-ish."

"Ah, my savior." Greedily Katy reached for one of the glasses. "Your timing is perfect. I was just beginning to notice a purple tinge around my fingers and toes. The first signs of prune-hood, if my science training serves me correctly."

She took a huge gulp, then said, "Seriously, though. Pull up a chair—or a beach towel, if you're so inclined—and keep me company. I'm finding out that it's kind of boring, doing nothing."

"So I've heard." Wes sat down on the edge of her chaise lounge. "Well, it looks as if things are going pretty well for you these days."

"Well enough, I suppose." Katy eyed her brother critically. She was getting the feeling that there was something on his mind, something he wanted to talk about other than this mindless small talk. "How about you, Wes? Everything hunky-dory up in old Beantown?"

Wes glanced over at her for a second, then fixed his gaze on the rim of his lemonade glass. "Not exactly. You know, uh, I wasn't exactly telling the truth when I told everybody last night that it was business that was keeping Barbara in Boston." He was trying to sound casual, but his voice was strangely thick.

"Oh, really? Don't tell me good old Barbara has taken a lover or something."

The look on her brother's face immediately made Katy regret what she had meant to be a joke.

"Hey, I was just kidding." She stared at her brother intently. "Wes, are you two having some kind of problem?"

"Yeah, I guess you could say that." Wes still kept his eyes

down, feigning interest in the ice cubes that were bobbing around in his drink. "She's left me, Katy."

"What?" Katy sat upright. "What are you talking about?"

"You heard me. She moved out."

"Whoa. Wait a minute." By now she had realized that her brother could well be refusing to meet her gaze because there were tears in his eyes. "What happened exactly, Wes? Can you tell me about it?"

There was a long pause, as if Wes were trying to regain his composure before going on.

"Well, I thought things were fine. You know, we'd both fallen into a pretty comfortable routine. We'd get up early every morning and rush out of the house, put in long days at our jobs. . . . By the time we got home at night, we were pretty bushed.

"Even so, we always managed to find the time—and the energy—to really *talk* to each other, you know? All about the stuff that had happened to us during the day, office politics and all that. . . . Hell, sometimes it felt like we were best friends more than anything else."

Katy felt a twinge of jealousy just listening to her brother describe the relationship he had with his spouse. But then she reminded herself that all was not quite so sunny—at least, not anymore. She kept silent, anxious for him to go on.

"We felt like we had it all, Katy. I mean, *I* did, anyway." He laughed self-consciously. "I guess Barbara didn't."

"Hey, I'm sure it's just a temporary thing," Katy insisted with false heartiness. "It'll blow over. Every marriage has its rough spots, from what I understand. What happened? Did you two have an argument?"

"Hardly. As a matter of fact, I had taken her out to the Parker House for dinner. It was her birthday, three and a half weeks ago." Wes took a deep breath. "Before I got to the part about how I felt it was high time we went away on a little vacation together, that we should spend some time away from our jobs and all that day-to-day stuff so we could just *relax* for a change, she told me it was all over between us, that she'd be gone by the next morning.

"And sure enough," he finished, his voice heavy, "she was."

"Hey, she was just upset about something. That kind of thing happens to everybody sometimes. You get to the point where you just can't take your own life anymore, and so you need to find a way to take a break.''

"She was so matter-of-fact about it that it made my blood run cold.'' Wes swallowed hard. "You should have heard her. It's funny; I've always admired Barbara for being so logical. So much in control. She's great at thinking things through and then drawing the right conclusion. I guess I always figured it was something she and I had in common. That the two of us thought the same way and that was why we got along so well.

"But while I was sitting there at the dinner table in this posh restaurant, staring at the bottle of French champagne I'd just ordered and listening to her saying she had to go, that it was the only thing for her to do, sounding as if she were telling some—some *client* that his stock had just split or something . . .''

"Mom know about this?'' Katy's voice was gentle, but in reality she was feeling frustrated by her inability to be consoling. It was apparent that Wes was upset—and that he had every right to be. It sounded as if Barbara really meant business—yet she couldn't think of a single thing to say. Continuing to insist that she would be back would sound hollow; telling Wes that he'd get over it would sound as if she were already resigned to the failure of what Wes had obviously thought was a very satisfactory marriage. So suggesting that he enlist the aid of someone else—anyone else—seemed like a much safer bet than making her brother feel even worse.

"No, I haven't told Mom,'' Wes said softly. "Actually, I'm kind of afraid to. I think she'd feel really bad.''

Hah! thought Katy. What he's afraid of is that she'd end up blaming the whole thing on him. And to be perfectly honest, I'd be afraid of the same thing.

"As a matter of fact,'' Wes went on, "I haven't told anybody except you.''

"Aw, Wes.'' Katy reached over and hugged her brother. He put his arms around her, too, and the two of them stayed locked together for a long time.

"I'm so sorry,'' she said, her voice muffled as she kept her face pressed against his shoulder. "I wish there were something I could do. . . . Look, why don't you just give it some time? It's still possible that everything will work itself out. There's always a chance of that.''

As she continued to hold him, she kept wishing there were something she could do or say that would help, and her inability to put things right for him frustrated her. But at the same time, she couldn't help looking at her brother's sadness from her own perspective.

Poor Wes—but at least it's not me, she thought. See that? There *are* some benefits that come with being a loner. Here's just one more example of why it's better not to take a chance with that crazy little thing called love. Wes and Barbara were always like some kind of perfect couple or something; even Wes thought so. But now, it turns out that there's trouble.

This was not the first time Katy felt relieved—and lucky— that she was exempt from this kind of heartache.

Chapter Nine

"*C*ome on, Beth! By the time we get to the beach, the *sun's* gonna go down!"

"I'm coming, Chrissie," Beth called downstairs crossly.

It was Sunday afternoon and, over lunch, the female contingent of the Gilbert clan—with the addition of Josh—had concluded that, just as Pat had suggested, going to the beach would be the ideal way to spend the rest of the day.

Now it was time to leave. Everyone was gathered by the front door, bathing suits donned, suntan lotion packed, towels folded—everyone, that is, except Beth. She was still upstairs in the bedroom that she and her sister had been sharing with their Aunt Katy, staring morosely at her reflection in the full-length mirror that lined the back of the door.

What she longed to see staring back at her was a lithe, tanned, teenaged girl with long blond hair and a perfect complexion. A younger version of Chrissie. What she actually saw, however, was enough to bring tears to her eyes—which was precisely what happened. Because looking back at her was a butterball. A *short* butterball, no less, complete with bulging thighs, a thick waist, and a round protruding stomach made even more pronounced by the pink one-piece bathing suit that was stretched around the expansive flesh, girlish and cute with its small white polka dots and a ridiculous ruffle around the hips. Then there was the limp brown hair that did nothing but hang down lethargically around her shoulders, a startling contrast to her pasty white skin.

I know; I won't go to the beach, Beth decided then and there. I simply won't go. Especially since Danny Burtis could be there. Besides, nobody will care—not really. I'll just tell Chrissie and Katy and everybody else to go without me. I'll say I'm not feeling good. Or else I'll just say that I'd rather stay home and read. . . .

"Be-eth, come *on!*" Chrissie squealed. "God, you're always making us late for *everything!*"

That did it. Now that she had been accused of holding everyone up, she *had* to go. Desperately Beth wiped away her tears with her fists, then grabbed the man-sized white T-shirt she had brought along for an occasion just like this one. She knew it wouldn't really hide anything. But at least it would make her feel better.

Someday, Beth thought as she raced down the stairs tugging at the hem of the shirt in a futile effort at making it cover up even more of her than it already was, someday, I'll show them all—Julie, Mom, Grandma, and especially Chrissie. I'll be thin, and beautiful, and I'll dye my hair blond, and I'll be famous and successful and make lots and lots of money, and there'll be a hundred guys in love with me, rock stars and famous movie actors and millionaires. . . .

She expected her older sister to grumble about her slowness for the rest of the day, or at least as they all walked over to Crescent Beach. Fortunately, Chrissie had already forgotten about it. She was too busy showing off her new bikini, turquoise blue and so skimpy that its purchase had precipitated a huge fight with her mother. Meanwhile, she was totally monopolizing Julie, chattering away a mile a minute, telling her all about the fabulous tan she'd been working on all summer and how these two weeks were her last chance to get even darker so she'd look great when school started.

These two headed their little parade, with Josh between them, plastic sand pail and shovel in hand as he eagerly let them lead him off to the giant sandbox he loved so much. Behind them strolled Beth's mother and her grandmother, lugging bright canvas tote bags.

Beth chose to walk halfway between the two groups as they all tromped down the road toward the beach like a caravan of African natives, once again lost in her daydreams about what a wonderful creature she would be one day, when she grew up. She expected to walk the entire way to the beach alone, and so she was surprised when Katy, who had been trailing way behind, caught up with her.

"Hey, kiddo, glad you finally got around to joining us!" she said with a grin.

"I'm *sorry*!" Beth lashed out. "I can't help it if I'm slow sometimes! Gosh, will everybody just get off my case for a change?"

"Hey! I was only kidding, Beth! Don't get so upset!" Katy held up her hands, signifying her surrender. "It's just me, remember? Your old pal, Katy?"

"Sorry." This time Beth's apology was rueful. "It's just that—oh, I don't know. My stupid sister is always making me feel as if there's something terribly wrong with me." She glanced over at her aunt. "Oh, you wouldn't understand."

Katy snorted. "Are you kidding? You're talking to another younger sister, remember? Believe me, I know *exactly* what you're saying."

"You do?" Beth blinked. "You mean Julie used to make you feel bad sometimes?"

Katy was silent for a minute. She was remembering all the times that Julie had made her feel inferior, just in the same way that Chrissie had the power to affect Beth. By making her feel fat, slow—as if she were *not good enough*. More often than not, it wasn't even intentional. Just by witnessing Julie being Julie, Katy had felt inadequate, constantly comparing herself and invariably coming in second.

Yes, she knew what Beth was feeling. More, probably, than the younger girl would ever know.

"Listen," she said, her voice suddenly soft. "Today is a gorgeous day, and the first real day of this vacation of ours. How about if you and I forget all about big sisters for now? Instead, let's talk about something pleasant. Something fun."

"Okay. Like what?"

Katy's mind raced. What could she talk to her thirteen-year-old niece about? Not clothes, not boys, not school, not food—what was left?

"Movies. Let's talk about movies. What's the best film you saw this summer?"

By the way Beth brightened, she knew she had hit upon the right topic. The two of them immediately became absorbed in an animated discussion, with Beth relating the plot of the last movie she'd seen, one whose story had centered around having as many teenagers murdered, as creatively and gorily as possible, within the space of two action-filled hours.

"So, Lynn," Pat began conversationally, hoping she sounded friendly.

She always found it such a strain, trying to make conversation with her older son's wife. There was something so—so timid about her. It was as if she lived in constant fear that something—or someone—were going to pounce on her. Whenever she did talk to her, Pat found herself proceeding with great caution, acting as if talking too loudly or too quickly, or even making a statement that was the least bit controversial, might cause her to burst into tears.

"I'll bet this is a nice break for you. Getting away from home, I mean." She sighed as she passed her canvas bag from one hand to the other. It was a bit too heavy for her, but she wasn't about to admit that to the younger woman. "Living in a house with two teenaged girls can be quite trying."

"I can manage them all right," Lynn said defensively. "Why? Has Michael said anything?"

"Why, no, dear." As always, Pat ended up feeling like a great lioness attacking a poor, vulnerable zebra. And she was only trying to make conversation. "I just meant that—well, it seems as if Chrissie is going through a rather difficult stage right now. She's so wrapped up in herself these days!"

Just like her father, Lynn thought, biting her lip. And knowing that she could never, ever say the smallest negative thing about Michael. Not to his mother. No, he was her pride and joy. Perhaps Lynn needed to talk to someone about the unrest she had been feeling lately—but that "someone" was definitely not her mother-in-law.

Not when Lynn suspected that the reason for all the peculiar changes in her husband's behavior as of late were due to the fact that he was having an affair. That had to be it. She had figured the whole thing out: he had gotten tired of her, finally recognizing her weaknesses, once and for all seeing what she really was.

Besides, what else could it possibly be? All the signs were certainly there: the way he acted so distant all the time, withdrawing into himself, hardly showing any interest at all in making love. . . .

Not that there were any definite indications, of course. No hastily scribbled telephone numbers discovered as she went through his pants pockets on her way to the cleaners; no late-night telephone calls behind closed doors; no mysterious listings on the MasterCard bill made at fancy restaurants or florists or jewelers.

No, it was all just a hunch. But after living with someone for seventeen years, weren't one's hunches virtually foolproof?

She tried to put aside the uneasiness she felt just thinking about this subject, an uneasiness that she had grown better and better at hiding as time wore on and it became more a part of her life. She reminded herself that she was supposed to be making pleasant conversation with her mother-in-law—a woman she found so intimidating that even doing something that simple required every last bit of her concentration. Especially since, this time around, Pat seemed to be criticizing her abilities as a mother.

"Chrissie's going through a very difficult period right now," Lynn said in response to Pat's comment. "It's not easy, being sixteen."

"Yes, I know, dear. But sometimes it seems as if that granddaughter of mine hasn't a thought in her head besides what color nail polish she should be wearing. As for Beth— well, you really should do something for her, you know."

"What do you mean?" Her tone grew sharp, for she knew full well what she meant.

"Why, her weight, of course. You know, Lynn, Beth is about to begin a very difficult time in her life. Why, you just said yourself that it's not easy being a teenager. And having the other children set her apart certainly isn't going to make it any easier. You know how cruel children can be. And soon she'll be interested in boys."

"Perhaps *you* should speak to Beth." Lynn immediately hated herself for having said that. She was squirming under what she perceived as the woman's criticism, and her way of fighting her off was trying to divert it onto someone else. Her daughter, no less. Her baby. The one person in the world who she saw as being even more timid, and more insecure, than she was.

"What I meant to say was," she hastily corrected herself, "Beth is very sensitive. She is about everything, but especially about her weight. Frankly, Pat, I don't think it would do any good for either of us to try to help her. Maybe someone else could influence her, someone more objective. . . ."

Someone more diplomatic, she was thinking. Somebody

who won't make her feel as if she's worthless just because she's a few pounds too heavy. Somebody who doesn't always make a person's weaknesses seem as if they're all her fault, something over which she should have total control. . . .

My, what a strange bird, Pat was thinking with irritation. Every time I try to have a conversation with Lynn, I find myself wondering what on earth Michael ever saw in her. He's so bright, so self-confident, so competent. Yet the wife he chose is afraid of her own shadow. Why he ever picked out such a mousey woman to be his bride is beyond me. . . .

By that point, the parade of six women and one little boy had reached the half circle of sand that was Shelter Island's most popular beach. They laid out their beach blankets and towels, arranging them as carefully as a group of backpackers setting up camp for the night.

"Oh, shoot!" wailed Chrissie. "I forgot the zinc oxide! My nose is gonna burn! Oh, I'll look so geeky by the end of the day! Mom, what am I gonna do?"

"I had a feeling you'd forget," Lynn said matter-of-factly. "Here, I packed it for you. I also brought a sun hat for you, Beth."

"My, my, you're certainly organized," Julie commented admiringly. She peered into Lynn's tote bag. "Goodness, what else have you got in there?"

Lynn wasn't sure whether to be proud or embarrassed. "Well, I suppose I'm just one of those people who plans ahead. I try to be prepared, that's all. I brought a few extra magazines for everybody, and some tissues and some of those premoistened towelettes, and this little toy, in case Joshie gets bored." She laughed self-consciously. "I guess I'm just a packrat at heart."

"Not at all," Julie insisted. "I'm telling you, if one-third of the people who I work with at the studio were half as organized as you, well, I can't imagine. That's a real skill you've got there. If you ever want a job producing my show—"

Just then, Josh broke into a run, his pail and shovel still in his hand as he headed toward the water.

"Ooh, the ocean!" the little boy chortled. "Big waves!"

"Don't go in the water!" Julie yelled, already jogging after him. Over her shoulder, she called to the others, "We really have to watch him. I don't want him going in too deep."

"Does he know how to swim?" Katy asked. "I've read

about these swimming programs for really little kids. They start teaching them when they're still only infants.''

Julie shook her head. Her first inclination was to apologize, to explain that she hadn't had time to take him to weekly swimming classes when he was tiny. But she remembered that this was one instance in which it wasn't her busy career that had stopped her.

''No, Josh can't swim. I know those programs are in style these days, but frankly I could never get too excited about taking a two-month-old baby and plopping him into six feet of water.''

''I'm a great swimmer,'' Chrissie was boasting. ''You should see me do the Australian crawl, Julie. There was this really cute lifeguard at the pool last summer, and he said . . .''

Beth turned away, not wanting to participate in this discussion at all. She had taken swimming lessons, of course; who hadn't? But, unlike her sister, athletics had never come very easily to her. She was a terrible swimmer. Her arms were weak, her breathing was always off. Just one more area in which her sister surpassed her.

Katy seemed to read her mind. ''Hey, Beth. Come on over here with me. I want to ask your advice about something.''

Beth was only too happy to pair off with her aunt. Especially since everyone else seemed to be too busy to pay any attention to her. Her grandmother had immediately hid beneath a big straw hat and sunglasses, her face buried in a thick novel, the one about Hollywood scandals that everyone was reading that summer. Her mother was smearing sun block all over her arms and legs. Josh, meanwhile, was prancing in the foam along the shore, attended by both Chrissie and Julie.

Those two women happened to be absorbing the attention of every male on the beach who was between the ages of twelve and ninety. They were quite a sight as they stood together, two blond goddesses who were lean and tall and brown, Chrissie in her tiny turquoise bikini, Julie in a strapless white maillot, the two of them together looking like a swimsuit ad in a fashion magazine.

''Yes, Katy?'' Beth turned her attention back to her aunt. ''What is it?''

''You know, I've been giving a lot of thought to what Grandpa said last night. You know, about having one of us come into the business with him.''

"Why don't you do it?" Beth suggested brightly. "You'd be great! You're so smart, and—and you're never shy. . . ." I bet Katy wouldn't have any trouble talking to a boy, she was thinking. I wonder if maybe she could give me some advice.

But Katy didn't seem to be taking her suggestion very seriously. "I don't think so, Beth. I'm not cut out for that kind of thing."

Besides, I have enough options these days, Katy was thinking. Let's see. I could decide to make Foodstuffs and the catering business my life—at least for a while, until I get bored with it. Or I could embark on a passionate affair with Nicholas Somers. That would certainly give me something to get excited about. Or, of course, I could just chuck the whole thing and run off to California. Start all over again, in a place where nobody even knows me . . .

"Actually, what my father said at the barbecue last night got me wondering about what *you* want to do when you grow up."

"Me?" Beth looked up at Katy, sitting on the sand beside her, and blinked. "Gee, to tell you the truth, I haven't thought about it very much."

"Well, if you haven't thought about what you want to be, have you ever given much thought to *how* you want to be? You know, what kind of person you'd like to be?"

Beth frowned, giving the question some serious thought. That was certainly a strange question. Now that Katy had brought it up, she had to admit that she had given even less thought to what kind of person she wanted to be when she grew up than to what kind of career she might like to have. As a matter of fact, she had always just assumed that those kinds of things just *happened* to people, not that they sat down and made decisions about them.

"I know!" she said suddenly, flashing her aunt a sunny smile. "I know what kind of person I want to be!"

"Okay. Hit me."

"When I grow up, I want to be just like you, Katy!"

A few feet away, Chrissie was kicking mindlessly at the waves that were flowing around her ankles. She remembered having read somewhere that this was a good exercise for the inner thighs. Meanwhile, she surveyed the people on the beach, looking for someone tall, dark, and handsome—or even some variation on any of those three.

"Hey, Julie?" she said all of a sudden, her voice dreamy and distracted.

"Yes, honey?" Even as she spoke to her niece, Julie kept a sharp eye on little Josh.

"Did you ever have sex with anybody besides Brad?"

Julie's eyes flew to Chrissie. "Uh," she said with a gulp, "well, I had boyfriends before Brad, of course. . . ."

"I know that." Crissie sounded impatient with her circuitousness. "But did you ever sleep with any of them?"

"Uh . . ." Instead of floundering for an answer, Julie decided to take a different tack. "May I ask why the history of my love life is suddenly so important to you?"

"Oh, I don't know," the girl said with a shrug. "I was just wondering."

Chrissie pretended that she had already lost interest in the subject. "Hey, Joshie! Look at the pretty sand castle those kids over there are making! Want to go see it with me?"

Making certain she sucked in her stomach and held her chin up high—just in case—she went bounding up onto shore, with her little nephew in tow.

Chapter Ten

*D*espite Julie's hopefulness that her niece's questions about her sex life were based purely on girlish curiosity, Chrissie's intentions were much more than a desire to make casual conversation. Late that night, after everyone else in the Gilberts' house had gone to bed, she snuck into the kitchen and dialed a long-distance number. Sure, it would show up on her grandparents' telephone bill within a few weeks. But by the time it did, she'd be long gone, back in Lawrenceville, far away from here.

"Hello, Heather?" Chrissie kept her voice as low as she could.

"Chrissie! What are you *doing*? It's almost *midnight*, for heaven's sake!"

"Oh, Heather, it's so good to hear your voice! God, I miss you, like, *so* much!"

"Me, too. How is it, anyway? Is it awful?"

"Oh, yuck. You can't imagine. It's like *jail* here!" Chrissie perched on top of a high wooden stool, having decided that she might as well get comfortable. After all, this could well turn out to be a rather long conversation. "My mother watches every move I make, my stupid little sister keeps following me around. . . . And then there are a million other relatives here besides, aunts and uncles and grandparents all over the place. I can hardly *breathe*!"

"It sounds just awful. Oh, Chrissie, what are you going to *do* for two whole weeks?"

Chrissie smiled, curling a strand of her long dark blond hair around one finger. "As a matter of fact, Heather, I've come up with an idea for a rather interesting . . . project."

"What do you mean, a 'project'?"

"Well, you know. Something *worthwhile* to do while I'm being tortured, held prisoner here at my grandparents' house for the rest of the summer.

"Heather," Chrissie breathed, lowering her voice just in case anyone happened to be awake, "I've decided to lose my virginity."

"You've *what*?"

Chrissie giggled. Sure enough, her announcement had elicited exactly the reaction she'd wanted—especially from Heather Larson, who just happened to be one of the most popular girls at school, and had only recently accepted Chrissie Gilbert into her special clique.

"I mean, I'm *sixteen* already, Heather! Don't you think it's *time*, for goodness sake?"

"But who's it going to be, Chrissie? The guy, I mean."

"We-e-ell . . ." Chrissie was enjoying this even more than she had expected. She felt so *important*, even compared to someone like Heather, who could get just about any boy she wanted. "That's the fun part. The *challenge*. The idea is to find somebody while I'm here on Shelter Island."

"Are there many guys around?"

Heather's doubts rattled Chrissie a bit, but she managed not to lose her cool. "Are you kidding? Of *course*! There are *thousands*! And they're all cute, and tan, and they have their own cars. . . . I mean, this *is* a resort island, don't forget." She sighed. "If anything, I'm going to have a hard time deciding which one is going to be the lucky boy."

"Wow!"

Chrissie was gleeful over the envy she could hear in Heather's voice.

"Well, one thing's for sure," she went on. "Whoever I pick, he has to be very special. I mean, this is a pretty important occasion, after all, and I don't intend to choose just *anybody*. He has to be gorgeous, of course, and a lot older."

"Really? Like how much older? Like—like eighteen?"

"Oh, older than that, even," Chrissie said loftily. "Probably a college man. Of course, this place is simply *crawling* with guys like that, juniors and seniors from Harvard and Yale and Brown."

"Gee. You sure are lucky, Chrissie! Boy, as a matter of fact, right now I wish I were *you!*"

Chrissie just giggled. That was precisely what she'd been hoping Heather would say.

"It was nice that you and I had a chance to spend some time together this morning, wasn't it, sweetie?"

Julie had just emerged from the shower, pink and smooth and floating in honeysuckle fragrance, the result of the new bath soap and shampoo she'd bought just for this little get-away. Oh, she knew it was silly, believing that a little thing like that could make a difference. But she had high hopes for these two weeks on Shelter Island, when she and her husband were far away from job obligations and pressures and the lackluster routine her marriage had drifted into, without her even having seen it coming.

So far, however, she and Brad had scarcely had a moment to themselves. They'd both been here for over forty-eight hours, yet they'd spent virtually every minute in the company of her family. But now, it was late, and the house was quiet. As Julie slipped into bed, she had big plans for turning what was left of this evening into a romantic interlude.

She sat down on the edge of the bed, over on the side that Brad had staked out as his own, the one next to the good reading light. She was naked underneath her flimsy robe, satiny silk the color of daffodils. It was no coincidence that she was wearing her one-year anniversary present from Brad.

He, however, didn't seem to notice what she was intending as a blatant invitation. In fact, he barely looked up from the real estate section of the *New York Times*, spread out before him so that it spilled over to her side of the bed, as if to suggest that there might not be enough room in there for her, as well.

"It was fun playing golf this morning, wasn't it?" she said, this time leaning over and placing a soft hand against his cheek. As she did, her robe fell open slightly.

Brad's reply was a grunt. His eyes remained fixed on his newspaper.

"Brad, honey," Julie said gently, "I was hoping that being away from the city like this would give us some time to talk to each other. Look, we've got three meals a day prepared for us, clean sheets, free babysitting. . . ." She rested her head against Brad's chest.

"Hey, watch it!" Protectively he grabbed the newspaper. He hesitated, then chucked it onto the floor. "You're right—as usual. It's time to turn off work. We do need some time together—alone." He put his arm around her, and she snuggled up against him.

"Listen to how quiet it is out here," she murmured. "No cars honking, no sirens. You can actually keep the windows open without going deaf or crazy."

"Sure, if the crickets don't get to you."

The two of them were silent for a few moments, listening to the peaceful sounds of the night: the rustling of the trees, the crickets that Brad had complained of cheerfully, the occasional *whoosh* of a car passing by outside the house. Julie sighed contentedly.

"I'd forgotten how nice it was out here. Brad, do you ever think about moving out of the city?"

Brad snorted. "Are you kidding? With our schedules? You're up before dawn every morning as it is!"

"I know. But maybe one day, in the future, our lives won't be quite so hectic." She turned her face toward her husband's. "Hey, I can dream, can't I?"

She kissed him then, feeling his mouth melt into hers. She tingled all over as he slid his hands under her robe. So he had noticed, after all.

Even as her body seemed to be coming alive, something deep inside Julie relaxed. It was as if sweet moments like this, when she and Brad were close and loving, made up for all the arguments, all the times when she felt as if they would never experience anything but disharmony for as long as they were together. At moments like this, she could remember why it was she loved Brad.

The next morning, Julie was still in her dreamy state. She lay in her empty bed, stretching and luxuriating in the sunshine streaming in through the window, the smell of fresh-brewed coffee wafting up from the kitchen, the smooth coolness of the sheets against her bare skin, still vibrant from the memory of Brad's lingering touch.

Downstairs, she could hear Beth and her mother trying to coerce Josh into eating something other than Count Chocula cereal for breakfast. She smiled, wondering if they'd have any better luck than she usually did. Actually, this morning she didn't feel like playing the role of mother. Not after her long, delicious night with Brad. Instead, she wanted to be a *wife* today: a lover, a friend, a partner. She lolled in bed a while longer, trying to decide what she and Brad might do with this glorious day that lay ahead of them.

And then, she could no longer stand the anticipation. She slipped her eyelet-trimmed pink cotton nightgown over her slender frame and went downstairs to the kitchen.

Her mother's greeting words snapped her out of her hypnotic state immediately.

"If you want to say good-bye to Brad, you'd better hurry."

"Say good-bye? What are you talking about?"

"He's about to leave for the city. Wes is driving him to the ferry. They both just shot out of here a couple of minutes ago, right after Brad made some important phone call."

Without bothering to grab a robe or even slippers, Julie tore out of the house. Sure enough, Wes's car was revving up, and Brad was sitting in the passenger seat. She flagged them down just as they were ready to pull out of the driveway.

"What's going on?" she demanded, poking her head inside the open car window. "Mom says you're going back to the city!"

"Sorry, hon. I called Cliff Eber first thing this morning, and something's about to break on the new Colony Building. He set up some meetings for early this afternoon."

"But what about *us*? What about you and me spending some time together? . . ."

"Hey, I said I'm sorry." Brad's voice softened when he saw how upset she was. "Look, I'll just be gone for a couple of days. Three, tops. I'll be back before you know it. And I promise that we'll do something special then. Okay?"

Instead of being appeased as she watched Wes's blue Volvo drive away, however, Julie was filled with rage.

How *could* he? she was thinking. How could he possibly put business ahead of his marriage one more time—and after last night, no less!

She felt betrayed as she slunk back to the house, and more than a little foolish for having trusted him, for allowing things to turn out this way—again.

After pouring herself a cup of coffee, Julie retreated to her bedroom. To *their* bedroom, she reminded herself as she glanced at the unmade bed, its disheveled sheets and blankets a testimony to the passion those covers had witnessed the night before. On the floor beside the bed, in a tangled heap, lay the yellow silk robe. Instead of picking it up, Julie reached over with a bare foot and kicked it.

It was at that moment that she realized what she was about to do. Of course, she had intended to do it all along; it was simply a matter of waiting for the proper time. And this, she decided without reservation, was definitely the proper time.

There's nothing wrong with telephoning an old friend, she was thinking. Just to say hello, of course. I mean, it's not as if Paul and I would necessarily even have to *see* each other. . . .

And what if Sally answers? a taunting voice asked. A dagger of bitterness immediately pierced her heart. The mere thought of hearing the voice of Sally Horner—now Sally Dereksen, as she knew only too well—filled her with resentment. And a kind of dread that made her realize that even though nearly twenty years had passed since that episode, more of that pain than she cared to admit to still lingered.

Still, I suppose I could just hang up if she answers, Julie insisted to herself. Sure it's childish, but there are worse things someone could do.

She sat down on the edge of the bed—on Brad's side. And then quickly, before she lost her nerve, she picked up the receiver of the beige telephone on the nightstand and dialed the number she'd memorized from Paul's business card. Her heart was beating so loudly that she felt like a teenaged girl—although once that thought occurred to her she realized that someone like Chrissie probably wouldn't think twice about making a call like this.

The telephone rang once. It rang a second time.

Oh, dear, I'll probably get an answering machine, Julie suddenly realized with chagrin. After all, this is a business number, and it's nine-thirty in the morning. Paul is probably off talking to some clients, or working in his shop. . . .

That possible twist set off an entirely different set of decisions that would have to be made. But before Julie had a chance to ponder the question of whether or not even to leave a message, much less what that message might be, a male voice that she recognized only too well answered with a friendly, "Hello?"

She froze for a few seconds, suddenly not sure if she could handle this. Or if she was making a mistake. Or if she really even *wanted* to be doing this, dredging up her past. But when he said "Hello?" a second time, she swallowed hard and said, "Hello, Paul? This is Julie Gilbert."

There was a long pause. Julie was holding her breath. Had she done the wrong thing, after all?

"Julie! Julie Gilbert!" The softness in his voice quickly appeased her fears. "I'd been hoping you'd call."

That was the last response she'd been expecting. "But how did you even know I was out here?"

"You're forgetting what a small place Shelter Island is," Paul replied with a chuckle. "Especially if you've got your ears open."

As soon as she heard him laugh, Julie could tell that Paul Dereksen hadn't changed a bit. He was still open, still warm. Realizing that simple fact made her heart ache.

But he *has* changed, she reminded herself. He's married now, with a child, perhaps even more than one. And you're married, too, don't forget. Neither of you is the same as you were twenty years ago.

Why, then, did it feel to her like they were?

"Actually, a friend of your mother's, somebody I did some work for last winter, happened to mention that the Gilberts were having a little family reunion at the end of August." Paul chattered away congenially, as if the two of them were the best of friends. "I ran into her at Bliss's a couple of weeks ago. Apparently she'd told your mother that I was on the island now, and your mother happened to remember that I was someone her daughter used to know."

How casual he sounded! Was he mocking her, teasing her—playing with her by sounding so lighthearted, so matter-of-fact? Julie squeezed her eyes shut against the tears that were welling up in them. Is this what it comes down to? she wondered. The closeness, the plans for a future together, the love . . . is it possible that it now seems as if none of it counted for anything?

"Well, I just thought I'd give you a ring and say hello," said Julie. "See how you were doing, after all these years." There, I can be just as flippant as he can. But trying to do so was only making her feel worse.

"Everything's great. Let's see, I moved out here about— what is it now, seven years ago? Yeah, hard to believe. Anyway, I've managed to build up a nice carpentry business for myself. Renovations, additions, stuff like that. I've got a great little house. And I even bought a boat. Oh, sure, it looks like a piece of driftwood compared to what else is out there—y'know those big yachts that look like floating condominiums. But at least it gets me out on the water on Sunday afternoons. So I guess I really have nothing to complain about," he went on cheerfully. "How about you, Julie?"

"Oh, things with me are fine. I'm doing some work on TV now—"

"That's a real understatement!" Paul teased. "Don't you think we hicks out here get 'New Day, New York'? Believe me, I make a point of catching your show every chance I get."

"Really? That's nice to hear." Julie could have kicked herself for sounding so formal. Yet she didn't know how else to react. "Anyway, I'm living in the city, and I've got a wonderful little boy, who's two now."

"Hey, that's terrific. Kids are great, especially at that age, when they're still too young to have gotten all screwed up."

"How's your child?" She bit her lip.

"Whoa! Becky's hardly a child anymore! She's almost eighteen, do you believe it? Just graduated from high school, and she's starting college in the fall. She's fantastic. Of course, I don't get to see her nearly as much as I'd like."

"What do you mean?"

"Well, Sally and I split up almost ten years ago. You mean you hadn't heard?"

"No," Julie said softly. "I hadn't heard."

"Yeah, well, I've been a swinging bachelor ever since. Well, a bachelor, anyway. I'm afraid that the most 'swinging' I'm doing these days is going over to the Dory for a couple of beers after work." He chuckled self-consciously. "So, uh, are you married?"

"Yes. To a wonderful man." Her words sounded hollow, even to her. "He's a real estate developer in Manhattan and, um, we've been married for—let's see—six years now."

"I hope he appreciates what a lucky guy he is." As soon as he'd gotten the words out, Paul seemed to realize what he'd just said. A barrier rose up between them instantly.

"We're pretty happy, if that's what you mean," Julie said in a strained voice.

"I'm glad to hear it. Really, I am. So, listen, how about us getting together, while you're out here? Maybe going out for a drink?"

She didn't hesitate. "I'd love to, Paul." Julie chose to ignore the guilt that was nagging at her. Instead, she began thinking about what was on for the next few days, when would be the best time to get somebody to baby-sit for Josh—and how long Brad was likely to be tied up in the city. "Maybe we could meet somewhere."

"Or you could just come over. Actually, I'm pretty proud of this place. Sure, it's small, and probably not much compared to a city slicker's standards. But I've done a lot of work on this little house of mine. I figure when you're trying to make it as a carpenter, the very least you should do is turn your own house into sort of a showplace. I've done a lot of building, and experimented with some solar stuff. . . . Anyway, why don't you come around for the grand tour?"

He made the whole thing sound so innocuous, so innocent. . . .

And it *is*, Julie insisted to herself.

"How could anyone turn down a sales pitch like that?" she replied, laughing. "I can't wait to see your house, Paul."

I can't wait to see you, either, she thought, without daring to say it.

They decided that Wednesday afternoon would be the best time to get together. Paul had no pressing work scheduled for that day, and Julie was pretty sure she could get Beth to baby-sit. Besides, there was a good chance that Brad, even if he'd come back, would be otherwise engaged; showing off at golf or tennis, or making a fool of himself attempting to sail the Sunfish, or drinking himself into a state of such belligerence that he would be best left alone, anyway. . . .

Stop it! she ordered herself, growing flushed when she realized the direction in which she'd been letting her thoughts drift. You're falling into a real trap, turning Brad into the bad guy—and Paul into the good guy. Don't forget that you haven't seen Paul Dereksen for almost twenty years. A lot's happened to him since then—and a lot's happened to you. You're not the same people you were back then.

Despite her attempts at protecting herself, however, Julie was already planning her little reunion with Paul. She was deciding what to wear, what to say, how to act. And even though it frightened her to admit it, the prospect of seeing him again made her more excited, more gleeful and lighthearted and free, than she had been in months.

Chapter Eleven

"*Hi, Katy.* Is Chrissie home?"

Katy leaned in the front doorway of the Gilberts' house late on Monday afternoon, making a halfhearted attempt at concealing the copy of *People* magazine she had been devouring, her forefinger marking the cover story on Cher as she held it behind her back. She blinked a few times, slightly confused as she eyed the boy standing before her.

"You mean *Beth*, don't you? I mean, you *are* Danny, aren't you? The kid from next door?"

"Well, yeah." His cheeks turned pink and he looked down at his well-worn Reeboks, the confidence with which he'd started out having already vanished.

Katy immediately felt sorry for him. "I guess you should know who you're looking for, right? Besides, it just so happens that they're both here. Come on in." She swung open the door. After hesitating for a few seconds, he stepped inside.

"Chrissie! Company!" Katy yelled. She climbed up two steps toward the second floor, then came back down right away, having decided that she had already dedicated sufficient physical effort to her niece's social life.

But she remained sympathetic to Danny. Turning back to him, she offered, "Why don't you come into the kitchen? You can wait in there. Want a Coke? A diet Coke? A cherry Coke? A beer?"

Danny chuckled. "A Coke'd be fine. The regular kind."

Katy was relieved to see he'd regained his cool. After all, she'd been a teenager herself, once. Hell, she still felt like one, most of the time.

Katy and Danny were engaged in a halfhearted discussion of the Mets' prospects for the new baseball season when Chrissie came bounding into the kitchen, her eyes bright over the prospect of an unexpected visitor. For some unknown reason, she was dressed in her turquoise bikini and a white oversized T-shirt with the CAMP BEVERLY HILLS logo emblazoned across the front in pink and green.

But her face fell the moment she spotted Danny, sitting at the kitchen table with Katy, guzzling a can of soda.

"Oh. It's you."

"Hi, Chrissie. I was afraid you wouldn't remember me."

"Oh, sure. I remember you."

"Well," Katy said cheerfully, "guess I'll leave you two kids alone." She suddenly felt as if she were about eighty years old.

"So how've you been, Chrissie?" Danny asked brightly.

"Oh, okay, I guess." She thought about grabbing a diet Coke herself, but decided that she didn't want to drag this out any longer than necessary. "Listen, I'm kind of busy right now. I, uh, told my aunt I'd do some babysitting for her this afternoon. . . ."

"That's all right. I just wanted to ask you one quick question. Uh, some of the kids who are out here for the summer are having kind of a beach party tomorrow night, and I was wondering if you'd like to come. . . ."

"Why, that sounds lovely!"

Chrissie and Danny turned to see Pat standing in the kitchen doorway.

"A beach party—what fun! I'm sure that Chrissie would love something like that. Wouldn't you, dear?"

"Grandma, I can't," Chrissie whined.

"Well, why on earth not? If Danny here is nice enough to invite you . . . ?"

"Because I, uh, I told Beth I might take her to the movies tomorrow night."

"You did not." Beth, too, came into the kitchen then. She had been hanging around outside the kitchen door, listening to every word, just as she had ever since Danny had stepped onto the Gilberts' property. "You never said anything like that."

Her grandmother's presence was making her unusually bold. Totally ignoring her sister, she turned to Danny and said, "Do you think maybe I could come along to the beach party, too?"

Danny looked surprised for a moment. But then he smiled. "Sure, Beth. I bet you'd have a great time. There's gonna be lots of kids there—some of 'em even your age."

"Thank you so much for thinking of the girls," Pat said, beaming. "What time should they be ready?"

Great, Chrissie thought after Danny had left, disappearing into her bedroom and wishing she could disappear into a hole in the ground just as easily. I just got roped into going to a stupid beach party with that cretin Danny Burtis. Oh, yuck. If Heather ever finds out, I'll just die.

And if *that's* not bad enough, my creepy little sister is gonna tag along. . . .

But on second thought, maybe that wouldn't necessarily be such a bad thing. After all, Beth could act as a sort of chaperone. Having her around would keep it from seeming like a real date.

Besides, Chrissie realized, actually beginning to look forward to going to the party, it's not as if Danny will be the only boy there. There'll probably be *lots* of guys hanging around. . . .

With that, she trotted into the bathroom in search of her jar of depilatory.

Might as well give this my best effort, she decided, already thinking up ways to make this beach party sound like the social event of the season the next time she snuck in a long-distance telephone call to Heather.

As she got dressed for an evening with her husband—dinner at the Ram's Head Inn, Shelter Island's finest restaurant—Lynn was surprised to find she was actually nervous. True, there had been quite a bit of tension between Michael and her lately—the short words and the long silences, the hurts and frustrations and disappointments that were left hanging in the air with no way of being dissipated, like the cigar smoke from a business meeting trapped in a small, windowless room. And it was also true that they hadn't spent an evening alone together, without the distraction of at least one of their daughters, for as long as Lynn could remember.

Even so, the fact remained that Michael and Lynn had been

married for seventeen years now, ever since he was twenty-three, a bright young second-year student at the University of Pennsylvania Law School, and she was twenty-two, a starry-eyed romantic who had given up all aspirations of her own, wanting to believe that what she had found in Michael Gilbert needed nothing else to complement it—aside from her full concentration, lest the happiness she'd discovered slip away when she wasn't paying attention.

Seventeen years. Lynn looked in the mirror above the dresser of the bedroom that Pat had designated as theirs, like a camp counselor handing out bunk assignments. She had lived with Michael for seventeen years. Shouldn't that mean that she should be able to *talk* to him by now? Approach him without fear or self-doubt, as a sympathetic ear if not actually a helpmate?

Yet the look of resignation on the woman before her, putting on lipstick that she suspected was too dark even as she applied it, told her that she was, indeed, a woman who was unable to take the bull by the horns, even when that "bull" happened to be the man whose bed she had shared for almost two decades.

It was impossible to tell how things had gotten to this point. Why, it didn't seem that long ago that this woman in the mirror with the slightly thick waist and the mousey gray-streaked hair had been Lynn McGoldrick, smart, energetic, and sure of herself as she'd enjoyed her first year on her own.

After being graduated from Rosemont, a small, mainline Catholic women's college, she had taken an apartment in west Philadelphia, a closet-sized studio that anyone else would have considered a tenement, but which she absolutely adored. Happily she poured every cent she could afford into decorating it. After buying some basics—an oatmeal-colored sofa bed, bright fabric for curtains, simple white dishes and mugs that would go with everything—she scoured the city for additional touches that would make it hers. And her efforts paid off. Everyone who came by complemented her choices—the colorful handwoven throw rugs, the yellow and orange folk art pillows, the unusual batik wall hangings that brought the single boxy room alive.

During the day Lynn worked as a bookkeeper for a small import firm. It was hardly the kind of glamorous career she had always dreamed about, but at least it paid the rent. Besides, she considered her job only one small part of her new, independent life-style.

Two evenings a week, she took courses at Penn's special adult education program, planning to get a master's in social work, having vague aspirations of someday launching a career in which she could help people. She was also taking a pottery class on Saturday mornings, something she discovered right away she had only a minimal aptitude for, but finding the experience of trying something brand new exhilarating nonetheless. All in all, it was a time of experimentation, of being on her own, of approaching each new day as a chance to bask in her own independence, to be her own person, and to find out, once and for all, who Lynn McGoldrick really was.

It was at that point in her life that she had met Michael Gilbert. She was at Penn's student bookstore late one Saturday afternoon, having finally scrounged up enough money to buy a few of the thick, erudite-looking paperbacks that one of her professors had suggested as additional reading for his course.

She could still remember that day in October 1969 clearly. The first rush of autumn weather seemed to have electrified her very soul. Her eyes were bright and her cheeks flushed as she stopped to browse at a display of art supplies on her way to the cash register, admiring the paints and colored pencils and wondering if, next semester, she might dare to try her hand at still another art class. Her hair was long then, flowing almost down to her waist, a shiny chestnut brown. All in all, she looked like just another student, dressed as she was in jeans tied at the waist with a beaded macrame belt and a purple-and-white batik T-shirt.

But as Michael Gilbert was to confess a few weeks afterward, to him, the sparkling-eyed beauty that he almost tripped over as he was making a beeline for the law section was anything but "just another student."

"Excuse me," he said, frantically trying to think up a way of engaging this stranger in conversation without sounding as if he were delivering a line, "but, uh, weren't you, uh, at the peace rally last weekend?"

Lynn looked up, startled. But as soon as she saw the handsome, intense-looking man planted next to her, looking as if he had absolutely no intention of moving on until he'd gotten what he'd come for, she smiled.

"Actually," she said, grinning shyly, "I've never been to a peace rally in my entire life."

"Really? Me, either!" As soon as he realized what he'd said, Michael clasped his hand over his mouth.

But Lynn just laughed. While she had only been in this young man's presence for some thirty seconds, she had already decided that she was in no hurry for them to go their separate ways, either.

That was the beginning. She paid for her paperbacks, he bypassed the law book section altogether, and they went to a student cafe nearby for espresso. The next day, they went to the Philadelphia Art Museum. The night after that, to dinner at an inexpensive Indian restaurant. They both found it so easy, so natural, to spend hours together, talking and laughing and baring their souls, that they drifted into a tight relationship before either of them had even had a chance to think about it.

The following summer, they were married. Lynn felt just a twinge of regret as she gave up her apartment, her eyes welling up with tears only momentarily as she took down the purple silk batik wallhanging and packed it into a cardboard box. Besides, she had little time to dwell on the end of this chapter of her life. She was too busy helping Michael decorate the new apartment they had found together, one that was big enough for two. Soon she was absorbed in buying curtain fabric and rugs for *their* place—although the colors she chose this time around were subdued, much more fitting for the residence of a brilliant young lawyer-to-be and his new life with his adoring wife.

Now, after all these years, it was difficult for Lynn to believe that she had ever been that young woman. Somewhere along the line, she had lost that spark, that energy—ironically, the things that had drawn Michael to her in the first place. She had abandoned the night classes in social work the autumn after they'd married, having decided the tuition money could be better spent in other ways. The experimentation with art courses had also fallen by the wayside when she found herself pregnant with Chrissie just a few months later and was exhausted all the time, even as she was climbing out of bed in the morning.

Yes, she had changed a great deal since getting married, hoping all the while that having lost much of what had once set her apart from the others would slip by unnoticed by Michael, that, somehow, it wouldn't matter that these days all she could find to talk about was meat loaf recipes and Beth's

weight problem. Yet now, as she contemplated being alone
with her husband in a quiet, intimate restaurant, she was
afraid that her shortcomings would stick out like some gro-
tesque physical flaw, there for everyone to see clearly, with
no way of being concealed.

Well, thought Lynn with a sigh, I can't put off having
dinner alone with my husband for the rest of my life. I'd
better just finish getting dressed and get on with it. Who
knows? Maybe the music in the restaurant will be so loud that
we won't be able to talk to each other, after all.

She was ready to add the finishing touch to the simple pale
blue dress she was wearing: the sapphire and diamond earrings Michael had given her on her thirty-fifth birthday. She
opened the top drawer of her dresser, wondering if adding
something so dazzling might help perk up her own appearance.

But her carefully made-up face quickly tightened into a
frown. She couldn't find the earrings. They weren't in the
tiny box she'd brought along especially for storing her jewelry. She looked in a few other places, but they weren't to be
found anywhere.

Oh, dear, she thought, deflated by dismay. I guess I forgot
to pack them. Although I could swear. . . Oh, I'm getting so
absentminded these days. I probably left them right on top of
my dresser at home.

Disappointed, she picked up her purse, checked her lipstick
in the mirror and decided the shade was just fine, and headed
for the door. She wasn't about to let a small thing like
forgotten earrings get in the way. After all, Lynn McGoldrick
wouldn't have let something that trivial upset her. So perhaps
it was time for Lynn Gilbert to stop letting that sort of thing
bother her, too.

Lynn was hurt, and a little bit surprised, by Michael's
silence as he drove to the Ram's Head Inn. After all, going
out to dinner, just the two of them, had been his idea. She
had been hoping that this was a sign that he was ready to start
acting like half of a husband-and-wife team once again. She
was pleased that he had taken the initiative, suggesting that
they do one of the things they never seemed to find enough
time for in the course of their normal lives.

Yet from the way he was acting as they drove to the
restaurant, from the way he had withdrawn into that annoying
little shell of his, she could see that she had been overly

optimistic. But aside from the way he was distancing himself, as he did more and more all the time, she thought she detected some nervousness in him. Given her own apprehensions about their dinner together, it was probably inevitable that he, too, dread the evening ahead at least a little bit. So the two of them sat in silence, their tension alleviated somewhat by the soft rock station Michael switched on, filling the car with Crosby, Stills and Nash, an ironic reminder of the past they had shared, a past that had, somehow, evolved into this confusing, painful present.

Both their moods improved markedly, however, once they were seated on the terrace overlooking the sparkling blue waves of Coecles Harbor. It was a lovely evening, and it was relaxing just sitting there, sipping white wine and watching the osprays from the nearby Mashomack Preserve glide gracefully over the water.

"Gee, this is nice, isn't it?" he said after a few minutes. "How come you and I don't do this more often?"

"We really should, shouldn't we?" Already Lynn could feel the wine affecting her, infusing her with a sense of optimism and well-being. Michael was right—it was nice. And having him notice made it even better.

She was surprised to find that they chatted easily over their broiled scallops, about how much Josh had grown since the last time they'd seen him, how well the Mercedes was running since its tune-up, how much more crowded the island seemed this summer. Then they moved on to how they really had to get some kind of anniversary present for Ben and Pat.

Mentioning her father-in-law prompted Lynn to say, "You know, I felt kind of sorry for Ben the other night. While he was talking about how much it'd mean to him if someone from the family was interested in taking over Benjamin Gilbert Associates, I mean."

"Really? How come you felt sorry for him?"

"Because I can't imagine any of you ever taking him up on his offer. Not Julie, not Wes, not Katy—who's left?"

"Me, of course." Michael grinned. "You look surprised. What's the matter, don't you think I could manage to fill Ben's shoes?"

"Oh, Michael, I have no doubt that you could do anything you set your mind to. It's just that—well, you're a lawyer. You're all settled in at Pearson Willoughby. One of their shining lights, I might add."

"Yes, but maybe it's time for a career change." Michael sat back in his chair, his eyes half-closed, only half joking. "Maybe giving up law and moving on to something new isn't such a bad idea. I mean, I've already devoted, what, fifteen years to the same damned thing, day after day. People do get burned out, you know.

"And here's a golden opportunity, just falling into my lap. Stepping into the presidency of a successful firm, having total control of my own business, one where everything's already set up, running smoothly, turning a handsome profit year after year . . . Hell, we wouldn't even have to move. New York City's only an hour's commute from Lawrenceville."

Lynn giggled, not certain of whether or not he was just teasing her. "And just think: it would give you a chance to work side by side with your father for the next few years, while you learned the business. Wouldn't you like that, Michael? I know that he would."

He opened his mouth—but whatever it was he had been thinking of saying just wouldn't come out.

Lynn could sense that he was holding something back. She wanted to ask him what it was, she wanted to so much—but she couldn't. Not when she was so terrified of what the answer might be.

"Actually," Michael was saying, "I already told Dad I wasn't interested. Sure, joining B.G.A. would have its benefits. But somehow the idea of following that closely in my father's footsteps just doesn't sit right with me. I've worked too damned hard, going to law school and paying my dues and all that, to allow myself to become nothing more than Ben Gilbert's clone."

The vehemence with which his words were spoken took Lynn aback. Even so, she couldn't really complain. She had to admit that, for once, they were *talking*. Maybe not about their marriage, about the uneasiness that had been haunting them for so long, but at least about something of substance, something that was important to Michael.

"Poor Ben," she said, turning back to her dinner and feeling just a tiny bit guilty that she was relieved they were talking about her father-in-law's problems rather than nothing at all—or worse yet, *her* weaknesses. "I do hope that somebody comes through for him. He deserves it."

How silent the world is, thought Lynn, climbing out of bed

and tiptoeing across the sand-colored carpet of the bedroom, having decided to admit, after an hour's tossing and turning, that this was simply one of those nights when sleep insisted upon eluding her. She was still thinking about her evening with Michael.

The quiet of the house was oddly comforting as she made her way downstairs, noticing for the first time how soft the carpeting on the stairway felt beneath bare feet. She headed for the living room, then sat down on the couch without turning on a light. It was pleasant just sitting in the dark like this, all alone.

She was lost in thought, going over every moment of the evening she had just spent with her husband, running through her mind each word, each gesture, each smile, and analyzing them like a student preparing for an exam, when a light was suddenly snapped on.

"Lynn! What are *you* doing up?" she heard Ben ask in a surprised voice. "And what are you doing, sitting here in the dark?"

"Oh, hi, Ben." Lynn smiled wanly, embarrassed at having been caught. She was still blinking hard, trying to get used to the light. Once she managed to focus on her father-in-law, she saw that he was holding a plate on which was a generous slab of leftover peach pie from dinner. He was looking a trifle embarrassed himself. "Guess I couldn't sleep."

"And you thought sitting on the couch without any lights on would help?"

"I was thinking. I don't need lights to think."

"Ah. I see." Ben sat down next to her, offered her some pie by waving his fork in her direction, and, when she declined, helped himself to a mouthful. "And what's so important that you need to be awake past midnight to think about it?"

"I could ask you exactly the same thing, you know."

"Yes—except you look like somebody who was being kept awake by something important. All I had on my mind was this pie."

"Actually . . ." Lynn cleared her throat. "Ben, what do you think is the secret to a good marriage?"

"Well, I don't think there's any *secret* involved. In fact, the first thing I thought of when you asked me that question was the word *honesty*. I think that if two people are willing to be honest with each other, to open up and talk about anything that's on their minds, just about any problem or difference of opinion can be worked out.''

"You really think that's the key?''

"There are some other things, too, of course. Like trust. And commitment. And I think it doesn't hurt if each person in the marriage likes him- or herself.''

A sad smile crept over Lynn's face. "You're talking about *me* now, aren't you?''

"And here I thought we'd been talking about you all along,'' Ben replied gently. "You know, Lynn, sometimes I wish you could see yourself the way those of us who love you do.''

"You mean like Michael?'' The bitterness in her tone surprised even her.

"Michael's a tough one. Not the easiest person to read. He's never been very good at showing his feelings—not even when he was a little boy. But there's one thing I do know, and that's that he loves you very much.''

"I guess I haven't been feeling very loved lately.''

"Is it possible that perhaps you just haven't been feeling very *lovable* lately?''

"Both, I guess.'' Lynn thought for a few seconds, then said, "The two are pretty closely related, aren't they?''

"Like that.'' Ben held up his hand, with two fingers crossed together. "Hey, you sure you don't want any of this pie? It's a lot like marriage: it seems to get better and better, the older it is.''

Lynn laughed. "No, thanks. I'm getting tired. Think I'll go back to bed.''

"Sweet dreams, Lynn.''

She stood up and stretched. "Sweet dreams, Ben.'' And then, almost as an afterthought, she leaned over and gave him a quick peck on the cheek. "And thanks, Ben. Thanks a lot.''

Chapter Twelve

Well, kid, you've done it again, thought Katy, pulling the sheet up over her head. So much for Randy Palmer. One more attractive, available man does a disappearing act. What is it, Tuesday morning already? And not a single word from Mr. Prep, not a peep out of him in the last thirty-six hours.

How many times have I been through this before? she wondered, already lapsing into a foul mood even though she'd been awake for less than five minutes. I mean, I meet some guy, usually when I'm not even trying, like that guy Mick or Dick or whatever his name was, over at the Volkswagen place, or—or that guy at the bus stop that time. And they act like they're interested, and I believe them.

I even talk myself into thinking they're actually what I've been looking for all along. I wake up humming in the morning, I wash my hair every single day, just in case they decide to pop over unannounced, I make sure I'm never away from the phone for very long. . . . And then, little by little, as the days go by and the phone does nothing but get dusty, I finally start admitting to myself that I'm never going to hear from the guy again—that good old Katy's been duped one more time. Welcome to the world of Gullible's Travels.

Boy, you'd think I would've learned by now. But no-o-o. Instead, I just added one more name to the list: Randall Palmer. Stuffy, full of himself—and he even has a bit of a beer belly. Another Class-A jerk. Or maybe it's *me* who's the

Class-A jerk. At any rate, lying around in bed all day isn't going to accomplish anything. . . .

"Sh-h-h! Katy's sleeping!" Beth's stage whisper was so loud as she tiptoed into the bedroom that it was guaranteed to wake anyone who wasn't either drunk or dead.

"Be-eth, I have to get my bathing suit!" Chrissie, right behind her, hissed.

"It's okay, guys. I'm up." Katy dragged herself out of bed and stretched lazily. "Good morning—I suppose. What time is it, anyway?"

"Nine twenty-two," Beth replied. "About."

Katy groaned. "Oh, God. Is it that late? I'm sleeping my whole life away."

"I've got to get outside while the sun's still hot," Chrissie complained. "I've got less than two weeks left to perfect my tan."

Katy vaguely remembered having come up with a similar plan ages ago. "Don't you read *Glamour*?" she countered with a yawn. "Ideal tanning rays are out between eleven and three. And here you kids think reading's a waste of time."

But Chrissie had already dashed out, no doubt frantic over the possibility of missing out on even a minute of some activity geared toward improving her looks. Katy marveled over the vanity of teenagers, then pondered how odd it was that she had never really passed through a stage like that herself. Of course, when she was sixteen mascara was considered counterrevolutionary and anything dressier than a blue work shirt, or perhaps an embroidered Indian blouse for formal occasions, was denounced as deplorably middle class.

On second thought, she supposed that she had obsessed over her appearance back then. But given the social climate in those days, she would have been embarrassed to let on how much she really did care. Chrissie, on the other hand, just accepted the fact that it was her duty to strive for physical perfection—and very little else.

Beth, of course, was another matter entirely.

"What about you, Beth? What've you got lined up for this morning?"

"Oh, I don't know. I guess I'll just . . . read." Meekly Beth held up a battered paperback, one of those thick romances whose title was an absurd feminine name and whose cover showed a raven-haired beauty in a white ruffled gown who was about to be ravaged by a handsome rake—and loving it, of course.

Katy was tempted to question its suitability for a thirteen-year-old, then realized how terribly old-fashioned a comment like that was bound to make her sound.

Instead, she said, "Personally, I'm not much for baking in the hot sun, either. Sure, I'd love to come out looking like a bronzed goddess. But no matter how I try, all that ever happens is that my freckles get a tan. Hey—I just had a great idea. Maybe you and I can find something to do together."

"Thanks, Katy. But I'd rather spend the day reading." In a conspiratorial tone, she added, "This book has a lot of really juicy parts."

"I'll bet it does. Well, then, I guess I'll just have to be resourceful. See you later."

As if to prove that she was done waiting around for one Randy Palmer, hoping he'd appear on her doorstep at any moment with a bouquet of wildflowers in one hand and a ticket to paradise in the other, Katy put on a pair of faded cutoffs and an electric yellow T-shirt, printed with FOOD-STUFFS GOURMET SHOP AND CATERING SERVICE on the front and FOR A GOOD THYME, CALL 555-2323 on the back. She couldn't wait to hear what her mother was going to have to say about this morning's fashion statement.

Then she pulled her unruly brown hair back and forced an elastic band around it, creating an effect that had, in her estimation, about as much charm as a squirrel's tail. She had decided to dedicate herself to gardening today, to sublimate all her erotic impulses into converting her father's side garden into a *House and Garden* cover.

An hour later, she was furiously engaged in doing exactly that. She knelt on reddened knees, with cool soil under her fingernails and sweat running down her neck, pouring her very soul into weeding and tilling and mulching. She had tied a purple bandanna around her hair, and her cheeks were streaked with dirt and perspiration. She knew she looked like a hired hand, but she felt good, really good, as if she were doing something worthwhile for the first time in as long as she could remember.

"Hey, Katy, there's some guy here to see you." Beth had just sauntered out of the house, carrying her book but for a change looking as if she were actually more interested in what was going on in real life than in the action going on within the pages of a novel. "He's kind of cute, too. He said his name is Randy."

Katy gasped. "Oh, my God."

She glanced down at her T-shirt, her grimy arms, her raw knees peculiarly bumpy from the impact of the pebbles she'd been kneeling on. Her mind raced as she tried to come up with a way of making herself presentable before seeing Randy: sneaking into the house through the back door; taking a thirty-second shower that would eliminate at least some of the odor emanating from her every pore; throwing on some absolutely marvelous outfit, probably one she'd steal from Julie's closet. But she gave up even before she began. Instead she wiped her hands on her cutoff jeans, whipped off her purple bandanna, and fluffed out her hair.

"Good thing beauty's only skin deep," she quipped, winking at her niece.

"You look okay to me, Katy."

"Let's just hope that Randy Palmer is as much of a visionary as you are, kid."

"Huh?"

But Katy was already halfway inside the house.

Sure enough, Randy was sitting on the living room couch wearing khaki Bermuda shorts and another Izod sport shirt—this time, navy blue. He looked nervous, so much the stereotypical "gentleman caller" that Katy had to laugh.

"Hi, Randy."

Gone was her self-consciousness about the unkempt state in which he had found her, as well as her anger over not having heard from him for what had seemed an eternity but which, she realized now, was in reality a mere three days.

"Hi, Katy." He looked relieved to see her, as if sitting there in the Gilberts' living room was just as painful for him as it appeared. Then his expression turned into one of alarm. "Oh, gee. It looks like you're in the middle of something. I guess I came at a bad time, huh?"

"No, not at all. I was just messing around in the petunia patch." She grinned shyly. "Actually, I'm really glad to see you."

"Oh, yeah?" Randy's cheeks turned just a little bit pink. "I just thought maybe you and I could, I don't know, go for a drive or something."

"It just so happens that I'd love going for a drive or

something. All I need is about thirty-two seconds to change my clothes.''

Randy surprised Katy by being the owner of a convertible. Not just any convertible, either—this one was a turquoise 1956 Chevy Bel Air in mint condition, such a funky piece of machinery that she wondered if perhaps she had judged this man a bit too hastily.

"Funny. I would've pegged you as a BMW man," she teased as they drove off in a swirl of dust. "Or maybe a Volvo."

"See that?" He looked over at her and grinned, obviously pleased that he had impressed her. "Underneath this façade of the successful, upwardly mobile super-yuppie, super-preppie banker, there lurks an alter ego that borders on zany and madcap."

"Oh, that's right. You mentioned that you work for a bank."

"Right. I work for Chase—you know, the Chase Manhattan Bank? I'm a lending officer."

"You mean you lend money to happy home owners who want to add on a new dormer?"

"Not quite. Actually, I lend money to happy car manufacturers who want to add on a new factory."

Randy Palmer, Katy was delighted to discover, was full of contradictions, the most obvious ones—his chosen career and his chosen mode of transportation—being only the beginning. While he appeared stodgy on the outside, he was one of the few people Katy had ever met who actually possessed the ability to laugh at himself.

Although he put in long hours playing the game and making lots of money, he wasn't someone who saw that as an end in itself. Instead, he was hell-bent on using that hard-earned cash to enjoy himself. As for his occasional gawkiness, she was beginning to see it as merely a manifestation of his underlying sensitivity, his willingness to please—and, above all, his wanting desperately to be liked.

"So tell me, Randy. How does the owner of such a snappy car get to be a banker, anyway?" Katy teased as she took a big bite of her cheeseburger. Their drive around Shelter Island had led them to the Inn Between for a lunch break, after they'd both agreed that they'd already had enough of admiring nature for one day.

"What, does it bother you that I'm a banker?"

"It doesn't *bother* me, exactly. It's just that I always thought Wall Street types were boring."

"I take that as a compliment. That you find me an exception to the stereotype, I mean. As for how I got into it—it was just one of those things. I graduated from college, and I didn't want to put in two more years getting an MBA. I needed a job. Then somebody told me about this credit-training program at the Chase Manhattan Bank . . . and voilà."

"And do you like it?"

He pondered that question for a few seconds, as if it hadn't occurred to him to ask himself that for some time. "Yeah, I guess I do. It's a job that's treated me well enough."

Katy grimaced. "Boy, my mother would sure love it if I saw things that way."

"Don't you and your mother get along?"

"Ha!" Katy snorted. "Let me put it this way. Last year, when I called her on Mother's Day and said, 'Hi! Happy Mother's Day!' she paused for a minute and then said, 'Who is this?'"

Randy laughed. "So I take it she doesn't really approve of her daughter making her living by giving people 'a good thyme'?"

"Actually, when it comes to my mother, I don't think she'd approve of me if I were the president of General Motors."

"Aw, that job's been filled, anyway."

"Well, you of all people should know." Pensively Katy chewed on a French fry. "You know, it's funny. I had already given up on you, before you stopped over today. I figured you'd just disappeared into the woodwork, never to be heard from again."

"Since we're being honest here, I guess I can confess that it took me a couple of days to get up the nerve to come by and see you. You've got to admit, Katy—you are a little bit intimidating."

"*Me?*" Katy squealed. "Queen of the Marshmallows? I happen to be the least intimidating person east of the Rockies!"

"Are you kidding, Katy? You're so—so *sure* of yourself."

"*Moi?*"

"Sure. I couldn't tell if you were really interested in seeing me again, or if you were just playing with me. Heck, I even thought maybe you were married, that picking me up at the garage sale was nothing more than a morning's entertainment."

I've found myself a man who uses the word *heck*, Katy marveled, having already decided to pass on dessert and instead suggest an afternoon at the beach. Not only that: I have a sneaking suspicion that this is a man who can even handle seeing thunder thighs here in a bathing suit.

"Just look at these two!" Pat put down the copy of the *Ladies' Home Journal* she had been thumbing through while she waited for "Wheel of Fortune" to come on and clapped her hands together. Chrissie and Beth had just come into the living room to wait for Danny Burtis to pick them up. "My goodness, don't you both look nice. And so grown up! Why, I'm so proud I could burst!"

"Oh, Grandma, it's only a stupid beach party." Tonight, however, Chrissie's sullenness was short-lived. The opportunity to be admired was too tempting to let pass. "Do I really look okay?"

She twirled around on long bare legs, shown off to maximum advantage by the fact that the only garment she appeared to be wearing was an oversized pastel pink T-shirt with the word ESPRIT printed boldly across the front in yellow.

"Aren't you afraid you might get cold?" Pat asked cautiously.

"Grandma, it's a *beach* party! You're *supposed* to wear a bathing suit!"

"You mean there's a bathing suit under that shirt?" Wes sauntered into the living room with the magazine section from the previous Sunday's *Times* under his arm and his tortoise-shell glasses perched on his nose. "I thought you were about to join a nudist camp."

"Oh, Wes, not you, too!" Chrissie wailed. "God, why is everybody *against* me?"

"I think you look great, Chrissie."

Beth had been hovering in the background, not nearly as anxious to be noticed as her big sister was. She, too, was wearing a baggy T-shirt over her bathing suit, but she had also put on a pair of loose-fitting cotton pants designed to hide rather than to show off. She had come downstairs with a speech prepared about how she didn't want to risk getting mosquito bites. Now, however, she found herself feeling like the paragon of good sense as she took off for a beach party covered from head to foot.

Her compliment went unacknowledged. "Everybody around here is so old-fashioned," Chrissie whined. "I mean, you'd probably all love it if I dressed like a *nun*."

"Just remember," Wes said, "sometimes men find it intriguing to have to use their imaginations a little when they're with a woman. You don't have to make things so easy for them, you know."

"Is that how Barbara acted when you first met her, Uncle Wes?"

He put down the magazine section and smiled. "When I first met Barbara, I thought she was the most beautiful, the most *mysterious* woman I'd ever seen in my life. . . ."

He lapsed into silence then. The others, however, were too wrapped up in themselves to notice.

Danny Burtis showed up right on time, proudly toying with the keys of his father's shiny red car, loaned to him for the evening.

"Hi, Mrs. Gilbert, Wesley. Hiya, girls. All set?"

And they were off, Danny and Chrissie in the lead, Beth lagging behind a few paces, not yet certain of whether this was going to turn out to be the best night of her life or the worst.

The party was being held at Crescent Beach, a well-lit stretch of shore in front of the Pridwin Hotel. As the threesome drove up, they could hear loud music blaring from blocks away. There was a bonfire burning, and the kids who were already there—thirty or forty, Chrissie estimated as she and the others walked over from the parking lot—were dancing or sitting on the beach.

Most of the girls, she noticed, were wearing pants and shirts.

She felt horribly naked as she trailed after Danny and Beth. Already she'd lost all her enthusiasm for the evening ahead. She was back to dreading it, to hating being there, to wishing she'd never set eyes on stupid Danny Burtis.

"Come on, Chrissie. I'll introduce you to some of the kids."

She was miserable as Danny took her by the hand. But being on her own, here in the middle of a bunch of strangers, dressed all wrong as she was, would have been even worse than being with Danny. As she let him lead her along, she stuck out her chin and tossed her head so that her long hair swung dramatically.

Who cares what these creeps think, anyway? she thought as she forced herself to smile at the boys and girls that Danny introduced her to.

They were all nice enough, she supposed, and some of the guys looked mildly interested in checking her out further. That was a nice feeling. But since she'd already decided that she wanted absolutely nothing to do with any of Danny Burtis's friends, all she had to do was get through the evening.

This is the most exciting party I've ever been to in my life, Beth was thinking, meanwhile. Her eyes were wide, positively glowing.

True, all the kids seemed much older than she was—fifteen or sixteen, at least. But that was fine with her. Just being able to hang out with them was a treat. Especially since her big sister never let her come near her and her friends when they were over at the house.

Even so, it wasn't the party she was interested in. It was Danny. She planned to watch him tonight, to try to read his signals more clearly. After all, he *had* invited her to come along . . . sort of.

Maybe it's me he's really interested in, Beth thought, taking a swig from a can of diet Sprite and noting with delight that, for once, she was dressed just fine. Maybe he was just being nice to Chrissie because—because he felt sorry for her. Yeah, he probably felt bad that she's so conceited that none of the other kids want to be friends with her. Sure, I bet that's it. See that? He's even nicer than I ever thought.

"So what do you think, Chrissie?" Danny planted himself next to Chrissie, way over at the edge of the beach where she'd retreated as soon as she'd had a chance to get away. He offered her one of the two Cokes he'd brought with him. "Pretty nice bunch of kids, wouldn't you say?"

"Yeah, I suppose."

"I guess you must have a lot of friends where you live, right? Where is it, again?"

"Lawrenceville. It's in New Jersey. And, yeah, I've got, like, a million friends there."

"Got a boyfriend?"

Chrissie looked at him for the first time since he'd sat down. "What business is it of yours?"

She was hardly about to admit that ever since she and Keith

Simon had broken up that spring, she hadn't been going out with anybody. Especially after the fool she'd made of herself, making such a play for Stephen Clyde when everybody in the world knew full well he was madly in love with Jennifer Powell—except for her, that is. . . . Well, after all that, she wouldn't be surprised if nobody ever asked her out again.

Still, there was no reason why anybody here on Shelter Island had to know anything about that.

"I don't know," Danny replied, his eyes fixed on his Coke. "I just figured that somebody like you, who's probably the best-looking girl I've ever seen in my life—"

"Hey, Danny! There you are!"

For once in her life, Chrissie was actually glad to see her chubby sister trundling toward her, pink-cheeked and breathless, her stringy hair hanging down limply around her shoulders.

"I was looking all over for you," she puffed. "Listen, one of the kids just told me that everybody's going over to the Tuck Shop for ice cream later on. Want to go?"

"Sure, I guess." He turned to Chrissie. "Unless there's something else you'd rather do after the party."

"Actually, I think I'd like to go home early, Danny. I've got kind of a headache. As a matter of fact, I think I'll go take an Advil or something. I left my purse in your car." She scrambled away, gladly leaving Danny to her sister.

Two of a kind, she thought, relieved that she'd found a way to escape. I'll let the two of them *bore* each other to death.

"This sure is a neat party, Danny. Thanks for inviting me." Beth had already sat down in the same spot that only seconds earlier had been occupied by her sister. She could scarcely believe her good fortune: Chrissie dashing off that way, leaving the two of them alone together. And it was so romantic sitting here on the beach like this, listening to the water lapping up against the shore, watching the bonfire's hypnotic light—all of it in the moonlight, no less.

"No problem. Hey, what's the story with your sister, anyway?"

Beth had almost forgotten all about her. "Chrissie? What do you mean?"

"She's kind of—I don't know, quiet, don't you think?"

Beth shrugged. "Oh, don't worry about her. She's just stuck up."

"Chrissie? Nah, I don't believe that. Maybe she's just shy."

"No, I'm telling you. My sister thinks she's God's gift to boys or something. Hey, hear that song? That's Whitney Houston. I *love* that song. Want to dance?"

"No, thanks. I'm gonna go look for Chrissie. I hope she's okay. She said she had a headache. . . . I'd better make sure she's all right."

He scrambled across the sand toward the parking lot, leaving Beth sitting alone. She watched him hurrying off, running away in search of her sister. And then, after a few seconds, she turned away, suddenly finding that the ache in her heart made it hurt too much to look at him.

Chapter Thirteen

By Wednesday, Brad still hadn't come back from the city. In his place he sent a dozen red roses, with a card that said simply, "Sorry."

He also telephoned late that morning.

"I still feel bad about the way I just took off like that," he murmured. "I was a real jerk, not even saying good-bye. The truth is, at the time I just didn't have the heart to wake you."

"Oh, it's okay," Julie cooed. At the moment, as she gently fingered the soft petals of one of the most graceful long-stemmed roses she had ever seen, she couldn't even remember what she had been so upset about. Instead she felt selfish, as if she'd made no attempt at all to step back and look at things from her husband's perspective. "I know how demanding your business is, honey. And I know how important the Colony Building is to you."

"I knew you'd understand, sweetie."

When it was time to get ready to drive over to Paul Dereksen's house a few hours later, Julie wasn't even sure she wanted to go anymore. All of a sudden, it seemed like a waste of time looking up an old boyfriend like this. Why, she hadn't seen Paul for twenty years. What would they ever find to talk about? And it was a beautiful day—why waste it talking to someone she would probably never see again when the afternoon would be much better spent taking Josh to the beach?

"Beth, are you sure you don't mind babysitting?" Julie

figured she'd take one last stab at backing out before climbing into the car and taking off. "It's so gorgeous out. I'm sure you could find something better to do than take care of Josh. What I'd planned for this afternoon isn't really all that important, and it's not too late to cancel."

But Beth just looked hurt. "Don't you trust me, Julie? I'll take good care of Joshie, I promise. Look! I even put him in his bathing suit already!" Proudly she pointed to her little nephew, looking like sunshine personified in his little yellow bathing trunks, made absurdly puffy by the diaper underneath. "I can manage, really! And you don't even have to pay me or anything. . . ."

Ten minutes later, the red BMW was pulling up in front of a small but well cared for house, set apart from all the others surrounding it by its handcrafted wood trim, the sleek deck at the side, and the workshop out back, a converted garage with huge sheets of plywood leaning against one of its sides. Nervously Julie smoothed the skirt of her lavender cotton sundress, then glanced at her wrist, wondering if she was late or early. But she wasn't wearing a watch. She had planned to wear her gold one, but when she'd gone to take it off her night table, it wasn't there. Probably fallen under the bed somewhere . . .

Well, Paul Dereksen, she thought ruefully, ready or not, here I come.

By the time she'd made her way up the short front walk, he was at the front door, smiling shyly as he watched her through the screen. She had wondered how time would have affected his appearance, yet she could see that he was better-looking than ever. Still the same wheat-colored hair, the intelligent hazel eyes, the handsome features that had made him the most popular boy at Harrington High. And he was tan and muscular, both of which were shown off by the tight jeans and black T-shirt he was wearing.

As for his reaction to her, there was no reason for her to have been apprehensive. The moment she saw him, she knew that it was still there. She could see it in his eyes, the way they lit up when he looked at her, making her feel as if he could see into her very soul. Suddenly she was seventeen again, her eyes and her heart filled with nothing but Paul.

"Hi," she said, swallowing hard. Then, not wanting just to stand there, she added, "I hope I'm not late."

"Come on in, Julie." Paul's voice was strangely husky.

She brushed against him as he held the door open for her, and a jolt of electricity seemed to pass through her.

Oh, God, was it a mistake coming here? she wondered. And what would he think if I just turned around and ran right out of here, right now, while everything that was once between us is still buried? . . .

But she knew full well that it was anything but that. And that no matter how she may have felt, she wasn't about to bolt out of there without saying another word. So she simply sat down on the edge of a chair and said, "My, isn't this a lovely house."

The funny smile Paul was wearing as he sat down, a safe distance away, told her that he recognized what she was doing and that he, too, was willing to go along with her little charade of formality—at least, for now.

"Thanks. This house is my pride and joy. I can't wait to show you all the work I've done on it. . . . But tell me, Julie, how *are* you?"

"Oh, fine. I'm just out here for a couple of weeks, visiting my folks. Actually, the whole family's out here, Michael and Wes and Katy. . . ."

"I always liked Katy. What's she up to these days?"

They continued their stiff conversation for a few more minutes, with Julie chattering away about her sister and her brothers and her parents. He, in turn, kept feeding her questions that enabled her monologue to continue.

When the telephone rang, before she'd been there even ten minutes, she was relieved. Somehow, this whole thing was going all wrong, and she welcomed a chance for them to start over again, after she'd had a chance to get over the initial shock of seeing him.

"The phone," said Paul apologetically. He stood up and shrugged. "Sorry. The rest of the world thinks I should be working today."

"Oh, don't worry about it. I'll be fine."

Paul strode over to the dining room and picked up the phone. "Hello?"

Julie stayed glued to her chair, just watching him.

"Oh, hi, Skip. Thanks for returning my call so fast." With his hand over the phone, in a stage whisper, Paul said, "It's the lumberyard." Then, he was all professionalism again: "Listen, Skip, I'm going to need to add to that order. I'll be needing a hundred and fifty, not a hundred and twenty feet of

that African mahogany. And make sure none of the pieces are
under five inches. Wait, there's a couple more things. Hang on
a sec.''

As he rummaged through the haphazard pile of drawings
and catalogues and handwritten notes that covered what was
obviously supposed to be a dining room table, he cast an
apologetic glance in Julie's direction. "Sorry about this, but it's
important. I'll be off in a minute.''

"That's okay. Take your time.'' She stood up then, wandering off in search of the bathroom, with a vague notion of
checking her appearance in the mirror. In actuality, she wanted
to find something to do other than sitting and waiting for Paul
to get off the phone, or wandering, uninvited, around his
house.

She found the bathroom at the top of the stairs between two
small bedrooms. It instantly struck her as being very male.
She immediately felt out of place in there—but curious, too,
about this private side of Paul Dereksen. Brown and beige
towels, a bit frayed at the ends, some folded on a small shelf
in a lopsided fashion, some flung over towel racks with
refreshing carelessness. A dirty shirt had been left hanging on
a hook on the back of the door.

She couldn't resist peeking inside the medicine cabinet.
Only a few items were stashed away on the shelves. A bottle
of aspirin, an Ace bandage, a bottle of alcohol, two boxes of
Band-Aids, a bottle of Mercurochrome. There was also a
bottle of Old Spice aftershave—how corny! That was what
her father had always used, ever since she was a little girl.
But that wasn't how Paul had smelled. Ah, there it was: a
small bottle of Aramis, hardly used at all. Probably a gift,
perhaps even from a woman. The realization that it may well
have been opened expressly for her visit made her blush. She
hadn't felt she had such power over a man since—well, since
Brad had begun pursuing her so doggedly almost nine years
earlier.

Julie knew she should be feeling at least a little bit guilty
for spying on Paul. But once she got started, she found it
difficult to stop. There was something so intimate about
looking at the things this man used as a part of his everyday
life. When she had known him as a boy, she hadn't been
privy to such things. She had never even seen the inside of his
bedroom when they were going out in high school. Funny;
despite their closeness, a certain distance was always there

between them, imposed on them by what was then considered
a sense of propriety. Back in the early sixties, nice girls
simply didn't go inside boys' bedrooms. The fact that their
intimacy had gone far beyond such arbitrary limits made the
whole thing even more ludicrous.

"Oh, before I forget, Skip, have those Austrian recessed
hinges come in yet?" Paul's voice drifted up from downstairs. He sounded so confident, without the slightest twinges
of the becoming boyishness that Julie remembered in him so
clearly. He existed in a world that was so separate from hers,
so foreign to her. But instead of feeling alienated by that
realization, as she would have expected, Julie was actually
finding it enticing.

Since he was still absorbed in his telephone conversation,
she ventured into the room next to the bathroom. It was his
bedroom. Large windows overlooked the water, and the view
of colorful sails on the boats that lolled around in the afternoon sun, punctuated by bursts of sunlight sparkling on the
water, was calming.

Again, there were those signs of maleness—or, of bache-
lorhood, she reminded herself with an indulgent smile. The
clothes strewn across the bed and on the chairs, the books
piled up haphazardly in a corner, the shoes left in the middle
of the room all said that the person residing here had no one
else to consider, neither a wife nor a lover who had to share
this space and therefore deserved some semblance of order.
Despite its comfortable chaos, it was a pleasant room, painted
a pale shade of blue and furnished with simple wood pieces
that Julie surmised Paul had made himself.

She was about to turn away and go back downstairs when
she noticed the picture hung next to the door. The moment
she saw it, she drew in her breath sharply. Was it possible
that he had saved it all these years? And was it possible that it
still meant something to him—so much, in fact, that he kept
it hanging on the wall of his bedroom?

It was a simple watercolor, a painting of a bunch of
daisies. Julie's high school graduation present to Paul. But it
was more than just a pretty floral design. A month or so
before graduation, he had given her a bouquet of daisies on
her birthday.

"I'm sorry they're not roses," he had apologized with a
grin. "Afraid the old budget doesn't allow for that kind of
extravagance. But you wait: one day, I'll be able to afford to

buy you roses. And I'll have a dozen delivered right to your door, every single week."

She hadn't minded that the flowers he gave her were only inexpensive daisies. What was important was that he expected they would still be together long afterward, that he was thinking about that "one day" in the future when he would still be buying her flowers. Of course, they had both believed that, had wanted it so badly, had just assumed that their fates would forever be bound up together. . . .

Suddenly, she couldn't bear to look at the painting for another minute. She turned and fled down the stairs. Paul was just finishing up on the phone when she came back into the living room.

"Sorry about that. It took a little longer than I expected—Hey, are you okay? You look a little shaken."

Julie forced a laugh. "And here you were just telling me how great I look. No, really, I'm fine. Just a little warm, I guess."

"Yeah, it is pretty hot in here. I still haven't worked out all the kinks in my thermister controls for the vent fans. Oops—sorry. What I mean is, the energy-efficient cooling system I'm trying to install still has a ways to go yet. Listen, let me get you something cold to drink."

He disappeared into the kitchen. When he emerged a few seconds later, he was grinning apologetically. "All I've got is beer. Is that okay?"

"That's fine." Gratefully, Julie reached for the ice-cold glass.

"Funny, you don't impress me as being your typical beer drinker."

"When I get hot enough, I'm your typical *anything* drinker." She looked around the airy front room after taking a few sips. Between the cold beer and her pleasant surroundings, she was finally starting to relax.

They talked a bit more, mainly about life on Shelter Island and some mutual acquaintances from high school who they'd each kept in touch with.

And then, Paul asked casually, "So, Julie, how are you finding married life?"

"Oh, it's great. Just great."

"What's your husband like?"

"Brad is every mother's dream of who her daughter should marry. First of all, he's very successful. He develops commercial real estate in Manhattan. He's also charming, witty, bright. . . ." That is, whenever he wants to be, Julie was thinking. "And as if all that weren't enough, he's even tall, dark, and handsome."

Paul was looking at her earnestly. "Do you love him?"

"Of course I love him!" Julie snapped.

A funny half-smile crossed Paul's lips. "Well, then, you're pretty lucky. Not everyone has the good fortune to hook up with somebody they really care about." He laughed coldly. "You're looking at a prime example of that."

Suddenly Julie felt extremely uncomfortable once again. She looked down at her glass of beer, now almost empty. "I guess you're talking about Sally."

She expected him to launch into a dispassionate monologue about everything that had gone wrong with his marriage, a recitation of all the things that were, in his eyes, wrong with the institution of marriage. Instead, he rushed over to her side.

"Look, Julie, I never even had a chance to explain what happened."

She looked at him then, her soft green eyes clouded with hurt. And holding back, pretending that everything was fine, just fine, was no longer possible. "You and I were *engaged,* Paul." Her voice was practically a sob. "And the next thing I knew, you were getting married to somebody else. To that— that—to Sally Horner, of all people."

"It was all a mistake. A horrible, nightmarish mistake."

"Was it . . . something I did, Paul?"

"God, no, Julie. It was me. It was just me, being stupid." He sighed deeply, suddenly sounding very tired. "Do you remember that weekend you were supposed to come up, and then you canceled at the last minute?"

She nodded. "It was Homecoming Weekend. The first week in November, during our junior year of college. I was all set to come up to your school. I'd even bought a new dress. I still remember it." She smiled wanly. "It was that shade of purplish blue you always liked so much. Remember? I had a sweater that color."

"I remember."

"Well, anyway, all that's not important. What turned out to be important, I guess, was the fact that I changed my mind at the eleventh hour, and we had that terrible argument over the phone. I decided, at the last minute, that with midterms coming up, I'd better buckle down and get some work done instead of flitting off to the local boys' school for a decadent weekend of fun and frolic.'' She bit her lip. "And when Christmas vacation finally rolled around, I found out you were about to be married. I never did understand it.''

And I guess I never really got over it, either. Julie let that last confession go unspoken.

"There's not much to understand.'' Paul was speaking softly, being careful not to let his eyes meet Julie's. "I was pretty disappointed when you canceled out at the last minute. Hey, face it: I was mad as hell. And it just so happened that Sally was around that weekend.''

"I always wondered if the reason she decided to go to Binghamton, of all places, was because you were there.''

"Well, at any rate, she was there at one of the frat parties. And I was feeling pretty sorry for myself, so I drank a few too many beers, and she kept coming on to me. . . . The whole thing had such a bad feeling about it, right from the start. But the next thing I knew, she came to me and told me she was pregnant. When I suggested an abortion—illegal in those days, you may recall—she went nuts.

"So,'' he continued with a melancholy shrug, "I did what in those days was optimistically referred to as 'the right thing.' I dropped out of college, got a crummy job, and married her.''

"And after Becky was born?''

"Well, for a while it looked as if things might actually work out. I mean, we were both so caught up in the excitement of having a new baby around. But it wasn't long before the whole thing got to us both. I felt really trapped, you know? And I guess that once old Sally had me where she wanted me, she decided I wasn't what she wanted, after all. And she wasn't exactly the easiest person in the world to live with. Not that that came as any great surprise, of course. Anyway, we finally split.''

There was a long silence. Julie was the one who finally broke it.

"It must be hard, not seeing your daughter as much as you'd like. Where do they live now?''

"They're both still upstate. They never left that area, right around Binghamton. I go up there a couple of times a month, and Becky comes out here on some of her vacations. Of course, once she goes to college, it'll be even harder to see her. She's going out to Ohio State.''

"I guess it's inevitable that they all grow up, sooner or later." For a moment, Julie was almost smug about the fact that Josh was still just a baby. She still had his entire childhood ahead of her, something to look forward to, something to savor. Paul, on the other hand, already had all that behind him.

"Yeah. So, anyway, after Sally and I split, an old friend of mine was doing some work out here and he told me it was a booming area. I needed a change, so I thought I'd check it out. And, well, that was seven years ago." Paul chuckled. "I'm practically an institution around here by now."

"It looks like it's not a bad life," Julie said, looking around her as if the house itself gave testimony to that fact.

"No, it's a great place. Real quiet in the winter, but I kind of like that. And I've got my work, which keeps me busy." He hesitated, as if wondering if he should continue going off on tangents or make a point of going back to what they were originally talking about. He decided that opting for formality wouldn't do either of them a bit of good in the long run. There was still too much that was unfinished between them.

"So, Julie, do you think you could ever forgive me for the way things turned out?" he asked gently.

"Oh, Paul, we were both so young then. And it seems so far away now." It was a lie, pretending that she didn't care anymore, that so much time had gone by that she no longer felt devastated. But the fact was that a lot of time had passed, and dwelling on things that couldn't be changed seemed like it would only cause more pain.

"Well, maybe it all worked out for the best then, after all. I mean, look at you. You're a big celebrity, you've got a fancy car . . . and you're married to a man you really love. Someone you really care about."

Julie just smiled weakly. "Yes, I guess I can't complain about the way things have turned out for me."

She stood up then, without even realizing that she was about to. "Well, I guess I'd better get going."

Paul looked at her in astonishment. "So soon? But I haven't even had a chance to show you around the place."

"I took the liberty of doing some snooping while you were on the phone. It's a terrific house, Paul. I can see that you've really done a lot with it, and that you love your work. You're very lucky that way. But I really do have to run. My niece is babysitting, and I feel bad sticking her with Josh for too long. After all, it's her vacation, too.''

Paul resisted the urge to protest. Instead, he just nodded. "Well, okay. But you're going to be out here for a while yet, right? Maybe we could get together again. It really is great seeing you, Julie. Besides, I promised you a drink, and I still owe you a night out.''

"It depends on my husband's plans," she returned. The coldness in her voice surprised even her. But all of a sudden, she felt an inexplicable anger toward Paul. Not so much for what had happened twenty years ago, but more because he was of no use to her now, no use in helping her deal with the things that were bothering her, tearing her apart. He didn't belong in her life anymore, and the thought of spending even another minute with him made her restless.

"Okay." He sounded deflated, and more than a little surprised by her sudden change of tone. "Whatever's best for you. But I'd like to see you again, if it works out. Just give me a call. I'll be around.''

The good-byes that followed were stiff and hurried. Julie could hardly wait to get to the safety of her car. She just wanted to be alone, away from all the complications of life, the emotional upheavals that threw her into such turmoil that she could hardly think straight. She felt so confused—about Paul, about Brad, about what she was feeling, about what she really wanted. She felt as if she wanted to drive and drive, just get away from everyone and everything.

But, of course, she couldn't. She had to get back to Josh; perhaps not as quickly as she had pretended, but she was responsible for him. It was her son she should be spending the afternoon with, not some old boyfriend, a man who had once meant a great deal to her but now had no place at all in her life. She tried to think about Josh as she sped away from Paul's house, glad that the empty roads provided her with the chance to be just a little bit reckless. But even as she tried to concentrate on an image of his angelic face, how gleeful he would be to see her, she felt a miserable heaviness in her heart. Tears were streaming down her cheeks by the time she got home.

Chapter Fourteen

It was not often that Barbara Boucher Gilbert was nervous.
That tight feeling in the stomach, the barely perceptible
trembling of the hands, that awful sensation of being just on
the edge of panic, of losing control—these were all quite
foreign to this woman who, at thirty-four, was one of the
most successful stockbrokers at Kinney, Mays & Dayton,
Boston's oldest and most prestigious investment house.

Yet today, as she stepped off the Shelter Island ferry,
already scanning the crowd for her husband, studying the row
of cars waiting at the edge of the parking lot as she tried to
make out Wesley's Volvo, she was actually experiencing
those signs of anxiety—just as she had ten minutes or so
earlier when she had telephoned Wesley from Greenport,
unannounced and completely unexpected, to say that she had
had a change of heart and decided to join him and the others
out here on Shelter Island, after all.

"Barbara? Is that you?" At the mere sound of her voice,
she had observed dryly, Wes had gone from sounding like a
mature, confident man to sounding like a high school sophomore who couldn't quite believe that the head cheerleader
was actually calling him on the phone.

"Hello, Wes," Barbara had returned evenly. "Yes, it's
me."

"It's so good—I'm glad you called. Is—is everything okay?"

"Everything is fine." She paused, not quite sure of what to

say next. She decided to keep it simple. "Wes, I'm in Greenport."

"Greenport! You're out here?"

"Yes. I came down from Boston last night. I spent the night in New York, at Melanie's apartment. You remember Melanie, don't you? My old roommate from Wellesley?"

"Vaguely."

"Well, anyway, I caught the nine o'clock train out this morning. I'm about to take the ferry across."

"Fine! Great! I'll come pick you up."

After a few hasty exchanges to clarify where and when they should meet up with each other, Wes's voice had suddenly softened.

"Hey, Barbara . . . ?" he said, his voice strained.

"Umm?"

"I, uh, I'm so glad you're here. I can't tell you. Why— why did you change your mind about coming?"

At that point, Barbara had been relieved to be presented with a convenient distraction. "Oh, the ferry's about to pull out. Listen, Wes, we'll talk about it when I get there."

The uncertainty she had felt then about her sudden decision to come out here lingered throughout the short ferry ride. Now, it was erupting with more and more ferociousness as she caught sight of the Volvo pulling into the ferry dock's parking lot.

Not that anyone would ever have guessed. As usual, Barbara looked as if she'd just stepped off the pages of a fashion magazine. She appeared to be perfectly relaxed as she stood leaning against a low fence, dressed entirely in white: tailored pleated pants, clingy tank top, blousey jacket. Her thick, straight black hair, cut blunt just above the shoulders, was neat and shiny; perched atop her head was a pair of dark sunglasses. Over one shoulder was an oversized straw bag that looked more like a fashionable purse than a suitcase. Everything about her was fresh-looking, even though she'd just spent three hours on a train and everyone around her looked hot and wilted.

She was perfectly aware of the many glances that were cast in her direction as she stood waiting—approving glances, envious glances—but they didn't faze her in the least. After all, Barbara was used to it by now. It seemed to be her lot, being admired by others, just as much as it seemed to be her lot to remain slightly apart from everyone else. That was how it had always been for her, partly because of circumstance, partly because she wanted it that way.

When she was a little girl growing up in Alexandria, right outside Washington, D.C., she had had no time for the other little girls with whom she attended private school, girls who were preoccupied with dolls and birthday parties and hair ribbons. Instead, she had preferred being alone, reading or studying or playing the harp.

Both her parents were serious about whatever endeavors they undertook, and their successful careers—her father's as a diplomat, her mother's as an internist—were proof that such dedication paid off. And so it seemed only natural that their only child follow in their footsteps, revering the concept of hard work and backing it up with tremendous self-discipline.

Ironically, her aloofness had always made her even more attractive to others than she might have otherwise been. As a young woman—poised, beautiful, intelligent, talented—she had been invited to all the "right" parties. The most desirable boys had always asked her out, even though she never went out of her way to catch their attention. She constantly won prizes and awards and honors for music and academics and all the other achievements that came to her so easily.

After graduating from Wellesley College summa cum laude, with a double major in French and economics, she spent two years in Paris working in the marketing department of IBM. Then she returned to Boston, where she continued with the same firm, this time in a management capacity. She had never expected to go into finance, but when she met one of the partners of Kinney, Mays at a cocktail party and he was totally bowled over by her, she found herself being wined and dined and finally lured into the employ of the highly respected investment house.

Now, almost ten years later, she was, as her boss was fond of saying, so important to the firm that it was surprising that the IRS didn't require their accountants to list her name under "Assets." Even so, today she was feeling like quite a different person from that self-assured dynamo that the nine-to-five world was so used to seeing—especially as she spotted the familiar blue Volvo heading over in her direction.

Once it had pulled up right in front of her and Wesley leaned across the front seat and opened the car door for her, she slid in promptly, without giving a thought to that little courtesy. Her posture was regal, her movements confident yet graceful as she arranged herself beside her husband, feeling his eyes upon her.

"Hello, Wes," she said with a small smile.

"Barbara, it's so great to see you. . . ."

"I thought that train ride would never end." She was suddenly cool, finding herself withdrawing from him without even realizing it. She pulled her sunglasses down from the top of her head and put them on, as if to keep her distance. "I took the Eastern shuttle down last night. It's amazing that it's three hours from New York to Shelter Island, but I got to New York from Boston in less than an hour. It was wonderful seeing Melanie again, though. We put our heads together and figured out that it's been three years since she and I last got together."

Slowly she crossed her long legs. "So how has your stay out here been? Nice to see the rest of the Gilbert tribe, I imagine." Barbara didn't even try to keep the sarcasm out of her voice.

"It's been kind of fun, actually." Wes sounded only a little bit defensive. "Katy and I have had a chance to catch up—and you should see Josh. He's practically grown up."

But Barbara could barely bring herself to listen. "I can't wait to take a shower," she said, staring out the window. "And I desperately need something to eat. I'm starving."

"Both can be arranged easily enough. In fact, you're in luck: Chrissie and Julie spent the entire morning in the kitchen, whipping up some kind of fancy curried chicken salad."

How odd, she thought as she and Wes both lapsed into a rather uncomfortable silence. There must be a million things that Wes is dying to say to me. . . . I know that I feel as if there's still a lot that needs to be said.

Yet here we are, talking about lunch.

When in Rome . . . thought Barbara, pulling a jade green one-piece bathing suit up over her narrow, well-toned torso. Everyone at the office knows I'm spending this week and a half on a resort island, so when I show up at the office the day after Labor Day, I'd better have a decent tan. Not that I consider lying around in the sun the most enthralling way of spending my first morning here on Shelter Island. . . .

Actually, it wasn't the prospect of baking in the heat that was making her so pensive as she tugged at the top of the bathing suit, then the bottom, and then scrutinized her reflection in the mirror. No, there was something else on her mind as she leaned forward and peered at the tall, slim woman looking back at her.

She looked just fine, she was pleased to see, as sleek as ever. But then it was time for the true test. She turned ninety degrees so the slender body in the mirror was in profile. She studied her own image with a merciless eye—and let out a sigh of relief.

It was about eleven weeks now, according to her own calculations and Dr. Cadman's confirmation, but she wasn't showing yet. Her silhouette, as sleek as a jaguar's even in this tight-fitting bathing suit, was not about to betray her secret.

As for the six pounds she'd put on in the last couple of months—well, no one would ever notice. No one, that is, except for Wes. After all, he was the only person who saw her frequently enough to pick up on something like that. Besides, he knew how compulsive she was about watching her weight, going on a virtual starvation diet every time the digital scale in their bathroom warned her that she had put on even a pound.

Bearing that in mind, Barbara grabbed an oversized cotton shirt to wear over her bathing suit, resolving to remove it only when her husband was out of sight. As she slipped into it, still studying her reflection in the mirror to see just how good a job it was doing of concealing the ever so slight thickening around her middle, she found her thoughts drifting back to another slinky outfit she had once owned, the one she had been wearing the very first time she and Wes met.

She had been barely out of her twenties, yet Barbara Boucher was already a phenomenally successful businesswoman with her own one-bedroom condominium overlooking Boston Harbor, a sleek white Porsche, and a platinum American Express card. Her work was her life, leaving her little time or inclination for very much of anything else. That is, until a week or so before Christmas, when her boss invited her over for a small holiday party—an evening of "drinking eggnog, singing corny old Christmas carols, and networking," as he put it.

It was just a coincidence that a few days earlier she had overheard one of her male colleagues snickering to another, saying that underneath those pinstripe suits of hers, Barbara Boucher had "balls of steel." She had been mildly amused at first, then quickly became determined to make a point. She showed up at Carter Dayton's Christmas party in a slinky red dress slit up the thigh and the highest pair of heels she owned. And while she got the reaction she had been hoping for, it turned out that the effect was noticed by more than just the men she worked with day in and day out.

Wesley Gilbert, as the brainy dynamo behind Tek-Life, was someone Carter Dayton had decided was worth getting to know better. He was expecting great things from that company, and he knew full well that Wes Gilbert *was* Tek-Life. As soon as he walked in the door, Carter sicced his top broker on him.

"He's all yours, Barbara," he said with a grin. "There's a man who's really going places. At the very least, try to get him to invest with us."

As soon as she laid eyes on him, Barbara knew she wanted to do a lot more than that.

"Hi," she said in her throaty voice. "I'm Barbara Boucher. I'm a broker with Kinney, Mays."

When Wes looked up from the rum eggnog a waiter had just handed him, he nearly dropped his glass. He was completely taken aback by having been approached by such a beautiful woman, especially since she had been the first person he'd noticed when he walked in the door less than five minutes earlier. "Hello," he managed to say with great difficulty. "I'm Wesley Gilbert."

"Yes, I already know all about you." Beyond her usual businesslike manner, there were undertones of flirtatiousness as Barbara spoke. "And my boss tells me that you're someone worth knowing," she went on, her dark brown eyes fixed intently on his green ones. "How about us getting out of here? I'd love to buy you dinner. And it just so happens that my favorite Italian restaurant is only a few blocks away from here."

Wes was charmed right from the start. As for Barbara, she was pleased, and even a little bit relieved, that now that she had finally found someone she considered worth pursuing, her abilities in that area were proving to be more than adequate.

Their love affair seemed too good to be true, right from the start. They could talk for hours, both of them enjoying the chance to show off how smart they were—and have it be appreciated, too.

And it turned out that they loved so many of the same things: going to classic films or newer, offbeat ones at the Orson Welles Cinema in Cambridge; shopping for fresh ingredients in Haymarket Square and the North End and then whipping up a fabulous dinner for a small group of friends or even for just the two of them; attending lectures on erudite subjects like Trends in Contemporary Japanese Art or Decorative Pieces from the *Art Moderne* School at one of Boston's universities or the fine arts museum.

Their decision to marry seemed a logical next step. And for a while, the apparent perfection of their relationship continued. They had their careers, their common passions, their compatibility.

But then, out of the blue, it all fell apart. Barbara discovered she was pregnant. Her marriage was no longer just one more achievement, a pleasant diversion she had more or less fallen into, something else for everyone on the outside to envy. She was no longer trying it out, comfortable in the feeling if it proved to be too confining for her, if she missed her independence too much, she could always slip out of it with the same ease and grace she had maintained all her life.

All of a sudden, it was for real. And that, she had recognized right away, changed everything.

Well, no use ruminating over all that now, Barbara insisted to herself, shaking her head as if trying to rid herself of the thoughts that had been obsessing her for the past three weeks, ever since she had left her husband, unable to deal with the conflicting emotions that were suddenly overwhelming her. I might as well let myself take at least a little break. Long enough to go downstairs and get myself some breakfast, if nothing else.

With that, she buttoned up the last button, checked her silhouette in the mirror one more time, and headed downstairs.

She had been hoping to enjoy a cup of coffee, and maybe an English muffin, in peace. Instead, on her way to the kitchen she was spotted by a group of Gilbert women outside on the patio having what looked like an early morning *kaffeeklatsch*.

"Good morning, Barbara!" Julie called to her gaily, with a little wave. "Why don't you grab a cup of coffee and join us?"

"Sure." Barbara forced a smile.

So much for a solitary morning, she thought wryly. I should have known better than to expect more than two minutes by myself while I'm out here.

But it was just as well, she knew. Joining the others would

give her an excuse to stop trying to figure out her reasons for having come, as well as trying to decide exactly what to say to Wesley now that she was here.

She was ravenous, she discovered as soon as she went into the kitchen and was confronted with the half-eaten tray of cinnamon-pecan rolls that was sitting on the counter next to the coffeepot, still warm and emitting an irresistible spicy fragrance.

Little Miss Homemaker Lynn's doing, no doubt, she thought cynically.

But as she helped herself to two, arranging them on a small plate, then wolfed down a third after glancing around to make sure no one was watching, she realized what a hypocrite she was being, criticizing her sister-in-law even as she greedily took advantage of the woman's domestic abilities.

I'm probably just jealous, she thought, heading out to the patio. The only thing I ever bake is Aunt Jemima's coffee cake from a mix, and even that usually comes out dreadful.

As she approached the others, gathered around the table and appearing to be having a merry time together, she forced herself to smile, hoping that acting the part would help her ease into a more sociable mood.

"It looks like it's going to be a perfectly gorgeous day," Barbara said breezily as she slid open the glass doors and joined Lynn, Katy, and Julie out on the patio. "I'd almost forgotten how beautiful it is out here on Shelter Island."

"Especially this early in the morning," said Julie. As Barbara headed over in her direction, she pulled her chair over to make room for her sister-in-law to sit down.

It was no coincidence that Barbara chose to sit next to Julie. Out of all the Gilberts, she was the one she felt closest to. After all, the two women had quite a bit in common. They were both extremely successful in their careers, and they had both chosen unusually demanding, competitive fields in which to make their mark—Barbara in finance, Julie in television. And they were equally attractive, Barbara with her dark, exotic beauty, Julie with her all-American blond, green-eyed sunniness.

Yet there were differences, as well. While Julie was a warm, outgoing woman, someone who thrived on being with people, Barbara was much more withdrawn, much more introverted. Even so, their contrasting styles had served each of them well enough as they strove to excel in their work. Julie had climbed to the top by making friends all the way up the ladder, winning everyone over with her friendliness and her lack of pretentiousness. Barbara, meanwhile, had never been comfortable acting buddy-buddy with her coworkers. Instead, she had made her mark by handling herself with impressive coolness and self-confidence, at the same time doing such a superior job that she was bound to get recognition.

While Julie and Barbara were aware of how differently they approached their jobs—and everything else, as well—they felt a kind of bond, a kinship that was based on their mutual understanding that they were both up against the same kinds of pressures, that they both wanted the same kinds of things for themselves.

"And here I thought I was to be commended for getting up so early," Barbara said as she helped herself to a healthy slab of softened butter, then spread a generous amount onto one of the cinnamon-pecan rolls. "Do you mean to tell me I'm the only one in this entire house who slept past eight?"

"I'm afraid that's pretty much the case. The members of this family don't seem to have much understanding of the concept of *leisure*," Julie said with a smile. "Let's see. My brothers are both out sailing already. Wes is in the Lightning, and Michael took out the Sunfish—"

"That sounds like something worth getting up early for," Katy interjected.

"Actually, I was thinking the exact same thing," said Julie. "As a matter of fact, I was wondering if maybe a whole bunch of us could get together and go out for a sail later on. Maybe this afternoon. It'd be fun, don't you think? Just like when we were kids. Gosh, I haven't been sailing in years. . . .

"Anyway, Barbara, to get back to my status report on the entire Gilbert clan," Julie went on, "Chrissie's already at the beach, Mom's in the shower, Dad's got Josh out on a nature walk collecting shells along the shore—"

"Beth's still in bed," Lynn said. "Now there's a late sleeper for you."

"By the way, Lynn," Barbara interjected, "these rolls are fantastic. I think they taste better every time you make them."

"That's funny, Barbara. I don't think I've ever seen you eat one before," Katy noted, interrupting before the blushing Lynn had a chance to thank her sister-in-law for her compliment. "As a matter of fact, you usually treat sugar as if it were cyanide."

Barbara smiled, a bit thrown by having been caught. "Must be old age creeping up on me. I'm losing my willpower."

"But certainly not your figure!" Lynn assured her quickly.

"Boy," said Julie, putting down her coffee cup and leaning back in her chaise lounge, "if you're worried about 'old age,' Barbara, where does that put me? You're—what, thirty-four? I'm thirty-nine. And you know what *that* means."

"Oh, Julie, you'll be a gorgeous forty." Barbara tried leaving the second cinnamon-pecan roll on her plate, just to make a point, but found that she simply couldn't. "Besides, look at Barbara Walters. She just gets better and better with time."

"Richer and richer, too," said Katy. "Maybe that's what I should have done with my life. Gone into broadcasting, like you, Julie." She sighed dramatically, then rested her chin in her hands. "If only I'd been planning my future when I was a little girl, instead of wasting all that time selling Girl Scout cookies."

"It's funny," Lynn said with a self-conscious giggle. "When I was little, I wanted to grow up and have a glamorous career. Become a fashion designer, or maybe an airline stewardess so that I could see the world. . . ."

"How about you, Julie?" asked Katy. Surprisingly, there was no malice in her voice. "When you were a kid, did you ever think you'd be a famous television personality *and* have a gorgeous husband and a beautiful child?"

The look of irony that flickered across Julie's face went unnoticed. She adjusted the straw hat she was wearing to protect her eyes and said, "Frankly, when I was growing up, I never gave much thought to the future. I was too busy living for the moment. You know, obsessing over whether or not I was going to make the cheerleading team, or who I'd go to the Junior Prom with."

She shrugged. "It wasn't until much later that it even occurred to me that people made plans. How about you, Katy? Surely you didn't spend *all* your time thinking about Girl Scout cookies."

"Oh, you know me. I wanted to join the circus, star in a rodeo, make a million dollars by the time I was twenty-one, and marry Mick Jagger." Katy let out a boisterous laugh, then immediately grew serious. "In some ways, I guess I have done a lot of things. Not those, maybe, but some that are almost as outrageous."

And I left a few of them unfinished along the way, too, she was tempted to add, thinking about the career as an anthropologist that she almost had.

"Well, at least you have your whole life ahead of you, Katy." Lynn suddenly sounded bitter. "You still have plenty of time to decide what you want, and then go after it."

"Why, no more than you do. I'm thirty-three, and you're thirty-nine. That's only six years' difference."

"Yes, but things are different for me. I've got two teenaged daughters and a husband who . . . and a husband." Lynn looked away from the others.

"Oh, dear," said Julie loftily, pretending she took Lynn's outburst as a joke. "Don't tell me that brother of mine has been giving you a hard time. What's Michael up to now?"

Lynn wished she could tell them. She wanted so badly to fit in with this group: beautiful, successful Julie; brilliant, outspoken Katy; cool, controlled Barbara. But she didn't fit in—she couldn't. She was the outsider again. Especially since she had her own suspicions about what Michael was "up to," and it was hardly the kind of thing she'd want to go around talking about, especially to his sisters.

"Oh, he's not up to anything. I guess we've just gotten into . . . kind of a rut. But don't worry," she rushed to assure them. "It's nothing, really. And getting away for a couple of weeks is bound to set everything right again."

Julie and Katy exchanged glances. But before either one of them could offer any encouragement or probe any further, Pat appeared at the sliding doors that separated the back porch from the living room. The congenial mood was broken, the spirit of closeness and camaraderie that had brightened up the women's morning was diffused.

"Guess I'll go get dressed," said Katy, feeling guilty about having had her mother catch her sitting around in her nightgown—just one more manifestation of her laziness, she was certain was Pat's interpretation.

Barbara, however, was relieved. She had had enough chatter for the moment, however entertaining it might have been. With secrets of her own, secrets she was bent on keeping, opening up even just a little was simply too dangerous.

Chapter Fifteen

"*This is just* like old times, isn't it?" Michael glanced over at his brother, who was busily setting the spinnaker pole in anticipation of the run downwind into Peconic Bay. The Lightning, an angular nineteen-foot Fiberglas sailboat that was known for its lightness and speed, was one of Ben's newest toys, bought only a couple of years earlier to replace his wooden model of the same design.

"What's like old times? You mean you sitting there and me doing all the work?" Wes returned with a grin.

"Michael Gilbert, are you still bossing your little brother around, even after all these years?" Katy yelled over from the Sunfish that she and Julie were sailing right behind them. "If you're not careful," she went on to tease, "you may find yourself up to your neck in water one of these days."

"It wouldn't be the first time," Julie joked. "What about that time Wes and Mike took the Lightning out—the old wooden one we had when we were kids, remember? The one the boys insisted on painting that ugly purple? And the wind suddenly came up . . . ?"

"Right," Michael remembered with a groan. "We made the mistake of practicing tying knots in the mainsheet while there was no wind. The next thing we knew, the wind got stiffer and, of course, we couldn't let the mainsail out because the knots get caught in the pulleys."

"And the boat tipped over." Wes chuckled. "I remember that day well. I lost my brand-new Topsiders. Mom had a fit."

"Oh, yeah? Well, I lost my radio. That was the last time I ever took anything valuable on board."

"Fortunately, you're both too mature to make any silly mistakes like that, right?" quipped Katy. "I sure hope so, because I don't particularly feel like saving two drowning water rats today. It's too nice out to waste the day practicing my water-saving technique—whatever's left of it, that is."

"Yes, it is nice, isn't it?" Julie observed. She was taking her turn at the tiller of the Sunfish, but with today's gentle wind, there was little for her to do besides adjust it slightly every now and then to make sure the women's smaller boat kept up with the much faster Lightning.

"Yeah, this was a good idea," said Wes. "Just the four of us, out on the water, hanging out together, like when we were kids."

"Except for the fact that now some of us actually *have* kids," Michael commented. "God, I can't believe that Chrissie is actually going to be starting college in another couple of years. And Beth—little Beth!—is already becoming interested in boys."

"Tell me about it," Julie agreed. "Look at Josh. I haven't even had a chance to give away my maternity clothes, and he's already talking!"

"Speaking of the passage of time," said Katy, "has anybody besides me noticed that Dad's looking a bit peaky around the gills lately?"

"I don't know about his gills," Wes replied, "but he does look kind of tired. I noticed that as soon as I got here. And he's been acting old, too."

Julie frowned. "What do you mean, 'acting old,' Wes? I don't follow."

"I do," Katy interjected. "Like if you suggest he do something the least bit strenuous, like play tennis or go for a swim, he looks alarmed at the mere thought. And he always says no, like he just doesn't have the energy—or like he's afraid he might not have the energy. He didn't used to be like that."

"Has Mom said anything?" asked Wes. "I mean, is he still his old energetic self at home?"

"I haven't heard her say anything," said Julie with a

shrug. "I think she would have told me if something was wrong."

"Well, he is getting on, don't forget," Michael pointed out. "I guess he's just starting to feel it a little bit, that's all."

"I don't buy it." Katy shook her head. "It's not like him. He's too much of a fighter."

"Even fighters get old," Julie pointed out gently. "Hey, look at those white caps. I think we're finally getting some wind here."

"All right! Let's reef the mainsail, Wes."

Michael slid over to help Wes bundle the bottom of the sail up around the boom, the horizontal wooden foot that formed the bottom side of the sail's triangle. It didn't take the two men long to make the sail smaller, to adjust for the sudden puff of wind.

"There. Just in time, too. This wind is serious."

"As I recall, that was one of the very first lessons from sailing class," Katy remembered. "The bigger the wind, the smaller the sail. Otherwise, prepare for a dunking." She, too, was busy trimming the sail, having learned well the lesson that leaving too much surface area in a strong wind was bound to capsize a small boat like the Sunfish or the Lightning.

"No, thanks," Michael called back. "But how about racing?"

"No way!" she protested. "This is supposed to be a pleasure sail, remember? Not a cutthroat drag race with two hoodlums in some macho boat!"

"Look, if you two want to go off and take advantage of this wind, feel free," Julie offered. "Don't feel you have to wait around for us. We could never catch up with you, anyway."

"Due to the differences in our boats," Katy was quick to explain, "not because my sister here and I aren't both master sailors."

"Well, ex-master sailors, anyway." Julie smiled. "I think we're all a little bit rusty."

"I'm ready to take to the open seas," said Michael. "How about you, Wes?"

"Sure. Let's try out the old sea legs."

After the men had taken off, leaving the women behind in the Sunfish, Katy turned to Julie and grinned. "What is it

Mike and Wes were saying? That this was like old times? Guess they were right.''

"Yes, here we are, left behind by our rabble-rousing brothers," Julie agreed with a chuckle. "But it's kind of nice being out here alone like this, don't you think? I'd almost forgotten how much fun sailing was."

"Yeah. Too bad there doesn't seem to be much time for this kind of thing in grown-up life."

The two women were silent for a few minutes, absorbed in coordinating their movements as they zigzagged the Sunfish back and forth, tacking against the steadily increasing wind.

It was Julie who finally spoke. "Hey, Katy?"

"Umm?" Katy was now at the tiller, and the stronger winds were keeping her busy.

"You were right before. What you said about Dad, I mean. I did notice that he looks . . . I don't know, tired. Older, I guess.''

Katy shrugged. "Well, like Michael said, he is getting on."

"Yes, I know. But I guess knowing that and wanting to believe it—I mean really accepting it—are two entirely different things."

"I know what you mean."

For a long time the women were silent, just staring out at the sea. Yet they were both aware, each in her own way, that they were sharing a special closeness, a common bond rooted in the fact that no matter what their differences, they were, after all, still sisters.

Chapter Sixteen

There's nothing more deadly than a rainy day on Shelter Island, thought Katy with a deep sigh.

She was standing in front of the sliding patio doors, her breath making little bursts of fog on the glass as she watched the steady rain falling over the bright yellow-and-white-striped awning. As she let herself be nearly hypnotized by its comforting rhythm, it occurred to her that it was acting as if it were actually enjoying the way it was making a mockery of the very concept of summer fun.

Around her, the level of boredom was so high that she could feel it pressing in on her, almost as oppressive as the stagnant summer heat that was today made even worse by the extreme humidity. Being cooped up inside all day was like a test—and according to the informal anthropological analysis she was making, the various personality types within this tiny society were each responding to the challenge differently.

The first group—the troopers, as she'd labeled them—had banded together, determined to make the best of it as boisterously as possible. The four of them were sitting at a folding bridge table set up in the middle of the living room, huddled around the Trivial Pursuit board. As Katy stared out the window, pulling the white acrylic sweater she'd borrowed from Lynn more tightly around her, she was half listening to Michael, Lynn, and Dad guffawing over Wes's inability to remember the names of Lucy and Ricky Ricardo's next-door neighbors.

She had nicknamed the second group the fainthearted. They were the introverts, the ones who had retreated into pursuits that were more personal—and considerably more quiet. Beth, sitting apart from all the others, was watching soap operas on television. Barbara was upstairs in her room, forging through the latest humongous James Clavell novel. Chrissie had been shut up in the bathroom ever since lunch. Josh was taking his afternoon nap. Pat, as usual, was tucked away in the kitchen, slaving away as she chatted to Julie, who, she guessed, was helping her prepare an elaborate dinner that this crowd would no doubt gobble up in seven minutes flat.

And as if this scene on the home front weren't bad enough, Katy was thinking, this obscene rain means that I won't be seeing Randy today. He is, after all, only a houseguest at the Cotters', so that doesn't give him a whole lot of freedom to entertain lady visitors. And I sure could never bring myself to invite him over to this madhouse, not today when all the inmates are locked in. So what's left? With this weather, both picnicking at the beach and miniature golf are definitely out.

She was surprised just thinking about Randy filled her with a warm feeling, one that was entirely unrelated to the damp heat hanging over the room. No, this one was making her feel almost as if she were glowing.

Uh-oh, she warned herself. Watch out, kid. Sure, he likes you; that's obvious. But don't for even a minute lose sight of the fact that you're nothing more than a summer fling—if that. Good old Randall Palmer is still Mr. Corporate, don't forget, complete with the one-bedroom co-op in Brooklyn Heights, in which he is firmly rooted. Somehow that image just doesn't mix with a funky Foodstuffs' employee from upstate New York, a long distance away in more ways than one.

Nah, we've got no future, me and him, Katy concluded, insisting to herself that she didn't really care. Besides, once I get back to Real Life, I've still got that dashing Nicholas Somers waiting in the wings. So, I'll have a couple of laughs with Randy, take it for what it is—and with my usual skill, simply walk away, unscathed, once it's all over. . . .

"Look, everybody! Don't you just *love* it?"

Chrissie had just come prancing into the living room, wearing Julie's yellow silk bathrobe and very little else. But this time, it wasn't the teenaged girl's outfit that everyone in

the room immediately focused on: it was her hair. While only
that morning the thick mane of long straight tresses had been
a pretty golden brown, it had, through the magic of a few
chemicals and a short bout with a blow-dryer, been trans-
formed into a dramatic champagne blond.

"Isn't it the most gorgeous color you've ever seen in your
life?"

"Oh, my God!" Automatically Katy's eyes flew to Lynn's
face.

"Chrissie, I thought we had already talked about you
bleaching your hair." Lynn's words, though even and controlled on the surface, emerged from between clenched teeth.
The magnitude of her anger was also reflected in her eyes.

"Oh, Mom, I didn't *bleach* it! I just *colored* it! And I think
it looks fantastic. Just because you're so old-fashioned—"

"Chrissie, whether or not you agree with me is not the
point. What is the point is that we already discussed this, not
two months ago. And as I recall we decided that you would
wait until you were older before you started ruining your
hair."

"I didn't *ruin* it! Boy, Mom, you think *anything* I do is
terrible! You're always against me! You *hate* me, don't you?"

In the face of all this family tension, Beth quietly picked up
her book and slipped away virtually unnoticed, retreating to the
safety of her bedroom upstairs. Only Katy saw her stealing away.
The girl's pain tugged at her as sharply as if it were her own.

Without giving it a second thought, she tore after her
younger niece, taking the steps two at a time.

"Hey, kid," she said brightly, "how about you and me
doing something fun?"

Beth had already settled into the soft upholstered chair in
the corner, right next to the window, with her book placed
firmly in her lap. As she glanced up, she kept her finger on
the line she had been reading, Katy observed, as if wanting to
keep an immediate escape nearby in case this intrusion proved
to be too much for her.

"What do you mean, 'something fun'? Like what?" She
looked doubtful.

"Oh, I don't know. Surely two geniuses like you and me
should be able to come up with something if we put our heads
together."

"I have an idea," said Beth. "Maybe we could try dying
my hair blond, too."

Katy couldn't tell if she was kidding or not. "Nah. Women like you and me, with our coloring, look best when we leave things as Mother Nature intended them to be. Although I have considered dying my hair purple. . . . To tell you the truth, I was thinking more along the lines of . . . oh, I don't know. Baking cookies, maybe."

"Peanut butter chocolate chip?" For a moment, a flicker of joy shone in Beth's eyes. But it faded as quickly as it had appeared. "No, I'd better not. If I make them, then I'll want to eat them."

"Yeah, I know what you mean. The good stuff is always bad for you, right?"

Katy's sympathy was sincere. She understood only too well the frustration of wanting—of *craving*—what could only end up turning against you. The desire for the sweet, short-lived fix derived from devouring a fistful of chocolate chip cookies was the perfect example of the debate that raged inside her constantly. The temporary cure for what ailed her—feeling lonely, feeling blue, feeling fat and unattractive—would only compound that condition even further, not too far down the road.

"Hey, I know!" Katy snapped her fingers. "What a brainstorm! How about if we go upstairs into the attic and poke around a little bit? Come on, it'll be fun to do some exploring."

Beth frowned. "I didn't even know there was an attic in this house."

"Just a dusty, musty little place. You have to lower a ladder out of the ceiling to get up there. You know, I don't think anybody's bothered to scrounge around in it for ages. But I bet we'll find all kinds of neat stuff packed away up there."

"Yeah? Like what?" Beth still wasn't totally convinced.

"How should I know? If I knew, we wouldn't have to go exploring. All I know is, Mom and Dad practically emptied the attic of our house in Harrington when they converted the third floor into that extra guest room. And they ended up putting most of our old junk up here."

"But aren't there spiders . . . ?"

Katy groaned. "What a worrywort! Where's your sense of adventure, child? Come on, get your ass in gear!"

While Beth's apprehensions about creepy-crawly things proved unfounded, Katy's description of the attic as dusty and musty turned out to be uncomfortably accurate.

"This is like opening an Egyptian tomb!" Katy began to cough uncontrollably as soon as she opened up the attic door and stuck her head up inside it. She sneezed a few times, then blinked away the tears that had sprung to her eyes. But when she looked down at Beth's hopeful upturned face, she decided to forge ahead. "But I guess a little dust never hurt anybody."

Crawling around on their hands and knees, balancing flashlights as best they could, they began peering inside trunks and cardboard cartons. Overhead, the rain pelted down hard on the roof, just a few feet above their heads. But they quickly forgot about all worldly matters as they became lost in uncovering little pieces of the Gilbert family's past.

"Hey, check this out!"

Katy held up a strapless gown with a straight skirt, made from white satin interlaced with strands of gold. It was the kind of dress that a lounge singer might have worn thirty years earlier—except that this dress was only six inches long.

"My Barbie doll used to wear this! That is, before she had her consciousness raised, dumped that turkey Ken, and put herself through law school working as a carpenter. And here's all her other clothes. A ski outfit, an evening gown, a tennis dress. . . . Wow, look at these red plastic shoes! Boy, with this bimbo as my role model, it's no wonder I turned out as screwed up as I did."

"What's this?" Blinking in puzzlement, Beth held up another tiny dress, this one a short white shift trimmed with five tiny rows of fringe.

"Oh, my God. That, my dear innocent lamb, is a twist dress."

"A *what*?"

"It's a dress you wear when you're doing the twist. You know, the dance? Chubby Checker, the Peppermint Lounge . . . ? You have no idea what I'm talking about, do you?" Katy shook her head and sighed. "I'm starting to feel like it's time for me to sign myself into the Little Flower Home for Senior Citizens."

But Beth wasn't listening. "What's this?" She had just opened a small cardboard carton. In it was nothing but papers, some tied up in bundles, some just tossed in haphazardly.

"Oh, wow." Katy had already abandoned the doll clothes and was sifting through the contents of the box. "Look at this! It's all our old report cards and awards and class pictures. . . . Whoa! There's your father, when he was in the third grade! Check out that crew cut! And get a load of those ears! I'm surprised he wasn't recruited by the Mickey Mouse Club!''

"That's my *father*?''

"It sure is. Whoever would have thought that that geeky-looking kid would ever grow up to be a handsome hotshot like your father, huh?''

Beth just stared. "He looks so—so *ordinary*!''

"Yeah, well, I'm sure that when this picture was taken, they had to drag him out of the corner, where he was being punished for, oh, I don't know, putting gum in some girl's hair or something.''

"Really? You mean my dad used to do weird stuff like that?''

"Are you kidding? All the time. When Michael was a kid, *trouble* was his middle name. We always figured that, given his personality, he'd either turn out to be a lawyer or a criminal.''

She chuckled. "I remember this one time, his class was having a bake sale, and all the kids were supposed to bring in something, right? Well, he forgot to tell Mom about it, so the morning of the bake sale, he rode over to this tiny little mom-and-pop deli on the edge of Harrington, someplace where they wouldn't know him. He went up to the man behind the counter and gave him a big sob story about how his father had lost his job and he and his brothers and sisters were all starving. Anyway, the next thing you know, he's walking out of there with two dozen chocolate cupcakes that the guy had given him, free!''

"Really? My dad did that? Tell me more, Katy!'' Beth's eyes were shining as she listened, hanging onto every word, scarcely able to believe that her father had ever been anything but the model child. She seemed to find it fascinating that he, like her, was just a regular kid once, getting into trouble, dis-appointing teachers and parents—in short, failing to be perfect.

Katy, meanwhile, was more than happy to comply, giving her niece quite an earful about the pranks that Michael and all the Gilbert children had played as kids. As she talked, she continued with her exploration, peeking into boxes and shop-ping bags.

And then she came across a real treasure.

"Oh, boy, Beth. You're not gonna believe this. Here, help me drag this box out of here. . . .''

"Hey, look what I found!" A few minutes later, Katy came parading downstairs into the living room, carrying a large cardboard carton. "Home movies! There must be a couple of dozen reels here!"

"Goodness, I'd forgotten all about those." Pat had come out of the kitchen, and was now wiping her damp hands on a cotton apron. "I stuck those up in that attic ages ago, along with all the other old things."

"I see you've got the projector, too." Ben nodded toward his granddaughter, who was struggling to lug it down the stairs. "Here, Beth, let me help you with that. So does this mean we're being treated to a film festival this afternoon?"

Julie let out a wail of protest. "Oh, no! You're not going to show those awful things, are you? I look terrible in all our home movies!"

"You never looked terrible a day in your life, sis," Katy said matter-of-factly. "And, yes, I am going to show them. Every blasted one. That is, if I can get this creaky old film projector to work. God, it's practically an antique, isn't it? Maybe the Smithsonian would be interested in putting it on display one day. That is, if we can ever bear to part with it."

"I'll tell you what: I'll go make some popcorn in the microwave," Pat offered. "Come on, Julie, you can help." The two women disappeared back into the kitchen, leaving Katy and Ben behind to try to figure out how to get the old piece of machinery to work.

"Boy, I hope these things held up," Katy said as she threaded the brittle eight-millimeter film, now almost thirty years old, into the projector. "They're probably kind of faded . . . Wow, I don't even *remember* the last time I looked at these!"

"I do." Wes had just sauntered into the living room, grinning. "It was Christmas, about three years ago, right after Barbara and I got married."

"That's right. I'm pretty sure that that was the last time we used the camera, too. We shot a roll of film at your wedding reception, remember? Let's show that roll, too."

"Oh, I want to see the really old ones." Chrissie came bounding into the room, still looking shockingly blond, this time carrying a hairbrush. "Are there any of Julie when she was my age?"

"Only a couple of thousand feet. Now if I can only figure out how to use this thing. . . . Here we go. You just hit this switch, and . . .

"Ladies and gentlemen, please take your seats," Katy boomed. "The show is about to begin!"

The lights were snapped off, the projector turned on. Along one white wall of the living room appeared a grainy, pale image.

"Now, what is this? . . ." Katy wondered aloud, leaning forward as she tried to get a better look. "The labels on the reels were so old and dried up that they fell off. . . . Oh, my God! That's *you*, Julie! Whoa, don't you look like something out of a time warp! I mean, are we talking major 'Twilight Zone' here or what?"

On the screen, a radiant seventeen-year-old Julie was gliding down the stairs, all decked out for her Senior Prom. Her blond hair was teased slightly on top, with the ends curled into a crisp flip. The stiff organdy bow fastened in the back was the same soft shade of baby pink as her floor-length gown. From underneath the ruffled hem peeked white high-heeled pumps with dangerously pointed toes. Her makeup, however, was what was the most laughable: pale pink lipstick, almost white; thick black eyeliner that came to tiny points; a heavy smear of green eye shadow coating each eyelid.

"Was this your prom or a Halloween party?" Katy chortled.

"I think she looks beautiful," Chrissie insisted.

"Thanks, but Katy's right. I do look pretty weird."

Despite her attempt at levity, Julie's voice sounded strained. After all, she had already seen these old home movies dozens of times, and by now she was familiar enough with them to know what was coming next.

Sure enough; just as she expected, the smiling teenaged girl on the screen waved self-consciously at the camera, then moved across the living room until she was next to her date for the evening, standing in front of the fireplace. She glanced up at him with moist eyes that made her feelings completely transparent, then took his arm.

Seeing Paul Dereksen like that, back in another time when they had both been so much in love, made her heart ache.

We were supposed to stay together, she thought bitterly, amazed at how much it still hurt. We were a couple, Paul and I. The way we looked at each other, back then—the picture up there on the wall tells it all.

Fortunately, another image popped up before she had a chance to succumb to the tears that were threatening to fall. A grinning Katy had appeared before them, pudgy but buoyant as she scampered around for the camera's benefit, racing around the backyard with their neighbor's good-natured mutt.

"There we go," Katy said. "Beth, there's your Aunt Katy at just about your age."

"That's *you*?" Beth squealed. "Oh, boy! You look just like *me*!"

Katy looked over at her niece and was surprised to see that the observation she had just made had pleased the little girl no end.

The images continued to light up the wall, carrying the Gilberts back into the past as they sampled little bits of the children's pasts. Michael at his junior high school graduation, tripping over his gown; Wes winning the Westchester County Math Award when he was just twelve, the youngest recipient ever; Katy and Wes frolicking in the snow, aged eight and eleven. There were even some baby pictures, including one of all four Gilbert children stuffed into the bathtub, along with a couple of dozen bath toys and a huge mound of bubbles that nearly covered them.

They were about to call it a day, having had about all the reminiscing they could handle at one sitting, when Katy insisted upon showing just one more reel.

"Come on, it's a short one," she pleaded. "Besides, it's the very last one. We might as well finish them off. Then we can stick them all back into the attic for another couple of centuries."

The last reel was the most recent one, the film of Wesley and Barbara's wedding ceremony and reception. The couple happened to be sitting together on the couch as shots of that special day appeared on the wall: Barbara, in an elegant white dress, gazing into the eyes of her groom, a somewhat younger version of Wes, who was looking rather silly in his rented tux but, at the same time, obviously so happy that he was about to burst.

Katy couldn't help glancing over at her brother. She saw that Wes had taken his eyes off the screen and was instead studying his wife's reaction. Barbara, meanwhile, watched in silence, her mouth drawn into a tight little line, giving no clue as to what she was feeling.

And then, it was over. The lights were back on, the scenes of the past had vanished, and the present hung over them all like some kind of challenge.

"Okay, guys," Katy said heartily. "The show is over.

Please pay on your way out. And remember, the tipping of ushers is permitted.''

Even as she was joking, however, picking up the roles of film and placing them back in their thin square boxes, she kept stealing glances at her brother. She watched as Wes leaned over, starting to reach for Barbara's hand but then stopping himself.

Then, in a soft voice, he said, ''That was some wedding we had, wasn't it?''

Barbara forced a smile. ''Yes, it was lovely. Now if you'll excuse me for a minute, I really have to put in a telephone call to my boss. I know I'm supposed to be on vacation, but there are still a couple of loose ends I really should tie up. . . .''

And she was gone.

Katy's heart went out to her brother as she watched him sitting alone, looking as if he were only vaguely aware of the teasing chatter going on around him as the rest of his family kidded each other about the clothes and the hairstyles of the past. She suspected that he had been hoping if Barbara saw the film of their wedding, it might remind her of the love they had shared in the past, the vows they had taken, the promises they had made, and that it might help restore some of those feelings.

But from what she was observing as she mindlessly stacked up the boxes of film, preparing to exile them back up to the attic for another long stretch of time, it seemed as if it had simply driven the two of them even further apart.

Chapter Seventeen

"**G**randma, are you having something fixed around the house?" Beth stood up on tiptoe and peered out the kitchen window, so curious about the dilapidated pickup truck that had just come lumbering into the driveway that she forgot all about the silver butter knife she had been polishing.

Her grandmother, sitting at the kitchen table with service for twelve spread out in front of her like the cards in a game of solitaire, glanced up. "No. Why?"

"Because a guy in a truck just pulled into the driveway. Wait—there's writing on the side. It says, 'Paul Dereksen, Home Improvements.' "

"Paul!" Pat dropped her polishing cloth on the table and pulled off her eyeglasses. "Paul Dereksen, here? Why, that's Julie's friend."

"Julie's?"

"That's right. He was one of her old boyfriends. They went together in high school. And I told her he was living on the island. Oh, dear, I hope the breakfast coffee is still decent. Are there any of your mother's rolls left?" It was as if Pat, not Julie, was the one about to receive a visitor. She tore off her apron and draped it over the back of her chair, then patted her hair.

Beth didn't notice. She was too busy staring out the window, trying to get a look at this old beau of Julie's—an old beau who was apparently still interested in looking her up, even now, twenty years after high school.

She wasn't disappointed. Despite his unimposing mode of transportation, the man who was strolling up the walk, toward the front door, was very good-looking, with shaggy blond hair and craggy features.

"Boy, he's cute!" Beth breathed.

She wondered if she'd ever have some handsome young man coming up the walk to visit her. But then she caught sight of her reflection in the glass of the window. What she saw there—the round face, the limp brown hair, the beginnings of a blemish—made it difficult for her to believe that any boy, or any man, would ever pay attention to her. It was no wonder Danny preferred her sister to her, even though Chrissie was boring and dumb. At least she was pretty—almost as pretty as Julie.

Apparently Beth was not the only one who had noticed Paul Dereksen's arrival. Julie was already tripping down the stairs with a peculiar flush on her cheeks. She was at the front door before Beth had a chance to answer it and get a better look at this gentleman caller. But Beth wasn't about to let an opportunity like this slip away. She sauntered into the living room, where she could get a better look at what was going on without being noticed.

"Hello, Julie," Paul said quietly. The gentle smile on his face was almost conspiratorial.

"Hello, Paul."

Even though their words were hardly out of the ordinary, Beth sighed over the romantic undertones of this meeting. From where she was standing, she could see the look in their eyes, and she surmised immediately that there was something more between Julie and her "old boyfriend" than mere memories.

Julie was blushing like a schoolgirl. Already she was calculating the likelihood of her husband showing up today. And, she was pleased to realize, the chances were slim indeed.

Yes, she felt guilty about thinking that way—and guilty about being as pleased as she was to see Paul again. But her guilt was not strong enough to prompt her to decline when he said offhandedly, "It's such a great day today—much too nice to work. I woke up this morning and decided that Sylvia Dorfman's new kitchen cabinets could wait. So how about it, Julie? Want to keep me company while I play hooky?"

Beneath his easy grin, Julie could see that he was a little bit nervous about how she might respond to his invitation. So she knew he'd be pleased when she said, "I'd love to."

"Great." He glanced at what she was wearing, a jade green tank top and a pair of white shorts. "Listen, why don't you bring along a bathing suit? You never know when you might get an irresistible urge to jump into the water."

Julie was surprised to discover that she, like Paul, was a little bit nervous as she climbed up into the cab of his pickup truck.

"Sorry about this little buggy of mine." Paul cast her a sheepish glance. "The Honda's been in the shop all week."

"We could take my BMW." As soon as she'd made the offer, Julie regretted it.

"No, thanks. That's okay." Paul kept his eyes fixed on the rearview mirror as he pulled out of the Gilberts' driveway. "Besides, I don't plan to keep you captive in this heap of junk for very long. I've got a much more luxurious ride in mind."

Fifteen minutes later, Julie was following Paul down the dock at the Dering Harbor Marina, clutching the bag of groceries he'd picked up, still puzzling over what he had in mind.

"Where on earth are we going?"

"Just come with me. I have somebody I want you to meet."

She didn't catch on until he stopped in front of one of the boats bobbing alongside the dock and looked over at her with shining eyes.

"Julie, meet *Scheherazade*." He gestured proudly toward a twenty-six-foot wooden sloop, an unassuming vessel that was dwarfed in both size and grandeur by the rows of considerably more impressive yachts flanking it.

"Paul! Is this your boat? It's wonderful!"

"Yeah, I think so." Paul looked at it fondly, almost as if he were about to reach over and pat it.

"And I love the name. *Scheherazade*. Now, let me see. . . . Wasn't she the legendary storyteller? That's right. She managed to save her own life by telling her captor—an Indian sultan, I think—a story every night, one that was chock full of adventure and romance. But she left off the ending until the next night. Yes, now I remember. She kept on for a thousand and one nights, right?''

Paul was pleased. "That's the one. Come on board. I'll show you around.''

The *Scheherazade* was modest, but so well-designed that it had everything a boat owner would require. The front deck was just large enough to spread out a picnic lunch, and Julie understood now why he had made such a point of bringing sandwich makings along. Inside the cabin there was a compact stove, a sink, and even an icebox. Along the two sides were berths that doubled as couches. All in all, Julie was charmed—not only by the boat itself, but also by the obvious pleasure Paul derived from it.

"It's a terrific boat, Paul! And it's got everything. A little kitchen, a place to sleep . . .''

"It's even got a head,'' Paul informed her proudly. He patted the steering wheel as if it were a pet he were particularly fond of. "Yup, she's really something. Every time I climb in, I feel as if I'm beginning a new adventure. I just head off in whatever direction I feel like going without a single plan or a care in the world, and then sit back to watch what happens. And it always turns out a little bit differently.'' He chuckled, suddenly self-conscious about his enthusiasm. "I guess that's why I named her *Scheherazade*.''

"It's a lovely name. It fits perfectly.''

"So, are you ready to take her out?''

Julie laughed. "I thought you'd never ask!''

By the time they were sailing across a particularly benevolent Dering Harbor, Julie felt as if all her worldly concerns were a million miles away. All that mattered were the delicious sensations that were lulling her into a state of bliss: the cool breeze, the rocking motion of the waves, the pleasure of steering the *Scheherazade* into the wind as Paul was busy hoisting the sails.

"Funny, I don't remember you being interested in sailing back in the old days,'' she called to Paul as he tightened the jib halliard, causing the sail to billow out dramatically.

"Nah, it's a relatively recent obsession. The way I figure it, everybody's entitled to have at least *one* vice, don't you think? You know, it never even would have occurred to me to get into boating—until I moved out here, that is. I kept seeing these people who seemed perfectly sane otherwise making these babies the center of their lives. Wasting all their hard-earned money, spending their Saturdays and Sundays scraping off barnacles, just so they could spend a few hours a week floating around on the waves. Well, finally it got me curious. So I figured I'd give it a try myself, just to see what the fuss was all about.

"And here I am, four years later, already on my third boat." With a shrug he added, "Nobody ever told me how addictive it was."

"Yes, I've always enjoyed sailing. And I can see why gunkholing about in a boat like this could become a habit quickly."

As she gazed around at the sparkling water, glistening against a dramatic backdrop of cloudless blue sky, Julie felt a sense of peace that she couldn't remember having experienced in ages. And, she realized, it wasn't just the beauty of the scenery and the hypnotic motion of the boat that was making her feel that way.

It's being with Paul again, just the two of us, out alone, she thought. We still seem to belong together, to fit—the same way we did back in high school.

It was easy to pretend she was seventeen again. She even constructed a fantasy about the two of them, going so far as to pretend they were spending the summer together after having just graduated from college, a scene she had once imagined almost constantly but which had never actually come to pass.

Almost as if he had read her thoughts, Paul asked offhandedly, "So, where's hubby today?"

His question snapped her quickly back into reality. "Oh, Brad's in the city. He had to go back for a few days. Some big business deal that's about to break."

"Gee, that's too bad." Despite the obvious insincerity of his words, neither of them chose to acknowledge it, not even in a teasing way.

"So tell me, Julie Gilbert Kane." Paul abandoned his skillful manipulation of sails after coiling and securing the lines, then came over to sit next to her. "What's it like, being a big TV star?"

"Oh, come on, Paul. Give me a break!"

"No, really. I'm serious. How does it feel, turning on the television and seeing your face plastered all over it?"

"How does it feel walking into a room that you built single-handedly?"

"It's not the same thing. Building bookcases for people, or adding decks onto the back of their summer houses, is hardly the same thing as having millions of people watch you on the boob tube every morning."

"Well . . ." While Julie was embarrassed by Paul's question, she was also enjoying his flattery. "Actually, it's pretty exciting. I keep waiting for the novelty to wear off, to become matter-of-fact about the whole thing—but to tell you the truth, I still get a kick out of it. Most of it, anyway."

"Really? What parts don't you like?"

Julie wrinkled her nose. "Getting up with the chickens, for one thing. And always having to be aware of how I look. That gets to be a drag, even though we have a whole truckload of people on staff whose job it is to make sure I look presentable.

"But there are other, more important things, too. Like never being able to spend as much time with my son as I'd like."

"Yeah, that's something I can understand. I feel exactly the same way. About Becky, I mean."

A dark look came into his eyes—then vanished as suddenly as it had come. "Listen, let's make a pact, okay? For the rest of the day, let's not even think about anything any more serious than—oh, I don't know, whether or not to bother putting suntan lotion on."

"It's a deal!"

Indeed, sticking to their agreement proved to be no hardship at all. Not while there was so much beauty around them to admire, not while being out on the open seas created a dreamlike world in which nothing seemed to be the same as it was on land. Finally, around noon, they anchored, changed into their bathing suits, and jumped into the brisk water for a refreshing dip. They horsed around like children, splashing and dunking each other and playing silly games.

"No, don't!" Julie shrieked, diving under the water to avoid Paul's teasing attempt at grabbing her, giggling so hard she could scarcely breathe.

"Gotcha! You're it! Uh-oh, look out! Here comes a shark!"

"Forget the shark! Here comes a whale! It's coming after you!"

It still feels good, Julie reflected over and over, taking a step back from all the fun they were having. Nothing has really changed, even after all this time. It still feels right.

By the time they climbed back into the boat, they agreed that they were both starving. With shameless abandon they plunged into Paul's picnic lunch.

"Hey, listen to this," Julie said gaily, having just devoured half of the huge ham and cheese sandwich she had made herself in five bites. "You'll never guess who I saw last night. Not in a million years."

"Let's see. This must be someone we both know." Paul frowned as he ran through in his mind all the mutual acquaintances from high school that Julie could conceivably have run into out here on eastern Long Island.

Julie decided not to prolong the guessing game. "It was you, Paul. A seventeen-year-old version of you."

"I don't get it."

"Our prom night." She looked down at him and grinned shyly. "Home movies. Katy found a whole carton of them yesterday. We spent hours watching them all."

"Oh, no! I'm almost afraid to ask, but how did I look? Crew cut? Acne?"

Julie chuckled. "As a matter of fact, you looked pretty good." Julie could feel her cheeks turning pink. "Of course, your hair is a bit longer now. . . ."

"A bit grayer, too, I bet." Paul grimaced. "How about you? I bet you looked exactly the same then as you do now. I even remember the dress you wore, as if it were yesterday. It was long, all the way to the ground, and it was a soft shade of green, the same color as your eyes."

"Paul, it was *pink*!"

"It was not. It was green!"

"Paul!" Julie laughed as she swatted at him playfully. "Don't tell me you've forgotten!"

"Hey, watch it! I'm the captain of this seaworthy vessel, remember? There's a big sign up in the cabin that says, 'Striking the captain prohibited.' "

And then she was caught up in the moment she had been hoping for, dreaming about ever since she had first heard Paul was here on Shelter Island, she now realized. They were face-to-face, separated by only a few inches, their eyes locked together in a gaze so intense that it took her breath away.

But instead of moving closer toward her, Paul broke the magic spell by looking away. "You know, Julie," he said in a husky voice, "I'm seeing someone now."

Her body stiffened. As much as she hated to admit it, Paul's words stung. She was jealous. It was absurd, she knew, but there it was.

"Oh, really?" She tried to keep her voice casual. "Is it anything serious?"

"I don't know yet."

A faraway look came into his eyes. It was clear to Julie that he was thinking about *her*, this mystery woman who was a part of his life. And she was the one who belonged there, not Julie. She could feel her stomach tightening, her heart aching as she saw the effect that thinking about this woman had on him. And knowing that she had absolutely no right to feel that way did little to alleviate the intensity of her reaction.

"Her name is Susan. She just moved to the island last winter. She's a potter. She's got a little pottery studio, right behind this house she's renting." He hesitated, staring out at nothing in particular. "We have a lot in common. You know, we have the same kind of life-style, we want the same things. . . . We have fun together."

"Well. Aren't you lucky."

Julie hadn't meant to sound so sarcastic, so bitter, yet the words had insisted upon coming out that way. She turned away, watching a sea gull soar down from way up high, dip into the water, and head back up to the open skies once again, a prize tucked protectively in its beak. But it wasn't the beauty of the bird that she was thinking about.

She was so confused. She actually felt rejected by Paul's sudden distancing of himself, even though she knew that that was the way it had to be.

After all, she reminded herself, you're a married woman now. You have no right to go around throwing yourself at men, even someone you're in love with. . . .

No! she was quick to correct herself. You're not in love with Paul. You *were*, once a very long time ago, but it's all over now.

She tried to convince herself that it was only the memory

of what had once been between her and Paul that she was finding so enticing, that their love had been dead for almost two decades. It was Brad that she loved now. He was her husband, the man with whom she had had her wonderful son. That was where her loyalties belonged.

But as she turned back to look at Paul as he tightened the downhaul of the mainsail in response to the stiffening breeze, as she watched him move with confidence and even a kind of grace, it was difficult to believe that the feelings that were overwhelming her—this craving to be with this man, to touch him, to share with him everything that mattered to her—were nothing more than memories.

Chapter Eighteen

"*Hey, I* just had a great idea! How about going for a bike ride?"

Barbara glanced up from *U.S. News and World Report*, pretty sure that her husband had to be talking to Beth or Chrissie. And so she was surprised to discover that his suggestion was directed at her.

"A bike ride?" she repeated, blinking.

"Sure. Look, I was just down in the basement, bringing some stuff up for Mom, and I noticed that there are a bunch of old bicycles stashed down there. They're a little bit rusty—nobody's used them for years. But I bet if we put some air in the tires, they'll work just fine. I'd love to try out my old ten-speed, and I'm pretty sure that Julie's Schwinn is down there."

Barbara surveyed the living room and saw that it was littered with various members of the Gilbert clan, lingering over coffee or leafing through magazines—looking, for the most part, as if they intended to stay put. The thought of spending the morning in their company, in a similarly lethargic manner, was too boring to bear, so much so that even pedaling around the quiet back roads of Shelter Island, admiring scrub brush and sand dunes, sounded attractive to her.

"Sure," she replied, already closing her magazine and setting it down on the coffee table. "I'm game."

Once their plan was actually underway, the two slightly out

of practice cyclers weaving across the Gilberts' circular driveway and toward the road, Barbara was surprised to discover
that she was pleased in another way, as well. It was going to
be fun spending some time alone with Wes for the first time
in weeks. While she was the one who had initiated this
distance that now existed between them, even she was finding
it frustrating to have been in the same house with him for two
whole days now without having had a single conversation any
deeper than a discussion of who would take which side of the
bed or how high the temperature was expected to rise that
day.

What made it all feel even more peculiar was the fact that,
up until lately, the two of them had been together virtually
every moment that wasn't being gobbled up by the demands
of their jobs. Coming home early in the evening, enjoying a
quiet dinner of take-out food or something quick and easy like
omelettes, sharing the details of their workdays. Frequently
they ventured out of their newly purchased brownstone in one
of Boston's changing neighborhoods to try a new ethnic
restaurant in Somerville or catch a movie around Harvard
Square. On weekends, they relished their time together, lounging in bed and reading, seeing friends, or, more likely,
working on the house.

It was the house, in fact, that had become their shared
passion. Two years earlier, their accountant advised them that
it was time to seek out better ways of investing their growing
incomes. Around that time, the lease on their one-bedroom
apartment in Brookline was about to expire, they were beginning to crave more space—and they stumbled upon a small
brownstone on Columbia Street, one that needed major renovations but whose potential promised to make it much more
than simply a sound financial investment.

Right from the start, Wes and Barbara were enthusiastic
about their find. It had a stone fireplace, a view of the
Charles from the third floor, hardwood floors that promised to
be marvelous once they were refinished. The kitchen was
huge; there was even a breakfast nook. With the addition of
another bathroom, with a little bit of scraping and sanding,
with some creative use of color, it wouldn't take much to turn
it into a real home.

It was true that renovating the brownstone was turning out
to be much more work than either of them had ever dreamed.

Even so, they threw themselves into this project with the same enthusiasm and energy they devoted to everything else in their lives that they cared about. Not only was it fun choosing linoleum and interviewing contractors and fantasizing about what the ideal kitchen should include, they also felt as if they were *building* something together, putting their heads together to construct their own future, pooling their ideas to come up with something brand new, something that was exclusively *theirs*.

At least, that was how it all seemed to be going. Now, however, as Barbara snuck a glance over at the intense young man coasting beside her on a slightly rusted black ten-speed bicycle, she wondered if perhaps she had been misinterpreting her feelings all along.

She knew that she was painfully confused; at the same time, she was totally cognizant of how her ambivalence was affecting poor Wesley. Her announcement that she was leaving had, after all, come to him as a total surprise. He hadn't even had a chance to see it coming, since her decision was so sudden that even she was amazed by the speed and certainty with which she made it.

Barbara was fully aware that Wes lived in a constant state of awe over having found her in the first place. While on the outside Wesley Gilbert may have appeared to be the picture of success, self-confidence, and intelligence, she knew him well enough to realize that on the inside, part of him still felt like the gawky egghead who didn't fit in anywhere, who retreated to a world of mathematical logic and brain-twisting puzzles and, finally, computers, to a world where everything was clear-cut and there was almost always one single answer.

All that was easy enough to understand, given his history, one that he had told her about with some timidity, as if he were afraid that the Wesley Gilbert of the past might still rise up once again to haunt him. When he was growing up, the fact that he was the smartest kid in town, with an IQ that easily put him into the genius category, was a hindrance. The other students shunned him, for the most part, taunting him with nicknames like "The Brain" that were meant not to flatter, but rather to make him an outsider by emphasizing those differences that were envied or mistrusted.

Having an older brother like Michael didn't help, either, Barbara knew. He was constantly being compared to the older boy, known throughout Harrington for his popularity and his charm. What was winning the Westchester County Math Award, for example, when his brother had just been elected president of the senior class? What did a solid-A average in math and science mean compared to Michael Gilbert's touchdown that won the pennant for Harrington High?

Despite all the odds seemingly being stacked against him, however, Wes was never too disheartened by being a social outcast. For one thing, he always managed to find at least one good friend, someone who shared his love of math and science, someone with whom he could wile away afternoons after school building models or Saturday afternoons collecting different specimens of leaves.

Girls were an entirely different matter. By junior high school, the tendency to be a loner had evolved into deep shyness. Meanwhile, Wes was still categorized as a nerd. Those things, combined with the scrawniness that kept him looking boyish long after his peers were developing into hulking young men, placed him way at the bottom of the popularity list. His lack of invitations to boy-girl parties came as no surprise to him, and from early on he avoided school dances, knowing he would only come home humiliated. Through it all, he bided his time, waiting until that vaguely defined "someday" when he would be appreciated.

That time did arrive. During his first week as a freshman at M.I.T., he discovered that there were boys—and girls, too— all over the country who had been experiencing childhoods that were remarkably like his. He had a host of friends, an immediate circle of cohorts who were as enthusiastic about Möbius strips and Boolean logic as he was. The classwork challenged him, the teachers inspired him. At last, he felt he belonged.

The Wes Gilbert who emerged from M.I.T. with a Ph.D. was a different person from the one who had entered seven years before. Not only had his intelligence been developed, making him one of the top computer experts in the country. He had also grown up to be a self-possessed, good-looking man who, aside from being appreciated by others, now appreciated himself.

It was only when it came to the opposite sex that his old insecurities snuck up on him. Not that he had much of a chance to meet very many women. Tek-Life snapped him up right out of his graduate program, and he immediately immersed himself in his work. Those infrequent times when he did come up for air, he found that there weren't very many women around. Those at his workplace he considered off-limits, and with his new career the center of his life, he had little time to go out of his way to meet and greet. Sure, he felt the loneliness, the emptiness, the longing. But getting up the nerve to do something about it was another matter entirely.

He was in this frame of mind when he met Barbara at a Christmas party, an event that his boss had teased him into attending. Not that he'd really minded going. It was simply that he didn't expect anything more than an evening of holding up the wall, sipping sickly-sweet punch, and listening to smarmy versions of holiday carols.

The appearance of Barbara Boucher on the scene was like an unexpected Christmas present. She was more like a fantasy come to life than anything bordering on reality, at least the reality that he was used to dealing with. She was beautiful, brilliant, cool, self-assured—and on top of all that, she even went so far as to fall in love with him. He felt like he had been rewarded, as if all those years of pining away for a woman to love were some bizarre kind of joke, and that having Barbara to love, and having her love him back, was the punch line.

Their three years of marriage easily constituted the most blissful period of his entire life. Not only were Wes and Barbara truly happy together, still enjoying a sense of smugness over having found each other—their future together was teeming with all kinds of possibilities.

That is, she thought ruefully, until I took it upon myself to destroy it.

Almost as if he had been listening in on her thoughts, knowing how bad she felt for the rift she had caused between them and wishing desperately for the return of at least some of the closeness that had once been something they had both taken for granted, Wes suddenly glanced over at her and said, "So, how have things been going? Is it working out all right, staying with Elizabeth?"

"Well, getting into the city from Newton every morning is no picnic, as you can imagine. But otherwise, it's been okay."

Wes nodded. "That's good. How are things with Elizabeth, anyway?"

"Things are going very well. She expects to be a partner at

her law firm in another year or so. Her work does keep her pretty busy, of course, but she seems to love it.''

''Ah. I see. Same old Elizabeth.''

Barbara recognized the fact that he was making a point of remaining polite and in control, making it sound as if they were simply having a casual discussion of one of Barbara's closest friends from her college days, without referring even indirectly to the fact that the reason she had become her roommate in the first place was that she had walked out on Wes. She also appreciated the way he was placing so few demands on her, when there must have been a million things he was dying to say to her, realizing that this was a time when she really couldn't handle any pressure from him.

''So how about you? Is everything all right?'' Barbara used that same civilized tone.

''Oh, sure. The same old thing. You know me.''

''And the house?''

''I haven't had a chance to do much on it. Oh, there was something I wanted to tell you: the decorator called last week to say she'd gotten ahold of those upholstery fabric samples. I told her to hold off for a while, that we weren't ready to make a decision yet.''

Barbara just nodded. She was fully aware of how contrived all this was, yet at the same time she was grateful to her husband for allowing their formality to continue.

''Hey,'' he said all of a sudden, his voice soft and filled with tenderness, ''how about if we dump these bikes for a while and take a little walk along that stretch of beach over there?''

Without a word Barbara acquiesced, following his lead. She leaned her lavender Schwinn against the trunk of an impressive oak, right alongside Wes's battered up old bicycle. They walked together, side by side but without touching, off the road and onto the sand.

The beach was empty, almost eerie in its isolation. Neither Barbara nor Wes spoke, almost as if they were respecting the tranquility of their surroundings. Despite their silence, however, there was a cloud of unacknowledged tension hanging in the air, words unspoken but heard nonetheless.

Finally Wes turned to Barbara and, without any of the hesitation she would have expected, took her in his arms.

''Hey, you know I love you,'' he whispered, burying his

face in her hair. "No matter what happened, no matter what happens from here on in, I still love you, Barbara."

They stood locked together for a long time, clinging to each other with a kind of desperation. And when Barbara finally lifted her head from Wes's shoulder, letting her eyes lock into his, she knew that what he was seeing reflected in them was none of the things he probably would have expected, neither anger nor arrogance nor indifference. Instead, she knew that what he was seeing there was fear.

Chapter Nineteen

"*Oh, God,* don't you just *hate* her?" moaned Chrissie, having suddenly halted her casual skimming of the latest issue of *Glamour.* "I mean, just *look* at her!"

"Who's that?" Katy looked up from the bowl of leftover carrots she was covering with plastic wrap long enough to cast a quick glance at her niece, perched on the stool next to the telephone as her aunt and uncle cleaned up after that night's dinner. "Who are you looking at, Chrissie? Imelda Marcos?"

"Who? No, I'm looking at a picture of this model who's, like, totally gorgeous." She held up the magazine, flashing a photograph of a leggy dark-haired beauty who looked as if she hadn't had a decent meal in months, modeling a ridiculous draping of fabric and leather that was trying to pass itself off as a dress. The look on Chrissie's face was one of pure envy.

"Don't hold it against her," Katy quipped, turning back to her carrots. "She's probably bulimic. And she probably hasn't had a date in six months because she's so shallow that none of the men she meets can stand to spend more than ten minutes with her."

Chrissie rolled her eyes, then went back to her magazine, oblivious to the chaos around her: the stack of dirty dishes waiting to be scraped, rinsed, and loaded into the dishwasher; the various platters and bowls of leftover food; the pots and pans that would require a substantial amount of scrubbing before the night was through. And in the middle of it all was Katy, setting about each task with determination, her workload lessened somewhat by the helping hands of her brother, Wes.

"What are you doing in here, anyway, Chrissie?" Katy asked good-naturedly. "Shouldn't you be—oh, I don't know, curling your eyelashes or painting your toenails or something really important like that that's guaranteed to make our world a better place?"

"I already did those things today," Chrissie replied, without looking up from the Revlon lipstick ad she was studying, as if staring at the sensuous-lipped model whose face covered the entire page would somehow force some of the woman's glamour and sophistication onto her. "Actually, I'm hiding. I don't want anybody to find me."

"Hiding!" Wes exclaimed. "What about Katy and me? Aren't we 'anybody'? I know that I, for one, like to believe that I'm *somebody*." He looked over at Katy and winked.

"I'm hiding from my *mother*."

"Ah." Wes nodded knowingly. "Good move. She'd never think of looking for you in a place where people are working."

Chrissie glared at him, then swept her newly blond hair over one shoulder, stroking it lovingly as she spoke. "She's upstairs, talking to Grandma. So this isn't such a dumb place to hang out, after all."

"Unless she suddenly becomes overwhelmed by a Big Mac attack," Katy interjected seriously.

"Don't worry," said Wes. "If that happens, we can hide Chrissie in the blender."

"Or in the food processor," his sister suggested. "Might as well be as high tech as we can." Turning to Chrissie, she asked, "May I be so bold as to ask *why* it is you're hiding from the woman who gave you the gift of life?"

"Because," Chrissie whined, "if she sees me, she's gonna come up with some horrible idea, like why don't I take Beth to the movies tonight."

"Oh, no!" Wes gasped. "Not the Movie Torture! What a cruel, heartless woman!"

"Come on, you guys." Chrissie was growing increasingly exasperated by her aunt and uncle's unwillingness to appreciate her plight. "I don't want to get stuck hanging around with my *sister*!"

"I don't know." Wes grinned. "I've always kind of enjoyed hanging around with my sister."

"Chrissie!"

"Oh, shoot. Here she comes." Chrissie looked imploringly at Wes, then Katy, but found not a glimmer of sympathy in either of their faces.

"Chrissie," Lynn said as she sailed into the kitchen, beaming, "I just had a fantastic idea. Why don't you and Beth do something together tonight? Pat just reminded me that there's a miniature golf course here on the island."

"Uh-oh," Wes whispered to Katy. "The Miniature Golf Torture."

"Mom, I *can't*!" Chrissie wailed.

"Why not? Have you made other plans already?"

"Well, not exactly, but . . ."

Suddenly one more person appeared in the doorway.

"Hi, Mrs. Gilbert!" said Danny Burtis brightly.

He looked as if he had just spent a goodly amount of time primping. His hair, still damp from a shower, was combed neatly. His green-and-white-striped rugby shirt and khaki pants were clean, and there was a small nick on his chin, evidence that he had even gone so far as to shave, an effort that was no doubt not entirely necessary. He smelled faintly of deodorant and mouthwash. Wes had to look away, feigning interest in unwrapping a brand-new Brillo pad in order to keep the teenaged boy from seeing the smile on his face, even though it was one of empathy, rather than ridicule.

"Hi, Katy, Wes. Hi, Chrissie!"

"Hi, Danny!" Chrissie had brightened the instant he came in. Not that she was genuinely pleased to see him, of course—except that his timely entrance afforded her the perfect opportunity to wheedle her way out of the contemptible evening her mother had taken the liberty of planning for her.

Her reaction to his appearance was not wasted on him. His already wide smile grew about two inches wider. "Listen, I was wondering if you were free tonight. My dad loaned me his car— "

"Why, how nice!" Pat Gilbert had just come into the kitchen, her interest piqued by the strange voice she had overheard from her bedroom upstairs. "How are you, Danny? How are your folks?"

"They're fine, Mrs. Gilbert." Danny beamed at the older

woman, then turned his attention back to Chrissie. "So how about it, Chrissie? Want to go out for ice cream or something?"

Pointedly Chrissie glanced at her mother. Then, her eyes upon her grandmother, who was still smiling approvingly, she said, "I'd love to, Danny. Just give me about two minutes to change my clothes."

"Chrissie, what you've got on looks fine." As always, Lynn was chagrined over her daughter's obsession with her appearance—not to mention all the laundry that her numerous daily changes of clothing generated, the bulk of which Pat was doing, insisting that her houseguests shouldn't have to bother with something like that during their vacation.

"Mom!" Chrissie protested, already bolting for her room, "I *have* to change! I'm going out on a *date*, for heaven's sake!"

Danny turned so red that both Katy and Wes were forced to bury their faces in the dishwasher in order to keep from succumbing to uncontrollable laughter.

True to form, it took Chrissie almost twenty minutes to make herself presentable. She had been torn between trying to look her worst, so as not to encourage Danny, and looking her best, just for the fun of taunting him with something he could never have. In the end, her vanity won. First she put on as much eye makeup as she thought her mother would allow her out of the house with, without making a big scene. Then she pulled on her shortest white shorts and a sleeveless peach-colored top that allowed the bottom two inches of her midriff to peek through. Its clingy knit fabric also accentuated the roundness of her breasts, as well as the fact that she was going braless. Before dashing out the door, she sprayed a healthy spritz of Julie's Obsession down the front of the low neckline.

"What the hell," she muttered with a giggle, giving herself the once-over in the mirror and concluding that she looked fantastic before hurrying back downstairs. "Might as well have some real fun."

Indeed, while it had been fun dressing for the part of *femme fatale*, actually playing the role was considerably less rewarding, Chrissie discovered as soon as she climbed into Danny's father's Cutlass. Sure, it was nice to know that the guy she was with adored her. But every time she looked over at him and was reminded that the boy casting longing gazes at her across the front seat was only Danny Burtis, she was so frustrated she could have cried.

If I'm going to . . . accomplish what I told Heather I was going to accomplish, she reminded herself grimly, I've got to start looking out for bigger game than creepy old Danny Burtis.

It wasn't long before her spirits brightened, however. After some stilted conversation, screamed over the loud Whitney Houston that was blasting on the radio, Danny pulled into the parking lot of the Tuck Shop. Chrissie remembered coming here for ice cream other years, usually with her father or Julie. But she had never noticed that it was a popular hangout for kids her age. The parking lot was filled with teenagers, leaning against back fenders and flirting as they indifferently consumed the ice cream that was allegedly their reason for being here in the first place. Chrissie's heart was pounding as she leaned forward in her seat, trying to get a better look.

"They have great ice cream here," said Danny. "What's your favorite flavor? Hey, Chrissie? I said, what's your favorite flavor?"

"Huh?" Chrissie was annoyed that Danny was bothering her with stupid questions. She'd forgotten, for a moment, that he was even there. "Uh, I don't know. Chocolate, I guess." Remembering that she didn't want to get pimples, she added, "But I usually have peach or coffee or—hey, who's that?"

One boy, in particular, had caught her attention. He had white-blond hair and exceptionally broad shoulders, with that preppie look that she always found so appealing. Besides, at first glance he reminded her of Stephen Clyde, the boy she'd made such a fool of herself over.

"Who, that guy over there?" Politely Danny made the effort to pick out the boy in question. "I don't know. I don't think I've ever seen him before."

"Oh." It didn't matter, after all. When she'd gotten a better look at him, she'd seen that he wasn't so cute. Besides, he was with someone, a tall, really beautiful girl with jet-black hair that reached practically to her waist.

Chrissie continued to scan the crowd that was sprinkled throughout the parking lot, checking out each face as if she were looking for someone in particular. But in the end, she came away feeling disappointed. There were no prospects here, after all.

She turned back to Danny, who was looking better than

ever—at least, for the moment. ''Let's go inside,'' she said
sweetly, flashing what she always thought of as her Christie
Brinkley smile.

The Tuck Shop was small and rustic. The front room, into
which Danny proudly led his date for the evening, was nothing more than an ice-cream stand. It contained an L-shaped
glass case displaying a dozen different flavors, melting and
coagulating in their cardboard five-gallon drums.

The blond boy and his raven-haired girlfriend were in line
right in front of them. Chrissie was chagrined to see that, up
close, he was pretty good-looking, after all. She was equally
perturbed by the way the girl with him was falling all over
him, not even pretending to be interested in the butter pecan
ice-cream cone the girl behind the counter had just handed
her.

Chrissie looked over at Danny, who was studying the list
of ice-cream flavors posted up above. Not wanting to feel left
out, she took his arm, then leaned her head against his
shoulder, just for a moment.

''It was nice of you to invite me out for ice cream tonight,'' she purred. She glanced over at the blond boy,
wondering if he'd even noticed her. But he and his girlfriend
had already left.

Danny, however, was thrilled. ''Sure, Chrissie. Any time.''

He was about to put his arm around her, but Chrissie deftly
ducked away before he had a chance. ''Oh, I think I'll have a
coffee cone,'' she said.

While Danny's chocolate mint chip was being scooped up,
Chrissie wandered over to the wood-frame screen door that
led to the other section of the small shop, a game room. She
saw that this room, like the parking lot, was full of kids, the
boys ravishing the video games and pinball machines, the
girls, many of them younger than she was, standing together
in clusters, watching the boys and giggling—and acting just
plain silly, as far as she was concerned.

''Let's go in here,'' Chrissie insisted. ''Hey, got any quarters? I feel like playing one of these.''

Danny was already fishing in his pockets. Chrissie grabbed
a few of the quarters he offered her, spread out in the palm of
his hand, and headed for one of the few video games that
wasn't already in use. The truth was, she was generally pretty
terrible at this kind of thing. She rarely bothered wasting her
time with them, but tonight, she was bored. She wanted to do

something, and this was as good a choice as any, given the limited possibilities.

It was a driving game, one that showed a road on the screen, giving the player the opportunity to test his or her skill at maneuvering an imaginary vehicle over a curving cliff-side highway studded with treacherous obstacles. She grasped the black plastic steering wheel firmly in both hands, already starting to get into it. She licked her lips and riveted her eyes to the screen.

"Okay, Danny. Watch this."

She had decided to throw herself into this challenge wholeheartedly, concentrating all her efforts on getting as high a score as possible. And as the various images popped out on the screen—a reckless oncoming car, a small animal darting suddenly across the road—she found herself getting really involved. She gasped as each new challenge arose, then squealed with glee as she successfully conquered it and the points of the digital scorekeeper mounted up with a triumphant *ping*ing sound.

"Oh, no!" she moaned, rocking her hips back and forth as her invisible car collided with a YIELD sign, setting off a barrage of condemning bells and lights. Biting her lip, she continued navigating with even more determination, forgetting that Danny was beside her, aware only of how she was using her entire body to play this game. She thrust her pelvis against the machine, then felt her breasts jiggle as she jumped up and down with impatience at the slow truck that had just moved in front of her on the screen.

And then, her concentration seemed to vanish in an instant. She looked up, having suddenly become aware that somebody was watching her. Sure enough, over to the left, in the corner just a few feet beyond the video game, there was a young man leaning against the wall, staring at her from behind a pair of mirrored sunglasses, the expression on his face and the posture of his body letting her know exactly what he was thinking.

Her interest was piqued. He was alone, for one thing, without anyone hanging on his arm or whispering in his ear. He also looked older than the other guys here—twenty, maybe even twenty-two. And he was kind of cute, with black hair that was just a little too long in the back, a rugged-looking face behind those mirrored sunglasses of his, and a stance that said he thought he was hot stuff. He had a great body, too, she couldn't help noticing, lean but muscular, shown off to its best advantage by the tight jeans and olive green T-shirt he was wearing.

"Look out, Chrissie!" Danny suddenly yelped, reminding her that she was supposed to be controlling two tons of steel speeding along at seventy miles an hour.

"What? Oh, this stupid thing." She looked back at the screen and saw that she had just crashed into a train. While the video machine was screaming at her, she couldn't have cared less.

"Come on! What happened? You were doing great there, Chrissie!"

"Huh? Oh, I don't know. I guess I just lost my concentration or something. Hey, why don't you give it a try?"

Timidly she peeked back at the corner of the room again, but the boy was gone. While she was tempted to go looking for him—or rather, move around the room so that he could go looking for her—she couldn't very well leave Danny just standing there, no matter what she thought of him. So instead she slid over to the side of the video game, bending over and leaning against it, her chin resting in her hands. She knew that bending over like this was guaranteed to cause her short-shorts to hike up in the back—after all, wasn't that why she had bought them?

She watched the screen, pretending to be interested as Danny's make-believe car traveled the same route that hers had, meeting up with the same obstacles.

"Great—you missed it!" She actually managed to sound enthusiastic. "Oh, no—watch out!"

But her attention was attuned to the people coming and going in the room around her. Where could that boy have gone? Had he just *left*? How could he, after looking at her like that?

She was beginning to feel deflated when she suddenly felt someone brush up behind her, just a little bit too close for it to have been entirely accidental. She whirled around and found herself face-to-face with that same boy.

"Sorry," he said, taking off his sunglasses. His dark eyes burned into hers with an intensity that could only mean one thing. He was grinning at her, but Chrissie saw his smile as a dare. He leaned forward, very slightly, and said in a soft, mocking voice, "Things can get a little tight in here."

He turned and took off then, swaggering across the room,

not looking back. Chrissie watched him, her heart aching. She longed to follow him, to come up with some clever, challenging retort. . . . But Danny had just grabbed her arm.

"Look, look! I broke a thousand!" he cried, pointing to the scoreboard beside the video screen.

Chrissie looked over at him contemptuously. "What a stupid game," she said, her eyes narrowed. "Even *I* got eight hundred, and I've never played one of these dumb games before."

She looked back in the same direction the boy had taken, her yearning escalating to an excruciating level. But he had vanished. Through the window, out in the parking lot, she could see him sauntering over to a blood red Corvette. After glancing over his shoulder, back at the Tuck Shop, he climbed into the front seat.

"Boy, that was fun," Danny was saying, beside her. "That's a pretty neat game. Hey, what do you say we take a drive? Go to the beach or something?"

"Sure, Danny, if you want to," Chrissie said listlessly, her heart clenched as her eyes followed the red Corvette, gliding out of the parking lot and out of view. "Whatever you want is fine with me."

Chapter Twenty

"**G**oing out with that guy again?"

"If by 'that guy' you mean Randy," replied Katy, pausing in her painstaking application of mascara long enough to glance over at Beth, who was lying on the bed watching her, "yes, I am going out with him again."

"That's the second time this week."

"Third, actually, if you count the day we met," she corrected her niece gaily. "But who's counting?"

"I guess you two really like each other."

Katy smiled at the mirror. As she did, she noticed that the woman she saw reflected there actually looked pretty. "Yeah, I guess we really do."

"Well, if he likes you so much, Katy, then how come you have to put on all that makeup and stuff before you go out with him?"

Katy thought for a few seconds, then looked over at Beth and grimaced. "That's a good question, Beth."

As the two of them were enjoying a good laugh, Julie suddenly poked her head in the door.

"Hey, you two, what's so funny?"

Katy immediately stiffened, but Beth exclaimed, "Oh, we were just talking about Katy's new boyfriend."

Julie's eyebrows shot up. "Oh, really? You mean there's been a romance going on right under my nose and I haven't even noticed? Tell me! Who's the lucky guy?"

"His name is Randy," Beth replied, pleased at being an insider for a change. "He drives a really neat car, he makes gobs of money—and he's crazy about Katy!"

"Wow! Sounds too good to be true. Is this guy really as perfect as he sounds?"

"Well, he's a banker." Katy saw in the mirror that she was blushing.

Julie laughed. "Katy, you're the only person in the world who would consider that a negative!" Sensing immediately that what she had meant as a teasing remark had hurt her sister, she went on, "So is this serious?"

Once again, Beth was ready with an answer before Katy had a chance to reply. "I think I may hear wedding bells in the distance."

"Oh, good! I haven't been to a wedding in ages!" Julie was already caught up in the fantasy. "I'd love to get a new dress. Something slinky, the kind of thing we old married ladies don't get the chance to wear very often."

"Come on, you guys!" Katy groaned, even though she was secretly enjoying this little game. "I haven't even kissed the guy yet, and you've already got us living in suburbia with 2.2 sheepdogs and a station wagon in every room."

"Let's leave Miss Sourpuss alone, Beth," Julie teased. "Come on downstairs and help me teach Josh how to use his new tricycle. Actually, it belonged to Wes once, about a million years ago, but Mom found it in the basement this morning, and I know that Joshie is going to go wild over it."

"Have fun on your date!" Beth called gaily over her shoulder as she bounded out of the room after Julie, showing more enthusiasm than she had in days.

"If I ever get out of this house," Katy muttered, noticing that Randy was due to pick her up in less than five minutes. She opened up the top drawer of her dresser, having decided to wear one of her less outrageous pairs of earrings, the plain gold hoops, during today's excursion to the town of East Hampton. As she pawed through the jumble of jewelry pieces she had brought along packed in a Zip-Loc bag—hot pink porcelain earrings and bright enameled bangle bracelets and a few strings of beads—she was surprised that the hoops were nowhere to be found. It wasn't as if they were valuable, of course; none of her jewelry was. But it was annoying, since she had decided that they were the ones she wanted to wear today.

"Good old scatterbrained Katy," she muttered, disgusted by her own lack of organization. She grabbed a pair of silver earrings studded with turquoise that dangled halfway down her neck—not at all the kind of look she had been striving for as she dressed in a simple purple T-shirt dress that was the closest thing to conservative that she owned—but they would simply have to do.

"There," she said with a nod, taking one final look at herself in the mirror. "That's as good as I can make myself look. Take it or leave it, Randall Palmer."

As Katy came tripping down the stairs, as excited as she always imagined teenaged girls were supposed to be before a date, she saw that Randy had already arrived. He was sitting on the couch, thumbing through the new issue of *People* that he had picked up from the coffee table, looking just a trifle uncomfortable—one of the things that Katy liked about him.

"Hey, sailor! Looking for a good time?"

"I sure am," he returned with a grin. He tossed the magazine back onto the table and stood up. "And it looks like I've come to the right place."

"You sure have. Especially since today we're offering a special discount for guys with flashy cars."

It was the ideal day for an outing: temperatures in the eighties; low humidity; a cloudless baby blue sky punctuated by a friendly, rejuvenating sun. And as if all that weren't enough, Randy had the top down.

"I always feel like Annette Funicello whenever I get into this car," Katy quipped as she arranged herself in the front seat. "Or at least like I should put one of those chiffon scarves over my hair."

"The really flimsy kind, right? Pink, studded with rhine-stones."

"Or pom-poms."

"Well, then, how do you like these shades?" Proudly Randy whipped out a pair of sunglasses, the lenses tinted so dark she could scarcely see his eyes, the frames bright blue plastic.

Katy laughed. "I wonder what they'd think over at the bank if they could see you now?"

The ride to East Hampton was a pleasant one, across Shelter Island, onto the ferry to Sag Harbor, then across the South Fork of Long Island to the shore. Along the roadside was lush greenery, dotted with neat tiny houses that bordered on rustic. The small towns they passed through were quaint seacoast villages, with the same feeling to them as Shelter Island Heights—lots of nautical paraphernalia in hardware store windows, fashions in boutique displays that incorporated boats into their design as frequently as possible, restaurants that featured fresh clams and bay scallops, served against a decor that capitalized heavily on the underwater theme.

The town of East Hampton, by comparison, was positively cosmopolitan.

"Gee, I haven't been here in years," Katy observed as she climbed out of the car, after Randy parked it on one of the two intersecting main streets of the large, posh resort town. "They sure have spruced this place up."

"What you mean is, the yuppies have moved in, full force," said Randy. "I bet that ninety-nine percent of the people that can be observed right now with the naked eye are from Manhattan, yuppies every one. In this town you can get Reeboks, BMW parts, and tri color pasta salad just as easily as you can get milk and bread."

"Gee, that sounds pretty good to me," Katy returned. "Maybe if I spend enough time here, some of it'll rub off and I'll become a yuppie, too."

Randy and Katy spent a good hour browsing in the dozens of shops downtown: bookstores, clothing boutiques, antique stores, gourmet shops. By noon their enthusiastic exploration had rendered them tired, hot, and ready for lunch. At Randy's insistence, Katy chose the place, an outdoor café that appealed to her more because of its charming appearance and the chance to observe some of the street life than because of any special intuition she may have had about the quality of the food.

Once they had ordered, Randy looked over at Katy with a glint in his eye. "I got you a little present," he said. He was trying to sound offhanded as he reached under the table and pulled out a small bag that she hadn't noticed before, but Katy could tell he was pretty pleased with whatever it was he had found.

"You little sneak! When did you get this?"

"Oh, while you were paying for your parents' anniversary present in that trendy little gift shop. Open it up."

Katy didn't need a second invitation. It was a white T-shirt, she discovered as she unfolded the small bundle. As she read what was printed across the front, she burst out laughing. "It's perfect! I love it! Thanks a lot, Randy."

"Here, hold it up. Let me see how it looks."

Dutifully Katy held it up against her chest. NO CONDO, NO BMW, NO MBA," the bold black letters read.

"Yup, it's you. It's definitely you."

Katy cocked her head flirtatiously as she folded the T-shirt up again. "You seem to know me pretty well, Randall Palmer, considering we only met a week ago."

"Well, sure. You're pretty transparent. I mean, I knew right off that you were the kind of person who has at least five kinds of tea in her house, right?"

"No! Well, maybe. . . . Let's see. Earl Grey, English Breakfast . . ." Her voice trailed off as she took a mental inventory. "Seven," she reported, blushing slightly. "I have seven kinds of tea in my house right now."

"Aha! And I bet you have a cat, too."

"I live with five cats."

"Five cats! And roommates?"

"Would you believe four?"

"Four! See that, you're even more Katy-ish than I thought."

Katy laughed. "Yeah, well, you're pretty transparent, too, you know. I feel as if I know everything there is to know about you."

"Everything?"

"Everything."

"Okay, then. When I was a kid, what did I want to be when I grew up?"

"Let's see." Katy squinted, as if trying to see into the past. "You wanted to be . . . a fireman. And your favorite TV show was 'Zorro.' And every night you went to bed hugging your baseball mitt."

Randy was genuinely astonished. "How did you know all that?"

"See? I told you you were as transparent as glass."

"Okay. So tell me more."

"I bet you've been to Club Med at least once. One that's in a hot place, not one of the skiing ones. And every summer, you get a share in a house for the weekends—oh, somewhere on eastern Long Island—where you play tennis all day and spend every evening memorizing the answers to Trivial Pursuit questions."

Randy's self-conscious chuckle told Katy she wasn't that far off from the truth.

"All right. So tell me about the first major love of my life."

"Hmm. Not counting a handful of little girls in your elementary school days—blondes, no doubt, tending toward pigtails with ribbons at the ends—I'd say it was Buffy Hochschwinder, a sophomore at Simmons. A French major . . . No, a French *Studies* major. Am I right?"

"Pretty damned close. Her name was Bunny van Pelt, and she was a freshman at Skidmore. And if I remember correctly, she majored in Art History."

Katy laughed triumphantly. Then she grew more serious. Casually she said, "And what happened after you found out that Bunny van whatever-her-name-was wasn't your dream girl, after all?"

"You mean she wasn't?" Randy pretended to be shocked. "Hey, wait a minute. It sounds to me like you're trying to get me to spill my guts about the history of my love life or something."

"Well, I . . ." All of a sudden Katy was flustered. She was surprised when she heard Randy's voice soften.

"Actually, it's kind of funny you should bring this up. Because the truth is, Katy, I've been wanting to know every single detail about your life, too. Especially all about the men in your past. And," he added shyly, "any of them that might be in your present."

A wave of warmth flowed over Katy, and she could feel her cheeks burning.

"Well," she drawled, "there's no one serious in my life right now."

"Oh, really?" Randy said lightly. "Does that mean you're heavily involved with six different men right now, all of whom have a sense of humor? Get it? 'No one serious . . .?' "

Katy hesitated, seeing through Randy's attempt at joking, uncertain of just how honest she should be. She didn't want to make it sound as if *no* one was interested in her, that she was as unwanted as the things she and Randy had picked through at the garage sale where they'd met.

"There's this one guy I've kind of been seeing," she said. Wanting to make her half-truth sound even more convincing, she added, "His name is Nicholas Somers."

"Oh." Randy looked hurt.

"But it really isn't serious at all," she hastened to tell him. "Besides, we've just started going out together. I mean, I'm not really sure it could ever lead to anything. . . ."

Their waitress arrived with their lunch just then. Katy was

glad that her babbling was put to an end before she had a chance to talk herself into an inescapable corner. Overall, she was satisfied with the impression she had left on Randy: still available, but just barely.

It was still early when the two of them returned to Shelter Island, just after four o'clock. Katy was silent as the ferry pulled into shore and, once again, they were on familiar terrain, signifying that the day's excursion was over. She didn't want the day to end, yet she was afraid of pressing the point by saying anything to that effect. Maybe Randy was tired of her. Perhaps he'd had enough Katy Gilbert for one day.

She was trying to construct some offhanded comment that would indicate her interest in extending their day together while still giving him an easy out if he was inclined to have them both go their own separate ways when he said, "By the way, the Cotters are away for the weekend. They went into the city for a big wedding or something. That means I have the house to myself." He glanced over at her shyly. "Want to come home with me and raid their liquor cabinet and rifle through their underwear drawer?"

"Now there's an invitation I haven't had in a long time," Katy returned. She could feel herself glowing.

The Cotters' house was glamorous, the kind of place she would have expected to see featured in some slick home-design magazine. It was light and airy, with stark white walls, natural wood trim, and huge windows and skylights everywhere, giving the impression that one was actually a part of the spectacular landscape and seascape surrounding the house, rather than an intruder within it.

"Wow!" Katy breathed, wandering wide-eyed through the cavernous rooms on the main floor. "This is the kind of house I want when I grow up. What do the Cotters do, anyway? Rob banks? Sell cocaine?"

"You're close. They're both attorneys."

"So this is the house that law school built. Color me impressed."

"You ain't seen nothin' yet. Wait until you check out the second floor."

As Randy had promised, the cluster of four bedrooms upstairs was even more dramatic—the master bedroom, in particular. Two entire walls were glass, and overlooked Coecles Harbor. The other two walls were painted a watery blue-green that echoed the color of the sea. The room was large but sparsely furnished; two teak dressers, a sand-colored area rug on the hardwood floor, and, jutting out on the diagonal, a king-sized bed.

"Somehow, this is how I always imagined heaven would be," Katy commented, leaning in the doorway.

"Come on downstairs, now that you've had the grand tour. I'll make us some coffee. Talk about yuppies—Wendy and Mark must own every small appliance known to civilization. Wait until you see their high-tech coffee grinder. I swear, the thing looks like it could be used as the Pentagon's paper shredder."

Sure enough, the kitchen, like the rest of the house, was sleek and sensational. Everything was a bright white: the tiled floor, the walls, the cabinets, the appliances.

"Well, this place is probably easy to maintain," said Katy as she climbed up onto a stool and leaned her elbows on the tiled countertop that divided the room in two. "Every couple of months, you take a can of white spray paint, stand smack in the middle of the room, and *ps-s-s-st!*"

"Tell me: does this house look as if it's taken care of by the people who own it? No way. Mark and Wendy have a maid, and a gardener, and a pool man. . . ."

"Oh, no!" Katy groaned. "You mean they have all this and a pool, too? I should have guessed."

"Hey, how about some cappuccino? We might as well take advantage of all this."

"Sure. Sounds good."

Randy immediately began bustling around the kitchen, playing the role of the perfect host. "So," he said, taking cups that reeked of Conran's down from the shelves, "I told you what I wanted to be when I grew up . . ."

"Actually, I told you, remember?"

"Right. Anyway, how about you? What did you want to be when you grew up?"

"Not that I consider myself there yet—but would you believe I wanted to be an anthropologist?"

Randy looked up from the espresso beans he was measuring into the coffee grinder. "No, I wouldn't."

"Well, believe it. I was working on a Ph.D. in anthropology at the University of Wisconsin."

"No kidding! What was your research topic?"

"The Ramapo Indians."

"The *who*?"

"No, not The Who. The Ramapo Indians. They're a mixture of black, white, and American Indian, and they live in New Jersey, of all places, about an hour from midtown Manhattan. Yet they're totally isolated, living up in the Ramapo Mountains. . . . Like they have no TV, no shopping malls, no coffee grinders."

"No coffee grinders! Goodness, how on earth do they survive?"

"That's what I was researching. Actually, it was pretty fascinating. I mean, these people live right in the middle of civilization as we know it, yet they're totally cut off, living practically in another century, in another *world*."

"It sounds fascinating. How come you gave it up?"

"Oh, I don't know. Guess I just got bored."

"*Bored?* Are you kidding?" Randy abandoned his domestic duties and came over to her. "Look, I may not have known you very long, but I don't think I've ever heard you sound so excited about anything. What do you mean, you got bored?"

"Skip it, okay?" Katy was suddenly irritated. "I just decided it wasn't for me, all right? So let's just forget the whole thing."

Randy stared at her for a few seconds, then shrugged. "Okay, fine. If that's what you want." He turned back to the cappuccino machine. "Now, how do you suppose you work this monster? It looks like you put the coffee in here, and the water in here. . . . What's this thing do?"

"Here, I'll show you."

Katy hopped off her stool and proceeded to show the intimidating-looking appliance who was boss. Ten minutes later, she and Randy sat down at the counter, this time to a delectable spread of cappuccino and three different kinds of cake.

"Gee, nothing like a little designer coffee and cheesecake for a late afternoon snack." Katy hesitated only for a moment before helping herself to a second slice. After all, she rationalized, the first one had been so small. Besides, this was one of those desserts that was worth splurging on. "Sure beats peanut butter on Ritz crackers."

"It's nice to see a woman who eats like a human being, for a change," Randy said with a smile. "Most of the women I know, like the ones I work with, eat two lettuce leaves for lunch. And then they start complaining about how full they are.''

Katy grimaced. "Yeah, men always say that—at first. Then, before you know what hit you, they start giving you all these subtle hints about how fat you are. And by subtle, I mean lines like, 'Hey, Porky! Okay if I use your backside to show my home movies?' ''

She glanced over at Randy, but he wasn't smiling. "Boy, you sure sound cynical.''

"Life has made me realistic, that's all.'' Katy shrugged. "I've learned what to expect from people. Especially male people.''

"You make it sound as if every relationship is destined to end disastrously.''

Isn't it? Katy was thinking. But she decided not to say what was on her mind for a change. Especially since Randy's last comment had been made in a peculiarly husky voice. She saw that he was looking at her with an unmistakable intensity.

"Just tell me one thing. Do you still have enough faith left in men to give it one more try?'' Tentatively he reached across the counter and took her hand.

Katy just nodded.

"Good. Because if it's okay with you, I'd like to try to change your mind.''

After swallowing hard, she said, "Okay,'' her voice so low it was hardly audible.

Then, despite the solemnity of the moment, she couldn't resist cracking a joke. "So what happens now? Should we celebrate by going skinny-dipping in Mark and Wendy's swimming pool?''

"I have a better idea,'' Randy replied, deadpan. "Why don't we go upstairs and try out Mark and Wendy's king-sized bed?''

Chapter Twenty-One

The sight of Wes's car lumbering into the Gilberts' circular driveway on Sunday morning, after making a pick-up at the ferry, elicited two contradictory reactions in Julie: relief and fear. She was relieved that Brad was back because she would no longer be tempted to pretend she was a freewheeling single woman, galavanting about with old boyfriends on land and on sea. But at the same time, she was afraid—afraid that he would somehow know what was going on inside her, that he would recognize the ambivalence she was trying so hard to quell.

"Hi, sweetie! How's the Big Apple getting along without me?" Julie greeted her husband at the front door with a kiss. Despite all the charm she was pouring on, however, she could barely bring herself to look him in the eye. Not with all the guilt that was nagging away at her, not only over having spent such a glorious day with Paul on the *Scheherazade*, but also over being able to think about little besides him ever since.

"Broadway insisted that I give you its regards," Brad returned with a teasing and affectionate smile. "How about you? Been getting along okay out here in never-never land?"

"Oh, you know me," she said noncommittally. "I always manage to find something to do. And, of course, Josh keeps me busy."

"Where is the little guy, anyway? I brought him a present.'' He gestured toward the large shopping bag he had just deposited on the ground. Peeking out of the top was a white box which, according to the label, contained an erector set that looked like something out of a science-fiction movie. ''Saw it in the window of F.A.O. Schwarz, and, well, I just couldn't resist, even though he probably won't be able to appreciate it for another ten years. Have you seen the toys they're coming out with these days? I swear, they're more complicated than computers.''

''I'm sure he'll get the hang of it, sooner or later. Especially if you sit down with him and show him how it works.''

''Don't think I forgot about you, my dear. While I was in the neighborhood, I stopped off at Tiffany's.'' He reached into his pocket and pulled out a tiny blue box. ''Here you are, babes. Happy . . . I know, happy Labor Day eight days early. How's that for an occasion?''

''Oh, Brad! You didn't . . .'' Breathlessly she opened the box, so anxious to see what was inside that she couldn't wait another minute. And she wasn't in the least bit disappointed. The emerald stud earrings inside were tiny, but so radiant and so elegant that she knew just putting them on would make her look as if she were glowing.

''Oh, honey, they're *gorgeous*! I—I don't know what to say.''

''Then don't say anything. Here, try them on.''

Julie was tempted to give them back, to insist that she didn't deserve them. Why, it was possible that Brad had been picking out these exquisite earrings for her at exactly the same moment that she was gazing into Paul Dereksen's eyes, wishing she had the courage to lean forward and kiss him, and, when she realized she didn't, hoping he would take the initiative for her.

Wait a minute. You didn't do anything *wrong*, she argued with herself. There's nothing wrong with *wanting* something . . . is there?

But it was the wanting, Julie knew only too well, that was the part she felt so guilty about. What actually happened seemed to be secondary.

She was married to Brad. She loved him. She shouldn't be thinking about some other man, wishing she were with him, fantasizing about what it would be like to kiss him one more time. Those thoughts and feelings were supposed to be reserved for her husband. . . .

"There, now. You look even more beautiful than usual. Go find a mirror and take a look at what a knockout my wife is."

"Thanks, honey. This was so sweet of you." She leaned forward and gave him a light kiss.

"I just wanted you to know that I missed you, and that I was thinking about you. Now, where'd you say Joshie was?"

Once she was alone again, Julie could scarcely bring herself to look in the mirror. When she finally did steal into her bedroom, she saw that, just as she'd expected, the emerald earrings looked fabulous. And, also as she'd expected, the expression on her face was one of pure misery.

Oh, what am I *doing*? She sat down on the edge of the bed, her face buried in her hands. I'm so lucky, and here I am, behaving like a fool. Flirting with some old boyfriend who's ancient history, running around town like I was . . . *Chrissie*, for heaven's sake, and at home I've got a wonderful husband who loves me. My life is so perfect, yet I'm risking messing things up good.

From the room down the hall, she could hear Josh and Beth squealing over the elaborate new toy Brad had just given them. Predictably, it was the shopping bag that Josh was finding most enthralling. Julie had to smile. Brad was patiently trying to explain to his son that it was the erector set that was the "pwesent," not the shopping bag.

Yes, she thought, this is my family. These are the people who deserve my love—and my loyalty.

And from now on, she decided, I'm going to try a little bit harder to remember that.

As Barbara wandered into the living room with three or four sections of the Sunday *New York Times* under her arm and her second cup of coffee in her hand, she was looking forward to a few minutes of solitude. This was one of those rare occasions on which no one seemed to be around, the others no doubt having decided to take advantage of the excellent weather late on this Sunday morning to pursue more outdoorsy pastimes.

She needed some time to herself. The Gilbert family could be pretty overwhelming, not only in enthusiasm but also in sheer numbers, and after four days of dealing with an ongoing mob scene, a short breather would be just the thing.

So she was startled when her entrance into the living room was greeted with a hearty, "Well, well, well!"

She cast a grim smile in the direction from which the familiar voice had come.

"If it isn't the ever-lovely Barbara Gilbert, Boston's own financial wizard." Brad's tone was mocking as he got up from the oversized chair that had all but concealed him. With a drink in his hand and a smirk on his face, he leaned forward and planted a chaste kiss on her cheek. "What a treat."

"Hello, Brad," Barbara returned drily. "I had heard rumblings about your return, and here you are. You look as if you're in your usual top form."

"Always. Always." He retired to his chair, but not before giving her the once-over. The leering look in his eyes made it clear that he liked what he saw.

Barbara simply glared at him. By now, she was too accustomed to her brother-in-law's boorishness—his sexual innuendos, his rude jokes, the way he had of looking at her that left no doubt as to what he was thinking—to really be bothered by it. She made a point of turning her back to him as she arranged her newspaper on the table.

"So tell me," he went on, his bleary eyes still fixed on her, his tone still thick with belligerence, "how's life up in good old Boston?"

"Keeping me busy," she replied with more courtesy than she thought he deserved.

"That's good. And is my little brother-in-law treating you okay?"

"Just fine, Brad." She couldn't resist adding, "Believe it or not, some men actually know how to be nice to their wives."

"You know, Barbara, you really are some piece of work." Lazily Brad dragged himself out of his chair once again. He went over to the bar, splashed some more Scotch into the glass he was holding, plopped in two more ice cubes with his fingers, and sauntered over to her.

"Thank you, Brad. That is, assuming you meant that as a compliment."

"Oh, I did. I definitely did. I mean, just look at you. You're the woman that every little girl dreams of becoming. You're successful, you're cool as a cucumber, you're gorgeous." He slid his arm around her waist, letting his hand come to rest on her hip. "And you're a damn sexy broad, to boot."

Barbara just smiled at him coldly. "I don't suppose it's necessary to add that I'm also a lot stronger than I look, is it? Or that I'm perfectly capable of giving you a swift kick in a place that I suspect is quite near and dear to you?"

His response was a deep chuckle. "Did I mention that you also have a hell of a sense of humor? You know, Barbara, I've never been able to figure out how you ever ended up with a guy like Wes. I mean, I've always thought you deserved *better*."

"Oh, really? And how do you define 'better'? Richer? Louder? Or maybe more sober . . . ?"

"I think you know exactly what I mean." He tightened his grip on her, pulling her very close to him. "I've always gotten the feeling that you couldn't help wondering what it would be like if you and I—"

"There you are!" Wes said brightly as he came striding into the room. "I've been looking all over the house for you, Barbara. Oh, hi, Brad. Listen, honey, I just had a brainstorm. Listen to this, Brad, since it involves you, too. Barbara, how about if you and I spend the afternoon playing aunt and uncle?"

"I'm afraid I don't follow," said Barbara, her cold gaze still fixed on Brad. "What do you mean?"

"Let's volunteer to take Josh to the beach for a few hours after lunch. What do you say?" Wes was positively gleeful. "It'd give Brad and Julie a little break, and it'd be fun for us. What do you think?"

"All right. It does sound like fun." Barbara glanced at Wes, then turned back to face her brother-in-law once again.

"Well, then. I guess I'd better start getting ready. Sorry I have to drag myself away, Brad. It's always such a delight to see you." She patted him lightly on the cheek. "But I'm sure you and my husband can find something to talk about."

Brad slumped back into his chair as she glided out of the room.

"Hmph," Barbara heard him mutter angrily, more to himself than to Wes, after she had left the room and was heading toward the stairs. "*She's* a hell of a woman."

"Yeah, I know what you mean." Wes's voice sounded strangely soft by comparison. "She really is a hell of a woman."

Julie had virtually forgotten all about Paul Dereksen by

lunchtime. Ever since his return, Brad had been especially attentive toward her, making a point of taking her hand or touching her shoulder every chance he got, listening carefully to her reports of all the cute things their son had done in his absence. While she was with him, she came close to feeling the way she had back when she and Brad had first met: as if she were the luckiest woman in the world.

In fact, she had even gone so far as to start feeling a little bit smug.

Brad and I really do have a good, solid marriage, she had told herself over lunch, surveying the others who were sitting around the table. Even though we Gilberts all put on a pretty good show, acting as if everything in our lives is running perfectly smoothly, I know the members of my family well enough to pick up on those subtle little tensions in the others' relationships.

Barbara and Wes, for example. I'm beginning to feel that it was more than just business that kept Barbara from arriving with him last weekend. She seems so distant. . . . Why, look at her. It's as if she can barely look him in the eye. I can see that something is wrong.

Then there's Michael and Lynn. Now, there's definitely something going on there. Nothing I can put my finger on, maybe, but I can just *feel* it. Poor Lynn is trying so hard, and Michael keeps pulling back.

Oh, well, she thought with a sigh. There's always Ben and Pat. If only I could have a marriage that's as close and loving as theirs.

And for a while, she actually managed to convince herself that that was, indeed, the case.

Later, however, once she was on her own again, having volunteered to pick up a few things for her mother while Brad showered and Josh took off for the beach with Wes and Barbara, her perceptions changed.

As she drove down winding New York Avenue toward Shelter Island Heights, those same dark feelings returned, the ones that had been haunting her for days, ever since she had spent that glorious day with Paul. It was so confusing, trying to figure out not only what her feelings were toward the man with whom she had been involved twenty years earlier, but also toward the man with whom she was involved now. Nothing seemed clear anymore, and she was finding the whole experience disorienting.

I must still be in love with Paul, she decided as she put the car into Park and pulled up the emergency brake. But by the time she unbuckled her seat belt, the very notion sounded so absurd that she was embarrassed that she had ever even had such a thought.

Finally, she decided just to forget the whole thing, to avoid agonizing over the emotional seesaw that she was finding so draining. With a determined toss of her head, she strode into the Shelter Island Heights Pharmacy, sticking to her resolution by thinking about neither Brad nor Paul, but instead of the four or five items she had promised to get for Pat.

She was lost in thought once again—this time about whether to buy Nuprin or Advil or one of the countless other brands of ibuprofen on display before her—when she felt a light tap on her shoulder. She jumped, taken totally by surprise. Given her self-absorbed state, being touched by someone seemed like an unconscionable intrusion.

"Hello, Julie. Fancy meeting you here." He was holding a can of shaving cream, apparently his reason for having come into the store.

"Paul!" She gulped, feeling as guilty as if she had been caught shoplifting those little bottles of pain reliever instead of merely examining them.

"Uh-oh. Stocking up on the hard stuff, I see," he joked. "I guess the Gilbert family reunion isn't going quite as smoothly as it could."

"As a matter of fact, it's going fine. Just fine." Julie could feel her cheeks burning. "My parents' forty-second wedding anniversary is in a couple of days, and we're all looking forward to a big family celebration. And it's been great, spending lots of time with my favorite niece, Chrissie—and Joshie, too, of course. . . ." For some reason, she babbled on and on. Even as she listened to herself, she knew she sounded a trifle hysterical. But she couldn't stop herself.

"Sounds like you're all having a blast over there." Paul leaned forward, with what Julie was certain was a seductive glint in his eye, and said, "I hope that with all these festivities, you'll manage to find some time to sneak away and take another sail on the *Scheherazade*. Or, at least, come by the house for another visit."

Julie cleared her throat nervously. "Actually, Paul," she began, "I really don't think that'll be possible."

"Gee, Julie. I'm really sorry to hear that." Paul swallowed

hard. The confusion he was feeling was reflected plainly in his hazel eyes. "And here I thought that you and I had had a really good time together."

But don't you see? That's the whole point! a voice inside her shrieked. We had *too* good a time! I want to be with you too much, Paul.

All she said, however, was, "I had a wonderful time, Paul. It's just that, well, all of a sudden I'm so busy with family obligations."

"Ah. I take it hubby's back in town."

"As a matter of fact, he is." Julie hadn't meant to sound as cold as she did. But the truth was, she was playing a part: the part of the loyal and devoted wife. Perhaps if she acted that way, she could manage to actually feel that way. The fact that she wasn't having any success so far didn't keep her from trying. "But that's not really the reason. Things are just so hectic all of a sudden, over at the house. I doubt that I'll be able to get away."

Paul was suddenly stone-cold. "Well, whatever. See you around, then." He tossed the can of shaving cream into a bin, muttering something about how he guessed he didn't really need it.

As she watched him stride out of the store, it was all she could do to keep from calling after him, or even following him out. Her heart was aching in much the same way it had when she had first found out that Paul was going to marry Sally Horner.

She stood there without moving, until long after he had left, still clutching both a box of Advil and one of Nuprin in her hands. But even as she tried to force herself to focus on them, to go back to trying to make what should have been the simplest decision in the world, she found that all she could think about, all she could see, was the hurt look in Paul's eyes.

Chapter Twenty-Two

"**I** *sure hope* this doesn't turn out to be a mistake." Wes cast his wife a good-natured grin as he pulled the blue Volvo into the parking lot of Sagaponak, one of the public beaches that ran along the south shore of Long Island. This beach, in particular, had long been one of the Gilberts' favorites: while it was just a stone's throw from the Hamptons, it had nevertheless remained both uncrowded and uncommercial, still virtually undiscovered by the hordes of summer people who migrated to the South Fork every summer.

"I'm sure it can't be all that difficult," Barbara returned with a smile. Actually, she was hoping that she sounded a bit more optimistic than she was feeling. "After all, parents with just as little training as we have have been taking care of two-year-old children for years. And as far as I know, they've all survived."

Ruefully Wes peered into the rearview mirror. Behind him, Josh was strapped into his car seat, happily singing to himself.

"Yeah, I know," he said with a loud sigh. "But it's probably a whole different ball game when the kid in question is your own. Don't forget—Joshie here is just on loan to us for the afternoon."

"Oh, what could possibly be difficult about taking care of a little boy for a couple of hours?"

Once again, Barbara sounded much more confident than she really was. While she was used to looking at her nephew as a sweet, relatively harmless diversion, someone who it was fun to tickle for two or three minutes, or delight with some small plastic toy unexpectedly whipped out of a pocket, she was suddenly seeing him quite differently. This whole thing had been Wes's idea, not hers, and while she was not entirely opposed to his generous suggestion that the two of them take Josh off Julie's hands for a couple of hours on this hot, sunny Sunday afternoon, she was also not about to underestimate the challenge that this task presented, especially to two novices like themselves.

Even so, she was trying her best to look at the bright side of the situation. She mustered up every last shred of her imagination in an effort to share Wes's vision of the three of them laughing together on a beach blanket as they admired the tremendous castle they had all just built out of sand and shells and pretty stones, meanwhile sipping celebratory paper cups of lemonade—all in all looking like something out of a magazine ad.

Besides, she told herself bravely, maybe it will be good for us. In a way, we'll be replaying a part of our past. It will be just like the way Wes and I worked together, side by side, renovating that dilapidated old brownstone of ours on Columbia Street, wiling away all those long weekend afternoons stripping paint off doorjambs and laboring over the book of wallpaper samples. Maybe seeing us together this way again will help me see things a little bit more clearly. . . .

But she had to admit that, so far, their attempts at putting their heads together to cope with something a little bit out of the ordinary had been less than triumphant. In fact, the whole thing had been nothing but an exercise in frustration.

First, the two of them had spent a full half hour packing up the car, lugging across the front lawn a car seat, a stroller, a cooler for Joshie's milk and juice, a beach umbrella to protect him from the hot summer sun, about four thousand plastic sand toys, and a canvas bag, packed to bursting with towels, changes of clothing, diapers, and three kinds of crackers, that must have weighed at least as much as Josh himself.

Next, they had both been forced to memorize a list of instructions on feeding, diaper etiquette, and the prevention of sunstroke in small children. Then, they had endured a full five minutes of wailing as she and Wes dared to wisk Josh away from his mother. In the end, the two of them had resorted to singing at least fifteen choruses of ''Old MacDonald'' in a futile effort to convince Josh that they were on his side.

But still she strove to keep a stiff upper lip. "Besides," she went on, "there are two of us, and only one of him. Those are odds we can't complain about . . . aren't they?"

It didn't take her long, however, to conclude that a ratio of six to one might have been more reasonable. As Wes struggled with the umbrella, cooler, and all the other accoutrements that Julie had insisted were necessary for an afternoon outing at the beach, Barbara took charge of Josh. As the threesome began to make their way from the parking lot to the beach, a distance of only a few hundred feet, she reached for his hand, expecting him to walk beside her placidly. Instead, he immediately put up a fight.

"Want Wes!" Josh insisted, trying to extricate his pudgy little hand from her grasp. "No Bah-bah. Want Wes!"

"No, honey. Wes has his hands full right now. He can't—"

"Want Wes! Want Wes!" Josh was screaming now, twisting his arms in his struggle to break free.

"Josh, there are cars here! You can't—I'll tell you what. Come here, and I'll carry you." Already frustration, anger, and fear had risen up in Barbara. She bent down to pick him up. But the little boy was not prepared to be cooperative. He shrieked as Barbara tried to grasp hold of him, wriggling away so adeptly that grabbing him was nearly impossible. When she finally did manage to get hold of him and lift him up into the air, he began to kick.

"Stop it, you little beast!"

"Barbara, calm down. He's just a baby, remember?" Wes deposited all his possessions on the ground, then reached for his nephew. "Here we go, Joshie. Let me—"

"No! No!" Josh threw himself on the ground, waving his arms and legs violently in the air and yelling "No!" over and over again through his hysterical tears. When Wes bent over him, trying to retrieve him, the little boy's temper tantrum escalated.

"Great. What do we do now?" Wes mumbled.

"Don't worry about it. He's just a baby, remember?" In response to her husband's glare, Barbara said, "Sorry. I couldn't resist. Look, why don't we try bribery?"

"Good idea. Hey, Joshie. Want something to eat? How about some milk? Or a hot dog? Or—or—"

"Chips. Want *chips*!" Josh had already stopped crying. He

climbed to his feet, eyes wide, disagreements forgotten. "Chips. Chips."

"Does he mean potato chips?" Barbara whispered. "Or maybe French fries?"

"It's got to be one or the other. Here, I'll take him over to the concession. Can you manage all this stuff by yourself?"

"Believe me, I'll find a way."

"See you in a few minutes."

"Take your time. Meanwhile, I'll be keeping my fingers crossed, hoping that plying him with junk food will turn out to be the answer."

Barbara expected them to return within a couple of minutes. But she had time to spread out the blanket, set up the umbrella, slip out of her shorts and shirt, and lather up with suntan lotion all before they had showed up again. She was about to stretch out and relax when she jumped up with a start, propelled into action without even having had a chance to think about what she was doing. The sight of a tiny towheaded child, rushing into the sea, had her adrenaline pumping before she was even certain it was Josh.

Sure enough, the little boy who was chest-deep in the ocean and continuing out even further without showing the least signs of hesitation or fear was indeed her nephew.

"Stop! Where are you going?" She raced down the beach, oblivious to the scorching sand beneath her bare feet. It didn't even matter that the water was ice cold as she pursued him. All she knew was that she had to reach him, to overcome the infuriating resistance of the swirling water that reached her midthigh, fighting her every step of the way.

"Come here, you." She reached for him, expecting him to be grateful to her for saving him.

Instead, he yelled, "No! Stop it!" and dropped down under the water.

Panic rose up in Barbara. She pushed her way through the waves, trying to grab him, afraid of losing sight of him. And suddenly she felt herself toppling over, losing her balance and falling into the icy water before she had even had a chance to gasp for one last breath of air.

"I—uh—where . . . ?" As she stood up, coughing and sputtering as she tried to get reoriented, she discovered she couldn't see him at all. She whirled around, searching for him desperately, petrified of what she might see—or not see.

What she found right behind her, however, was a calm

little boy, standing calmly in waist-high water, looking a trifle bewildered.

"Wha' happened?" he asked. "Bah-bah all *wet*!"

"Oh, good. You got him." Wes came splashing through the water, a frenzied look in his eyes. "God, for a minute there I thought I'd lost him."

"What do you mean, you thought you'd *lost* him?" Barbara suddenly had the presence of mind to realize how furious she was. Now that it was evident that Josh was safe, and he was willingly being led out of the water, back to the safety of the sandy beach, she was able to focus on the fact that she was sopping wet, shivering from her tumble into the freezing water, and exhausted from what had been a totally draining experience.

"Look, it wasn't my fault. God, what an ordeal. First he knocked over this—this *tower* of paper cups they had on the counter next to the soda machine. Then he grabbed a huge handful of straws and dumped them all over the place. Finally, I had to put him down so I could pay for this stuff." Sheepishly Wes held up the cardboard container of French fries he was holding in one hand and the opened bag of potato chips in the other. "He was on the ground for a total of two seconds, and the next thing I knew, he took off. I went running after him, but, boy, that little guy is fast!"

"Chips!" Josh demanded, reaching both hands toward Wes imploringly.

"And I never did figure out exactly what 'chips' meant. So I just decided to play it safe."

"Both probably have about equal amounts of starch, salt, and grease." Exhausted, Barbara dropped down onto the blanket. "Oh, boy. Are we ever in for a long afternoon."

But much to their surprise, Josh sat down on the edge of the blanket and happily began stuffing junk food into his mouth, first three or four French fries, then a fistful of potato chips, then back to the French fries. As she watched him, Barbara couldn't help noticing how cute he looked. And when he began crooning a little song to himself, with the lyrics, "Chips, Fr'fries, chips, Fr'fries," she was affected in a way she never would have expected.

"Look, Wes. Isn't that the cutest thing you've ever seen in your life?"

"It's definitely one of the contenders," he returned with a

grin. "Kind of makes you wish you had a camera, doesn't
it?"

Or how about a child of your own? Barbara was thinking.
But before she had a chance to say anything, she noticed a
shadow crossing the blanket, then stopping. She looked up
and found a woman in a straw hat, probably around sixty,
peering down at the three of them, beaming approvingly.

"I was just trying to figure out which one of you he looks
like," she said.

"He's not ours," Barbara informed her quickly.

"Right. We're just babysitting today." Wes leaned over
and slung an arm around Barbara's shoulders. "We don't
have any of our own. At least, not yet."

The opening was all too perfect. As the woman moved
away, Barbara glanced over at her husband and said casually,
"Hey, Wes?"

"Umm?"

"I was kind of surprised by what you just said to that
woman. About us not having any children *yet*. You made it
sound as if it were something you just automatically assumed
we would do one day."

Wes thought for a moment. "Well, yeah, I guess it is. I
mean, I know we've never actually *talked* about it, but I
always figured that one day, when we both decided the time
was right— Hey, where do you think you're going, little
guy?"

Without any warning, Josh had suddenly sprung up from
the beach blanket, leaving a messy little pile of crushed
French fries and broken potato chips behind. He ran back
toward the water, announcing, "Joshie want t'go da water."

"Oops. Catch you later." This time, as Wes headed
toward the waves, he was smiling indulgently, looking as if he
were actually looking forward to romping in the waves with
his enthusiastic little nephew.

Barbara looked on without even realizing that she, too, was
smiling. She was totally charmed as she watched the two of
them playing together. Even more, she was struck by the fact
that she was witnessing a whole new side of her husband, one
she had never even suspected existed, as he lifted Josh high
up into the air, then slowly lowered him into the water, only
to scoop him up once again as soon as he'd gotten wet, a
game that Josh obviously found just as delightful as his uncle
did.

The two of them looked as if they were having a grand old time. They seemed to belong together, the little boy and the man, and as she watched them, it seemed to Barbara as if Wes were realizing for the very first time that there could well be an element that was missing from his life, one that a child like Josh could provide.

And what about me? Barbara wondered as she stretched out flat and closed her eyes, confident that now that they were beginning to get the hang of it, those two were perfectly capable of taking care of each other. Do I possess enough of a capacity to love to find room for a child in my life? All the sacrifices that it would require, all the compromises, all the things I'd have to give up . . .

But what about the things I would gain? Am I willing to shift my priorities so much, am I willing to let myself change in the ways I'd have to change?

Then there's my relationship with Wes. Having a baby would certainly change things between the two of us.

If we did go ahead and have this child, she thought, we wouldn't just be a couple anymore, selfishly going our own separate ways most of the time and then coming together only when we want to indulge our need for companionship. When we feel like belonging to a couple. When we're prepared to love. Suddenly, we would be a *family*. We would need each other in an entirely different way.

It was too overwhelming, too terrifying to contemplate. She needed more time, time to decide what she really wanted—and time to decide how much of herself she was really willing, and able, to give.

Chapter Twenty-Three

*B*arbara threw her head back and closed her eyes, relishing the sensation of the scalding water pelting her skin, massaging every one of her muscles, then took a small step forward so she was standing directly underneath the shower head. The pounding water, so hot that it was almost unbearable, cascaded over her head and her shoulders with such force that she couldn't breathe. She could scarcely think, in fact, as the deluge rushed over her eyes, her face, seemingly forming an impenetrable barrier separating her from the rest of the world.

Barbara felt as if she were able to relax for the first time in weeks. While the afternoon she'd just spent at the beach with Wes and Josh had been fun, it was tinged with tension, stemming mainly from her ambivalence about whether or not this was the right time to tell her husband. She had been on guard the whole time, feeling as if he were watching her, as if he were waiting for an explanation, meanwhile playing the part of the perfect husband—caressing her with suntan lotion, brushing sand off her back—as if hoping that he could lure her back into the intimacy they had once enjoyed.

But now, the afternoon was over, and she was alone. The long day in the sun had taken its toll, forcing every muscle to let go, dissolving all the tension, tiring her to the point where thinking about anything even remotely serious was next to impossible. The saltwater and the sun had conspired to smooth out all the rough edges, in the same way they might have worked together to hone a jagged rock on the beach. And now the hot water of the shower was finishing the job, anesthetizing her to a point where all her worldly problems seemed as elusive as the cloud of steam that surrounded her as she opened the glass shower door and stepped out onto the fluffy rose-colored rug, into the middle of the bathroom.

Plump drops of water were sliding off her slicked-back hair at an alarming rate, so she immediately grabbed a pink towel off the rack and bent over so she could wrap it tightly around her head, turban-style. When she stood up once again, she discovered that she was no longer alone. The door had been flung open; leaning against the doorframe, a glass in his hand and a leer on his face, was Brad.

"So, Brad, we meet again." Barbara stood before him completely naked, as shameless and as undaunted as if she were dressed in a snowsuit. "At the risk of sounding trite, we really have to stop meeting like this." She continued to look directly at him, her blue eyes stone-cold, her gaze unwavering.

It was Brad who looked away, suddenly embarrassed. For once in his life, he was at a loss for words.

"What's the matter, Brad? You're turning a rather unusual shade of red. Maybe it's the steam in here . . . or maybe it's something else. Oh, *I* know. This little game of yours didn't turn out exactly the way you'd expected, is that it? You thought I'd scream and run for the nearest towel and never be able to look you in the eye again, right? Or maybe you thought I'd fling myself at you. You know, tear off all your clothes and jump you, right here in the shower stall. Sounds pretty romantic, doesn't it?"

"Now that you mention it, that does sound pretty good," Brad said, regaining some of his bearings.

A lecherous gleam came into his eyes as he looked her up and down. He had to admit that her naked body was even more beautiful than he'd imagined: firm large breasts, a tiny waist, slim hips atop long slender legs, a thick triangle of dark hair in the midst of her creamy white skin. He could feel himself growing aroused.

"Well, Brad, if nothing else, it shows that you have some imagination, after all." Matter-of-factly Barbara reached for the white terry-cloth bathrobe that was hanging from a hook on the back of the door and slipped it on, tying the belt around her waist with a firm tug. Her chin was held at an arrogant angle as she sailed past him toward the door. "*Quite* an imagination, as a matter of fact.

"But to tell you the truth, I'm a little bit tired of talking about you. I think I'd rather go get dressed for dinner. Excuse me, won't you?"

It wasn't until she was in her bedroom, alone once again, that she realized she was shaking with anger.

A half hour later, as she and a handful of the other Gilberts who were at home this evening rallied together in the kitchen to put together an informal dinner, Barbara had calmed down. But the sordid incident with her brother-in-law had not been forgotten. And she was determined not to let him walk away from it unscathed.

She waited until Katy and Michael went down to the basement with Pat to help her search for some ingredient or other, leaving her alone with Julie.

"Julie, honey, I wouldn't say anything about this if I didn't feel it was in your best interest, but I think that husband of yours should think about having a lock put on his zipper."

"What are you talking about, Barbara?" Julie looked up from the pile of fresh mushrooms she was slicing and blinked, her confusion sincere.

Her dark-haired sister-in-law came over to her, speaking in a low, earnest voice. "If it had only happened once, I probably would have just let it go. I mean, sooner or later every woman's husband, no matter how saintly he may be, has one drink too many and makes a pass at somebody else's wife."

"And I take it that's what you're telling me Brad did."

"The first time—yes. But this afternoon, when I came in from the beach and went in to take a shower, he just happened to wander into the bathroom as I was coming out of the shower stall." A cold smile curled her lips. "Yes, old Brad got quite an eyeful. Exactly what he was hoping for." Barbara touched Julie's arm gently. "I'm really sorry, Julie. And as I said before, I wouldn't even have mentioned it if—"

"It could have been a mistake, couldn't it? I mean, maybe he just happened to walk into the bathroom by accident. . . ."

"I wish that'd been the case. Really, I do. But your husband has been coming on to me ever since I got here, and, well, I just thought you should know."

Julie forced a smile. "I appreciate your telling me, Barbara. And it's not as if I blame you for anything. But I'm pretty sure you've got it all wrong."

Barbara opened her mouth to protest, then snapped it shut

and thought for a few seconds. "Look, Julie. You and I have never been close. But I've always had a lot of respect for you. You're a woman who's got a lot going for her—including intelligence. Don't make the mistake of assuming your husband is Mr. Perfect, and that I'm just trying to stir up trouble. Look, what would I possibly have to gain from doing something like that, anyway?"

There was an odd look in Julie's eyes—one of pity, from what Barbara could see. "I know you really believe that Brad has been putting the moves on you, Barbara. But that's because you don't really know him. He just has kind of a funny way of relating to women sometimes, that's all. I mean, who could blame him? He's used to having women flirt with him all the time!"

Barbara was about to blurt out the first comment that came to mind, but she stopped herself. She realized that trying to expose that man for what he really was to a wife who simply refused to believe the truth was a losing battle.

"Maybe you're right," she said after a long silence, turning back to the sauce she had been stirring. Julie, working beside her, absorbed in her slicing of the mushrooms once again, was humming some unrecognizable melody. "I guess I just don't know Brad as well as you do."

Julie looked over at her and smiled sweetly. "There. Do you think I've sliced up enough mushrooms for the salad?"

Despite her refusal to admit to Barbara that her reports of Brad's boorish behavior could possibly be true, Julie's conversation with her sister-in-law left her with a heavy heart. She was quiet over dinner, too, absorbed in her own thoughts to contribute to the lighthearted conversation going on around her. She kept picturing in her mind the scenario that Barbara had described: Brad walking in on her just as she was coming out of the shower, going out of his way to create a situation meant to embarrass her. Or was she underestimating his true intent, preferring misreading it to dealing with the possibility that her husband was, indeed, making advances toward his sister-in-law—advances that he had every intention of following up on, given the chance?

The whole thing took away her appetite, and it was all she could do to force herself to pick at the veal dish she and the others had worked so hard to prepare. Maybe it was silly, but she didn't want anyone to see how upset she was—especially Barbara.

Even so, she couldn't help being preoccupied, involuntarily closing out the merry chatter of the people around her. It wasn't until Katy's statement about the disappearance of a pair of her earrings that she snapped out of her self-absorption.

"I know it was just carelessness," Katy was complaining, sounding almost cheerful, "but it still bothers me that I mislaid those stupid hoop earrings. They weren't all that valuable, but they were gold-plated. . . . At least they had some gold in them. But what really gets me is that I can be so damned absentminded. I mean, I could have sworn I packed them!"

Julie was surprised to hear Lynn chime in, "It's funny you should say that, Katy. I've been thinking the exact same thing. A few days ago, I lost some earrings of mine, too. Well, I didn't lose them, exactly. I guess I left them at home, probably right on top of the dresser. I must have forgotten to pack them. Gotten distracted at the last minute or something."

"This must be contagious!" Julie interjected, glad to have something other than Brad to think about. "I lost my gold watch. It's probably just stuck behind the bed . . . maybe it even fell underneath the rug. I haven't had a chance to do a really thorough search yet. But it's an odd coincidence, isn't it?"

"I think it's just a sign that we're all getting old," Katy concluded, reaching across the table for a biscuit, then remembering her latest pledge to start being more vigilant about the calories she consumed.

"Or else that we've got a lot on our minds these days." Lynn smiled wistfully. "I like my explanation a lot better."

"Well, at least we don't have to worry about misplacing really valuable stuff," said Katy. "Just think: if Liz Taylor were having the problems we're having, she could lose a pair of earrings worth France's entire defense budget"—she snapped her fingers—"like that!"

Suddenly the three women's absentmindedness seemed comical, and everyone at the table was laughing about it. Only one of the Gilberts had to force a chuckle, knowing full well that it was more than just a humorous coincidence that things were beginning to disappear mysteriously from around the house.

Chapter Twenty-Four

At first Katy was confused, struggling to figure out what the shattering ring of a telephone was doing in the middle of her dream, a dream in which she was back in high school, late for gym class but unable to remember where she had put her gym suit and sneakers. In the end, however, reality won out. She was dragged out of her sleep, into the realization that she was not about to incur the wrath of Miss Grundorf, her high school gym teacher, after all.

But her confusion over exactly where she was in time was replaced by bewilderment over who could possibly be calling at this ungodly hour—barely eight-thirty, according to the wristwatch she grabbed off the night table next to her.

Katy's eyes were still half closed as she stumbled downstairs, into the kitchen, and groped for the telephone receiver.

"Hullo." Just getting the word out was an achievement.

The voice at the other end, however, was alert and animated.

"Katy! Is that you? Hope I didn't wake you."

"Leslie?" Immediately she took a quantum leap into full consciousness. "Hi! Gee, what a surprise."

The last person in the world she would have expected to hear from during her two-week vacation was her boss. Leslie Marr was simply not the type to intrude upon one's private time. Unless, Katy thought, quickly leaping to an assumption, there was some kind of emergency.

"Listen, is everything okay?"

"Well, Kate, it's nothing catastrophic, if that's what you're thinking." Leslie's reassurance was delivered in her usual hearty manner. "As a matter of fact, what's bad news for me could very well turn out to be good news for you."

"So something *has* happened. What is it?"

On her end of the line, Leslie took a deep breath. "Last night, Carol and I had a long talk. I've known for a long time that she's been thinking about moving on. For months now she's been talking about going back to school, or getting into something new, another business, maybe. Anyway, to make a long story short, she's decided that she wants out of the business."

Katy was aghast. "But Leslie! You and Carol started Foodstuffs together! You two have been partners for, what is it, four years?"

"Almost five. But, as I say, she's decided she wants to move on to other things."

"Like what?"

"She doesn't know yet."

Katy decided not to pursue this line of questioning any further, since she was beginning to get the feeling that the decision to break up the partnership was more than just a business decision.

"I see. So, uh, what does all this have to do with me?" Katy's confusion was sincere.

"Well, Kate, I know this is really coming to you from out of the blue, but now that it's definite that Carol's leaving, I'm kind of freaking out over here. I can't run Foodstuffs by myself. Hell, I wouldn't even *want* to. One of the nice things about having a partner, I found out, is that you always have a backup. Not to mention," she added with a good-natured chuckle, "that if there's some dirty job that you really don't want to do, sometimes you can talk the other person into doing it instead."

Leslie paused. "Anyway, I guess you can figure out where all this is leading, Kate. You and I have always worked well together—you're more familiar with Foodstuffs than anybody besides me and Carol—and, well, I'd really like it if you'd consider coming into business with me."

Katy was speechless. This *was* coming from out of the blue! Here she'd been moseying along, thinking of herself as just an employee of what was pretty much a pleasant place to work—and all of a sudden she was being invited to become a partner!

"Wow," was all she could think of to say. "That's—that's quite an offer, Leslie. I have to think about it, of course."

"Oh, of course. That's why I took the liberty of calling you even though you're on vacation and Foodstuffs is probably the last thing on your mind right now. But give it some thought, Katy. I think it could work out really well, for both of us. Not to mention the fact that I'm *desperate*," she added with a self-conscious laugh. "Maybe by the time you come back to work next week, you'll have made a decision."

After Katy had hung up and was shuffling back to her bedroom, she realized that she felt like a whole new person. She was elated and petrified at the same time. What an opportunity! A chance to step into a successful business like Foodstuffs, to work with somebody neat like Leslie—to have some real definition of who and what she was for a change.

"Hi, I'm Katherine Gilbert," she muttered. "You know, the co-owner of Foodstuffs."

Just trying it on for size gave her goose bumps.

Already her mind was clicking away. She pictured herself sailing into the small shop, nodding approvingly at the wicker baskets piled high with oversized muffins, the glass platters of lobster salad, the golden Rock Cornish hens all lined up in neat rows. In her fantasy she was dressed in a silk dress, strappy high heels, and dainty gold jewelry—very much the kind of outfit Julie usually wore, in fact. Her extra weight had magically melted away; her hair had lost its tendency to frizz in the damp weather; she was more serene, more sophisticated, more *together*.

She was also thinking about the changes she would want to institute, little things that had occurred to her during the hours she had worked there. The desserts, for example. These days, the chocolate velvet pies and carrot cakes were unceremoniously stuck on the bottom shelf of one of the glass display cases, almost as an afterthought. Foodstuffs' magnificent desserts deserved better. They were worthy of their own case, set apart from the rest of the food. Maybe they could even build up an additional reputation for themselves as a bakery, rather than just an excellent gourmet food take-out shop with a couple of cakes thrown in for shoppers' convenience.

Then there was the basic layout of the place. The cash register should be back in the corner, not right out in front, the first thing the customers saw when they came in. . . . Yes, she had ideas. Plenty of them. More than she had ever been aware of, even, she realized as she sat on her bed and stared at her toes, wondering whether being the proprietor of such a classy establishment would warrant an occasional pedicure. Or at least a manicure.

That was her initial reaction. With a frown, Katy allowed a bit of reality to creep into her overactive imagination. The bottom line was that accepting Leslie's offer to become a partner in Foodstuffs was a real *commitment*. Aside from the glamour of the silk clothes that she would allegedly have the money to buy and the excuse to wear, despite the attraction of acquiring a definition for herself, once and for all, what it all came down to was deciding that *this* was what she wanted to do—at least, for a little while. Saying yes to Leslie would mean sticking to something, making a promise that she felt she could honor. No longer could she think of herself as being in transition, of not yet being fully-formed—of floating around, still considering the endless number of possibilities that lay before her.

The surge of adrenaline that only minutes before had elevated her to euphoric heights by now had disappeared, leaving in its wake a feeling of having been deflated. Yes, it was flattering having Leslie call her up like that. But it also meant that Katy would be forced to do the one thing that seemed to come to her with more difficulty than anything else: making a decision, and sticking to it.

"Anything wrong? You seem a bit pensive today." Randy reached across the table set out on the patio of the Dory, the informal restaurant across from the town dock where lunch was now being served, and gently pushed away a strand of hair that had fallen into Katy's eyes.

"And that's saying a lot, considering that having a single thought in my head is a rare occasion." Katy guffawed.

"Come on. You know I wasn't saying anything like that. You just seem kind of distracted, that's all."

"Yeah, well, I do have kind of a lot on my mind today." Katy hesitated, stirring her iced tea with a straw and watching the ice cubes swirl around the glass as if it were a truly fascinating sight. "I got a phone call this morning, and it really threw me."

"From that guy?" At the mere thought of Nicholas Somers, Randy's entire body had grown rigid.

"Who? Oh, you mean Nicholas. No, nothing like that." With a wave of her hand, Katy dismissed the very idea. Randy, she was pleased to notice, breathed a sigh of relief. "My boss, Leslie Marr, called me. Well, she *used* to be my boss, anyway. The reason she called was to ask me if I wanted to become her business partner. You know, become the co-owner of Foodstuffs."

"Whoa! What an opportunity!" Randy's enthusiasm left no doubt as to how he felt about the offer Leslie had made. "Katy, do you have any idea how many people out there are dying to run their own business? Especially one that's already doing well! And to have it just fall into your lap like this . . . Boy, you really lucked out, kid. Congratulations!"

"Wait. Hold on. Don't take my picture for the cover of *Business Week* yet. I mean, it's not as if I actually accepted."

Randy shrugged. "So what are you waiting for? Call her back, tell her the deal is on."

"Well, it's not that simple." Katy sat back in her chair and surveyed the scenic view of Chase Creek that was laid out before her. A few ducks skimmed the surface of the water, looking so placid that it was as if the Dory's owners had hired them to make the patio restaurant even more delightful. "If I *do* accept Leslie's offer—and mind you, I'm not sure I'm going to—it means agreeing to stick with the food business. You know, making a real commitment to hanging in there, no matter what happens."

The look on Randy's face told her that he didn't have the slightest idea what she was talking about.

"There's other stuff to consider, too," she went on. "Like it'd mean I'd have to stay around Albany."

"So what's wrong with that? I thought you liked that area." Another angle suddenly occurred to him, and his voice softened. "Hey, if you're thinking about you and me, don't worry about it. Albany's only, what is it, a three-hour drive from the city? My trusty Bel Air can certainly handle that. I can come up on weekends."

Katy was not too absorbed in thinking about the business decision that was facing her to appreciate what Randy was saying. So he didn't think of this as a harmless little summer fling, after all. He did expect that the two of them would continue to see each other, even after the summer had ended.

"If you put it that way, it makes it sound just plain *dumb* to say no to Leslie."

"Well, then, it's settled," Randy said with a quick nod. "What do you want to do first, call up—what's her name? Leslie?—or celebrate? Hey, do you think they serve champagne here?"

"Randy, it's *not* settled." Katy was beginning to wonder if there was something wrong with her. Here Randy was convinced that this was a terrific idea, a magnificent opportunity that she had just lucked into. And he was somebody who seemed to know a lot about the way the world worked. Why, then, was she still so reluctant?

"Look, it may seem cut and dried to you," she went on, "but it's a big decision for me. I have to decide if this is really what I want to do. I need to think about it." She looked at him pleadingly, hoping he wouldn't think she was being difficult, or that she was trying to be the center of attention, or that—God forbid—she was just wishy-washy.

But Randy was matter-of-fact. "You're right. No reason to rush into anything, no matter how good it might look on the surface. In fact, if you'd like me to take a look at the financials for Leslie's business, I'd be happy to do it."

"Okay. Thanks. I just might take you up on that offer." Katy puffed out her cheeks and blew out a slow stream of air. "You know, it's really amazing. When it rains, it pours."

"What do you mean?"

"Well, here this incredible opportunity has just fallen into my lap, from out of the blue. And as if that weren't outrageous enough, it's the second business proposition I've had this week."

Randy just looked puzzled. "Explain."

"Well, when all us Gilberts got to my parents' beach house, my father told us that one of the reasons he wanted to see us all together was that he's started thinking about retiring. And he was hoping he could pass the family business on down to one of us." Katy shrugged. "It could be me as well as anyone else."

"What kind of business is this?"

"Oh, sales promotion, basically. You know, coming up with ideas for contests and free offers and stuff like that, ways of promoting clients' products, then executing the plans."

"Sounds like fun. Is that something you might want to do?"

"Not particularly. The only thing is that taking Dad up on his offer to be the new president of B.G.A. means instant career. Instant success. I mean, it's not every day that you get to become president of a company that you've never even worked for."

"For you, it is," Randy teased. "So what's it gonna be, Katy? Are you going to become a food tycoon or a marketing magnate?"

Katy frowned. "Ever heard of having too much of a good thing?"

He reached over and took her hand, once again playing the role of lover rather than business consultant. "Well, look. Whatever you decide to do, I'm behind you one hundred percent, okay?"

"Your kind support is appreciated," Katy quipped, embarrassed by his intensity. "At this point, I could use a little help from my friends."

"I'm a little bit more than a friend," he said, leaning across the table and giving her hand a squeeze. "Because you know something, lady? I happen to be falling in love with you."

As if there weren't enough confusion in her life already, Katy returned to her parents' beach house that evening to find herself in the middle of a family crisis. As she waltzed in, still slightly dazed by everything that had happened to her that day, she found the entire Gilbert clan sitting down to dinner— not at all unusual, considering that it was seven o'clock, their regular dinner hour. What was unexpected, however, was the tension hanging in the room, so thick that Katy couldn't help picking up on it right away.

"Uh-oh. Maybe I should have accepted Randy's invitation for leftover franks and beans, after all," she joked as she sat down at the table. But her remark didn't elicit a single smile, not even from Beth. "What's up, guys? Did we lose the family fortune in a stockmarket crash while I was out?"

Since no one seemed willing to answer her, she turned to the person sitting closest to her, who happened to be her sister. "Julie, would you mind telling me what the hell is going on around here?"

"Barbara's diamond ring is missing." Her voice was barely audible.

"You're kidding! Her *engagement* ring? You mean that rock that's about as big as— What do you mean, it's missing?"

She looked around the table, searching for some explanation, but once again got little response. Then Lynn piped up.

"At first we thought it was just a coincidence," she said hesitantly. "Remember? We were talking about it just the other day. About how careless we were all getting, I mean. Julie said she'd misplaced her watch, I couldn't find my earrings—"

"And I lost my gold hoops." It was beginning to make sense to Katy. "And now it's Barbara's engagement ring. Something that cost a small fortune, to boot. Hmm, you're right. This *is* becoming more than a coincidence."

"I still think that you all simply misplaced your jewelry," Pat interjected firmly. "It's possible, isn't it? It's summer vacation, you're all living out of suitcases . . ."

"Mom, you just can't believe that anyone would ever do anything dishonest," remarked Michael.

"Wait a minute." Now things were getting even more focused for Katy. "Are we all inferring that somebody took all this jewelry—somebody as in a family member?"

"I don't know who else it could possibly be." Barbara's haughtiness seemed terribly out of place. It was clear that she was wounded—and that she was anxious to ferret out the culprit.

Even so, Katy thought, she's not *really* a member of this family, not by blood, anyway—and since things between her and Wesley seem to be so shaky lately, why is she so upset about her engagement ring, of all things?

Still, Katy had to admit that stolen jewelry was pretty heavy, something that couldn't just be ignored. Especially if Barbara's insinuation that someone at the table was responsible turned out to be correct.

"Okay, everybody, empty your pockets," she teased, desperate to try easing some of the tension.

Her oldest brother, however, was quick to reprimand her. "Really, Katy. This is hardly something to joke about."

"Well, then, I recommend that we get serious. I move that we find out who did it and then boil him—or her—in oil. But make it safflower oil. Might as well be healthy about it."

She looked around the table once again, searching for some kind of support. Sure, this situation was bad news, but dwelling on it like this, turning a few pieces of missing jewelry into a federal case, wasn't going to help. Fortunately, her usual ally was prepared to come through for her one more time.

"Katy's right," said Wes. "Unless somebody's willing to admit they've been lifting jewelry, this isn't going to get us anywhere. Let's leave it for a while, okay? Especially since that beauteous chicken that Mom spent all afternoon roasting is going to get cold if we don't start in on it soon."

Relieved to have the opportunity to abandon what was only becoming a more and more unpleasant topic, the others allowed themselves to be drawn into normal dinner conversation. Only Barbara seemed unable to let it go, and Katy couldn't help noticing that when Wes made a move to take her hand, she made a point of reaching for her wineglass instead.

Chapter Twenty-Five

*C*hrissie scrutinized the pouty, smudge-eyed young woman looking back at her from the mirror, then at the model pictured in the magazine, then back at her reflection once again. Yes, it was close—surprisingly close. She looked a lot like the woman in the Guess clothing ad. The shiny, dark red lips; the smokey blue eye shadow; the two sharp streaks of blush, one on each cheek—the same look, exactly. And since the woman in the makeup ad was old—at *least* twenty— then that meant *she* must look that age, too.

Once she was satisfied with the glamorous face in the mirror, achieved after a good half hour of painstaking work with makeup brushes and pencils, she turned her attention to her outfit. That, she had copied from another ad, a few pages beyond in the same magazine. Once again, she had to congratulate herself. A straight white miniskirt, a tight black tube top, no bra—she looked at *least* twenty-one, she decided smugly. No question.

That was the easy part. The hard part was going to be getting out of the house looking this way. Fortunately, her mother was out playing tennis with Katy, and her father was off sailing with Wes. The only person she would have to slip past was her nosey baby sister.

Sure enough, once she left the bedroom, she encountered Beth, sitting at the kitchen table, pouring over one of her thick paperback romances. She tried to slink past her without being seen—but no luck. That kid had radar when it came to her big sister's comings and goings.

"Hi, Chrissie!" she said brightly, her entire face lighting up as she looked up from her book. "Whatcha doing?"

"Oh, nothing, Beth."

"Hey, you're all dressed up. Wow, you look really great!"

"Thanks."

"So where are you going?"

"Oh, just out."

"Yeah? Can I come?"

Chrissie grimaced. That was all she needed tonight: her dumb little sister tagging along after her. "No, Beth, you can't come with me."

She would have preferred it if her sister responded by whining, "Why not?" or even demanded that she let her come. Instead, Beth flinched as if she had just been slapped across the face. Even as she forced her mouth into a pathetic smile, the hurt showed clearly in her eyes.

"That's okay, Chrissie," Beth said with unnatural heartiness. "I'm really enjoying this book and, um, I wouldn't mind just staying home tonight and reading." As if to demonstrate how absorbing her book really was, she immediately bent her head down and went back to it, her brow furrowed.

Chrissie was immediately stabbed by a sharp pang of guilt. But she fought against it—just as she always did. She tossed her head, then ran her fingers along her scalp, fluffing out her hair.

"Have fun, Beth!" she called over her shoulder as she sashayed out the door.

By the time she had walked the length of the driveway, out to the road, she had already forgotten about her sister.

She had never hitchhiked before, but she was pretty sure it would be safe. First of all, the people on Shelter Island were respectable enough. Boring, even. None of them would ever do anything bad. Then there was the fact that she wasn't about to make a habit of it. No, this was a one-shot deal, just to get herself over to the Tuck Shop.

Besides, she reminded herself, determined to banish whatever babyish fears were still nagging at her, Heather does it all the time.

There wasn't much traffic tonight. She started walking along the shoulder, wondering if she might be better off just walking the two or three miles to the Tuck Shop. But just as she was becoming resigned to showing up covered in sweat, her eye makeup no doubt totally ruined, she heard a car coming up behind her.

Timidly she turned around and stuck out her thumb. Chrissie wondered if Heather always felt this self-conscious when she hitched. She hoped the car would stop . . . she hoped it wouldn't.

When it veered to the right and slowed down, its front tires crunching loudly over the sand by the side of the road, her chest tightened in a combination of fear, excitement, and ambivalence. It was the same way she had felt as she watched the list of girls who'd made the cheerleading squad being posted, or just before walking onstage the year before, when she'd had that bit part in her high school's production of *Guys and Dolls*.

"Need a ride?" the driver asked cheerfully. He didn't look at all threatening as he leaned out the window and craned his neck forward—to get a better look at her, she ascertained.

The car was strange, one of those fifties' styles with the fins that everybody was always making such a big deal about but which she thought were just plain ugly. As for the driver, he was youngish—although not really young, more like the same age as Katy or Wes. Thirty-five, maybe. But at least he wasn't some old geezer.

At any rate, he looked safe enough.

Chrissie hoisted her pocketbook over her shoulder and climbed into the front seat. As she did, she was aware of how short her skirt really was. Most of her tanned, slender thigh emerged as she slid across the seat trying to be graceful, searching for a place that wasn't so close to the window that she would look as if she were scared or something, but still not close enough to this stranger that he might get the wrong idea.

"Where are you going?" the driver asked, sounding friendly.

Chrissie was a bit embarrassed. After all, the Tuck Shop was a kids' hangout. A teenage place. Why, anybody who knew Shelter Island at all knew that. Yet she couldn't very well lie, especially since there was nothing else nearby that she could claim was her destination.

"The Tuck Shop." She stared out the window, trying to keep her voice casual. "Know where that is?"

"Of course." The man shifted the car into gear and took

off. "Best place on the island to get ice cream. As a matter of fact, I think it's practically the only place."

Chrissie was grateful for his diplomacy. She looked over at the driver and decided that he was okay-looking, for somebody that age. "I hope it's not too far out of your way."

"Not at all. As a matter of fact, it's right on my way. I'm going over to the Inn Between to meet some friends of mine for dinner."

"Sounds like an exciting evening," she observed dryly.

"Oh, sure. Nothing like hanging out with a bunch of old friends." He peered over at her as if he were taking a really thorough assessment of her for the very first time. "Hey, you're all dressed up. Got a date?"

"Sort of."

"Sort of. Does that mean you're meeting one guy in particular, or just that you're hoping to get lucky?"

"Is this really any of your business?" Just because this jerk was giving her a ride didn't entitle him to know her entire life story.

"Just curious, that's all." He sighed, and Chrissie knew there was more to come. "Boy, I remember when I was your age . . . What are you, about fourteen?"

"I'm sixteen!" Chrissie was indignant.

Aw, he's just trying to get to you, that's all, she assured herself.

"Sixteen, huh? Well, anyway, I remember when I was a teenager, I was always in such a hurry to grow up. And now, I wish I'd slowed down a little bit. Enjoyed being what I was, instead of trying so damned hard to be something else."

"Thanks for the free advice."

"You know what they always say," he commented cheerfully. "You get what you pay for. Anyway, I just want to tell you to look after yourself. You've got to take care, you know."

"Look," Chrissie said impatiently, folding her arms across her chest, "can't you just drive without talking so much? God, why is it that just because somebody happens to be older than somebody else, that person thinks he has the right to tell the other person what to do all the time? You sound just like my mother. Or one of my aunts or uncles."

The driver looked over at her one more time. "Hey, wait a minute. What did you say your name was?"

"I didn't say." Chrissie glared at him. "My mother always told me not to give out too much information to strangers."

"Yeah, well, I thought you were just telling me you're not the kind of girl who pays very much attention to what her mother tells her. Your last name Gilbert, by any chance?"

Startled, Chrissie replied, "Well, yeah. How did you know that?"

"Oh, let's just say you and I have a mutual acquaintance."

"Who?"

Randy was smirking as he checked the rearview mirror. "My mother always told me not to give out too much information to strangers."

"Oh, come on. What, are you friends with my father or something? Or Wesley? Hey, wait a minute. I know who you are. You're that guy that Katy's been mooning over all week."

"That's me."

Chrissie rolled her eyes. "Oh, brother. From the way she's been acting, you would've thought she'd snagged herself Robert Redford or something."

Randy pretended to be hurt. "You mean I've been fooling myself all these years, thinking Bob and I could pass for doubles?"

"Look, do me a favor, will you? Don't bother mentioning to Katy or anybody else that I was hitching, okay? Or that I was going out alone?"

"My lips are sealed." Dramatically, Randy locked his mouth with an imaginary key.

"Thanks. Maybe you're not such a bad guy, after all."

"But you have to do me a favor in return."

Chrissie eyed Randy suspiciously. "Yeah? What?"

"Don't do anything stupid, okay?"

"Look, here we are." She was only too happy to change the subject. "Why don't you just drop me alongside the road, okay?"

"Fine with me."

Actually, she had been hoping he'd drive her right up to the front door. There was real status in arriving in a car driven by an older man. The kids who saw her would either assume that he was one of her boyfriends or else someone she'd hitched a ride with. Either way, she'd be a winner.

But she couldn't very well tell him that. Especially after

the lecture he'd given her. All she wanted to do was get away.

"Okay, well, thanks a lot." As she hopped out of the car, she swung her head so that her long straight blond hair all fell over one shoulder. For some reason, it was suddenly very important that this dumb boyfriend of Katy's see how grown up and sexy she really was.

" 'Bye! See you around!" he called, leaning across the seat to give her a wave and a smile. "And don't forget all the terrific free advice I gave you!"

Chrissie just glared at him and strutted away.

It was a Tuesday night, yet the Tuck Shop was crowded, just as she'd expected. After all, even though it wasn't a weekend, there was no place else for the teenaged kids to go.

After debating with herself for a couple of minutes about which would be cooler, heading into the game room with an ice-cream cone or hanging around without one, she ordered a strawberry cone, one scoop. She hated to consume all those calories, but she decided that having a prop might be useful. Besides, a girl who was licking an ice-cream cone could be pretty seductive. She could remember Heather and some of the other girls joking around about that in gym class one day.

Just as she'd expected, things inside the dimly lit game room were hopping. Chrissie staked out a dark corner, in between Pac-Man and the driving video game, casing the joint and licking her ice cream, wondering exactly what it was she was supposed to do with it in order to look sexy. After the initial thrill of being there on her own had worn off—which took about ten seconds—she was disappointed. Upon closer scrutiny, the guys hanging around tonight looked pretty creepy, just a bunch of pimply-faced fourteen-year-olds more interested in scoring Pac-Man points than in picking up girls. A couple of scrawny guys in denim jackets were giving her the eye, trying really hard to be cool, but she made a point of not making eye contact. There were a couple who looked as if they might be possibilities, but they already had girls hanging on their arms.

Besides, the one boy she was really looking for was nowhere in sight.

Chrissie was beginning to wonder why she had even bothered to come when she noticed someone come into the front part of the Tuck Shop, the section where the ice cream was sold.

Her heart began to pound. It was him! He hadn't seen her yet, but she knew that it was no coincidence that he was back here again tonight. Without thinking about what she was doing, Chrissie dumped her strawberry ice-cream cone into a trash can and strutted out of the game room. Her heart felt as if it were going to burst out of her chest. Was it nervousness? Excitement? She didn't know, and she didn't care. She wasn't thinking straight. She was running on automatic.

"How about buying me an ice cream?" she cooed, strolling over to him, cocking her head flirtatiously and looking at him with such arrogance that her question sounded like a dare.

Slowly he removed his sunglasses. But after letting his eyes meet hers for only a moment, he made no effort to hide the fact that he was looking her over. Studying her, evaluating her. She held very still, suddenly very self-conscious as his eyes drank in her silky blond hair, her round breasts beneath the tight flimsy fabric of her tube top, her long tanned legs covered only by the skimpy cotton miniskirt. Yet she felt an unprecedented elation, the kind that comes only from feeling one's own power.

Then the boy turned away and put his sunglasses on again, as if he had seen enough. "Sure," he said casually. "I'll buy you an ice cream. Just tell me exactly what you want."

Chrissie blushed. "Strawberry," she said.

"I would've thought a girl like you preferred cherry," he said offhandedly, glancing over at her with a smirk.

She didn't understand the joke, so she just smiled, hoping he would just assume that she did. The clerk handed him her cone, and he pretended he was about to pass it along to her. But as she reached for it, he suddenly snatched it away.

Grinning and holding it just out of her grasp, he said, "You've got to eat it in my car."

"Okay." After all, she didn't want him to think she was a baby or anything. Besides, wasn't this what she had come here for? She swallowed hard as she took the ice-cream cone from him, his fingers brushing lightly against hers as he relinquished his hold. "Thanks," she mumbled, and she followed him outside into the parking lot.

Chrissie didn't know much about cars, but she knew enough to be impressed by the gleaming red Corvette he led her toward, the same one she'd seen him driving the last time.

"Wow!" she breathed. "Is this yours?"

The boy just grinned. "Hop in. Just be careful you don't get anything sticky."

Without waiting for her, he climbed into the front seat. Chrissie hesitated for a moment, then walked around the front of the car, knowing he was watching her. As she got in, she was aware, once again, of how short her skirt was, of how much leg showed. This time, however, she made sure the skirt hiked up just a little bit further as she wriggled into the car.

"So, you like ice cream, huh?" he said, his mouth pulled back into a leer even as he ate his ice cream in little bites, never taking his eyes off her. His arm was draped across the seat, and he was slouched down as if he couldn't have been more relaxed.

"Yeah, I guess so." Chrissie crossed her legs, then looked away from him, at her ice-cream cone. She stuck out her tongue and licked the strawberry ice cream slowly, starting at the bottom and working her way up. God, it felt wonderful playing this game! And it was turning out that she was good at it, better than she would ever have expected.

"What else do you like?" His voice was languorous, its taunting edge barely perceptible.

"Oh, I don't know. Music, I guess. Going to the beach."

"Yeah? I bet you look great in a bikini. Got a boyfriend?"

She cast him a sidelong glance. "Maybe." She stuck the entire scoop of strawberry ice cream into her mouth, then slowly pulled it out. She swore she could feel the electricity emanating from his body. And the sweet tension that was building up inside of her was nothing short of intoxicating.

"How old are you?"

Chrissie paused, but not for long. "Eighteen," she lied. "I'm starting college in the fall."

"Ah, a college girl, huh? Hey, what's your name, anyway?"

"Chrissie." She immediately regretted saying that. She should have said Chris, or Christine. Chrissie suddenly sounded so babyish. "At least, that's what my friends call me."

"Chrissie. I like that." Apparently he didn't think it sounded babyish at all. "My friends call me Rick."

"How old are you?" It was an awkward question to blurt out, but she was dying to know. It would be important, after all, when she reported this exciting little adventure to Heather, the very first chance she got.

Rick leaned his head back and smiled. "Well . . . a little

bit older than eighteen. Hey, listen, you want to go for a ride?''

"Can't." Like just about everything else she had done and said this evening, Chrissie answered automatically. She needed more time. Aside from wanting to savor her newfound role, she was finding that keeping him waiting was part of the fun. "I have to get back soon."

"Ah. Mom's waiting up for you, huh?"

"No, of course not. It's just that . . . I'm expecting a phone call. From my best friend."

"I see. Well, is this best friend of yours gonna be calling you Friday night, too, or are you free then?"

"No, I'm free."

"Good. I'll meet you here about, oh, I don't know, say nine-thirty. We can go for a drive or something. How's that sound?"

She cocked her head to one side. "Oh, I don't know. I guess it sounds . . . like a possibility."

She could feel her adrenaline pumping. This was too good to be true! It was all happening just the way she'd imagined it would. She couldn't wait to tell Heather.

"Sounds like a possibility, huh? Well, then, I guess maybe I'll be seeing you Friday."

Chrissie looked over at him and smiled seductively.

"Sure," she drawled. "See you Friday—maybe. Unless something better comes along."

As she climbed slowly out of the car, she could feel his eyes on her. She headed back into the Tuck Shop, her head held high, her hips swinging from side to side, taking care not to look back.

Chapter Twenty-Six

*F*ive Gilbert women lingered at the breakfast table on Wednesday morning, long after all the others had taken off, anxious to get the new day underway. Yet as they sat inside the kitchen, nursing their coffee and finishing off the rest of the English muffins, they remained silent, each one absorbed in her own thoughts.

Julie, slowly sipping her second cup of coffee without even tasting it, was thinking about Brad—and, despite the guilt nagging away at her, about Paul. She and her husband had argued again the night before, her simmering anger over Barbara's report of his boorish behavior causing her to let what started out as a simple disagreement over what kind of present to give Pat and Ben for their anniversary escalate into a full-fledged fight.

The bad blood between them prompted her to begin daydreaming about Paul. She found herself regretting her decision to steer clear of him for the rest of her stay on the island. Indeed, she could hardly stop obsessing about what he must be thinking, worrying about how he must feel about her now.

Katy, too, was feeling confused as she poured herself a third cup of coffee from the white Corning thermos housing the third fresh potful of the day. She knew all that coffee could well prove to be more than she could handle, that there was a good chance that it would make her crazed for the rest of the morning. But she didn't really care. She needed all the help she could get, even in the way of artificial stimulants that would hopefully help her think a little bit more clearly.

After all, as if the sudden and unexpected appearance of one Randall Palmer in her life weren't enough to throw her into an emotional turmoil, she still hadn't made up her mind about Leslie's offer. She had never seriously considered Ben's invitation to his children, his plea for a new B.G.A. president from inside the family. But Leslie's offer—that was something else altogether. She savored each mouthful of her coffee with great deliberation, hoping that the infusion of caffeine would help her straighten some things out in her own mind.

Lynn was picking mindlessly at the crumbs of yesterday's leftover cinnamon-pecan rolls, a treat that even she had to admit was becoming a bit tired. As she did, she ruminated about her husband. Michael seemed to be growing more and more distant, even though this vacation was supposed to bring them closer, give them time together as a couple, without all the distractions of the kids and the house and his job.

She was supposed to be having fun, here on this idyllic resort island. Instead, she was beginning to count the days until she could return to her normal life, where at least she was on her own familiar ground. Her feelings of loneliness and isolation were escalating, and she was wondering just how much longer she could stand it.

Chrissie, meanwhile, was thinking about Rick. Sure, she was excited about her date with him, now only two days away. But at a moment like this, when she was deep in thought and able to let down her defenses, even those she generally kept up for her own benefit, she was able to admit that she was just a little bit scared. And it was already too late to change her mind. After all, she had told Heather all about him . . . and her plan. There was no turning back now, a realization whose finality was bound to have some impact, even on someone as determined as she was.

Beth, on the other hand, was seething with anger, thinking about her sister's telephone call to Heather the night before, the one she had eavesdropped on. She had gotten quite an earful as she lurked in the hallway, right outside the bedroom, overhearing Chrissie telling that stupid girlfriend of hers all about this "really neat guy" she had "picked up" at the Tuck Shop.

Why, what about Danny Burtis? It wasn't bad enough that

he, for some incomprehensible reason, seemed to prefer obnoxious Chrissie to Beth. But now she was two-timing him, the witch, sneaking around behind his back with some other guy. Beth didn't know whether to feel bad that poor Danny's feelings were bound to get hurt, or glad that once and for all he would see what a creep she really was. If that happened, he might start to appreciate Beth a little bit more. . . .

So the silence surrounding the little cluster of coffee drinkers was hardly a contented one, no matter how it may have appeared to an outside observer. Instead it was one that was fraught with guilt, ambivalence, anger, and self-doubt.

It was Chrissie who finally broke it. She let out a loud sigh that, without her realizing it, spoke for all of them.

"Well, I might as well put on my bathing suit and head over to the beach," she said lazily. "There are only a few good tanning days left."

"Sounds like fun," Julie observed, without very much enthusiasm.

Katy grimaced. "Somehow, the idea of spending the entire morning doing absolutely nothing but drying out one's skin and cultivating a faceful of premature wrinkles sounds like plain *boring*, if you ask me."

To Beth, however, it sounded like an excellent idea. "Can I come, Chrissie? Please?"

"No, you can't come."

As if the mere suggestion of having her baby sister accompany her on the day's outing agitated her no end, Chrissie picked up her blue Sportsac pocketbook, lying nearby on the counter, and began scrounging around inside it. "Where'd I put that stupid hairbrush?" she mumbled, irritated.

"Please, Chrissie. Don't brush your hair at the table. It's rude." Her mother's reprimand was only halfhearted, as if she'd already given this same warning too many times in her life.

"There are about twenty-six thousand hairbrushes in the bathroom upstairs, on the top shelf of the closet," Katy informed her niece. "If you can bring yourself to walk up an entire flight of stairs, that is."

"Oh, yuck. I don't want to use a brush that somebody *else* used." More determined than ever, she continued her search, pulling out a wallet, a change purse, two lipsticks, some photographs, a half-eaten pack of sugarless breath mints—but no hairbrush.

"Chrissie, you really should clean that thing out one of these days," her mother commented, casting a disapproving glance at the wad of tissues streaked with black her daughter had just pulled out of the shoulder bag, presumably the victim of either a wayward ballpoint pen or mascara that had exploded.

"I *will*," she whined. "I just haven't had a chance yet. . . . Oh, rats. I know it's here somewhere!" In a last ditch effort, Chrissie held the large blue purse over the table, turned it upside down, and dumped out the remainder of its contents.

Sure enough; there was the hairbrush. There were a few other items of interest inside, as well.

"My earrings!" Katy shrieked. Her first reaction was to be overjoyed over finding them again. Eagerly she grabbed the gold hoops from among the clutter in the middle of the table.

"My watch!" Julie was more reserved. She simply stared in amazement at the little cache of jewelry that had just come tumbling out of Chrissie's pocketbook. "And if I'm not mistaken, that's Barbara's engagement ring."

"And those are definitely my earrings." Lynn's mouth was set into a tight frown that made it clear just how furious she was.

Chrissie was aghast. "What's that stuff doing in *my* pocketbook?"

"That's a very good question, young lady," her mother replied. "And I'm waiting for the answer. I think we all are."

"How should *I* know? Hey, wait a minute. You don't think *I* hid them in there, do you? You don't think I'm the one who took them?"

"They are in your purse," Julie pointed out dryly. "Don't you find that a little bit odd?"

Chrissie turned on her with fire in her eyes. "Julie! What are you saying? You, of all people, are accusing me of having stolen this stuff?"

Julie just lowered her eyes.

By now the sixteen-year-old was close to tears. "Do you really think I'm a thief? I didn't take these! Honest! I didn't!"

"Chrissie," said her mother, "I think you and I will have to sit down with your father and have a little talk as soon as he gets back."

"But I didn't *take* them! I *didn't*!" Chrissie shrieked, jumping out of her chair. "Do you really think I'd be dumb enough to dump all this stuff out on the table if I had stolen that jewelry and hidden it in my purse?''

"Now that you've been caught," Lynn countered, "you could at least be honest about it.''

"Mom, you're always accusing me of everything! Everybody in this family *hates* me! You're all against me!'' Breaking into uncontrollable sobs, she dashed out of the room, leaving the incriminating evidence smack in the middle of the kitchen table, along with her purse and all her other possessions.

Julie, Lynn, and Katy just exchanged silent glances. Beth, whose presence everyone seemed to have forgotten about, shrank down into her chair, her eyes wide as she observed the scene around her without comment.

It was almost a relief when someone else came parading into the kitchen.

"Oh, good. It looks as if I'm not too late for a second cup of coffee." Barbara stopped in her tracks as it suddenly became apparent to her that she had walked in on some dramatic moment. "Goodness, is something wrong? What's going on?''

As she glanced at the mound of clutter in the middle of the table, trying to figure out just what was going on, Lynn spoke up.

"Well, I guess you could say it's good news, in a way," she said in a thin voice. "Barbara, your engagement ring's been found.''

Chapter Twenty-Seven

That evening, the mood around the Gilberts' beach house remained tense. Chrissie stayed out of sight, for the most part, sulking upstairs in her bedroom. Whenever anyone did cross her path, she was barely able to say a civil word. Lynn, meanwhile, maintained an icy silence, her lips drawn together in a tight frown, her eyes clouded with anger and confusion.

As for the others, they made a point of avoiding the principals. The cheerful tone of voice they spoke in whenever they did meet up with Chrissie or Lynn or Michael was almost theatrical.

Despite the bad feelings hovering in the air, however, the fact remained that it was Ben and Pat's forty-second wedding anniversary. It was the night of the celebratory dinner that Julie and Katy and the others had been planning for days. And so they all made a tacit agreement to adopt a lighthearted mood. Even if it wasn't one hundred percent sincere, at least it was enough to get them all through the evening.

Pretending that nothing was out of the ordinary was made easier by the arrival of gifts every few hours throughout the day. The first one came right before lunch. A stunning bouquet of long-stemmed red roses was delivered by a van printed on the side with SHELTER ISLAND FLORIST. The card, predictably, was signed, "To my wife Pat, with forty-two years of love, Ben."

An hour and a half later, a gum-chewing delivery boy

handed over a dozen helium-filled balloons, a colorful collage of pastel blues, greens, pinks, and yellows. The card accompanying this "bouquet" was signed, "To Grandma and Grandpa, Happy Anniversary! Love, Chrissie."

Then, in the middle of the afternoon, UPS arrived with a huge package. Everyone gathered around it with shining eyes. They were like children on Christmas morning, confronting one of Santa's most dramatic surprises.

"What on earth is *this*?" Pat was so delighted that it scarcely mattered what was inside.

"I don't know, but it's so big that we might have to add on an extra room just to accommodate it," Ben chortled.

"Open it." Michael's pride over the reaction this gift had already elicited made it clear that it was from him and Lynn.

"Why don't you help them?" Lynn suggested. "Here, I'll get some scissors."

"Get a knife, too," Michael called after her. "A sharp one."

After a laborious unwrapping process that contributed even further to the growing anticipation, Michael and Wes dragged out from an impressive mound of cardboard, molded Styrofoam pieces, and balled-up wads of newspaper two oak Adirondack chairs. With their simple design, the natural wood finish, and the obvious skill and care with which they had been constructed, they would be the perfect addition to the second-floor deck.

"Oh, Michael. They're beautiful!" Pat cried, throwing her arms around her son's neck. "Thank you so much. Ben and I will enjoy these for years."

"Get a lot of use out of 'em, too. I plan to do a lot of sitting from here on in. And what better place than up on the deck, where I can look out and see the most beautiful view in the world!" Ben winked at his oldest son as he lowered himself into one of the chairs, then eased back. A look of contentment lit up his face.

As evening approached, however, preparations for the special dinner became the focus of activity. Julie arranged the roses in a glass vase and placed them on the buffet at one end of the dining room, where everyone could enjoy their fragrance as well as their beauty. Even Chrissie came out of hiding long enough to tie a balloon to the back of each chair. Meanwhile, Katy and Wes labored in the kitchen while Lynn set the table, taking to new heights of creativity what was normally a mundane task.

"There. Now if *that* doesn't look like the cover of *Better Homes and Gardens*, I don't know what does."

Feeling a surge of satisfaction, Lynn stepped back to survey her handiwork. On the table was laid a freshly pressed white linen tablecloth, a wedding present to the newlyweds more than four decades earlier, hand-embroidered by Pat's grandmother. Lynn had used her in-laws' "good" china, gold-rimmed Lenox decorated with dainty pink flowers. The cloth napkins were pale pink linen, the silverware freshly polished.

In the middle of the table was a graceful crystal bud vase, in which she had placed one single perfect rose from the bouquet Ben had given Pat. Surrounding the vase were four pink candles, one to symbolize each of Pat and Ben's children, towering above elegant silver candlestick holders.

"It looks lovely, Lynn." As Julie came out of the kitchen and saw how nice the table looked, she placed an appreciative hand on her sister-in-law's shoulder. "You certainly have a way with decorating."

"Why, thank you, Julie! Gee, maybe my art background hasn't gone entirely to waste, after all."

Katy came bustling out of the kitchen then, wiping her hands on the apron she'd thrown over her jeans. Her eyes were aglow with the excitement of doing one of the things she enjoyed most: orchestrating a gourmet meal.

While she was only one of the chefs, officially in charge of salad and dessert, her two specialties, she couldn't help being involved in a much more personal way than any of the other contributors to tonight's feast: Julie with her grilled chicken in mustard sauce; Wes with his vegetable mélange sprinkled with cheese and seasoned with fresh spices; Lynn with her herbed batter bread; Michael with his deliberate selection of wine.

To her, this was more than a chance to sit down to a leisurely meal, even more than a celebration: it was a work of art, an end in itself. Even more than that, it was her chance to shine, to show off to her family, to present for their approval one of her most glorious creations—the ultimate cheesecake.

"Lookin' good, Lynn," Katy commented with an approving nod. "I only hope the food tastes half as wonderful as the table looks. Oh, that reminds me." She snapped her fingers.

"I'd better take my cheesecake out of the fridge. Give it a chance to warm to room temperature."

As she scurried back into the kitchen, she was already looking forward to the last course of tonight's dinner, the moment that her cheesecake would be brought out in all its glory, the crowning touch that was bound to elict oohs and aahs all around.

Indeed, Lynn's table and the impressive menu, not to mention the importance of the occasion, succeeded in setting a festive tone right from the start. Even Chrissie was in a good mood, cheered by the promise of a special meal, as well as the glass of wine that Ben declared would undoubtedly be most acceptable for both his granddaughters on a noteworthy evening like this one.

"My goodness! Everything looks so beautiful!" Pat exclaimed as she took the chair down at one end of the table, assisted by Wes.

"It certainly does," agreed Ben, sitting down at the other end. "And the best part is that our children did it all for us."

"Before we get started, I propose a toast." Michael stood up and held his wineglass in the air. "To Ben and Pat, the best parents in the world."

"The best grandparents, too, don't forget," Beth piped up.

Wes chuckled. "Hear! Hear! To Ben and Pat. Wishing you many more years of happiness together. Happy anniversary!"

"Happy anniversary!" the others chorused, raising their glasses and drinking a toast.

"Thank you, thank you. Now, do I have to make a speech?" joked Ben. "Or is it okay if we dig in to some of this good-looking food?"

"Oh, by all means, let's dig in," insisted Julie.

"Katy, your salade niçoise looks fantastic," commented Barbara. "Wes, do you want to start?"

They were quick to discover that the spectacular appearance of the food was only secondary to its taste. All the dishes had been prepared with such care and such love they were truly delicious. Indeed, the principal topic of conversation was the fine taste of each dish, with its creator modestly pointing out some barely perceptible fault—a bit too much pepper in the mustard sauce, eggplant cubes that were a trifle undercooked—then finally admitting that it was, after all, fairly close to perfection.

"Hey, how about opening the rest of your presents?" Wes

suggested when the last of his vegetable mélange had been scooped up out of the casserole dish and Lynn's herbed batter bread was nothing more than some crumbs strewn across a breadboard.

"Good idea. I'll get them." Lynn disappeared into the living room, reappearing a few seconds later with a small stack of prettily wrapped packages.

"My, this is just like Christmas! Now, which one should I open first?" Pat began opening the gifts, stretching out the process to an almost excruciating degree, slowly smoothing out each ribbon, pulling off each piece of Scotch tape, folding each piece of wrapping paper.

Julie and Brad's gift was a Steuben glass paperweight shaped like a small round bird. Pat immediately pronounced it the sweetest thing she had ever seen in her life. Wes and Barbara gave them a silver sugar and creamer set. As for Katy, her find from her day of browsing in the shops of East Hampton with Randy was pink ceramic salt-and-pepper shakers in the shape of flamingos.

"For the kitchen," Pat declared with a weak smile, setting them side.

The final gift, from Beth, was a blown-up photograph of herself, her seventh-grade school picture. It was displayed in a wooden frame she had painted herself and decorated with shells.

"My, my. So many lovely things! Thank you all so much," Pat said. "I can tell that you put a lot of thought into picking out each present."

"Yes, thank you," said Ben. "It means a lot to us that you all went to so much trouble to make this day special."

"Now," said Lynn, standing up, "who's ready for dessert?"

It was the moment Katy had been waiting for. She was actually nervous as she watched Julie and Wes take away the dinner plates and serving dishes, then bring out the dessert plates, the cups and saucers, and the coffeepot. She was about to stand up, to go into the kitchen to get her masterpiece, when she suddenly noticed Pat standing in the doorway—carrying a cheesecake of her own.

"Here we go. I know this isn't on the menu, but I just couldn't resist picking up this cheesecake for dessert."

Immediately Wes, Lynn, and Julie looked over at Katy.

All the color was drained from her face. "Mother, what are

you doing? You know full well I spent all day yesterday making a cheesecake for tonight's dessert.''

"Well, yes, I know. But I wanted to do *something* to help out. You all went to so much trouble—shopping and preparing the food and setting the table—well, it seemed like the least I could do.''

"Mom, I was supposed to be in charge of dessert.'' Katy's eyes flashed, giving away her growing anger.

"Well, dear, I suppose we'll just have to wrap yours up and eat it another time. Now, who wants the first piece?'' She had moved aside some dishes and placed the bakery-made cheesecake in the middle of the table. Already she was busy slicing it. "Ben, how about if I give you this one? It's much too big for me.''

"I can't believe you did this! Mother, what could you possibly have been thinking?''

Pat finally looked over at her daughter. "Katy, you're behaving like a baby. Now pass this piece over to your father.''

"Or I have a better idea. How about if I just leave the table? That way, you can enjoy your anniversary with the people you care about, the people you love, without the rest of us getting in the way!''

Pat placed the knife down on the table. Her body was rigid, her expression hard. "I don't understand you, Katherine. I never have. Ever since you were a child, you were always different. You were never like . . .''

"Go ahead. Say it.'' Katy's eyes narrowed. "Say that I was never like Julie. Say it!''

"Well, you weren't. And I don't know why you can't be more like her now.''

"Oh, I see. Still the Golden Girl. She's done all the right things, hasn't she? She's got the husband, the baby, the career. . . . Everything you ever wanted for your daughters, right?''

Pat bit her lip. "All I ever wanted for any of my children was for them to be happy.''

"Then why won't you let me be happy?'' Katy screamed. "Why won't you let me just be myself?''

Suddenly all the tears she had been struggling so hard to hold back came flowing out uncontrollably.

"You're my *mother*, for God's sake! You're supposed to love me the way I am!''

"Oh, Katy, you're being ridiculous. I do love you! Of course, I love you!" By this point, Pat, too, was on the verge of tears. And being so close to losing control was making her even more frustrated.

"Oh, really?" Katy spat out the words. "Then why is it I haven't felt it? Not once, in my entire life!"

She stood up and stormed out of the dining room. Her footsteps were fast and heavy as she ran up the stairs. The others sat in silence, not uttering a sound, not even moving. Pat's cheesecake sat in the middle of the table, its very presence seeming to taunt them.

Finally, Michael cleared his throat. "Gee, I'm so stuffed, I don't think I could eat another thing."

"You know, me, either," Wes agreed. "I think I'll just call it a day. Maybe I'll have something later."

Slowly they began to get up from the table, some of them retreating to other rooms of the house, some clearing the table, all of them careful not to meet each others' eyes. And then, little by little, they began talking, making conversation in hushed voices, talking about the tasks of cleaning up as if it were a much more interesting topic than it really was.

Pat stayed at the table for a very long time, even after all the others had left, her eyes fixed on some unknown point on the table. And then, all of a sudden, she stood up. Carefully she picked up the cheesecake, grasping the plate firmly in both hands.

"I'd better put this back in the refrigerator," she said softly, to no one in particular. "If it's out too long, it's apt to spoil."

Before heading into the kitchen, however, she took a moment to lean over the table. Her head held high, she blew out each of the four candles, one by one. She was glad that, as she lifted the cake up slowly from the table, there was no one around to see how her hands were trembling.

Chapter Twenty-Eight

"*Well, I guess* there's one thing you can always count on," said Brad with a wry smile. "There's certainly never a dull moment around the Gilbert house." He kicked off his shoes, stretched across the bed, and downed the last of the Scotch he had poured himself before coming upstairs.

It was still early evening, much too soon to be winding down for the night. But as soon as the catastrophic dinner party had abruptly disbanded, leaving a fog of bad feeling hovering in the house like a storm cloud, he and Julie had retreated upstairs to their bedroom. It seemed like a good idea to lie low for a little while, until things had had a chance to settle down. Fortunately, Josh had been unusually cooperative for a change, actually demanding to be put to bed with a bottle of water and his favorite teddy bear right after dinner.

Julie looked up from the magazine she had been leafing through listlessly and sighed. "It's been kind of a tough week and a half, with all of us packed together under one roof. I suppose that sooner or later, things were bound to erupt."

"Hmph! You make it all sound so innocent."

"I'm afraid I don't know what you mean."

"What I mean is," Brad explained, the tiniest hint of a sneer on his face, "this whole damn thing was Katy's fault."

"It's not just Katy—"

"Come on. That sister of yours has been a troublemaker ever since Day One."

"I don't think that's fair, Brad. She was just upset, that's all. There's always been a lot of tension between her and Mom."

Brad laughed coldly. "I should have known that whatever I said, you'd find a way to disagree with me. Look, you know damn well she was just being her usual obnoxious self."

"Wait a minute. You're not—"

"I really don't see what she got in such a huff about," Brad went on. "Making such a big scene, ruining the evening for everybody . . . That fat little bitch just doesn't know what the hell she wants."

Julie was shocked. "Brad, that's a terrible thing to say! And who are you to go around calling Katy such awful names?"

"Aw, you just can't see her for what she is because she's your sister. But the truth is, she's a spoiled little brat."

A strange look came into his eyes. "Yeah, I can remember the very first time I ever met her, back when you and I had just gotten engaged. You invited us both to dinner, at your apartment. Then, at one point, you left us alone for a few minutes." He shook his head slowly, and a strange smile played at his lips. "Hell, I was just trying to be friendly. Trying to get to know my future sister-in-law a little bit better. But then she went ahead and misinterpreted the whole thing, making a big deal out of nothing."

Julie could feel the color draining from her cheeks. "What happened that night, Brad?"

"Oh, nothing. Really, it was absolutely nothing." Suddenly a look of fear crossed his face. "Why? What did she tell you about that night? What did that little liar say?"

The room seemed to be spinning around as Julie grasped the back of the chair, struggling to maintain her balance. It was growing all too clear. First Barbara's warning, the accusation about Brad making passes at her. Now, this, with Brad saying a little bit too much—about her own sister, no less! Or was it simply the Scotch talking? . . .

But all that was just the beginning. However forgiving Julie might have been about her husband's inappropriate behavior toward other women, whatever possible excuses or explanations could be found, the fact remained that Brad simply was not much of a husband to Julie. Or much of a father to Josh, either. His family was one of his lowest priorities in terms of how he spent his time. And whenever he did deign to be with them, whenever circumstances forced him to be an active part of the threesome, he was angry.

It's not that he's tired from working so hard, Julie admitted to herself, biting her lip to keep the stinging tears from rolling down her cheeks. It's not that he's tense from his high-pressured career. The truth is, he doesn't want to be with us at all. He resents us.

She understood it all so clearly now! Brad was the kind of man who had always gotten through his life, sailed through it with impressive success, by keeping himself apart from his emotions. That was how he remained so cool while making those multimillion-dollar deals, deals that would have caused anyone else almost intolerable anxiety. He was used to cutting himself off. And when he was with his family, the only situation in his life in which people demanded that he refrain from separating himself, the only one in which *love* was demanded of him rather than cleverness or coldness or nerves of steel, he balked. It was not how he was used to playing the game.

And Julie saw, for the very first time, that his reaction to being told that he couldn't play by his own rules was that he wasn't going to play at all.

"Well, whatever Katy told you about that night," Brad was saying as he downed the last of his drink, "I'm sure she blew it all out of proportion. Made a mountain out of a molehill, the way she usually does."

"Katy didn't have to tell me a thing about that night," Julie said, her voice so controlled she almost sounded calm. "You've told me enough yourself."

With that, she turned around and started for the door.

"Hey! Where do you think you're going?" Brad grabbed her by the wrist, just a little bit too roughly.

Julie's eyes flashed with anger. "Brad, let go of me."

"I said, where are you going?" Instead of loosening his grip, he held her even more tightly.

"Brad, stop it! You've had too much to drink! You're hurting me!"

Suddenly remorseful, he let go of her. He stepped away as if he had only then realized how powerful his anger was, how dangerous he could be. "I'm sorry. I—I don't know what happened to me. I just thought . . . You started walking out . . . Please, come back and sit down, Julie.''

"I'm going out." When she saw how her words affected him, almost as if she had slapped his face, she softened her voice. "I want to take a walk, that's all. Maybe go for a drive. I need some air.''

"But it's almost dark.''

Julie actually felt sorry for him. He looked so pathetic standing there, pleading with her. The ferocious lion was gone; left in its place was a creature who was meek and penitent, one she found almost pathetic.

"Let me go, Brad,'' she said gently. Then, she added, "I won't be gone long. I promise.''

But as she took off in the car, careening down a dark empty road at an uncharacteristically reckless speed, she felt as if she never wanted to go back. It was as if she had seen her husband for what he was for the very first time, and what she had seen was so sad that it made her feel physically weak. And it wasn't the drinking, it wasn't the womanizing, it wasn't even the cruelty with which he sometimes treated her. No, it was realizing that beneath the brash exterior, the suave partygoer, the competent businessman with admirable sang-froid, there was nothing but an empty shell, a sad little boy who had never learned how to love.

She never actually made a decision about where she was going. Even so, she was not at all surprised to find herself driving down West Neck Road, toward Paul Dereksen's house, slowing down the car as if she'd suddenly realized that it was no longer necessary to act as if she were running away.

When Paul opened the front door, his face registered puzzlement at first, then delight.

"Julie! What a nice surprise! Come on in.''

"I hope I'm not disturbing you.''

"Not at all. I was just sitting here with a can of beer and a frozen dinner, trying to decide whether to go out back and do some work on the Riesers' bookshelves or call it a day and turn on the tube.''

It wasn't until she had come inside that he saw the stricken look on her face.

"Julie, what's wrong?''

She forced a wan smile. "I didn't know it was so obvious. I guess maybe I am a little bit upset.''

"Want to tell me about it?" Already he had led her over to the couch, sat her down, and settled in next to her.

"How about getting me one of those first?" With a nod of her head, she gestured toward the can of beer on the table.

"Uh-oh," Paul joked, retreating into the kitchen and returning a few seconds later with another can of beer and a glass. "Must be something pretty heavy going down." Underneath his teasing tone, however, was real concern.

Tiredly, Julie ran her hand through her hair. She took the beer, ignored the glass, and gulped down four big swallows.

"Feel better?"

She shook her head. "I wish it were that simple. No, I'm afraid that even getting dead drunk isn't going to help."

"It's not Josh, is it?"

"No. It's Brad. My husband—remember him?"

Paul frowned, but said nothing.

"You may recall that the last time you asked me about him, I insisted that things between Mr. and Mrs. Bradford Kane were fine. Well, I lied. The truth is, our marriage stinks."

"Hey, listen, if you two just had a fight . . ."

"I really wish it were nothing more than some silly argument about, oh, I don't know, what color the new drapes should be. But it goes a lot deeper than that." She looked over at Paul and blinked. "It's not working, Paul. I don't think Brad and I are going to make it."

Paul opened his mouth as if to protest, then closed it again, shaking his head sadly. "I remember that feeling. From when Sally and I broke up. It's like a black cloud, a fog or something, that comes over you all of a sudden. Hits you in the stomach."

Then, as if suddenly remembering that his role was to be supportive, he said, "What about marriage counseling? You've got to at least try to work things out between you."

"Brad would never agree to go. I'm sure of that. And as for me, well, I'm not so sure I'd even want to hold this marriage together. Not now, when I'm finally beginning to see the kind of man my husband really is."

Paul stood up and began pacing around the room, his hands jammed into his pants pockets. "Julie, I'm beginning to get a really bad feeling."

She looked up, startled. "What are you talking about?"

"I don't know. I can't help feeling that you and me seeing each other again has something to do with all this."

Julie could feel her face reddening. "I can assure you, Paul, that what's going on between Brad and me has absolutely nothing to do with you, or anybody else, for that matter."

"How can you be so sure? Isn't it possible that you're romanticizing things just a little bit?" He rushed over to her side. "Look, I've been feeling that way, too. Just seeing you again . . . it's filling me with regrets, and fantasies about what could have been."

"You mean, what *should* have been." Julie's tone was bitter. And then, all of a sudden, her anger exploded.

"Damn you, Paul Dereksen!" she shrieked, standing up and hurling her half-empty beer can across the room. "Damn you for screwing up my life!"

"Me? Ruin your life? You, with the career as a big television personality and the fancy New York apartment and the kid who looks like something out of a Walt Disney movie? You've got to be joking! What's that expression, 'Charmed lives'? If anyone ever had a charmed life, it's you."

"But I *loved* you!" she sobbed. "My God, Paul. Do you have any idea what you did to me, back then? Do you have any idea how much you *hurt* me? I loved you, and I expected to spend the rest of my life with you. And then, all of a sudden, I heard about you and Sally. . . ."

Her anger dissipated into choking, and she couldn't go on. Nor did she need to. Paul knew exactly what she was saying, what she was feeling, and from the look in his hazel eyes she knew instantly that he felt the same way, too. He bounded across the room and took her in his arms with a sureness that showed how certain he was she wanted him to.

"It wasn't fair, Julie. I know that. I hated what happened. Hell, I hated myself, too, for the longest time. I tried to go through the motions with Sally, to make the marriage work. And I don't know what was worse, pretending it could work or knowing all along that I was just fooling myself."

"It's not too late for us, Paul." Julie's voice was hoarse, her words barely audible. But Paul knew exactly what she had said, and what her words meant.

With great tenderness he cradled her face in his hands. Then he leaned forward and kissed her, gently, at first, almost as if he were teasing her, then with more and more ardor, holding her closer against him. Julie was breathless, finally able to satisfy the longing she felt, the desire that had been tormenting her ever since she had first learned that Paul was on the island.

"I want to stay with you tonight," she murmured.

She could feel him stiffen. He pulled away—not only with his body, but with his emotions, as well.

"No, Julie. It's not a good idea."

"Why? Because of that other woman? Because of Susan?"

She expected him to deny it, to insist that this other woman had nothing to do with his decision. So his words hit her like a blow when he said, "It's partly because of Susan. But even more than that, it's because I know it's not really what you want."

"Oh, really? And who are you to know so much about what I want?"

"Julie, I know you're hurt right now. And believe me, I know how hard it is to go through what you're going through. I've been there, remember? But spending the night with me, or anybody else, is not the answer. Look, I know what I'm talking about."

Suddenly Julie burst into tears, ashamed at how needy she was feeling, humiliated over letting Paul see her like this. "All I wanted was for somebody to hold me all night. To make me feel like I matter!"

"Julie, you matter. You matter so much, to so many people." He put his arms around her once again, this time motivated by the desire to comfort her. "There's Josh, and your parents, and your sister and brothers. . . ."

"I know it's ridiculous," she sobbed. "But I feel like such a failure! I can't even make my own husband love me."

"I'm sure he loves you, Julie, as much as he's able to love anybody. And I still believe that you two might be able to work things out. Hell, I believe that Julie Gilbert is capable of doing anything she sets her mind to. At least, the Julie Gilbert I used to know."

"And what about us, Paul? Or is there no *us* anymore?" Her question came out in a whisper.

"It's been such a long time. Too long a time. Too much has happened, to both of us. We've got to stop living in the past. Sure, when I first saw you, I began to wonder if we could, you know, pick up the pieces, right from where we left off. But it's too late for us, Julie. It simply can't be. And do you know what? I think that's really for the best."

Julie looked up at him through wet eyes. "Do you really believe that, Paul?"

"Yes, Julie, I do. We've got to move on. Cherish what happened in the past, learn to live with the regrets, and just go on from there."

Julie averted her eyes. "I've been feeling as if I'm still in love with you, Paul."

"Maybe what you're in love with—maybe what we've both been in love with, for all these years—is really the fantasy of what we could have become together. And of the way our lives could have turned out, if only we'd done things a little bit differently."

Julie laughed. "You sound so wise. As if you've got the whole thing worked out."

"Do I? I guess I must be getting pretty good at faking it, then. The result of years and years of practice."

The mood was broken then, and Julie suddenly felt silly clinging to Paul, sobbing into his shoulder. She stood up straight and took a deep breath.

"Well. It's getting late. Maybe I should be getting home." She glanced around the room and caught sight of her smashed beer can, out of which had spilled a tiny pool of foamy yellow liquid. "Gee, too bad about that beer. I could've used the rest of it, right about now."

"I've got more in the refrigerator."

"Thanks, but that's okay. I really do want to get home. I've got some pretty important things to do there."

She picked up her purse and started toward the door. But before she left, she turned back.

"I'm not sure if I owe you an apology or my thanks."

Paul shrugged. With a lopsided grin, he said, "Who knows? Maybe both, maybe neither. But I think you and I know each other well enough to be able to dispense with such formalities."

"Does that mean we're still friends?"

"I sure hope so."

"Good. You know, I'd like to meet Susan, one of these days."

"Uh-oh. I hope you're not going to tell her about all the stupid things I did when I was a teenager."

Julie smiled and shook her head. "No. As a matter of fact, what I want to tell her is what a lucky woman she is."

As she drove home, back to her parents' beach house, Julie felt a calmness, and a sense of certainty that she couldn't remember having experienced in ages. Her mind was so clear. It was as if she had just been awakened from a long sleep, feeling relaxed and well rested and prepared to go on. As if to acknowledge her new clarity of purpose, a new moon was smiling down at her from the dark cloudless sky of late summer. There was a crispness in the night air that just barely hinted at the change of weather to come, a reminder that summer would soon be leaving and a fresher, more lively season would take its place.

She rolled down the car window, suddenly anxious to breathe in the invigorating air. She inhaled deeply, appreciating the sensation of letting something fresh, something new, become a part of her.

At last, she had made her decision.

Chapter Twenty-Nine

"*Come on,* Joshie. Let's play ball." Beth's tone was sweet and gentle as she knelt down beside the little boy. "Get the bat—that yellow one over there. And where's the ball? Oh, here's one of those Nerf balls. We'll use that."

Dutifully the two-year-old retrieved the plastic bat that was lying on the lawn, then scampered over to get the ball. But when his Aunt Beth tried to pry the spongy red ball out of his determined little fingers, he resisted.

"*My* ball!"

"Yes, I know it's your ball, Josh. But let me have it, and I'll throw it to you. . . . Here, you can hit it with your bat. Now go stand over there."

"*My* ball!" He was pouting now, clutching the ball even more tightly in his pudgy little fist.

"Let *go,* Josh! Come on! I'm trying to play baseball with you!"

"Mine! Mine! *My* ball!"

"Josh, you have to learn how to play nicely," Beth told him firmly. "Otherwise, nobody will want to play with you, ever. Don't you want to grow up and have lots of friends? You want everybody to like you, don't you? You don't want to end up spending all your time reading because nobody wants to play with you. . . ."

"Josh giving you a hard time, Beth?" Katy stepped off the porch, where she'd been standing all along, observing the telling interaction that had just gone on between Beth and her baby cousin. She tried to sound jovial, having no intention of letting her niece know how what she had just overheard had torn at her heartstrings.

"Where's Julie, anyway?" Katy went on. "Doesn't she ever take care of her own kid?"

"Oh, but I *like* playing with Josh!" Beth insisted.

"So do I. But that's not the point. This is supposed to be your vacation, remember? You're supposed to be having fun, not being Julie's au pair."

Beth looked at her and blinked. "There's nothing else to do, anyway."

"Nothing else to—girl, you happen to be on a luxurious resort island that most people would kill to visit. Well, maybe not *kill*, exactly, but— Listen, I have an idea. How about if you and I spend the whole day together, doing anything you want?" While for the most part Katy's intentions were altruistic, she did have a few ulterior motives. The tension in the house was unbearably thick—particularly between her and her mother—and she needed a distraction, especially one that would get her out of the house.

"What do you mean, 'anything I want'?"

"I don't know. You tell me. We can go to the beach, or take the ferry over to Greenport, or take the other ferry to Sag Harbor. . . . Just name it."

"And you'll come with me?" Beth still hadn't managed to digest fully the munificent offer that was being made to her by her aunt.

"Not only that. I'll pay for everything, drive you anywhere you want to go. Elizabeth Gilbert, this is your special day!"

"Okay!" Beth jumped up, looking so happy that Katy kicked herself for not having made a point of spending lots of time with her favorite niece all along.

"So what's on the agenda for today?" she asked again, once Josh had been put into his willing grandmother's care. "Which one of your dreams can I help come true?"

Even as Beth laughed self-consciously, it was clear to Katy that she was tickled over the idea of having a whole day to do whatever she pleased—and having someone to keep her company. But it was clear that such royal treatment wasn't something with which Beth was comfortable yet.

"Gee, I don't know. I guess we could go somewhere." Beth frowned, trying to think of something spectacular—

something that Chrissie would be impressed with. But then
she realized that that was a stupid thing to worry about. She
thought long and hard, struggling to recognize what she really
wanted. And then, slowly, almost painfully, ideas began to
surface. "I know. Let's go out to lunch. Someplace really
fancy."

"Okay. Lunch it is."

"And after that, let's go shopping. Yes, shopping! I can
get some back-to-school clothes, if you'll help me pick them
out." Beth usually hated shopping. A trip to the stores for
clothes invariably meant lumpy-looking dresses and bulging
jeans that resisted mercilessly when she tried to button them,
and in the background, a look of pity on her mother's face.
But shopping with Katy . . . that might even be fun.

"All right. That sounds like a trip to the Smithhaven Mall.
It's a bit of a trek, but my offer stands."

"And then—then we could go to the beach. If there's time,
I mean."

Katy laughed and put her arm around her niece, whose
eyes were bright as her mind clicked away, searching for
things that appealed to her. "We'll make sure there's time,
Beth."

Careening off the ferry, driving onto the mainland of Long
Island and leaving Shelter Island behind, made the outing
seem like an adventure. Katy was astonished at how relieved
she felt, just to be getting away for the day. She was equally
astonished at how different Beth was, once she was away from
her family—and, Katy observed, proud of her astuteness,
away from the role the dynamics of her family forced her to
play.

She had become cheerful and animated, chattering away
about the plot of the book she was reading and the little girl
she had been babysitting over the summer and the new puppy
the people across the street had gotten just that spring. As she
bubbled over, there was a rosiness to her cheeks and a glint in
her eyes that were telltale signs of how excited she was to be
spending the day with Katy, doing exactly as she pleased.

They stopped for lunch at an elegant little restaurant.
With a little encouragement from her aunt, Beth threw caution to the wind. Instead of the cheeseburger she was inclined
to order, she abandoned the familiar and at Katy's suggestion
tried her very first lobster salad.

"This is *good*!" she declared after her first mouthful, her eyes as bright as if she'd just discovered penicillin. "I like this! It tastes like—well, I don't think it tastes like anything I've ever had before! Thanks for making me try it, Katy."

Her aunt just waved her hand in the air. "Sometimes you've got to take a chance, kid. You know what they say: 'Nothing ventured, nothing gained.' You've got to step away from what's familiar to you and take a few risks every now and then."

To prove even further how rewarding that attitude could be, Katy went on to introduce Beth to guacamole and crème brulée, as well.

Beth was so stuffed after lunch that she insisted she'd never be able to spend the afternoon walking around a shopping mall—especially one as big as Smithhaven, with Macy's at one end, A&S at the other, and a hundred stores in between. But as soon as Katy dragged her into Macy's junior department, she forgot all about her full stomach.

"I don't usually shop in this department," she said, stopping at the edge of the carpeting that defined the limits of this wonderland of teenage fashion and dreams.

"Where do you shop?"

"My mother always takes me to the Pretty Plus department."

"Oh, great." Katy groaned. "That's always good for the old morale. When I was a kid, a trip to the Chubbies department—as we called it in the less-enlightened good old days—was practically guaranteed to make me gain another five pounds. I'd get so depressed that the minute I got home, I'd drop all those new size 12½ dresses in my bedroom and head for the refrigerator."

"Really? You used to shop in those departments, too?"

"Until I dared to try on a Bobbie Brooks sweater one day and discovered I could also fit into a junior size. Hey, look at these neat shirts. Oh, Esprit. Great colors! I like their stuff, don't you?"

Beth's eyes were wide. "Chrissie always wears their clothes."

Katy grimaced. "We'll try to forget the negative associations. After all, it's not Esprit's fault."

Sure enough, much to Beth's delight, the oversized jerseys in bright colors did indeed fit her—and they looked fantastic.

"Hey, I look really good in these!" Beth observed with amazement. "But now I don't know which one I like better— the green-and-pink stripe, or this purple one."

"In that case, we'll get both."

"But Katy! You can't buy me both! They're too expensive!"

"Look, let me worry about that. You look so terrific in both these shirts that I simply won't let you leave the store without them. Besides, when I told your mom where we were going today, she said she'd pick up the tab for any new clothes."

Money was hardly what Katy was thinking about, however. She was too busy being pleased at how giddy Beth was becoming as she watched her old "ugly duckling" image of herself slowly becoming obsolete in the mirrors of Macy's dressing room.

Once the two shoppers had acquired a peach cotton sweater, a pair of black corduroy pants, and some wild socks with pictures of cats and flowers woven into them in addition to the two shirts, Katy said, "Okay. Time to hit the makeup counters."

"Makeup?" Beth looked as if Katy had just suggested shoplifting a stereo.

"I know, I know. Philosophically, I disagree with it. Why should women have to put on expensive gooey stuff just to look decent enough to go out on the street? But what the hell? You're going into, what is it, the eighth grade this year?"

Beth nodded.

"Well, if I remember correctly, that's not exactly the easiest time in a woman's life to start becoming a revolutionary. Charles Revson, Estée Lauder, Maybelline, batten down the hatches, 'cause here we come."

At the Bonnie Belle counter, Katy and the saleswoman put their heads together and picked out a subtle pink lipstick for Beth, along with smokey blue eye shadow, pale peach blush, and a wand of brown mascara.

"Here, just put on a little," Katy instructed, demonstrating cosmetological skill she had never dreamed she possessed as she brushed a few light strokes of pink across Beth's cheek. "You're not trying to look like Dolly Parton here. Just a little bit, to highlight what you've got."

"Wow! I look *gorgeous*!" Beth stared into the mirror, scarcely able to believe that the radiant young woman looking back at her was really Beth Gilbert.

"Yeah, you do." Katy sounded matter-of-fact, but in reality she was surprised at how pretty and grown up her niece looked. She wasn't a little girl anymore, she realized, not without a pang of sadness. She was a young woman.

Their shopping spree continued. At the shoe department, Beth got a pair of mint green Reeboks. At the costume jewelry counter, she picked out a Swatch wristwatch, egged on by Katy's contention that any teenager worth her salt in the 1980s simply had to have one.

Finally, in lingerie, Katy insisted upon picking out some lacy underwear for her niece, who was at first so mortified by the bras and girdles and camisoles surrounding her that she kept her eyes glued to the carpet. In the end, however, she started to get into it, and she confided that she would save her new underpants—one pair of peach, one aqua, one a daring black—for gym days.

Despite Beth and Katy's sincere belief of only a few hours earlier, that neither of them would ever eat again, their tired feet and shoppers' droopiness around four o'clock necessitated a stop for a soda. Happily they collapsed onto a wooden bench near a fountain, armed with a large-sized diet Coke.

"Well, we did okay," announced Katy with great satisfaction. "We managed to get you a lot of loot. You're all ready to go back to school next week."

Beth wrinkled her nose. "Oh, yuck. I'm never ready to go back to school. I hate school."

"Yeah, well, I guess that's par for the course. If it's any consolation, I'm not exactly looking forward to getting back to my regular life, either."

"You're not? How come?"

"Oh, it's a long story." Katy sighed tiredly. "Much too long to go into right now."

"Does it have anything to do with that guy Randy?" Beth teased.

"I'm not sure. Yeah, I guess so. Well, not really. It's just that . . . I don't know."

Beth laughed. "You sound like me! Especially when I'm talking about some boy I like."

"Beth, I have kind of a confession to make. You know 'that guy Randy,' as you insist on calling him? Well, I think I'm falling in love with him."

"Oh, wow!"

"As if that weren't complicated enough, I think he's in love with me. At least, he says he is."

"Ooh, that's so romantic! A summer romance!"

"It's the part that comes once the summer is over that determines whether or not it's 'romantic.' "

"Hey, Katy?"

"Yeah, Beth?"

"I have kind of a confession to make, too. I've had a crush on Danny Burtis ever since we got here."

"Oh, really? And here I thought—well, I could be wrong, of course. . . . Hasn't he been hanging around Chrissie a lot?"

Beth frowned. "Well, I never said that he liked me back. Maybe—maybe he likes me, you know, as a *friend*, but he thinks I'm a little bit too young to be his girlfriend."

"Sounds reasonable. And I'll tell you something: contrary to popular belief, friends are nothing to scoff at."

There was a long pause. "Katy, there's something else I have to tell you." Beth was keeping her eyes down, and Katy had a feeling that this time, her confession wasn't going to be about some schoolgirl crush.

"What is it, Beth?"

"I'm the one who took the jewelry. Your earrings and Julie's watch and Barbara's diamond ring . . ." Her voice broke, and she had to pause for a second before she could go on. "I stuck them all in Chrissie's pocketbook on purpose. I knew that sooner or later she'd get caught."

While Katy wasn't entirely surprised by what her niece had just told her, she wasn't prepared for her own reaction. Her stomach tightened into a painful knot—almost in fear, as if she, herself, were the one responsible, as if she were the one who was in trouble.

She knew it was important not to act too shocked.

"I see," she said calmly. Instinctively she placed a comforting hand on Beth's shoulder. The thirteen-year-old girl responded by bursting into tears.

"Oh, Katy! I'm so sorry! I know it was a horrible thing to do, and I'll never, ever do anything so awful again, not for the rest of my whole life!" She threw both arms around her aunt, clinging to her as she sobbed into her shoulder. Katy hugged her back, oblivious to the curious shoppers who were staring at them. At the moment, she couldn't imagine how she had ever seen Beth as a young woman, when it was so clear to her right now that all she was, was a little girl.

When the sobs had subsided, when the tense shoulders had

stopped shaking, Katy cradled Beth's head in her hands. "How come, Beth?"

"Because I *hate* her!" came the vehement reply. But then Beth drew away slowly and raised her tear-streaked face up toward Katy's. "I don't really hate her, Katy. I just wish . . . Oh, it's not fair! Why can't I be more *like* her?"

Katy bit her lip as she gazed down at the chubby little girl looking up at her, completely torn apart and in desperate need of someone to tell her she was not a wicked girl, after all. And what she saw was not Beth, but herself, some twenty years earlier.

"You must think I'm awful," Beth said morosely, her words more a question than a statement.

"Not at all. And do you know what, Beth? It just so happens that I know exactly how you feel."

"*You*, Katy?" Beth thought for a few seconds. "Oh, you mean because of Julie. But you never felt the way I do—did you?"

"Hah! You saw those stupid old home movies. You know what Julie was like when she was a teenager. She was gorgeous, she was popular, she was brilliant—she was everything every girl ever wanted to be. And you saw what I was like. Clumsy, fat, ugly . . ."

"But you weren't fat, Katy! I *saw* you! You weren't ugly, either!"

"You want to know something, Beth? You're not ugly, either. Or fat. Or any of the things you're probably convinced that you are."

"Well, maybe I'm a *little* fat. . . ." Katy was gratified to see that Beth was actually smiling. "But I'm still not like Chrissie."

"That's right. You're *not* like Chrissie. You're like *Beth*. You're sweet, and smart, and sensitive, and caring. . . . And you know what, Beth? All that stuff is *better* than being like Chrissie. And you know what *else*? One day, you're going to wake up and realize it!"

"How old were you when you realized it, Katy?"

Katy's mouth dropped open. She looked down at her niece, expecting that she was teasing, but saw that the little girl was in dead earnest.

"I, uh, well . . ." And then, Katy started to laugh. She laughed and laughed, so hard that tears formed in her eyes. She laughed as if she'd never be able to stop.

"Katy, are you okay?" Beth was growing concerned. "Are you laughing or crying? Katy?"

"I'm not even sure," Katy gasped, barely able to talk. "I think some of both."

"Come on, kid," she said, tossing her head as she slung her arm around Beth. She felt as if she'd just stepped out of a haze, one that had been surrounding her for as long as she could remember. "We've had a long day. How about heading home?"

Once they were in the car, a mood of peacefulness that could only come from relief settled over them both. Beth turned to Katy and asked, "So what happens now? About the jewelry, I mean."

"Well, first of all, I think you owe your sister an apology."

"Yeah, I guess." She cast a nervous glance at Katy. "I bet she's gonna be really mad at me."

"Oh, I don't know. Maybe old Chrissie will surprise you, this time around." Especially if I talk to her before you do, thought Katy, with a newfound resolve to start looking out for her niece a little bit more—even when they weren't together on vacation. "Then, I think you'd better have a talk with your mom and dad."

"Oh, great."

"Listen, if you think it'd help, I'll be there with you, okay?"

"Really? You really mean it, Katy?"

"Hey, kid, it's the least I can do. Anyway, besides that, you'll have to apologize to Julie and Barbara, too."

A look of horror crossed Beth's face. "Barbara?" She gulped. "Katy, would you come with me when . . . ?"

Katy laughed. "Of course. I don't blame you for not wanting to face Barbara the Tigress alone. She can be pretty scary, can't she?"

"You really think so? Oh, wow!" Beth flopped against the back of the seat in a dramatic demonstration of how relieved she was. "And here I thought I was the only one who thought that!"

"Are you kidding? Every time I run into her, I end up eating at least two Sara Lee fudge cakes!" Thoughtfully she added, "But I'm not going to do that anymore. At least, I'm going to *try* not to."

But Beth hadn't heard her. She was too lost in thought as

she stared out the car window at the passing scenery. "Hey, Katy?" she finally said, her voice sounding oddly mature.

"Umm?"

"Thanks a lot. I mean, I think that little talk we had before did me a lot of good, you know? Thank you."

Katy kept her eyes on the rearview mirror, but she reached across the front seat and gave her niece's hand a squeeze. "No, Beth," she said. "I'm the one who should be thanking *you*."

Chapter Thirty

"**H**ey, Michael! Let me give you a hand with that!"

Michael glanced up from his fruitless struggle with the Lightning's centerboard, so thickly covered with barnacles that it was stuck in the centerboard trunk. Squinting in the bright afternoon sunshine, he saw his sister Julie coming toward him, looking fresh and healthy in her white running shorts and a navy blue T-shirt printed with the WCBC logo in front.

"That's okay, Julie. I think I've just about got it."

"Here, let me have a try. Believe it or not, big brother, there are some things that I just happen to be better at than you."

She cast him a teasing smile, then stepped off the dock, into the small boat. Without giving it a second thought, she grabbed the sail batten, then slid the thin piece of wood down inside the trunk, using it to scrape off enough barnacles to free the centerboard.

"There you go. That should take care of it."

Michael cast her a startled look. "Hey, you sure made that look easy. I'm impressed."

"Don't be." She patted his shoulder. "You may have forgotten, Michael, dear, but when you and I were teenagers, hanging out at the town dock, while you were busy flirting with every girl in Harrington, I was actually listening to what our sailing instructor was saying."

"Aw, you make it sound like I was some kind of twelve-year-old Don Juan or something."

"Are you kidding?" Julie jabbed him playfully in the ribs. "If I remember correctly, at least two-thirds of the female population of our high school was madly in love with you. After all, you went out of your way to make sure of it!"

Suddenly she grew more serious. "Speaking of your love life, Michael, there's something I've been meaning to talk to you about."

"Uh-oh. Don't tell me you've got some girlfriend who needs some advice on how to charm a man. Or worse, that you want me to dig up some poor single guy so that you can sic your single friends on him."

His attempt at turning the tone of their discussion back to a joking one was completely wasted on his sister, however.

"I'm talking about you, Mike. You and Lynn. Don't you think I know you both well enough to be able to see that something is wrong?"

"Hell, Julie. It's nothing. What, are you upset because I couldn't deal with a few barnacles? Just chalk it up to a combination of laziness and poor hand-eye coordination."

"You know perfectly well that's not what I'm talking about."

"Oh, Julie, don't worry about it. Really. The only thing going on between me and Lynn is the occasional domestic squabble about whose turn it is to do the dishes or—or spend all day Saturday chauffeuring the kids around, that's all."

Lightly he added, "You know, it's no easy thing trying to keep my three ladyloves happy. Of course, that's not counting you!"

But Julie refused to be put off so easily. "Listen, Michael, I know you probably think I'm being a busybody, and that we'd all be much better off if I just minded my own business. But you're my brother, for heaven's sake, and I can see that something is bothering you. And I want you to know that if there's anything I can do to help you or Lynn out, anything at all . . ."

"I'm telling you, Julie, there's nothing wrong. I wish you'd stop worrying about me. Besides," he added, flashing her his most charming grin, the one that had broken so many hearts back in high school, "I'm older than you, remember? If anything, I'm the one who's supposed to be worrying about you."

Julie smiled wryly. "Okay. I'll try to keep that in mind."

She leaned back against the fence that separated the back-yard from the dock, her expression softening along with the tone of her voice. "You know, Michael, these past two weeks, all of us being together again like this, have really been great. This was a wonderful idea, this family reunion—or whatever you want to call it. Oh, sure, there's been a little tension, every now and then, but that's to be expected."

She chuckled. "There are so many of us, for Pete's sake, that we're bound to have some arguments. I mean, that was pretty much a given when we were all growing up."

"Yeah, I guess it has been kind of fun." Michael's agreement was only halfhearted.

"It's been so nice being able to spend some time with everybody," Julie went on. "Wes and Katy . . . and you, too, of course. I've really enjoyed seeing how much Chrissie and Beth have grown up. And I always appreciate the chance to see Lynn." She paused, thinking for a few seconds. "You know, I still remember the very first time I met Lynn as if it were yesterday."

"God, Julie. That seems like such a long time ago. It was, what, almost two decades ago?"

"I guess it was. Even so, I remember it well. You two came up to Harrington from Philadelphia for the weekend. You'd been going out with Lynn for some time, and for months your letters and phone calls to all of us had been full of little else. Then you started hinting about how the two of you were thinking of getting married, and how you wanted us all to meet each other."

"Yes, I remember. We all went up to Mom and Dad's for Easter. It was right after you first found out you got a job with WCBC. You were on cloud nine the whole time."

"That's right." Julie chuckled as she thought back to that time. "I remember how Mom was all in a tizzy beforehand. I went up a day or so early, before you two got there, to help her get ready for the big weekend. Gosh, she was so excited about meeting her future daughter-in-law. Dad was, too."

"And did they approve?" There was a slight edge to Michael's tone.

Julie hesitated. "Mom had her reservations, as I recall. But you know how she is. Always so cautious, always wanting only the very best for her children. Especially you, her num-ber one son."

"How about Dad?"

"Oh, he was quite taken with her, from what I recall."

"And what about you, Julie? What was your first impression of the woman I was about to marry?"

"You know, Michael, I knew right from the very first time we met that there was a lot more to Lynn than most people could see. Sure, anyone could see that she was bright and energetic, even if she was just a little bit unsure of herself sometimes. That she was someone who tried hard to make people like her. But there was so much more underneath."

She looked over at her brother, the intense look in her eyes reinforcing the earnestness of her words. "She's a strong woman, Michael. That wife of yours is a lot tougher than she looks. And don't you forget it."

Michael shook his head slowly. "I'm afraid I don't follow, Julie."

She stood up straight, then placed her hand gently on his shoulder. "Lynn loves you, Michael. You're lucky to have a woman like her. She's not nearly as fragile as you think. I have a feeling that you have to start remembering the way she was when you two first met. She's still that same person, you know. I know it's easy to forget that, when you get caught up in all the details of day-to-day life."

Michael furrowed his brow, unable to look his sister in the eye.

"You know, Michael," Julie continued, "she wants to understand you, to be close to you. You're hurting her by closing her out. You need her now, and she wants to be needed. Don't be afraid to draw on her love and her strength. Especially when you need it most."

After his sister had gone back into the house, Michael continued sitting there, leaning against the fence for a long time. And when he finally got up and strode toward the house, there was real determination in his step.

Upstairs in the bedroom, Lynn was enjoying herself as she sat cross-legged on the floor sorting through a shoebox filled with old photographs. Her hair was pulled back into a girlish ponytail, and she was dressed comfortably in a baggy T-shirt and a pair of jeans.

What fun it was, looking through these stacks of pictures that captured the lifetimes of people she knew. Here was Michael as a teenager, his hair so long that he was wearing it in a ponytail, much like the one she herself was wearing today. Here were Julie and Katy, wearing black patent leather shoes and identical frilly dresses with full skirts and puffed sleeves, probably dressed up for Easter or some other such spring occasion. And here she was with Michael, the two of them proudly showing off their six-week-old daughter who, while at the time they had thought her the most beautiful child in the world, she now had to admit looked as pink and wrinkled as a rosebud.

That last photograph made her chuckle. She was putting it into the small pile to her left, the pictures she was planning to bring home with her, when she heard someone say, "Hi, honey."

"Oh, hi, Michael." She was surprised not only by her husband's sudden appearance, but also by the gentleness in his voice. "How's the boat? Did you figure out how to fix the centerboard?"

"Yes, finally—with a little help from Julie, that is. Sometimes I forget that she's almost as at home on the sea as she is on land. Too bad she doesn't find the time to get in much sailing anymore. How about you? What have you been up to?"

"Oh, I've just been going through these boxes of old photographs. Pat got them out for me. And she told me I was welcome to help myself." She shrugged as she added, "Actually, I was thinking that it might be fun to put together a scrapbook of pictures of you when you were growing up. The kids would probably get a kick out of it. I found some pictures of them, too, that I think they'd enjoy."

"Great idea." Gingerly Michael sat down on the edge of the bed. "Hey, Lynn?" he said, that same softness in his voice.

"Yes, sweetie?"

"I—I think we need to talk, you and I."

Lynn put down the handful of black-and-white photographs she had just started arranging on the floor in front of her like the cards in a solitaire game, then looked up, her eyes clouded with concern.

"Okay. Let's talk, then."

"Look, I don't know how to say this gracefully, so I'll just spill it out. I hope you'll bear with me, however this comes out. . . .

"I'm afraid I've done something really stupid. It's been on

my mind for months now, but I just haven't had the guts to come out and tell you about it.''

"Go on," Lynn prodded gently. "I'm listening." Only the stricken look on her face told how fearful she was of what he was going to say.

"Okay, here goes. A few months ago, Greg O'Leary—you know, he's one of the new associates at the office—came to me and told me about this speculative real estate deal he had some inside information on. Some brother-in-law of his or something, or at least that's what he told me. 'A sure thing,' he called it.

"Well, I was feeling a little bit pressured back then—it was right after those stocks of ours had done so poorly—so I figured that making some extra money wouldn't be such a bad idea.''

As he spoke, he was growing more and more distraught. Ironically, Lynn, still sitting on the floor beside him, could feel her tension dissipating as she listened.

"Anyway, buying into a piece of the action required a little more money than we had on hand at the time. So . . . I borrowed some from the company. It was no big deal. It was simply considered an advance on my salary. Not that it even mattered to me at the time, since I expected to make it all back within a couple of weeks. . . .''

He took a deep breath. "But to make a long story short, Greg's 'sure thing,' turned out to be a total fiasco. I lost everything, Lynn—practically all our savings, plus the twenty thousand dollars I borrowed from the firm.

"And as if all that weren't bad enough, it turned out that this deal was not exactly on the up-and-up in the first place. Not that it matters all that much, since the whole thing ended up falling apart anyway. But the fact remains that I was a part of it, and, well, aside from what anybody else might think, or what might eventually come out about the whole deal, I don't feel too good about that. I just never bothered to look into it that carefully—mainly, I think, because I wanted to believe it was an easy answer. You know, that no-fail, get-rich-quick scheme that everybody dreams about.'' He laughed coldly. "Instead, it turned into a nightmare.''

"Oh, Michael," Lynn breathed, taking hold of his arm. "Is *that* all?''

"*What*? What do you mean, is that all?'' Michael looked at her, incredulous. "Am I hearing you correctly, or have I finally gone bananas? Lynn, this thing has been tearing me apart for months! I just didn't have the guts to tell you about it. Instead, I've been acting like a complete lout."

"Yes, I know you have," Lynn agreed matter-of-factly. "But don't you understand? Don't you have any idea what I've been thinking all along?"

Michael was still baffled. "No, I don't."

"Oh, Michael! I thought you were tired of me, that you'd gone out and found somebody else. I thought you were having an affair!"

"What? *Me?* Why in hell would I ever do a stupid thing like that?"

"Come here, you idiot." Laughing, she pulled him down onto the floor. "I know it's terrible. But it's just so much *less* terrible than what I thought you were doing!"

"God, Lynn, an affair! I could never do that to you! Hell, I'd never even *want* to! Why would I? You're the only woman I've ever loved."

"I love you, too, honey." She gave him a big hug, then folded her hands primly in her lap. "All right, Michael. Let's start at the beginning. Tell me about this 'deal,' and exactly what went wrong. . . . You know, I've got a little money saved up, a few thousand dollars I've managed to stash away over the years, without ever bothering to mention it. Why don't you tell me exactly where we stand right now in terms of dollars and cents?"

Michael grimaced. "It's pretty bad, Lynn. We've lost just about everything."

Lynn took her husband's hand and gave it a squeeze. Then, with a shy smile, she corrected him.

"No, we haven't, Michael. Not at all. After all, you and I have still got everything that matters."

"How are you feeling, Ben?" As she slid into bed beside her husband late that night there was real concern in Pat's voice, an undertone that made it clear that her question was more than just small talk. "I hope having so many people around isn't turning out to be too much of a strain on you."

Ben closed the book he had been reading, the latest bestseller about improving one's management skills. "Not at all. Sure, it's been a little bit tough, but that's to be expected." He glanced over at his wife and grinned. "After all, over the past two weeks I've put in more time playing horsey with a two-year-old, acting as referee between two teenaged girls, and drinking beer with a couple of men a fraction of my age than I have in years.''

Pat laughed. ''Yes, it has been great, hasn't it? Having all the kids around.''

''It's been wonderful. I only regret that we haven't been doing this kind of thing more often. Can you believe how fast the girls are growing up? Not to mention little Josh.''

''Actually, Ben, it's not Josh's aging process that I've been worrying about lately.'' She frowned. ''You know, Ben, I've been wondering if maybe you owe it to the kids to tell them about . . . you know, about what happened back in June.''

''Nonsense. Why worry them? They've got troubles of their own.''

''I think you should tell them, Ben,'' Pat insisted. ''After all, they are your children.''

''Exactly. They're my children—and I'm their old man. With the emphasis on the word *old*, I might add. Hell, they're not interested in hearing the details of every ache and pain a man in his sixties has to complain about. That kind of thing is to be expected, after all, once a man reaches my age. The only reason I would even consider telling them about what happened is the business—and the unfortunate fact that I have yet to have any volunteers to take over at B.G.A.''

Ben sighed, then placed his book on the night table beside him. ''As much as I hate to admit it, Pat, it really looks as if I'm going to have to start thinking about selling B.G.A. to an outsider. Not yet, of course . . . but soon.''

Pat remained silent. But her mind was racing. She knew how it would hurt him to have to do that.

Why, B.G.A. is almost like his fifth child! she was thinking, her heart breaking as she thought about what this realization he was making must be doing to him. What a disappointment it would be for him not being able to pass his company along to someone in the family.

She yearned to comfort him with some soothing words, to pipe up with some cheerful contradiction to his statement. More than anything, she wished she could insist that he shouldn't yet give up on his dream of having a member of the next generation of Gilberts replace him as president of the firm.

But she couldn't, since she had come to the same conclusion as her husband: that B.G.A., the family firm, was about to move out of the family.

As they both leaned over and snapped off their bedside lights, then said their rather formal "good nights," Pat rested her head on her soft down pillow, expecting to fall asleep quickly. After all, it had been a long day, and she was tired.

Instead, her mind continued to churn, wrestling with all her contradictory emotions. In a way, she would be glad once Ben retired. It would be good for him to slow down; besides, they would finally be able to spend some time together. Maybe they would even start traveling, something they had always dreamed about. But at the same time, she knew know difficult it would be for her husband to leave B.G.A. behind—especially if in doing so, he had to let go of it forever.

And the worst part was that she was powerless to do anything. Once again, the love she was feeling, the desperate desire to help someone she cared about, had no outlet. All she could do was stand by and watch, just as she had on so many occasions with her children—Katy and Wes, and even Michael and Julie, she now admitted to herself—feeling frustrated by her own inability to reach out to them, to solve their problems for them. It was no easy thing, recognizing her own limitations.

Especially, she thought, turning over, determined to force sleep to come and save her from the intense sadness that had fallen over her, when those limitations make it impossible to lessen the load of the people that I truly care about.

Chapter Thirty-One

"*O*oh! *I love* this song! It's so hot. . . . Oh, shoot!"

As Chrissie reached over to turn up the volume on the radio, having just heard the new Madonna song coming on, she accidentally bumped one of her freshly lacquered fingernails against the dial. Sure enough, much to her horror, she found that the dark burgundy nail polish on the right index finger now had a smudge, right smack in the middle.

"Oh, no! Just *look* at this stupid . . . !"

Anxiously she glanced over at the clock on the night table next to the bed. There wasn't enough time to do anything about it now. She was meeting Rick in front of the Tuck Shop at nine-thirty—a deliciously, dangerously late hour—and if she was going to get over there on time, she had to start recruiting a ride right away.

She had pegged Wes as her best bet. He was the least likely to start asking questions. And even if he did, he'd see nothing wrong with her going out on a date.

"Hey, Wes?" she cooed, checking out the living room and seeing that she had been fortunate enough to catch him alone. "Would you do me a teensy little favor? Please?"

"Does this favor happen to include the exchange of any legal tender?"

"Nope. I just need a ride somewhere."

"Well, that sounds easy enough— Whoa! Check this out!"

278

He had glanced up from his newspaper to discover that his little niece looked like the kind of girl he had only fantasized about when he was that age. She was wearing a short, tight white miniskirt and a clingy hot pink tank top. Over it was a denim jacket that had obviously been thrown on for effect, since the warm weather on this Friday evening before Labor Day made it entirely unnecessary.

Her long hair, still shockingly blond, had just been washed, a full and fragrant mane that framed her face like an aura of light. Dangling from each ear was a pair of long silver earrings. Her makeup looked just a bit heavy, but then again, he reminded himself, he was hardly a qualified judge of that kind of thing.

"Got a big date?"

"Yeah, sort of." The grin she flashed was seductive, yet at the same time girlishly self-conscious.

"Well, then, let's hit the road." He put down the newspaper and checked his pants pockets for his car keys. Then he looked over at his niece through narrowed eyes. "Hey, wait a minute. Isn't it kind of late to be going out?"

Chrissie groaned. "Oh, Wes. Don't be so old-fashioned!" Laughing, she pushed him toward the front door.

"Do I sound old-fashioned? Really? Oh, no." Melodramatically, he slapped his hand against his forehead. "God, what's happening to me?"

As she stood alone in front of the Tuck Shop, feeling just a tinge of nervousness as she watched her uncle drive away, she wondered if perhaps Rick wasn't going to show up, after all. Maybe he'd been teasing her, or maybe he forgot—or maybe he changed his mind.

But it was barely past nine-thirty when the familiar red Corvette came careening into the parking lot. Chrissie's heart raced as she watched Rick pull up in front of her and stick his head out the window.

"Here she is," he murmured.

She strutted over to the car, certain she could feel a dozen pairs of envious eyes upon her.

"Hi." She climbed into the front seat.

"Hey, there, Chrissie, baby. You're lookin' good tonight."

She could feel herself blushing. "Oh, I just threw on any

old thing, you know? I mean, I just wasn't in the mood for getting dressed up or anything.''

"Whatever you say." He looked at her appraisingly, then backed out the car so suddenly that she had to grab on to the seat to keep from toppling over.

"So, where are we headed?" She was trying to sound casual, as if she went driving around in red Corvettes with older men all the time.

"The beach. You said you like the beach."

She had said that, of course—but she had meant she liked the beach during the day, when she could lie in the sun and work on her tan. The beach at night was an entirely different matter. Suddenly she felt uneasy.

"How about someplace more . . . exciting?" Someplace with other people around.

"Oh, the beach can be plenty exciting, believe me."

As if to demonstrate how well versed he was on the topic of excitement, Rick stepped on the gas a little bit harder.

You can take care of yourself, Chrissie told herself firmly. Whatever happens, you can manage. Besides, this is what you wanted, isn't it? To meet an older guy, somebody worldly . . . to find out what it's like?

Even so, now that it was happening, she felt just a little bit frightened, even in the midst of her exhilaration. It was as if she were riding on a roller coaster she wasn't quite sure was safe.

Rick drove in silence, something Chrissie found disturbing. She would have expected him to be making conversation, trying to find out what she was like, getting to know her. Instead, it was almost as if he didn't really care.

But it was a clear night, accented by a big friendly moon, so Chrissie tried to enjoy herself. She concentrated on what she would report to Heather about this momentous night— very possibly the most important one of her entire life.

For the sake of research, she glanced over at Rick so she could get a better look at what he was wearing. Tight jeans, a T-shirt—not very thrilling. But she'd find a way to *make* it sound thrilling.

Well, at least his car is really hot. . . .

"I really love this car."

"Yeah, I know. Isn't she a beauty?"

"How long have you had it?"

"Yeah, well, it's not *mine*, exactly. It belongs to a friend of mine." He was quick to add, "But he lets me borrow it, anytime I want. All I have to do is take it."

"Oh. You two must be pretty close friends."

That's one detail I won't bother mentioning to Heather, thought Chrissie. Not that it's important.

She could feel herself growing just a little bit deflated.

"So, Rick, do you go to college or something?"

"Me? Nah. Dropped out."

He's taking a year off, to—to pursue some of his interests. Yeah, that sounds good.

"What college were you going to?" Taking a year off from Harvard, after all, would sound positively glamorous.

"Oh, you probably never heard of it. It's a technical college, over in Jersey."

"I'm still in high school," Chrissie offered lamely.

"Hey, didn't you say you were eighteen?" Rick gave her the once-over, then grinned. "You sure look pretty grown up. Anyway, you're old enough to drink beer, aren't you?"

"Sure. I love beer."

"Great. There's some right behind you. Help yourself. Hey, grab me one, too, will ya?"

Chrissie had had no idea that her fib would be tested so soon. While she sipped a can of beer, treating it like a glass of champagne, struggling not to make a face with each miniscule mouthful, she noticed that Rick wolfed his down in just a few gulps.

"Get me another one, okay?"

Silently Chrissie complied. She was concerned about how eagerly he attacked his second beer, but then it occurred to her that it would be amusing to complain to Heather about how Rick tasted like Rolling Rock when she kissed him.

Almost as soon as she'd had that thought, he turned off the main road, onto an overgrown path that led to an isolated patch of beach.

"Gee, I never even knew this place existed." Chrissie's cheerfulness sounded painfully forced.

After turning off the ignition, he leaned back and smiled, looking her over once again.

"I'll tell you what. We'll keep this our little secret, okay? Make it our special place."

"The water looks really pretty from here, doesn't it? With the moonlight and all?"

"Yeah, well, I'm sittin' here thinking that *you* look really pretty from here."

"Thanks." Chrissie smiled weakly.

"Hey, let me see those earrings you're wearing."

He slid across the front seat until he was close to her, his shoulder touching her shoulder, his thigh pressed tightly against hers. His leg felt so hot, so *close*, it was as if it were somehow invading her body.

Her heart felt as if it were in danger of exploding, and she was tempted to draw away. But she couldn't, not now. What would he think of her?

Besides, this is what you wanted, she reminded herself. You're the one who set this whole thing up in the first place.

"Yeah," Rick was saying, "these are pretty. Real pretty." He fingered her earlobe gently. His breath was warm on her neck, his nearness creating an intimacy that was as terrifying as it was intoxicating. Chrissie sat perfectly still, her eyes fixed on the silver knob of the glove compartment.

He moved even closer. She was overwhelmed by his presence, by the heat of his body.

"You got pretty hair, too," he muttered, his fingertips traveling across the line of her jaw, along her neck, gently, slowly. His light touch was giving her goose bumps. More than that, it was causing a sweet tingling in the pit of her stomach, or somewhere deep inside her. It felt good, so good. . . .

"Why don't you just relax?" His voice was hypnotic. He pushed aside her hair and began to massage the back of her neck, his face getting closer and closer until his lips were brushing against her.

God, it feels so wonderful. . . . She closed her eyes and tried to let go, as he'd instructed. His other hand was on her shoulder, so light that she was barely aware of it at first. Then it traveled down to her breast, a tender caress that electrified her.

When he kissed her, his tongue seemed disproportionately large as it pushed its way inside. His mouth was pressed hard against hers, demanding and sure, leaving no room for resistance. Still his hand caressed her breast, but the sweet tender touch had become so forceful that it almost hurt. Her first impulse was to protest; instead, she kept still.

He leaned against her with all his weight, practically lying on top of her. His heaviness was oppressive, especially with his muscles so strangely tensed. His breaths were coming hard and fast. Suddenly her growing fear could no longer be quelled.

Meekly she tried pushing his hand away. "Hey, wait a second." It wasn't until she talked that she realized she could hardly breathe.

"What's the matter, baby?" His voice was filled with concern. "Is something wrong?"

He began kissing her neck lightly, moving his hand from her breast to her shoulder. But the fear in the pit of her stomach remained.

"N-no, nothing's wrong, exactly. You're just going a little too fast, that's all."

"Okay, baby. I'll slow down, then."

This time his kisses were more gentle. Still, it wasn't exactly what Chrissie had meant. She had hoped they could just talk for a while, get to know each other a little bit better. But she was afraid of sounding stupid. She didn't want to keep making such a big deal about everything.

So when he slid his hand under her shirt and let his fingers come to rest on her nipples, by now embarrassingly taut, she just let him. She even tried to enjoy it, to recapture that tingling deep inside her. But she was just too nervous.

But you'll get to tell Heather all about this, she reminded herself. She'll want to hear every detail. I'll be the experienced one, acting cool as I tell her about every single move this guy is making. She'll be hanging on to every word. . . .

This is what I wanted. I wanted to find out what it was like to be with a guy who could show me the ropes.

Despite her internal argument, it all felt wrong. It was going too fast, happening too soon. . . .

When Rick reached for her hand and pulled it down firmly toward his groin, Chrissie suddenly jerked it away.

"Hey, listen," she said, her voice hoarse. "I really think maybe we should, uh, cool it for a while."

"Aw, what are you talking about?" He tightened his grip on her.

"No, really. I just realized that it's getting kind of late, and, uh, I have to get home."

"Hey, wait a second. What is this 'It's getting late' shit? You're not going anywhere."

Panic began to rise up inside her. "Come on, Rick. I don't want to." While she had wanted her words to sound forceful, they instead came out as a whine.

"Oh, you don't want to, huh? That's sure not how it seemed over at the Tuck Shop."

He pushed her down and climbed on top of her. She was close to panic as she realized there was no way she could get away from him.

"Hey, cut it out!" she pleaded. "Come on. You're really being stupid. Don't, Rick!"

"You know what I think? I think maybe you're just playing hard to get, that's all." More insistent than ever, he jammed his hands between her legs, pushing her miniskirt up almost to her waist.

"Stop it!" she shrieked. She tried to squirm out from under him, but it was futile. He was just too heavy. She tried hitting him, but the way he had her pinned down made it almost impossible for her to move at all.

And then she noticed that jutting out of his back pocket was the stubby end of a pencil. She managed to grab it and, without a moment's hesitation, jabbed it into his hip.

"Ow!" he yelped, immediately backing off. "What the hell was that?" He sat up abruptly. Bewildered, he looked around, rubbing his side. And then he realized what had happened. "You little bitch!"

He lunged for her one more time, but it was too late. Chrissie had made full use of his few seconds of confusion. Already she had opened the door and was scrambling out of the car.

"Get back here you! Aw, the hell with you! You can walk home, for all I care!"

From behind her came the sound of a car door slamming, an engine being revved up, a car taking off with such speed that the tires screamed their resistance. But Chrissie didn't turn around. She kept running, not stopping until she saw the red taillights of Rick's car vanish around a turn in the road.

She held on to the branch of a tree as she struggled to catch her breath. And then, even though all she wanted to do was curl up somewhere and have a good cry, she forced herself to start walking. Tears were streaming down her face, now streaked with makeup. Her nose was running, too, and she desperately needed a tissue. She reached for the pocket of her denim jacket, and realized that she had left it in the car.

It was a good two-mile walk back to the Gilberts' house. Some stretches of the road were pitch-black, since streetlights were scarce and it was late enough for the windows of many houses to be blackened. Despite the ominous shadows that surrounded her, however, despite the threatening clumps of trees and bushes, Chrissie wasn't afraid. She felt safe now, certain that the worst was over.

"Boy, that's the last time I ever drink two cups of coffee after dinner!"

Katy knew it wasn't really the caffeine that was keeping her awake tonight. But when she padded into the living room just past midnight, hoping that the inevitably lulling effects of The Johnny Carson Show would help, she discovered that her sister had gotten there first. And she wasn't about to admit to her that the source of her insomnia was internal.

"Can't sleep either?" Julie looked up from the mindless banter between the talk show host and his guest, a bleached-blond starlet she vaguely remembered as being associated with a popular sitcom.

"Oh, who wants to sleep, anyway? Sleep is boring."

"Well, then, pull up a cushion."

"Isn't there anything better than this on?"

Julie handed her sister the *TV Guide*. "I'm afraid not. It's either this or a sci-fi movie. Take your pick."

"Gee, I would've thought this *was* the sci-fi movie."

On the screen, the giggling actress was gushing about how wonderful everyone was on the set of her show, all the while tugging at the ridiculously low neckline of her tight evening gown.

"Hey, I know her. That's my old Barbie doll, come to life."

Julie laughed. "Might as well be."

"Why don't we just can this?" Katy looked around the living room, searching for something to distract her. "I wonder if Mom has any old magazines around."

"Nope. I already checked. If I know her, she probably spent weeks cleaning up before we all got here, and they all got thrown out with the trash."

"Good old Mom." Katy grimaced. "It never would have occurred to her to save something like that for us, would it?"

Julie leaned forward and snapped off the television. Turning to face her sister, she said, "Katy, how come you're always so hard on Mom?"

"*Me?* Hard on her?" Katy was indignant. "What about the way she treats *me*?"

"I think that a lot of the time, you read things into what she says. She doesn't mean to sound critical, you know."

"Oh, really? And how would you know? I mean, she's never criticized you once in your entire life. Not once!"

"Oh, come on. You're making it sound like she thinks I'm nothing but wonderful, and that you're nothing but trouble."

"But it's true, isn't it? Look, you may never have noticed—or bothered to notice—but practically my whole life she'd been on my case."

Julie sighed. "Well, one thing I have noticed is that you two have bickered constantly ever since I can remember. And to be perfectly honest, I've never really understood why it had to be that way."

By this point, Katy was really riled. She had reached a point where she could no longer hold in words she had been swallowing for years, ever since she was a little girl.

"Well, maybe that's because you never had the kind of pressure I had to be somebody I wasn't. Somebody *perfect*. Somebody like my big sister."

"Oh, Katy. That's not fair. I'm not 'perfect.' I never have been. I've always had problems, just like everybody else. You just never wanted to see it, that's all."

"Really? You had problems? Like what? Like which of your eighteen million boyfriends to go to the Junior Prom with?"

"No. Like how to live up to the high expectations that Mom had of me, too. The only difference between us, Katy, is that you opted out, a long time ago. You didn't want to put up with the heat, so you got out of the kitchen. I, on the other hand, felt I had no choice but to hang in there, always forcing myself to work harder than anybody else, to be the most popular . . . to be the *best*.''

''Oh, come on. A lot of that stuff came to you easily. Don't try to convince me that being captain of the cheerleading squad was a major cross to bear.''

''No, of course not. Doing well always has its rewards. But don't you see that I always felt the pressure from Mom just as much as you did? And Michael and Wes, too. We all did. She's very demanding, in her way. Rigid, too. Her kids have always had to be superior—period.

''And I'll tell you something else: I was the oldest daughter, so I felt it a lot more strongly than you ever did.'' Julie bit her lip. ''And I'm still feeling it, Katy.''

Katy snorted. ''You? Julie Gilbert Kane? Woman of the Year? Tell me one thing about your life that's not incredibly wonderful.''

Even as she said the words, however, Katy knew what her sister was referring to.

''Speaking of the less than perfect aspects of one's life,'' Julie said, her voice so soft that Katy could hardly hear her, ''how come you never told me about Brad coming on to you that night? You know, the very first time you two met each other? . . .''

Katy couldn't meet Julie's eyes. ''I don't know why. I guess that, in some weird way, I was trying to protect you.''

Julie's reaction was one of astonishment. ''But Katy! Why on earth would you want to protect me when you said yourself that you resent me?''

Katy shrugged. ''I suppose it's because, underneath all the other stuff, I love you.'' Timidly she looked over at her big sister.

''Oh, Katy. I love you, too. I just wish that my existence hadn't always caused so many problems for you. I certainly never wanted it to be like that.'' She threw her arms around her sister and hugged her. ''I always wanted us to be close. To be friends. But there was always all this other garbage in the way.''

''The competitiveness, you mean. I know. It seems like Mom set it up like that, right from the start.'' Katy drew away, a sheepish look in her eyes. ''Well, maybe that's not entirely fair. Maybe I'm guilty of feeding into it a little bit too much. I mean, it was always easy, using you as an excuse for the things I was afraid of, things that really had nothing to do with you.''

"What do you mean? What things?"

"Like allowing myself to be serious about a man. Like being a success. Like making a decision, even—any decision— and sticking with it. Finishing the Ph.D. program at Wisconsin, or deciding to become a partner at Foodstuffs—"

"Katy! I didn't know you were thinking of becoming a partner!"

"Well, the whole thing just kind of fell into my lap. My boss called me last week and asked me if I was interested.''

"And what did you say?"

"Oh, the usual Katy Gilbert response: 'I'll think about it.' '' Katy laughed. "But do you know what? I'm finally done thinking about it. I've made my decision. And do you know what else? It feels really good.''

"You mean you're going to do it?"

But before Katy had a chance to reply, both women started at the sound of a key turning in the front door.

"Who on earth is that?" Julie frowned.

"Well, burglars rarely come in through the front door— and they rarely have house keys.''

"Chrissie! What are you doing out so—Chrissie, what happened? My God! Are you all right?"

Their niece had just straggled in, looking as if she had just been through a terrible ordeal. Her makeup was streaked all over her face, her skirt town, her sandals coated with dust. But even more telling was the look in her eyes.

"What happened?" Julie repeated, rushing over and putting her arm around her shoulders. "Are you okay?"

"Yeah, I'm okay. Just barely, but I'm okay." Tiredly, Chrissie sank onto the couch.

"You look like you could use a good stiff drink," Katy offered.

"Thanks, but no thanks. I just want to sit down. I'm fine, really.''

But within a few seconds she had burst into tears. Katy sat down on one side of her, Julie on the other, then proceeded to attempt to comfort her. Despite their good intentions, however, they were hampered by the fact that they still had no idea what had happened.

When her tears finally dissipated into quiet sobs, Julie asked gently, "Are you ready to talk about it?"

"Julie, I don't think I'll ever be ready to talk about it. Let's just say that I did something really stupid tonight. I mean, like *really* stupid."

"Join the club," Katy breathed.

"You don't understand. This was something totally dumb."

"What exactly did you do, Chrissie?" Julie reached over and stroked her hair. "You can tell us. We're not going to judge you."

Chrissie took a few deep breaths. Then she looked up and shook her hair out of her eyes. "I guess what I did was try to be somebody I'm not." She leaned over and buried her face in her hands.

"Yeah, I see what you mean," Katy said gently. "That is pretty dumb. But do you want to know something?" Over Chrissie's head, Katy cast her sister a rueful grin. "Realizing that that's what you've been doing is half the battle."

Chapter Thirty-Two

The moment she awoke, Katy was surprised by how good she felt. She lay in bed, marveling over the luxurious sense of serenity in which she was bathed.

At first, she was afraid to think very hard about what was behind it. After all, it could turn out to be a mistake, a mere delusion that would be quickly and cruelly crushed by the first hint of reality. But then, tentatively, timidly, as if walking across a gravel driveway in very high heels, she allowed herself to think harder, to tread into dangerous territory—to try to figure out if there was, indeed, a concrete reason why she should be feeling so good.

Then she remembered. All the things that had been happening lately came back to her in a rush, the thoughts that had been smouldering in the recesses of her mind suddenly emerging into a bright light of understanding. And she felt positively giddy.

Yes, this feeling of lightness was real. It was something she had earned.

"Good morning," she said cheerfully a few minutes later, bouncing into the kitchen with such enthusiasm that it was immediately suspect.

"You're up early—for you, I mean," her mother observed, glancing up from her newspaper.

"That's right, Mother, dear. It's a new day, full of promise.'' She leaned over and gave her astonished mother a peck on the cheek. ''Is there any coffee?''

''A fresh pot.'' Pat eyed her suspiciously. ''There are some English muffins, too.''

''No, just coffee will be fine, thanks.''

''What's this? No English muffins?'' Wes came into the kitchen, still in his pajamas, yawning and stretching. ''Are you really my sister Katy, or are you an alien living in my sister's body?''

''Ah, so now you know my secret. The real Katy Gilbert *is* an alien.''

''See that? I knew it all along.''

''You know what they say: 'Like sister, like brother.' Well, my dears, it's been fun, but I'm afraid I must run.''

''Goodness! Where could you possibly be going at this hour? It's barely eight o'clock.'' Pat was still having trouble adjusting to what she was seeing.

''Probably a secret love tryst.'' Wes gave his sister a wink.

But her response was matter-of-fact. ''Not far from the truth, Wes. Not far at all.''

Just as she'd expected, Randy was outside on the Cotters' deck having breakfast with a man and woman so glamorous that they simply had to be the inhabitants of the dream house that had become Katy and Randy's love nest. Mark was blond, as tan and muscular as some daytime soap opera's version of a tennis pro. Wendy was dark and sleek, the kind of woman who looked as if she had never once perspired in her entire life.

Ordinarily, Katy would have been at least a little bit intimidated by a couple like the Cotters. Today, however, she barely blinked, even when she noticed that it was caviar they were spreading on their croissants.

''Hi, Randy!'' she called brightly, waving as she came up the wooden steps to the deck.

''Katy! What a surprise!''

''Sorry to interrupt your breakfast.''

''No, not at all. Katy, meet Mark and Wendy Cotter. Mark, Wendy, this is a friend of mine, Katy Gilbert.'' As if to alleviate any fears his hosts may have had about the probable length of her visit, he added, ''Her folks have a beach house here on the island.''

''Glad I finally had a chance to meet you.'' Grinning, Katy

extended her hand. "I love your house." Without missing a beat, she added, "Especially the bedroom."

"Why don't you join us?" Mark offered. "There's more coffee."

"No, thanks. I really wanted to talk to Randy." As he got up from the table, she added, "Don't worry. I'll return him in a few minutes."

"So what's going on?" he asked once Mark and Wendy were out of earshot. He and Katy were walking together on the beach, kicking at the sand along the shoreline. "Nothing's wrong, I hope? . . ."

"Nope. Not at all. As a matter of fact, I'm beginning to feel as if there's a whole lot of stuff that's *right*." She paused. "But first, a word from our sponsor. Randy, I've been doing some thinking, and, well, I thought it was important that we talk. Or, really, that I talk and you listen."

"All right. Shoot."

She took a deep breath. "Well," she began, "I'm afraid I haven't been completely straight with you. And, well, there are a couple of things I want to get off my chest."

"Okay." Randy tried to keep his expression neutral, but the unmistakable flicker of fear in his eyes made it clear that he was a little bit afraid of what he was about to hear.

"First of all, you know this guy Nicholas Somers I keep talking about?"

Randy swallowed hard. "Yeah, sure. What about him?"

"Well, I'm not really going out with him. What actually happened is that he said a couple of things that let me know he wanted to go out with me, but I never actually said yes. Because, you see, there's one minor complication I never mentioned. Nicholas Somers happens to be married."

When she saw the shock in Randy's eyes, she was quick to add, "Not that I ever really thought about saying yes. Not seriously, anyway. I mean, I wasn't in a hurry to get involved with a married man. I'm not *that* dumb!

"But it was good for my ego, you know? It made me feel as if somebody wanted me. And, well, I never bothered to tell you the details of the situation because I wanted you to think somebody else was hot for my body. I thought it would make me seem more attractive to you."

"Aw, Katy. You didn't have to do that."

"I know. That is, I know now. But back when we first met

. . . Anyway, that's the true story behind your supposed competition.''

"Well, I guess I'm a little bit relieved." Randy smiled shyly. "Maybe even a whole lot."

"Wait. I'm not finished with True Confessions yet."

"Go on. I'm listening."

Katy bent over to pick up a stone, then hurled it into the sea as far as she could. Long after it had disappeared into the waves, she continued staring off in that same direction. "Oh, boy. This is going to be even harder than I thought."

"Whatever it is, Katy, I'm sure—"

"No, it's not that it's going to be hard for you to hear this, Randy. But it is going to be hard for me to admit." She looked back at him. "Remember when I told you about that Ph.D. program I dropped out of?"

"Of course. The Ramapo Indians."

"Right. The Ramapo Indians. Well, you may recall that when I told you about why I dropped out, I said it was because I just sort of lost interest. Remember?"

"Sure. You said you got bored."

"Yeah, well, I lied. I didn't leave the program because I was bored. I left it because I was *scared*."

"I don't get it."

"Look, I was okay as long as I was taking courses and doing my little research assignments—you know, being led by the hand. And when I started studying the Ramapos, that was fine, too.

"But as soon as I had to face the reality of writing a thesis—of really testing myself for the first time in my life, for putting myself on the line and letting other people decide whether or not I had the stuff it took to make it—well, I just couldn't hack it. I was too afraid of failing.

"So I took off. I left the program. I came up with a million excuses—and eventually even *I* got to believing them."

"Would it have been so terrible if it had turned out you couldn't have hacked it?"

"Hah!" Katy snorted. "Are you kidding? After having spent my whole life competing with my sister? Trying to live up to the great Julie Gilbert? You're damn right it would've been terrible! It would have been devastating!

"But do you want to know something? I finally realized one important thing, Randy. It's time for me to grow up. To stop thinking of myself as Julie's little sister—or, to be more accurate, Julie's fat, dumb, ugly, inferior little sister. Because that's not what I am. I'm just *me*, that's all. And I've got to start accepting that, or else I've lost the battle before I've even started to fight.

"And you want to hear something else? I'm beginning to realize that being me, Katy Gilbert, isn't such an awful thing. I've got a lot more going for me than I've been willing to give myself credit for. Up until now, that is."

Randy reached over and took her hand. "And here I've known that ever since the very first time I laid eyes on you. I don't suppose I had anything to do with all this self-revelation? . . ."

"Let's just say that meeting you at this time in my life didn't exactly hurt." Katy squeezed his hand. "But it's funny: the person who really helped open my eyes the most was Beth."

"Beth? Your niece? Isn't she, what, twelve years old?"

"She's thirteen."

"Same difference. So tell me: what miracles did this *wunderkind* perform?"

"Oh, it's a long story. Maybe I'll tell you about it one of these days."

The gentle, almost dreamy smile that had been playing at Katy's lips suddenly vanished.

"But wait—there's more. There's something else I want to tell you."

"Okay, hit me."

"Well, I've made a major life decision. I've decided what I want to do when I grow up. Or at least for a little while, anyway."

"Don't tell me. You've accepted your boss's offer. Leslie, or whatever her name is. You're going to become a partner at Foodstuffs."

She shook her head. "No, afraid not. That was something I just fell into, not anything I ever decided I really wanted. I plan to call Leslie this afternoon and tell her thanks, but no thanks."

"Let's see, then." Randy frowned. "Oh, I know. You're going to take over the family business. Become the new president of B.G.A."

"No, not that, either. I'm not cut out for the corporate world. That, I've known all along."

"Well, then, I give up."

Katy looked at Randy with an impish gleam in her eye. "I've decided to go back and finish the Ph.D. program at Wisconsin. Get my degree in anthropology—finally."

"Wow! That's great! 'Dr. Katherine Gilbert.' Yeah, I like it." Randy's enthusiasm faded as quickly as it had appeared. "But wait a minute. The University of Wisconsin. Isn't that . . . in Wisconsin?"

Katy laughed. "That's where they're keeping it these days. But don't forget—I've finished all my coursework. All I have left to do is complete my research and write my thesis. And that means going back to New Jersey—a mere stone's throw from Wall Street, I might add. Oh, occasionally I may have to fly back to the Midwest, to talk to advisors or something, but basically I'll still be around."

Randy looked over at her through misty eyes. "I'm glad, Katy."

They were silent for a long time. It was Katy who finally spoke, her voice hesitant, making it clear that she had continued ruminating about her decision as they walked, her mind churning as she labored to digest the new perspective she was forming—and to convince herself that the jubilant feeling that had come with it was real.

"So what do you think? We're talking two, maybe three years of my life here, obsessing about the Ramapo Indians, living in libraries, carrying those colored index cards everywhere I go, maybe even buying myself a word processor. Are you willing to wait for me?"

"Just as long as you promise not to make me move in with a crowd that has no TV, no Twinkies, and no K mart," Randy replied, deadpan. "But seriously, Katy, that's only a couple of years. What happens after that?"

"I don't really know, Randy. That depends on a lot of things. I might decide to go into teaching. Or I could do research, applying for grants and all that. Or, knowing me," she added with a grin, "I might turn around a hundred and eighty degrees and open up a catering business.

"What matters for right now is that I've decided to finish up what I started. That I'm not going to be afraid of failing—or succeeding, for that matter—because of this stupid inferiority complex I've been weighed down by for all these years, using it as a—a *crutch*, an excuse for not doing the stuff that everybody's afraid of, but that I've been just letting pass me by."

"Good for you. You know, as dumb as it sounds, I'm proud of you."

"It doesn't sound dumb, Randy. Not at all." Katy sighed. "You know, I feel fantastic. It's like I've finally given myself permission to let go of some of the stuff that's been dragging me down, getting in my way ever since I was a little kid. And all it took is the simple realization that I don't have to be Julie in order to be a deserving human being who's just as good as everybody else."

"For what it's worth, I sure am glad you're not Julie. I'm glad there's a Katy Gilbert in the world."

They stopped walking then, instead turning to face each other. All around them there was a calm beauty that Katy felt she had never bothered to appreciate before, that she had never even really seen: the fine clean sand, the turquoise water, the soft blue sky.

And above all there was Randy, who suddenly seemed to her even more of a miracle than anything else.

"Yeah," she said, her voice soft and husky, "and I'm glad there's a Randall Palmer."

Isn't this something? Katy thought with amusement as she turned her face up toward the sun and felt Randy's lips touch hers. For once in my life, I'm living a scene that's just like something out of the movies.

Chapter Thirty-Three

The Sunday before Labor Day, unofficially the last day of the last weekend of summer, was a disappointment. Instead of the intense sun and balmy breeze that beachgoers, sailors, and joggers had been counting on, feeling that they deserved one final taste of summer at its best, the day was overcast, its hazy grayness a warning that it was only going to get worse.

As if that weren't bad enough, there was something ominous in the air, an eerie stillness that couldn't quite be trusted, something reminiscent of the eye of a storm. At least that was what Beth was thinking as she sat cross-legged on the floor of her bedroom after lunch, playing with her little cousin Josh.

She had chosen to stay behind while most of the others went out to pursue one last bit of fun, to take their chances despite the uncooperative weather. Katy, Barbara, and Chrissie were playing tennis, hoping to get in a couple of sets before the rain descended upon them, completely spoiling whatever was left of the day. Wes and Julie, meanwhile, had taken their father up on his invitation for a round of golf. Her mother, Lynn, had gone off to Fedi's, wanting to pick up the ingredients for a picnic in anticipation of the next day's long car trip home. Even Pat was out, breaking away from her unending sense of duty to indulge in a leisurely walk on the beach with Michael.

Beth didn't regret her decision to stay behind, however,

297

declining all the invitations to join in that had been extended
politely by the various members of her family. Nor did she
mind being left more or less alone. She was used to that.
What was annoying was the fact that she felt as if she were
hiding, holed up in the bedroom with Josh and his "Sesame
Street" jigsaw puzzle even though the rest of the house was
empty.

Or, to be more accurate, it was *almost* empty. Downstairs,
in the living room, her uncle Brad was drinking away the
afternoon. She could hear the quiet clinking of the ice against
the side of his glass, the creak of the floor as he paced around
the room, and, now and then, his barely audible muttering.
And every few minutes, all those sounds intensified as he
went over to the bar to make himself still one more drink.

Not that she was scared. After all, Brad *was* her uncle. He
was family. Yet there was something about him sitting around
like that, acting so—so angry, that made her feel uncomfortable.

So it was easier just to stay put. And it looked as if that
were exactly what she'd be doing all afternoon—that is, until
Josh decided he wanted something to drink.

"Beth? I want juice."

Beth pretended she hadn't heard the little boy's request,
knowing that responding to it would require going down to
the kitchen and interrupting the boy's father—when it was
pretty clear to her that he was much better off just being left
alone. Instead, she bent over the puzzle, neatly fitting in the
orange piece that completed the face of the "Sesame Street"
character of Ernie.

"Look, Joshie! I did it! See, Ernie's all done. Now, let's
see if we can find the piece that will finish off Bert's shirt."

"I want juice. Apple juice. In the red *Superman* cup."

Beth eyed him uneasily. "Joshie, can't you wait? I'll bet
your mom will be home soon. . . ."

"I want juice! Juice!" Already the little boy had started to
cry, uncontrollably frustrated by having voiced a desire and not
having had it fulfilled within seconds.

"Joshie, can't you . . . ? Oh, okay." Despite her reluctance, Beth knew that there was no distracting him now. The
issue had become more than just a question of simple thirst. It
had instantly escalated to a battle of wills. And she was only
too aware that two-year-olds were hardly known for their
willingness to negotiate. "I'll get you some juice. You wait
here while I run downstairs to the kitchen."

"I want to come!" As if to demonstrate the sincerity of his demand, Josh threw his arms around her neck and clung to her tightly.

Beth sighed. "Okay, Josh. We'll just go down to the kitchen, get your juice out of the refrigerator, and come right back up here, okay?"

As soon as Josh spotted his father, however, Beth's hopes for a quick getaway dissolved. Brad was standing in front of the sliding glass doors that opened up onto the patio, gazing out.

Automatically, Beth, too, glanced outside. She saw that while the view from the patio doors was usually a scenic one, the kind of thing that unfailingly elicited oohs and aahs from first-time visitors to the house, today it was all pretty gray. Dreary, even. The sky was dark, the water choppy and uninviting. The houses across the bay, usually friendly and appealing, looked distant and forbidding, as if no intruder was welcome there today. The only thing that looked even remotely friendly were the two boats that were tied to the Gilberts' dock, the Sunfish and the Lightning. They stood out on this gray day, their white color oddly cheerful.

Beth saw Brad's face ease into an odd smile as he mumbled, "Hey, I didn't get a chance to go sailing once this whole summer. And tomorrow I'm going back to the city."

She realized then, watching him peer outside as if he were trying to see if there was actually any rain falling yet, that he hadn't heard them come into the room. In fact, it wasn't until Josh cried, "There's my daddy!" that he turned away from the window, startled—and, from what she could see, a little bit annoyed, as well.

"Daddy! Daddy!" Josh cried as he wrested himself from Beth's halfhearted grasp. He ran toward him, his blue eyes bright as he scrambled across the thick carpeting.

Brad's expression softened just a bit. "Hey, there's my little fella." He paused to set his drink down on a table, then crouched down and opened his arms.

Beth was just a few feet behind as Josh ran up and gave his father a big hug. "Hi, Uncle Brad. I was just going into the kitchen to get Josh some juice. Then we were going back upstairs to work on the "Sesame Street" puzzle we're doing." As if to make an excuse for the fact that she was spending the afternoon playing with her cousin, she added, "I'm babysitting him this afternoon, while Julie plays golf."

"Aw, you kids spend too much time indoors. But do you know what, Joshie? Your daddy just had a real brainstorm. How about going for a little sail? Want to go for a ride in a boat with Daddy?" Brad looked over at Beth. "You, too, Beth. How about it?"

She glanced out the sliding glass doors at the clouds above. Sure, it would be fun to go for a sail, even if it wasn't the nicest day of the summer. She hadn't been out once since she'd gotten here—no one had thought to invite her. On the other hand, the bad weather was making her just a little bit nervous.

"Are you sure, Uncle Brad? I mean, the weather isn't all that great today."

"Hey, why not? So what if it's not sunny? People go sailing in all kinds of weather. That's part of the fun."

She hesitated only a moment longer. "Okay, sure." After all, she decided, she didn't want her uncle to think she was a baby.

"Great. You can hold Josh while we're out on the water. Here, why don't you put a sweatshirt or something on him first? I'll meet you out at the dock. Move it, though. We don't have all day."

"Okay. I'll just get him some juice first. It'll only take a second. I'll have him back here in no time, I promise."

But Brad didn't seem to be listening.

By the time Beth came out to the dock, Josh skipping beside her excitedly, dressed for the outing in a sweatshirt and a pint-sized yellow slicker, Brad had the Lightning rigged. She glanced around uncertainly. Had it really gotten darker, or was she just imagining it?

"Are you sure about this, Uncle Brad? I mean, it really looks like it's gonna rain soon."

"Oh, come on. We have plenty of time before the rain," he growled. "Besides, a little rain never hurt anybody. Let's go."

Beth hesitated. She had to admit that she was a little bit scared. But if she refused to go, Brad might think she was accusing him of being careless. Besides, then Josh wouldn't be able to go, either. Next to her, he was jumping up and down, chirping, "Joshie go inna boat! Joshie go inna boat!" No, she couldn't back out. Not now.

"Okay. We're ready." She tried to sound cheerful as she handed the little boy to his father, then stepped onto the boat herself. As she slid past Brad, she could smell liquor on his breath. Without asking him, she reached under the deck and took out two life preservers. She put one on Josh first, then herself.

"Hold on, crew," Brad called over his shoulder heartily. "We're going to cast off!" As he released the last dock line, simultaneously tugging at the sail, the Lightning bolted away from the dock. "God, this is great, isn't it? What a feeling!"

Beth sat cross-legged on the floorboards, which seemed to her the safest place. Beside her, Josh's eyes were wide as he began to realize exactly what "going inna boat" entailed.

"Now you have to sit very, very still, Joshie," she said to him in a soft voice, hoping that Brad wouldn't overhear. "And you have to hold on very tight, okay? Don't let go. And stay close to me, no matter what. I'll look out for you. I promise."

She shivered slightly in the cool wind, telling herself that it was only early September and she had no excuse to be cold. As the Lightning headed out further into the bay, she watched the Gilberts' house growing smaller. The water was choppy enough to make the ride uncomfortable. Protectively she kept one arm firmly around Josh's tiny shoulders. With the other, she held on to the cockpit combing along the edge of the boat.

Brad sat alone at the stern, seeming to have forgotten all about the others. He was absorbed in adjusting the mainsail and admiring the speed with which the little boat was skimming the water, never once looking over to see how the children were doing. Occasionally he exclaimed, "Isn't this great? Nothing like a sail!" But even then, he seemed to be talking only to himself.

When a fat drop of rain fell on Beth's cheek, then another and another, she leaned over so that her face was very close to Josh's. "Don't worry, Joshie," she said quietly. "It'll be over soon. It's raining now, so we'll be going home in a little while."

"Want to go home *now*!" he demanded.

"I know. It's cold, and it's bumpy. . . . But I'm sure your daddy will start home soon."

But Brad was showing no signs of turning back. Instead, he continued on the same course, heading further out into the rough waters of the bay.

Beth was getting scared. She regretted her decision to go

along with her uncle, to put aside her own common sense in her effort to please him. Josh, meanwhile, had begun to whimper.

"Joshie *cold*! Joshie want to go home! I want Mommy. I want my mommy!"

"It's okay, honey. We'll go home soon. We'll see Mommy." In a much louder voice, she called, "Hey, Uncle Brad! Can we start back now? Joshie's getting cold!"

"I told you to put a sweater on him!"

"I did, but he's just a baby, and—"

"Aw, he's okay. Look, it's really starting to blow now. This is the kind of wind a Lightning was made for. We're really taking off! We can't stop now!"

Beth opened her mouth to argue further, but quickly snapped it shut. She didn't want to sound like she was whining. Besides, she had already realized that Brad wasn't about to listen to anything she had to say, anyway.

"Beth! Want go *home*! Want Mommy!" Josh was crying now, clinging to her in fear and misery. For his sake, if not her own, Beth knew she had to try a little bit harder. The rain was no longer just a drizzle. It was falling harder and harder, with no sign of stopping.

"Uncle Brad? We really have to go home. Look, Joshie's crying."

But before he had a chance to respond, there was a particularly strong gust of wind. He hurried to let the mainsail go—but it was too late. The poorly tended line at his feet snagged in the jam cleat, and his attempts at responding to the sudden change of wind were futile.

And then he was losing his balance. He tried to grab hold of something, but the boat was turning over and they all tumbled into the cold water.

"Whew! That was quite a game!" exclaimed Julie, storming into the kitchen with her younger brother and her father not far behind.

"I'll say. Boy, you really beat the pants off us, Dad!" Wes pulled open the door of the refrigerator and surveyed its contents. "Oh, good. There's some beer left. I guess summer's not quite over, after all. Want one, Dad? Julie? I think we all deserve something cold after a workout like that!"

"Thanks. I'll have a soda. That is, if there's any left."

"Here, try this on for size." Wes tossed a can of diet Pepsi to his sister, who had already plopped down into one of the kitchen chairs. "How about you, Ben?"

"Sure, son. I'll have a beer." Ben dropped into the chair opposite his daughter, admitting to himself that this was one of those times when he was feeling his age. "And don't think for a minute that I don't know that you two whippersnappers let this old codger win. What was that, anyway, your good-bye present to your old man?"

"Are you kidding? You won, Dad, fair and square," Julie insisted.

"That's right," Wes agreed. "And the strange part is that I'm really wiped out. Guess it was the stress." He leaned against the kitchen counter and greedily brought the icy can to his lips.

Ben took a more modest gulp of his beer. "Pooping out on me, are you? And here I was hoping I'd be able to talk you into helping me get the boats out of the water. You, too, Julie, I could use all the help I can get."

Wes sighed. "Well, sis, what do you say? I guess a little bit more exertion isn't going to hurt us. Especially if it's for such a good cause." He took a few more gulps of beer, then said thoughtfully, "You know, I've always found that that's kind of a sad thing to do. To me, putting the boats inside has always meant the real end of summer."

"I know what you mean," said Julie. "But I guess this really is the end, isn't it?"

Glancing over at her brother, she noticed that the mere mention of the fact that the arrival of tomorrow morning would mean climbing into the car and heading back to Boston, back to his real life, plunged Wes into a state of sadness. And she couldn't help feeling that his reaction was due to the tension between him and Barbara that she had seen all week. Even so, she didn't feel she could bring it up.

Besides, his expression had already changed, as if he had pushed whatever was upsetting him out of his mind. "Well, then," he said heartily, "let's get those boats." He set his half-finished beer down on the counter. "We might as well get them under cover before this rain gets any worse."

"Yup. It's really coming down now," Ben noted, glancing out the kitchen window. "Either of you want a slicker?"

"No, thanks," said Wes. "I'm waterproof."

"Me, too," Julie agreed. "Besides, I'll just jump in the shower the minute we're done."

When Ben and his two children crossed the living room on their way to the dock, however, they all noticed at the same time that the Lightning was no longer docked outside the house. From what they could see, it was gone.

Ben frowned. "What the . . . ? That Lightning couldn't have come untied, could it?"

"I don't think so," said Wes. "Mike and I were the last ones to take it out, and we're always pretty conscientious about tying up the boats."

His father still looked confused. "You don't suppose anybody was foolish enough to take a sailboat out on a day like today?"

"Nobody with any sense, anyway."

While Julie remained silent, her mind was already clicking away as she took a mental inventory of the members of her family. Barbara and the others had just come in from their rained-out tennis game and were upstairs changing. That let them out. Lynn was probably still at Fedi's. Minutes before, she had passed Mike and Pat on their way back from the beach.

That left Beth, who didn't know the first thing about sailing, and Josh . . . and Brad. Brad! No, even he would never try a stunt like that, not in weather like this!

"Oh, no," she breathed. Already she was halfway up the stairs, heading toward the second-floor deck, where she would be able to get a view of the water.

"Julie! Where are you going . . . ?" But even before Wes had asked the question, both her father and her brother understood. They bounded up the stairs, just a few steps behind her.

Sure enough, as soon as Julie reached the deck, she spotted the Lightning. It was way out in the middle of the bay, maybe half a mile away. Even through the mist, she could see that something was wrong.

"Oh, no!" she cried, only dimly aware that Wes was at her side, with Ben right behind him.

And then, all three of them realized within the same split second precisely what had happened.

"Holy shit," Wes breathed, already turning away. "The Lightning's capsized."

"Oh, my God!" Julie lingered at the railing only a moment, still filled with horror. The sight of the white underside of the small boat, reminding her of the vulnerable belly of an animal, filled her brain. What horrified her even more was the sight of the blurs of orange bobbing beside it, the bright color of life jackets that told them all the whole sickening scenario. Immediately she, too, was catapulted into action.

As she raced down the stairs, her brother was already way ahead of her, pulling off his sweater as he hurried across the living room toward the patio doors. While she struggled to keep up, Wes was faster than she was. Within seconds he had dashed outside and was heading down the beach, never missing a step.

Julie never lost sight of him. Her adrenaline was pumping violently as she raced along the sand trying to catch up with him, wanting to get as close to the boat as she could before ascertaining the best way for the three of them to attempt a rescue. The currents were in their favor, at least: from what she could tell, the Lightning appeared to be drifting closer to the beach.

Finally she managed to catch up with Wes when he had reached a point at which the capsized boat was only a hundred yards or so offshore. He had stopped, and was struggling to catch his breath.

"God, Wes, what should we do?" Julie cried, frantic. Her own boating experience and training told her that the safest plan would be to go over to the Burtises' house and borrow their motorboat. But if her suspicions were correct, if it was, indeed, her little Josh who was out there, in doing that they could be losing precious seconds.

"Get a boat," Wes barked, his thoughts obviously having followed the same path. "I'll go out and keep them all afloat."

"Wes! You can't do that by yourself!"

At that moment, Ben caught up with them both. In a breathless voice, he demanded, "Who is it? Can you see yet?"

"I'm pretty sure it's Brad," Wes called over his shoulder. "And he may have Beth and Josh with him."

"Oh, my God!" Ben exclaimed.

But Wes didn't hear him. He had already jumped into the water and begun swimming as fast as he could, never once looking back toward the shore to see how far he had come. The few times Julie did see him come up, it was only long enough to make sure he was headed in the right direction and to see how much further he had to go.

Watching from the shore, she could see that it was a struggle wrestling with the waves and battling the current. She was just glad that her brother was young and in such good physical shape.

But his swimming out like that was only half the battle. She turned and began running toward the Burtises' house, hell-bent on getting ahold of their motorboat. She concentrated on doing just that, not even for a moment daring to let herself think about how terrified she was.

It seemed to Beth an eternity before the swimmer finally got close enough for her to be certain that it was, indeed, something real, and not just something she had invented in her nearly hysterical state.

Yes, she decided, finally willing to believe what she was seeing, he's real.

As she watched the figure swimming steadily toward her, she felt a great surge of relief. At the same time, however, she felt afraid in a different way. She and Josh were so close to being rescued . . . yet what if she couldn't hold on? What if she panicked, or found that she was too weak to keep going?

But for now, at least, she was still all right. She had managed so far, and she was strong enough to last a little bit longer, she insisted to herself as she bobbed up and down in the hostile waves. Her face was stricken with exhaustion and fear, her eyes wild, her lips blue. She held onto the side of the boat, keeping one hand around the ankle of the terrified Josh, perched on top. Despite the hellishness of the situation, however, she knew she was managing to appear perfectly calm, keeping up a running monologue for the little boy's benefit.

"See, Joshie?" she cooed, her eyes fixed on the approaching swimmer even as she never stopped talking to the little boy. "I told you someone would be coming for us right away. Here comes Uncle Wes. He's going to save us. He'll get you home before you know it, and you'll see your Mommy."

"Thank *Christ*!" The sound of Brad's voice came as kind of a shock to Beth. In her attempt at concentrating on Josh, she had almost forgotten about him. But there he was, over on the other side of the boat, his look of despair already becoming one of great relief. "We're all okay. I couldn't pull in both kids, so I just waited. . . . Hell, I didn't know what to do."

"I'll leave you to fend for yourself, Brad," Wes called. By now he had reached the boat and, like Beth, was holding on to the side. "Are you okay?" he asked the little girl, looking at her searchingly and then studying Josh with the same concern. "It looks like you've got everything under control."

"We're okay, Uncle Wes," Beth replied through chattering teeth. "But please, get us out of here."

"I'll do just that," Wes returned in a soothing voice, "just as soon as I figure out how to do that single-handedly."

"Hey, isn't anybody getting a boat?" Brad demanded. "I don't think I'm strong enough to get back on my own."

Beth glanced at Wes and saw a look of anger and disgust on his face that she had never seen before.

But his voice remained controlled. "Julie's trying to get a boat, but I don't know if she'll be able to." Wes looked at Josh, then at Beth, then back at Josh again. "I could get one of you back to shore," he said, "but since there are two of you . . ."

And then, suddenly, they all heard a calm voice say, "Here we go, Joshie. Come to Grandpa. That's it. There's my boy."

Beth blinked, not really believing what she was seeing. Yet she knew it was true—and, understanding that now it was going to be all right, she found herself nearly collapsing with gratitude that it was. Ben had swum up behind Wes at a slower pace but with enough strength and steadiness to cover the entire distance. Now he was taking the frightened little boy into his arms, already positioning him to be towed back to shore.

And then the sound of a motor, accompanied by excited yelling, prompted them all to turn around. They were greeted by a most welcome sight: Julie heading toward them in the Burtises' small motorboat, with Barbara already preparing to drop a rope overboard so that the children, and then the others, could climb aboard.

Deftly Julie pulled the motorboat up alongside the capsized Lightning and, with Ben's assistance, pulled the terrified Josh aboard. She clasped him closely against her, suddenly succumbing to violent sobs even as she tried to comfort her baby and stop his tears.

Next, it was Beth's turn. She didn't realize how exhausted every one of her muscles was until she collapsed on the hard wooden floor of the motorboat, too tired to cry.

Once both children were inside the boat, and Brad was making his way slowly to its side, Wes turned his attention to his father, still treading water beside him.

"My God, Ben! Whatever possessed you?" he scolded, only now fully appreciating the risk his father had just taken. "A man your age—"

"Save it, Wes," Ben interrupted. " 'A man my age?' Hell, I've never felt better in my life."

Chapter Thirty-Four

It wasn't until early that evening that the Gilbert household finally settled down. Once everyone had returned safely to shore, the entire family had gathered around to inspect the children. Then, Michael and his family, as well as Julie and Josh, headed over to Greenport Hospital's emergency room.

"Josh and Beth are both fine," Lynn reported to Pat over the telephone a few hours later, her voice tremulous with relief. "They're still a little bit shaken, of course, but the doctors have assured us that there's nothing to worry about."

"Thank God!" Pat breathed, her response communicating to all the others listening to her end of the conversation as they waited together anxiously in the living room for the doctors' report, that the children had survived the accident without injury.

"We're going to stay here on the North Fork and have dinner," Lynn continued. "Maybe it'll help get the kids' minds off things a little bit."

Once the children had received a clear bill of health, Brad took it upon himself to vanish. He had changed out of his clothes first thing, then holed up in his room. As soon as Lynn's telephone call came, however, he got in his car and just took off, without saying a word to anyone. It was just as well: while everyone had quite a bit they would have loved to say to him, none of them was about to take the liberty of doing so.

An angry silence continued to hover in the house. Those who had stayed behind lay low, preferring to be alone for the rest of the day, staying in their bedrooms or talking together quietly, as if someone in the house were ill or sleeping.

Barbara, however, took advantage of the relative quiet by staking out the living room. She lit a fire in the fireplace, not only to ward off the day's chill, but also in an attempt at banishing the emotional iciness that permeated her bones. She couldn't seem to banish the vision of those small children in the water, Beth bobbing up and down, Josh perched precariously upon an overturned boat with her husband floundering beside him, that look of desperation on his face. Even now, even sitting inches away from the fire, it made her shiver just to think about it.

She poured herself a glass of red wine, wrapped one of Pat's hand-crocheted afghans around her shoulders, and sank into the corner of the couch. She just stared at the fire, mindlessly sipping her wine and thinking. Then, all of a sudden, she sprang up and headed upstairs, knowing exactly what she needed to do.

She found her husband sitting in a comfortable chair, holding an open book in his lap but gazing out the window. There was a glazed look in his eyes, as if his thoughts were anywhere but in this room.

"Busy?" Barbara asked by way of a greeting.

Wes glanced over at her, startled by the unexpected intrusion. "Oh, hi, Barbara. I was just . . . reading."

"So I see. Feel like some company?"

He looked surprised by her invitation. More than that, he was pleased to see her leaning in the doorway, her expression tender, with just the hint of a question in her eyes. Her long black hair with its rich red highlights was loose, cascading down around her shoulders. She was wearing jeans and a baggy oatmeal-colored sweater. It was one of the rare occasions on which she looked soft, vulnerable . . . approachable.

"I'd love some company," he replied. "Pull up a chair."

"Why don't you come downstairs? I've got a fire going in the fireplace, and I opened a bottle of wine."

He followed her downstairs, then sat down on the couch.

"Now, how about some of this wine?"

"No, thanks. Maybe in a while."

"Okay." She picked up her own glass, then sat down on the couch, a safe distance away. Then, after a moment's hesitation, she slid over next to Wes and nestled her head against his shoulder.

She was more than a little relieved when he put his arm around her and drew her even closer. She set her wine down and snuggled next to him. They were comfortable and relaxed, both of them aware that it had been quite a while since the last time they had sat together this way.

"So you and Ben turned out to be real heroes," Barbara said lightly, her eyes fixed on the flickering flames of the fire.

Beside her, she could feel Wes stiffen. "That bastard. I feel like—I don't know what I feel like doing to that brother-in-law of mine, but something terrible, believe me. I can't understand for the life of me why Julie puts up with a jerk like him."

"Hey, it's over." The gentleness in her voice immediately had a calming effect on him. She could feel him relax once again.

"Yeah, I guess you're right. At least Beth and Josh are okay. Boy, if that had been my kid that idiot took out on a sailboat on a day like today, not to mention in the condition he was in—"

"Wes, there's something that you and I have to talk about."

She could feel him shrinking away from her, not physically, but psychologically, quickly putting up an emotional shield to protect himself from whatever she was about to say. Not that she blamed him. In fact, for the first time since she had decided to leave, she understood exactly what he was going through, and felt those very same feelings of loss and sorrow herself.

Telling him how she felt, however, would be another matter entirely.

"I—I know this has been a hard period for you, Wesley, that you haven't understood what's been going on with me. . . . Or maybe what I should say is that I haven't let you understand." She bit her lip, keeping her eyes fixed on the fire, unable to look at him. "It's just that . . . you and I have been drifting along together for years, playing the role of the perfect couple, living together happily ever after and all that. We've never had to stop and think about what it means, what it *really* means, to make a commitment." She shrugged. "Up until now, it's as if you and I have just been playing house."

"Playing house?" Wes sounded hurt and angry. "I certainly never thought of it that way. I believed that when we took those wedding vows, as corny as they may be, that they really meant something. At least, I know that they did to me.''

Barbara paused. "I know. They did to me, too. At least, I thought they did. But I never realized until recently just how afraid I really was, underneath it all. I always figured that if things didn't work out between us, I could just walk away.''

"Is that what you wanted? A way out, just in case? And here I thought that you and I had always been pretty happy together.''

"Yes, we were. We *are*. But I needed to know I had an out, if I ever needed it. It was as if I had some kind of emotional claustrophobia. It isn't that I ever actually wanted to leave, but I wanted to know that I could if sooner or later I changed my mind.''

"Oh, yeah? So what happened?'' Wes demanded coldly. "How come you suddenly decided that you needed to go flying out the door?''

"Because,'' Barbara replied, trying to keep her voice calm, "all of a sudden, it wasn't so simple. It was more than just trying it out, seeing if it would work. It became a commitment to a family, to a life together, one that would go on forever. I—I guess I just panicked. I'm not saying that I was right, just that that's how I reacted.''

Wes was growing impatient, and he had no qualms about letting it show. "Look, I'm afraid I don't get it, Barbara,'' he said, folding his arms across his chest. "It's been a long day, and after all that's happened, I'm not exactly in the mood for riddles. Why don't you just say whatever it is you're trying to say?''

She sat up straight, pulling away from him so that they were no longer touching. "Wes, I'm pregnant.''

He looked over at her with wide eyes, her words not registering at first. And then, once he realized what she had said, he wasn't sure if she was serious.

"What?'' His voice was nothing more than a whisper.

"It's true, Wes. Dr. Cadman confirmed it a few weeks ago. On my birthday, as a matter of fact. Of course, I'd suspected for a while, but I didn't want to believe it. . . . I was too scared to believe it.'' She blinked hard, banishing the tears that were blurring her vision. "All of a sudden, everything changed. It became so real, so serious. It wasn't just a game anymore. The days of 'playing house' were over.''

"Barbara, I—I don't know what to say. A baby! That's—that's such wonderful news!'' Gradually, Wes's confusion was giving way to a rush of happiness, happiness so profound, so overwhelming, that it was unlike anything he had ever experienced before.

"I've been so frightened,'' Barbara continued, spurred on by his positive reaction to the news she had been so frightened of sharing with him. "I've been so ambivalent. I wanted to tell you. It was all I could do not to tell you. But first I wanted to figure out how I really felt about it . . . and know, for sure, whether or not I could really go through with it.

"And then today, after the Lightning capsized, when I rode up with Julie in the motorboat, my heart was in my mouth. All I knew was that there had been some kind of boating accident, and that you'd been involved in it somehow. . . .''

It was all she could do to keep from sobbing as she struggled to go on. "Oh, Wes! I was so afraid that something had happened to you! It was as if until that moment I had never realized just how much I loved you. And then when I saw little Josh sitting there on the boat, looking so cold and so scared, I felt such a strong pull toward him, and toward our own baby. I felt so protective, in a way I never have before, not toward anyone. I guess that was the first moment I realized how it would feel to have a child of my own to love. And I knew then how badly I want us to be a family. The three of us . . . you, me, and our baby.''

Without a word, Wes reached over and took her in his arms. They clung to each other for the first time since that day at the beach when he'd seen fear in her eyes.

Now, when he pulled back to look at her, he saw love.

"A baby, huh?'' he whispered. "I'm going to be a father?''

Barbara just nodded, a small, uncertain smile on her lips.

"Wow. A father. Me, a daddy.''

She laughed, partly from the relief she was still experiencing, partly from joy.

"And what about you? You're going to be a mother! A mommy!''

"I know. It does sound kind of funny, doesn't it?''

"Naw, it doesn't sound funny at all.'' Wes's face lit up in a tremendous grin. "As a matter of fact, if you ask me, it sounds pretty damned terrific.''

*   *   *

Even though it was late and the house was quiet, Lynn was still awake, too keyed up to sleep. The events of the day replayed over and over again in her mind, like a videotape that automatically rewound itself the moment it was finished and started up all over again.

As she had returned home from Fedi's, she was innocently lost in thought ruminating over nothing more important than the two bags of groceries she was hauling, wondering how many sandwiches to make for her family's picnic lunch for the trip home the following day. And she had walked in and found the entire household in chaos. A capsized boat that was the result of her brother-in-law's deplorable judgment; her younger daughter up to her neck in cold choppy water for a frighteningly long time; her nephew, still a mere baby, kept alive by a terrified thirteen-year-old girl.

And then a frantic trip to the emergency room over in Greenport, the endless waiting for the doctors' report. . . . None of it seemed real to her, somehow; yet at the same time, she knew she would be haunted by the memory of this day for the rest of her life.

But the horror of the boating accident was only one of the reasons she was finding it impossible to fall asleep tonight. There was something else on her mind, something she had been mulling over for a full two weeks now, ever since the night she had arrived here at Ben and Pat's house. During her whole stay here, she had been pondering it, carrying on a nonstop internal debate, not able to put it out of her mind for even a moment.

And now, she had to make a decision, once and for all. Tomorrow she and Michael and the girls were leaving Shelter Island, all the members of the Gilbert family going their own separate ways. Summer would be over. This unique time, a time when all of them had forgotten their differences and instead struggled to remind themselves of their blood ties, would be nothing more than a memory.

If she waited any longer, it would be too late.

She knew she would find Ben downstairs, that he, too, would be unable to sleep tonight. She was right; when she wrapped herself up in her pink bathrobe and went downstairs, she discovered that he was sitting alone in the living room, watching the fire that Barbara had built earlier that day burn itself out.

"Excuse me, Ben," she said softly, not wanting to startle him. "Mind if I join you?"

He turned around, the expression on his face showing that while he was surprised by this unexpected late night visitor, he was pleased to have some company.

"Lynn! Are you still awake? Well, of course, I'd love it if you joined me. Come on in and pull up a cushion." Gesturing toward the fire with his chin, he added by way of explanation, "You know, lately I can't seem to manage to fall asleep knowing there's still a fire burning in the house. I guess that once you get to be my age, you figure it's your job to worry about things like that."

Lynn chuckled, then said seriously, "Do you really expect me to believe that's the only thing keeping you awake, after all that happened today?"

"Well, you've got a point there. I guess I do have a lot on my mind." He sighed deeply. "Thank God those kids are all right."

Lynn nodded. "In a way, I think it's good that we're all going home tomorrow. Hopefully getting away from here will help Beth get over it faster."

"Yes, I suppose so. Are you and Michael planning to leave early?"

"I think we'll have to, if we want to avoid the worst part of the Labor Day traffic."

"That's the smart thing to do." Ben thought for a few seconds. "You know, I've been sitting here thinking that there's a fair chance this could be the last time I'll have you all together like this. My entire family, under one roof."

"Oh, no," Lynn protested, knowing even as she did that he was right. "We all had such a good time, I'm sure everyone will want to get together again as soon as we can. Maybe even for Christmas."

"Well, tomorrow it'll all be over. You'll all go off, taking with you all your little secrets and inside jokes and all those parts of your lives that I, as a parent, will never be privy to."

"Children grow up," Lynn said gently. "They move on to their own lives, their own families. It's all part of the never-ending cycle."

"I know. But I still feel as if there's something unfinished. There are so many things that a father yearns to say to his children, but either he doesn't have the words to express himself, or else he doesn't dare to. He's too afraid of being misunderstood. Or what's even worse, discounted." He shrugged. "But I guess all that's just part of the deal, isn't it?"

"Yes. Even so, you're right; it is a little sad. Separations always are."

"So," Ben said, his tone suddenly brisk, as if wanting to move on to a more cheerful topic, "I guess in a couple more days, Beth and Chrissie will be back in school, Mike'll be back at work . . . and what about you, Lynn? Where does all that leave you?"

"It's funny you should ask," Lynn replied in a strange voice. "That's exactly what I've been wanting to talk to you about."

Ben looked at her quizzically. "Me? What do I have to do with it?"

Lynn proceeded slowly, measuring each of her words with great care. "Ben, I don't believe I've ever asked you for anything."

"Lynn," he interjected, only half teasing, "I'm pretty well aware that you're the kind of person who finds it hard to ask anybody for anything."

"Maybe so. But I'm about to ask you for something. And, well, I hope that before you turn me down, you'll think about it, at least a little bit."

Ben frowned. "All right. I promise to give serious consideration to whatever you say."

"Good. Okay, here goes." She took a deep breath. "Ben, I want to take over the family business. Learn it all, from the bottom up, and one day be the one to fill your shoes as president of B.G.A."

His eyebrows immediately shot up.

"Wait." Lynn held up her hands. "Before you say no, let me finish."

"I'm listening."

She stood up then and began pacing around the living room, gesturing histrionically as she spoke. "It's not as crazy as it sounds. Think about it. I've got some business training; I was a bookkeeper, after all. And I've had some art training, too. Surely something like that's bound to come in handy. . . .

"Okay, maybe neither of those are much, and that part of my life was a long time ago. But you know I'm someone you can trust. And I'm willing to learn, and I promise you that I'd work really hard.

"Besides," she went on with a self-conscious laugh, "I need a job. Not only because of . . . well, let's just say because of some financial problems that Michael and I have run into lately, but also because I've come to realize that if I go back to a life of staying at home all day, staring at the dust forming on the coffee table and watching soap operas whose plots I can't even follow, I'm going to go . . ."

She stopped pacing and turned to face her father-in-law. "Ben," she demanded indignantly, "why on earth are you laughing?"

"Because, Lynn," Ben replied with a chuckle, "I think you're wonderful. And I think your idea is fantastic."

"You do?" Lynn blinked.

"Yes, I do. It's the perfect solution. And do you know what? I could kick myself for not having thought of it myself! I guess it just never occurred to me that you'd even be interested in learning to run B.G.A."

"To tell you the truth," Lynn said sheepishly, "it never occurred to me, either. At least, not until you mentioned that you were looking for a replacement. That's what got me started thinking about the company . . . and myself. Where I was going—or maybe I should say where I *wasn't* going."

Ben just nodded. "You know, you're a strong woman, Lynn. Stronger than you think. I've always known that about you. I even wondered at times if my own son was smart enough to see it. And, yes, I agree that you're the perfect choice for my replacement."

"Really? You're serious?" Now that the whole thing seemed to have been decided—more easily and certainly more quickly than she ever would have dreamed—Lynn was positively gleeful. "Oh, Ben, I know I'll do a good job!"

"It's going to mean long hours, you know. And the commute to New York City from Lawrenceville is going to be at least a good hour, every single day."

"I know. But I already talked to Julie, and she agreed that I could spend a night or two at her place every week."

Speaking almost to herself, she went on. "I think it'll be good for the girls to have a little break from their mother, too. Especially Beth. She needs to start developing some independence. Having to make some decisions on her own will help her grow up a little bit."

Thoughtfully, she added, "Maybe if she'd had the guts to

say no to Brad today, that stupid boating accident would never have happened.''

"Now, now. Don't go blaming Beth."

Lynn looked up at her father-in-law, surprised. "I'm not blaming her, Ben. Not for a minute. I'm blaming myself. Somehow, I've never managed to instill in her a sense of her own self-worth. Maybe because I've never really had very much of my own. I realize now that in that way, I've been failing her. Even that business with the disappearing jewelry . . . it's just one more example. I really think that by giving her a little room to breathe, by forcing her to start making her own way in the world a little bit, instead of trying to protect her all the time, I'll be helping her in the long run.

"That goes for Chrissie, too. I know she puts on a good act. But for all her showing off, underneath all the makeup and the trendy clothes, she's really just a scared little girl."

"You know, Lynn, this is all working out so well. I'm just tickled that you're interested in coming into the family business. In fact, I'm so thrilled that I'm tempted to wake everyone in the house and tell them."

Lynn laughed. "Somehow, Ben, I don't think they'd appreciate your enthusiasm at this hour."

"No, I guess you're right." Ben let out a deep sigh. "I have every confidence that this is one decision that I'm never going to regret. And do you know why that is?"

Lynn just looked at him with wide eyes and shook her head.

"Because," said Ben with a knowing smile, "you, Lynn McGoldrick Gilbert, happen to be a very wise woman."

Chapter Thirty-Five

"*W*here's my blue bathing suit? Has anybody seen my blue bathing suit?" Chrissie's voice, emanating from one of the bedrooms upstairs, was a nearly hysterical shriek.

"Try the dryer," Pat called back from downstairs in the living room. "Or maybe I put it in Julie's room by mistake. . . ."

"Whose socks are these? They're sure not mine!" Another voice rang through the house.

"Should we take the sheets off our beds?"

"Where do you want these used towels, Mom?"

And then, a plaintive wail from somewhere in the upper reaches of the house: "Oh, no! I'm *never* gonna get all this stuff to fit in my suitcase!"

Throughout the household, the Gilberts were scurrying about, preparing to leave, getting ready to make the transition back to real life. It was Labor Day, the end of the summer. Some of them were by now impatient to get back, while others were reluctant to leave behind what had, after all, been a refreshing respite.

Wes and Barbara were the first to leave, packing up the car early, claiming that the six-hour trip back to Boston was bound to take at least eight, what with all the holiday traffic. They had never before looked quite as happy as they did that morning. Wes was beside himself, totally delighted by the news he had so gleefully reported to the others the night before, the announcement that he was going to be a father. Meanwhile, Barbara was glowing as the others all gathered around, congratulating her and wishing her the best.

Michael and his family began their own preparations for departure soon afterward, with Michael hurrying them along all the while, expressing concerns about Labor Day traffic that were similar to Wes's. Finally they, too, were ready to go.

"Hey, Dad, thanks a lot." As he stood by the front door, with one arm around his wife and the other resting on Beth's shoulder, Michael's dark eyes glistened. "You, too, Mom."

"It was so lovely to have you, Michael, dear." Pat leaned forward and gave him a big wet kiss on the cheek. "It was lovely to have all of you. Chrissie, too—wherever she is."

"Yes, where *is* she?" Michael wondered, glancing at the staircase with some annoyance.

"Lynn, don't forget that you and I have an appointment next Monday at nine sharp. My office. Or," Ben added with a conspiratorial wink, "I guess I should say *your* office!"

Lynn smiled. "All right, Ben. I'll be there, raring to go."

"I should certainly hope so!" Pat cried. "Joining the family firm is no small thing!"

Instead of being insulted, this time Lynn turned to her mother-in-law and smiled. "Don't worry, Pat. I'm not going to let you and Ben down. You've got my word on it."

Just then Chrissie came bounding down the stairs looking distraught. "Mo-o-om, I still can't find my blue bathing suit! I looked everywhere!"

"Relax, Chrissie. I packed it already," said Lynn. "I found it in the bathroom, curled up in a tiny ball in the corner, underneath a towel."

"Oh, yuck!" Beth wrinkled up her nose in disgust. "I bet it had *mold* or something growing all over it."

"It did not!" Chrissie was indignant.

"Huh! I bet it did!"

"Come on, girls. Chill out," pleaded Michael. "We've still got a long drive ahead of us. Lynn, I don't suppose you packed any earplugs . . . ?"

"Daddeee!"

Beth turned to her grandmother. "By the way, if Danny Burtis asks you for my address, it's okay to give it to him."

"Oh, brother!" Chrissie rolled her eyes upward as her father ushered her out the door.

Katy was outside, loading up her car. She, too, was on the way out. She would be leaving with pretty much what she had brought, with one addition: a photograph of herself at age thirteen—plump, sloppily dressed in a sweatshirt and a worn-out pair of jeans, wearing a big grin—a reminder of the little girl who was so full of dreams and plans for her future.

" 'Bye, Michael.'' She slammed the hatchback door of the Rabbit, then turned to give her brother a big hug. "Take care of all your females.''

Michael grinned. "Yeah, more likely they'll be taking care of me.''

Katy turned to her niece. "Now don't forget, Beth. You're coming to see me Christmas week, remember? I'm taking you to Times Square on New Year's Eve.''

"Okay!'' Beth's blue eyes were shining. "There's one thing, though. . . . Is it okay if I bring my boyfriend? If I have one by then, I mean,'' she was quick to add.

Katy laughed. "If his mother lets him. But you can tell her that there'll be a male chaperone present at all times. And he's a pretty responsible, trustworthy guy. I mean, he's a *banker*, for heaven's sake!''

Julie watched from her bedroom window as the blue Mercedes and the white Rabbit pulled out of the driveway. It was almost time for her to be on her way as well, heading back to the city with Josh and Brad. The suitcases were all packed, Josh's toys were in the trunk of the car, all the accessories needed for a long auto trip with a small child were in place. But first, there was one more thing she had to do.

She found Paul exactly where she expected him to be: at the town dock, readying the *Scheherazade* for a day's outing. She was taken aback only for a moment when she saw that there was someone else on board, a pretty young woman with liquid brown eyes, closely cropped chestnut hair, and a shy smile, who was carrying two large grocery bags. She just had to be Susan.

"Julie! What are you doing here?'' Paul looked as pleased as he was confused when he spotted her. "I thought you were leaving this morning.''

"I am, in about half an hour. But I wanted to talk to you one more time.'' She glanced over at Susan who, after giving her a friendly nod, gestured that she had her hands full and then retreated inside the cabin. "I've thought a lot about the conversation we had the other day, and I . . . Well, I realized that I owe you both an apology and a thank-you, Paul.''

"Really? What for?"

"As far as the apology goes, let's just say that over these past two weeks, I've been using you, in a way.''

He was still puzzled. "I don't get it.''

Julie gazed out at the tranquil water of Dering Harbor. "I was unhappy, Paul. I had been for a long time. But I was afraid to admit just *how* unhappy I was . . . or to take a really serious look at why.

"Then, when I ran into you again, I was forced to remember some of my dreams. To think about what I had once wanted—expected, even—from a marriage." She bit her lip. "Everything you said I was doing."

Then she smiled sadly. "I guess that day we were out on your boat, I began to wish that our running into each other again, after all these years, would end up like one of those Scheherazade stories. You know: romance, intrigue . . .'' Her voice cracked, but she went on. "And, of course, a happy ending."

Julie shrugged. "And maybe, like Scheherazade, what I was trying to do was save my own life.''

"Nobody could ever blame you for that," Paul said softly.

"Maybe. But wait; there's more. The way I used you was by fantasizing about you and me getting back together again, about having you replace Brad." She hesitated. "That's when I began to realize how much I needed to get Brad out of my life.''

She turned to face him. "I've decided to leave him, Paul. I realized the last time I saw you that that was what I wanted to do. But it wasn't until yesterday that I was certain I'd actually have the strength to do it.''

"Have you told him yet?"

She shook her head. "No. I'll tell him tonight, as soon as we get back to the city. Which brings me to the thank-you I owe you. If it hadn't been for you, the way you bothered to understand me so completely—''

Paul stopped her by placing his finger lightly against her lips. "No 'thank-yous,' no 'I'm sorrys.' You don't owe me anything, Julie.''

She laughed self-consciously. "And here I've been feeling that I owe you so much.''

"I haven't done anything that you wouldn't have done by

yourself, sooner or later. You're the one who deserves all the credit, not me. You've got a lot of courage, Julie. Don't ever forget it.''

''I won't.''

As she turned to leave, Paul reached out and grasped her arm. ''Hey, Julie?''

''Yes?'' She turned back and was surprised by the intensity in his eyes.

''Don't ever forget me, either,'' he said in a hoarse voice. ''Okay?''

''No, Paul,'' she replied. ''I won't forget you. Not ever.''

Epilogue

The Greenport offices of Dr. Robert Barnes, cardiologist, were not at all what Ben was used to. Those few times he'd stopped by his buddy Dave Jennings's office, back in Harrington, he'd sat in a homey waiting room with dark wood paneling and Early American furniture.

Dr. Barnes's office was another story altogether. It reminded Ben of a hospital, with its clean, simple lines. No personal signature here, no well-worn magazines on the mock-colonial end tables, no granddaughter's finger paintings decorating the walls. Here, everything was modern and impersonal: glass and chrome furniture, dove gray carpeting, bright posters of museum exhibits. Even the magazines were slick, he noted as he glanced at the covers of the latest issues of *Geo* and *Psychology Today* on the coffee table in front of him.

So Ben was more than a little relieved to find that Dr. Barnes himself did not make him uncomfortable. Though considerably younger than Ben and very self-assured, the doctor was not at all pompous. It was a combination that was guaranteed to inspire both confidence and respect in his patients, even a reluctant first-timer like Ben.

"Interesting." Dr. Barnes frowned as he studied the results of the lab tests that had just been performed by one of his nurses, a young woman with an identical no-nonsense manner, the same assured way of doing things. Now, with the physical examinations completed, the two men were sitting in

Dr. Barnes's office, a large room with the same streamlined feeling as the waiting room. "The EKG shows no sign of a heart attack."

"But that's impossible," Ben protested. "I tell you, last June, while I was out jogging—"

"Tell me about it again, Mr. Gilbert. Start at the beginning. You were out running . . ."

"Right. It was early in the morning. I had run about two miles, when all of a sudden I felt a stabbing pain in my chest. I lost my breath, I doubled over. I was sure it was a heart attack."

"But you didn't see a doctor."

"Well, I . . ." Ben was sheepish. "Look, Dr. Barnes, when you get to be my age, there are some things you don't want to hear about. Especially from a doctor."

"I see. So what prompted you to come see me today?"

"Two days ago, Sunday, there was a boating accident right outside my summer place, over on Shelter Island. I swam a pretty good distance in some rough water—and it didn't faze me. I found out I wasn't so fragile—so *old*—after all." He shrugged. "Once I came to the conclusion that I was probably pretty healthy, I decided to have it verified by a pro."

Dr. Barnes closed the file that housed Ben's medical records. "Tell me a little bit about yourself, Mr. Gilbert. Not just the medical facts—I've already got all that, right here." He gestured toward the manila folder on his desk.

"Let's see. I've always been pretty healthy. In college I was on the swimming team my first couple of years. Then I got interested in track. I was quite a star," he couldn't resist boasting. "Broke my school's record for long-distance running. Of course, all that ended when I got an injury. Bruised my neck and shoulder pretty bad. They healed amazingly fast, but even so that kind of put a damper on things. Anyway, that was all a long time ago."

"Tell me more."

"Well, since then I've tried to stay in shape. None of those fad diets or exercise kicks for me. I had always been involved in athletics, so I knew how to maintain a fairly healthy life-style. Kept my weight down, stayed active. Then, fifteen years ago, I took up the jogging. Insurance against the approach of old age, I suppose." Ben smiled. "See that? I guess I wasn't completely immune to what I saw on TV and read about in the magazines, after all."

Dr. Barnes returned the smile, but it faded as quickly as it had appeared. Ben could see that his mind was clicking away, already moving on to other territory.

"Mr. Gilbert, I think I understand what happened to you back in June. It sounds to me like that old track injury of yours was behind what you thought was a heart attack. I suspect that a pinched nerve in your neck or your shoulder acted up, giving you the same kinds of symptoms someone would experience from heart failure. Given your history, as well as the results of your tests, it all seems to add up."

Ben sat very still, having not yet fully digested the doctor's diagnosis.

"Wait a minute. Let me make sure I've got this straight. What you're saying, then, is that I didn't have a heart attack."

"That's right. From what I can see, you're as fit as a fiddle. It was nothing more than a false alarm, another condition entirely fooling you into thinking you'd had a heart attack.

"There's nothing wrong with you, Mr. Gilbert. I just hope that when I'm your age, I'm in such good shape." Dr. Barnes smiled warmly, for the first time allowing something of himself to emerge. "Come back in six months for another checkup. In the meantime, keep on doing whatever it is you've been doing."

He stood up then, paused only long enough to shake Ben's hand, then hurried out of his office, already thinking about his next patient.

Outside, the streets of Greenport were quiet. Ben strolled toward his car at a leisurely pace. He was still feeling a bit dazed, but not so much so that he didn't take the time to breathe in the fresh salty air.

The very mood of the seaport town had changed. The summer people were gone, having taken with them the feeling that real life had been suspended for a while. The stationery store window now displayed spiral notebooks and pens for kids going back to school; sweaters and sturdy shoes had replaced the sundresses and sandals of the clothing shops; the hardware store was already featuring a variety of rakes for the inevitable onslaught of autumn leaves.

As Ben drove back to the ferry, his senses were strangely alert, heightened to a new degree. Eagerly he took in everything around him, seeing it all with a new appreciation. He noticed things, little things, he had never taken the time to see before. The beauty of the sun on the water; the charming trim on the Victorian houses; the friendly smiles of the people he passed, going about their business as if it were simply another day. Above all, he found himself relishing the feeling of just being alive.

Yes, summer was over, and a new season was about to begin. The kids were back home, scattered north, west, and south, already involved in their own lives once again, no doubt having picked up the pieces so smoothly that it was almost as if they hadn't even been away.

As for Ben, it was time for him to get back home himself. This afternoon, he would put up the storm windows while Pat packed. Then, tomorrow morning, after one final check around the house, it would be time to head for home.

As always, he would hesitate before leaving, taking a moment to review some of his fonder memories of the summer and to wish it didn't have to end. But before long, he would join Pat in the car, his mind already shifting to the future, gradually letting go of the past, no matter how sweet it may have been. After all, he would remind himself with a smile so secretive that even his wife wouldn't notice it, he had his own life to get back to.

About the Author

CYNTHIA BLAIR grew up on Long Island, earned her B.A. from Bryn Mawr College in Pennsylvania, and went on to get an M.A. in business from M.I.T. After a four-year stint of writing part-time while working as a Marketing Manager, she abandoned the corporate life in order to concentrate on her novels. She has had more than twenty published, including Young Adult books such as THE BANANA SPLIT AFFAIR, THE DOUBLE DIP DISGUISE, and THE POPCORN PROJECT.

Ms. Blair lives on Long Island, N.Y., with her husband, Richard Smith, an architect, and their son, Jesse.